EVE
OF
Endless
Night

Other books by S D Simper:

The Sting of Victory (Fallen Gods 1)
Among Gods and Monsters (Fallen Gods 2)
Blood of the Moon (Fallen Gods 3)
Tear the World Apart (Fallen Gods 4)
Eve of Endless Night (Fallen Gods 5)

Carmilla and Laura

Beneath the Dark Moon (Sea and Stars Prequel)
The Fate of Stars (Sea and Stars 1)
Heart of Silver Flame (Sea and Stars 2)
Death's Abyss (Sea and Stars 3)

Beneath the Loch

Forthcoming books:

Chaos Undone (Fallen Gods 6) – *TBA*

Fallen Gods: Series 2 – *TBA*

Unnamed Phantom of the Opera Project - *TBA*

S D SIMPER

Eve of Endless Night

Cover art by Jade Merien

Cover design and interior by Jerah Moss

Maps by Mariah Simper

ISBN (Hardcover): 978-1-952349-20-1

Visit the author at www.sdsimper.com

Facebook: sdsimper
Twitter: @sdsimper
Instagram: sdsimper

For LJ

Publisher's Note: Eve of Endless Night is a fantasy horror novel intended for adults and may contain material upsetting to some readers. Please visit sdsimper.com to view a list of spoiler-free content warnings.

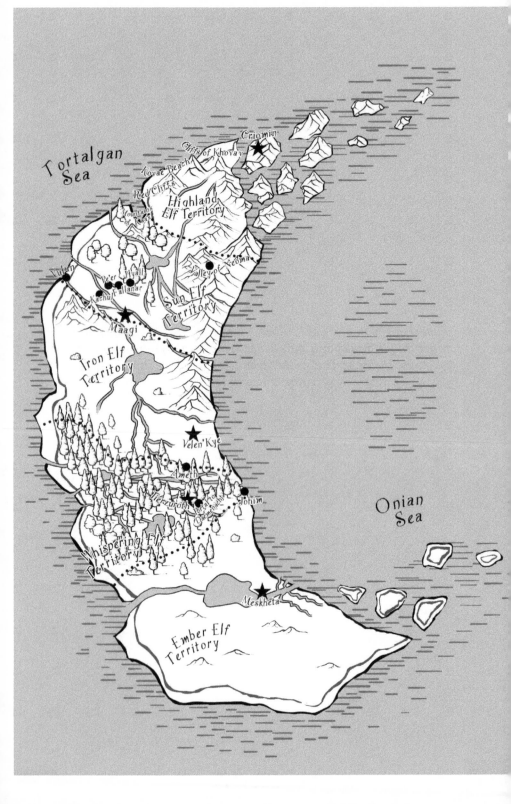

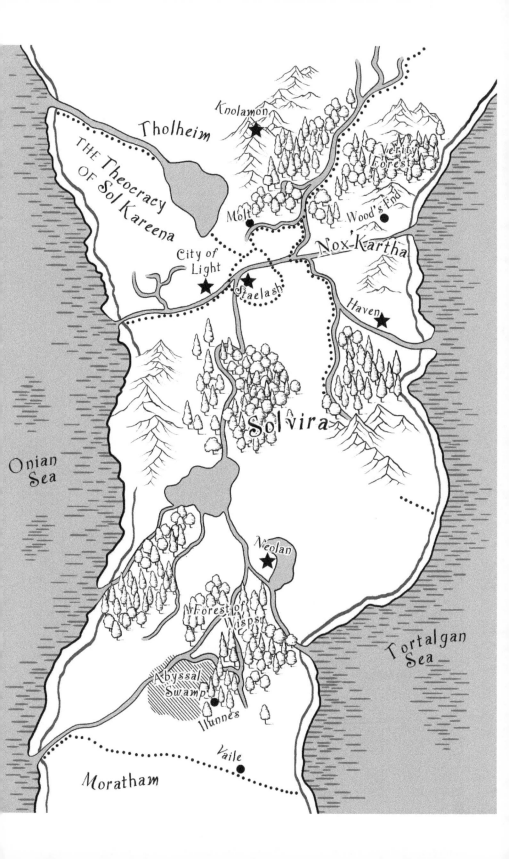

Names

THE COUNCIL OF NOX'KARTHA

Casvir – Kas-**veer**

Murishani – Mur-eh-**shah**-nee

Khastra – **Kas**-truh

THE ROYAL COUNCIL OF SOLVIRA

Etolié – Eh-**toh**-lee-ey

Zoldar—**Zohl**-dar

FIREBORN FAMILY

Sora Fireborn – **Sohr**-ruh **Fire**-bohrn

Mereen Fireborn – Mer-**een** **Fire**-bohrn

Tazel Fireborn – **Taa**-zuhl **Fire**-bohrn

Sarai Fireborn – Suh-**rye** **Fire**-bohrn

FOREIGN DIGNITARIES

Marielle Vors – **Mair**-ee-el **Vohrs**

Zorlaeus – Zor-**ley**-uhs

OTHER PLAYERS

Flowridia Darkleaf – Floh-**rid**-ee-uh **Dahrk**-leef

Ayla Darkleaf – **Ai**-luh **Dahrk**-leef

Demitri – Dih-**mee**-tree

Odessa – Oh-**des**-uh

Kah'Sheen – Kuh-**sheen**

Uluron – **Oo**-luh-ron

Soliel – Suh-**lil**

VARIOUS GODS, ANGELIC AND DEMONIC

Sol Kareena – Sohl Kuh-**ree**-nuh

Eionei – **Eye**-uhn-eye

Alystra – Ah-**lees**-truh

Staella – **Stey**-luh

Neoma – Ney-**oh**-muh

Ilune – Eye-**loon**

Morathma – Moh-**roth**-muh

Izthuni – Iz-**thoon**-eye

Ku'Shya – Koo-**shy**-uh

Onias – Uhn-**eye**-uhs

Within his decorated war chamber in the capital city of Velen'Kye, Executor Luc Stormforged, elected leader of the Iron Elves, read a disappointing report.

A large table spread before him, filled with maps and models of weapons he knew well, some of which he had even helped to design. His high general stood to his right, along with various lieutenants, a few aviators, and his spymaster, who delivered yet another failure: "There is not even a whisper of her presence, Executor Stormforged. Ayla Darkleaf continues to evade us."

"I shall consider making a more public call," Luc replied, though the idea irked him. Not an attractive look, and the Scourge of the Sun Elves would take note of it.

He called for the lieutenant next.

"The reports said the imperator meant to march across the Plains of Rosh, but we know now that was false. The Bringer of War destroyed six of our airships at the Red Cliffs but was stopped by the cliffs themselves. Whispers suggest they'll be striking at Kovae Beach, but the imperator has deceived our spies before."

"So long as we do not allow him inland," Luc said, "Executor Yewblade can keep him entertained in the north for some time. But I will send a few gliders to the beach to assist. The towns beyond are vulnerable, and if I must call for an evacuation, I would rather Velen'Kye be prepared to receive them."

Next came an engineer, who relayed ill news. "Unfortunately, the prototypes for an airship capable of ocean travel continue to be uninspiring. More funding is required at the university."

"You shall have it."

Luc stopped when the great doors of the war chamber opened. Resplendent light followed, along with the shadow of a new and magnificent interloper.

Every elf, including Luc, bowed before the Deity who entered—the Old God of Order himself, whose presence cast an aura of light around him. He wore the armor gifted from the Iron Elves, forged from steel and decorated in gold; a match to his hair, blond and flecked with grey. Luc had personally overseen the crafting of the massive sword at his hip, had approved the artwork engraved into the hilt.

"It is an honor to stand in your presence, Great Father," Luc said, for though he was not pledged to this man, it did not diminish his power and strength. "What can we provide for you?"

When the God straightened his stance, he towered above them all. "I have come to Velen'Kye for rest and supplies." Such odd gentleness in the God of Order's voice, yet it could not be ignored; thunder could whisper, but it was heard across the land. "My quest for the dragon continues. Uluron has hidden herself well. I came to inform you of that and to ask how your efforts go in slowing Nox'Kartha."

Luc kept his posture, kept his pride, but inside, his stomach churned to deliver grim news to a God. "I suppose if I say it is a stalemate, that is good for your goals and our own, long term. But it does not do well with keeping up morale among my citizens. Spies say the imperator has put a hold on the war on Tholheim, keeping watchers on the border instead, to better focus on Zauleen. For months now, the outlying towns have feared their destruction, and even Velen'Kye never sleeps lest the imperator strike. I know all is better than it seems. I know we await you finding the remaining Convergence Orbs, but they do not. Respectfully, we instigated at your word—might there be any direct aid you could offer?"

"Perhaps I might speak to the populace."

"It would be appreciated. Our plan to boost morale was to enlist an old celebrity of ours to assist, given she may also be able to provide legitimate aid. I doubt you have heard of the Scourge of the Sun Elves, but there is bad blood between her and Imperator Casvir."

Nothing shifted at all in the God of Order's countenance, yet something in his words set Luc's instincts, honed from many years as a politician, on edge. "I know Ayla Darkleaf."

"Then you understand why she might inspire morale among the populace. Be that as it may, she is not an easy woman to find."

The God became thoughtful, the aging lines of his face deepening. "Have you sought Flowridia?"

Luc frowned. "I am afraid I do not know the name."

"Flowridia Darkleaf is Ayla's wife."

"Her wife?"

"If Ayla never wants to be found, she never will be. It is her greatest strength as a creature of the night. But perhaps Flowridia Darkleaf will be easier to track down. She is not nearly so subtle."

The idea was too strange to even give weight to, yet it came from the Old God himself. "Forgive me for clarifying," Executor Stormforged said, "but do you mean to say that Ayla Darkleaf, Scourge of the Sun Elves, is married now?"

"She is, to a necromancer from Solvira."

"Surely not an elf, then?" When the God of Order shook his head, Executor Stormforged failed to hide his scoff. Sun Elves were strange mongrels, but even they were not known for marrying outside their blood. Surely there was something more to it. Besides, Ayla had proven in the most dramatic and violent of ways that she was different from them. "Strange times. But if this 'Flowridia' truly is the missing piece, I shall overlook her parentage. I have never heard of an unimpressive necromancer—"

A necromancer from Solvira, he had said? "Was Flowridia not the name of the woman who married the late Empress Alauriel? The one from Staelash?"

"She is the same woman."

"And now she is married to Ayla Darkleaf?"

"That is correct."

Flowridia of Staelash was a name thrown around in the past, when rumors that the imperator might take a bride had come to Velen'Kye. The affairs of humans and De'Sindai were rarely concerning, but the name had circulated again when Solvira announced the engagement of their late empress—to Flowridia Solviraes, paving her path to be Consort of Solvira.

And now this? "She is either a hussy or a diabolical sociopath," Luc said, "but the latter might be useful for the war effort. Would she assist?"

He feared he had misspoken, given the notable shock on the God's face. But the God of Order collected himself, resuming his even tone. "If she can be convinced, then yes. She was once a pawn of the imperator as well, but if she has disappeared with Ayla, she is no longer loyal to him."

Luc looked to his spymaster. "Resume your search across the sea. Inquire of Flowridia Darkleaf."

On a moonless night, Flowridia Darkleaf paced the outskirts of a grand estate, studying the foliage and defenses. Clever, to construct a thorny hedge of roses for the perimeter. She touched upon the plants with her magic, finding the flowers healthy and well nourished. A twinge of regret filled her for their fate, but thorned vines were a powerful force.

Shadowing her, Demitri was less silent on his large feet, having to duck to not be spotted over the top of the hedge. Though his growth had slowed, the wolf remained an imposing force, matching the tallest of steeds. Even in the absence of danger, her familiar was a comforting presence.

When she reached the entry gate, the great iron bars radiated a subtle bit of magic—an alarm should anyone try to pass. And so Flowridia stood a ways apart, unwilling to risk discovery. Crisp air and adrenaline kept her senses alert as she waited for darker company to join them.

The shadows shifted before her, and the world became colder when Ayla Darkleaf rejoined it. An errant grin twisted her slight lips as she emerged from Sha'Demoni, pride in her stance—as tall as the clouds, though she stood a head shorter than Flowridia. Such grace in her gait, such allure, yet she was as petite as the knives she wielded. Elves were naturally lean, and Ayla especially so. "I counted fifteen vampires in all," Ayla said coolly, her voice a dark luxury, "though it is unclear which are a part of the coven and which are slaves."

"Do vampires often have slaves?"

"Of course they do. Do not forget that vampires are helpless to their creators. Few resist the temptation to turn mortals into undead pets."

"I see," Flowridia replied, the idea less than gratifying. "So, we kill all of them?"

"Less risk that way. Think of it as putting them all to rest." She took Flowridia's hand and led her to the enchanted gate, her calculating mind surely noting what Flowridia had already seen. "Do you know what the spell does?"

"It'll sound an alarm if we try to pass."

"Best to get rid of that, then."

Ayla held up a hand, and from the pores of her skin came smoldering flame. In shades of silver, it overtook her hand, rising to engulf her arm. She grinned at the dynamic magic, then grasped the iron bars.

For a mere moment, the gate's aura burned bright, flashing before fading, the magic absorbed. Ayla glowed in its stead, but when she clenched her fist, the fire and light disappeared. "We should not have any trouble now. Are you ready, my love?"

Flowridia gathered herself, breathed to find equilibrium, and with her exhale came a rise of purple smoke from her hand. "I'll request your assistance in cleaning up the damage. This hedge is beautifully put together; I hate to ruin it."

"My darling, you have my solemn vow." Ayla stood on her toes to meet Flowridia's mouth, their lips touching lightly. They did not part; instead, their kiss deepened, amorous intentions laid bare in Ayla's sigh. When her magic-imbued hand caressed Ayla's face, her wife gasped, her ensuing groan the grandest delight.

Euphoria filled Flowridia, both for the kiss itself and for knowing what the necrotic magic did to her undead love. She prayed the sensation never faded—not today, not tomorrow, nor a thousand years from now. No amount of time would be enough with the woman she called her wife.

They parted, though the promise of more lay in Ayla's enamored gaze. "We shall celebrate our victory with passion and blood. But first, we must earn it."

Only then did Flowridia realize her sweet boy had been watching all along. "Sorry, I—"

I'm used to you and Lady Ayla.

Though his shoulders met the top of her head in height, Demitri had a child's voice. Flowridia's motherly heart hoped it remained for all his days. "Will you be safe out here?"

The worst things out here are other wolves, and I'm bigger.

She kissed her familiar's nose. "I'll fetch you once we've

won."

I won't be far.

Half her heart went with, as she watched her dearest Demitri go. She worried; she always did. But Ayla took her hand and squeezed, reminding her of their quest. If they succeeded, they could rest.

"Fear not, Flowra. He will be fine."

Flowridia's magic expanded, purple smoke seeping from the pores along her arms. She breathed, and it ebbed from her lips with each exhale, for it brewed deep within. Most potent when angry, but even in times of calm, she could summon an impressive storm.

She gripped a single rose, which withered in her grasp. The blight spread rapidly along the hedge, the roses wilting, desiccating at her command. The magic disappeared into the darkness, but as it spread, the stolen life filled Flowridia, infusing her with energy. Oh, such exhilaration; a moan sought to escape her lips, but she bit it down, silently reveling in the power.

When death had fully circled to the opposite side of the gate, the entire hedge lay brittle and brown, all semblance of its lush growths gone away. Flowridia held the stolen life inside her, savoring its pressure a few moments more, then released her breath—

And faster than it had been stolen, the hedge burst with false life. The roses rejuvenated, overflowing with vibrancy. The thorns became softer, supple, their greenery surely spectacular by day. When Flowridia beckoned, a single vine grew toward her, delivering a gorgeous blossom. The scent bore the sweetness of floral life, but with it came a dash of necromancy, the cloying intoxication of death.

"You are incredible," Ayla whispered. That smile accentuated every muscle in her gaunt face, highlighting both her cheekbones and the hint of fangs behind her lips—proof of her excitement. "Ready?"

Flowridia snapped the stem of the undead rose, finding it an attractive accessory. She placed it between her teeth as she gathered her hair into a thick tail, then stole the rose back and bid it to wrap around the auburn locks. Functional, yes, and pretty, if Ayla's softening gaze was any indicator. "Ready."

When Ayla pushed the gate, a faint *crack* sounded within the locking mechanism. It swung open smoothly, well maintained. No fear in Ayla's strides, whereas Flowridia crept

7

cautiously behind. The branches on the ground grew to follow her, creating a sea of thorned beauty.

Ayla announced their presence with the iron doorknocker. Ever grandiose, she placed herself in a haughty pose and froze like a stone gargoyle—prepared to come to life when the moment came.

Ayla held so much more ease in the face of danger, though being immortal and theoretically unkillable likely had something to do with it. Flowridia did not have the luxury— yet.

'Yet' remained a silent impasse between them. It was not a war, no, but a worry. They were at peace, but Flowridia's mortality steadily ticked past, day by day.

From the window, a flicker of light appeared at the seam of the curtains. The door swung open, revealing a deceptively human-looking woman, candlelight reflecting against her pallid features. "Good evening . . ." Her words faded as she stared first at Ayla, then Flowridia, then the creeping roses behind them.

"My name is Ayla Darkleaf, perhaps better known to you as The Endless Night. I am claiming this house."

Recognition froze the young woman's features.

"I assume you are not the lord of the house," Ayla continued, smoother than a serene sea, "so bring him here, or run away—I don't care."

"I-I would run, but I cannot. His lordship commands me." The girl, a vampire, looked to Flowridia, a plea in her predator eyes. Her voice lowered. "You are Flowridia Darkleaf, then? They say you are merciful. If I bring his lordship here, will you spare me?"

Flowridia did not know her name or story, but her willingness to betray her master spoke volumes. Surely the very walls listened, so she whispered, "Yes."

The girl raised her voice. "Please, come in. I shall tell Lord Avalon he has esteemed guests."

She did not shut the door behind them, instead leaving room for Flowridia's creeping vines. With a snap of the girl's fingers, the chandelier above them burst with light, illuminating the massive entry room. Ayla would have already seen it with her keen eyes, but Flowridia now absorbed the magnificent space: luxurious décor, velvet curtains, a grand staircase at the end of the entryway, with doors placed along the walls and above on the second floor. A worthy home for a disgraced empress consort and her monster wife.

The girl ran to a nearby door and knocked before disappearing.

"You are making promises on my behalf," Ayla said, clear annoyance in her tone. "Spare her? I intended to kill everyone, remember?"

"You offered to let her run."

"Yes, but then I would have hunted her down."

Flowridia's terse words became quieter, lest they draw attention. "She's clearly a slave, Ayla."

"Slaves can talk."

"She won't."

"Do you want to have to move again?"

They had been nomads for months now, wandering the continent with wanton abandon, but if work were to resume, they needed a place to operate. That, and travel was exhausting. Flowridia yearned for a place to call home.

So when rumors had come of a coven of vampires in the mountainous woods beyond Wood's End, they had decided to stake their claim.

"No, I don't," Flowridia said, resigned, "but she clearly has no love for the vampire lord and is frightened enough to believe you if you say you'll tear her head off if she speaks."

"Assuming she isn't warning him now."

"Just let her walk away, please."

"Fine, fine, if you insist," Ayla said, no bite to her ire.

The door opened. No sign of the girl, but a man who must have been Lord Avalon emerged, clothed in rich furs and glittering gems. Two women stood at his side, their dresses equally rich, and Flowridia felt their hungry eyes surveying her.

Yet their intrigue fell upon studying Ayla, interest was replaced with confusion. "Good evening, fair ladies," Lord Avalon said. "I'm told—"

Flowridia did not believe in small talk—his words were stolen by vines bursting through the doorway, controlled by her will. They wrapped around each vampire, who fought the unnatural bonds, their shock shifting to rage.

Ayla drew a knife from her belt. "Thank you, Flowra."

Within seconds, three heads were on the floor, their bodies limp beside them. "Take them outside," Ayla said, "but be sure their heads are nowhere near the bodies. They will catch fire at sunrise."

9

Flowridia gave the silent command to her plants to drag them away, the gesture as innate as moving her arms.

"Keep them readied, but leave a path for the girl," Ayla continued, smoothly approaching the door Lord Avalon had appeared from.

Within, a fireplace held a luxurious flame, casting warmth through the sitting room. The same girl waited, nervous as she curtsied. "I feel my mind clearly again. He is dead?"

Pity filled Flowridia. The girl looked younger than even she. "He is."

Ayla spoke up, her words curt and short. "Are there any other nobles, or are the other eleven of you slaves as well?"

"We are all only slaves, Lady Darkleaf."

"You have one hour to vacate this home. Gather your fellows and run. If you return, I will kill you. If you tell anyone we are here, I will find you—and I do know how to torture vampires, don't you worry."

The girl gave a swift nod, a muttered *"Thank you"* on her lips as she ran.

Ayla locked the door behind her. "One more hour, and this place is ours forever."

Flowridia had nothing to say to that, still fixated on this strange mercy. "You're letting them all go?"

"I am. What of it?"

Flowridia took her wife in her arms and kissed her softly, Ayla's tension fading in the gesture. "You are something, my love."

"It is what you would have done, and you inspire me." Wickedness turned her once-kind smile. "And it does pay to have a few vampires owing us favors."

"That sounds more like you." Flowridia laughed when Ayla stole her lips anew. "We have an hour before we can explore our new home."

"And we have this wonderful fireplace to bask in." Ayla led her to the couch, and when Flowridia sat, she straddled her lovingly, embracing her on the plush cushion. When she cupped Flowridia's cheek, the chill touch of her hand sent a shiver down her spine. "Welcome home, Flowridia Darkleaf."

With a kiss, the celebration began.

Across the sea, within a once-tranquil clearing, Sora Fireborn stood alert and watching.

A palpable aura of magic pervaded the space, the river pure serenity. Willow trees hung low, hiding secrets within their leaves, and flashing fireflies flew on, oblivious to the screaming in their domain.

Sora wasn't so lucky. She clenched her fists, surveying for predators—as though any predators would dare approach with those wrenching cries echoing about.

"Please, Mereen! I don't know—!"

The screaming resumed, and on Sora's shoulder, her bird trembled, clearly agitated. Sora's stomach clenched at the continuing cries. A flock of birds scattered from the trees, surely startled by the agonized voice.

Amid the tortured wailing, she offered a silent prayer: *Sol Kareena, grant mercy to her, whoever she is.*

There came no reply. Leelan rubbed softly against her. *Loosen her tongue so this can end.*

Beside her, Tazel didn't fare much better. He held Ferseph, the sweet little bird, in his hands, as though it could protect her from the torturous sounds. Handsome and scarred, his face held thinly veiled disgust. His short blond hair, once maintained, now curled around his ears, conveying the passage of time since they'd sailed across the Tortalgan Sea from Nox'Kartha.

"It would be nice if she warned us," Sora offered, her jovial smile failing to alleviate the tension.

Bitterness showed in Tazel's reply. "Mereen has the mentality of someone who best works alone, despite having the charisma to rally others to her cause. You get used to being left in the dark. She doesn't tell me anything either."

Sora glanced back when the screaming quieted, leaving soft whimpering in its wake. Blockaded by thick foliage, they stood too far away to see it—by Mereen's command—though her senses went on high alert at the wispy cloud of purple seeping out.

The fog spread toward them, slow as a lava stream. Ferseph flew high into a tree, followed closely by Leelan. "In

11

hindsight," Tazel said, "of course Flowridia's mother is a necromancer. When they can stop bickering long enough to actually communicate, Mereen and Odessa are a terrifying duo."

In the ensuing silence, Sora waited on edge for the screams to resume. "The witch shares her flippant morality. But I'll be honest—I don't like this. I don't endorse torture."

"Sometimes the greater good demands sacrifice." Yet regret showed in Tazel's features, his eyes wide and weary.

"What kind of torture can a necromancer do?" Sora asked, but an entire flood of ideas followed at the thought. Necromancers were creative by nature.

And often sadistic.

"I once met a witch who could slowly unravel years of your life. It felt like she'd dragged a knife across my veins." Tazel kept a permanent eye on the necrotic magic, though it seemed to have halted its approach. His hand settled upon her waist, his other arm void of a weapon yet held in a defensive stance.

Sora didn't know what protection it would provide against a cloud of death, but kept close, nevertheless. "She took your life?"

"A few years, probably. She steals it from the end, so I wouldn't know how much. Perhaps you know that story, actually—Helfira, the Witch of the North. She was a plague upon the Highland Elves."

"My mother told me, yes. But you defeated her by cursing her."

Distant sorrow settled upon Tazel's features. "Yes. Cursed in death to protect the very lands she once oppressed. Adira sacrificed herself for the curse's components."

"Adira?"

"My partner, at the time. Together, we made a name for ourselves breaking curses and killing monsters in the elven lands. But she slit her own stomach for the final piece—blood of the dying."

Sora had heard something of it as a child but had hardly known Tazel then. She hardly knew him now, despite four months together on boat and land. "What's special about blood of the dying?"

"Different spells require different components. To literally seal a being away—or seal them to a cause, as was the case—requires sacrifice."

"Couldn't you have healed her after?"

Tazel's grave features conveyed the answer first. "No. Spells are fickle. Had Adira lived, the spell would have failed—"

"*Mereen!*"

The screaming resumed. Sora tried to stay stoic and brave, but the sheer anguish struck her deep, her soul tainted to be near it. Fresh billowing purple swirled into the air, spreading once more. Yet with it, as the discordant voice grew louder, something shifted beneath her feet. The ground trembled; branches cracked and fell. Trees split down the center of their trunks. The river rose, becoming turbulent.

Sora covered her ears, yet the sound threatened to split her skull. "What is that?!"

Tazel wrenched her back before a falling branch could crush them both.

A blast of necrotic energy burst like lightning from the trees. The screaming stopped.

Silence settled. Every nerve in Sora's body buzzed as she watched the unnatural smoke, an omen of carnage.

"This is either a person who controls nature," Tazel whispered, his grip tense around her, "or a creature with some sort of vocal magic. Perhaps a banshee or a specialized witch."

From afar, Sora heard conversation, though only Mereen's voice cut through the fog of anticipation: "*You've held to that lie for a thousand years.*"

A whimper came, indecipherable, nearly a sob.

"*Go on.*"

Sora strained to listen, curious beyond measure, and managed to hear a few pained words: "*... don't know where ...*"

And then Mereen's outburst: "*How am I supposed to—!*"

"*He said ...*" Gentle weeping filled the clearing, a haunting refrain. "*He said ...*"

Next Odessa's quiet ire. "*... the letter of the law and the spirit of the law, Mereen ... could have saved us months of travel if you had just ...*"

"*... you have a better plan?*"

"*I do. But we mustn't be overheard.*"

The eerie silence of the clearing raised the hairs on the back of Sora's neck. Nothing but the babbling of the river beside them showed any life, until trudging footsteps revealed the return of Mereen and Odessa. Tazel released her, and Sora forced herself to stand at attention as two silhouettes cut through the necrotic cloud, immune to its effects.

Mereen Fireborn wore leather dyed pure white, a ghostly figment in this ethereal realm. Eternally youthful, vampirism had perfected what had surely been beautiful in life, her blue eyes bright, her pale blonde hair pristine in its braid. With swords on her back and a revolver at her hip, Mereen was as imposing as ever, ingrained in Sora's memory as a woman to respect—and fear.

Even by her own mother. *"There's a reason I kept you and your father far away from her..."*

At her side, Odessa smiled prettily, looking like the cat who'd found the cream. Though her doe eyes played innocent, a conniving, brilliant mind rested behind her lovely face—not unlike her daughter, but Sora hadn't ever dared to compare her to Flowridia aloud. She didn't know what magic Odessa had wrought, only that Mereen looked pleased by the results.

"Our quarry has said enough," Mereen said. Her grin showed no fangs, merely perfect white teeth, but deception made the predator all the more frightening. "We move on."

Sora peered past Mereen's shoulder, yet saw nothing but the expansive pond, the rich foliage, and the cloud of smoke. All the fireflies had scattered, repulsed by the choking magic. "Is she all right?"

Displeasure turned Mereen's smile into something virulent. "Anything you can offer will only leave her worse off."

"Where are we going?" Tazel asked, but it was Odessa who answered.

"You need a monster to fight a monster," the red-haired woman replied, her beauty duplicitous—a mortal puppet pulled by literal ghostly strings, "or at least a monster's weapon. The location of Staff Seraph deDieula is no secret to those of us who study demons and death, though that doesn't make it any easier to get."

When Tazel's face bespoke horror, Sora asked, "What is that?"

Unlike her vampiric counterpart, Odessa never looked at Sora with derision. For all her wicked flaws, Odessa treated her as a person. "For thousands of years, the God of Death ruled Solvira with her godly mothers. She wielded a staff of unparalleled power, created by herself from ingredients unknown, but it allowed her to amplify her unique magic. I believe it . . ."

Mereen held up a hand, stilling Odessa's words. "No need to worry their gentle hearts."

Tazel held his hands stiffly behind his back. "Do we at least get to know where we're going?"

"*Daemenacht*—Goddess Ku'Shya's realm. She keeps a personal eye on it."

Dread filled Sora. "We're going to sneak into the Goddess of War's castle and steal an ancient artifact?"

"Oh, no," the witch replied, unnervingly flippant as she chuckled. "Well, yes, but no—Goddess Ku'Shya lives in a cave, not a castle. They don't call her The Great Spider for nothing."

Sora bit her tongue, uncertain of how to explain why that wasn't better.

"It's south. Far south," Odessa continued. "We'd be better off setting sail again."

Mereen led their exit, followed closely by Tazel and Odessa.

Yet Sora hesitated when quiet weeping sounded beyond the trees. She did not know the tortured figure, and so it should not have mattered to leave her behind, yet Sora's apprehension rose. This cruelty . . . it was not what Sol Kareena preached.

Sora's senses prickled. She spun around—just in time to catch Odessa about to place a hand on her shoulder. "Didn't mean to frighten you, dear. But you'll be lost if you're left behind."

Despite her distress, Sora stepped with her, chanting a prayer in her mind. *Sol Kareena, harden my heart . . .*

At best, she managed not to cry. Sora withdrew her pipe and stash from her satchel, praying it quelled her nerves.

Etolié, Daughter of Stars, Savior of Slaves, former Magister of Staelash and current Empress of the Fucking World, sat among piles of boxes in a cottage surrounded by eternal stars. She coughed at the swirling puff of dust cast into the air when she opened the next box, revealing an array of likely useless trinkets. She illusioned a handkerchief, holding it against her mouth as she waved away the dust. Not the most illustrious task for the Empress of Solvira, but even recently crowned monarchs were weak to their momma's polite request for help cleaning out an old closet.

"Are you all right, Starshine?" came a voice outside the room, which managed to both be softer than starlight and carry all through the house.

Etolié heaved a few final coughs into her handkerchief before dispelling the magic. "I'm fine!"

Etolié's wings cast golden light throughout the cluttered room, and the shift in light meant Staella, Goddess of Stars and Mercy and Motherhood and a whole slew of other things had returned. Her own lustrous wings put Etolié's to shame, her skin casting the same golden light—a true angel, whereas Etolié was only mostly one. Rather than navigate the sea of boxes, Staella floated on her gentle wings. "I brought more tea. I find it helps me focus. Does tea help you focus?"

"I don't drink enough to have an opinion on the matter," Etolié replied, though she accepted the offered cup and saucer with a smile. The first sip was bliss, because Momma's tea was fucking perfection. "Anything useful in this box?"

Staella was small, far less lanky than her daughter, and had little trouble finding a spot to land and sit. "Oh goodness, yes!" With palpable joy, Staella lifted what appeared to be a tiny painting from the box. "I made this for Ilune when she was six years old. She was inconsolable when her favorite mouse was too disintegrated to keep animating into a pet, so I painted a rendition of it for her to remember it by."

Staella smiled wistfully at the painting before turning it around—showing off an artistic rendition of a half-rotted mouse with creepy glowing eyes.

Etolié couldn't say she understood nostalgic love to this degree or envision summoning any sort of love for drawings of dead animals, but she faked a smile, nevertheless. "Very charming. I assume you're keeping that one too?"

Staella's musical laughter filled the room. "You don't have to understand, Starshine. Yes, I intend to keep this one."

As Staella returned the painting to its place, Etolié spared a glance for the single box filled with things her momma was actually willing to part with, currently consisting of a jar holding a pile of dust—apparently some 'failed experiment' of Ilune's, which Etolié did not ask any more about—a broken teacup, and a matchless sock. Hours of work had culminated in . . . that.

"Oh, and look at this—isn't this sweet?" Staella offered Etolié a wooden box, revealing what appeared to be a dried lily. "A gift from Neoma. Can't believe it's survived this long."

"Yes, fine. I won't argue with keeping that."

Etolié began searching in a new box, sighing internally as Staella gave a dissertation on the pair of dirty baby shoes inside, and while Etolié would never insult her mother by calling her a hoarder, she definitely had a habit of holding on to every little thing that passed into her life and never letting go.

"And what is . . ." Etolié voice trailed off at her spiking headache. From a padded crate within the ancient box, she held up . . . a teapot? A perfectly normal fucking teapot, fashioned from clay of some sort and painted by clumsy hands, likely a child. Except, despite appearances, it wasn't perfectly fucking normal. "Momma, this reeks of evil."

"An evil teapot? Let me see." Staella stared quizzically at the offered teapot, even going so far as to peer inside. "How strange. Likely cursed. I'll take care of it."

Staella floated back up, teapot in hand. Etolié might've summoned a few swears, but curtailing her tongue in Momma's house was one of her good traits. "You're very blasé about a cursed teapot in your house."

"I'm the Breaker of Curses, Starshine. What's the worst it can do?"

Staella left the room, and Etolié rolled her eyes because Momma was a big girl who could make big-girl decisions about gods-damned cursed objects.

From the other room came Staella's voice. "You haven't stopped by Sha'Demoni lately, have you?"

Grateful her empathic mother was out of the room, Etolié felt no need to hide her eye roll. "I told you, Momma—the scroll isn't in Sha'Demoni. It was destroyed in the blast."

"You can't be too careful."

"Well, if you'd tell me what's in it, we could have a better conversation about this."

Staella said nothing at that.

Etolié wouldn't call it a sore point between them, but Momma was being suspiciously tight-lipped about a certain mysterious scroll she'd gifted to the fake Empress of Solvira.

Every once in a while, Etolié mulled over the fact that she'd watched false Empress Alauriel tuck it into a shadow. Or an extra-dimensional space. Or something. But surely it had been destroyed in the blast that had blown up half of Neolan. ... Right?

When Staella returned, Etolié was arms-deep in the next box. "I think the stew is about ready," Momma said. "Would you like to take a break?"

Hyperfocus brain said stay, which Etolié had learned over the past few months she and Momma both suffered from. So if Momma was exhibiting self-control, so could she. "No, but I will."

Admittedly, it was nice to breathe air that wasn't filled with dust. In the kitchen, Etolié's stomach rumbled when Momma placed what appeared to be perfectly normal beef stew in front of her. "Thank you."

As Staella served herself, she asked, "Do you need to be going back to Solvira after this?"

Etolié swallowed her bite, countenance settling somewhere between bliss and a grimace. The food was fantastic; the question was not. "Bureaucratic bullshit can wait."

"I presume Khastra isn't back yet?"

Her heart sank at the question—yet another confusing emotion when juxtaposed to her second bite of stew, the deliciousness of which was increasingly suspicious. Then again, Momma usually enchanted her food. "No. And she doesn't know when she will be."

General Khastra of Nox'Kartha led the greatest army in the world, combating the Elven Alliance with a sea of undead at her beck and call. But being across the sea meant there was little time for her to detour to Solvira.

"I'm so sorry, Starshine." When Staella offered a hand across the table, Etolié accepted, grateful for the comfort. Given the nature of her momma's godly powers, the comfort was likely magical, but Etolié wasn't going to complain about what was technically emotional manipulation.

"The things she describes in her letters are insane," Etolié said, managing to smile at the memory. "Ships that fly in the air—can you imagine? And carriages that shoot fire! The cynical part of me hopes Casvir has met his match, given there are virtually no dead people to raise and add to the army. It's all machines. So, no, I'm not worried for Khastra, but I miss her. As neat as it is to hear about, I would like the war to be over now."

18

"I always hated it when Neoma had to interfere in mortal wars," Staella offered, her thumb stroking soft lines across Etolié's skin, "even though there was rarely any danger to her. I understand."

Not the most comforting statement, given that Neoma had one day not come home. But Etolié didn't say that, for any mention of the late Moon Goddess from her momma still welled up old fears. "This is the longest Khastra and I have ever been apart. Even when I thought she was dead, it was only for a few months. And I feel awful for being so bitter about it. It's not like I'm alone. I have friends in Solvira, but it's been six months, Momma." The final word choked in her mouth. Mist blurred her vision when she blinked. "I'm so tired."

Staella came to Etolié's side, and in her hand appeared a brush. Likely also an illusion, though Momma's weren't nearly so powerful as her own. "May I?"

Etolié nodded, managing to smile despite her threatened tears. Momma pulled the string holding her bun together, and when Etolié's hair unraveled, she made tender work of it. For someone who generally hated physical contact, Etolié had a weakness for having her hair touched, and Momma was always so gentle.

"Will you tell me more?" Staella asked. "Or would you rather not?"

"There isn't much more to say. I miss her, and I'm tired of waiting." No, it wasn't all, though Etolié's next words were stilted by the chills running across her body, evoked from the brush. "So I appreciate you letting me come here. It helps me not think too hard."

Vulnerable words, but Etolié was finding her momma kept delicate care of vulnerable words. "There is always a place for you here, my Etolié."

Etolié's lip trembled, wondering if she would always be raw when faced with motherly words. When she didn't trust herself to speak without bursting into sobs, her momma began to sing.

Eionei was known for his songs, for crafting crass insults to gods and love songs to soften the hardest of hearts, but even he sang of the legendary beauty that was the voice of the Goddess of Stars. As pristine and pure as moonlight, as luxurious as fine wine, and while all his words were barbed with poison now, it did not mean they were lies.

Etolié had lived more of her life than not without Staella, but though she feared she would be forever healing, in these moments, she felt true hope.

Chapter 2

When they had journeyed across the Tortalgan Sea to the continent of Zauleen, Sora hadn't worried much about developing sea legs. The smooth ocean had caused her no issues.

Now, faced again with the sea, Sora leaned against the side of the boat, her stomach threatening to spill out her throat as she stared upon the distant, dark horizon. In one hand, she held her beloved pipe, huffing at its contents. Something about the Onian Sea made her ill, even on so serene a night. A breeze caressed her face. She pulled her coat tighter around her. "Sol Kareena, grant me health."

"You doing all right, dear?" came a familiar, feminine voice.

Odessa sauntered up, terribly pretty with her fashionable dress and hair, her eyes bright as they reflected the moon. Sora wondered daily if she used magic to enhance her clothing, given her own were dirty from travel, as were Tazel's. Mereen remained immaculate, but Mereen was undead, and though Odessa was a ghost, her body was warm and alive.

"Just feeling ill," Sora muttered, not trusting her stomach.

"I've got a spell for sea legs. Let me—"

Sora caught the witch's wrist when Odessa reached for her face, reflexes faster than even her mind.

Odessa stared, starkly surprised, but her countenance softened as she took her hand back. "No? I promise, there are no tricks with this one. It'll settle the liquid in your ears, help you to stop feeling so dizzy."

Sora gave a cautious nod, her sickened stomach overpowering her distrust of the wicked woman. Odessa touched both her ears, each a brand of her heritage, but cast no judgment on them. Instead, Sora gasped when slight pressure filled them, along with a silent *pop*.

In slow measures, the sensation of nausea faded, leaving Sora much lighter. "Thank you."

"I'm something of an expert in bodily manipulation," Odessa replied, her tone suggesting nothing of the subtle horror behind the statement. "Sorry you're suffering. If I *weren't* the aforementioned expert, I would also be suffering. Though I meant to ask you about those mushrooms you love smoking. Do they help with nausea?"

Sora was already partway through a breath, letting the cloying sweetness infiltrate her lungs. Relief coursed through her. Her nerves settled. "A little."

Odessa's cackling unraveled at the seams, straight from the storybooks Sora read as a child of evil witches and sorceresses and their demonic powers. "Sora, dear, you're stubbornly independent. You are allowed to ask for help."

Sora shook her head. "I prefer to draw as little attention to myself as possible."

"So instead you'll teeter on the edge of throwing up on the side of a ship?" Odessa's *tsk tsk* held the affection of a motherly chide. "To be fair, if I were dangling on the edge of a cliff, I wouldn't ask Mereen for a hand."

Sora bristled at Odessa's words. "She'd help you. You're on her team. She's loyal."

Odessa leaned against the ship's railing, her gaze curious as it fell upon Sora's long blonde locs, following their length down her back. Typically they were bound in a tail, but Sora appreciated the feeling of the salty air through her loose hair, content to let it spill freely around her shoulders.

"I did once tie her up a bit—well, a lot. She broke into my house to steal the late Empress Alauriel's body, you see. Tied her up with enchanted chains, and to be honest, I don't think she's ever forgiven me. And then what about you? She tried to kill you in my house when we first met, and you'd defend her?"

Sora set her jaw, fighting her rising contempt for the witch and her words. "It's my business what I think about her."

"No need to be defensive. Though I do wonder why you're here. Fireborn is a famous name, but is that enough?"

"I'm here to kill Ayla Darkleaf." Again, Sora brought the pipe to her lips. "It's the right thing to do."

EVE OF ENDLESS NIGHT

"Then you're a much stronger person than me. I'm here for revenge; Ayla tried to kill me. She tried to kill Tazel when he was a boy. And she succeeded in killing Mereen."

Odessa's pretty face held nothing of enmity, but Sora did not have to be intuitive to feel her skepticism. Another puff of her pipe, and she felt nearly mortal again. Sora forced the words, despite her reticence—and dread. "She killed me too."

"Yet you stand here huffing on that pipe?"

The question was layered, and Sora felt the invitation to unburden herself. It was a story she had told before, to priestesses and other confidants, but Odessa knew far more players than she realized. "Years ago, when Flowridia lived in Staelash, she began sleeping with Ayla Darkleaf—which should have been impossible, because I thought The Endless Night was dead. I assumed her name was an unfortunate coincidence. I kept my distance at first, but when she appeared as her demonic self, I knew. And I knew Flowridia was in danger. When I made it my business to help, she thanked me by asking Ayla to kill me."

Though her anxiety threatened the rise, the smoke did its duty of keeping her heart from pounding. "At which point," Sora continued, "Ayla ripped out my tongue to shut me up and dragged me into Sha'Demoni. Knowing what I know, I suppose I'm grateful she slit my throat so quickly, given the state my body was left in. But what matters is Sol Kareena herself apparently saw it fit to give me a second chance."

A strange memory. Fear, pain . . . then light.

She held the next part close to her heart, words she hadn't shared with anyone—vague memories of a warm embrace, a whisper in her ear: *Sora Fireborn, you will not die this day. Rise, and be my new champion.*

Perhaps simply a dream, but she had awoken at Sol Kareena's feet upon the cathedral steps, heaving desperate breaths.

Odessa's jaw hadn't raised. "You must be a celebrity, right? Sol Kareena herself resurrected you! You know she is the only god capable of true resurrection."

"I became the high priestess in Staelash, but I've distanced myself from any fame."

"I think we can count on one hand the known times in history that Sol Kareena has performed that particular miracle. Do you know who paid the cost?"

Sora hadn't felt particularly enthusiastic before, but the

question caused her shoulders to slump. Her gaze fell upon the dark waves, nearly indiscernible beneath the night sky. "My mentor, Meira. She was the original high priestess in Staelash. Instead, she died to host Sol Kareena's body and bring me back."

"Incredible, truly. All of it. And so you seek revenge?"

Despite the question, Sora dwelled upon Meira, the eccentric blind woman having left a void in her life. "No. Not like how you mean. When Flowridia went on her trip with Imperator Casvir, I took the time to pray and meditate, and I could never shake the impression that I was meant to forgive her. So I did. I truly held no animosity toward her until everything that happened in Solvira."

Thousands dead after a catastrophic explosion. Sora had witnessed such a tragedy only once before—less than two months prior, in the Theocracy of Sol Kareena. Flowridia had let a monster sit on the throne, complicit in this heinous crime.

"But Sol Kareena must have resurrected me for a purpose," Sora continued, "and I believe that purpose is to put an end to Ayla, whom she slew on the cathedral steps seconds before giving me new life. Between you and me, Mereen said Tazel was Sol Kareena's Champion in the past, but the goddess, she . . ." Her words trailed away, for to speak it aloud turned her tongue to lead. "The walls have ears."

"No walls here, but I catch your drift."

"I won't squander what my goddess has given me."

Silence settled between them, the waves filling the lull as they lapped against the ship.

"May I ask something?" Odessa asked. "Gossip for gossip?"

"Sure."

"You and Tazel—am I imagining the starry eyes? Are there feelings there or is it hero worship?"

Sora scowled at the question. "He's my cousin."

Odessa's horrid laughter filled the deck. "Historically, elves barely care about that. But fine, fine—I apologize for offending you."

"Tazel's kind to me. That's all."

"Adorable."

Sora returned her gaze to the sea. "I suppose I do have a bit of hero worship. Growing up, I heard countless stories about him. My mother adored him. Considered him her dearest friend. So it's strange, getting to know him. He's quiet, but . . . you'll laugh, but he reminds me a little of my father."

"Why would I laugh about that? That makes far more sense. Besides, Mereen has some deep claws in that boy, but I don't think she'll bite your fingers off for that attitude. Usurping him as Sol Kareena's Champion, sure, but not passing reminders of your father." Odessa's scoff became the preamble to crueler thoughts. "Though I hope your father treated you better than that."

"Tazel is good to me."

"Good, sure. But these Fireborns are so cold, and all he does is spend his day placating that bitch leader of ours. Unless Mereen is like your mother, but you're much too sane for that."

Sora made no attempt to hide the contempt in her voice. "I would appreciate if you didn't speak about my family that way."

Odessa's smile remained, something clever in her wicked gaze. "Perhaps that's your problem. You love people who show you the bare minimum of decency. Though what do I know. I kill my children and eat them."

Again came her cackling laughter. Sora's discomfort rose, though the reminder of Odessa's character was important. The witch could be charming at times, but she could not be a friend. Sol Kareena would not approve.

"Oh, I'm jesting," Odessa said, coming to match her pose as she leaned against the ship's barrier. "Well, not really, but I forget most people aren't so keen to jest of cannibalism. But no, I don't advocate for love—except self-love, which you are clearly not practicing."

Sora forced her smile, seeking to be polite. Once more, she breathed in the cloying fumes of her pipe, her thoughts finally settling. "Have you ever loved anyone?"

To her surprise, Odessa gave no immediate answer or any sardonic quip. Instead, her good humor softened, something dreamy in her gaze. "Yes, though a very long time ago. His name was Elyas, just the most darling man. He came to Ilunnes to sell eclectic wares to the shop in town. He was a merchant, you see, traveling all across the southern parts of Solvira. And he would always stop by my little cottage at the edge of the forest to bring me a gift. Usually flowers, though sometimes he would bring some rare fruit. Once he brought a whole cow." Her smile became gentle, shadowed with sorrow.

"I even confided in him about Rulan."

"Rulan?"

"My familiar. This was nearly eight hundred years ago, in the era of the Solviran Witch Hunts, so Rulan had to be a secret."

"Forgive me if this is not my place," Sora asked, sensing a tragic end, "but what happened?"

Odessa's sorrow came to eclipse all else, though so little in her lovely countenance changed. "My story is not different from any other witch of that era, except that I lived. Prince Azrael Solviraes swept through Ilunnes with his hunting party—killed Elyas, killed Rulan, and would have killed me if I hadn't been beautiful."

"And you're still here," Sora remarked, for Odessa had magic yet no familiar. Leelan was away in Sora's room, asleep for the night, but she felt the connection to the bird still—the link from her magic to Sol Kareena herself.

"I have and always will survive, Sora Fireborn." Odessa's smile became cruel, the only mar to her beauty. "After the prince had his way with me, he decided I'd make a fine addition to his collection of whores and sought to bring me to Neolan. But my benefactor—the demon who gave me Rulan—granted me one final boon. Rulan's spirit was returned to me; now we're never apart. And so the story is happy, I suppose. I slew the prince. I slew his party. I returned to Ilunnes, but they knew me without my mask now—I was a witch, even without a familiar. They even blamed me for Elyas' death, denied me the right to know where his grave was. And when word spread that the prince was dead, they hunted for me. But no one traverses the Abyssal Swamp and lives, so there I went. I built a home through magic, maintained it through spite, and I'm a legend they fear, even now."

An incredible story, inspiring in its own way. Still, it left a foul question unanswered, and Sora braced herself. "So how did that lead to you eating infants?"

"Oh, baby steps."

At Sora's groan, Odessa again gave that awful laugh.

Sora recalled a memory of years past, a passing comment she'd heard as she tended to the horses in the stables in Staelash. Flowridia had been a new presence in the manor, a quiet, shy soul who Sora had decided to leave in peace.

"*The orange trees are particularly* fruitful *this time of year.*"

Sora had paused because it couldn't have been on

purpose. She remained invisible at the juncture of the stable and the outside world, but there was Flowridia, bantering with Thalmus.

"*I* seed *what you mean.*"

"*I will be* juice-*tifiably annoyed if they're left to rot.*"

Apparently, poor humor was an inheritable trait.

Seeking to derail it, Sora asked, "Rulan is always with you, you said?"

Odessa wiped her eyes, her amusement at her own jest leaving her wheezing. "Don't you know that witches can absorb their familiars? It makes us more powerful than you can ever imagine. The proof is in the shadows."

Sora glanced to the lit torch beside the stairs leading below deck, but Odessa's shadow was lost to the sea. "Did you ever find Elyas' grave?"

"I did," Odessa said, that wistful look returning. "I raised his body and brought him home. You'll find the rest horrifying, but let me remind you I had recently absorbed an owl spirit—and owls aren't exactly known for having ethical palates. I had so many new and odd compulsions inside me. It isn't common, but did you know owls are known to engage in cannibalism?"

Sora merely blinked.

"You can guess the rest. And you can judge all you want, but I found it comforting, in a way. Something about my own body being his final resting place brought me peace."

Such outlandish words, yet Odessa seemed so sober. "I do find it horrifying—" Sora's words stopped at Odessa's scowl. "B-But I don't have to understand it. He was already dead, and you had to do what brought you peace."

No sense in commenting on the fact that Elyas was only the first of Odessa's cannibal endeavors. Therein were her aforementioned 'baby steps.'

"If there's any moral to my story, it's that Elyas wasn't only 'good to me.' He adored me, and I him. He loved me because I was different, not in spite of it."

Sora kept her elbows to the edge, knowing a plunge into the darkness would mean death. She mulled over the statement, for Odessa's message was clear. "I think I'm just a fool who looks for her father in all the wrong places. He died a long time ago."

At least, she hoped he did. In truth, he had simply disappeared, but explaining that she'd rather her father be

27

dead than the alternative was a difficult conversation.

Because if he were not dead, he abandoned her. She smothered the thought with a puff from her pipe; doubts led only to pain.

"I'm sorry to hear that," Odessa said. "My parents are dead too, though don't weep for me. At my age, it's to be expected. I'm here if you need to vent about it, but otherwise, I think I've done a fine job at making this little chat properly depressing. If you aren't going to bed, would you like to play cards?"

Sora sought a catch, but there was nothing more than earnest inquiry upon Odessa's face. "No, thank you. I-I should sleep."

"Understandable. You have a wonderful night, Sora."

Cards sounded enjoyable, but Sora could not. Odessa offered vulnerability in exchange for . . . for what? Friendship?

"Sol Kareena, guide me," Sora muttered as she stepped down the stairs, uncertain of what to do with any of it.

Etolié rarely slept.

But there were rare moments of succumbing to exhaustion, wherein she buried herself in enough blankets to be a shallow reflection of something comforting and warm, a shadow of an embrace capable of crushing her to dust yet gentle as a bird's touch.

Loneliness followed wherever she wandered. Sure, she had Momma and Zoldar and others—she was hardly alone—but it was a very different thing to not know when you'd hold someone's hand again.

Khastra would return. Khastra always did, even when Etolié thought her dead—though in Etolié's defense, she had fucking *died* and had a *funeral* once, so this was hardly an irrational feeling—but Etolié, always floating, missed her anchor.

Solvira kept her busy, but when she had no work to bury her worry with, she spent her days cheating money from her friends in the Nox'Karthan Library.

"I'll raise you four gold pieces, Zoldar," Etolié said to her little circle of companions: a De'Sindai servant named Kyla who kept coming back to lose more money, an equally demonic guard named Luca who Kyla had brought along, Zoldar, and Zorlaeus, who Etolié suspected was lonely. Being the husband of a traitorous hussy had its drawbacks.

The green-hued Skalmite placed his gold in the pool. More mantis than humanoid, Zoldar was her best employee and one of her few companions who understood that sometimes verbal abuse was how friends showed love. He blatantly relayed instructions with his mandibles, but no one except Etolié could understand his insectoid clicks and chirps. *Zorlaeus is sweating again,* Zoldar said, which meant Zorlaeus was about to lose a whole lot of Murishani's money.

The rest of the group dropped their matching funds in the pot. Kyla placed a card and withdrew a new one, a flash of devious delight crossing her features. "I'll raise ten."

The girl had a good hand. Time to end this.

They continued down the circle, each ensuing bet smaller and smaller, when Etolié made an exaggerated frown at her own hand. "I'm calling it," she said, and she laid down her cards, exposing an absolute dud of a hand. Zorlaeus followed after, displaying his own shitty ensemble, followed by Luca, who wasn't doing abysmally, but then Kyla laid hers down, looking as smug as a fucking peacock.

Having seen Kyla's hand, Etolié waited for Zoldar to hold the cards away from his maldectine necklace and made a casual flick with her finger. It didn't matter what the cards were—simply what they appeared to be, and Etolié's illusions were the best in the business. Zoldar laid his cards down, immediately clouding Kyla's sunny mood.

As Zoldar hoarded what would be their shared wins, Etolié gathered the cards and withdrew her spell to shuffle an untampered deck. A servant came into the library—the very servant who Etolié had paid a handsome sum to keep on the lookout for one specific thing. "Empress Etolié?"

Etolié's breath caught.

"Imperator Casvir has returned to the palace, as have his lieutenants."

Her hope surged, but she couldn't let it soar, not yet. "And his general?"

"I haven't seen her, but I presume so."

Excitement radiated off Etolié's skin like static. She dropped the deck and leapt into standing, her wings appearing as all semblance of propriety and control vanished. Her hands fluttered like a bird's wings, glitter bursting unbidden in her joy upon all except Zoldar, who wore his pendant of maldectine. "Zoldar, cancel all my meetings. This may be the best day of my life this year." To the servant, she said, "Find General Khastra. Tell her I'm in the war chamber."

When the servant nodded and left, Etolié twirled about in her illusionary dress. Perhaps later she'd find her head and think it childish, but fuck propriety. She ran from the library, unable to contain her bliss as she plotted how best to greet her favorite beefcake.

And that was how, not five minutes later, Etolié found herself lounging entirely nude on the massive table in the imperator's war chamber.

Visibly naked, rather, given she was always naked. But Khastra was the general of the most feared army in the world, which meant the worst that could happen was Etolié was laughed at and kissed, and the best-case scenario involved celebrating the general's return with some unconventional fuckery right here on the table.

As she waited, Etolié artfully rearranged the pieces on the table to conspicuously hide her more scandalous features—the buds of her breast and the flower between her legs, so to speak—grateful that Casvir had apparently invested an impressive amount of money on figurines. Perhaps it was a hobby. Even ageless demonic tyrants needed those, but Etolié only cared that it covered a decent amount of the aforementioned flower.

The doorknob turned. Etolié pursed her lips, lounging to best amplify her breasts, and said, "Hello, there—!"

Etolié squeaked. In her desperate attempt to hide her assets, she rolled off the table, knocking the figures down in her panic. When she stood, she wore an illusionary gown, something black and boring and entirely opaque.

Standing in the doorway, Imperator Casvir looked deeply unimpressed but, to his credit, certainly not like he'd expected to walk in on a naked Celestial. With his daunting horns and corpse-blue skin, it's not like he ever looked particularly pleasant anyway—the opposite, really, given how fucking massive he was in that armor. But, by Eionei's Asshole, she had stunned him into silence.

Etolié would have to remember to be proud of herself later—assuming she lived through the next few minutes instead of dying of embarrassment. The typical disdain that filled her at the sight of his stupid face paled to how desperately she wanted to shed her skin and melt. She forced a smile. "This didn't go how I planned. I'm going to leave now."

"Are you going to put my troops back in order?"

Etolié shuffled herself toward the door. "Well, I don't actually know where they go."

"Then why did you rearrange them?"

"Because I wasn't thinking."

"Clearly."

"If you'll excuse me, I'm going to go throw myself off the roof—" He didn't move from the doorway, standing firm as she peered past him. "In polite society, that sort of statement precludes you fucking move."

"Sit down. We need to talk."

Too embarrassed to argue, Etolié obeyed, sitting on one of the sturdy chairs along the wall.

Casvir shut the door behind him, his stoic features annoyingly indecipherable. "There was an incident."

Between those words, the lack of Khastra, and her lost pride, Etolié's stomach dropped.

"While pursuing a fleet of airships, the Bringer of War leapt off a cliff and plummeted into the ocean."

Despite the inherent comedy in imagining the gargantuan, transformed half-demon sinking like a rock, Etolié's breath caught in her throat. "I-Is she . . . ?"

"Her body has been recovered." A pause, but right as Etolié's eyes filled with tears, he added, "Though it took time to drain her lungs of water, she is fine—"

"*You could have opened with that!*" Etolié cried, relief and rage filling her in tandem.

"It was not chronological."

Rather than scream in his face, she released a breath as hot as flame, illusioning real fire to punctuate it. "Sensitivity training really isn't one of your strong points, is it."

An understatement, given his history of enslaving foreign monarchs, destroying entire cities in a night and turning their entire populace into undead, and just generally being a dick.

"In conversing with General Khastra," Casvir continued, doing a spectacular job at ignoring Etolié's tantrum, "she has expressed dismay about this occurring again. I wished to ask if you had any suggestions."

Etolié frowned, this whiplash of emotions frankly exhausting. "The Bringer of War is infamously, uh, chaotic," she managed, still processing the fact that Khastra wasn't dead forever. "They always kept a cow on hand during training in Staelash in case she tried to eat anyone. My wings tend to draw her attention, but she's not known for cognitive thought, you know? She's known for violent rampages."

Casvir remained silent for a time, and while it was probably mere seconds, to Etolié it was a small eternity to dwell on the fact that he'd seen her tits and wish she could light herself on fire. "Would you consider accompanying my army?"

It took Etolié a few blinks to return to the present. "I beg your pardon?"

"I will allow you a choice, as this is an unconventional request for an empress. But if your wings are as useful as you claim, it would save me a significant amount of time and headache."

Her mind finally caught up, weighing the idea of spending time with Casvir's undead army versus bickering with Zoldar. "You're asking me to leave my stuffy castle duties, go to the battlefield, and babysit an unruly half-demon?"

"Yes."

"And by that, I mean you're actually asking me to choose between spending more time with my favorite lady or less time with my favorite lady."

"Will you do it or not?"

"Of course I will. When are we leaving?"

"I intend to stay in Nox'Kartha for a few days to settle some affairs, but you will be given notice."

"Just give me time to let Zoldar know his new job duties and pack a few gowns." She stood and smoothed her illusionary dress, hoping it served to better convince him that it was real and she wasn't still currently naked, despite always being naked. "So where is—"

The door opened. Etolié lost her breath.

General Khastra cast a magnificent presence wherever she went, her stature surpassing even Casvir's. Her musculature was enhanced by the stunning silver tattoos covering every bit of her exposed blue skin—and unexposed, Etolié knew—and today her clothing was not armor, nor meant for travel, but cut to suit her massive figure, bearing intricate embroidery and room for her digitigrade knees.

Utterly inhuman in every perfect way, and her horns served to punctuate her godly heritage, a crown worthy of her title: *Daughter of Ku'Shya, Bringer of War.*

Khastra's thousands of years of life had granted her a stoicism to rival statues, but Etolié's heart fluttered at the light flooding those glowing, pupilless eyes. "Imperator Casvir," Khastra said, offering a slight bow. To Etolié, her smile came easily. "Empress Etolié, I was told I could find you here."

Ever professional, and Etolié admired that, sure, but her own excitement radiated, buzzing across her skin. Her hands vibrated, sparking glitter. "Hi."

Casvir looked between the pair, then to Khastra, he sternly said, "Do not copulate on my table."

He left. Khastra frowned at his departure, clear bafflement in her elegant features. "Why would we copulate on the—"

Her words were stolen when Etolié leapt into her arms. Khastra caught her with ease, her large frame hoisting Etolié up as she spun them around and laughed. Despite her undeath, Khastra remained warm; blood pulsed through her veins through an unholy amalgamation of science and magic, and while Etolié would love her if her skin was ice, there was comfort in the illusion of life. Tears prickled in Etolié's eyes, her happiness brimming, overflowing to feel those strong arms, to have her anchor returned.

"I missed you, ya big lug," she said, choking on the final word, and when she met Khastra's gaze, the half-demon's eyes misted.

"I dreamt of you every night and longed for you each day."

"Shut it, you poetic fuck."

Forever unflappable, Khastra's laughter resumed. Etolié managed only a single kiss before her sobs overcame her. "Did you dress up just for me?" she managed amid her tears.

"Of course I did. My armor stank of seawater. I would not subject you to that."

"Cassie told me what you did, dumbass." Tears fell upon Khastra's tunic, surely marring the expensive threads, but the half-demon was richer than most gods and could deal with it. "He wants me to babysit you."

One arm had settled beneath Etolié's bottom, where she straddled Khastra's waist. The other came up to cup Etolié's cheek, the rough callouses on her fingers familiar and

33

soothing. Shock furrowed her brow, but Etolié saw no anger. "You will be coming?"

"If that's all right with you, General." Etolié winked, apprehension rising at the words. What if she objected? It's not like battlefields were a recommended point of operation for empresses.

"It worries me. I will need to make preparations for your safety." Khastra's tension fell away with her sigh, leaving a graceful smile. "But you would be a valuable asset to the war. Though . . . I do not know if machines can respond to illusions."

"They can't, but I'm there for you. Not for combat."

Etolié pressed their lips together anew, this time able to appreciate the sensation without the fear of snot running down her weepy face. Her fingers slid through the short locks of Khastra's hair—once magnificent, nearly down to those amusingly goat-like hooves, but lost in the battle against Soliel.

Hair was a spell, and Khastra *could* hire a hairdressing sorceress to grow back her epic lavender strands, but instead it grew in natural measures—until Soliel's hopefully inevitable death, that was. Such was Khastra's misplaced sense of honor. But after a few days of having to interpret a face with no eyebrows, Etolié had cracked and dragged the half-demon to the aforementioned sorceresses by her metaphorical pointed ear. Initially, Khastra had visited weekly to sustain a 'natural' hair growth, though the war had stagnated that.

Khastra could not grow it on her own in her undead form, but they had happily settled on that compromise.

"Well, since Imperator First and Last has spoken, can we find somewhere else to be alone? We don't even have to fuck if you're tired. I just want you to crush me."

"I am not too tired for you." Such adoration in Khastra's gaze, and Etolié melted beneath it.

"You could always let me pamper you."

"I would accept pampering."

"Then take us to your room, Beefcake."

Khastra did not release her, though she did move Etolié to a less amorous position, cradling her with ease. Silly half-demon—Nox'Kartha and Solvira knew they were in bed together now, but Khastra remained demure in public.

She was hardly a freak in private either, too hung up on 'love' and 'devotion,' but Etolié had learned what buttons to press to get a rise out of her.

Admittedly, though, it was nice to just be cherished sometimes.

Despite what nostalgia might preclude, Etolié had spent little time in Khastra's new private chambers. The half-demon all but kicked open the door, leading to a space far more prison cell than room, but privileges had been taken after Khastra had squished Imperator First and Last like a spider. Because she was the child of a literal Goddess, and because *technically* he had violated the agreement to never harm Etolié, Casvir had foregone enacting any real punishment—this time—but, like an asshole parent, decided she needed to earn back the right to luxury.

Stone walls, a boring though appropriately sized bed, a chair, and a plain chest of drawers made up the entire space, but with a wave of Etolié's hand, it became something new. She cast an illusion of rich fabrics to decorate the walls, a four-poster bed covered in plush comforters and pillows, even a fountain for good measure—of a naked stone Etolié blowing a kiss.

Khastra chuckled at the display, and Etolié's heart soared at the validation. "You are spoiling me," the half-demon said, setting Etolié down when she beckoned.

"The spoiling hasn't even started." Etolié gestured to the now-cozy armchair. "Have a seat, but take off those clothes first."

Again, Khastra laughed at Etolié's words, smoothly slipping her tunic over her head—with absolutely no trouble despite the horns, a fact that forever boggled Etolié's mind. She wore nothing beneath, revealing the beautiful, slight curves of her breasts and that chiseled stomach. In her time away, she had lost a small bit of mass, replaced with definition that Etolié could have mapped for hours, analyzing every curve and line of the biological marvel she had the honor of loving. Those endless tattoos created symmetry, silver runes carved into her skin. When Khastra removed her trousers, Etolié bit her lip at those massive thighs, the plump curve of her ass, and blushed at the small hint of vulva.

"Sit down, you said?" came Khastra's voice, jarring Etolié from her study. "Anything else?"

Etolié shook her head, a large part of her still in disbelief to be in Khastra's presence. This was no dream or fantasy— simply a perfect day.

Khastra sank into the cushion. Elegance lay in her

posture, the proud lift of her jaw, for Khastra had been born into godly blood, born to inherit the largest kingdom in all the known realms. With an idle flick of her fingers, Etolié's own clothing disappeared, excitement pulsing through her as Khastra's gaze studied her up and down. She came around to the back of the chair and draped her arms over Khastra's front, near enough to her breasts to make clear implications. At the touch of their skin, Khastra's silver tattoos illuminated, not unlike the glow of Etolié's wings, magic responding to magic.

Etolié kissed her, the sensation of Khastra's lips sending butterflies through her stomach. She gently trailed her lips to Khastra's pointed ear, then whispered, "Pampering, huh? Any requests?"

How gratifying, to feel Khastra's shiver beneath her. "Anything you want to give, I will be grateful for."

"Careful. You know I like being nasty."

Blood rose to Khastra's cheeks, a soft blush filling them. "Be nasty, then."

"Fuck yes."

With a bit more focus, a second entity sparkled into view—a perfect likeness of Etolié, down to her little pink nips. The only exception was her missing wings; past experience said they obscured the view. Then came a third, identical in appearance. She blew a kiss to Khastra, but the first of the illusions groped her doppelgänger's breasts, evoking a true-to-life moan.

Khastra's breath hitched. Etolié's lips caressed her ear. "You just relax, Beefcake. I'll take care of everything."

The illusionary Etoliés kissed, taking great care to keep their bodies on display as they touched each other. Behind Khastra, Etolié herself placed her mouth upon her demon's neck, one hand falling to caress Khastra's breast. She took the tender nipple between her fingers, savoring the moan from her companion. "They'll join us in a minute. Any requests in the meantime?"

"Um, well." Khastra struggled with words, her awkward laugh not conveying discomfort, just sex brain. "Whatever they want."

"They don't have brains, Beefcake."

"This is nice."

"Stop being coy, you passive fuck. We're being nasty, remember?"

How easy Khastra's smile was when she met Etolié's

gaze, amusement in her enamored features. "Fine, fine—I like it when they fuck."

"Position?"

"Anything with the strap."

Etolié snapped her fingers for show, and one of the figments suddenly wore a large protrusion between her legs—fake, glittery, and pink. She feigned surprise, even bounced it with a laugh, until her companion got on her knees and took it in her mouth.

With the face fucking on full display—Doppelgänger One was showing no mercy—Etolié returned her attention to Khastra's nipple, reaching around to tease the other. It took all her will to not laugh when it glowed, because glowing nips would never not be fucking hilarious. "I admire her gag reflex."

Khastra chuckled, something starry-eyed in her gaze as she met Etolié's once more. "That is what fantasy is for."

Etolié gasped in mock offense. "Was that a challenge? Because I'll fail it."

"I would not fail," Khastra replied, her wink pulsing heat through Etolié's body.

"Just watch the show, temptress."

Khastra obeyed, and her soft sigh at Etolié's touch was worth the world.

The figment getting her face fucked pulled away, staying on her knees as she turned around. Doppelgänger One wasted no time in grabbing Two's hips, resuming her pounding from a different side.

With full intercourse displayed, even Etolié felt warmth well between her legs. She turned up their sounds, pleasuring Khastra's breasts to the chorus of her own impassioned moans—which, yes, was weird, but Khastra liked it, and Etolié liked that Khastra liked it. Plus there was something ridiculously flattering about it, watching yourself get railed by yourself and knowing the woman you loved was getting off on it.

"Do you want to keep watching or do you want them to join?"

Khastra took a moment to respond, her blood clearly far from her head. "Can we not have both?"

"Well, fuck me—you're right." Etolié snapped her fingers; two more appeared. "Well, fuck *you*, as the case is going to be."

The original Etolié doppelgängers continued to fuck, with Etolié herself adding a tiny bit of extra bounce to those tits. The two new ones immediately swarmed to Khastra, one seating herself on the arm of the chair to suck on her nipple, the other kneeling between her legs.

"Spread 'em wide, Beefcake," Etolié commanded, and Khastra obeyed, unveiling her glistening cunt. The Etolié illusion licked a line up her vulva, her submissive gaze a pleasure to witness—even to Etolié.

Look, it wasn't a crime to get off on yourself. At worst, it was technically masturbation.

At Khastra's gasp, Etolié stroked her finger up her love's chest, then removed her touch completely. She sat herself on the opposite arm of the chair as her figment and set her lips around Khastra's nipple, savoring her demon's amorous moans. Khastra's rough hand trembled as she cupped Etolié's cheek, directing her mouth away from her breast and to her lips. They kissed to the chorus of Etolié Two's screams of pleasure and Khastra's building moans.

As they kissed, Etolié massaged Khastra's breast, adoring the touch and unabashedly stealing glances of it glowing beneath her hand. But her split focus fell primarily to Khastra's lips, savoring the affection while the illusions largely maintaining themselves. Khastra chose to believe them, and so they remained.

At Etolié's silent command, the figment with her mouth on Khastra's cunt slipped her fingers inside. Khastra's breath hitched, her ensuing gasp pulling her lips from Etolié's. "Just enjoy it," Etolié cooed, her hand trailing down to touch the tender bud atop Khastra's vulva, as the doppelgänger fucked her harder than Etolié's mortal strength would have allowed.

Khastra unraveled within minutes, Etolié's touch never ceasing. The doppelgängers did slow in their actions, however, and when Khastra stilled, exhaustion filling her eyes, they sparkled out of view—both the ones near and the duo fucking.

Real Etolié crawled into her demon's lap, skin vibrating from the joyous sensation of Khastra's embrace. "I can bring them back, but it's creepy when they stare."

Khastra slumped over her, breathing labored. "They can return later."

"Look at you—you're dying right in front of me." Etolié winked, her jest not funny even one bit. "Go to bed. I've got a song to get that undead brain of yours to fall asleep."

With ease, Khastra lifted Etolié as she stood and brought her to bed. The half-demon laid her down, then crawled in beside her. "Is there anything I can do for you?"

Etolié kissed her cheek, adoring her lingering blush. "I want you to rest. Ask me again once you've woken up."

Typically Khastra would argue against such an unfair distribution of pleasure, but the half-demon's eyes fluttered and shut, her breathing immediately slowing.

Etolié set Khastra's arm over her like a blanket, the security of her embrace the greatest pleasure of all. Around her, the illusion of her fancy room disappeared, revealing the dungeon she was condemned to. But from Etolié's lips trilled a luxurious tune, laced with magic she only barely understood, while Khastra slept in perfect peace.

And that made everything worth it.

In Solvira, the reconstruction of Neolan continued.

Etolié walked through the city streets, the bulk of which had blessedly survived the castle's explosion months ago. The wall and gate had been repaired after Alystra's contribution, though the fields beyond would be ravaged for years to come, the charred earth overgrown with untamed foliage.

The castle was more of the same.

Nothing new had been built. Instead, digging continued in the massive pit that was once the Glass Palace, the black sand fine enough to clog one's lungs without magical intervention. But the excavation continued. Remnants of the library had been dug from the debris, and Etolié saw no need to cover the hole for vanity's sake when priceless knowledge might still be found. Of course the vast majority was gone, but the maldectine crystal had absorbed the blow—and so a few scrolls had been found, a few books here and there. Days would pass without a find, but right as Etolié contemplated scrapping the project, there would come some joyful announcement that another scroll had been dug up from the grave of knowledge.

At midnight, Etolié stood beneath a sea of stars and stared upon the black pit, contemplating its loss and all that had fallen with it.

"Thinking of you, Moonbeam," she whispered to the wind, but she prayed Lara didn't hear it. The girl deserved to be far away from this cursed realm and find peace in the Beyond with her mother and father. Instead, Etolié took a gulp from her flask and dedicated the brew to the late Empress Alauriel Solviraes, the last true empress of Solvira.

Etolié was a piss-poor replacement, but when only one person could stand between an entire kingdom and the 'justice' of a neighboring tyrant actively moving in, you settled for piss. Twenty-four or so years left of her servitude, and all there was to look forward to at the end was the dissolution of Solvira.

At least no one else would die. Etolié still hated herself daily.

Only when the sunrise loomed on the horizon did Etolié return to her new home, a manor built in the city's richest district.

The gates swung open at her approach, the guards offering respectful bows. No matter how many times she had told them to stop, the news never spread, so Etolié had eventually swallowed her frustration and chose to bear it. So different from Staelash—and gods, she missed it. She could not believe she missed it.

White stone made up the magnificent manor, bearing silver emblems and edges. Though it was far from a castle, Etolié thought it much more prudent, if still outlandish. Twice the size of the rebuilt manor in Staelash, which Etolié supposed was at least one '*fuck you*' to Marielle.

Thoughts of the duplicitous Duchess of Staelash made her blood boil.

The doors opened before she could touch them, the constant doting of servants aggravating. She ignored their greetings, instead heading straight for the semi-secret basement—semi-secret because while everyone knew of its presence, absolutely no one was allowed inside.

Except one.

Down in the underground world, Etolié found a fancier recreation of her beloved library in Staelash. No skylight, much to her chagrin, but Zoldar preferred it that way, so at least someone was happy.

"Bug! How goes transcribing those Demoni documents?"

She was met with a series of clicks. In the center of the

room, Zoldar sat with a pen in his spindly fingers, his penmanship shockingly precise for someone who was biologically incapable of speaking Solviran.

"She has shitty handwriting? Well, the Goddess of War probably has better things to do than develop proper penmanship. There's no hurry. Just get it right."

Whatever Zoldar signed, it was sassy.

"Khastra wants this letter on record. I'm just impressed you're polyglot enough to figure this shit out. What does it say, anyway?"

Zoldar gave a few noncommittal clicks.

"Something about the God of Order? I don't like that."

Zoldar set down his quill, rapidly signing at a pace Etolié knew he only maintained when annoyed. *Khastra's mother says the God of Order is across the sea and that she's ready at any time for Khastra to host her so she can bite his head.*

"Bite his head?"

Bite his head.

"Well, that's a visual."

She sat down across from him, the mention of that monster filling her with fresh grief. "Is it bad that I sorta wish Khastra *would* host her mom and let her kick the God of Order's ass?"

What if she loses?

"I suppose it's possible, but . . . I don't know. I feel fucking useless and at least it would be something."

Zoldar's slender insect hand took hers and squeezed. He made a few clicks. *Moonbeam?*

"It was her quest. And I'm doing what I can, but my time is constantly torn between Solvira and Casvir and bureaucratic bullshit—and now the war! Uluron is the safest bet we have for protecting the damn orbs, but is it inevitable for him to find her? I don't know."

Instead of replying, Zoldar perked up like a hound dog with a scent, which meant someone had violated the prime directive of *not* entering Etolié's private domain.

"If you're an assassin, I can and will illusion a dragon."

"Oh, please. They let me in."

She knew that bougie voice. At her shared glance with Zoldar, the Skalmite mimed the universal gesture for throwing up—which was hilarious, given he was incapable.

Viceroy Murishani entered, striding as tall as his pompous aura would allow. His scarlet robes dragged on the floor, the deep cut in the front revealing a substantial amount of his hairless, chiseled chest. His blond hair was perfectly straight today, reaching past his shoulders. "This is so much cleaner than your last library."

"Yes, and I like it eleven times less. Now, bow." She withheld punctuating it with '*bitch*,' but it was implied.

Their mutual hatred had an understandable foundation, in Etolié's opinion. He hated her because she had stolen Solvira's throne from his bastard hands, claiming half the blood of Ilune—literally, given he was a bastard Solviraes, Silver Fire wielding and everything. And she hated him because he was a fucking creep. All was fair.

Murishani's smile could have cast curses on lesser folk, his sweeping bow exaggerated but technically proper. "Greetings, Empress Etolié. I have been sent by Casvir from the battlefield. He requests your aid in distracting the Bringer of War. She is unruly. Apparently this has been discussed."

Etolié's heart soared at the words, and despite the slime the viceroy's mere presence seeped, she could have hugged him. "Lead the way, pretty boy."

His derision oozed, but Etolié suspected he was contractually obligated to not kill her. With a snap of his fingers, a portal split the air. Etolié's stomach lurched, but she swallowed the bile, lest she show any weakness in front of this sleazebag. "Does this lead to the front end of a tank flamethrower?"

"Only in my dreams, Empress Etolié."

"I love it when you're honest." Etolié stepped through the portal.

The first few moments felt like flying without wings, helplessly suspended, dragged through space and time.

She collapsed into a grimy field and puked inside the gory flesh of something that had been dead a long time.

The heavy hoofbeats beside her signified the imperator's presence, but he had recently seen her tits, so who gave a fuck about propriety anymore. She finished vomiting into the ghoul's remains, then rinsed her mouth with booze—which was a horrible flavor combination, yes.

The taste was so nasty, in fact, that she nearly didn't notice the retreating storm.

The Highland Elves had gained their name because of their homes built in and upon cliffs, and Etolié recognized the sensation of thin air, saw the distant drop into what she

EVE OF ENDLESS NIGHT

presumed was the Tortalgan Sea. Sparse vegetation lay scorched and splattered with undead parts, but held an equal amount of scattered gears and metallic scraps.

In the distance, the undead swarmed a metallic monstrosity surrounded by the corpses of its fellows. It expelled fire from some sort of pipe, burning the dead it came in contact with. More rose to consume it, the thing—the tank flamethrower, she assumed—not standing a chance when Etolié's favorite monster appeared just in time to smash it with her fists, then grab it with her oversized claws and *slam* it into the ground.

It exploded in a fiery storm, but the Bringer of War laughed in the face of fire—unlike her smaller, untransformed counterpart, which Etolié was *very much* inclined to remember. The half-demon rushed to another and tore away the flame-spewing pipe, then bashed the machine with its own severed piece.

She held out a clawed hand; her hammer flew into her grasp, making a mockery of the makeshift weapon she'd torn away. Magnificent, her finesse at wielding the gargantuan hammer. The crystal head reflected the sunlight in blinding shades of purple, its sturdy base enhanced by a magic not of this world—for it was a weapon of Sha'Demoni, forged by the Goddess of War herself.

She battered back the massive onslaught of machines, only hindered when one of the lingering airships poured what appeared to be molten metal from high above. The Bringer of War evaded, then ran as fast as her bulky legs would allow, circling back toward the airship as she leapt—

And grabbed its wooden frame, dragging it down with her sheer mass. In the air, she ripped it apart, fearless despite the great height. Etolié watched a few fortunate elves manage to jump from the ship, saved by . . . parachutes, if her memory served her correctly. When the Bringer of War climbed in through the hole she'd torn into the hull, Etolié knew it was only a matter of time.

Despite the inevitable death of its crewmates, something about watching the monster she loved go fucking crazy on a machine really got Etolié's heart fluttering.

Soon enough, smoke poured from the ship, and when it descended, the half-demon burst through the adjacent wall, the earth surely cracking where she landed.

"The threat is subdued," Casvir muttered from atop his

steed, a skeletal horse taller than any living one Etolié had ever seen. "But she will attempt to pursue those final airships."

Etolié gawked at the sight in the distance, like stagnant dragons flying away. Her curious brain longed to know more, but there were greater issues at hand. "Stop her before she can reach them. Can do."

"It would not matter if I thought she could reach them in time. I worry about her launching herself into the sea again."

"Got it."

With her wings spread wide, Etolié shot up into the air, allowing the breeze to catch and carry her. Angel wings were slow, like a dandelion's pace, but Celestial wings bore a bit more substance. Etolié was no bird, but she could swoop and direct herself a little better than her angelic progenitors. "Khastra!" she yelled, but the Bringer of War did not react. "Beefcake, look up!"

Instead, the Bringer of War ran toward the airships.

Damn the Highland Elves and their cliff islands. She soared downward, plummeting toward the half-demon.

She landed squarely on the Bringer of War's shoulders.

Etolié's victory was short lived; she shrieked when the Bringer of War tried to swat her like an errant insect. "It's me, asshole!"

Her demon grasped her more gently—and tossed her away.

Etolié tumbled through the air like a feather, landing just as softly. "Fucking dammit." She sprinted, cursing athletics as a concept, and grabbed the Bringer of War's digitigrade knee before she could launch herself at the ships. "Casvir wants you back, and I want you un-drowned!"

Clawed hands gripped her wings. As Etolié was swung toward the half-demon's face, she resorted straight to drastic measures—and unillusioned her clothing.

At the sight of Celestial tits, the Bringer of War did pause. Etolié grinned, taking her breasts in hand as she dangled in the air. "Oh, you like that, huh?"

Whatever the Bringer of War muttered, her Demoni words still a struggle to decipher, it was certainly not about the war, the cadence just smooth enough to be taken as . . . sultry, in her monstrous way.

Etolié's demon smelled of smoke and fire, but she could not have cared less. The realization that she got to see her favorite beefcake *and* potentially get fucked senseless on the battlefield sparked excitement inside her. "I'm just saying, I'm much shinier than those airships."

In the far distance, Casvir waited atop his horse, and Etolié bid him a silent apology as she grabbed the Bringer of War's horns and brought her breasts to the half-demon's mouth. She trusted Casvir in few things, but knowing he wouldn't be a pervert about her public display of sexy times was one of them.

However, at the first swipe of that long tongue across her breasts, Etolié lost all thoughts or cares about anyone watching. "Fuck, I love that mouth of yours."

Fangs? Irrelevant. Those lips easily engulfed an entire tit.

Etolié gripped her demon's sweeping horns for support, groaning at the blissful sensation coursing through her body, as well as the contentment upon the Bringer of War's features. She caressed Khastra's scalp, adoring the shorter locks of hair, and kissed whatever she could reach, uncaring of the taste of smoke.

The advantage of fighting machines meant there was no blood, which would be a far different concern.

When the Bringer of War took her in her hands, Etolié lay as helpless as a doll. Though barely a third of the half-demon's size, Etolié felt safe in those massive hands. Her demon placed her on a clean patch of grass, tender when her lips grazed Etolié's pale skin.

She neared Etolié's ear, smothering all other sensation; Etolié remained buried beneath mounds of armored muscle, assaulted by the scent of fire, her gaze only for those glowing blue eyes—and then came a whisper that pulsed hot through Etolié's blood. Oh, those Demoni words made her wet between her legs, for amid the foreign words came a few she knew: *"Love Etolié . . . fuck Etolié . . ."*

"Oh, please fuck me." Sunlight blinded Etolié as the Bringer of War kissed down her body once more, grinning as she neared her hips. Her mouth opened; out came her massive tongue. Etolié gasped in anticipation, then cried at the first caress against her wanting cunt. She turned her head to kiss the Bringer of War's fingers, hands numbing as her demon teased her entrance, tasting her, worshipping her—

She pushed inside, and Etolié screamed.

Her mind fell utterly apart, stars blinding her vision as the sensation rose to consume her. She felt nothing save for the pulsing pleasure, tinged with the pain of stretching to be filled with *her*.

At her cry, the Bringer of War chuckled, the only sound Etolié cared for. Though she touched her demon's hair, she barely felt it, gasping when that tongue began fucking in and out.

She tried to find her words, some tease, some jest, but all that came were more inarticulate screams as her demon's tongue stroked deep inside. In and out, and her body steadily adjusted, any discomfort falling far away. Instead, she settled into a lull of pure stimulation, the fire within her blazing hot.

At the moment of orgasm, she swore the world went white, her cries echoing across the battlefield. The Bringer of War did not relent, savoring the time between her legs, and Etolié shook in her hands, protected by her monstrous presence.

Some bit of sanity returned as her spirit fell back down to earth. "I'm done," she managed, but her demon did not stop, instead bringing her thumb to rub Etolié's breast. "Never mind."

Her arousal rose anew, and Etolié lay happily helpless in her demon's hand.

Chapter 3

They arrived at a port in Johim. Even with her nausea soothed by Odessa's spellwork, Sora ran from the dock, fell to the solid earth, and sent a prayer of gratitude to Sol Kareena, feeling it reflected in Leelan. The warm sunset cast blessed light upon her face, and Sora savored it, for it was of her goddess' domain.

Sora wouldn't say Sol Kareena had ever spoken to her, not like she had to Meira. But when Sol Kareena personally came to the realm to return your spirit to your dead body, well, that certainly meant she knew you. But while Sora had often felt that presence in the past . . . not anymore.

Sora's mind fell upon the Theocracy's destruction, the horrors she and Etolié had witnessed. In nightmares, she recalled Etolié's singing, her tears as the Celestial had struggled to control her voice for the children. Still, death had risen around them. Sora had never quite collected her own shattered pieces, of having seen her goddess' city destroyed.

Now, Etolié worked for the man who had wrought it. She had told Sora the tale with tears in her eyes, how she had signed herself to Casvir's services for the noblest cause, to save thousands of Solviran lives—even if many of those lives had been lost anyway, at the hands of the monster Sora now sought to slay.

But how dare he. How dare he enslave the child of the goddess whose kingdom he had stolen, the niece of the kingdom he had toppled. Etolié had wept, but Sora knew it was surely just a droplet of her pain.

Perhaps when this quest to kill Ayla had concluded, Sora would dedicate herself to avenging the fallen Theocracy.

The final hints of sunlight faded, leaving only night. "We are leaving, Sora," came Mereen's taciturn voice, and Sora gathered herself and followed.

The small city held an older style of elven structure, though Sora had not seen anything new in long enough to be a proper judge. Brick homes lined the streets, with her distant cousins, the Whispering Elves, hard at work both inside and out. Night meant nothing to them; they were considered nocturnal by most, though many wondered if they slept at all. Their pale skin rivaled Mereen's, tinted in hues of purple and blue, and the few who noticed them gave cold glares to Sora's warm skin, to Odessa's human body, even to Tazel's obvious Sun Elven glow.

But from Mereen, they averted their eyes. Some even went indoors. It seemed they knew the Dark Slayer.

"We will not need accommodations or supplies," Mereen said as they neared the edge of town. "Once we are out of Johim, we will phase into Sha'Demoni. If you separate from me there, you won't be found, so stay close. The demons will not be happy to have visitors, so don't draw attention to yourself."

Fortunately, the only one of them not attuned with stealth was Odessa, though Sora knew enough of both witches and ghosts to know invisibility was a real possibility. "You each need a partner who can navigate the demonic realm. Tazel, stay by Sora."

Odessa sidled up to Mereen and looped her arm around hers, not unlike how she might to a gentleman. "That leaves you and me."

Mereen's surprise was not quite angry, but she certainly did not look prepared. "Yes, fine."

The man was not nearly so forward, but he did stick near to Sora's side. "You can step into shadows?" Sora asked.

"Not as well as Mereen, but she taught me years ago."

"That's incredible."

"It's something. At least on this continent, it will be safer for us. The demons are alive on this half of Sha'Demoni, which means we aren't susceptible to demonic possession."

Chills rose along Sora's skin at the thought. The farther they walked, the sparser the buildings became, steadily leaving civilization behind.

"But we will face different problems," Tazel continued.

"Anything in particular to know?"

"Instead of possess you, they'll simply kill you outright."

The urge to smoke never fully went away, but Sora's

brain screamed for it. "How charming."

"I have no doubt you'll protect me," he said kindly, but Sora scoffed at the notion.

"I'm a poor replacement for Mereen."

"You're incredibly capable, Sora." Tazel's smile was shy and sweet, bearing reminiscence of her mother's blood. But she could not help but compare it to one she had lost—for her father's countenance had become the sun with even the smallest of smiles.

"Besides," he continued, "Goddess Ku'Shya and her demons hold no grudge against you. They might kill Mereen on sight."

"What?"

"Huddle up!" Odessa suddenly chimed. "Mereen says we're near enough to phase into Sha'Demoni, so let's discuss. The heat of Sha'Demoni is sweltering to us mere mortals, and the air is so thick and wet, we'll be having strokes within a few hours. So we must move quickly. Once we're underground, we won't be in danger from bodily shock—instead, we will be in danger of being eaten by Ku'Shya."

Sora prided herself on wilderness survival. She rarely shied from a challenge, but what Odessa described was suicide. "And if any of us start having convulsions, what plan do we have?"

"Drink water. We all have waterskins."

It wasn't that Odessa was wrong. It was that Odessa had missed the point.

"This is espionage," Odessa continued cheerily, as though this were something to be cheery about, "and while you're all very stealthy, there is only one entrance to *Daemenacht*, and Ku'Shya literally sits on her throne and stares at it for most of her day. Fortunately, you have me. Now, my powers of invisibility are . . . finicky. It's based on self-perception. You have to think so little of yourself that you disappear in everyone's gaze. If you're like me and struggle with overconfidence, consider latching onto some horrible memory. Something to make you feel like shit while we walk beneath Ku'Shya's nose.

"Once we're past the entryway, we must make it to the deeper sectors of her catacombs. Unless she has done some modifications in the last century, my maps should be accurate. You follow me downstairs, and we pray very hard we aren't caught and thrown into her dungeons. One wrong turn, and it's an eternity of torture and flame—assuming you aren't immediately eaten."

For not the first time, Sora wondered if this really were the simplest solution, as Odessa had oft called it.

"Assuming we don't get caught in her dungeons," Odessa continued, "we end up in the vault. All sorts of artifacts there, and I need you to swear to me now that you'll keep your grubby hands to yourselves and not trigger any alarms. Got it?"

No one responded, and Sora suspected it was because none of them were kleptomaniac children.

"I shall accept your silence as a yes," Odessa said. "I anticipate magic but no guards in the deeper reaches of the cave. The staff is down there; I won't pretend to know how it's kept safe because absolutely no one knows that. But I'm going to operate under the assumption that we are able to find and secure it. From there, we send final prayers to our deities and hope we can leave the same way."

Again, this 'simple' solution became increasingly convoluted. Sora braced herself to be berated. "Perhaps I'm missing something, but we could simply ask for it."

Odessa shared a look with Mereen, then burst into laughter. "Sora Fireborn, I like you," Odessa said, "but that's so very stupid."

"Doesn't she also want Ayla dead? We can't forget that Ayla technically killed Khastra."

"Well, between that and Ku'Shya's grudge with Izthuni, I don't doubt she would eat Ayla alive and shit her out again and again for all eternity if given the chance . . ." Odessa looked again to Mereen. "Perhaps it isn't so stupid."

Mereen had done little more than glance at Sora since setting foot on the ship, but now she studied her like a cut of tenderloin at the butcher. "You might be onto something," Mereen said, suspiciously serene. "We should ask. And who better to ask than you?"

Sora bristled at the proposal. "Why me? I'm the most vulnerable of all of us."

"Consequentially, you are the least likely to be labeled as a threat. And don't forget—she has a taste for elves, but her children are half-elves."

Sora merely blinked.

"I want you to plead our case before Ku'Shya," Mereen continued, a frightening sincerity to her smile. "She will likely say no, no matter how dearly she wishes for Ayla's death, because she won't part with the staff to do it—this is simply fact. But you are the former High Priestess of Staelash, and she currently bears no grudge with Sol Kareena. Use your station to negotiate leaving her throne room alive."

"I appreciate your faith in me," Sora replied, finding it difficult to fathom the magnitude of this request. Stand before the demonic Goddess of War? Famed for eating those who displeased her? "But what's the use if you're convinced she'll say no?"

"Because while you speak to her, we will sneak in. A perfect distraction."

Sora's hands trembled behind her back; she preferred the perpetual nausea of the sea to this. But when given the task of facing the Goddess of War instead of embarking on an impossible feat of espionage . . . There was no winning, but it was the safer part. "What if she does say yes, though?"

"Then our quest gets much easier."

Sora considered herself courageous, though she recalled the shadow of the Goddess of War at Khastra's funeral, her size and aura daunting even as a specter. How would it feel to be in her physical presence? "I'll do it. But if I die, please send a message to Etolié."

"Oh, that Celestial you broke into my house with?" Odessa said. "I will take personal charge of that, assuming I live as well."

A fair response.

They resumed their walk into the eerie woods. Sora's periphery created images of dancing shadows and demons amid the darkness, her nerves sparking under her skin. When Sora was tempted to summon holy light for sight, Mereen finally stopped them. "Tazel, take the girl. We go to Sha'Demoni."

Sora had witnessed Ayla Darkleaf phase out of the shadow realm before, so to watch Odessa and Mereen disappear into darkness was far more fascinating than alarming.

"Stay in this realm, Ferseph," Tazel whispered to his little bird, and with a kiss, he released her into the dark woods.

Sora repeated the ritual with Leelan. "Keep Ferseph company."

She did not expect Tazel to reach for her hand—but at the touch, darkness overtook them.

On the night of Sora's murder, Ayla had dragged her into Sha'Demoni. She recalled so little, delirious from shock and blood loss, but the chill had been inescapable, and all the world had become corporeal shadows.

This was not the same.

The dark night disappeared into a world of vibrant colors. High above, the purple sky reflected ambient light with no discernible source, no sun or clouds. Stark vermilion rocks supported them, too vivid to be mistaken for anything resembling home. The oppressive weather felt more sticky than hot, and the gargantuan plants ahead of them promised it would be a moist journey. The very air hung thick, clogging her lungs as she breathed. Yet it was the plants themselves that were the most alien of all, with their juicy, yellow leaves speckled in that same scarlet tone. Sora watched in horror as the plants' roots withdrew from the ground of their own volition, creeping like tentacles to evade Sora's party.

Odessa covered her mouth from alarm. "Are they creatures?"

Mereen shook her head, unbothered by the scene. "Something in between plant and creature—wait!"

Too late—Odessa ran toward a fleeing patch of them and plucked a growth with no hesitation. The roots flailed, then latched onto her arm. Odessa gasped; from her hand came a flash of crackling purple.

The plant ceased its motions, withering as it released her. "Fascinating," Odessa mused, then she tied the desiccated leaves to her belt. "I'm changing the terms of the agreement. I want revenge *and* a sampling of Demoni plants to bring home."

Unquestionable incredulity showed in Mereen's stare. "Yes, fine. After we've killed Ayla, I will bring you here to harvest as many as you'd like."

Odessa gave a delighted clap as she followed along.

Tazel lingered behind. Following his gaze, Sora beheld a vast black ocean consuming the horizon, far closer than the ocean in the mortal realm. "Amazing," he said, "to see where the world begins to die."

The distant beach held monochromatic shades, all color desaturated as it neared. Sora sought an edge, but it was simply a perfect ombré. "I suppose it stands to reason that the most powerful deity in Sha'Demoni would claim the best plot of land."

"Some say it's because of her power that the land maintains its structure," Tazel replied, and when he followed after Mereen and Odessa, she joined him. "Ku'Shya is wicked by our mortal standards, but she is a hero to the demons here. She is the ultimate enforcer of Demoni Law, which some say is the most perfect, though callous, justice system of any realm. Better than even Solvira—no mercy to obstruct justice."

Distaste welled in Sora's mouth. "How is eating her worshippers justice?"

"She doesn't eat her worshippers, unless they're sacrifices. She eats slaves and foreigners."

"That's still barbaric."

Tazel's chuckle held warmth. "Be careful with those words. She is the supreme ruler of this continent."

Sora nodded, supposing he was right. "I will be tactful in our meeting."

"You'll be incredible, I'm certain."

At least someone believed in her.

As they hiked, the jungle-like atmosphere became denser, the air thicker, but the smaller plants scattered wherever they went. Colossal trees remained fixed in place, however, and Sora feared to think those roots could also detangle from the ground. She kept her distance. She saw no animals, no other variety of creature, but Odessa's assessment of the terrain was as predicted; the deeper they hiked, the heavier the heat became, piling upon them.

Sweat poured down Sora's face, her clothes drenched in both perspiration and moist air. Tazel didn't fare much better, his lithe body equally soaked, and even Odessa patted her sweaty face with her handkerchief—as well as her cleavage, her neck, anything exposed. "Gods, this is worse than the swamp," she muttered, breathing notably labored. "It's wet, but not like this."

"We are near," Mereen said, her vampirism keeping her pristine. The rest stumbled along behind her.

Soon enough, half an hour at most, the path dipped into a wide canyon.

Mereen stopped at the crux of the swoop downward. Farther along, the path turned, revealing hints of a structure carved into the canyon walls. "Sora, you will want to go alone from here. Odessa will lead us when she deems the time is right."

Odessa fanned herself with her hand, every part of her

53

drenched. "Sooner than later, I promise. I'm feeling a bit dizzy." Sora forced a confident smile but was stopped by Odessa's pat on the back. "I have faith in you. If you do die, I have remedies for that."

Sora's false smile faded. "No, thank you."

"You'll do fine," came Tazel's voice and, with it, a glimmer of confidence.

The canyon walls rose as Sora stepped along the sloping path. Though exhausted, she managed to keep her pace, generously helping herself to her waterskin. If she lived, she could bathe, and there was no greater reward than that.

The walls were thirty feet across at least, wide enough to build a respectable home inside. With each step, the world beyond faded away, the silence of this place weighing heavily upon her.

Deep carvings appeared in the walls, first of Demoni characters but then of figures: demons, elves, and a few surely of Ku'Shya. Sora slowed to study them, wondering if she might find Khastra among them—there!

The Bringer of War herself had been carved into the wall, her depiction in the red stone a worthy mirror to her likeness. So enamored was Sora with the art that the sudden hollowness beneath her feet startled her. She glanced down, only to stumble back as she realized . . . she stood upon skulls.

A whole path of them, embedded in the ground. Surely it was magic, for they had aged far too much to not have crumbled beneath her feet if their coloring was any indicator.

Alone, Sora fumbled with her pipe and dried mushrooms, igniting the concoction with a match—and at the first inhale of cloying smoke, it cut through her brewing anxiety, letting courage fill the gap.

She turned a corner, and before her was the unmistakable entrance to *Daemenacht*.

A massive cave veered downward, and Sora froze as the first living creatures she had seen approached: two demons, or so she assumed, with spindly legs in contrasting shades of yellow and blue. They did not hold weapons, but their claws were sharp enough for it to not matter. Despite their arachnoid shape and eight legs, their resemblance to anything from the mortal realm ended there; their physiques held more in common with Zoldar than any spiders from home. Their many eyes glowed in shades of blue, not unlike Khastra's, and when one opened its maw, Sora was reminded of The Endless Night.

Guttural Demoni words filled the canyon's walls. Sora did not know their meaning. "I'm here to see Goddess Ku'Shya," she said, the pipe held mere inches from her mouth. "I have a proposal for her."

The demons exchanged quick words, leering as they debated. One finally beckoned.

Sora sent a silent prayer to a goddess far away. *Sol Kareena, protect me. Inspire my tongue.*

Difficult to say if she felt any different. Her blood ran too cold to know. After another puff from her pipe, she covertly dumped its contents on the ground, then followed the Demoni guards into the vast cave, preparing for an unknown abyss.

The underground tunnel was as wide as the canyon, the art in the walls depicting more horrifying scenes—of the Goddess of War consuming tiny figures, wielding various weapons as she faced armies, even shown in battle against a gargantuan figure with countless tentacles and a single eye. Sora had no time to appreciate them, instead keeping alert. As they walked, the heat tapered off. Still warm, yes. The air choked, but Sora's head cleared, allowing her to think.

The guards did not ask for the knife at her belt. They did not inspect her at all, which could mean many things—that Sora was not a clear threat, that the guards were indifferent, that this was standard procedure . . .

Though the most likely option was that Ku'Shya didn't care.

The tunnel ended at an enormous amphitheater, and there, the Great Spider appeared.

Goddess Ku'Shya, a deity of war and pure power, did not sit upon a throne, no, but a pile of bones massive enough to accommodate her gargantuan self. Forty feet tall at least, her four legs were something akin to both knives and tree trunks, slightly curved, and perhaps would be thinner were she small, but instead matched her bulk. Four enormous arms bulged from her exoskeletal torso, nothing human or elf about her. Her head nearly resembled a dragon, yet was not scaled but armored like an exoskeleton, with fangs as long as Sora herself jutting from her mouth. Four yellow eyes blinked in succession, no pupils or soul within them as they narrowed upon her.

Sora stopped in her tracks to absorb the sight, knowing

far fewer had left this place than come.

She nearly didn't notice the smaller entities around the Goddess of War, so shaken she was to face the beast. But more Demoni guards stood around her, some nearing half Ku'Shya's height, though none could be compared to her bulk. Behind Ku'Shya were three pedestals, two of which displayed large crystal weapons: a bow of amethyst—an impossible creation yet gorgeous, nevertheless—and an eerily familiar hammer. The third remained empty.

The outlier was a comparatively small creature, who Sora presumed was also a demon, but less alien. Her torso, though it bore four spindly arms, was unquestionably elven, ending in an arachnoid lower half. With her needle-thin proportions, her age was indeterminable, and her four yellow eyes held a stark resemblance to the goddess beside her.

Khastra had siblings. Perhaps this was one of them.

Harsh, booming words tore Sora from her observations, spoken by the goddess herself. She did not know them, only recognized the guttural accent. Yet the Demoni tongue did not sound so harsh in this foreign world, melding with the ambience. Sora had heard the Bringer of War speak, had felt how the words grated against the natural world.

Here, they were simply words.

The ageless demonic girl came forward, her voice girlish and bright. "You are speaking elven?"

"I speak elven, yes."

"Very good. Goddess Ku'Shya is asking you to introduce yourself."

"My name is Sora Fireborn, former High Priestess of Sol Kareena, and I come with—"

"Sora Fireborn, like *Mereen Fireborn?*"

No sense in lying, given how famed the name was. "Yes. I'm her great-great-great-granddaughter."

To her surprise, the demon girl did not repeat the words to Ku'Shya. The demon goddess simply replied, though in Demoni.

"Goddess Ku'Shya is not liking Fireborns," the girl translated.

Tazel had alluded to that, and Sora internally cursed for forgetting to follow up. Still, she fought to soothe her burning blood at the remark. "I didn't realize you knew my family so well."

"Why are you coming here?"

"I come with a plea for aid and a proposal."

Whatever Ku'Shya said held the stain of mockery, which Sora decided was not a comforting sound. "Goddess Ku'Shya will be listening," the demon girl translated, "but she is not expecting to be impressed."

Sora gritted her teeth, every instinct screaming to grab her knife and run. "I come on behalf of my party. We have a single goal—slay Ayla Darkleaf, The Endless Night, for good."

The mood of the room shifted, for though Goddess Ku'Shya was difficult to read, Sora swore everything in her stance became as stone.

"I do not ask for your assistance," Sora continued, "but there is an item in your possession we require for our plan to be successful: Staff Seraph deDieula."

All amusement left Ku'Shya's words as she spoke, slow and succinct.

The demon girl said, "Goddess Ku'Shya is wishing to know where the rest of your party is."

"They sent me alone—"

Ku'Shya barked harsh words to the guards, who scattered the large tunnels leading away from the amphitheater. And then a few more to the demon girl, who said, "What is your plan?"

"Truthfully, I don't know. I wasn't trusted with the information. But Odessa—"

Again, Ku'Shya interrupted her.

"Goddess Ku'Shya is not giving you anything without knowing."

Had enough time passed for Mereen and the rest to sneak inside? Sora wished she had been given a time frame. "I understand."

"And she is wondering why the rest of your party is being cowards."

The conversation returned to Sora, yet she knew not what to say, realizing how woefully unprepared for this encounter she was. She spoke the truth once more. "Mereen thought I was the person you were least likely to eat."

Horrible heaving erupted from Ku'Shya, her laughter more akin to a donkey's bray than to mortal delight. "Oh, so it is Mereen you are working for," the demon girl said, her own amusement apparent. "We are understanding now. Not the first time she is sacrificing her own to murder Endless Night."

Sora knew so little, and certainly not whatever the

demon girl referred to. Before she could speak, there came bellowing elven from Ku'Shya.

The words were unnatural—clear in their conception though heavily stilted. "You are leaving now. Tell Mereen I am not helping her. I am hating her." The language seemed forced, as though her tongue could not quite form it. Perhaps demon mouths struggled with mortal vernacular the same way mortals struggled with Demoni. "She is hurting my baby. I am never forgiving. You are reminding her."

At the word 'baby,' Ku'Shya brought a large hand to the demon girl and gave a tender stroke to her long braid.

"I will tell her," Sora replied, shaken to realize . . . she might yet live. "Thank you for your time, Goddess Ku'Shya."

Sora backed away, knowing better than to remove the demon from her sight, but damnation came in a scream echoing across the distant tunnels.

Ku'Shya yelled some dreadful thing; demon guards rushed to Sora, their piercing claws gripping her arms. The demon goddess grabbed the crystal hammer with one arm and the large bow with two, and with a speed sickening to behold from the colossal beast, she darted down the hall with a demoralizing battle cry. Sora's ears ached at the noise, but sounds of violence soon joined it. Another cry, and the demons holding Sora dragged her along.

The demon girl followed curiously behind, though kept her distance.

Crystal sconces lit the tunnels, casting them in eerie yellow light. As Sora feared, there were Odessa and Tazel, held by Demoni guards, evidence of necromancy wafting from the dead demons before them. Ku'Shya herself held Mereen in her free hand—crushed her, most likely, for how limply Mereen's neck lay.

Ku'Shya glared at Mereen. "Trickery," she spat. "I am knowing."

Whatever Ku'Shya yelled, it held unparalleled fury, a horrid, deafening rumble. They were dragged deeper into the cave, Ku'Shya in the lead, through winding, giant tunnels, many of which split away. This labyrinth held countless corridors, and Sora feared she'd never see the sun again.

Deeper underground they went, the ground sloping haphazardly. Distant shrieks chilled Sora's blood, becoming louder the farther they walked.

They entered a room of horror unbound.

The smell of burning flesh and hair assaulted Sora, along with screaming. At the far end boiled a pool of what might have been lava. Above it hung multiple cages, most bearing prisoners slowly roasting alive. Devices of torture were laid out in organized rows, many of which Sora knew, while others were entirely alien. Old blood stained the floors, while some spots looked freshly coagulated.

Several paths branched away from this large amphitheater of torture, but with the exception of the prisoners burning above the pit of lava, Sora saw no one else. She was stuffed into a cage along the side wall, with Tazel shoved in beside her. Odessa was thrown into her own. All were dotted with small green crystals—maldectine, to nullify magic.

However, Ku'Shya held onto Mereen. The Goddess of War disappeared down one of the separating paths, leaving her guards behind.

Though bruised from the demons' grips, Sora managed to stand. "What happened?" she asked Tazel, who lay on the ground, clearly pained.

"It was like they were looking for us," he said with a groan.

Odessa spoke from her cage. "They were. The guards said Ku'Shya instructed them to search the caves for intruders. She was suspicious when Sora came that there was a trap—smart. Much smarter than I would prefer."

Sora gazed beyond the cage, upon the many torture devices, envisioning Tazel being stretched along the rack, or Odessa plucked slowly apart by metal shredders. "What about Mereen?"

"I don't know. No one said."

From her boot, Sora withdrew her smallest knife—a letter opener, technically—and cautiously slipped it through the bars. When nothing tried to cut her hand off, Sora poked the tip into the locking mechanism—

Only for it to spark, sending a jolt through her arm. She gasped and dropped the knife, then scrambled back when one of the guards scurried over. Sora narrowly ducked when it shot one of its appendages through like a sword, the tip sharp enough to impale her. It spat something virulent, and Sora instinctively nodded at its warning, only breathing once it withdrew, taking the knife with it.

Damn.

Lightheaded from adrenaline, Sora sat beside the injured Tazel, but Odessa gave a light clap.

"Good effort," the witch said. "I appreciate the thought. Pity about your knife."

"I have another one," Sora muttered, though she struggled to concoct a new plan. She looked to Tazel instead. "Where are you hurt?"

"I-It's nothing. Simply bruising."

But when he coughed, blood flecked onto the cage's floor.

Damn it all. *Sol Kareena, give him strength. Please.*

From the entrance came the demon girl.

Inquisitive, she approached, ignored by the guards. Her many legs moved smoothly beneath her, graceful despite her great height—as tall as Khastra at least. Though she had appeared tiny next to Ku'Shya, she towered above them all. "Are you understanding Solviran?" she whispered in the language. At Sora's nod, she glanced to the guards. "Very good. They are not understanding, but Mother is, so you must be quiet. You are seeking to kill Endless Night, who is slaying Khastra, my sister. I am hating her very much and want to help. You are needing Staff Seraph deDieula?"

Hope filled Sora. "We are. You know where it is?"

"I am sometimes knowing things I should not."

"Who are you?"

"I am Kah'Sheen, youngest of Ku'Shya." Kah'Sheen looked more closely at Sora. "Sora Fireborn, I am thinking you are familiar. Where am I seeing you?"

"I can't say I've had the pleasure of meeting you before. I grew up in Solvira and lived in Staelash until—"

"Oh!" Kah'Sheen perked up, her eerie smile nearly cute despite her pointed teeth. "Yes, yes, in Staelash! I am seeing you before in shadows. I am coming to visit Khastra sometimes, to deliver mail. You are knowing Etolié?"

Though the idea of a half-demon daughter of a goddess delivering mail was too strange for words, Sora instinctively smiled at the endearing mispronunciation of Etolié's name— exactly as Khastra did. "She's my friend."

"Oh!" Delight filled Kah'Sheen's countenance, her hands clapping to match. "She is my sister."

The statement made Sora pause. Had Etolié and Khastra married? Not an outlandish idea, but news to her.

"Friends of Etolié are my friends too," Kah'Sheen

continued before Sora could ask. "Are the rest of you knowing Etolié?"

Odessa raised her hand. "I don't know that we're friends, but she was delightful."

'Delightful' was one way to describe someone who had illusioned setting your home on fire, Sora supposed.

"Yes, yes, very good. Stay quiet. I am investigating. Mother is not hurting you yet, so you have time."

"Thank you," Sora said, uncertain of what to make of this new friend—who was apparently Etolié's sister.

"Sincerely," Odessa added, gracious as ever.

Kah'Sheen left down the same corridor as Ku'Shya.

Hours passed, shown only in the dwindling screams from above the lava pit. Sora felt sicker with each one, but she could do nothing for them. She could only protect what was hers.

She stroked tender lines through Tazel's hair, the gesture softening his pained features. Sora knew enough about bandaging superficial wounds, but his deep bruising required something stronger, and the maldectine glowed ominous and cruel.

She had not felt this muted since before her resurrection. Magic was a habit now, and it hurt to be apart. The longer they waited, the slimmer Tazel's chances of healing were.

"Is he breathing?" Odessa asked from her separate cage.

Sora nodded, unwilling to wake him. At least in dreams, he had some respite.

"If he stops, let me know."

Sora gave no reply.

Hope waned with Tazel's labored breaths, but finally Kah'Sheen returned to the massive room. She yelled Demoni words to the lurking guards, who paused, answered, then skittered away.

The half-demon came near the cage and whispered, "I am risking my station in doing this, and so you must agree to two things. One, I am coming with you to help. My mother's anger is dissolving when I return. I am knowing her temperament. And two, you are returning the staff to me."

"We would gladly accept The Coming Dawn's aid," Odessa said, and the title pinged familiar in Sora's memory— though she could not quite place it.

"I am not happy to be seeing Mereen. But our mission is killing Endless Night—it is that way before, and it is that way now."

"Why, though?" Sora said, unable to stop the words. "I thought you and Mereen were partners."

Kah'Sheen's indifference became false, purposefully neutral. "Long story. No time now. When we are free, you may be asking."

From a hand hidden behind her back, Kah'Sheen produced a ring of keys and unlocked both doors. Sora gently shook Tazel, mindful of his hidden bruises. "Can you stand?" she asked.

Tazel balanced on his elbows and winced, but when Sora offered her hands, he shook his head. "I can do it."

Though clearly pained, he pulled himself up with the cage bars for assistance. When he stumbled out, Kah'Sheen caught him before he fell. After a few breaths, radiant light glowed within his body, bright enough to illuminate his clothing. With each gasp, his breathing steadied, and soon he stood on his own.

Strange, to step beyond the maldectine and feel the sensation of magic return. Leelan was a world away, safe in the forest with Ferseph, but the bird's presence remained in her head.

"Mereen is in a special cage beyond," Kah'Sheen whispered, beckoning them to come. "I need assistance to reach her. You are invisible in entering *Daemenacht*, yes?"

"Correct," Odessa said, "and I will happily cast the spell again. However, for it to be effective, you must think as little of yourself as possible. The spell is not true invisibility, but the ability to not be noticed."

"What went wrong before?" Sora asked.

"Your grandmother, bless her heart. Apparently her ego is too much."

Try as she might, Sora had no rebuttal to that.

"Yes, yes," Kah'Sheen said, her four eyes alert to every motion. "I am agreeing. But we must stop wasting time."

A faint flash of purple shone in Odessa's eyes, then a

translucent bubble expanded around her, enveloping them all before fading. "The spell affects the area around me, but you won't feel yourself step out, so stay near."

Sora brought up the rear, keeping close. To think little of herself . . . to conjure a memory of feeling small . . .

"I have no place for half-breed bastards in this house! Crawl back to your swine of a father!"

Those were the last words Mereen had thrown at her before ripping her from her dead mother's arms.

Sora's breath hitched, but she clenched her fists to stave it off. And though she'd normally shove it down, swallow that pain, it was as Odessa said—to feel small.

Fifteen years later, and the memory could certainly do that.

Sora's heart beat in her throat as she followed behind Odessa, nearing a pair of Demoni guards standing at attention at the entrance of a new amphitheater. Yet they did not stir at their approach. Sora kept near but absorbed these new, horrid confines.

Darker, this space, lit by faint sconces. A longer series of cages lined the walls, most empty, thank the goddess. But a massive pit was the centerpiece, the downward ramp wide enough for Ku'Shya herself to traverse. Sora could not fathom its depth, but she flinched at the faint screams from below.

She looked to Kah'Sheen, who offered no explanation. Instead, they walked along the row of cages, and at the end, one shone illuminate.

A single prisoner lay crumpled within. The white-blonde braid was unmistakably Mereen's. Whatever light shone upon her was unnatural, yet Sora knew what magic it must be—harnessed sunlight.

Filtered enough to not be lethal, but still debilitating to vampires.

Kah'Sheen glanced around, noting the guards back at the entrance. "Is your spell making things silent?" she whispered, hardly a breath. From her cage, Mereen shifted but held no strength to stand.

"No," Odessa replied. "But if I stand near the door, it will encompass her too."

Kah'Sheen's grimace spoke volumes. With her keys, she cautiously unlocked the metal bars, the *click* like gunfire in the quiet space, but nothing stirred.

Kah'Sheen entered the prison, careful as she placed

three of her hands upon Mereen and rolled her over. The vampire covered her eyes but did not fight as Kah'Sheen dragged her out. "Quiet."

Mereen said nothing, merely stood when assistance was offered. Confusion marred her perfect face as she looked Kah'Sheen up and down, but the half-demon put a finger to her lips and beckoned them all to the ramp.

After their first few steps, Odessa whispered, "How deep will we be going?"

"To the bottom."

"Would it be faster for me to levitate us down?"

Sora followed Kah'Sheen's gaze as she studied the pit. The enormity of the ramp meant it would surely take hours. "Yes," the half-demon replied.

"Remain calm, everyone."

Had Sora not been warned, she might've gasped. Her feet rose unbidden from the ground. On instinct, she reached out for stability, settling instead on clutching herself. She shut her eyes, but already her stomach heaved.

A slow descent, but far quicker than walking. The lighting remained constant, sconces situated at every spiraling floor. Foreign beasts locked in cages passed them by, some roaring at their passing, but Kah'Sheen did not react.

"My mother is keeping dangerous and important prisoners farther down," Kah'Sheen said, louder now. "Keeps them far enough away from others so they are not plotting. It is why they are so spread apart. But artifacts are at the bottom, including Staff Seraph deDieula."

"Is the God of Death kept here?" Sora asked, for all of it was fascinating. What sort of prisoners did a demon goddess keep?

Kah'Sheen's many legs suspended oddly, like a spider on its silk. "No. Mother is not foolish enough to keep God of Death near the staff, or near her children. She is somewhere secret, far away."

An alarming statement, and a testament to Ilune's power—that she was so much worse than the rest, even Ku'Shya would not keep her here.

She was, after all, a god.

"In Sha'Demoni?" Sora asked.

Suspicion came with Kah'Sheen's frown. "Why are you wanting to know?"

"Curiosity."

"The more who know, the more who can seek to free her. Very few are knowing—only Sol Kareena and my mother. No one else."

Sora held her tongue, unwilling to risk angering their guide.

Down they went. Soon, Sora saw the bottom.

She was surprised to find it was merely dirt. Her stomach churned from the lingering sensation of falling slowly. Tazel fared little better if his chagrin was any indicator, but the dead and demonic needed no recovery.

Kah'Sheen escorted them to the single tunnel leading away. "We will find no guards here. Magic is guarding this place. Only Ku'Shya's blood can deactivate the wards, so you are fortunate I am helping."

They walked with no hindrance. "What would have happened if we didn't have you?" Sora asked.

"Unless you are deactivating the magic, there are alarms."

Behind Kah'Sheen's back, Odessa pointed to herself with an arrogant grin. "I could have done it," she mouthed, and Sora swallowed the urge to balk at her audacity.

The tunnel held crevices of varying shapes and sizes, some sort of transparent barriers between them and whatever artifacts were held within. They passed armor meant for alien species, weapons Sora had never seen, as well as a few she recognized—swords and maces and such. Some items were incomprehensible—piles of gems, strange metallic objects with spikes and even flesh—while some seemed inconsequential—a significant amount of jewelry, though Sora supposed they could be cursed.

But at the end, their quarry awaited.

She did not have to know Staff Seraph deDieula to feel the dark aura it radiated. A small ramp led to a pedestal, where it stood behind a translucent barrier, shined and smoothed at the stave, but at the top was a De'Sindai skull—with magnificent horns to rival Casvir's, and within the eye sockets there emitted a faint, purple glow.

Odessa hurried ahead, radiating excitement. "Oh, it's magnificent! More beautiful than I imagined!"

Sora despised even standing near it, but she had stopped seeking sanity in Odessa's judgments.

Yet when Odessa took the first step toward the pedestal, she flinched, stumbling back as though struck. "What in—"

"It is warding against undead," Kah'Sheen said, "so God of Death cannot claim it, even if she is coming this far."

Odessa pouted, far more childish than Sora found acceptable, but Kah'Sheen passed the magical barrier with no issue. Mereen stayed back, casting silent judgment upon the witch.

The barrier held a pink sheen, shimmering when Kah'Sheen deftly touched the center. It vanished.

The half-demon lifted the staff from where it floated, gazing fondly upon it before taking it down. "You are now meeting Ko'Khan—my brother."

"Really?" Odessa asked, wonder in the word. "So there is Demoni magic in the staff. Incredible. Of course it would enhance Ilune's power."

Sora stared in horror. "Your dead brother powers the staff?"

"In a manner of speaking, yes. I am never meeting him; he is dead before I am born. But it is why Mother is given stewardship of the staff. She is laying Demoni claim, and no one is questioning that she keeps it safe."

Odessa reached for it, but Kah'Sheen took a step back up the ramp. "You will agree once more, or I am sounding the alarm: you are returning the staff to me when we kill Ayla Darkleaf."

Despite Odessa's pout, Mereen remained stalwart and extended her hand. "I will not break my word. The staff shall be returned to you upon the completion of our quest."

"Which is slaying Ayla Darkleaf," Kah'Sheen added, suspicion in her glowing eyes.

"Which is slaying Ayla Darkleaf."

Kah'Sheen's stance remained wary, extending only a hand past the warded area to accept Mereen's. "This is not forgiveness."

After shaking, Mereen withdrew her hand, not a twitch in her countenance. "I did what I had to."

Kah'Sheen clutched the staff, giving Odessa a wide berth. "I will be keeping it until it is time."

Tension welled between them; Odessa's good humor faded. "With due respect, I will need to practice."

"Then I will be keeping it until it is time to practice, and then you are returning it."

Odessa looked again to Mereen, who said nothing of it. Instead, the vampire sauntered behind Kah'Sheen. "It will be useful to have you along. Like old times."

Ice filled Kah'Sheen gaze, her words bearing shards. "I am only so loyal, Mereen. You are not sacrificing me too."

Sora did not know their history, but blood clearly stained their falling out. As Kah'Sheen had said—she would ask when there was time.

Tazel had said nothing through it all, simply held the same wary stance as the staff passed by him. "How will we get it out?"

"I am taking care of this."

They followed Kah'Sheen out as they'd come, levitating up the massive tunnel. Sora's heart pounded all the while. Given Kah'Sheen's old grudges, Sora suspected the half-demon would not be their advocate if they were caught.

Sol Kareena, please let me see the sun again.

She felt nothing.

Kah'Sheen crept ahead, beckoning when she peeked around each corner. When they reached the tunnels, she whispered, "You must do the invisible spell again. When we are reaching my mother's throne, you wait. You are running when it is clear."

Sora nodded, grateful she held the least responsibility here.

"Mereen, dear, this time just think about how many times you've failed to kill Ayla Darkleaf," Odessa said, cruelty in her wink.

Mereen sneered but followed silently along.

Though visibly wary, the half-demon offered the staff to Odessa. "If you are using it, I kill you. But I cannot be seen holding it."

With delight, Odessa accepted the wicked staff, pursing her lips to suppress her squeal. "Oh, this feels wonderful."

"I am telling you—"

"I won't use it." She did, however, caress the skull, her affection akin to facing a lover.

Moving remained slow and bitter work, and at times, Kah'Sheen ran ahead to spit quick orders to unknown entities around the corners, sometimes frantically pushed their party back, leading them away from whatever threat approached. Sora swore she did not breathe all the while, her brain desperate for smoking as much as survival.

It seemed like hours before the throne room, as Kah'Sheen had called it, came into sight. A unique sort of throne, that pile of bones. It certainly made an impression. But they faced it from a new direction.

Kah'Sheen held up two of her four arms, stopping them. "You are waiting here. When Mother leaves, run."

With no other explanation, she scurried ahead.

They lingered in silence. Sora matched eyes with Tazel, his confusion clear, but then came booming words from beyond.

A conversation ensued, and soon footsteps shook the earth, disappearing to the opposite side.

"This is our cue," Odessa whispered, and all of them bolted ahead.

Tazel and Mereen sprinted with ease, Sora following in matching strides, but Odessa fell behind, weighed down by the staff and her lack of athleticism. Sora slowed; the others did not. "Come on," she whispered, placing her hand to Odessa's back.

"Oh, don't worry about me."

"But I do," Sora replied, though it was strange to admit.

They ran together, and Odessa managed to match Sora's slower pace. Panic gripped her heart, especially at the sight of that mountain of bones, but there were no guards and no Goddess of War.

Whatever Kah'Sheen had done, she deserved a damn medal.

The uphill sprint out of the cave pumped adrenaline through her veins, even as Odessa faltered. Sora pulled her along, determined for them all to live—

Hands grabbed Odessa.

With no thought, Sora withdrew a knife—only to face The Coming Dawn. Kah'Sheen aided in hauling the panting witch, and soon they emerged into an oppressive, humid jungle.

But they were safe.

Tazel and Mereen waited at the top of the canyon, their relief notable. "You had me concerned," Mereen said, though her gaze rested upon the staff. "Excellent work, all of you."

Sora looked to Kah'Sheen and asked, "What did you tell Goddess Ku'Shya?"

Before the half-demon could answer, Odessa sat on the ground, breathing heavily as she clutched the staff. She did not fight when Kah'Sheen took it away, the witch's face flushed and beading with sweat. "My goodness. A few months on a boat and seven hundred years of never leaving your house really knocks the wind out of you." But she laughed, apparently in good spirits.

"I am telling Mother about a malfunction in second dungeon."

"A second dungeon, you say?" Odessa said.

"Yes, yes—second dungeon. You are kept in fifth dungeon. But there is a malfunction in second dungeon because I am making one. Mother will be busy." She offered Odessa a hand, who stared at it pitifully. "Sorry to push, but we must be leaving. We are making a camp in mortal realm."

Odessa accepted the gesture, clinging when Kah'Sheen did not immediately let go. "I could use a good dinner. In fact, I refuse to resume tracking my Flower Child without one."

"I am escorting you to a safe place," Kah'Sheen said, though wariness showed in those four glowing eyes, hesitant as she spared a final glance to the canyon behind.

But Kah'Sheen forged ahead, Odessa in tow, and Sora followed them back into the jungle.

Chapter 9

The world clung to the chill of night when Flowridia awoke in a plush nest of comfort. Demitri's faint breaths from the foot of the bed set her at ease, a beautiful constant in her world. As she sat and stretched, the barest hint of light shone on the horizon.

Sunrise would soon come. Flowridia had much to prepare for.

She dressed, and while Ayla had a stash of gorgeous gowns set aside just for her, today called for something simple, something for work.

She emerged after a kiss to Demitri's sleepy head, who stirred and proclaimed he needed another six hours at least. The balcony across the second floor led to several different rooms—mostly bedrooms, though a few sitting spaces—as well as a grand staircase.

Sunlight illuminated the massive first floor through lacy curtains, and Flowridia parted them one by one. How peaceful, their beautiful home, slowly gaining personal touches as the months passed. Ayla had created serene works of art—done in paints, she insisted, not blood—and a few drawings of Flowridia herself dotted the walls. A bit outlandish, especially the nude tapestry, but they never had visitors, and while Flowridia was shy from the attention, every bit of it was proof of her eccentric wife's love. She could only blush for that.

After opening the windows, she opened the large double doors, letting fresh air permeate the home. She left them ajar as she stepped out, cherishing that first breath of crisp, fresh air.

Birds sang to chime in the morning, and Flowridia savored every sensation—the scene of dew and floral life, the fluttering of birds and bees—and bid good morning to the undead monstrosity making its rounds.

An experiment by her wife, stitched together from multiple corpses, this four-headed nightmare saw the world from literally every angle and made a perfect guard for their beloved home. It did not respond to her tidings but instead mindlessly lumbered along.

In the trees, the chirping birds avoided the impostor among them—an undead raven, a stalwart spy amid the leaves. She passed another macabre creation bearing six arms and legs, a rival to even the most arachnoid of De'Sindai. Ayla had insisted he could fight, but Flowridia remained skeptical, knowing how fragile these monsters could be. She'd attached its excess limbs herself, her magic instrumental in all their unnatural creations.

She could not say it was her first choice in date-night activities, but watching Ayla's enthusiasm was its own reward. Ayla regularly shadowed her while she gardened, so all was fair.

They just as often spent time apart as together, content both in each other's company and alone. Marital bliss was everything she had hoped and so much more, yet . . .

Unfinished business plagued her. But no need to mar her morning dwelling on wicked contracts, even if the shadow haunted her each and every day.

She passed a few more undead creations, all instructed to stay away from her garden, lest their mindless bodies damage the gentle growths. She entered her floral sanctum, euphoria filling her at the sweet scents around her. In Staelash, her garden had been a small, sacred sanctuary, a place for her to feel safe after a turbulent three-year storm of abuse and fear. This one was larger, though not so large as the one she had tended in Solvira, but it was no less a place of peace.

As she passed a patch of hybrid plants, a recreation of the gift she had grown for Ayla long ago—moonlilies and gardenias—distant thoughts of her old life in Staelash passed through her head.

Strange, to call it her 'old life.' Thalmus had said he tended to her garden there, kept it safe for her return—a return that had never come.

Thalmus had loved her until the very end. Forgetting would be easier, but forgetting disregarded the purest love she had experienced in all her days. A father in all but name, and she had never deserved him. Forgetting would be easier, for she still cried on quiet nights. Gods, to feel his life extinguish in her arms remained a nightmare. A thousand times, Ayla had held her and soothed her boundless guilt.

Flowridia stepped beyond the trees just as light flickered above the horizon, blessed and blinding. She whispered, "Good morning, Kedira."

Perhaps his death was cruel, perhaps a mercy. But Flowridia refused to let him go, and any morning she could, she named the sun for the daughter Thalmus had loved and lost.

Today was not meant for the garden, however. Today, she was promised to town, but not until she greeted her love.

At the back of the manor, aged cellar doors led downward. How beautiful, the grounds of the manor, her garden an exquisite point of pride, but in the underground, Flowridia entered an entirely new and macabre world.

The pungent scent of blood struck her as she descended the stairs. Boundaries had been placed regarding *who* Ayla brought into her little realm—no children, no mothers or fathers unless they deserved it, preferably criminals with proven crimes—but it twisted Flowridia's stomach nevertheless whenever she found living victims awaiting their mistress' attention. The stairs ended in an expansive stone room, meticulously organized to keep Ayla's books and papers far from any potential bloodstains. A makeshift wooden wall stood between Flowridia and the shelves of notes and diagrams, blockading her from the horror beyond. No screaming today, but it did not mean her love was alone.

Flowridia stepped past tables and shelves, the vile scent assaulting her. Here lay Ayla's workshop of horrors, less magnificent than her cathedral beneath the Nox'Karthan Palace, but the laboratory had been essentially recreated, with cages stained in blood—one containing a whimpering person, who Flowridia kept her gaze far away from—and a surgical table, cleaned and sanitized. Macabre diagrams covered the walls, detailing the inner workings of various races—elves, humans, and more. Hooks hung from the ceiling, chunks of dried flesh caught on their sharp tips, and far too near it was a wooden table covered in strips of leather, some bearing chalk markings.

Ayla herself sat at a desk, a quill in hand, the sudden sparkle in her eyes at complete odds to the gruesome scene.

72

But Ayla was many things, and inexplicable had always been the top of the list. She set aside her work and practically danced into Flowridia's arms, her contented hum that of a woman in love. "Good morning, darling."

Flowridia kissed her, never fully at ease in the horror-filled space but not at risk of panic either. It was the smell she would never be used to—death and chemicals were a vile mix. "I'm heading off to Wood's End. Do you need anything before I go?"

"Oh, is that today? Damn." Ayla pouted, then glanced back to her workspace. "No, no. Go have fun. This will give me time to finish up with that one."

Flowridia looked to the person in the cage, not daring to humanize it any further than that. "Can I be of assistance? I can put them to sleep if you'd like."

Ayla shook her head; humane was not a concept she understood. "No need. But if you have time to look at something, I always appreciate your wisdom."

With their fingers intertwined, Ayla led Flowridia to her desk, revealing more of the grotesque basement—specifically her small collection of flesh dress forms, each in one of two sizes, most with half-completed dresses pinned to their persons. But Ayla drew her attention to the piles of books and scrolls on her desk, as well as her notes. "Did you know a Solviraes once turned himself into a lich?"

"Their progenitor also did, so I'm not surprised."

"Well, he did not last long," Ayla continued, offering an open book. Flowridia saw circled passages in the text, marked by Ayla's own exquisite penmanship. "He created a phylactery of gold, placed his heart inside it, and displayed it in the throne room of the Glass Palace. Vain, that one. Kept the box open so visitors could see it and tremble, apparently. Needless to say, his daughter stabbed it and then him so she could become empress."

Flowridia scoffed as she handed back the book. "I can't say he didn't deserve it."

"Agreed. What an idiot." Ayla returned her attention to her notes. "But disregarding notable exceptions, most necromancers who cross the barrier into lichdom have a bit more common sense than that. A few thousand years ago, there was a lich who kept her heart behind a tunnel of ice in the far north—she might still be alive, had the tunnel not collapsed and crushed it. Another enchanted hers to be invisible and kept it on her person at all times, but she was burned at the stake during the witch hunts, phylactery and all. I think my personal favorite is the one who put it in a box in his attic and never told a soul, let it collect dust. We only know because he wrote that information down before he stabbed it himself, apparently bored with immortality."

"Ghastly," Flowridia replied, the idea disconcerting. "Forgive me, but it's strange to think someone would kill themself after going through such lengths to live forever."

"Flowra, you're twenty. Typically I would never lord my age over you, but at one thousand seven hundred and thirty-eight, I'm well over twice the age of the average elf and can see how boredom would drive someone mad."

The thought prickled uncomfortably. Flowridia placed her hand on her wife's waist. "Are you bored?"

The moment of hesitation wrote chapters of unspoken dialogue. "A little, but you shall keep me here a few more years before I'm restless." Ayla smiled, and there was nothing predatory in it at all. Instead, genuine delight. "Besides, I have something precious to live for. I would tell you well before I came to a suicidal state."

Flowridia kissed her, lingering this time. When she pulled away, Ayla's striking gaze became her whole world, and she questioned the use of going to town when all she wanted was here. "You'll never get bored of me, right?"

"Darling, it took me how many hundreds of years to find someone to love? Do you really think I would lose you over something so petty as boredom? I know intellectually that the desperate longing of new love fades with time. Perhaps we have already come to that, given our separate hobbies. But poets would not pen epics of lifelong loves if it were so shallow, so easily lost. I intend to love you for all eternity if you'll let me."

And then, though Flowridia swooned for her beautiful words, Ayla's expression fell. "Besides, it is much easier for mortals to be bored. You're the one with the constant need for growth and purpose. It is in your nature, as a human, and especially as young as you are—"

Her words vanished when Flowridia placed a finger to her lip. "I am growing," Flowridia said, willing her love's thoughts to settle, "and more importantly, *we're* growing—together." She cupped her wife's face in her hand, her cool skin familiar and treasured. "How can I help you be less bored?"

"You cannot," Ayla replied firmly, a certain resignation in her tone, "because I am only willing to entertain a certain level of excitement until we've secured your immortality."

Guilt filled Flowridia, though it was misplaced—Ayla had forgiven her broken promise, her tearful plea to remain mortal a while longer, and had never held it against her. But Flowridia held resentment toward herself, that she'd allowed the time leading up to their wedding to be filled with fear instead of joy. "I suppose that's fair," Flowridia said, because she knew even allowing her the freedom to go alone through the forest and into town caused Ayla dread—but with Demitri at her side, she had accepted there was little danger. Even without him, Flowridia was a formidable foe. "Perhaps you could find entertainment without me."

"Is that not what I'm doing?"

"Yes, but we just established that you need something more. What of Izthuni? Perhaps he has something for you."

Ayla's grimace said enough. "He has attempted to communicate with me a time or two, but I know I won't like what he has to say. I have no interest in drawing attention to myself, and he and I are not exactly subtle together. Perhaps once we have no need to hide, I might play at being The Endless Night again, but in the meantime, I would rather keep a quiet life with my wife, bored or not.

"Besides," Ayla continued, "I *do* have a quest, and that is to study lichdom and figure out where in this godforsaken realm Casvir hides his phylactery. Best we live a boring life for a time."

Yet another source of guilt, but at least the final goals didn't conflict. Ayla had always wanted to slay Casvir, and now she had a reason. They had a few years yet before he would come to collect his debt. "I'll leave you to that," Flowridia said. "But I'd love your company tonight."

"In what capacity?" Ayla winked to punctuate it, and Flowridia couldn't help but grin.

"You know I love your games."

They parted, but Flowridia's touch lingered, their hands still held. "I love you, wife."

"And I love you," Ayla replied, looking far more like an enamored youth than the fearsome monster of legend.

Flowridia heard screams on her way out, reminding her of the real and far more damning truth.

She stopped at the top of the cellar doors, the magnitude of their task as heavy as slogging through a bog. Kill Casvir, her once-dear friend—a father and mentor too.

But he was too selfish to feel real love. Perhaps Flowridia was too, but it did not make the betrayal of his character hurt any less.

Yet Ayla did not hate her for what she had done, for what she had signed away in order to save the soul of a woman Ayla would sooner see burn than feel peace. Her firstborn child for an empress' soul . . . Alauriel Solviraes—yet known so much better as Lara—deserved peace, and though Flowridia had made peace with selfishness, there were loyalties that transcended monstrosity. Lara, who had given her life to save Flowridia from Soliel. Lara, who had been ripped from the afterlife to serve as an undead slave to Casvir yet had risked it all to save Flowridia once again. Lara, who was a friend and nothing more, but whose soul had been freed for that unbearable price . . .

Flowridia's hand fell upon her empty womb and prayed it remained so, cold to think of the cost.

The walk to Wood's End was little more than an hour. Flowridia had quickly fallen back in love with the small mountain town—who had embraced her as well, to her surprise. Though over a year prior, her visit with Casvir had not been forgotten.

Especially by the family who owned the inn.

Flowridia carried a satchel filled with clinking vials over her shoulder. As she neared, a familiar voice cried out her name, and then came the pitter-pattering of small footsteps as four-year-old Leddie ran down the path. Once upon a time, Flowridia had saved her life from a parasite, and though the De'Sindai girl didn't remember, she had been charmed by Flowridia's company. "Lady Flowridia!" she yelled, waking the entire town, and Flowridia knelt to catch her and swing her around.

Demitri, too, greeted the girl, indulging her need to pat his head. Leddie had a familiar shadow—Atia, no longer a gangly adolescent but nearly fully grown. Her skin held a red hue, clear hints of her De'Sindai heritage, though subtle hints of elven blood showed in her lithe physique and pointed ears. "Lady Flowridia, I hoped you'd come today!"

When offered, Flowridia accepted her embrace, split between the child on her hip and the young woman by her side. "I wouldn't miss my weekly visit. Tell me everything that's new."

As Atia spoke of youthful things and gossip—of the miller who had fallen mysteriously pregnant despite her husband being out of town, of the boy who visited the inn daily to find some excuse to talk to her—Flowridia cherished the child in her arms, adoring the attention. Leddie held the same features as her sister, though in miniature form. Children were invigorating, a warm change from her quiet life, and while she and Ayla were at peace with keeping their family small, it did not mean she couldn't treasure the children she was blessed to know.

As they went together into the town proper, Flowridia was greeted by a plethora of people, offering waves and the occasional greeting.

"Lady Flowridia," one middle-aged woman said, "if you can offer any remedies for a fever, my son has been in bed for two days."

Flowridia set Leddie down, first handing the girl a large jar of healing balm. "Deliver this to your mother, would you?"

Leddie ran off, overjoyed to have a quest.

From her satchel, Flowridia withdrew a vial filled with opaque yellow liquid. "This is ginger root, with a little extra magic. It should help."

The older woman thanked her, and when Flowridia rejected payment, she offered bread instead—which was graciously accepted.

A strange arrangement, Flowridia and Wood's End. Flowridia had become something of a friendly witch in the woods, offering aid to the town. In return, they offered goods, as well as a blind eye to any missing criminals. Ayla had come to town exactly one time and said absolutely nothing at all. Instead, she had loomed silently behind as Flowridia greeted the townsfolk, the quiet threat conveyed—that if anyone breathed a word of their presence to the imperator, the consequences need not be spoken aloud. They knew who Ayla was, and they knew who Ayla was to Flowridia, more importantly. All had gone smoothly thus far. If anyone rejected them, they wisely kept it to themselves.

All was well, until Leddie returned, hand in hand with her mother. "Lady Flowridia, it's a delight to see you," the woman said, yet something furrowed her brow.

"Is everything all right?"

The woman's hesitation stirred worry in Flowridia's gut. She withdrew a letter from her apron. "Two days ago, a man came asking for you."

Flowridia didn't recognize the wax seal, but there in precise penmanship was the name *Darkleaf.*

"I told him you were a difficult woman to find but offered to deliver the letter. He agreed, though he alluded he would come check that the deed was done."

"Did he say who he was?"

"No, but he certainly wasn't from around here. He was elven, and we don't get many elves in this part of Nox'Kartha."

Flowridia gave a quick *"Thank you,"* then stepped away to study it. It took no energy at all to ascertain that there was no magic in the letter—not a trick, merely paper. She ripped the seal, hands shaking, and suddenly lost feeling.

Ayla Darkleaf,

This was not a mistake. But it was not for her. Ignoring the sudden sinking in her stomach, she read on. It bore elven script, but she managed to plod through and understand.

> *Congratulations on your recent nuptials. The news came as both a surprise and a convenience. You are a difficult person to find, but your wife is not, assuming this letter reaches its intended target.*
>
> *The following is an offer we of the Four Kingdoms hope you will consider: join us in the war effort against Nox'Kartha. Your knowledge of their political machinations would be invaluable, and rumors have spread of your grudge against their imperator. In exchange for his head, we would offer a great many things.*
>
> *Should you wish to negotiate an offer, we ask that you attend a political summit on a date convenient for you in the great city of Velen'Kye. Each summit is held on the final day of the month.*

Accommodations shall be put in place for you, your wife, and her familiar.
We anxiously await your arrival.

Regards,
Executor Luc Stormforged
Executor Vale Yewblade
Executor Euron Faeborn
Executor Bree Desertblessed

Each signature was unique and flawless.

"Forgive me," Flowridia managed, breathless as she spoke, "but I must return home. I-I'm terribly sorry."

With Demitri in tow, Flowridia stumbled down the cellar stairs, too numb to care about the shrieking down below. "Ayla!" she called, then she peered past the makeshift wall.

The chained hooks on the ceiling were in their proper use, with a wailing, half-flayed man dangling above the ground, the hooks securely embedded in his underarms—Ayla had once given a rant on what flesh was useless and what wasn't, and thus the ideal places to hook a potential victim. Blood splattered Ayla's entire figure, coating her monstrous visage in sickly shades of red. She stood upon a stool, a knife in hand, surveying Flowridia with colorless eyes. Black consumed the ring of silver and blue, and fangs marred her perfect, small lips. "You're home early."

Stubbornly compartmentalizing the screams, Flowridia ignored the ghastly scene and thrust the letter forward. "An elven man came into town asking for me. He dropped off this letter."

Ayla took it, giving no mind to her bloodstained hands. She studied it intently, saying nothing at all.

But then . . . she grinned. "Oh, this is wonderful."

"It smells like a trap."

Ayla handed it back. Flowridia carefully touched only where there wasn't blood, unwilling to stain her fingers. "I doubt it," Ayla said. "The only part that reads as strange to me

79

is that they knew about you. This all makes perfect sense; I'm only surprised they waited this long—" She shut her mouth, suddenly thoughtful. "Except, they didn't. They had to find me through you, which implies they tried to find me and failed, because of course they did."

"Do you want to do this?"

Ayla returned her attention to the half-flayed man, indifferent to his whimpering. "My instinctive answer is yes. But I will have to think on it."

On her stool, Ayla resumed her torturous work, cutting a line with perfect precision, then slowly slitting down, ignoring the man's shrieks.

"What would it entail?" Flowridia yelled, for the man's cries filled the entire chamber.

"I might be asked to go literally retrieve Casvir's head, but I would turn them down. You and I both know the impossibility of that plan. It isn't so simple." Having shaved another strip of flesh, as wide as Flowridia's hand, she stepped down to carefully lay it on the nearby table, where it joined the other bloody pieces of skin. The man wept, but Ayla appeared pensive. "I don't quite know what the day-to-day would entail, but they mean no harm to me. They sincerely want my aid."

Flowridia stood frozen as she watched Ayla work, a certain wistfulness to her wife's smile. She stepped back to avoid a sudden spray of blood, and caressed Demitri to ground her unease. "You should go," she said softly, but Ayla's keen ears heard her despite the screaming.

Ayla paused in her slicing. "Should I?"

"You said yourself that you're bored, and this could be a wonderful opportunity for you. If you're confident this isn't a trap, then this only helps our goals."

Though she'd only cut halfway down the man's back, Ayla stepped down from her stool, knife in hand, the flap of flesh hanging open. "Elven aid could be invaluable. Even if I can't give them Casvir's head, we can always find a way to trap him until we think of something better. Perhaps we can torture the location of his phylactery out of him. But what about you?"

"What about me?"

"I don't know how long I would be gone. Would you be all right alone? I don't know that I would have any fun at all without you. I would simply worry."

80

"The letter invited me too." Flowridia tapped the evidence, confident enough in her elven to believe she hadn't misinterpreted. "I'm coming with you."

Despite the fangs and the blood, and even her enlarged pupils, panic flashed across her wife's features. It faded into a grin—which, if it weren't for the fangs, Flowridia suspected would be unquestionably nervous. "Oh, no. No. You would hate it."

Flowridia let the letter flutter to the ground as she crossed her arms. "Would I?"

"You would be miserable."

Ayla's expression was one Flowridia hadn't seen since Solvira, when she still held her habit of lying. "I don't know if that's your decision to make for me."

"Don't you trust me, darling? I think I know what you love and don't love at this point."

"Whether or not I would love it, someone has to save you when it all goes wrong."

At that, Ayla frowned. "All right. If it's all the same to you, I will take Demitri. He would be a feather in my cap and a believable companion for someone like me. Would that appease you?"

Given that Ayla was desperate enough to take away Flowridia's only protection, this bespoke a plot. Memories surfaced of their time in Solvira and, with them, a deep frown. "If Demitri is a feather in your cap, what am I?"

"You're my wife—"

"Actually, per your anecdotes, I'm your cow. Isn't that what you said once? That an elf and a human together is like a man and his cow?"

With some stiffness, Ayla placed the knife onto the bloody table, a curt smile on her face. "I know what you are thinking, and it's not quite the truth."

"So I'm not *quite* your cow—"

"You are being unfair, and you know it." Behind Ayla's gore-splattered face, Flowridia saw hurt. "I am not ashamed of you. I love you, sincerely and truly, and I would not have married you if I thought you were lesser because of your parentage. But across the sea, you won't be given that same luxury. You will be looked upon as a servant at best, never as my equal. Yes, I shall be mocked, potentially to my face if these executors are brash enough to call upon The Endless Night for help. And yes, I care very much, because my pride and reputation are unfortunately of high importance. It's a weakness, I know. But you . . ." Ayla looked to the ground in a rare moment of vulnerability, visibly struggling for words. "You have seen the treatment of half-bree—*elves*. You are a step above, but that's not particularly high. We could claim you are a Celestial and salvage something of my reputation, but it would not do much for you. You are as beautiful as a sunrise, but you still look human."

Ayla's sober tone held only sincerity, yet Flowridia's pride still bristled. "It's probably irrational that I feel so offended."

"I don't think you can fathom it. They won't care that you are a witch; they will care about something far pettier. I am worried you will only be hurt."

Flowridia nodded, scorned but swallowing it down. "I understand." Subdued, she turned on her heel to leave.

"Flowra—"

"You should finish your project," Flowridia said, unwilling to cry in front of her wife—not for this. It would only make Ayla feel guilty.

As she traversed the stairs, the screaming resumed. Behind her, Demitri's voice spoke in her head. *What are you thinking?*

She waited until they stepped into the sunshine. Fresh air invigorated her, stealing the memory of stagnant blood and gore. "I'm thinking I should process this away from her because my real feelings are irrational and will only make her . . . sad." She spat the final word, still angry despite herself. "It's stupid. I'm being stupid. But claiming I'm a Celestial to salvage her apparent reputation? How am I supposed to react to that?"

Poorly, because that's a rude thing to do.

"Thank you." Soothed by the sun and the afternoon air, Flowridia went to her garden, ignoring the patrolling undead around their manor home.

Summer neared, so all was in bloom, a vibrant rainbow of colors enclosing her and Demitri, welcoming her return. Spots of blight existed within it, sentinels set to keep a watchful eye. Another undead bird spied from the branches of a tree, unseeing yet seeing all—ready to fly and report if anything breached what she hoped were impenetrable wards. But if she had learned anything in the presence of demi-deities and their ilk, it was that nothing was unstoppable.

In the shade, Flowridia sat on the grass. "She should go. She's bored. And it wouldn't be forever. Not even close."

There's a huge 'but' at the end of this, isn't there.

"*But* it isn't fair." Flowridia laid upon the ground, her hair splayed against the thick grass, cushioning her head. "We finally have this moment of peace. It's been a blissful year for me. But how can I keep her trapped here if I know she's unhappy? She wants purpose, and there's nothing wrong with that. But I don't think she knows what 'purpose' means anymore—yet here come her people, offering it on a silver platter. It will only help our goals. She should go." She stared at the sky through the thick covering of trees. "I love her so much. I just wish we could find a life that made us both equally happy. She isn't meant for quiet moments of peace; she talks about me needing a purpose, but she's projecting. That could've been this opportunity, but it's difficult to stomach the idea that her own people would mock her because of me."

It's extremely rude of them.

"It really is. I'm delightful company." Demitri's shadow covered her as the massive wolf settled at her side. "And I'm angry that she'd lie about it."

You should clarify that. She won't feel less guilty, but she'll feel the correct type of guilty.

Flowridia sighed, knowing he was right.

Flowridia napped in the shade, and when she awoke, the sun was near setting.

She returned to the manor with Demitri close behind, surprised to find dinner on the table, cold but still edible.

And a single white tulip in a vase—asking forgiveness.

Once she'd sat and eaten a bite, Ayla emerged from the shadows, looking contrite. "I have decided to tell them no. I shall stay here in the mountains."

Flowridia swallowed and set down her cutlery. "Ayla, no. You should go. Even aside from it being what you want, it may help our mission to kill Casvir."

"Then you will come with me. I'm not ashamed of you, Flowra." Ayla sat across from her, her eyes reflecting the dim light. "But there are so many unknown factors. I'm afraid."

"They specifically said they would have accommodations for me and Demitri both."

"And that isn't strange to you? It's not common knowledge that you and me are wed."

Flowridia had nothing to say to that. Instead, she stared at dinner, contemplative as she took another bite.

"If my research has taught me nothing else," Ayla said, "it's that Casvir's phylactery could be anywhere from the center of the earth to a pocket behind his codpiece. I have no leads, no place to even begin searching. The shadows have said nothing, for they know nothing." Sorrow settled upon Ayla's countenance, and Flowridia took her hand, desperate to console her. "Darling, we may have decades before he comes to collect his debt, and that is what I tell myself when anxiety tries to consume me. But it may take me just as long to scour the realms, and even then, I worry. I have made no progress. That terrifies me."

It was a terrible truth, what precious thing Flowridia had sold. She had done the righteous thing . . . but she feared it had not been the right thing. The guilt lingered in the dark corners of her mind, and moments like this shed a vibrant light on it. "I'm sorry."

"Hush. We have been over this."

"I know, but—"

"There is no 'but,' and it will make me sick to dwell on it."

Flowridia nodded, returning her attention to dinner.

"The last day of the month is in only three days' time. If you are going to come, you should pack. Not clothing—you will need an entirely new wardrobe. Their fashion is different, and you will want to stand out as little as possible. We can return, but it won't be on a whim."

"Won't we journey through Sha'Demoni?"

"Yes, but just as there is a sea here, there is a sea to cross there. It is not a simple thing. There is a ferryman to pay, and a god to appease."

The words were hardly soothing. "How much money do we need?"

"Not money. The ferryman is a herald of Onias. We need sentiment. Something unique. Something his limitless mind has never beheld. I was thinking one of your warded flowers. Would you be willing to sacrifice one to the cause?"

Flowridia nodded, uneasy at the thought. "I'll pick the prettiest one."

"That will work for you. Bring one of your hybrid flowers as well, won't you? The one you made of moonlilies should pay for Demitri."

"And what will you bring?"

Ayla thought a moment, still holding Flowridia's hand. "I shall embroider him a gift."

"Has he never seen embroidery?"

"Of course he has, but I doubt he has seen embroidery of his all-seeing eye sewn into human leather."

Flowridia couldn't argue with that, the notion as charming as it was horrifying. "I'll warn you that I'm terrified."

"It won't need to be, so long as we are prepared." Ayla released her, then came around to embrace her from behind. "I need you to trust me. I need you to jump if I say jump and run if I say run. I know these people; I know their politics and their minds. Elven culture is very different from Solviran. Elves live long lives and have evolved a powerful ambition to match. Their leaders are not *good*, but they are efficient and useful to have as allies."

Flowridia recalled that these were the same people who turned a blind eye to Ayla's slow genocide of their Sun Elven neighbors. "I trust you. All will be well, Ayla."

"And I don't mean to suggest that you will have a miserable time. I think it will be far different than you can imagine. If nothing else . . ." Ayla planted a kiss on her head. "You will appreciate their vegetarian palates."

Flowridia smiled.

Ayla's grip remained tight, her posture slumping, protective and vulnerable both. "I am sorry, Flowra," she whispered, and Flowridia's heart hurt for her, as it always did. "I did not think. I . . ."

Her words trailed away at Flowridia's touch on her hand. "I forgive you. Please don't feel guilty."

Another kiss fell upon Flowridia's hair, her love's head then resting upon her shoulder. "Did you still want to be intimate tonight?"

Flowridia stilled at the question, but not for herself. "I would be happy to, but are *you* sure? We can wait if you're still feeling tender."

Ayla remained quiet, having been admonished more than once for giving thoughtless replies in moments like this.

It was rewarding and beautiful, watching her love slowly build a foundation of self-worth. She had not changed, no. She was still Ayla—still prideful and vain, still fragile. Self-destruction had defined her for almost two millennia, and if Flowridia could do only one thing for her . . . She would help her see her worth.

"Yes," Ayla finally said, warmth in the word, "I am sure. But I don't have the fortitude to put on a show. Simple is good, tonight."

Flowridia stood, Ayla's hands drifting from her body, and stole her wife into an impassioned kiss. "Let me lead," she whispered, their lips grazing gently together.

Ayla's smile was so tender, so mild, so starkly different from the monster in the basement who would skin a man alive. But Flowridia savored the precious moments where the monster was hers, and as she led Ayla to their bedroom upstairs, Ayla became a vulnerable shell for Flowridia to fill with affection.

Flowridia paused in the doorway, leaning down to kiss her. No hesitation in Ayla's stance or kiss, but soft revelry. Flowridia swept her inside, content to lead, hands already fumbling with the ties on the back of her dress. It slipped down with ease, revealing Ayla's body, her subtle curves and sharp lines, her slight, perfect breasts. She was hairless from the neck down, as all elves were, her smooth skin a joy to touch, and she laughed as Flowridia removed her own outerwear, though not nearly so gracefully.

How golden, her laughter. A small manifestation of joy.

Naked and free, they kissed anew, the sensation of bare skin welling warmth between Flowridia's legs. With wandering hands, they explored familiar territory, Ayla's body a comfort, a pleasure, from the lithe muscles of her back to the alluring shape of her ass. Flowridia gasped at Ayla's touch, melting at the subtle threat of her nails.

They fell into bed. In a rare show of dominance, Flowridia pushed her down, kissing Ayla's neck as her hand fell into the fine locks of her hair. Ayla embraced her, sighing at the tender affection.

Ayla's slight gasps brought Flowridia back to the present, to the soft touch of skin beneath her lips. A salacious idea filled her head, and with a summoned breath, she exhaled the first release of purple smoke, its glow illuminating her lover's skin in like hues. Each kiss left an imprint of lips. They faded in seconds, but she adored the sight. The smoke emanated from the pores of her skin, casting the whole room in light, and Ayla's gasp said she had done right. Lethal to mortals, but Ayla was far from one, her vampiric form coming alight at the invigorating touch.

Flowridia brought their hips together, smoothly grinding against Ayla, her own sigh coming unbidden. Ayla returned the motion, their conjoined pleasure a perfect chorus of moans. Flowridia left her neck and sat up to reveal herself, blushing at the smile on Ayla's lips as her eyes fell upon her body and breasts. Flowridia kept her grinding, her hips leading the motions, the sensual show precisely what her love craved. And how beautiful she felt to be gazed upon, how soft Ayla's worship as cold hands grabbed her breasts. Ayla's thumb grazed across her nipple, and Flowridia melted at the touch, cunt seeping against her love's body.

"Enjoying yourself?" Flowridia asked, the slow pace burning hot.

In response, Ayla pinched the sensitive buds, evoking a cry. "I love watching you work for me."

Flowridia increased her pace at that, bidding her breasts to bounce in Ayla's hands. The purple glow lingered within her skin. "My love, what better work is there than to nec-*romance* you?"

Flowridia laughed at Ayla's sudden glare. She returned to Ayla's neck, kissing softly as she whispered, "*Neck*-romance."

"It's somehow worse the second time."

Flowridia kept her giggles as she kissed down to Ayla's collarbone, removing her hips, though the feeling of friction lingered. At Ayla's breast, she blew a gentle breath upon the tender nipple, the necrotic magic swirling around it. She took it in her mouth, relishing the groan from her wife's lips. Flowridia cupped the other and squeezed, her own sigh escaping when Ayla tangled her fingers into her thick locks of hair, bidding her to stay.

Time passed leisurely as Flowridia romanced her wife's body, noting the subtle, slow rising of Ayla's moans. Ayla's nails made pleasurable work of her scalp, sending chills down her spine. Only when Ayla quivered against her did Flowridia release her breast, instead slipping her hand down to the sleek space between her legs.

Ayla's cunt twitched at the touch. She gasped when

Flowridia slipped inside her, magic wafting. With her mouth invested in Ayla's breasts, Flowridia gently fucked her, savoring the smooth ridges, the wetness a manifestation of her want.

How strange, for a creature of darkness to desire a tender touch. Ayla inflicted pain and pleasure both, her dominance all Flowridia desired, yet she melted beneath sweet kisses, became soft in quiet moments, placed all her trust in Flowridia's hands.

Flowridia vowed to never betray it.

"Oh, Flowra," Ayla managed, her oft luxurious voice little more than a pitiful whine. "Oh, harder please, *please* . . ."

Flowridia obeyed, adoring her wife's escalating cries. Torn between replying and the nipple in her mouth, she simply hummed instead. Ayla's obscene cries countered the sacred touch, the occasional release of *"Fuck"* enough to keep Flowridia's burning bicep moving.

Ayla tensed beneath her, her orgasm nearing. Flowridia kept her motions, the precious cry of her name pulsing fresh heat through her blood: *"Oh, Flowra, Flowra, Flowra—!"*

Ayla shuddered and clenched around her, body rocking as her pleasure peaked. Flowridia fucked her through her orgasm, only slowing when Ayla did. She remained inside as her love returned to earth. "Hello, beautiful," Flowridia whispered.

Ayla sat up on her elbows, jutting out her gorgeous breasts. "Give me a moment."

"Take all the time you need," Flowridia replied, but instead of withdrawing, she rubbed inside her love's cunt, careful as she studied Ayla. "Unless you want more."

Ayla needed no breath, yet somehow seemed to lack it. "What about you?"

"We'll get to me. In the meantime, I'd love nothing more than to take you again."

At Ayla's nod, Flowridia brought her other hand to touch the tender places around her entrance, heart swelling at the first fall of Ayla's tears.

Chapter 5

Flowridia took only a small bag. Her payments for this apparent ferryman were already tucked inside.

She tidied their room out of habit, forlorn as she tucked her crown into a drawer, hoping it would be safe. The filigree design evoked a bittersweet joy, six golden prongs and six gems each their own beautiful marvel.

Sometimes she dreamt of Lunestra, the woman whose mark on her life was a scar that never healed. A grandmother of sorts, her literal blood, and Flowridia thought often of the connection they'd shared, the family she had found—and the name she had been given.

Though she'd shed the name upon her marriage, *Flowridia Makosa* was her birthright. As Ayla had once said, nothing could take that away.

In idle moments, she thought of her father, a man she'd never known, and wondered about the mystery of his life. That he'd loved in secret—a woman she only knew as 'Mariam.'

She had never spoken of it, keeping it a quiet curiosity in her heart.

In many ways, her life had paused. Now, it resumed, a sleeping giant roused and forced to rise.

She gave a final check to her appearance, her dress attractive but suited for travel. Her final act was to slip on her wedding ring, beloved and imbued with magic, though not a magic she had ended up needing. Protection against compulsion—the wearer could not be controlled by magical means. But though its enchantment did not serve her, Flowridia adored its graceful design.

When she went outside, Demitri and Ayla waited, the latter of whom was dressed in one of her finer gowns, black and silver, cut to her navel. Flowridia knew it to be a Nox'Karthan style and said, "You mentioned that we would find new clothes in Zauleen." She gestured down to her simple ensemble, fine for travel but not for meeting elven executors. "Should I change in the meantime?"

"No, no," Ayla replied, and she took Flowridia's hand. "All shall be well, Flowra. Are you ready?"

When Flowridia nodded, Ayla led her and Demitri into the shadow of the manor, her pale hand gripping the wolf's fur.

All the world shifted and changed. Sha'Demoni embraced them.

Flowridia had become accustomed to the oppressive cold of the demonic realm, but never quite felt at ease amid the shifting shadows and monochromatic shades. Ayla appeared as one of them, her monochrome coloring matching the grey atmosphere. Demitri, too, though he walked stiffly, looked at home here.

Flowridia, meanwhile, with her auburn hair and amber skin, stood out like a lighthouse on the horizon. She kept a wary hand forward, looking for distant, blinking eyes, but followed where Ayla led, her other hand kept on Demitri. "How are you feeling, Demitri?"

Like if I get lost, it's forever, so please don't let go.

She slowed her pace enough to kiss his cold nose. "Ayla, love, would you mind reassuring Demitri that if ever he was lost in Sha'Demoni, you'd tear apart the realm to find him."

Ayla released her, her stare void of any humor as she stopped directly before the gigantic wolf. "Demitri, you are dear to my wife, and so you are of infinite value to me as well. She has told me you call her mom, and while I would never presume myself a stepmother, I would slit my own throat to save your life. The least I can promise is to tear apart Sha'Demoni if you were ever lost. Does that reassure you?"

Lady Ayla is very extreme, but I appreciate it.

Flowridia fought her urge to laugh and said simply, "He says it does."

So strange, to watch the shifting scenery. Dizzying even, after a time. Flowridia felt irrevocably lost but trusted Ayla to know the path.

Yet it was only half an hour at most before the scenery seemed to solidify in ways truly . . . different. Flowridia did not see hazy visions of her home realm, but instead, corporeal greys. Sha'Demoni was more solid here, bearing its own strange and rocky architecture.

The horizon spread before them as they came out of what Flowridia could only presume was a winding canyon—facing them was what appeared to be a massive plane of ice in shades of black.

She released Ayla's hand and ran across sand, where she realized nothing was frozen at all. It was merely stagnant—an expansive ocean. She knelt, and when she touched it, the ripples expanded until they breached the horizon, nothing to hinder them.

"Strange, isn't it," Ayla said as she approached, a certain awe to her tone. "For all my years here, it never ceases to astound me. Look over there."

Flowridia followed her pointing finger and saw . . . a dock?

In the distance was a pier. She accepted Ayla's aid to rise, and followed. Their footsteps slowly filled in behind them, erasing evidence of their passing—even Demitri and his plodding tracks. Though it appeared far away, the scenery rapidly approached, as was the nature of the shadow realm.

The dock stretched far into the sea, and an odd hooded figure stood still upon the end. Tentacled appendages spilled from its form instead of limbs, yet it held a humanoid shape. Too many eyes followed Flowridia as she and Ayla approached, and beside this strange demon was a simple raft, made of what appeared to be wood and ropes.

The figure spoke a strange, guttural tongue. Flowridia recognized it in passing, having heard the Bringer of War speak in similar tones. Yet Ayla's response made her queasy—despite her smooth voice, the harsh language sounded unnatural from her throat, an unholy blending of worlds.

Her wife withdrew the promised piece of embroidery and offered it to the ferryman. "Flowra, won't you present this fine gentleman your payment?"

From her pouch, she took two flowers, one bearing an ancient sigil in its roots and the other a silly gift to Ayla from long ago. When the demonic ferryman offered a tentacle, she placed her gifts into his grasp. He gestured for them to step upon the raft.

Flowridia feared Demitri would topple it, yet it hardly swayed at all from their weight. The ferryman joined them, carrying a strange, thin paddle, which he used to push them from the dock. The gentle dripping of water sounded like thunder in the silent world. There was nothing else—no breeze, no waves—and Flowridia sat as near the center as she could, feeling helpless. "I see why you don't cross the sea often," she whispered, praying the demon didn't understand Solviran Common. "Is this the only path?"

Ayla placed an arm around her, perhaps sensing her fear. "Yes. The sea surrounds this continent. To leave, we must pay homage to the sea's most . . . *prevalent* inhabitant. But Onias follows Demoni Law in its most perfect form. He will not harm us."

Behind her, Demitri trembled; she felt his fear as acutely as her own. She reached back to soothe him. "I don't know much about Onias."

"Oh, he's a frightful being. A massive void with no beginning or end, they say, and to stare into his eye means to succumb to insanity. Lost souls within his domain float for eternity in pure oblivion."

Flowridia's terror must have shown; Ayla's chuckle held gentleness. "Darling, do not fear. He does not leave his domain. You will never stumble upon him by accident."

The idea was soothing, though chills raised the hair on her arms. "Is he a friend to Izthuni?"

"Neither friend nor foe. Onias will not leave the sea, and Izthuni will not take it, so they remain neutral. My own god remains the king of a desolate land, while Onias rules something a little more formed. I should warn you, though— the elves coexist with Ku'Shya's kingdom, and she is no friend to either."

Flowridia recalled years ago, seeing the Great Spider at Khastra's funeral. That monstrous shadow had been forever emblazoned in her memory, certainly something to fear. "Will you be in danger?"

"If I'm caught in her realm, certainly. So while I can still cross through the planes, I will need to be more selective. She always despised The Endless Night. Viewed our actions as trespassing."

Flowridia leaned against her, hardly comforted by the revelation. "At least she's indifferent to me again."

"True. I should warn you of something else."

Flowridia braced herself for awful news but instead was met with biting amusement.

"Ku'Shya's Realm is nothing like Izthuni's. As I said, he

rules a broken world. Her kingdom is nearly whole. The beauty that was once Sha'Demoni before the Convergence of Planes still holds in most of Zauleen. There is even color."

Somehow, that was the strangest revelation of all.

Ayla prattled on about geography and demonic history, and Flowridia clung to the distraction from the endless void of sea.

Flowridia couldn't have guessed if it were one hour or six or even more, but the sky did steadily turn purple.

The horizon appeared, color striking her senses after so long seeing only black and grey. "It's beautiful," Flowridia said, and those were not words she ever expected to use to describe Sha'Demoni.

"Unfortunately, we shall not be exploring it for long," Ayla replied. "I don't dare march you around Ku'Shya's domain, as much as I adore showing you off. We will be traveling in your realm once we've arrived. It is not much farther."

When they finally reached the shore, relief flooded Flowridia to step onto solid land. The beach extended from the black water, steadily gaining color and substance—and what a beautiful sunset palette it was, the beach becoming a marvel of warm, vibrant hues. The distant plants were unlike any she had ever seen before, and her curious mind wished to know them all. "Are the demons here not shadows?"

Ayla appeared beside her. Demitri collapsed onto the sand and released a whine. Behind, the ferryman slowly floated away. "No, they are as alive as you. Hopefully, we slip by unnoticed."

Ayla took her hand and led her toward the copse of . . . trees? Spacious tree-like growths covered the land beyond the beach, yet their leaves were fleshy and speckled. "Brace yourself," Ayla said, and she took Flowridia and Demitri into a deep shadow—

Only to plunge them into Flowridia's world.

The alien territory vanished, replaced by a blue sky and sparse greenery. The flat terrain was so different from Solvira, the vast grassland spreading far and wide. In the distance were beginnings of what she presumed were high towers, but the landscape held little else.

Strange, to think she was thousands of miles from home. "It's quiet," she whispered, the light breeze stealing her words away.

Childish joy sparkled in Ayla's gaze. "Welcome to Zauleen. Sun Elven territory—or what remains, that is—is north of here. We are in Iron Elf territory, and the capital city of Velen'Kye is only a few hours away. We will make it well before nightfall."

With hands clasped together, they walked along the trailless path. Clear skies welcomed them. The day promised to be peaceful, but then Flowridia saw a strange bird in the sky. She stopped, wary of any bird large enough to stand out so vividly, until it struck her—it was not a bird at all.

Some sort of monster, shaped like a sailing vessel yet bearing strange protrusions on the top. Fin-like projections extended from the sides, rippling in the wind. Fear filled her. "Ayla, we should run."

Ayla followed her gaze in the sky and proceeded to laugh. "We are in no danger. That is an airship."

"A what ship?"

"An airship. Elven technology is vastly superior to Solvira's. With no magic comes heightened ingenuity."

Flowridia kept her stare, too shocked to move. "It's a machine?"

"Yes."

So strange and new, the idea that one could build a machine to traverse the sky like they would the sea. "Can I see one up close?"

"Of course, darling. They'll have plenty of docks in Velen'Kye."

Breathless, Flowridia followed, her smile glowing as she watched the great machine float along in the sky.

The sun hung low in the sky when they approached the massive stone wall surrounding Velen'Kye. Nothing stood beyond its boundaries—no homes, no farms. Nothing. Flowridia held Ayla's hand as they walked along a dusty road.

The grassy field continued in all directions for miles, though Flowridia saw evidence of a forest to the south. But ahead was the wall, and between the road and the city was a gate—and what an odd contraption. It appeared to be made of metal, a variety of interlocking gears visible in the grates covering it.

As they neared, Ayla squeezed her hand and whispered, "Let me speak."

"If they don't let us in, we could always use the shadows, right?"

"Yes, but . . ." Ayla's grin overtook her features, the hint of a laugh twisting her smile. "I so rarely get the opportunity to be scary in front of you."

Flowridia blushed, stomach fluttering to see her love so enthused. Enthused over impressing *her*, even. "Fair enough."

The two figures standing outside the gate looked nothing like the guards in Solvira. They seemed to wear only cloth, perhaps silk undershirts, but at their hips were rapiers and a frightful weapon, one Flowridia had only seen a time or two—revolvers were feared wherever you went.

One of the elven men looked warily at Demitri. "Is the wolf tame?"

"Yes, he is," Ayla said, releasing Flowridia's hand. "He is a witch's familiar and thus no danger to your populace."

The man spared a skeptical glance for Flowridia, then looked back to Ayla. "And what business does a human witch have in Velen'Kye?"

"She and I were personally invited by Executor Luc." Ayla offered the man her invitation.

Disgust showed on the guard's face as he accepted the blood-stained parchment—but stark horror fell upon him as he read its contents. "Lady Darkleaf, of course you and your guest may enter." He frantically handed it back. "So sorry to have wasted your time."

Ayla looked as pleased as a cat staring upon her conquest. "I am known to forget insults eventually."

The second of the guards pulled what appeared to be a lever. Flowridia stopped when the gate came to life, all the gears within turning in sync. So mesmerizing—even more so when it split in grid-like degrees, parting horizontally.

Flowridia's jaw dropped as she entered Velen'Kye.

A marvel, truly—a vast populace of people, yes, but the buildings swept up to impossible heights. She had only seen such grandeur in castles, but these appeared to be homes, businesses. Some were of brick, others of metal, many increasingly eclectic as they rose to touch the sky, new buildings built upon what already was instead of expanding out. It left her breathless but not so much as the airship high above. She stopped to witness it lower and land upon a dock well above the line of buildings.

"Come along," Ayla said, her own joy apparent. She led them to a sidewalk beside the road, where small carriages were pulled by horses, and where people briskly walked.

Their fashions surprised Flowridia. She felt starkly out of place to see their hair, for none of them wore it down. Instead, there were an array of elaborate buns, and she wondered if her own thick locks could possibly mimic them. Only children wore their hair down—and those were a rarity, she realized, the longer they walked. Parents never seemed to have more than one, perhaps two identical ones if she peered closer into the crowd, but those were even rarer.

The men favored vests and boots, but the women's skirts were meticulously shaped with gathered fabric on their posteriors, and each seemed to have impossibly thin waists— or perhaps that was simply a norm for elven bodies. Ayla seemed comparatively human, and with the thought came the realization that any elf she had ever met looked different than these. Never had she seen so many in one place. All were elongated to her human eyes, thin and tall.

Any elf she had ever met was a Sun Elf, so perhaps they held more genetic diversity than most.

Yet for all her self-conscious musing, not a single person seemed to give her mind; instead, their eyes went straight for Demitri, who was a gigantic wolf, or to Ayla, for whom the crowds parted.

"So are the buildings built how I think they are?" Flowridia asked. "They build up over time, right?"

"Correct. The city has certainly expanded since my last visit—upward, that is. But that was nearly five hundred years ago."

Remarkable, to consider.

Another airship passed overhead, stealing Flowridia's breath. "The offer still stands to see one of their ships, right?" When Ayla affirmed it, Flowridia added, "Would there be any way we could ride one?"

Amusement twisted Ayla's smile. "I don't see why not." "They're incredible."

Delicious smells wafted through the air as they passed an eatery, and the fact that she could unquestionably eat whatever they served filled her with a profound sense of freedom.

All was brick and stone and metal. And so when they reached what must have been a town square, the stark greenery was a surprise—but not so much as the grand display in the center.

A burning statue rose high into the air, rivaling some of the buildings, dominating the scene. Yet the fire was *blue* and showed no sign of fading. The longer she stared, the more clearly Flowridia could make out a figure—a female form forever surrounded by this strange blue flame. Whether it was made of metal or stone, she couldn't say. The fire burned too bright.

She tugged on Ayla's arm, bidding her to stop. "That's Goddess Chaos, right?"

"Correct. They all worship her here."

Flowridia stared upon the magnificent display, uncaring if it hurt her eyes. Enough stonework and greenery had been placed between the statue and the road to prevent the heat from becoming dangerous, or even uncomfortable. "She's incredible. Why is the fire blue?"

"They are burning wood saturated in salt water. There are priests and priestesses paid to keep the flame alive at all hours."

"But why not use regular fire? It would be easier."

"Easier, yes, but not true to legend."

Flowridia gazed upon Goddess Chaos' statue, astounded that so much dedication would be paid toward the long-dead Deity. So much attention to detail in her features, obscured by flame as they were. "She's beautiful."

"Her legends are beautiful too. Despite the negative connotations of the word 'chaos,' she is revered as an agent of change and creation, of the unpredictable nature of life. Art and inventions are dedicated to her, and she is even now prayed to for inspiration here in Zauleen. Death did nothing to stop her influence."

Memories of Soliel bombarded Flowridia then, along with the horrid vision he had shown her in the woods. She wondered, still, what this Godly woman would think of what her counterpart had wrought. "I think I'd enjoy studying her while I'm here."

"This is the best place for it." Ayla placed her hand on Flowridia's waist. "Come on. We're expected."

Flowridia followed, enamored by every new sight the city brought. Ayla's destination seemed to be a large bunker—a hexagonal masterpiece of brick and metal. The walkway was void of other buildings, decorated instead by plants trimmed into elaborate shapes. "What is this place?"

"This is the Executor's Summit," Ayla replied, "where gatherings are held and foreign dignitaries are hosted. It will almost definitely be where we are invited to stay." There were guards within sight, and Ayla stopped and surveyed Flowridia. "Brace yourself, darling. Solviran politics hold not a candle to this cesspool."

With that comforting statement, they approached the summit.

Ayla relayed a similar set of words to the guards here as she had at the gates, who reacted precisely the same—including giving Flowridia no mind at all.

"Wait just a moment, please," one of them said as he escorted them indoors. "I shall fetch someone who will know where to take you."

He left them in a lush reception room filled with art and statues.

Flowridia left Ayla's side to admire the canvases on the walls. Some were depictions of whom she assumed were previous executors, but many were of the Goddess of Chaos, some even featuring Soliel. Some showed fighting; others showed peaceful scenes, but all had one odd thing in common.

"Why do they never show Chaos' face?" Flowridia asked, her whisper loud in the vacant room.

"You'll be reprimanded if you refer to her without her title here," Ayla said, though her words were nonchalant. "Across the sea, you'll see the occasional depiction of her face, though usually veiled in some way. But here, they follow the tradition of obscuring her true form. Truthfully, I don't know why. I cannot say if anyone does anymore. Elves are the sort to question everything, but also to accept when no answer can be found—and given she is long dead, there is no one to ask. Some texts, though they're ancient even by elven standards, say she is disfigured, but that would be blasphemous to display without proof. Elves take their worship *very* seriously."

"Soliel would know if she's disfigured or not."

"Assuming we ever come across him again, I suppose you could ask."

As Flowridia stared upon a painting, one of a shadowy figure wielding six orbs of light, she recalled something from long ago. "She was an elf, wasn't she?"

"Per elven tradition, of course. Why would she be depicted as anything else?" Ayla's wink softened the words, but it brought an important reminder.

"Soliel is shown as a Celestial, though."

"They don't worship Soliel, even if they respect him."

Their conversation fell away when a well-dressed servant appeared in the doorway and bowed. "Lady Darkleaf, it is an honor. The executor has been informed of your arrival, and accommodations are being prepared as we speak. He understands if you are tired from travel but would happily welcome you personally."

Ayla's excitement practically oozed, though Flowridia suspected it was obvious only to her. "We would be delighted to meet with Executor Stormforged."

"Your servant will be provided a space as well," the man added, and Flowridia only recognized what he'd just implied in the seconds following, "though I would like to know—will your wolf be staying with you, or should he be cared for separately?"

Anxiety brewed in Flowridia's gut, and she braced for whatever explosion she was about to witness. For her part, Ayla's smile became stale, her eyes spelling murder. "Were you informed I would be coming?"

"Yes, my lady." Confusion marred his features, and Flowridia fidgeted with her skirt. "Executor Stormforged was very clear that you would be arriving, possibly accompanied by a spouse."

"Kindly repeat what you said but slow enough for your idiot mind to comprehend how *terribly* you have insulted me."

The man stared as though struck, his posture growing stiff. "My lady, I'm afraid I don't—"

"Get out."

To Flowridia's horror, he merely froze. "I-I beg your—"

"*Get out*! The next person to enter this room will be Executor Stormforged, otherwise I am taking my leave!"

He rushed away.

Ayla stood still, palpably seething.

Flowridia embraced her. "I'm impressed you didn't blow fire."

"He is fortunate I let him walk away without tearing off a limb," Ayla spat. "I knew this would happen, but the stark stupidity of it infuriates me! To not even *think* for a *fucking moment*? The executor insults me by sending his most moronic servants."

"I think this is something we may have to adjust to, my love," Flowridia said, still bristling—and she couldn't say if it were from Ayla's outburst or her own insulted ego. "Whatever they think, it doesn't change the truth. I love you, and you love me. We are married, and there's nothing they can do to change that."

"They can disregard it, though."

The door opened, and the approaching man could only be the executor. He held himself as a monarch and dressed the part, the fabric of his waistcoat luxurious and expensive. His hair was cropped short, suited for his handsome face, but most telling was his confidence when faced with The Endless Night. "Lady Darkleaf, I am Executor Luc Stormforged." He offered a hand. Ayla did not accept. "I want to reassure you that the gentleman who insulted you will be corrected and disciplined. You and yours have been disrespected while under my care, which is a slight on my honor. I extend a personal apology."

The air remained tense. Ayla finally took his outstretched hand. "Executor, if this remains the tone of my stay, I will not hesitate to disappear in the night."

"I would expect nothing less from someone of your esteem. It is an honor to meet you." When he turned his attention to Flowridia, she gave a small curtsy—which she hoped was the proper course, given his title. "You must be Flowridia Darkleaf. Your name precedes you. Do you prefer the title of Empress Emeritus or Lady?"

At times, Flowridia forgot she was the former empress consort of Solvira—and that the people truly thought she had wed Lara, then run away with Ayla. What it meant for her reputation had yet to be seen. "Lady is fine."

"Surely you are impressive, to have stolen the heart of someone so accomplished."

'Accomplished' was a strange word to describe someone who had committed genocide on an entire neighboring populace, but Flowridia decided not to comment. "I am a woman with many talents," she said, unsure of how else to answer, but judging by Ayla's neutral expression, she supposed it was the right thing. "I look forward to seeing more of your city. It's absolutely beautiful."

"Thank you. We Iron Elves pride ourselves on appearances."

The words were polite, but somehow Flowridia felt it was an insult.

"I would be remiss to not praise this fine creature," Luc continued, gesturing to Demitri. "I am told he is yours, Lady Flowridia. A noble companion. I am told he is intelligent."

Before Flowridia could comment, Demitri's young voice sounded in her head. *He's stuffy, but I want to hear more about me.*

"Demitri appreciates the compliment," Flowridia replied, resisting the urge to roll her eyes. "He is a conduit for my magic and as intelligent as any humanoid."

"Intriguing. Now, if you would not mind following me, there are two bedrooms prepared. We did not know if your familiar required his own space but thought to err with caution. It is next to yours, Lady Darkleaf."

"We will happily accept two rooms," Ayla replied, "as well as food for my wife and her esteemed companion. Bear in mind, his appetite is a bit bloodier than hers."

"I will relay the message myself. Will you need sustenance as well?"

"Why not."

They followed Executor Stormforged through winding halls, and Flowridia found it unnervingly maze-like. The room he escorted them to was beautiful, though it lacked any windows. A large bed stood as a centerpiece, but an entire lounge area had also been set, as well as a washroom beyond.

"The door there," the executor said, gesturing to a closed one, "leads to the wolf's bedroom. Dinner will be sent within the hour. If you need anything at all, ring this bell." He pointed to a button by the door. "I look forward to your appearance at the summit tomorrow morning. I would also like to extend a personal invitation to a fundraiser at the end of this week. A masquerade. If you would be willing to speak, your appearance would certainly generate funding."

"I shall consider it."

"Again, Lady Darkleaf, I apologize for the insult to your household."

"It will be remembered," Ayla replied, and the executor

101

bid them farewell.

Once the door had closed, she rolled her eyes and traipsed dramatically inside, throwing herself onto the bed. "Gods, I forget how insufferable these people are."

"He was a bit cold," Flowridia said. "At least this room is lovely."

"It's lovely because of me. Not you." Ayla's sneer relayed what she thought of that. "Understand, when their words cut me, I can cut them back. But when it's you, all I want is to tear their heads off."

"I can cut them back myself." Flowridia sat beside her seething wife. "I'm not a precious maiden in need of protection."

"No, but you should not have to need it."

Flowridia stroked a soft line across her wife's face. "The way I see it, I have to earn their respect. You're Ayla Darkleaf, The Endless Night, whereas I am an enigma. I have to show them who Flowridia Darkleaf is and whether I can stand on my own two feet. You said once that elves don't often marry for love, so perhaps they don't understand."

"No, they understand. Honestly, I need to be as insufferable as possible, lest they think I've gone soft."

"You've made an excellent display so far."

The executor thought I was noble. I always knew I was important, and now there's proof.

Flowridia had all but forgotten Demitri's presence. "Don't let it go to your head."

Too late. Already did. But I want to see my room, and I need an escort.

"Because you're very important?"

Yes. Also, I can't open doors.

Flowridia relayed the request, and Ayla took the reins, leading Demitri out.

Upon her return, Ayla's hands settled upon Flowridia's hips, then slid behind to grope her ass—which Flowridia put a gentle stop to.

"Dinner is soon." She giggled at Ayla's pout. "When the executor asked about sustenance for you, did they mean . . ?"

Ayla nodded, as though providing blood for your guests was perfectly normal. "It would be extremely rude if he did not. But I do need to ask . . . ." She grinned, sending a nervous shiver down Flowridia's spine. "Are you comfortable making love in this terrible place?"

"How else will we assert our dominance?"

Ayla laughed, divinity made manifest, and Flowridia kissed her lightly on the lips.

A knock sounded at the door.

Wordlessly, Ayla answered and was greeted by a different, but similarly dressed, servant than the one who had insulted her. "Lady Darkleaf," the elf said with a bow, "I come with dinner and a respectful inquiry—are we in any danger from the wolf? He must be fed as well."

Ayla glanced to Flowridia. "No," Flowridia replied, then impishly added, "not if you're coming with food."

To his credit, the servant held iron stoicism. "If there is anything more you need from me, please do not hesitate. Otherwise, I will leave the two of you to dinner."

"We will let you know," Ayla said. She gave no goodbye to the man as he left.

While the elf had clearly been in uniform, there was a stark difference in quality between his clothing and those worn by the girl who entered next. Flowridia supposed 'girl' might not be accurate, given that elves were largely ageless by her perception, but the softness in her features set her apart from her angular counterparts, her figure a little fuller, her eyes more familiar—and her ears betrayed the rest.

She was a half-elf, not dressed in rags, but her uniform was older, no richness to the fabrics. The girl said nothing, simply placed a tray of food upon the small table, then gave a low curtsy. As she turned, she revealed her opposite ear— mutilated, or *blunted*, as the crime was called, the tip cut off to appear more human.

She kept her head down, fear revealed in her trembling lip as she lingered.

Only then did her purpose become clear. "Thank you," Flowridia said, the statement a habit, safe enough to hide the rise of sickness in her stomach.

The half-elf did not look up, but she did nod in acknowledgment.

Ayla sauntered with all the dramatics the disdainful vampire she played here might need, her gaze studious. Already, darkness overtook the silver in her eyes, the first hint of fangs peeking from her mouth. "You will do. Sit down."

The girl obeyed, meeting no one's eye, even as Flowridia stared from afar. Incredible, to see the shift in Ayla's stance, from politician to predator, hunger in her gait. Yet unlike her encounters with Flowridia, those sensual, intimate moments they shared, there was no beauty in her desire—simply callous hunger.

Tears welled in the girl's eyes, and Flowridia swallowed her own. "I'm going to check on Demitri."

She prayed her steps were not too quick, too desperate. Of course Ayla hunted. Of course Flowridia had seen her feed. But this sickened her to her very soul.

She entered Demitri's room in time to face a bloody sight. Demitri, however, looked to be having the time of his life.

Two entire deer carcasses had been brought, freshly killed given how they stank of blood but nothing more. Though placed on an enormous tray, blood seeped into the rug, stained the wooden floor, covered Demitri's face, but her precious boy looked up with only innocent eyes. *Why are you sad?*

Flowridia's arms wrapped around herself. She trembled as the first of her tears fell. "These people are awful," she said, content to leave it at that.

The door opened behind her. Ayla entered, shrinking as a child might, seeking reproach. "I don't understand why you're angry."

"I'm not angry."

"Flowra—"

"It's not anger." Despite herself, Flowridia failed to quell her tears. "It shouldn't matter, but she was so scared."

"They always are. But she will live, if it soothes you at all."

"She's not a faceless prisoner. She has no crime except birth. And I know she means nothing to you. I don't have to understand your biases to acknowledge them."

"Flowra, this is not about—"

"Isn't it though?" Flowridia snapped, unwilling to hear it. Not today. "It shouldn't matter. You have to eat. But I think you forget that I'm human."

"I have never—"

"I think you forget that I romanticize little half-elves for all the same reasons I romanticize little dhampirs, which I know you equally look down upon." Gods, it stung to say it. Flowridia hated to wound her, hated to speak these tender, bruising words. "I'm sorry—"

"Stop." Ayla held up a hand, her stance small as she fell

into silence. How uncharacteristic, her hesitation, and Flowridia watched in wonder as she became a closed book once more, shutting her feelings away. "Wait here. Please."

Ayla swept out of the room, the arrogance in her stance returning.

I would kiss you, but I'm covered in blood.

Flowridia gave a pained laugh at that. "I love you, Demitri."

I love you too. I'm sorry these people are rude.

"We knew they would be."

Yes, but knowing they're rude and knowing they'll let Lady Ayla eat a half-elf are two different things.

At times, Flowridia still wondered if Demitri held fully sentient thoughts or if he simply mirrored her own. He remained validating, nevertheless.

Ayla entered, the open door showing a glimpse of the fleeing half-elf. "I'm insulted, Flowra," she said loudly, her audacious tone nearly humorous. "How dare they offer me a meal of anything but pure elven blood. I have instructed her to tell them of this slight. They will send me something new."

Guilt settled in with relief. "You didn't have to do that. You have to eat—"

"This city is filled with people far less innocent than her." All the dramatics in Ayla's aura faded, leaving only her wife. With care, she took Flowridia into her arms and whispered sweet words against her neck. "I don't want to hurt you. Food is food to me. It is not personal, but . . . I understand."

Flowridia held her tight, finding comfort in her wife's embrace. "I think if we have a fatal flaw as a couple, it's our continued habit of swallowing feelings we think will hurt the other."

"I must agree, unfortunately."

Flowridia kissed her hair, adoring her subtle, clean smell. "I'm hungry. Might we go back?"

Ayla led her out. "Tonight, we should rest. The executors meet tomorrow. Depending on how exhausted we are after, I think you would enjoy a tour of the city. There are libraries filled with books on airships."

Ayla's wink held a kind sparkle, and Flowridia smiled to see it. "I would love nothing more."

They returned to their room and spoke of lighter things.

Chapter 6

Warmed by a flickering fire, Sora kept at the edge of shadow, envisioning how to best use her knitting needles as knives. As it was, the repetitive pattern was soothing, her stocking coming along nicely.

By the fire, Odessa leisurely stirred the pot of mysterious stew, which Sora only trusted because she herself had slain the deer that made up the meaty portion. The witch took to her role of 'group mom' with pride and casually hummed a made-up tune.

"Mereen and Kah'Sheen, the vampire-slaying dream team . . ."

Mereen, for her part, glared from the corner of her eye, though whether it was at the singing witch or to Kah'Sheen, it was difficult to say. The half-demon held the cursed staff with the same protection of a mother bear to its cub, and Sora did not doubt she would tear Odessa's head off if she tried to take it. During their one night of rest, Kah'Sheen had gone as far as to sleep with her arms wrapped around it like a child's doll.

Tazel was reading, as he did most nights. Seated near Mereen, he seemed content in his little world.

Despite the tension it brewed, Sora was grateful for Odessa's rambling song, lest the scene be silent. The witch was immune to sour moods, she had learned, infectiously positive.

Sol Kareena, grant me clarity.

"Stew's ready!" Odessa chimed, and she took it upon herself to serve the masses. With a wave of her hand, a serving of soup poured itself into the bowl—and Sora noted the broth changed shades in the bowl. "First one's up. No meat or meat residue for the elves."

Mereen, of course, did not partake, but Tazel gave a gracious response upon being handed his bowl. "I've never had such fine food while adventuring. You really are too kind to us."

Odessa put a hand on her heart. "Tazel, you are a true gem among men. Had I allowed my son to live, I hope he would have turned out as precious as you."

She said it so sweetly, but even Tazel failed to hide his grimace at the words. Mereen, however, flexed her gloved hand, even brushed it across the gun at her hip, the twitch in her eye a glimpse into something far deeper.

To Kah'Sheen, Odessa offered a much larger bowl—which seemed appropriate, given the arachnid girl was at least nine feet tall. "Thank you," the half-demon said, her smile showing sharp teeth. "I am not often eating food that is not elf. A nice change."

"Pity, for I so rarely get to eat elves. Not many passed through my swamp."

"You are not hunting?"

"I was more like a spider, lurking on my web while I waited for unwitting prey to come to me." Odessa winked. Sora glanced to Tazel, finding her appall mirrored.

A good reminder of who this monster truly was.

Odessa came to Sora next, holding two bowls. Sora set aside her needles and half-formed stocking and accepted the offering with gratitude.

Odessa joined her on the log, beaming as she smelled the stew. "You have no idea what a blessing it is to eat after so long going without."

"I suppose it would be," Sora said, then blew on her first spoonful. It smelled delicious, uncannily so. "Do you use magic to cook?"

"Not at home, but when traveling, yes. Easier than keeping a load of spices on hand."

Odessa's glee manifested in a girlish hum upon her first sip of broth. Sora, however, stared once more upon her flickering shadow. It was not of a carefree, albeit wicked woman. No—something far more monstrous. Strange horns protruded from its head; the arms waved as wings.

"The proof is in the shadows," Odessa had said regarding her familiar's presence.

"May I ask . . ."

At Sora's hesitation, Odessa burst into laughter. "You're an inquisitive little lamb. Whatever you wish to ask, it will come out of your mouth eventually, so go on."

Sora blushed at the words. "Your shadow. It's different.

Is it Rulan?"

To her relief, Odessa gave a soft smile. "Yes."

Leelan kept his normal perch in Sora's hair, oblivious to the morbid topic. "Is it comforting?"

"Yes, though the constant reminder can be difficult. I do not forgive or forget."

"I've heard witches have powerful bonds with their familiars."

"Losing him felt like they took a hot knife to my heart." The firelight enhanced Odessa's eerie shadow. "You love your little bird, don't you? Leelan?"

Sora reached up to caress her bird, for yes, she loved Leelan, his morning chirps and the way he simply knew her thoughts and feelings.

"Imagine if he could talk. Imagine if he were a very extension of yourself. Your center. Your world. A child and a sibling and a parent, all in one. A mentor, even. Imagine you could hug your own soul and cherish it as a friend. That is what a witch's familiar is.

"So many say I'm mad," Odessa continued, but for all her antics, all her eccentricities, Sora had never seen the woman look more sober. "It is the title men cast upon women who do not fit their mold, who behave in ways that startle them. Rulan was my compass; he was my heart and soul, and to lose him cruelly broke me—I know that. I know that I'm evil. I know that my deeds are a dark legend. I don't care. But I don't believe I'm mad. I believe I am mourning."

Sora delayed her response behind a sip of stew, uncertain of what anyone could say to that. Odessa irked her in so many ways, but was it merely reflexive?

No, no—she could not like Odessa. That would be wrong.

"You know, I admire Flowra," Odessa said, jarring Sora from finding her reply. "She managed to move on. Though she also did not absorb her late wolf. She could actually mourn."

Sora often forgot that this woman had birthed Flowridia, but in any moments of remembrance, she had to admit this explained quite a bit about the girl's character, as well as her questionable taste in women. "Did she lose Demitri?"

"No, she had one before him. I have also never heard of a witch granted a second familiar, though admittedly, very few manage to lose theirs and not die in the same event. I'm alive due to the weakness of men and nothing more."

Sora again studied this odd woman's countenance, for that was the cruelest word she could think of her in the moment. "I'm so sorry."

Odessa's smile held sardonic glee, a glimpse of the malevolence lurking within her soul. "Someday you may meet Rulan. I hope so. He puts on an impressive performance."

"Do witches often absorb their dead familiars?"

"No. It is generally impossible, but my patron offered him back. I've never known how. Witches who absorb their living familiars are never the same. I'm mad enough, and Rulan is only a silent presence."

"What do you mean?"

"I once read an account from a De'Sindai witch south of Moratham who absorbed her spider's soul to save them both from slavers—and she described it as moments of lucidity in a constant stream of consciousness from her familiar's presence inside her. Souls were never meant to splice. It morphs your bodies and minds into one and drives most mad eventually."

"Bodies too?"

"They combine into something unnatural. I only absorbed Rulan's soul, and so my body was spared the price. Most are morphed into something in between. That witch and her spider? She left the transformation with more eyes and arachnid limbs."

Sora said nothing as she processed this horrible new knowledge.

Mischief twisted Odessa's grin. "Priestesses can do it too, you know."

Startled, Sora sought a reply as Odessa drank the remaining broth in her bowl. But the witch stood and wiped her mouth on her sleeve as she approached Kah'Sheen. "May I?"

Though clearly begrudging, Kah'Sheen offered the staff with two of her four arms, the others preoccupied with stew. "You are bringing it back."

"Did I not return yesterday? I have no doubt you would hunt me to the ends of the earth if I ran away with this. And sadly, I am not so adept at running as you." Still, Odessa gazed covetously upon it, caressing the skull like a lover. "Have you ever wielded it?"

"No."

"It is attuned to the God of Death alone."

Sora perked up at that, curious. "What does that mean?"

"There are magic items, and then there are magic items meant only for their creator," Odessa explained. "Items meant only for their creator can be wielded by others, but rarely without consequence. There seems to be some minor feedback on anything I attempt to subjugate." She looked to Mereen. "May I demonstrate?"

"Absolutely not."

Odessa shrugged. "It is difficult to say the extent because my experience only goes as far as woodland creatures. They don't have many thoughts, but I feel, at times, a rush of panic, the instinct of fight or flight. Little things. Makes me wonder. But I have only had one night with it, so perhaps I'm mistaken."

She wandered into the woods, leaving Sora unnerved.

But though curiosity compelled her to follow, she kept to her stew instead. Interest in necromancy was the first step toward that dark path.

Kah'Sheen watched until Odessa was but a memory in the dark. "She is making me nervous."

"I trust her to fulfill her part in this game, and that is what matters," Mereen said, seemingly idle, but that did not fit her character. Sora had no doubt she plotted something. She was always plotting something. "I don't have to trust her personally to trust her motives. Ideally, she would keep her mouth shut, however."

"Hmm." Kah'Sheen stood to refill her bowl, the steaming broth a marvel of delicious scents. "She is cooking very well."

Sora held back her gut response, not wishing to contemplate what sort of practice the cannibal witch had.

"Sora Fireborn," came the half-demon's voice, "you want to know why I am hating your grandmother, yes?"

Sora caught an icy exchange—Kah'Sheen's four eyes upon Mereen, who rolled her own. "You need to move on."

"No. I do not." Kah'Sheen smiled pleasantly at Sora, her teeth like a shark's. "You are knowing your ancestry, yes?"

"I am, but—"

"Raziel Fireborn is your great-uncle. You know he is dying in the fight to lock Endless Night into the coffin." Her gaze shifted once more to Mereen, murderous intent gritting her jaw. "Because Mereen is locking Raziel in the coffin with Endless Night—"

"He was in the wrong place at the wrong time," Mereen muttered.

"You are not hesitating to shut the lid."

"He knew the risk and was willing to die for the greater good."

"Convenient that you are hating him."

"It was not personal."

"No?" Kah'Sheen's chuckle was pure hatred. "Because you are trying to poison him before."

"You cannot prove that."

"No? Funny, he is so sick in your care, and he is better in mine."

Again, Kah'Sheen returned her attention to Sora, her smooth motions eerily arachnoid. But though her smile remained stale, her eyes softened. "Mereen is hating Raziel because he is making love outside his species. To me."

Not how Sora would have phrased it, but she blamed the language barrier. But her mother had committed the same crime in Mereen's eyes—no question of that. "I'm sorry for your loss—"

Her words were stolen by Kah'Sheen's girlish giggle, though malice stained the edges. "So diplomatic. I am admiring that. Do not mistake my calm for acceptance. I am loving him very much, and Mereen is fortunate we are sharing a blood quest, otherwise—"

Mereen stood. "We have discussed this. Let it go or leave."

"You need me—"

Click.

Mereen's weapon rose in a mere blink, aimed unflinchingly at Kah'Sheen's face. The half-demon rose to her full height, towering several feet above. Shadow melded in her four hands, daggers of pure energy appearing in her grips.

Sora's hand fell to the dagger at her hip, prepared to dart if Mereen shot. Tazel appeared beside Mereen, placing placating hands upon her. "Mereen, it isn't worth—"

"Is your little grudge going to interfere with this mission, *Kah'Sheen?*"

"No, *Mereen.* I am simply reminding you that you are a terrible bitch. In case you are forgetting."

"Stop this," Sora said, holding Kah'Sheen's eye. "It was a long time ago. We don't know what happened."

"Do we not?" Kah'Sheen's frightful teeth were revealed

in her smile, her attention to Sora now. "When he is reaching for her hand, she is shutting the lid."

Again, Mereen's eye twitched. "You are not the only one who's lost someone in this war."

Footsteps interrupted the rising conflict. When Odessa emerged from the trees, her unflappable smile stood at stark odds to her comrade's anger. "Is there a mutiny?"

Kah'Sheen's daggers dissipated. Mereen lowered her gun. "No," the half-demon said. "We are simply being honest."

"I have news," Odessa said, clearly perturbed. She held up a few strands of hair, which reflected the firelight in shades of dark orange. "Flower Child has apparently moved."

In the morning, at Ayla's insistence, clothing was brought to Flowridia and Ayla's bedroom.

Elven fashions were strange. The skirts were not nearly so layered as Flowridia had thought; instead, they wore small hoops beneath their gowns to give them volume, which she found rather . . . fun, actually. Still, her posture was stiff and forced from the corset around her torso, which seemed much more akin to armor than clothing. The idea that anyone except royalty wore something so confining was bizarre. It explained the outlandish waist sizes, however. The sight of herself in the mirror had caused a shock.

But she wore lovely shades of green and gold over this new undergarment, and while it was different, she felt attractive—especially to feel Ayla's admiring gaze, shameless in her adoration.

Ayla, meanwhile, flaunted something a little more outlandish, at least as far as modesty went. She had never been shy to show off her body, and her low-cut dress reflected that well. The gown was black, of course, which Flowridia found terribly humorous after two years together, but the corset did little for her; Flowridia suspected it was a blend of her petite size and developed core muscles.

But Ayla carried herself like she was on top of the world, a graceful empress overseeing her kingdom, her hair done up in an attractive bun. Flowridia's remained down, tucked away from her face with a jeweled hairclip. They walked hand in hand toward what would surely be a fateful meeting.

Demitri stole the show, however, walking tall with his bowtie—which he had insisted upon. *You get to look nice, so I get to look nice.*

Flowridia said nothing, not appreciating the double takes from passersby in the hallway at seeing her and Ayla's intertwined fingers. But Ayla seemed well, or at least she radiated enough excitement to cover anything else.

"What am I expected to contribute to this meeting?" Flowridia asked.

"Whatever you deem wise, darling," Ayla replied, though not without some conspiracy. "You and I both have our own unique insights into Nox'Kartha's military. You did, after all, help to defend against a siege. Simply be mentally present in the meeting. I promise it is not so daunting as you think."

Flowridia wanted to agree, but apprehension clutched her chest. She didn't have time to consider it, however; they reached their destination.

Ayla released her hand and opened the door with aplomb, not even allowing the attendant the honor of holding it for them.

A large table dominated the room, illuminated by a vast window revealing the brilliant sky. Nearly all the chairs were filled with elves, each with a glass before them. Pitchers of water were spread throughout. A few of the elves seemed more decorated than the rest—Flowridia presumed those were the visiting executors but couldn't claim to know enough of fashion to say for certain. Others must have been in the military, with their medals. She recognized Executor Stormforged at the head of the table, his keen gaze landing upon them. When he stood, the room quieted. Everyone sat.

There remained only one empty chair.

"We have a special guest today," Stormforged said, gesturing to Ayla, who appeared every bit the predator as she surveyed the scene. "Please welcome Lady Ayla Darkleaf, who after a long hiatus, makes a blessed return to our lands."

There was polite applause, but Ayla held up a hand, clearly reveling in the attention. "You are too kind, Executor Stormforged. I was flattered to receive your invitation and greatly look forward to what lies ahead. Our common goal is beneficial to us both—you wish to subdue the Nox'Karthan threat, and I wish for Casvir's head. I am confident this will be the beginning of a wonderful partnership."

"Before I introduce the rest, uh . . ." He finally looked to Flowridia. "Lady Flowridia, I can ask one of my employees to direct you toward entertainment in the city, if that's what you need."

"Oh, no, I . . ." Flowridia struggled to find words.

"Perhaps there has been some miscommunication," Ayla said, and Flowridia knew that lyrical lilt—the one she only did when hiding anger. "My invitation did specify that my spouse would be attending as well."

"For accommodations, yes," Stormforged said, with all the steadiness of a practiced politician—leaders were elected here, Flowridia recalled. "There was no expectation of having her provide input."

Ayla's face kept perfect neutrality, thinly veiled ice. "Then I'm confident she'll be a delightful surprise addition to our meetings. Perhaps you didn't know, but she used to live beneath the imperator's roof, and that was before she assisted in defending Solvira against his forces. Empress Emeritus, remember?"

"Of course. She is welcome to sit and observe, then." Stormforged gestured to one of the employees and whispered the word 'chair.' "And the wolf—"

"Stays."

"Of course."

A chair was brought, awkwardly breaking up the perfect pattern as it was placed beside Ayla. Flowridia remained uneasy as she moved to sit in the provided chair—only for Ayla to slide out the one intended for herself and gesture smoothly.

Ayla's pettiness might get them thrown out. That, or she recognized that they wanted her more than she wanted them. Flowridia offered a small smile as she sat, some apprehension fading as Ayla pushed it in politely.

Executor Stormforged introduced the other three executors, more clinical and curt than Flowridia had ever heard a politician be. But no one seemed offended, and Flowridia made a note of them and their names and mannerisms—how Executor Bree Desertblessed of the Ember Elves, who ruled the southernmost tip of Zauleen, had a darker hue than the rest, though not so dark as Flowridia, and quietly snacked beneath the table when no one was looking.

Euron Faeborn, she swore, bore the faintest of purple hues to their skin and wore silks as ethereal as their name. As Executor of the Whispering Elves, their lands sat between the Ember and Iron Elves, nearest to the entrance to *Daemenacht*—and so feared Ku'Shya more than they feared Nox'Kartha. Vale Yewblade had work-worn features, tanned compared to Luc Stormforged's pale, and ruled the Highland Elves in the far north—who Flowridia now knew bore the brunt of Nox'Kartha's onslaught.

Each unique, each known for their feuds, but all willing to unite for the cause of crushing Imperator Casvir. Somewhere between the Iron Elves and the Highland Elves, the Sun Elves lived their quiet lives. Of course, they would not be invited.

"Delightful, these introductions," Ayla said, each word saturated in luxury, "but before I hear another word, we will discuss my terms. My feud with Casvir runs deep, but it does not mean I will work for free."

"Nor are you expected to," Executor Stormforged said. "State your terms. We are honored that you would even consider us."

"I require no riches or material objects. As much as I wish I *could* accept Casvir's head, it would be to no avail. The man is a lich and cannot be killed through any conventional means. Be that as it may, I do want him dead. I want your promise to assist in my quest for his phylactery, so that I might kill him for good."

Approval swept through in hushed tones. Executor Stormforged scrawled quick notes upon a blank parchment. "You will have it."

"Alas, there is an addendum, and not one I relish. He cannot know we are here."

Flowridia frowned at that, though she realized she was alone.

"Casvir dangles a sword above my dearest wife's head, and if he catches a whiff of our involvement, I fear he would retaliate."

"I cannot account for gossip," Stormforged replied, "but officially, you can remain off the books."

"I accept that."

Flowridia gently touched her wife's arm, a question in her gaze.

Ayla mouthed a single, precious word: "Demitri."

Oh, damn Casvir. He truly had given her everything.

"But aside from accommodations for me and my wife, as well as an allowance of gold, that is all I ask."

"These are reasonable terms." Executor Stormforged drew what could only be described as a gaudy signature at the bottom, then handed the document to a waiting servant. "And so it shall be, with these prestigious fellows as our witnesses."

"Excellent," Ayla said. "With that stated, I do have some thoughts for how to subdue the imperator. But first, tell me of the war."

The generals relayed tales of the war thus far. Flowridia had feared she would be able to offer nothing, knowing so little of warfare, but she understood more than anticipated.

She listened as they discussed plans to transport weapons across the sea, amazed at how seamlessly Ayla integrated herself into their conversation. Though Ayla had done well in Solvira, she had been acting, playing the part of the empress. Here, she was Ayla Darkleaf, Scourge of the Sun Elves, able to reveal the darker parts of her mind.

"Haven would fall to your flying machines, assuredly," Ayla said, "though their gargoyles would wreak havoc upon them. You would need to account for that."

"We have yet to perfect an airship capable of flying across the sea," one of the generals said, as Stormforged took meticulous notes. "This presents a unique challenge."

Flowridia finally summoned the courage to speak up. "What if you built a sailing ship and transported the—"

"We already have those." Yewblade snapped as though swatting a fly.

The sting lingered. Beside her, Ayla seeped cold like a block of ice.

For half an hour, the elves gave their overview to Ayla Darkleaf—and only Ayla Darkleaf—until they spoke more in depth about troops, specifically those from Nox'Kartha.

"We thought we had managed to slay the Bringer of War," one general stated, "but apparently drowning is not a risk for such a beast. She returned to the battlefield within the week, though that is the longest the imperator was without her. She no longer pursues our ships across the cliffs. Our commanders have described her being distracted by a strange light source. We have yet to discern the cause."

It was so obvious that Flowridia could hardly believe Ayla didn't speak up first. "It's Etolié—"

"We wonder if we can harness this same magic to control her in turn. Perhaps mimic it with—"

"You can't," Flowridia said, but was, again, ignored. "It's the Empress of—"

"—frost blight and see if it is the magic or the light itself—"

"Pardon—"

"While the Bringer of War is not his key to victory, to defeat her would—"

"General Bellas!" Ayla said, fury enhanced by the horrid scraping of her chair upon the stone floor. Flowridia caught it before it toppled, but Ayla's statement had been made. She resumed, eerily soft and mild. "My wife has something to contribute."

All attention shifted to Flowridia.

Heat pulsed loudly through her ears. But now was her moment; she forced her own subdued words. "There is no magic. The light source is Etolié, Empress of Solvira. She is the only one who can exert any sort of control over the Bringer of War. Wasting technology trying to mimic the so-called light would be just that—a waste. You could potentially try to endanger her, but I fear it would only enrage the Bringer of War, and I suspect Casvir would let Etolié die before he risked defeat. Perhaps attempting to kidnap her would work, though I can't account for what consequences that would bring."

The ensuing silence burned worst of all. Ayla returned to her seat and placed a stiff hand on Flowridia's knee.

The conversation resumed, deviating from slaying the Bringer of War, but Flowridia's focus flittered away, centered upon not bursting into tears.

The sun had shifted in the window when Executor Stormforged proposed they take a break.

Ayla's face held forced neutrality as she helped Flowridia to rise. "Any preferences for lunch?"

From the corner of her eye, Flowridia watched most of the room slowly clear. "I don't know enough to have an opinion—"

"Lady Darkleaf, a moment?" Executor Faeborn stepped between them. "I have a few questions about the Silver Fire. I think our magic-fearing comrades are overlooking a potential asset."

Ayla glanced at Flowridia, unquestionable aggravation in her stare. "Flowra, are you hungry, or . . ?"

117

"I can wait a few minutes," Flowridia replied, then added, "but Demitri needs to go outside. I'll meet you there."

They left, she and Demitri. *You keep almost crying.*

Flowridia snapped her reply. "Wouldn't anyone?"

I don't like it. I don't like watching you be hurt.

Flowridia slowed, clinging to this small bit of validation. "Thank you."

Outside, the sunlight served to uplift her, at least by a few degrees. She stood beside a topiary, dwelling on the meeting, on how useless she felt. Nearby, a gardener trimmed the bushes, keeping them crisp and maintained.

Flowridia felt peace amid the sun and the scent of greenery, when voices approached, the door opening to reveal Executors Desertblessed and Yewblade, though they could not quite see her.

". . . cringed every time the rabbit spawn opened her mouth."

"Goodness, I was thinking the same! Classless little cow."

"I can't imagine what Lady Darkleaf was thinking."

"She's a pretty enough toy, and cows are known to let you fuck any of their holes."

Their ensuing laughter burned Flowridia's blood.

"And Empress Emeritus? Was she not previously seated on the Nox'Karthan throne?"

"No, no—she never made it that far."

"Still, the throne-hopping slut has her legs spread wide open for royals. I wonder who she'll abandon The Endless Night for."

They left earshot. Flowridia only then remembered to breathe.

Demitri disrupted her stupor. *These are the pettiest bitches I've ever met.*

"I don't disagree," she whispered, furious when her eyes misted.

She said nothing else, merely struggled to bite back her falling tears.

When Ayla appeared only moments later, Flowridia frantically tried to wipe them away.

"Darling, what's wrong?" Worry widened Ayla's large eyes. When she embraced her, Flowridia bit back a sob.

"What does 'rabbit spawn' mean?"

Ayla pulled back, revealing a glower. "It's a rude word for a human, referring to your tendency to, and forgive me, 'breed like rabbits.' Who called you that?"

"No one—"

"You wouldn't have asked if no one had."

"I overheard it." Flowridia sniffed, using her sleeve to blot her fresh tears. "I've been insulted before. I've made loads of enemies. But these people are so . . . so *mean*."

Ayla gently took Flowridia's face in her hands, guiding their gazes to meet. "We should go home."

"What? But you want—"

"What I *want* is a wife who isn't insulted at every turn."

Flowridia turned into the tender touch, managing to smile when Ayla's thumb rubbed against her cheek. "I feel childish—"

"Don't. I will not have you questioning your worth." Ayla pulled her back into her arms, and Flowridia felt, despite the cruelty around her, a bit of happiness. Ayla loved her; insults couldn't change that. "Lunch first. Then I'll inform Executor Stormforged that we're leaving. No need to burden him with our company any longer than we have to."

"Can't sully his reputation by being hospitable to 'throne-hopping sluts,'" Flowridia said, vindicated by her wife's sudden spike of rage.

"Who dared?"

"If I tell you, you'll just rip their heads off."

Ayla took her hand and led her to the city proper. "I can always err on the side of caution and kill all of them."

"Then Casvir wins the war."

"Fine, fine. We shall let them blow each other up for us."

Flowridia found this agreeable. "Perhaps this is better anyway, given how secretive we would have to be. I hadn't considered Casvir's power over me."

"A part of me doubts he would act, but if desperate, yours is the throat he would hold a knife to."

"He half-threatened it once."

The words still haunted her: *"I have given you everything, Flowridia, and I can take it away . . ."*

Ayla squeezed her hand, her soft acrimony assuring above all. If nothing else, Ayla would fight for her until the end.

In the late afternoon, Flowridia, Ayla, and Demitri returned.

Flowridia felt taller, in part because of her full stomach but also from Ayla's validation. A part of her looked forward to seeing the executors' faces when given with Ayla's rejection.

A part of her still worried this might set them back in their own small battle with Casvir. On sleepless nights, guilt plagued her, to think of what she'd sold. It would not come to pass—Ayla had assured it—yet nightmares still came. Not of the bargain itself, but of the little child who would suffer because of it, forced to be a weapon beneath Casvir's roof.

Gods, what had she done?

Though nervous to know their response, she trusted Ayla to deliver the verdict with style. Flowridia's heart palpitated as Ayla all but threw the door open—only to freeze.

The chairs had been rearranged to accommodate a new figure seated at the head of the table. Flowridia knew him well, though he'd cleaned up since their last interaction—his hair maintained and washed, wearing golden armor suited to his stature and title of God.

Soliel, the God of Order, stood at their entrance. "Flowridia Darkleaf," he said politely, his nod conveying respect. "Ayla Darkleaf. A pleasure to see you both again."

This man—who had murdered someone Flowridia loved, who had told her dark and dangerous truths of the future, who had, time and time again, taunted her with hints of her own demise—greeted them as pleasantly as the host at a dinner party. Flowridia couldn't summon words; shock stilled her tongue.

Ayla recovered far quicker. "And what have we done to deserve a personal reception by someone so esteemed?"

Two seats remained open at the table, perfectly patterned with the rest. Executor Stormforged had taken the seat beside Soliel, his face impassive as the God of Order gave a genuine smile. "The God of Order has been a resourceful advisor," Stormforged said, "whenever he graces us with his presence in Velen'Kye. The two of you were found because of his recommendation to seek your wife."

Flowridia remained transfixed, even as Ayla took her seat. This man, though there was little mortal about him, given his blatantly glowing aura and the four orbs casually floating behind his back, had been the cause of so much heartache—hers and many she cared for. Over time, she had seen him as both a man and as God, and here she was jarred to witness him back in his divine role. He held himself taller, no question of his importance, but more important to note were the elves seated closest to him; some scooted to the edges of their seats to give him a wide berth while others kept a wary eye upon him. He was not their God, but he was, indeed, a God.

"Lady Flowridia," Stormforged interrupted her inner monologue, "is something wrong?"

"No, sir." She took her seat beside Ayla.

Despite the Godly presence, they resumed exactly where they had left off, though Executor Desertblessed did deliver a brief summary of what was previously discussed. Flowridia could not quite relax. They had resolved to leave, yet Soliel's presence had utterly shaken her. Ayla seemed thrilled, thinly veiling her enthusiasm beneath her natural charm, but Flowridia felt trapped.

"I have thought a bit upon it," Ayla said to begin her speech, "and if Nox'Kartha has any fatal flaw, it is the sheer amount of power lying in its head. Murishani is fully capable of directing the undead, and the general holds some sway, but if you can defeat Casvir, the war will fall into disarray. And so I propose we redirect our focus from subduing the dead to capturing the imperator."

No one spoke. The immediate shift in gravity could have combusted a star.

"I understand the insanity of the notion, but the fact remains that if you kill him, he will return, but if you capture him, he is merely a man with a very specific skill. He controls hordes of dead—and who cares? He is a man of limited strength that would surely struggle to escape if encased in stone or dangled above a volcano."

"Encased in stone, you say," Executor Faeborn said, and of all the executors, Flowridia disliked them the least—they at least could look her in the eye. "Insane, yes, but the gamble is worth the prize."

Executor Stormforged spared a glance for the God of Order, who remained impassive for the exchange. "Can he be lured?"

"Unclear," Ayla said. "He is a man of no sentiment."

"What of the girl?" Executor Yewblade said, and Flowridia recoiled when she realized he meant her. "Rumor states they share a sexual history."

Flowridia could not even be angry, but she did wish to

fall into the floorboards.

However, Ayla bristled, lips drawn to reveal her teeth. "Those rumors were slander invented by the viceroy."

"My mistake. But my question remains—she stayed in his household for a time, or is that hearsay as well?"

Perhaps, Flowridia realized, but a bigger issue presented itself. "He would never—"

Executor Desertblessed seemed content to not hear. "If the girl is a supposed hostage, Imperator Casvir might—"

"I beg your pardon," came Soliel's pervasive voice, and all attention fell to him. His soft words held power unparalleled, the omen of a distant storm. "I believe Lady Flowridia Darkleaf was speaking." He motioned to her, every eye following suit.

"Casvir knows that Ayla would never let that stand," she said, her gaze set solely upon him. "He would immediately suspect a plot, because if you actually had me hostage, Ayla would stop at nothing to get me back. So either she's dead, which isn't possible, or it's a ploy."

"Unfortunate," Soliel said, then returned his attention to Executor Desertblessed. "As you were."

The discussion fell instead to what might entrap a man like Casvir, but Flowridia remained quiet, burdened with the knowledge that there simply was nothing. A man of virtually no sentiment, and even any attachment to her was less important than his aim for power. The thought was as hopeless as the quest for his phylactery.

There was one thing he desired, and she cursed her naivety just as she cursed his name. He wanted her to bear a child—any child—

And therein rose the beginning of a plot.

It would make her awfully vulnerable. Much more vulnerable than he would dare to risk. Casvir wanted a protégé to train and raise, and there was nothing sentimental about that. It was a power gamble arguably worth more than even the war.

She placed a gentle hand on Ayla's arm. As she leaned in, Flowridia met her wife's inquiring gaze and whispered, "I have a plan. Play along."

Ayla's face revealed nothing, but beneath the table, she squeezed Flowridia's thigh.

She politely listened, finding the thought of a stone prison both clever and cruel. Executor Stormforged proclaimed that a prison would be assembled in the meantime, ready to keep someone even as powerful as Casvir suspended in stone.

"Pardon me," Flowridia interjected when the subject came to a close, "but Ayla and I did speak of something else during our break."

Soliel claimed to know her future, but would he accuse her outright of lying? Would he even know? The gamble seemed worth it.

Funny, how confidence filled her only when she spun her words into lies. She placed a tender hand to her stomach, hidden behind the corset. "Ayla doesn't have to be nearly so secretive as we initially thought. She might even assist in the war itself, if a plan can be presented. The most important thing would be protecting me in my vulnerable state, given the baby."

Bless Ayla—despite the twitch in her eye, she became the very picture of a supportive spouse, her doting smile sincere to anyone who didn't know her.

Thankfully, Soliel spoke, alleviating her of the burden. His stark confusion lay apparent, a small deviation from Godhood. "The baby?"

"It's early enough that we've been keeping it quiet," Flowridia said, making a show of patting her stomach, "but I suppose the news will come out eventually. I'm pregnant. We're overjoyed, but Ayla worries that Casvir might try and use my safety as a threat against her. If you can assure my protection, her part in this can be public."

"It is the least we can do, in exchange for her service," Executor Stormforged said, his stoicism revealing nothing. The rest of the table displayed varying levels of shock and, in a few expressions, disgust. "This building is meant to provide protection from enemy weapons, and we can discuss placing guards at your door and a set to escort you."

"We certainly can discuss it," Ayla said, her hand joining Flowridia's, "just as we should discuss my use on the battlefield—or perhaps in assassination."

The conversation shifted, Ayla's demeanor with it, as they fell into violent topics. Vindication filled Flowridia at this new plot, however, because of all the rumors they could spread—and she had no doubt, given the reactions of the council, that it would spread across the whole world within days—Casvir would believe this truly, deeply impossible one.

And what a fool he would be, to risk the life of his future protégé. Just as much a fool as he would be for believing this outlandish lie. Flowridia held regrets miles deep, but the worst decision of her life now brought leverage.

"This is entirely too much," said Executor Yewblade suddenly, his glare narrowing upon Flowridia alone. "We are all thinking it, so I shall voice it—there is not a single word out of this woman's mouth that we can trust."

Ayla's hand tensed around Flowridia's. "Oh, explain yourself, Executor. Tell me of my beloved's crimes."

"This harlot has a reputation for sleeping with royals to gain power, only to abandon them for a higher throne. You deny the claim that she gave herself to Imperator Casvir, but six months under a man's roof is highly suspicious, not to mention she *married* the Empress of Solvira before blowing up her capital. And now she is with you, but pregnant with someone else's seed? Explain yourself, Lady Darkleaf, because you have clearly been cuckolded."

"Thank you for your words," Ayla said, and Flowridia froze beneath her cool tone. "I accept your offer of letting me snap your neck in your sleep."

Executor Stormforged held up placating hands. "Both of you, please. We can be civil and not resort to insults and threats."

"We are fools to place any credibility in Lady Flowridia's words! She will lead us to the slaughter, just as she led Solvira!"

Flowridia's anxiety spiked as Ayla scooted back her chair, far from casual. She stood, and not once did she raise her voice, her omen delivered in calm, sultry tones. "I am not a person to trifle with, nor is my wife someone you are allowed to insult. Let this whole room be my witness that you shall be dead before—"

"My love, wait," Flowridia said, rising to join her. She placed a hand on her empty womb for the act, then offered her most charming smile to Executor Yewblade. "I would like to speak for myself."

Yewblade kept his glare, a challenge in his gaze. Behind him, Soliel loomed like the vast presence he was, an intrigued furrow in his brow.

"Clearly, there is contention between us, though of your choosing. If it possible for us to discuss this in private and sort out any confusion between us—"

"No, I think we all deserve an explanation."

He left it at that.

Ayla's stance became pure predator as she took a step toward him, but Flowridia gently grabbed her forearm, stopping her in her tracks. "I am in love with Ayla Darkleaf and have taken her name. That is the truth. As for the rest, you may believe what you will, but I won't sit in what is supposed to be a professional meeting and be called a whore to my face. Save that for your private conversations with Executor Desertblessed."

She didn't miss the shift in the executor's posture, or the flick of Ayla's bright eyes.

"Of course, *Empress Emeritus*," Executor Yewblade said, the mockery of the title quite clear. "But this is not over. I think my fellows can agree to that."

The silence spoke of approval, except from one man.

From his seat, Soliel's ancient voice stole the air from the room like a void in space. "This is over. In matters of war, especially with Nox'Kartha, I would place my trust with Lady Flowridia. You should too."

He said nothing else. Ayla glared to burn through Yewblade's skin, even as Flowridia led her to her chair.

Flowridia squeezed her hand. "Trust me," she mouthed.

The conversation resumed, though awkwardly at first. Executor Yewblade, often outspoken, said nothing.

When Executor Stormforged announced they had discussed all they could, a pair of guards came to escort the God of Order. The elves stepped aside as he passed, not a single one daring to be within three feet of him, save for Executor Stormforged.

Flowridia tried to shrink into her chair, but he stopped near her and said, "Lady Flowridia, my sincere congratulations on the baby, to you and Lady Ayla both."

He remained indecipherable, but if he did not believe it, it seemed he held no wish to reveal it. "Thank you."

"Your input has been invaluable. I do hope you'll reconsider your conviction to leave."

So it had been a ploy. She remained small in her seat, knowing there was nothing at all to say, except that his alliance with the elves meant they either didn't know his quest or they condoned it—and her gut said it was the latter. They had looked the other way during the genocide of the Sun Elves. These were vicious people.

"What are you doing here?" she finally asked, acutely

aware of how Ayla studied him.

"The final two orbs are somewhere in Zauleen," he replied, not shy to say it—thus confirming her thoughts. "I shall be taking my leave this evening to continue my search."

Ayla spoke without fear, unfiltered glee in her gaze. "God of Order, I would delight in nothing more than a moment of your time. Perhaps we might take dinner together."

"I fail to see why my time would be of value to you."

The first hints of menace threaded into her words. "I think often of your words to my Flowra. You might find me a useful ally, should you assuage my curiosity. The shadows of Sha'Demoni do not whisper here as they do across the sea, but I can still be of use in tracking your quarry."

Ayla had not seen the vision, merely heard of it. Though Flowridia had yet to parse how she felt of it all, Ayla's easy betrayal of her realm—and others—was shocking.

Yet she did not speak up, for what was right and wrong anymore? Was it wicked to murder millions . . . only to save billions more?

"My victory is inevitable, Lady Darkleaf. The price you ask is not worth bringing it faster."

Ayla shrugged, apparently unbothered. "Your loss. I bid you luck in your quest to find the orbs. Flowra?"

Flowridia remained in her chair, ignoring Ayla's offered hand. "What game are you playing?"

Soliel paused. "My game is the one that keeps Nox'Kartha subdued for as long as possible."

"You're obsessed with me, and I'm tired of it."

Every remaining elf turned to stare. The air became cold, but Flowridia held her ground, glared upon this inscrutable man. Ayla failed to hide her delight at the sudden turn in drama, yet Soliel remained frustratingly stoic. "I'm afraid there has been a misunderstanding," he said.

"Why are you here? To talk me up?"

"Yes, actually."

Flowridia muffled her shock behind pursed lips.

"Executor Stormforged bid me to assist when you were overheard stating your intentions to leave. He is the one who wishes for you and your wife to stay, and I agree that you hold invaluable knowledge for the war against Nox'Kartha."

Flowridia sought a reply, refusing to feel like a fool for her outburst. The elves watched; they heard it all. "If you won't engage my wife in private conversation, would you speak with me instead?"

To her surprise, Soliel did not immediately dismiss it. "What do you wish to discuss?"

"I will tell you once we're alone."

Soliel looked to Executor Stormforged, whose stoicism held cracks. "Leave us," the Old God said. "I will speak to Lady Flowridia."

Luc immediately directed his fellows and guards to leave. Ayla met Flowridia's eyes, quite a few words said in her wink: *I'll be watching.*

Soon they were alone—Flowridia in her chair and Soliel looming beside her.

When she did not stand, he returned to his seat, the mantle of Godhood disappearing behind the tired man in the woods she knew. The exhaustion of his quest lurked in his slumped posture, even his words. "What did you wish to say?"

"Is this a trap?"

"No. The elves sought Ayla of their own accord. I simply informed them that you existed."

"And you agreed to come coddle my bruised ego after we were overheard?"

"Lady Flowridia, I was not always a god. As a mortal, I had many experiences as a human-looking man among elves, and those experiences were rarely pleasant."

Flowridia despised this engagement of empathy. To humanize this monster was too much. "Because of Chaos?"

"What of Chaos?"

"She was an elf. She was why you spent time among elves."

"You are technically correct."

"Technically—" She bit back her frustration, realizing there was no point in engaging. "Thank you for your answers."

"Is there anything else?"

Only a thousand questions—of the dragon Valeuron, his demise and cryptic words both—*I have seen your life. I know your death.*—of Lara's brutal end and Soliel's obsession with steering Flowridia's path, of every scene in their shared vision, of how Casvir became the greatest monster in the realms, of what Ayla became, for to know her future would break her heart . . .

And of course, Flowridia wished to know her own fate, but to know it would take it away—and Soliel would not risk that. He would say nothing of any of it.

She simply said, "No."

"Then I shall take my leave. Farewell, Lady Flowridia."

She gave no reply. Yes, it was rude, abominably so, but her shock from seeing him had not faded.

As he reached the door, however, a strange memory surfaced. "Wait."

He did.

"You told Casvir once that you would abandon this whole quest in exchange for his phylactery. Ayla and I are seeking it. Do you know anything? We would accept any aid."

"We never found it," Soliel said, an echo of his sentiment in the woods. "I wish I could help, truly, but I fear it is a waste of your time."

The words were a punch in her stomach. Perhaps he sensed it, lingering to hear more, but she had nothing else.

Upon his exit, Ayla stepped in through the shadow of the doorframe. "What a bore. You handled yourself well, my love."

"If he says it isn't a trap, I do believe him," Flowridia muttered.

"It does not matter. His presence is intriguing, but we can still take our leave. I do have a few questions for you, however." Ayla raised a quizzical brow, one hand falling to Flowridia's empty womb. "So we're to be mothers now?"

"If Casvir believes I'm pregnant, he wouldn't risk my life by taking away Demitri while I'm in this state, no matter how angry he is. And he *will* believe it, given everything."

Gorgeous glints of malice filled Ayla's gaze. "Darling, you are *brilliant*. Leave spreading the rumor to me. I know precisely whose ears to let it fall upon for Casvir to know as soon as tonight. In fact, I have an engagement planned for the evening—though do not fret. My night is for you."

"Thank you. I might as well salvage some advantage from my contract with Casvir." The word curtailed the high of her victory, bringing spots of anguish. Soliel's final words remained to haunt her. "All I want is to be free so that I can find a way to be immortal with you. Then when Soliel inevitably separates the realms, we can live amid the rubble— but at least we'll live."

Ayla knelt beside her chair and offered a tight embrace. "I shall protect you from all things, my love—even Soliel and his plot. Even Casvir and his bargain."

"But Soliel said—"

"I don't give a damn what he said."

"One of those things is my fault."

"Flowra, I told you I don't wish to discuss—"

"But we need to." Flowridia cursed her rising tears, swallowed them back. "Just because you don't hate me doesn't mean that I don't."

"Oh, darling—"

"I've been living in this wonderful bubble, hiding from the world while you've done the research and the work. That isn't right. Now that I'm back in the world and facing old remnants of my life, I can't help but fear. And I regret it all, yet I can't stand to take it back either."

Eternal slavery for Alauriel Solviraes. Or slavery for an innocent child. Her tears fell freely.

"We are going to kill Casvir," Ayla said, her vehemence soothing and frightful all at once. "You will not have to give him your child. You will *not*." Ayla kissed a falling tear upon the hollow of her cheek. "Instead, we use his own bargain against him. Executor Stormforged wishes to speak more in private of assassination plots, and I have high hopes." Ayla pulled them together, held her tight. "You really wish to stay?"

"It may be the only hope we have of buying time to find the phylactery."

"I suppose you have a point. It is why we are here, and we should not lose sight of it."

"We shall make the most of it."

"Yes, we shall. All will be well."

Ayla lavished kisses upon her, held her through her tears. "Is there anything at all I can do in the meantime?"

Yes, though it was utterly wicked. "I want you to bring me Executor Yewblade."

Ayla raised her eyebrow. "Right now?"

"Yes."

"Does it matter if he's willing?"

With her breath escaped traces of purple smoke. As she shook her head, that same potent power rose in her hand. "No. He won't be leaving quite the same."

Glee radiated from Ayla's malevolent smile. She disappeared into a shadow.

An evil thing, the blending of Necros and Flame, and Flowridia had not performed the act since her time in Solvira. But gods, the rush, the precious bonding it brought, and as

Ayla dragged a gagged man in from the shadows, excitement burned Flowridia's veins.

"Tie him to the chair."

Ayla obeyed, easily overpowering the struggling Executor Yewblade.

"Summon your fire."

Ayla did so, Silver Fire rising to coat her hand.

"I'm sorry we couldn't come to a peaceful consensus, Executor," Flowridia said, as impassively as she could summon. "But I think we may be able to persuade you."

She took Ayla's hand, Silver Fire and necromancy swirling into one. Together they touched the flailing man's forehead, and Flowridia sifted carefully through the delicate reaches of his head, seeking the bond of soul and body—

And severed it like the delicate string it was.

Executor Yewblade slumped over.

Though giddy at the display, Flowridia calmed herself and set her hand to his neck, relieved to feel a pulse. She coaxed his chin to rise. There showed a familiar vacant grin.

For a moment, she flashed upon High Priestess Jules' memory, the empty smile; this was the same.

With it came memories of Lunestra. She shoved those thoughts aside.

"Your name is Executor Vale Yewblade," Flowridia said, though it was far more a command. Magic boiled within her, burning her veins in every delicious way. "And you shall agree with absolutely everything I say."

"Yes, my lady," came his amiable reply.

"Is it worth attempting to reeducate him?" Flowridia asked her wife.

"I don't know enough of his daily life or habits. We shall simply leave his sudden lapse in personality as a mystery."

Whatever the depth of the crime, it could not be pinned to them. "Untie him."

Ayla did, and Flowridia counted the seconds for the man to walk stiffly away.

Once alone, she stole Ayla into a rough kiss. "Fuck me. Or I'll fuck you. I don't care."

Ayla's pupils held no color, a cat gone utterly mad. "Lie on the table. You're mine this time."

Ayla's fire extinguished, but Flowridia kept the potent necrotic energy flowing from her pores, knowing it was pleasurable against her lover's skin. The dress was like armor, difficult to remove for a quick engagement, but Ayla managed to remove her underthings, then crawled beneath her layered skirts to kiss the tender flesh.

At the first touch of Ayla's mouth upon her vulva lips, Flowridia groaned with relief, her body starved. Ayla's tongue explored the secret crevices, charting a map they both well knew, and when her fingers joined and fucked her hard, Flowridia fell into pure bliss, biting her tongue to not scream her pleasure.

She ought to be scandalized by the public display, the threat of someone finding them, but instead her heart raced wildly, the fear far outmatched by arousal.

Ayla knew her body well. Within minutes, Flowridia shuddered, her muffled scream contained by her hands.

When the final waves orgasm had quelled, Ayla made a salacious display of licking her fingers. "Absolutely decadent."

Flowridia sat up, legs still spread for Ayla, who stood between her skirts. She kissed her wife, adoring the familiarity of her lips and body. "Do you want something here or back in our room?"

"I want something later, unless it offends you."

Flowridia cupped her cheek, stroking the pale skin. "Later is fine. Something for me to look forward to."

"I need to speak to Executor Stormforged, but I have a project once the sun sets. Afterward, I shall be yours all night. Would you be upset if we planned on the library tomorrow instead?"

"Not at all. It gives me more to look forward to."

They kissed and sealed their love.

"*Pregnant?!*"

Etolié had never heard such bullshit before.

"There's no fucking way!"

With the permission to go between the battlefield and Solvira at her whim, Etolié sat in a canvas tent, seated in the lap of her favorite beefcake—naked, of course. Sex didn't have to be involved for naked cuddles to be comforting.

Not even the inherent distraction of watching Khastra's

many tattoos glow when their bodies made contact was enough to quell the fire of her disbelief. Etolié stared at the letter, seeking any sort of explanation, but no. The statement was stark and lacked any room for misinterpretation: *The elves claim Flowridia, wife of Ayla Darkleaf, is pregnant.*

"There's no way. It's a fucking ploy."

Khastra's voice rumbled against her back and wings, sending chills across Etolié's skin. "I do not know. It does seem strange, but they are married. Perhaps they are simply taking the next step in a human's life journey."

"You're telling me Ayla let some man fuck her wife? Have you met her?! There's no way!"

"I suspect the man is dead if that is the method."

"Khastra, that's *the* method. And speaking of—have you met *Flowers*?! Her interest in men is negative. Child of Neoma if I ever fucking saw one."

"Perhaps a spell?"

"Flowers is good, but she isn't that good."

Khastra's arms fell around her, trapping her in the best of ways. Though fire still pulsed through Etolié's limbs, she fell against one of Khastra's massive biceps, larger than the girth of her own thigh—by far.

"I am simply delivering what Murishani reported," Khastra said, her lips against Etolié's hair nearly enough to douse the flames. "He is telling everyone."

"That's in character. But it isn't true, Khastra."

"And I believe you, but Casvir is entertaining it."

The news jarred Etolié from her rant. "What?!"

"He seems to believe it could be true."

This irked her so deeply that she stood and illusioned a dress. "I'll be right back."

A blast of cool air filled the tent as she opened the flap, along with the stagnant stench of death. The starry sky filled Etolié with the happier memories of childhood, when her momma was well and would lay out a quilt beneath the desert sky and hold her as they named the constellations.

Momentarily disarmed, Etolié paused to study them, seeking the ones she loved the most—a mermaid's tail, a flaming sword, a castle spiraling up to the sky . . .

She missed her momma. It had been a few weeks. But she couldn't risk being gone when the Bringer of War needed her, and the time dilation between the worlds meant a day with Momma was a lot longer here.

She resolved to take time to dream. In the meantime, her quest awaited.

A literal sea of death surrounded them, their encampment small with the undead to protect them on all sides. Each tent was the same. Casvir's commitment to utilitarianism was a way to avoid assassination attempts, which Etolié would begrudgingly admit was clever. Not many tents. There were only so many living assets in the Deathless Army. But Etolié knew which tent belonged to the imperator and marched her way there.

Yet as she moved to tap on the canvas, something radiated across her otherworldly senses, her limited teleportation powers giving her an uncanny sense of when something traversed the parallel planes. Etolié froze, the hairs on the back of her neck rising in warning.

She whirled around, illusioned dagger in hand—and clanged against a weapon held by Ayla Darkleaf, aimed for her neck.

Etolié shrieked. She shot into the air, wings spread wide.

Khastra tore from her tent; Casvir burst from his, summoned weapon immediately bashing against Ayla—whose body glowed as it absorbed the magic. Her laughter held hostility and seduction both as she danced into the shadow of Casvir's tent and vanished.

Khastra was still naked, and Etolié immediately illusioned a set of armor over her vulnerable body—reminiscent of her old set, decorated with gems. Khastra cried, "You will show yourself, coward!"

Though menace emanated from Casvir's being, his voice remained calm. "Ayla Darkleaf, how unexpected."

Cast in shadow, a silhouette rose from the earth not fifteen feet away. She had no features, save for gleaming silver eyes and a wicked smile cast in red. "Good evening, Casvir."

"Congratulations are in order. I was surprised to hear the news that you and Flowridia were expecting so soon."

High in the air, Etolié balked at that odd statement.

"She's thrilled," Ayla replied, the words heavy enough on their own, though her sneer lay apparent.

"How fares her health?"

"Well enough, though she requires medical care. The elves are kind enough to provide it."

"The elves are not kind."

"Kind enough when given proper compensation."

"Is that why you tried to take Empress Etolié's life?"

Ayla's chuckle sent ice through Etolié's veins. "She was not my expected target, but who am I to not take advantage of opportunity. The Empress of Solvira, unaccompanied on a treacherous battlefield? For shame."

"When is your wife due?"

"Soon enough."

"If medical care is the price for your aid, allow me to present a counteroffer."

The Ayla silhouette remained silent, flickering at the edges. Etolié hated the sight of her in person, but she somehow became more nightmarish as a specter.

"I will gladly offer Nox'Kartha's brightest physicians to monitor your wife," Casvir continued, and everything about this made Etolié's mind reel. "She would live in luxury and be provided the highest care before, during, and after the birth—as would you, given your worth to her."

"As much as I would love subjecting myself to further time in your company, I will decline. She is well cared for."

"The Iron Elves were the first to report your presence and her pregnancy. Is that where she stays?"

"I cannot fathom why you would think I would answer that."

"Then why are you here, other than to present a counteroffer—"

From behind Casvir, the *real* Ayla Darkleaf leapt from the shadow—and stabbed a knife into the side of his neck.

Casvir's gasp cut off. The figment laughed as it dissipated. Black ichor seeped from the open wound, and Ayla was nowhere to be found.

Khastra ran to his side and clamped her hand down over the wound. "We must get you to Nox'Kartha."

Casvir's reply came as a gasping sort of gravel. Ayla must have severed his vocal cords.

A spark illuminated from within the sea of death, and Etolié watched in horror as Silver Fire erupted across the undead, turning orange as it caught. The dead rampaged as they sought her, larger abominations stomping the small ones. But Ayla was too nimble for that, and by the time the gargoyles swooped in to grab her, she had long since disappeared. The fire burned across the dead, those afflicted running from their peers, but it caught like bramble. The scent of burned flesh filled the air, wafting in sickening droves. A massive hole had been cut into the Deathless Army—theoretically limitless, yes, but Ayla had burned half a battalion in less than a minute.

Below, Casvir surely seethed, but for now, he remained on one knee.

Etolié deemed herself too fragile for this shit and stayed high above, surveying for any threats to her beefcake as Khastra wrote a frantic message to Murishani. But Etolié's gut said Ayla's point had been made.

She didn't have to kill Casvir to be the worst sort of nuisance.

And she would happily kill anyone in his service.

Night fell, and Sora came upon the town of Ameth. At the outskirts, Kah'Sheen took the staff and withdrew into the shadows, insistent that her presence would cause too much of a stir—as though the presence of a vampire, a half-elf, and a human would do much better. Tazel was the only inconspicuous one. However, Mereen kept hidden beneath the sturdy hood over her head, the rest of her body entirely covered in her white leather armor—perhaps enchanted to protect her from the sun.

Odessa muttered angrily, as she had done all day "This makes absolutely no damn sense. There is no way my Flower Child moved across an entire continent overnight. The spell must be broken."

"Can spells break?" Sora asked.

"First time for everything."

Ameth was a fanciful place, with guards and a proper cobblestone road. Sora held her head high as they passed elven citizens, but kept a hand near the knife at her hip. Elves held many prejudices, yet there was far clearer derision cast upon her than upon Odessa. She supposed a human was at least not a *half-breed.*

"*The whole world will tell you you're nothing,*" her father had said. "*The only way to prove them wrong is to live your best and happiest life.*"

"Tazel and I have our own quest," Mereen said, grabbing the man's arm; Sora's skin crawled to see it. "Don't go far, and don't draw attention to yourselves."

Odessa fawned over every new sight—the state of the buildings, the delicious smells, even the clothing. Sora had no interest in corsets or skirts, found them too difficult to fight in, though she knew elves who managed regardless. Most shops had closed, given the late hour, but a few subsisted off candlelight.

A great *hum* rose as a massive airship approached, flying low. It disappeared behind a collection of buildings. Sora supposed a city this large would warrant a dock.

"I'm unfamiliar with the mushrooms on this continent," Odessa said to one shopkeeper, her pretty self surely exotic to the elven merchant. She perused with scrutiny, nothing escaping her watchful eye. "Which would you say goes best with meat?"

"You'll be hard-pressed to find meat for sale in this town," the man replied, his derision wafting. "We elves don't resort to such barbarism."

"I had never considered the purchasing of meat to be barbaric. Though now that you mention it, I do prefer the hunt." Odessa withdrew a purse from the space between her breasts and made a show of counting her coins. "You'd be a delicacy."

"I beg your—"

"Hand me your most expensive mushrooms."

Soon, Odessa giggled with her sack of fungi. "Mushrooms are adaptable to anything, but a select few taste best with swine—pig swine or human swine, doesn't matter."

Sora did not laugh at the jest. "Did Mereen tell you where she was going?"

"No, but I can make a few intuitive guesses. Ameth is a large enough town to have a proper coffin maker."

"Coffin?"

"To hold Ayla Darkleaf."

"Why a coffin? Will Tazel be enchanting it?"

"It would be lovely if he could, but no. She has the Silver Fire now, so there's no point. But coffins are inconspicuous to transport and will fit an elven body." Her large eyes glinted with lust as they fell upon a nearby tavern. "I suppose we simply wait, though if they take too long I'm getting a drink. You don't know how much you miss alcohol until you're forcibly sober for a year. Incorporeal bodies have their disadvantages."

Sora's attention drifted off to the darkened printing press at the side of the road. A copy of a newspaper lay beside the front door, the name upon it unmistakable: *Ayla Darkleaf.*

She wandered over and brushed dirt and filth off the paper, noting it was dated for that morning.

Ayla Darkleaf Joins the War Effort
The Endless Night sleeps in Velen'Kye, according to reports from the Executor's Chamber. Executor Faeborn is quoted: "We, the executors of the Four Kingdoms, unanimously agree that Ayla Darkleaf will be an invaluable asset against the onslaught of Nox'Kartha and its imperator...

Convenient. And eerie, to think the Iron Elves were so readily accepting of a known mass murderess. "Odessa, come see this."

The witch scurried over, no concept of personal space as she placed her cheek against Sora's shoulder. "Well, well...won't you look at that." Odessa took the newspaper and skimmed the text. "A certain Lady Darkleaf is living in Velen'Kye. No mention of Flower Child—oh wait—"

Odessa's words stopped, eyes steeled as though she'd been bitten. She read aloud: "...Accompanied by her pregnant wife?"

"What?" Sora stole it back, the idea absolutely mindboggling. "This can't be correct."

"Perhaps she got fat and they made an assumption."

"That doesn't fit them. The elves pride themselves on truth. They wouldn't put it in the papers without it coming from a reputable source."

"So what I'm hearing is they heard it from Ayla or Flowridia themselves." Odessa's pout held contemplation. "That Darkleaf woman would never let a man fuck my Flower Child. Must be a spell."

"A spell? There are no baby spells."

"Are you a witch, Sora Fireborn? Do you know all the unnatural magics in the world? For goddess' sake, you would tell a Solviran citizen that there are no baby spells?"

"I feel like more people would do it if it were as simple as snapping your fingers."

"If you're so insistent, it's also possible they're lying."

Sora couldn't tear her gaze away from the paper, but there were no answers, no explanations—simply that one odd phrase. "Possible, but why?"

"No idea. That said, while this doesn't explain how she got here so quickly, at least we know my magic isn't broken." The boundless *hum* of an approaching airship thrummed through the air. "And I would bet a considerable amount of my sanity that the airship port will take us directly to Velen'Kye. When Mereen returns, we'll see what she says."

"I'm just shaken the elves would trust Ayla Darkleaf to help them, much less announce it."

"I don't know as much of elven history as I wish I did, but I recall hearing whispers of her gaining some semblance of power before she was sealed in that coffin. Despicable, their willingness to turn their backs on genocide, but there have been atrocities of that sort all through history. The Four Kingdoms have no living god to condemn their inaction."

Sora's hand brushed habitually across the hilt of her dagger.

"But why so blatant? Hope. It comes in an evil package, but if they believe Ayla can inspire the masses against Nox'Kartha, of course they would scream it to the world. And if they think news of a pregnant wife would ignite them further, well, why would they not say that too?"

Sora supposed there was logic in that, even if she found it abhorrent. "I don't have to support a woman who murdered my ancestors, even if she brings hope."

"Absolutely not, and no one is asking you to. None of this changes our plans. In fact, it speeds up our timeline, given they're just a few short days in the air away. With any luck, the monster who murdered your ancestors will be dead and gone soon."

Vindication did fill Sora at that. "Good."

"And if my Flower Child truly is pregnant, we can find a way to exploit that, I'm certain. Beyond that, nothing has changed."

Sora nodded, still reeling at the idea.

"Tazel will return soon with that coffin. Just wait until Mereen hears this."

When Flowridia set out to find dinner with Ayla, Demitri chose to stay behind, citing his inability to be around another person without snapping.

And I don't want to snap anyone, Mom. They'll take me away.

Flowridia laughed and said that was all right. It had been another long day of meetings, though Executor Yewblade had been mysteriously absent.

"We fear he may have caught some sort of fever."

It had taken all of Flowridia's willpower not to laugh.

Hand in hand with Ayla, Flowridia savored the sunset, though sadly found the stars to be less visible amid the lights of the city. Many eyes fell upon her, able to study her freely without the gargantuan wolf beside her, and Flowridia felt the quiet casting of judgment.

"Classless little cow . . ."

Flowridia had thought she was immune to insults by now, but here, everything felt heavy.

"We can fake a bump as the months go on," Ayla said, interrupting her musing. The world parted for her, granting her the respect only spilled blood could inspire. "And there are corsets for pregnancy."

Horror filled her at the notion. "There are corsets for pregnancy?"

"Yes, but they don't work the way you are thinking. More for support than for shape. You might even be more comfortable—or less, since there won't actually be a stomach to support. But if you're willing to put on the act, it would add to the effect."

"This was my idea. I intend to follow through as best as I can."

"And if too much time passes, you can tragically miscarry—at which point, we reevaluate my involvement in the war."

"It's not the most elegant plan, but Casvir believes it. It'll be worth it."

Ayla fell into silent thought, leaving room for Flowridia's own contemplation. Whatever discomfort she felt being in Velen'Kye, the idea of turning her contract with Casvir so viciously on its head made the hurt sting a little less.

"Would you still like to go to the library?" Ayla asked.

"I would, yes."

Ayla led her to a quieter district of the city, the path far clearer, largely devoid of elves. Most who did pass bore obvious signs of exhaustion, some holding piles of books, content to ignore the single human in their midst—and she supposed being ignored was better than being spat on. The dark streets offered spots of illumination, and in the distance, Flowridia watched a woman with a step stool going from lamp to lamp, lighting the path.

"The university here is the most prestigious in all of the

140

Iron Elves' land," Ayla said, "begrudgingly esteemed throughout the Four Kingdoms. They may not always get along, but scholars tend to be accepting of fellow intellectuals, regardless of their heritage. You might even be able to garner some respect. I believe the rare human has managed to be accepted."

A strange notion, but it did not immediately make her ill. "Are you proposing we stay long enough for me to enroll in school?"

Ayla's laughter filled the vacant street, joyful in the lamplight. "I suppose not. But you are incredibly intelligent, darling."

"I learned to read because of my mother," Flowridia said, rueful to admit any gratitude toward the woman. "And she only taught me because she wanted me to prepare spell ingredients for her."

"You managed to fool me," Ayla cooed, and Flowridia glowed beneath the admiration in her gaze. "I had no formal education either. When Eva took over the cathedral, she made certain all of us orphans were taught to read and write and given the basic tenets of mathematics. I suppose I can thank her for *something*."

Such derision in her words, and Flowridia squeezed her hand, voice low as she said, "I would love you even if you were illiterate, and if I could go back in time and slowly suck the life from Eva's veins, year by year, and leave her to linger on death's door for days before letting her succumb, only to thrust her soul back into her dead body and force her to watch herself decay in solitude and gradually go mad, I would."

Ayla stopped, the lamp above them shedding light upon her vulnerable visage. "I love you."

Flowridia kissed her, a statement far stronger than words. How perfect she felt, Ayla's lips filling her blood with soft heat and serene joy—

"Would you look at that—a cow and her keeper!"

Flowridia hardly heard the ensuing laughter, far too focused on Ayla becoming stiff in her embrace. "Ayla—"

A feral hiss left Ayla's lips, fangs bared as she faced the hecklers across the street—three young men; students, given their uniforms. She disappeared where the light ended and appeared in a blink at their sides. All semblance of a soul had vanished from her countenance, replaced with a monster's face. "Which of you said that?"

Panic flashed across their faces, perhaps realization too. They ran; Ayla withdrew a knife from her bodice and threw it—where it impaled one's skull.

He toppled. Ayla ran. Adrenaline spiked in Flowridia's blood, but she held her tongue, contemplating instead how best to hide this.

It was no trouble at all for Ayla to catch the other two, grabbing them by their shirts and slamming them down in tandem. One's skull split with a horrid crack upon the ground; blood seeped into cobblestone gridlines.

Flowridia ran, careful to keep her skirts clean of blood as she gently touched the broken skull—and felt the final vestiges of his life trickle away.

Ayla knelt upon the final one. "Do you know who I am?" Ayla seethed, her nail dragging a bloodied line across the last man's cheek. "Do you know who you've insulted?"

"A-Ayla Darkleaf," he whimpered, and Ayla set her hand over his mouth as her fangs plunged into his neck.

Though he struggled, it was to no avail, and Flowridia watched warily beside them. She breathed through her fright, frantically glancing up and down the street—but they were truly alone.

The lull of Ayla's throat as she drank her fill was almost peaceful, but the man's terror remained. Ecstasy showed upon Ayla's face, blood dripping from her pretty lips as she withdrew. "As much as I would delight in your final words being my name, I would have them be an apology instead."

"I'm sorry!" His voice remained weak despite his desperation. Tears spilled from his eyes, the blood on Ayla's fangs dripping to join them.

"To her."

His horror shifted to Flowridia. "I-I'm sorry. Please, don't—"

Ayla plunged her fingers into his throat, cutting off his breath.

Blood flowed down the street. Flowridia forced each shallow breath. Surely someone would come, someone would see.

. . . And do what?

Ayla stood and wiped her gory hand on a handkerchief, kempt despite the murders. "Idiots, all of them. Shall we?"

She offered an unbloody hand, but Flowridia struggled to move, each motion caught in a bog. "We can't just leave these here on the street. Can you hide them in Sha'Demoni?"

"And blame the demons? They wouldn't appreciate that. I can stuff them in an alley."

"I can do it." Flowridia summoned her power, swirling purple smoke escaping with her exhale. At her bidding, hardly a release at all, that same energy coiled around the dead men, fueling them with unholy magic. They stood on their own accord, leaving brain matter and bone behind, but they marched themselves into the nearby alley to collapse behind a large pile of wood, away from wandering eyes.

Blood remained in the streets. Perhaps The Endless Night would be blamed—but more than likely, Executor Stormforged would cover it up, considering Ayla's presence and fury the greater good.

With the return of her power, Flowridia's body came alight, invigorated by the intoxicating sensation. Before it snuffed from her mouth, Ayla pulled her down to seal their lips. Flowridia breathed, necromancy rising to caress her love before it dissipated with her exhale.

"What are you thinking, darling?" Ayla asked, her voice dripping with implication. "To the library, or . . ?"

Flowridia assessed herself, considered her mental state, and deemed herself mad for being so unbothered. "I would like to still go. But we should clean up first."

"Can't get blood on those books."

They set off to find a change of clothes.

Darkness had fallen by the time they reached the library, but Ayla insisted it never closed. "Research students come in at all hours of the day and night. Most Iron Elves operate by sunlight, but you'll find many a nocturnal worker or student, and there are plenty of businesses open for them."

The brick building held pillars of stone, as well as plaques etched with names Flowridia did not recognize. A building of prestige; Flowridia kept close to Ayla as they walked beneath the grand arches, memorizing every bit of it. They passed a few students laden with books and laughing with peers—who silenced upon seeing Flowridia and Ayla, their judgment turning to horror when they caught her eye.

But none of them said a word, and thank every god for that.

The soft lighting of the library held the faintest of flickering, revealing the candlelit source glowing within various lamps hung throughout. Flowridia hummed at the scent of old books, at the shelves reaching distant heights, at the endless rows of knowledge. Not so grand as Solvira's library, nor as deceptively boundless as Nox'Kartha's; instead, it presented its grandeur at the forefront, welcoming all.

An older woman at a desk kept her eyes to her paperwork, but behind her stood a great statue of the Goddess of Chaos. Cast in bronze, the fire did not flicker here, immortalized in metal, and she presented a book inscribed with the elven word for *judgment.*

Flowridia could not look away, fascinated by the mysterious figure—and thus was startled when a bored voice said, "Student papers, please."

"We don't need papers."

Though Ayla's words were not said with malice, Flowridia still braced herself for bloodshed.

The matronly woman peered up, and her apathy faded as she scrambled to put on her spectacles. "Lady Darkleaf and guest—"

"Wife."

"Wife, of course. The executor sent notice that you might be stopping by. Please, come in."

All things considered, the woman kept her calm awfully well in the face of a murderous vampiric monster, and Flowridia released a relieved breath when Ayla made no move toward violence.

Better to be a 'guest' than a 'servant.'

"My wife is Flowridia Darkleaf. Should she return on her own, she will be allowed the same favors granted to me. You will inform your staff of this."

"It shall be done, Lady Darkleaf," the librarian replied, an edge of anxiety to her words.

Flowridia followed behind her wife, captivated by the beauty of this ancient place. "How old is this library?"

"I am not entirely certain. It did not exist when I was born, but it was built sometime before I was trapped in the coffin."

Flowridia gazed back upon the Godly statue, memories of the blue flame and boundless art surfacing. The most intriguing aspect had been so commonplace . . . that it had hid in plain sight. "Goddess Chaos wields Silver Fire?"

"She does, yes. Ancient Priestesses of Chaos did too, granted by her power. It is well-documented, though not common knowledge across the sea."

"How is that possible?"

"Elves believe she was the origin of it. Neoma later gained it through worship. The Solviraes wielded stolen power, in their minds."

"What do they think of you?"

Ayla's chuckle held mischief. "They don't know about me."

Ayla led her onward, though occasionally stopped to study the signs. "Books about airships seem tangential to engineering. Perhaps we can start there."

"Lead on," Flowridia said, keen to watch the sultry shift of her wife's bustle.

A spiral staircase brought them to the upper floor, the wooden walls hiding them from the massive lower level. Smaller tables had been placed in secluded alcoves, perfect for studying, the ambience quiet save for their steps upon the creaking wooden floorboards. Dust and ancient texts ignited her senses; what a lovely place this would be to simply spend a day and read.

"Here we are." Ayla withdrew a book—an oft used one, if the lack of dust were any indicator. "*Modern Airships*. Seems promising."

She placed it on a table behind them, then resumed her quest.

They soon had a collection of maps and engineering textbooks—enough that, with proper study, Flowridia could likely build one on her own. "Obviously, we will take time to tour one soon," Ayla said. "Perhaps even set aside a day to take a trip. How does that sound?"

Flowridia smiled, enamored by the earnest affection in her wife's gaze. "I would love that."

It would never not be strange to see her monster wife in this way; a boorish creature to the world, but with stars in her eyes in quiet moments.

After a peek around to check for company, she placed an amorous kiss upon her wife's lips.

A stirring of passion filled the space between them. Perhaps it was the lingering adrenaline of murder, or perhaps the prospect of clandestine love in this library, but while Ayla was incapable of losing her breath, something in her gaze conveyed it, nevertheless.

Flowridia batted her eyelashes. "You know necromancy gets me terribly hot."

Ayla licked her lips, and all Flowridia's sanity unraveled. "Here, in the library? For shame, my darling."

"You can always toss me into the shadows if someone comes."

"Oh, someone will surely come," Ayla said, her grin holding vicious intent. "Though I might tie you up and leave you exposed if you don't behave."

The smallest piece of Flowridia, the part capable of contemplating self-preservation, sounded a warning at that, but the greater part of her lacked blood to her head. "Leave me wide open, then."

"If your body can handle just a few minutes of waiting, I can grab us the strap."

Flowridia seeped into her undergarments. "Yes."

And with that simple, powerful word, there came a shift in Ayla's demeanor. "State your boundaries."

The words were a chant, so often repeated. "No hitting my face. No breaking my bones."

"And what are mine?"

"Don't call you cute."

"And what will you say if you want me to stop?"

She could never *not* smile to say it. "Demitri."

"Take off your clothes."

No hesitation. Flowridia made swift work of the buttons at the front of her bodice, tugged her corset strings, stepped out of her layered skirts and crinoline. She slowed at her chemise, entranced to hold Ayla's gaze for the reveal of her body. Ayla's pupils dilated, the silver disappearing as the monster emerged—oh, any fear of being caught paled to the desperate want coursing through her.

"Stay silent," Ayla cooed as she plucked the corset from the floor. She pulled at the lacing, unraveling a length of ribbon from the eyelets. "Touch yourself."

Flowridia sighed but nothing more, hands skimming the curves of her breasts. How Ayla reveled in that, she knew, and how beautiful she felt beneath that gaze, desperate to succumb to all her wife's desires. She slid her fingers to the juncture between her legs and touched, making soft work of her clit as she groped her own breast, savoring the glint of lust in Ayla's gaze.

Ayla finally freed the ribbon. "Hands up. Sit down, pet."

Flowridia obeyed, setting her back to the shelf, brushing against old books. Though secluded between shelves, the threat of discovery remained, her nipples taut from intrigue. Ayla bound separate loops around her wrists, wrapping the rope between them in slow measures, and Flowridia ached all the while, agony in the artistry.

The other end tied all the way around the flat shelf above her, displacing ancient texts, forcing her arms up and leaving her top exposed. Ayla drew a line along Flowridia's chin, forcing their gazes to meet. "Be a good girl and wait here."

Ayla vanished into the shadows.

Golden lamplight touched her body, leaving her warm, but not so warm as the arousal lurking within her. Blood slowly drained from her arms, leaving her half-numb. Flowridia's rational mind screamed in warning, that any moment someone could walk in, but here she was no longer Flowridia Darkleaf. She was merely *pet*.

And *gods*, what a delicious thing—to belong so fully to Ayla.

The seconds ticked past, the anticipation torturous, every errant sound causing her to jump. Yet she swore the air grew colder to preface Ayla's return. Lady Darkleaf wore her same elegant black ensemble, though had removed her crinoline, the skirt less voluminous. She held velvet straps, sewn by her own expert hands and attached to a leather protrusion Flowridia simply adored. "You will be wearing it."

Helpless beneath her love's gaze, Flowridia responded to Ayla's touch as she slid the loops around Flowridia ankles, lifted her hips as Ayla slipped the velvet up her legs. She tightened the straps, leaving the phallic creation carefully positioned against Flowridia's clit before giving it a smooth rub with her hand.

Flowridia whined, then gasped when Ayla gripped her hair. "Quiet," her wife seethed, the warning made clear, before she released the thick locks.

Ayla made a show of gathering her skirts in the front, unveiling her shoes, her stockings, and finally . . . nothing. Gentler now, she tugged Flowridia's hair and guided her mouth to her cunt, already dripping from want. Flowridia savored the bitter flavor, just as she relished Ayla's dark moan. With her tongue, she made tender work of her wife's clit, shielded from any passersby by the voluminous skirts. She forgot herself, mind clear save for the touch in her hair, against her mouth, and the dampened groans from her wife.

Ayla stepped back, her pleasure coating Flowridia's

S D SIMPER

mouth, staining her face. When Ayla straddled her thighs, they shared a luxurious kiss.

"Be silent," Ayla mouthed, the repetition sure to haunt her pleasurable dreams. Ayla moved up to her hips, and pressure spiked against Flowridia's clit as her wife sank down onto her, taking her deep inside.

Flowridia bit her lip, her control quickly waning as she watched Ayla's face twist first in pain and then ecstasy, felt her motions as she fucked herself. "Gods, you're a delight," Ayla whispered, nearly innocent save for her slack jaw. Her dress hid her intimate parts, but Flowridia adored fucking with clothing—something so scandalous in the notion.

Ayla caressed Flowridia's breasts as she rubbed her body against her, squeezing the sensitive buds. Flowridia squeaked, mindful of Ayla's glare. She clenched her fists, her pleasure brewing even in the risky pose.

Despite the heat pulsing with each of Ayla's motions, her true enjoyment came from her wife—so often loud in her pleasure, now forced to curtail her cries in favor of soft groans. The slapping of skin became the loudest sound, and Flowridia sighed when Ayla's mouth went to her neck, kissing the sensitive skin. Her other hand remained on her breast, but when a sharp prick cut her skin, Flowridia lost all rational thoughts.

The heat within her turned cold, a new sort of pleasure filling her as Ayla drank. Gods, to feel the lull of Ayla's throat, the rising pleasure between her legs, to witness Ayla in ecstasy—Flowridia released a small cry—

Ayla's hand covered her mouth, and Flowridia gave a muted moan against her skin.

When Ayla withdrew, blood dripped from her mouth. They kissed, Flowridia's very life upon her tongue, and to taste it brought carnal joy. Ayla grinned, a macabre mess upon her lips. "Watch me," she mouthed, and to Flowridia's dismay, she removed herself from her strap.

Ayla gathered her skirts, revealing her glistening cunt, then turned, instead showing her ass. From her bodice, she removed a small vial. She popped it open and dripped the contents onto the strap, and Flowridia's blood boiled hot when she realized what was coming next.

Ayla stuck out her ass, returned to her knees, and held the strap as she positioned it at the smaller entrance in the back.

Flowridia whimpered at the first breach, Ayla's motions agonizingly slow as she slid herself down. They'd done this often enough, but Flowridia's gaze fell starkly upon her ass, which took the formidable strap with practiced ease.

Only when skin met skin once more did Ayla glance back, her expression hardly suited for the dominant Lady Darkleaf. Her control held by a mere thread, but at the return of her salacious grin, Flowridia simply fell apart.

Ayla fucked herself anew, slow at first, but each bounce of her ass coursed pleasure through Flowridia, this time with the added visual of the strap moving in and out of her body. Gods, she was erotic, this woman she was blessed to love, and when Flowridia bucked her hips to join, Ayla gave a leering grin.

The heat within Flowridia grew, burning at the gorgeous display, with each motion of Ayla's body, until it finally hit its peak. Her orgasm came silently, nails digging into her palms, tugging at her bonds as stars impeded her vision.

When she slowed, Ayla did too. "Look at you, you nasty thing. So shameless in this place. I adore it." Rather than withdraw, Ayla kept the strap inside her as she turned, the sensation strange and welcome upon Flowridia's sensitive clit. "Sit still, pet. I'm not quite done."

Facing her now, Ayla resumed fucking herself, this time with her skirts gathered up to reveal her lower half. She brought a hand down to touch herself, slipping her fingers inside her cunt as her ass leisurely took the strap.

Flowridia had already finished once, but fresh heat welled at the display, weak to Ayla's extravagance. She simply watched, writing the vision to memory for her to play on cold nights, until Ayla gave her own small shudder.

Ayla's pace increased at the coming of her orgasm, leaving her cunt to assault her clit, when finally, her motions ceased entirely. She fell listless against Flowridia, her head set against her shoulders. "You may speak."

"I can't feel my arms. Will you untie me?"

Ayla chuckled, only interrupted when the strap slipped out of her body. Her dress fell back into place, nothing amiss at all as she made swift work of the ribbon.

Flowridia rubbed her arms, coaxing blood through the agitated limbs. "Who knew we would be so productive."

Again, Ayla's laughter filled the room. She helped Flowridia to rise, though gasped when soft footsteps neared.

At Ayla's beckoning, Flowridia hid behind a bookshelf as her wife gathered her dress and underthings. Students filled the room, chattering about equations and upcoming exams, all while Ayla struggled with the unraveled corset strings and Flowridia suppressed giggles at her bafflement.

Once finally dressed, Ayla tossed the strap into Sha'Demoni, insisting she would find it later. They walked out arm and arm as though nothing had transpired, though Ayla did stop to grab the collection of books.

The moment they left the library's grounds, they fell into a fit of laughter at their close call. "Oh, darling, what a disaster that nearly was," Ayla said, but nothing in her words conveyed even an ounce of regret. "I did not think you would be keen for exhibitionism."

"Says the woman who once seduced me on a public altar."

"Poor Sora." Ayla pressed against her, an invitation in her gaze—which Flowridia readily returned, kissing her shamelessly upon the library steps.

Such beauty in Ayla's visage as they parted, akin to that perfect day across the altar. "Back to the executor's hall, then? We have some studying to do."

Flowridia took her hand. "Lead the way."

What a beautiful thing it was, to be loved by her.

"**L**ong story short—until Casvir's vocal cords grow back, the war is off."

In the ever-night of Staella's home, Etolié followed her momma as she flittered around her garden, tending to the glowing growths of stars.

"And look, he was insistent that he could lead without words. Necromancy doesn't require words. But all of us are in danger until we figure out how to mitigate the damage of one Lady Darkleaf. She's proven she can march in and wreak havoc on a whim."

Staella lovingly inspected all the stars along her path, whispering to each and every one. They cast ambient shades of pink, reflecting beautifully off the golden glow of Staella's skin. Staring closely, one might notice the spines along the branches, evidence of their desert heritage, but Staella gave them no mind, fearlessly cupping the little stone growths. "Can you not help him?"

Etolié placed her hand over one of the infant stars—an older one as large as her fist—intrigued by its faint warmth. "You're assuming I told him about my lackluster healing abilities."

"They're not lackluster at all. You're just learning."

"You're also assuming I give a shit about his well-being."

"A very good point."

The inherent warmth of Staella's Garden of Stars stemmed from more than simply the celestial growths. An unquestionable peace came over Etolié anytime she stepped within its bounds, more than even her mother's cozy home could provide. As a child, it had been barren. Now, it slowly regained a semblance of its once-legendary beauty, and Etolié loved seeing the progress with each visit—but more than that, she loved to see her momma so happy.

Inside, small signs remained of the difficult past they shared, but the garden was neutral ground. Though Etolié often wondered . . . if she were the only one of them who felt that way.

"Momma, I have to tell you—the fucking weirdest rumor is circulating, and Casvir seems convinced it's true. Flowers? Pregnant? Absolutely not."

Staella glanced up from her precious plants. "Which one is Flowers?"

"The wayward whore we do not speak of. But then after Ayla tried to fucking murder me, she basically validated the rumor to Casvir—which makes no damn sense."

Again, Staella turned away from her glowing stars. "So, to clarify, the wayward whore we do not speak of *is* Flowridia, right?"

"Yes, that one. But the part I'm not over is that Casvir seemed to be expecting this. He wasn't surprised. I have no idea what alternate dimension I've stepped into, but there is no bizzarro universe where Ayla sits back while some man fucks her wife."

"Sorry, sorry," Staella said, something unsettled in her features. "And Flowridia is the one who married the false Empress Alauriel who was actually that monster girl, right?"

"Yes, Momma. The monster is Ayla. I've told you."

"And Flowridia is the one who's pregnant?"

Etolié's bullshit senses began tingling, years of fighting in the political arena giving her a keen sense of when someone wasn't saying the whole truth. "That's the whole point of this story. But there's no way it's true."

"Oh, well." Staella turned back to her plants, her sudden spurt of nonchalance mighty suspicious. "Perhaps they found some sort of spell."

"Some sort of— Momma, people don't just cast magic baby spells. Flowers is a formidable witch, but you're describing god talents."

"You don't have to be a god to cast a magic baby spell."

Etolié resisted the urge to laugh, Staella's incredulity too much. "All right, but if you're trying to tell me that anyone can just stumble across a magic baby spell, you know way more exciting people than me."

Staella frowned, then returned to her work. "I suppose Neoma was an exciting person."

Though tempted to retreat at the mention of the name, Etolié pushed through the awkwardness. "This is fair, and no disrespect intended, but you and Neoma made a baby from the Silver Fire and not just anyone has the Silver Fire nowadays."

Staella said nothing, but somehow she didn't need to.

The suspicion returned, but Etolié still couldn't place it. "You're alluding to something."

"Well, not just anyone has the Silver Fire nowadays, as you said," Staella said, far more fixated on the stars than before.

"Momma, are you trying to tell me that Ayla and Flowridia made a baby out of the Silver Fire, because it sounds like you're trying to tell me that Ayla and Flowridia made a baby out of the Silver Fire."

Staella's voice came terribly small. "I wouldn't discount it."

"Momma, I feel like there's a learning curve for things like that, given there isn't a single known record of a Solviran impregnating someone with the Silver Fire—"

All rational thought left her as an idea as grandiose as the Bringer of War's hammer bombarded her memory. Once upon a time, at a particular wedding that Momma had attended, she had gifted . . . "Momma, you didn't."

"Empress Alauriel was the last of her line."

"Momma—"

"I did what I had to do."

"Momma, no."

"It's not my fault she ended up being a murderous vampire instead."

All Etolié's waning effort went into keeping her voice steady—and she failed miserably, but at least she wasn't screaming. "You mean to tell me that you gave the secret to creating life itself to *Ayla Darkleaf?*"

Staella's guilty smile confirmed it all. "I was hopeful it had been destroyed in the blast."

"*Apparently not*—" Etolié clamped her mouth shut, trying terribly hard to not have a complete meltdown in front of her sensitive mother, but she might as well have stuck one of those elven bombs inside her stomach, lit the fuse, and asked it not to explode. "So that's what was on the scroll."

"Correct."

No longer trusting her legs to work, Etolié sat in the dirt.

A thousand thoughts fluttered through her head, many of which were simply her own life flashing before her eyes as she contemplated a world with Ayla's spawn crawling through it. "None of this explains how Casvir knew, but baby steps."

"Baby steps."

"What the fuck do we do?"

Staella sat before her, looking equally lost. "We let people make their own choices."

"That's such a fucking mom thing to say."

Staella chuckled as she brushed earth and glittering stardust from Etolié's illusionary dress. "Good thing I'm a mother, then."

"So's Flowers, apparently." Etolié grimaced as another truth settled with it. "Oh shit, that's why she's with the elves. Silver Fire pregnancies kill."

"They can, yes," Staella replied, sorrow in the words. "But if she's as formidable a necromancer as you've said, she should be all right."

"It wouldn't be the worst thing if she died, honestly."

"Whatever the crimes of its parents, no baby deserves that."

Damn Momma, saying mom things again. Etolié's face fell into her hands. "This is a lot to take in."

"It's only a baby, Starshine."

"Only a baby?" Etolié glanced up, praying it conveyed her doubt. "The world is *not* ready for Darkleaf spawn. What's that thing that happens when a mortal and vampire have a fucking baby?"

"A dhampir, sweetheart."

"It's going to be whatever the fuck that is. Maybe it'll eat her from the uterus out."

Staella made no attempt to hide her distaste. "You understandably hold a grudge, but this is gruesome and you're above it."

Again, Etolié failed to hide her disbelief. "They blew up the castle in Neolan. I think I'm allowed to wish her a tragic childbirth."

"Please don't forget that I once lost twins."

"Don't even joke about them having twins—oh." Staella didn't have to rage to show her disappointment—and that was assuredly what it was, that scowl. Etolié wished to melt into the dirt. "I'm sorry."

Staella's countenance held uncharacteristic severity.

"Dead children will forever be a tragic topic for me."

Etolié fidgeted with her illusionary dress, struggling to thaw her frozen tongue. "Fine, in this hypothetical story, the baby lives. Are you happy?"

"I am."

Etolié could envision the tragedy perfectly well in her head without traumatizing her momma. And she did—on repeat, images of a nasty vampire spawn carving its way out of its mother's stomach.

Cathartic, honestly.

"I should tell you something," Staella said, returning her attention to the stars. She cupped one in her hands and wiped flecks of dust away with her thumb. "I've been in contact with your grandfather."

Etolié's exasperation with those bitches paled, by far, to this. "You what?"

"Alystra mediated a meeting between Eionei and me. I heard what he had to say." Staella's arms dropped, her whole body slumping with it. Momma was already small; to see her shrink lacerated Etolié's heart, a protective instinct rising within her. "He gave an apology, and I accepted. In fact, I gave one in return."

"You what?" Etolié repeated, because suddenly this was no longer her quietly vindictive mother who had once dubiously poisoned this same man.

"I believe that everything I said about his misplaced intentions, his love for you and me both, is true. I believe that he has loved me in his misguided way for far longer than your lifetime, but I fear it colored my own view of the past. I neglected to consider his point of view on a very important thing—my treatment of you."

"It's no excuse for what he did," Etolié said, stumbling to spit out the panicked words. "It's unforgivable. You shouldn't have spoken to him."

"Etolié, what do you want me to say? Eionei expressed regret for what he did, but he truly thought you could only heal and live if you were far away from me. And was he wrong?"

The words left Etolié cold, as any reminder of her childhood did. "Momma, I . . . Y-You apologized. You've changed. And I—"

The word caught at the tip of her tongue. That damned healing word. *Forgive.*

"He wants to see you," Staella said.

"Absolutely not."

"And that's all right, but please consider it, someday."

Etolié came forward, hating her rising apprehension. Heat coursed through her blood, fury causing her to shake. "Momma, I don't like that he made you feel this way. This is manipulation."

"No, it is not. The consequences of what I did don't end because you've come home. To atone means to make amends for every part of my mistakes, and the fact remains that he cared for you in Celestière when I could not and watched over you when you were in the mortal realm. For goodness' sake, he negotiated with Morathma on your behalf—"

"He what?"

Staella's face filled with grief. "And you didn't even know? Etolié, you, the daughter of a goddess, spent ten years fighting slavers in the desert. Not once did Morathma, ruler of the desert, personally interfere—and only because of Eionei, because he promised to never personally interfere either, lest there be a war between them."

"He always just said he'd watch in case I needed him," Etolié muttered, hardly audible at all. This was no small thing. Morathma was not a god to trifle with—especially as a Daughter of Staella.

"I hate to say I might've thought the same if I were Eionei," Staella said, "and I fear, in my own anger, that I was blinded to his true intentions. He has always loved me; that is simply fact. But he loves you too, and in the purest of ways. He thought he knew what was best for you, and should he have done it? No, but I understand. I hate it, but I understand."

"Momma, I just . . ." Tears stung Etolié's eyes, but she refused to cry. Not today. Not in front of Momma. "Let me just think about it, all right?"

Staella said nothing as she offered her hand. Etolié accepted, lip trembling as her momma held it tight. "I didn't mean to upset you. If you're ever ready, Eionei misses you. But you have your free will as well, and I will not push it."

Etolié nodded, for to speak would break her resolve.

"Anger can be healthy, but remember to not let it control you." Staella released her, anxiety revealed in how she played with her skirt. "May I make you tea? Some cookies? I'm sorry I've upset you—"

"No, no—Momma, it's not you. It's just that I've done

156

absolutely everything I can to not think about it, so it's . . . it's something."

The longer Staella studied her, the more exposed Etolié became, for her momma read her like a book no matter how hard she tried to keep her nasty feelings to herself. "Come inside, Starshine. I want to hear more about Khastra and the war."

Etolié followed as she led.

An eventful week passed of Flowridia absorbing the ambience of Velen'Kye. Such delicious food; such delightful sights. They returned to the library again and again—though engaged in less invigorating activities—where Flowridia memorized every map and passage about those mystical airships. When Ayla informed Executor Stormforged that they would be gone a few days following the masquerade, she booked a flight. Just a few more days, and Flowridia would see the world from new heights.

If it weren't for the people, she could've spent a lifetime here. Tonight she would be meeting a plethora of them.

"Flowra, I am afraid to admit I may have lost my mind on a particular something."

A suspicious phrase to utter, especially an hour before the masquerade. Within the executor's hall, Ayla stood deliberately between Flowridia and their bedroom door. Yes, Demitri could have barged past, but he listened as curiously as she.

"Is this related to your insistence that we don't need to go dress shopping for the masquerade?" Flowridia asked.

"It absolutely is."

Flowridia allowed her sly smile to come, amusement twisting her lip. "You haven't had time to sew something new."

"No, tragically. But I did have time to modify something I bought while you were busy reading about airships. And, well, sleeping." Her demureness rose, that same bashful purse of her lips whenever she had a gift to present, and Flowridia adored it. "I hope you like it."

She opened the door, and Flowridia gasped at the vision

displayed upon the bed.

Countless times, she had tried on beautiful gowns that Ayla had made or bought, sewn with lace or embroidered with gentle emblems like flowers or stars. Flowridia never sought to cast a large aura, content to fade into the background, but Ayla's gowns always brought her into the light—yet softly so, letting her become delicate art befitting an empress consort.

This was not delicate.

The colors were spring, white and pastel pinks, but while the dress adhered to elven standards, Ayla had added unusual flair. Jewels had been sewn onto the bodice in the shape of ribs, the gloves bearing bones of equally eccentric grace, and the mask might have been a wolf skull, but sturdier, surely fake but no less grand.

No, this was not delicate. This was a show of power by an accomplished necromancer. This was beautiful, and this was not a dress for the elves to dismiss.

She came forward in a daze, enamored by the sight. "Ayla, this is incredible."

Clear relief filled Ayla's words. "Oh, good. In my perfect world, I would have created this from scratch, but with only a week, I had to manage my time with care. Thankfully, I was able to use an old project for my own; no extra time needed."

"May I see it?"

From the wardrobe, Ayla presented a dark dress cascading with rubies—embroidered to appear as a wash of blood. "I think we will be an appropriate match."

Flowridia agreed, blushing as Ayla helped her to dress.

Once in her corset and underthings, Ayla assisted in fitting the elaborate dress to her body. But though Flowridia admired the sparkling jewels, her mind fell upon something else. "So this party is a ploy to spend money to gain more money?"

No matter how many times Ayla explained the concept of a 'fundraiser,' Flowridia struggled to comprehend the use.

"Essentially, yes." Ayla's deft fingers made quick work of the gown's lacing. Flowridia ran her hands along the bodice, the stones smooth against her fingers.

"Do their taxes not pay for the war?" Flowridia asked, and when Ayla's hands finished with the strings, Flowridia stepped closer to the vanity, absorbing her appearance. So strange, to look so highly upon herself, to see her body presented and feel sublime, but between the powerful dress and Ayla's adoring gaze, how could she feel anything less than perfect?

"You look gorgeous, my darling." Ayla adjusted her own corset, the black cloth a sight against her pallid skin. The strings did little to accentuate her waist—there simply wasn't anywhere for her tiny figure to go—but Flowridia thought her beautiful, nevertheless. "Their taxes do pay for the war, but investors can bring in mountains more. It's private money, so the executors can spend it however they want."

"So they're throwing an expensive party to appeal to the investors so the investors give them money?"

Ayla left the mirror to put on her elaborate gown. "Correct."

Flowridia thought it needless. Perhaps two months of ruling Solvira had gotten into her head. As she preened her thick hair, she said, "And they can't demand the money?"

"Not in this country."

"But the executors make the laws."

"Oh, darling, if I ruled this country, I would agree. But that would be easier said than done." Ayla soon returned in her own delicious gown, for that was the only word Flowridia could settle upon. By every god—she was gorgeous. "What do you think?"

"Beautiful is accurate, but it doesn't do you justice. Fearsome, perhaps. Magnificent?"

Ayla laughed, not shy one bit as she posed. But then she studied Flowridia closely, tucking aside a few idle strands of hair. "Will you be able to wear the mask with your hair?"

"You tell me."

In response, Ayla held up the skull mask. With care to mind the flighty individual strands, Ayla tied the ribbons around the tresses, then stepped back to survey her work. "Lovely. Thank goodness."

As Ayla tied her own mask—which Flowridia highly suspected was part of an actual elven skull—she whispered slow and sensuous, "Would you like to hear the best part about your dress?"

Flowridia bit her lip, her body responding to the alluring tone. "I would."

"It's long enough to hide your bare feet."

At Ayla's wink, Flowridia burst into laughter, joined by her beloved. "My love, you know me too well."

As their laughing fit ended, Flowridia spared a glance for

Demitri, whose golden eyes were intrigued. "Let me guess—you're too little to come. You'll get squished and die."

To her surprise, Demitri paused before replying, the voice in her head thoughtful. *I want to go.*

"Really? Why?"

Because I'm big now. If I'm there, it'll keep them nervous.

Flowridia laughed and relayed the message to Ayla, whose twisted grin spelled approval. "You're a handsome creature, Demitri," she said, coming to smooth the dark grey fur of his face and neck. "And anyone who objects will answer to me."

Mom, I need a mask.

"You really don't need a mask."

Yes, I do. It's a masquerade, and Lady Ayla says that means we all disguise ourselves.

As Flowridia questioned how to explain the dilemma of '*Dearest, you know you're a wolf, right?*' Ayla chuckled and spared her the headache.

"Let me see what I can conjure. Give me just a few minutes."

Ayla disappeared into a shadow.

She's going to be my favorite mom if you don't step up.

Flowridia rolled her eyes and continued preening.

"Are you fucking jesting?!"

Seated on her bed at the inn, Sora paused in her knitting to share a glance with Kah'Sheen, who held her own set of yarn and needles. She wore a small scarf to cover her breasts but was naked besides that, though Sora did not know enough of half-demon anatomy to find anything offensive in her lower half. Staff Seraph deDieula lay innocuously beside her, the skull propped on a pillow.

Sora would have thought, with her extra set of arms, Kah'Sheen might be well equipped for knitting. Alas, she struggled like anyone else.

They both stopped to listen to the outrage in the room next door.

"I'm insulted! This is my damn plan, and you would make me

an afterthought?!"

Sora set aside her half-made sock and pressed her ear to the wall.

"You know it would be suspicious if you were on my arm for the masquerade," came Mereen's calm response, but Odessa's rage rose anew.

"For gods' sake, I can manipulate minds! They won't even know I'm human. And you might need that too, given you're hardly inconspicuous yourself."

"That's why I'm taking Tazel who—"

"Is a celebrity?!"

Yelling ensued.

"It is funny to me," Kah'Sheen said, "that they are so similar and so different. I am thinking they are better working alone."

"I think Mereen and Odessa would do just fine with partners who aren't each other."

"Mereen is often working with partners, it is true, but she is not working with partners who speak up for themselves." Kah'Sheen glared at her needles. "Can you show me the purl stitch again?"

Sora sat at the edge of the bed, mostly level with Kah'Sheen, whose many legs were tucked under her abdomen as she rested on the floor, and resumed teaching.

Their peace did not last long before Odessa burst in, as haughty as a cat surveying her domain. "Who wants to join me in dress shopping?"

Sora did not, but she was the only realistic option, so she nodded anyway.

"Kah'Sheen, you are welcome to watch from the shadows and offer whispered opinions. In fact, it wouldn't be the same without you. I must insist."

"If we are infiltrating anyway, I can be stealing dresses for you."

Odessa pursed her full lips, her pretty face mulling it over. "Well, fine. I suppose that would be easier. My best color is green."

Kah'Sheen offered Sora her ill-fated project and ducked into the shadow of the bed.

Sora coughed in the awkward silence. "I may have overheard."

"Good. That said, I could not quite make an argument for you to join us as party patrons. Sadly we do need a few someones to pose as servants, but now you'll have Tazel to escort you. Gods, while I don't doubt he is a good man on his own, he is absolutely whipped by that woman. Tries to pad her way through life—disgusting."

"He's trying to help."

"Sora, dear, I know all the tricks for manipulating the people around me. I know I can't convince you that she's a mess, but your pandering is a little pathetic."

Before Sora could gather her ego and respond, Odessa held up two matching uniforms, each fitted with trousers but clearly shaped to accommodate breasts and hips. "Try this one. I need to modify mine to fit Tazel."

Sora bristled as she accepted the garment, her pride still battered, but with a snap of Odessa's fingers, a needle, a spool of thread, and the other uniform came to life and proceeded to modify itself. Sora stared, mesmerized by the motion, and was only pulled from the spell when Odessa coughed to move her along.

Sora quickly changed, having no qualms about disrobing in front of apparent friends, but was startled when Odessa began fussing over the buttons on the back of her vest. "Oh, let me. No need to wrench your arms." Odessa made quick work of it, then stood back to admire the fit. "I can modify it for you if you want. Help it be a bit more snug."

Sora tested the shoulders and found she could move with ease. "No, keep it as is. I need to be flexible."

"If it's any consolation, the party will be no fun at all, given elves have terrible taste in wine—if you can even call that watered-down grape juice alcohol. Elves and their fragile constitutions." Odessa glared once more at Sora's outfit, straightening her collar this time. "What about you? I've never seen you drink, but you love that pipe of yours."

"I'm definitely fully human in that regard. I can drink as well as anyone. Rarely sick."

"Good to know, in case I ever need to surreptitiously murder Tazel. A little poison in the stew—we'll recover; he will not."

Sora bristled as Odessa cackled, refusing to give her any validation.

As Odessa returned her attention to the enchanted garment and sewing supplies—a pair of scissors had joined the lot—Sora inspected herself in the mirror, adjusting the trousers and vest. She might've looked inconspicuous, but there was no hiding her hair.

She untied the leather holding it in place, then separated it into thick segments, content to braid it back.

Kah'Sheen soon returned, a bundle of dresses in her arms. "What are you thinking?"

Odessa tugged straightaway at a collection of green fabric highlighted with gold. "Something tells me this one is perfect."

Soon, they stood before a mirror, with Odessa scrutinizing her body as Sora tugged the corset strings. "Give it one more pull, Sora. My waist has nearly vanished!"

"Three, two, one—"

Odessa squeaked as Sora gave the final yank. "Perfect as it'll get," the witch said, then took a stabilizing, albeit shallow, breath. "If I were a betting woman, I'd say this body has never given birth. Look how smooth my stomach is."

As Sora tied the strings, she couldn't fathom where Odessa had found any sort of imperfection, her corset merely accentuating her flawless curvature. No, this was not her true body, stolen from an unfortunate human girl, but Sora swore it had slowly twisted the longer Odessa held it—the hair becoming more auburn, less fiery, subtle laughter lines appearing at her eyes to signify age.

Behind them, the enchanted thread and needle continued their work. Sora grabbed the dress—a gorgeous shade of green, surely flawless with Odessa's hair and skin—at which point, a realization struck her like a fist. "You can control inanimate objects with magic."

Odessa stared as though she'd commented on the weather. "Well, yes."

"So why am I tightening your corset strings?"

The dress levitated from Sora's grasp, all the buttons coming undone with a wave of Odessa's hand. "No need for accusation. I simply miss the ritual of helping my fellow women dress." She stepped into it, the dress adjusting around her figure with the ease of flowing water. "Look how much less fun that was."

Any implication of comradery set Sora on edge, but the bottom hem of Odessa's dress was folded. She knelt down to fix it, keeping silent lest she interpret her own discomforting feelings.

There came a knock at the door. "Come in!" Odessa sang.

Mereen entered, unquestionably stunning in her

ensemble of black and white. She oozed high society, every gesture dripping with grace and poise. Her blonde hair was in a bun, and her decorated hat held a veil, half-covering her beautiful face. "Are you decent enough for Tazel to join us?"

"I'm not naked, if that's what you're asking," Odessa replied, then resumed her girlish giggling in the mirror. "Isn't this color lovely?"

Sora went to work buttoning the back. When Kah'Sheen joined, her four hands proved perfectly dexterous even working in tandem.

"You're the best friends a lady could ask for," Odessa said, clapping with delight. "You spend a year as a ghost and forget how sumptuous a proper dress can make you look."

Tazel entered, still wearing casual attire. Mereen stared at Odessa with derision. "At least you clean up well. Do your hair."

"Getting to it, Mother Dear." Odessa's smirk could have spoiled meat, but she set her focus on her auburn locks.

"Is Tazel's outfit done?"

Odessa pointed at the bed.

Mereen thrust the garment at Tazel. "Tonight, we infiltrate the masquerade. They've made quite the spectacle of inviting The Endless Night. We survey the arena, see what the battlefield looks like, all while Kah'Sheen lurks in the shadows with the staff. When the time is right, Tazel will give a signal, and Kah'Sheen will emerge and toss Odessa the staff. She will subdue Ayla, who I don't anticipate going down without a fight, which is where Kah'Sheen and Tazel come in. Sora, keep your attention to Flowridia. Prevent her from causing too much trouble. Are we understood?"

Sora gave a quick nod. "What about you?"

"I know my part." Mereen left without further explanation.

Tazel, however, lingered at the door. "Thank you for the outfit. And don't mind Mereen. She's stressed over tonight."

"You are very welcome, Tazel." Odessa's attention didn't leave her hair. Fanciful pins were set throughout, and Sora suspected she had conjured them from the air. "Some of us just cope better with stress than others."

When Tazel left, Odessa released a seething breath. "I respect her talents. I respect her experience. When she has her mouth shut, she's a formidable ally, but gods. Has she always been this . . ." Odessa sought the word with her hand, waving until she settled upon the one she wanted. "Bitchy?"

Sora glowered, but Odessa turned her fuming attention to her, a warning in her glare.

"No," Kah'Sheen replied, defusing the tension between them. She resettled on the bed, which sagged beneath her size. No matter how slim she was, she was still exceptionally tall. "When I am first meeting her, she is very sad. She is heartbroken to give up her son. She is wanting to avenge her people, especially her sister."

"Her name was Sarai, right?" Sora asked, for her mother had spoken of a particular song, even hummed it a time or two.

"I don't think Mereen holds quite the same fondness anymore," Odessa said, her smooth words more akin to what Sora knew of the woman—sensuous and dangerous, "based on things she's said to me."

Sora waited for the witch to elaborate, but Odessa had disappeared into her own little world, returning to preening her hair.

"Mereen is mentioning her sister a few times," Kah'Sheen said. "Apparently she is silly but kind, with a voice to rival even Goddess Staella."

"That's high praise," Sora replied, for she had heard—or, more often, overheard—Etolié sing countless times, and she couldn't fathom a voice finer than that. The shared blood had surely evoked such beautiful talent. "I know there's a song she wrote that Mereen . . . clung to."

She struggled to find a better word for it, but some said undead were stagnant creatures—so of course Mereen would cling to one of her final mortal memories.

"Yes, yes—she is singing it once, a long time ago. Uh, something to do with death and to have redemption . . ." Kah'Sheen grimaced. "I am not remembering, and I am not adept at singing. But she is singing it to . . . to Mari? That is her pet name. Great-great-granddaughter."

Sora's heart lifted at the name, for any memory was precious. "That's my mom."

"Is she? You look very much like her."

Elation filled Sora, for she was not often compared to an elf—not even her mother. "What do you remember?"

"Oh, she is very sweet. We are only meeting a few times, but she is liking my knives. How is she?"

"She passed away about fifteen years ago, from a fever."

"Oh. Sorry to hear."

There was nothing more to say of it, for already Sora's stomach had dropped. She could not risk tears in front of this woman. "It is what it is. What else do you remember about my mom?"

Kah'Sheen told it all with a smile.

Flowridia stood at the cusp of an ocean of lights, glitter, and perfume as thick as fog.

"You are an absolute vision," Ayla whispered into her ear, their fingers intertwined. "Revel in it."

Flowridia suspected the partiers looked more to the giant wolf behind her, but Ayla's words still brought a blush.

With each graceful step into the ballroom, Flowridia felt increasingly daunted by the sea of masked partiers. Any one of them could be a friend or foe, and some were people she knew already but could not recognize. Surely the executors were here, easily able to spot her—a human witch with skin several shades darker than the tannest of elves, and accompanied by a wolf.

Ayla had said to revel, and she struggled, but she managed to breathe.

Already she searched for the table of food, as every party had, ready to stand in the corner with Demitri and say absolutely nothing, but Ayla entered the ballroom like a fighter in the arena, confidence in every stride. She greeted those who saw her—for she was unmistakable as well—and even drew Flowridia into those rapid interactions, charming all she met before pulling them away.

Demitri, too, parted the crowd, and Flowridia appreciated the empty space that naturally formed around him.

Strange, that she still had not spotted the table of refreshments, but she had seen a few servants carrying trays of small cakes and glasses of wine.

There are so many strange smells here.

"Well, let me know if any of those smells are dinner," Flowridia whispered, content to be a shadow at Ayla's side. She

EVE OF ENDLESS NIGHT

nearly wished Soliel had stayed—at least he was someone she knew.

"Lady Darkleaf, so delightful you could come. You must meet my wife."

Flowridia struggled a moment to connect the voice to the fanciful outfit and mask, the light blues perfectly tailored to the lithe man's physique. On his arm was a woman dressed more professional than outlandish, not a single curl out of place from her bun, her dress buttoned up nearly to her chin. Even the notable bump at her womb seemed deliberately decorated, structured despite the austere pattern of the gown. A second glance revealed the man to be Executor Stormforged himself, and Flowridia supposed only an intense woman would be married to someone so esteemed.

Ayla took the woman's hand, and to Flowridia's surprise, brought it to her lips and placed a kiss upon her knuckle. "I am charmed to meet you. As your husband said, I am Lady Ayla Darkleaf. This is my wife, Flowridia Darkleaf, and her familiar, Demitri."

"Elania Stormforged, inheritor of the Eventide fortune," the wife replied, and Flowridia did not know what it meant—but surmised it was of importance. "What an impressive creature, this 'Demitri.' If there is a price—"

"Absolutely not."

And thank every god Ayla spoke up; Flowridia feared she would not have been so polite.

"Of course. I would not willingly give up something so fine either. Wolves were once a sign of status in this country, did you know?"

"It rings a bell," Ayla said, and Flowridia genuinely did not know if she were lying.

"In the ancient days, our beloved Goddess of Chaos granted them as familiars to her priestesses, and there are accounts of executors keeping them as pets in our history books to show their devotion and power." She looked knowingly to her husband. "What do you think? I would fund it."

"Perhaps one a little smaller," the executor said, "but I see the appeal."

Elania turned her masked gaze to Flowridia. "Lady Flowridia, congratulations on the baby."

Flowridia placed a fond hand on her stomach. She supposed they would have to stuff it soon, but for now, she

167

feigned a protective gesture upon her hollow womb. "Thank you, Lady Stormforged," Flowridia replied, praying the title was correct.

Fortunately, the dilemma of whether it was rude to comment on Elania's own clear pregnancy resolved itself. "I'm due for my first soon as well. Halfway there. Only three more months to go." Flowridia apparently failed to hide her confusion at the stated timeline; Elania's chuckle held moderate condescension. "Do they not teach you that across the sea? We have much shorter pregnancies than you humans."

Flowridia swallowed her pride, though struggled to maintain her smile. "I was unaware, sorry."

The mood became discomforting. Elania kept her pompous tone. "My husband says you are a witch."

"That is true."

"Won't you do a little trick for us? I do love a performance."

She seemed sincere, though Flowridia didn't miss the twitch in Ayla's smile at the patronizing 'little trick' line. "My most impressive tricks tend to be dangerous. I can't say they would be appropriate in so . . ." She glanced about the crowd, struggling to relay the issue. "Populated a place."

"Oh, come now—surely you can conjure some entertainment?"

In Flowridia's brief search for something living, she spotted the corsage upon Lady Stormforged's breast. Mindful of the close crowd, she breathed and summoned the barest hints of necromancy, ignoring the gasp from the executor's wife as purple smoke wafted from her hand. At her bidding, the corsage withered and dried, only to immediately flourish with life. Absolutely perfect, void of all flaws, and Flowridia did stand a bit taller at Lady Stormforged's shock.

"And now, it shall never die."

"Amazing, truly," Elania said, then she turned to a couple beside her. "Ylandra, look at this, won't you? Lady Flowridia Darkleaf is a witch."

This new woman wore an entire hat laden with flowers, and Flowridia already plotted her next maneuver. "Won't you do it again?" Lady Stormforged asked, and Flowridia smiled apologetically at the other woman before casting her spell.

The flowers in her hat died like the corsage, then blossomed anew—but these ones she bid to move about like a snake, though gently so, lest the woman spook. The elf did remove her hat, her eyes as wide as the full moon to watch the flowers move of their own accord, purple smoke seeping from the leaves and petals. "How did you do it?"

"It's magic, as Lady Stormforged said," Flowridia replied, bidding the flowers to stop. "Necromancy, specifically. The flowers are dead, but it means they'll stay forever beautiful."

"I might need you to come to my estate. I can fire my gardeners." When she laughed, Flowridia sensed no mockery; it seemed she had done something right.

"But can you do it on people? On creatures?" Lady Stormforged asked, and Flowridia explained as well as she could for polite company—though these elves were oddly unbothered at the prospect.

They spoke for a time. Flowridia spared the occasional glance to Ayla to gauge how the undercurrents within the conversation were flowing, but she saw nothing but approval on her wife's face. Only when an announcer said the center would be cleared for dancing did their conversation end, and while Flowridia would not allow herself to be too cocky, she swore she saw a glimmer of respect in the executor's eye.

"You will dance with me, won't you?" Ayla said, her wink suggesting she knew full well that Flowridia was weak to many things—and this nearly topped the list. "We can show these silly rich folk how a true master does it."

"Yes, the master and her poor lacky struggling to follow along," Flowridia teased, but Ayla tugged her forward as the luxurious stringed instruments began a new tune.

"Hush. You've improved dramatically." Ayla placed her hands, then her feet. "Follow my lead."

Flowridia did, as though that could even be a question, content to twirl in time to the lovely tune. More refined than Solviran tunes, ineffably so, but time signatures were familiar wherever you went.

Every motion from Ayla's body was polished perfectly, from the points of her toes to the graceful pose of her hands. Flowridia felt comparatively clumsy, but Ayla would not lie if she truly had not improved. What mattered, however, was the touch on Flowridia's waist, the gentle way Ayla led. Dancing sparked memories of joy—of the embassy party where they had shared their first dance, their wedding and the afterparty . . . Flowridia's radiant joy flittered as laughter from her lips. They were the only ones on the floor, she realized, and a glance into the crowd revealed mostly apathy—

Though one masked woman watched intently. Something about her shape stood out from the rest. Flowridia blinked, and she was gone, but the oddness of her remained. Red hair, green dress—nothing strange about that. Flowridia tried to spot her again, but the song ended, and there came polite, bored applause.

They chuckled in the other's arms, but beckoning from the crowd interrupted them. Executor Stormforged motioned to Ayla, who gave a curt nod. "Seems it's time for me to inspire the masses."

"I have no question of your ability."

Ayla placed a small peck on her lips, then gracefully danced toward the executor, her steps light and enthralling.

Flowridia backed away into the crowd, to where Demitri waited. *That was the longest four minutes of my life.*

"You're the one who decided to come to the stuffy party."

Upon a platform, Executor Stormforged raised a hand behind a podium, calling the crowd to order. "I thank you all for coming. Velen'Kye is stronger for your support, and I look forward to the night's events."

Flowridia tried to listen, but from across the room, she spotted the auburn-haired interloper—or so she presumed, given she faced her back. The woman was with her own small group, moving vivaciously as she charmed an ensemble of nobles and looped around her arm was another woman's.

". . . without further ado, I present an esteemed guest—a woman known by many titles and legendary deeds, whose efforts to unify the Four Kingdoms centuries ago led to the prosperity we share today, and who has proven herself immune to death time and time again. Please give a round of applause to Lady Ayla Darkleaf."

Applause sounded, but Flowridia still stared upon the odd woman. Was her partner what stood out? Perhaps Flowridia was keen to accidentally spot other Daughters of Neoma. Not that she would use that term for an elf.

. . . But she was not an elf. That was the oddness of her.

"Greetings, guests of Executor Stormforged," came Ayla's words, her tone suspended between sultry and menace. "It truly is a delight to stand before you all."

The woman was as human as Flowridia, told by the

subtle differences in her curves. Flowridia was slim, but she was large compared to these elven women, and this woman could have been her twin in body type.

But why another human?

I don't like the smells here.

Demitri startled her from her musing. "What do you smell?" Flowridia whispered, eyes fixed upon the strange woman. Ayla spoke, but she did not hear it.

Gross perfume. It's the strongest stench.

"There's a balcony if you need to go outside."

Mom, I don't want to worry you, but I think there's something dead.

Perhaps it was chance that turned the woman's face toward Flowridia then. Her mask matched her dress, tied up into luxurious locks of auburn hair, and Flowridia was confident she did not know her face.

Yet that smirk left her cold.

"... Truly remarkable, how the Four Kingdoms have stood their ground against the onslaught of Nox'Kartha . . ."

The human turned back to her group, whispering something to her companion, but Flowridia's heart raced for reasons her mind had yet to catch up to. She knew it—by every god, she knew that smile, how she withered before it, how her heartrate spiked. But how? Why?

She shoved her way through the crowd, ducking past entranced partiers. Beside the platform, Executor Stormforged himself stepped in front of her. "What are you doing?"

"It's very important that I—"

"Darling?"

At Ayla's word, the entire room shifted to face Flowridia. Her attempt at words trailed off when in the crowd, the woman's elven companion spared her a glance—and Flowridia most certainly knew that pale hair and paler skin.

"Ayla—"

A blast of light filled the room.

Flowridia shaded her eyes, dazzled by the brilliance of it. Not fire, no. Nothing like Ayla's silver flame, but vibrant like the sun itself. Ayla flinched, shielding herself with more vigor, before pulling a knife from her bodice.

The crowd itself gasped at the minor unrest, yet most seemed eager, awaiting some other trick, some new performance. Instead, a large shadow suddenly loomed, and from the walls came . . . Kah'Sheen?

Flowridia knew her spidery figure—had once feared it, then considered it her savior. She was unmistakable, an acrobat as she flung herself through the crowd and landed in the center of the dance floor—and tossed a decorated staff to the woman in the green dress.

Partiers at the outskirts fled, but many lingered, split between panic and intrigue. From the ground rippled purple smoke, but it was not gaseous. Opaque, it morphed into tentacle-like tendrils and lashed across the crowd, grabbing some. Screams of pain arose. Many fell, desiccated in seconds. Flowridia did not burn at the touch, but it reeked of necromancy. A glance to the human woman confirmed her fear—and Flowridia suddenly knew her, knew the shadow she cast.

A monster. An . . . owl.

Her gut clenched with brewing bile—and dread.

In the split moment of Flowridia's realization, Ayla sparked to life. She ran for Kah'Sheen, who gleefully met her blade with her own. Flame burst from Ayla's body—which did seem to hinder the half-demon.

Demitri snarled, entangled by the dark magic. Despite the surrounding mayhem, Flowridia thought only of the impossible necromancer, but with that knowledge came something new—she had little to fear from her magic, at least. She forced a breath. With her inhale, she absorbed the potent necromancy. The tentacle holding her dissipated. She collapsed to the ground, but a strong grip wrenched her up.

Ayla fought Kah'Sheen, too distracted by her blood foe. Flowridia struggled against this new captor, swearing she knew them—the strength, the subtle sweet smell.

"I don't want to hurt you," came Sora Fireborn's voice, and Flowridia immediately combusted with necrotic power.

Sora recoiled at the blast of malignant energy. Flowridia yanked herself free. Instinct drove her to Demitri's side, where she absorbed the swirling death binding him.

Tazel Fireborn joined the fray, his rapier swinging with precision at Ayla. Flowridia could spare only a moment of anger for this apparent betrayal before he suddenly burned with energy. Holy fire bombarded Ayla, unnatural shades of gold meeting her silver. She flinched at the touch, then pounced—

Only to freeze and *scream*.

172

Ayla struggled against invisible bonds. She frantically swiped at Kah'Sheen, but her dagger dropped to the ground. The Coming Dawn did not engage, merely lashed at any in the crowd who dared to approach or run. Ayla screamed, every motion stiff, like slogging through mud. She stumbled. Shock stilled Flowridia, but the tears in Ayla's eyes pushed her to act.

As she summoned clouds of death, a bloodcurdling cackle ricocheted Flowridia into her own tumultuous past.

It could not be, yet she had seen the shadow herself. Mother's voice was unmistakable. The body was different, but there was no mistaking the approaching woman's sultry gait, the natural dramatics in her shoulders. The frightful skull upon the staff held glowing eye sockets, staring with the same menace as its wielder. "Hello, Flower Child," she cooed. "So wonderful to see you again."

Odessa held power, yes. But Flowridia had grown—and her mother reeked of death, but also fragile life. How convenient, for her quarry to have all come to her.

With a swipe of Odessa's hand, a few of the remaining elves screamed as they fell to her might, their life fueling her in literal glowing strings. Yet the skull faced Ayla alone, and Flowridia did not have to focus to know that it was the cause of her wife's pain. Crackling purple lightning rose from Flowridia's skin, dancing across her like a shield—

Until a swift kick to her ribs broke her focus. Tazel seized her.

"Demitri!" she cried, and the wolf fell not upon Tazel— but upon Mother.

The wolf latched onto her arm and thrashed her around like a toy. Amid Mother's screams, the staff clattered to the ground. Ayla scrambled to her feet, heaving as though she'd burst from deep water.

Power gushed from Flowridia's pores, and she shrieked as it grew—until Tazel released her, his cry of pain invigorating—

All the world slowed as Mereen emerged like a beacon.

She was gorgeous, precision in every curl of her hair, each curve of her figure, everything about her the perfect predator built to lure her prey. Her hand lifted, the gun steady, and Flowridia knew the sound like a rabbit knew a panther's footsteps.

Click.

Flowridia froze at the mechanical omen, the precursor

to certain death. Mereen's aim leveled with Flowridia's head.

Boom.

The explosion deafened her, yet Flowridia so precisely saw the bullet and, with it, a thousand memories of her twenty short years—of the orphanage, of Aura, of Mother, of Staelash, of Etolié and Casvir and Lara and Ayla and Solvira and Demitri—

It soared toward her . . . and missed.

So deliberate. It flew past her head, and she wondered if it were simply a warning, a threat, for Mereen would never be so sloppy.

But in the moment before the end of the world, the bullet stilled before Demitri, perfectly centered before one eye—wherein the gold reflected black death.

Wolves did not show emotion. Demitri merely emoted; he did not show emotion, yet she swore in her precious boy's eyes was terror.

Or perhaps it was simply her own.

Mom—

The bullet struck.

All the world became silent.

Chapter 9

"**K**ick his ass, Beefcake! Woo hoo!"

No, the resident beefcake couldn't hear her, but Etolié figured it was the thought that counted.

The battlefield stretched wide before them, filled with horror and mechanical marvels. There was little to be sickened by, except the undead themselves—but the lack of gore and screaming soldiers admittedly uplifted the entire mood of warfare. Sure, there remained the small fear for Khastra's well-being, but watching the Bringer of War lift an entire flamethrower tank and smash it into another flamethrower tank—or whatever the fuck they were called—certainly soothed a girl's romantic heart.

At the ensuing explosion, Etolié cheered, more so when the undead swarmed the remains. Beside her, Casvir cast his silent judgment, or perhaps that was the aura one naturally cast when seated upon a large skeletal horse. He said nothing, his gaze stoic and proud.

Etolié simply floated, her hatred of horses far surpassing her need for comfort—given it would not be comfort, by definition. She had no love for the monsters, and riding them was another matter entirely. There was only one monster she enjoyed riding, and the Bringer of War was a bit preoccupied at the moment.

A shadow passed over them. Etolié withheld a scream at the oncoming airship.

There was little finesse in how it dropped its spiked cannonballs, but finesse really wasn't necessary with this sort of heavy weaponry. The undead shrieked as they were crushed beneath their weight—larger than Etolié's head and, theoretically, solid metal—but the Bringer of War batted them aside like children's toys. Etolié might've spared a moment for applause were she not focused on keeping her own self un-crushed.

Thankfully, it was simply a matter of summoning an illusionary shield to float above her. Casvir looked more concerned, though he didn't seem to question why she didn't shield him too—good, because fuck him—but his flying gargoyles did a perfectly good job at protecting him, sacrificing themselves to bash the cannonballs aside.

Casvir froze. In his red eyes shone a thousand-yard stare of horror.

"Um, Tyrant Deathless—"

A cannonball suddenly smashed into the horse, scrapping a chunk of armor with it. The skeletal creature shattered. Casvir fell gracelessly, landing with a metallic thud. Etolié gasped and knelt beside him. "Imperator First and Last, are you all right?"

Unfortunately, he opened his eyes, staring as though she were a ghost. "We retreat," he said, attempting to rise—though he struggled to unearth himself from the pile of bones. "Immediately. Call General Khastra."

"Sure thing," Etolié said, but she made no move to go yet. "Are we losing?"

"No. Demitri is dead."

The words were so random, yet wrenching. "W-What?"

"You requested that I begin with the news instead of telling the story in order—"

"Yes, yes—I know!" She managed to stand, mind still racing to catch up to that awful phrase. "What do you mean, 'Demitri is dead?'"

"His presence has vanished from my mind. Not muted as though behind maldectine. Vanished. He is dead. My connection to Flowridia is severed."

Etolié had many grudges in life, rather proud of her capacity to hate so many people at once, but Demitri was not one of them. Never could be. "H-How?"

"I do not know. But we must find Flowridia immediately."

Wings spread wide, Etolié glided into the fray, numb as she went to fetch the Bringer of War.

At six years old, Sora had lost her first companion—a dog she had known since birth, who had followed and guarded her for her earliest years. When she buried him, her papa had knelt beside her. She still remembered the kind touch of his hand on her shoulder. *"It's healthy to mourn a pet, little huntress. Animal bonds are powerful. He was a true and proven friend."*

A semblance of pity panged in Sora's heart, to watch the weeping witch.

Flowridia's cries were muffled in the dead wolf's fur; she gripped him like a rock in a storm. While Sora had no love for her, she clutched Leelan close to her heart, watching the unfolding drama from the shadows of the room.

The scent of death rose slowly, the bodies of the revelers staining the floor in blood. Once a place of joy; now a massacre. And Sora hated it; hated the carnage down the depths of her soul.

These people had endorsed The Endless Night, supported her in her crimes. Surely it was worth it, these deaths for Ayla's. Yet even Leelan hid his face against her breast.

Louder than the witch's sobs was the furious exchange between Mereen and Kah'Sheen.

The half-demon seethed, her speech rapid, combative. "You are not telling me you are killing the dog!"

"It was the only way to—"

"I am here to kill Ayla Darkleaf, not dogs!"

The instinct rose to join the fight. Yet Sora stood frozen as she stared at the corpse of the wolf, for the cries of his mistress were inescapable.

Beside Sora, Tazel joined her in that same shadow, his weathered face not subtle in its grief. "Flowridia was just a kid when I met her. You struggle to break from that vision of someone."

Sora supposed she agreed, but to speak it was too much.

Odessa stole the scene, her voice dripping with cruel indifference. "Come now, Flower Child," she said pleasantly, managing to cut through the arguing duo beside them. Yet she gripped the wicked staff with white knuckles, a droplet of sweat the only sign of something amiss—though the coffin remained still and silent. "This is nothing you haven't experienced before, and we have a journey ahead of us."

Flowridia did not acknowledge her, did not move from

her weeping. Sora recalled holding her knife to the tiny pup years ago, uncertain even then if she could have acted.

It hadn't mattered. Sora did not hate Flowridia, though the memory of the girl making a wish for her doom did make watching her anguish a little easier. Death did sour one's attitude toward a person. But now the wolf was gone, and his mistress clung to his fur with desperate hands, willing him back to life.

But she was a necromancer no longer. She was nothing more than a little girl capable of cruel and terrible things.

It would never not be alarming to watch Odessa's shadow shifting of its own accord, revealing the secondary power lurking within. "I have a gift for you, Flower Child. A little something to prevent a, uh, *familiar* dilemma." Her cackling set Sora on edge, watching as the witch placed a green bracelet around her ankle—maldectine. Upon touching Flowridia, the stone began glowing. "Mereen says this belongs to you—"

Abrupt chaos ensued when Kah'Sheen suddenly screamed at Mereen, her words devolving into what Sora could only assume were Demoni curses. Mereen spat back a few, but Kah'Sheen's piled on her. Around her, dark shadows rose, spreading like tendrils along that wall.

All-consuming was her fury. So much that no one except Sora noticed Odessa make dainty steps toward her and touch her bare abdomen—

The half-demon slumped to the ground, her many limbs sprawling among the elven corpses.

"She's not dead," Odessa said cheerily. "Just eternal sleep—well, until something wakes her. A pity. I enjoyed her."

"Our party has no room for weak assets," Mereen said. She lifted one of Kah'Sheen's thin wrists, then stepped into the shadow Odessa cast, disappearing with the half-demon's body.

Mereen returned seconds later. "Ideally I'd cut the loose ends, but the risk of Ku'Shya's wrath is high enough already. We will let Sha'Demoni judge her. In the meantime, we move on. The airship awaits."

When Odessa grabbed Flowridia's arm, her daughter held tighter to the corpse. "You don't actually need both arms. If you're insistent on holding him in death, I'll leave one to do so."

Sora's gut twisted at those horrid words; they were no bluff. When Flowridia looked up, her face was swollen, her tears carrying evidence of matted wolf fur and blood. Helpless, she gazed upon her mother, and Sora was struck anew by her parentage, by how cruelly Odessa discarded the child she had long ago birthed.

Mereen came, having no reservation in wrenching Flowridia up by her thick hair. The girl yelped, grasping Mereen's hands. "We're going," Mereen said. "Sora, tie her up."

Sora drew a short length of rope from her satchel. With callous grace, Mereen threw her at Sora's feet, who flinched at the *slap* of Flowridia's body against the marble floor.

When Flowridia rose to her knees, Sora knelt beside her, cautious as she took the girl's hands, awaiting a blow, for her to scramble and run—*something*. But Flowridia complied as Sora tied her wrists together, leaving length enough to lead her. Before her was a broken person, stilled by shock and heartbreak.

"I won't hurt you unless you give me a reason to," Sora whispered, and when she stood, Flowridia followed. "Animals are innocent. Don't worry for his soul."

Paltry words, and Sora would fear a lonely afterlife were she the witch herself. But Demitri had not chosen to be used for wicked deeds.

Sol Kareena, protect his soul, Sora prayed and hoped it was absolution. Flowridia had forsaken Sol Kareena's continuous offers to join her, but the wolf was simply that. He was not damned.

Flowridia said nothing, merely kept her stare to Demitri until it would have broken her neck to continue.

"We will no longer have protection in Sha'Demoni," Mereen said at the edge of the ballroom, "and I can't risk our cargo—"

Screams erupted from the coffin. Odessa gasped, grip tightening on the staff as her face scrunched up. Within the box, small fists pounded at the wood—yet stilled when the skull's eyes flashed. Odessa's words came sensuous now, malevolence filling those large eyes. "Such violent imagery."

"There can be no accidents," Mereen seethed. "I will go." She looked to Odessa, vehemence in her words. "I won't be long. Kill anyone who tries to enter."

Odessa's smile held the sharpness of a knife. "Happily so."

Mereen disappeared out the door, as silent as the evening breeze.

"Are you all right?" Sora asked, for Odessa subtly swayed.

"It's a heavy burden," she said, speaking to the skull with clear affection. "I'm feeling...her. I blink, and I see...memories. They're not mine. They're hers."

Sora followed her stare to the box, ominous and quiet.

"Do you want help?" Tazel asked.

"Not yet, but it would do you well to learn to wield it."

"Sora," came a small voice.

Startled at the name, Sora matched eyes with Flowridia. Tears spilled from the girl's eyes, but she released no sobs now. "If we're to stay a few more minutes, will you let me sit by him?"

Sora sought trickery in her countenance, tried to imagine any spell she could conjure, yet maldectine dampened even any external tricks. Flowridia was helpless in every way. Sora released the rope. "Go ahead."

Flowridia shuffled to his shattered skull, his image reflected in her watery eyes. She rested her head upon his neck and simply breathed.

"Oh, Sora—look at you and your soft heart," came Odessa's sultry tone, but no mockery with it. "There's nothing she can do, don't worry. I don't know the method by which my familiar was returned to me, but the bracelet soothes that fear."

Sora said nothing, simply watched the bereaved girl shudder and whisper words she could not quite perceive, but it did not matter.

The wolf was dead, and all Flowridia had earned had gone with him.

Evening fell, and Etolié stood far away from evidence of mechanical carnage. The Bringer of War had finally calmed, replaced by General Khastra, and before them, Casvir spoke quick words to Murishani, who looked pompously out of place, as always.

"Let me be certain I'm understanding this," the viceroy said, and Etolié wondered if he'd curled his hair—he'd certainly done something, given its volume as it glinted against the setting sun, all soft and tousled. "You are abandoning the war to find a dead dog."

"That is correct," Casvir replied, without a glimmer of emotion.

Murishani's eyes managed to look more dead, despite his charming smile. "All right, I shall rephrase just to be certain I am truly, fully understanding your logic—you are leaving your army and conquests behind, as well as your dreams to expand Nox'Kartha across the world, to find a dead dog."

"He's not accepting constructive criticism," Etolié said, relishing any opportunity to be a nuisance.

"Viceroy Murishani, I am setting aside my current goals in hopes of salvaging what is left of a project I have spent twenty years cultivating. Do not forget, she is pregnant."

"Fine, fine." Murishani put up his hands in dramatic defense. "We can agree to disagree with your life choices."

To Etolié, Casvir said, "Empress Etolié, do you understand your part?"

"I keep you inconspicuous via illusion magic because I'm the best, and because you trust no one but yourself to get Demitri back."

"Correct. Are you ready to depart?"

"Almost. One final bow to tie."

Etolié looked to Beefcake—covered in ash, smelling of metal and fire—and floated up to meet her mouth. Their kiss lingered, and when Etolié snapped her fingers to illusion a velvet curtain between them and the imperator and viceroy, it deepened, tongues melding in their impassioned embrace. No, it wouldn't stop Murishani from seeing, but it made Etolié feel better.

Etolié supposed there was no real danger, no more than before, but when she pulled away to gaze upon Khastra's face, she was struck anew by those glowing eyes, the elegance of her face. "Don't die on me, ya big lug."

"I am already—"

"Oh, hush."

They resumed their kiss, which Etolié escalated with a vain attempt at groping Khastra's armored breasts, and she gasped when her demon gave a firm squeeze to her ass.

A slight *tap tap* on the curtain reminded them that the world was not theirs. Etolié and Khastra parted. The curtain disappeared. "I love you," Etolié said, savoring the feeling of Khastra's hand in her own.

Within Khastra shone the same precious adoration that always came in quiet moments, as though Etolié were worth the world. "I love you, Etolié."

Etolié let her go.

Murishani didn't snap his fingers this time. Instead, he tossed his hand in an impatient sort of way, and a portal popped into existence. Her stomach protested, but she swallowed back the rise of bile.

Casvir stopped before the portal. "General Khastra, the war continues at your command. I do not intend for this to be a long trip, but we will be in communication."

He stepped through.

Etolié blew a kiss at her demon and followed.

The journey through the portal was predictably vomit-inducing, and Etolié spent the split second in the span between worlds desperately trying to not lose her dinner in the starry void. When prickly grass touched her feet, she promptly fell to the ground and hurled. "This is normal," she managed after the first heave of half-digested chunks. A second stream poured out from her throat, bringing the nasty taste of bile. She prayed the dark night concealed the worst of it.

Imperator Casvir waited patiently as she gathered herself back together. He neither helped nor hindered, just waited, and Etolié supposed she couldn't hold it against him. "It is not a long walk to Velen'Kye," he said, the city's outline easily visible on the horizon. "I did not wish to risk being seen."

"Understandable." Etolié spat the last bit of upchuck from her mouth, then withdrew her flask from its extra-dimensional space, bracing for the putrid mix of alcohol and bile before rinsing her mouth with the vile liquid. She spat it out with a grimace. "I'm never drunk enough for extra-planar travel. Any requests for your disguise?"

"I do not care, so long as it will invite no questions."

"Valid." Etolié studied his hulking physique—not quite so tall as Beefcake, but broader—and chose simplicity. With a swipe of her hand, he became as nondescript an elf as she could conjure, though perhaps a bit sparkly around the edges where reality was told to stay invisible. With another, she, too, became a boring elf wearing boring clothing with a boring alibi.

"Why are you . . ." Casvir did not seem to know the word—that, or he was too proper to say it.

"Fat? I'm not fat. I'm pregnant." Etolié's hand went

182

straight through her illusionary pregnant elven stomach. "I'm your pregnant wife due to give birth in Velen'Kye's hospital. It's the best in the country, or so Khastra once said. If they try to turn us away, I'll go into labor."

"Clever."

The duo set off.

"All right," Etolié said, "the real question is—do you speak elven?"

"Very little."

"Well, I'm decent enough. How good are you at accents?"

"Not good."

"Then shut up and say nothing. At least I'll only sound like a hick instead of a demon. Worst case scenario, I can try to fly over the wall and teleport you over, but . . ." Etolié grimaced. "I can't promise that won't fuck with your disguise. Or potentially toss you into the wrong realm. Or leave you in multiple pieces. I'm still learning."

Casvir said nothing, but nothing meant he wasn't arguing.

As they neared the gates, Etolié was grateful her boring illusion included her face—her real face surely looked stupid, jaw dropping at the magnitude of the front gate. The intricacy of the gears reminded her of Solvira's destroyed one, but bigger, a spectacle. Likely on purpose, because elves were show-offs, but Etolié was truly enamored.

However, she did shy at the weapons on the two guards' hips. Guns didn't have to be magic to make her blood run cold. Bullets didn't believe in illusions.

"State your business," one said, the sheer apathy on his face inspiring.

"My sweetheart and I have been traveling for weeks to get to your little hospital," Etolié said, putting on her best country momma voice. To try and fail at a proper elven accent would get her exposed. To own that she had no idea what she was doing just might work. "The baby should have been here yesterday, so we're blessed to have made it this far."

Beside her, Casvir said nothing, glaring at the guards like the doting father he was meant to be. But though she prepared a follow-up, it proved to not be necessary—the gates opened.

At well past midnight, the streets of Velen'Kye were mostly deserted, though the occasional businessman hurried home, and a few guards made their patrols. The darkness hid the enormity of it, but Etolié still found it fascinating. The silent streets might've been ominous, but the greatest necromancer free to walk this realm stood beside her. Yes, the disdain was mutual, but she had twenty-four more years or so of servitude to finish up before he would let anyone kill her.

It was shockingly reassuring.

"Do you feel anything?"

"There is an inordinate amount of death here," Casvir replied, "including vampiric."

"Seems like a good lead. If Demitri is here, Ayla will be too."

Somehow, it hadn't occurred to Etolié until that moment that Ayla would be a part of the package, and even her illusion couldn't hide her sneer.

They came upon a convergence of roads, the cobblestone path meeting five others and splitting at the roundabout. Centered were statues of elven heroes—or something, given that Etolié wasn't sticking around to read the plaques—and the creaking of wheels upon stone approached as a covered horse-drawn carriage emerged from one of the paths. Not suspicious on its own, but driving the carriage was a shadow with an unmistakable mane of blonde, rope-like hair pulled back into a long tail.

Etolié was willing to bet there were only so many darker-skinned, blonde elves in the world. Her gut didn't know what it meant, but it fucking clenched. "Casvir, stop that carriage."

Something in her tone left no room for argument, and Casvir wasted no time summoning a mace of pure dark matter into his hands. He threw it with all his might at the wheel of the carriage, shattering the wood.

The horse screamed as it pulled along the haywire cart. The broken wheel skidded across the ground. Casvir and Etolié ran—the former much faster—as two figures leapt from the carriage's door.

One of which Etolié knew. "Mereen Fireborn?!"

Casvir apparently knew the other. "That man owes me money."

At the cry of her progenitor's name, Sora Fireborn glanced back and met Etolié's eye—but kept the horse moving. Muffled screaming came from inside the carriage.

At the window appeared fearful eyes and a mane of auburn hair. Flowers banged on the glass, only to be wrestled back by someone else within.

The carriage wasn't big enough for a dire wolf, but the

plot had certainly thickened. However, Etolié did not have time to think more on it before a nightmarish *click* drew her whole focus to Mereen. Her illusions vanished. "Etolié. Lovely to see you, sweetie."

"Thought we were friends," Etolié said, and not twenty feet away, Casvir swung his mace at the elven man, only to be met with a blast of holy fire.

"We are. Stay back."

Mereen set back the trigger, then ran into the battlefield.

With Etolié's illusions gone, there came the full might of Imperator Casvir. A summoned shield and mace became his weapons of choice against the elf who did what Etolié could only say was *dance*. So nimbly he sidestepped Casvir's blows, even managing to swipe the armored man with his rapier. Grace was his signature, beautiful to watch as light poured from his hand as fire. He blinked out of sight, only to reappear at Casvir's opposite side, and when Mereen accomplished the same task, dual swords in hand, Etolié realized the truth. "They're hopping in and out of Sha'Demoni!"

A split moment after Mereen nearly beheaded him, Casvir swiped the air. Out poured a battalion of undead.

Etolié soared into the sky, knowing her wings were slow, but it was better than trying to run through the fray. But as she flew above the battle, the carriage well in sight, a *bang* ripped across the silent sky—

Pain seared Etolié's wing. She plummeted toward the ground.

Etolié managed to coast well enough on her non-bloodied wing—well enough to not break her face when she hit the ground, at least. Her right wing, normally weightless, was weighed down by a bullet lodged in the ethereal tendril. Fuck, it *radiated*, like being stabbed in a nerve. Mereen busied herself with the dead, slashing foes left and right, her swords a blur in the darkness.

Etolié succeeded in standing, but her brutalized wing dragged on the floor, debilitated by iron. Bracing herself, she lifted the offending tendril and cradled it in her arms like a baby. "Fuck you too, friend," she muttered, and from Etolié burst fifteen identical doppelgängers, each wielding a different weapon.

Etolié herself sat at the base of the statues, invisible-ish as she plunged her fingers around the bullet. An amalgamation of flesh and light met her touch. The wing was shallow, so most of the bullet was visible, but goddamn if she didn't *shriek* as she ripped it out, tearing chunks of light with it. However, she had a wing that could float again.

The Etolié doppelgängers held their own against the two graceful combatants, circling perfectly around the juggernaut that was Casvir, who thankfully didn't question their presence. With maces and swords and daggers and even shields, they bashed their way through Mereen and her counterpart. Though her wing stung like a bitch, Mereen still had to reload, so Etolié flew once more. "Casvir!" she cried, noting that innocent citizens were definitely peering out their windows. "The carriage!"

It had gotten awfully far away.

Casvir heard and understood, charging through the fray. Etolié dove toward him, falling much faster than she could fly, and grabbed him by his pauldrons. "Can I just hang on?"

"Fine."

The man was fast, she would grant him that. They left the dead behind, though the doppelgängers disappeared once they'd run too far. "They're leaving the city!" Etolié cried, for in the far distance, the carriage crossed through a gate—

Into an airship dock. Fuck.

Footsteps signaled the return of their foes.

From Casvir's shoulder, Etolié summoned a throwing knife—which she pelted toward Mereen's head. The bitch deflected, of course, but Etolié summoned another, and another . . .

Until Mereen disappeared into the shadow of a lamppost.

The elven man kept running, but Casvir stopped abruptly when Mereen reappeared not two feet in front and clanged her sword against his armor. He bashed her with his shield after that frankly pitiful blow, but as the airship dock loomed, Etolié understood. "They're trying to slow us, not kill us!"

Casvir whipped his mace at the combatants and whacked the man in the face. The elf darted away, despite the blow to the head.

"Can't you control undead?!"

"Vampires are different," Casvir replied, not even winded—could he get winded?

There were more important questions at hand. Desperate, Etolié summoned a giant brick wall to block the path behind them.

Of course, Mereen and her companion simply ran through its shadow.

"I'll try to slow them," Etolié said, and floated up from his back. "You run!"

Etolié landed right as Mereen charged, realizing she hadn't thought this through. Mereen's sword swung to bisect her; Etolié screamed—

And warped into Sha'Demoni.

Very different on this side of the world. Not shadowy at all. Colorful, with warm hues beneath an indigo sky. It was a wonder Mereen could utilize it the same way, but Etolié had no time to contemplate it further because Mereen popped into the space right before her and swung again—

Etolié pushed herself back into the mortal plane. She shot into the air, narrowly missing Mereen once more. "What the hell kind of game are you playing?" Etolié yelled, but her gut clenched when Mereen dropped her swords and grabbed her revolver.

Rather than have matching wing scars, Etolié dove back to the ground, sending a flurry of illusionary snow—it was the first thing she thought of, all right?—at Mereen.

The male elf had continued running, as told by his renewed battle with Casvir up ahead. Nothing his fire touched caught flame, save for Casvir himself. Etolié arrived just in time for Casvir to swipe his hand across the air and summon more of his waiting dead.

She ran past them, past the man now burdened with fighting animated bodies, into the docking yard.

The gargantuan airships were docile in their slumber, no sign of the bombs or the flame they could carry. A single one hummed on a platform, and already Etolié heard the struggle below it.

Dim light revealed a frightful scene, of a human woman holding some sort of staff and skull who beguiled a levitating box to follow her up the ramp to the ship, and of Sora Fireborn dragging Flowridia forward even as the girl struggled and screamed. "Etolié!" Flowridia cried, but she stilled when Sora brought her elbow to her jaw.

"Sora Fireborn!" Etolié yelled, despite her heaving lungs. "I don't care what they're paying you; I'll pay more! Just put her down—!"

Click.

187

Etolié screamed when Mereen Fireborn appeared from the shadow, gun against her head.

Boom.

Etolié felt cold metal. She felt the ricochet of the blast, the vibration of the explosion, the heat—

And in the safety of Sha'Demoni, she touched her forehead to make sure she was in one piece.

Etolié's breath came in spurts. With trembling hands, she pinched herself to be certain she was truly alive, but if the sting in her arm didn't confirm it, the pulsing pain in her wing surely did.

Before reappearing, she flew up into the air, then warped back into the mortal realm.

Casvir had arrived, still in his fight against the dancing one. Etolié wouldn't say Casvir had met his match, but this elf had barely been touched. He sidestepped each move, anticipated each twitch, disappeared and reappeared at will. With Mereen at his side, they made a formidable team, but a scream of *"Etolié!"* pushed Etolié back into the moment.

The airship was lifting.

"Come on!" cried a woman's voice from the ship.

Mereen and her companion fully withdrew, the latter sending a final spray of flame as they darted up the ramp. A ladder was lowered as the airship floated up. Mereen and her partner narrowly grabbed it as it rose. Etolié ran, then flew to try and stop them.

Mereen, clutching the ladder with her other arm, pointed her gun at Etolié, and Etolié, not caring to find out if she was bluffing, popped back out of sight.

In Sha'Demoni, she floated to the ground, knowing she wasn't fast enough to have a hope of stopping them.

When she phased back in, she heard a desperate cry: *"Etolié, he's in the ballroom! He's in the ballroom!"*

And that was all. She stared upon the airship going ever higher, the fading hum of its motors settling like an omen.

Casvir appeared at her side. "This is unfortunate."

At that absolute understatement, Etolié looked back into the city, realizing there were angry cries coming from within, screams of terror and flame. Right—the undead. "Unfortunate, indeed."

"Flowridia said something about a ballroom."

"I bet that's where the boy is," Etolié replied, then she snapped her fingers; their disguises returned, though without

188

the pregnant stomach. "Now we're just your average frightened citizens. Let's go find Demitri."

They ran back into the city, the distraction of the dead enough to keep them covered.

Flowridia stared upon lost salvation until it was but a glowing pinprick in the darkness.

Mother had disappeared with the coffin. Flowridia had been knocked back when she'd tried to follow. Every piece of her hurt, the cold air whipping at the bruises and cuts she had garnered from wrestling Sora. Her shock had never settled; there upon her hands was blood, upon her dress was blood, clogging her senses was Demitri's precious blood . . .

Fresh tears welled in her eyes, gently falling against the wooden barrier of the airship.

More pressing than pain was numbness. She felt nothing of the world at all. Not magic, not death or life, and not . . .

Oh, Demitri. Anguish filled her anew, and with it a surge of tears.

"Sora, grab her."

At Mereen's command, rough hands tugged at the ropes binding Flowridia's wrists. No sense in fighting when they were a thousand feet in the air. Flowridia stumbled along, noting how Sora would not meet her eye, but more importantly the elaborate array of ropes, the sails, and the line of parachutes attached to the protective railing.

"There's a cell waiting for you, little girl," Mereen said, and Flowridia longed to crack the porcelain perfection of her face.

Flowridia followed at Sora's beckoning. "I'm not going to jump," Flowridia said, managing to keep her tears out of her steady voice. "What's the use of locking me up?"

Mereen's smile was as sharp as the swords on her back. "Flowridia Darkleaf, I have never once underestimated you. Quite the contrary—the moment I heard there was a girl loved by The Endless Night, I took you very seriously. Yes, your magic is gone, but you still have that clever head of yours. You're undoubtedly an idiot, but you're not stupid, which means I don't want to find out what you'll do if I leave you to wander freely."

Flowridia supposed the speech was a compliment, but she'd rather be thought of as daft.

She was taken below the deck, down a small flight of stairs to a narrow hallway. Torchlight filled the space, protected in some sort of case that allowed the light to flicker but not touch the wooden walls. She was shoved into an empty room, bearing no furniture nor lights—only a barred window, bolted from the outside.

"I'm expecting trouble, which is why Sora will be standing outside your door at all times." Mereen lovingly patted the gun at her hip, pulsing fresh rage through Flowridia's blood. "We will be here a few days, so best get cozy. You'll be fed in the morning."

Mereen left, leaving Sora in the doorway. The half-elf hesitated, gripping the door. The shifting light illuminated her amber face, casting her blonde locs in fiery hues. "If you need anything, just knock. I'll be listening."

Would Sora really insult her with kindness? Flowridia nearly laughed, the audacity too much. "That's not the comfort you think it is," she seethed, for though her heart lay shattered, how dare this woman look on with pity. "Leave me to mourn in peace."

Sora gave a curt nod. "I will offer a prayer—"

"Don't you dare—"

"—for the wolf."

"Your goddess has nothing to offer me."

Gratifying, to see the twitch in Sora's neutral countenance. "Perhaps not."

She shut the door, drenching Flowridia in darkness. A lock clicked.

Adrenaline pulsed through Flowridia, and she began surveying the sparse room by touch. Wooden walls, a wooden floor and ceiling, and a window barred with metal. She yanked on the barrier with all her might, but her minimal strength did nothing. Outside, a sky filled with stars greeted her, and her regret at being disowned by the daughter of the Goddess of Stars had never been so selfishly pertinent.

If she peered down, she saw a sea of black. There was nothing useful here. She clutched the bracelet at her ankle—it was, indeed, hers, created by Etolié and thought lost when she'd been taken by slavers a lifetime ago—but found it wouldn't budge. Surely nothing magical about it, given its nature. Perhaps Mother had jammed it somehow.

It was low on her list of worries at the moment. Instead, she felt around the wooden cage, mindful of splinters in the aging wood. The wood was not sealed, and the ship was quite old. Soon she found a broken piece, as thick as her thumb.

The saccharine scent of whatever Sora smoked wafted beneath the door. The half-elf listened. Flowridia willed her tears to flow, for sobs to overtake her as she tore at the splintered piece, breaking off a sizable chunk. Weeping, she touched the tips, finding them sharp enough to kill, and hid it among her layers of fine skirts.

But in truly weeping, the horrible truth of her situation fell upon her. Memories of Demitri's shattered life remained a nightmare she prayed to awaken from, but no—the bruises were too deep, her cuts stung too vibrantly. Flowridia was awake and alive but her dearest boy was not.

She took a gasping breath, willing herself to stabilize. She knew not what Mereen's wicked plot was, but somehow the worst had yet to come, she feared.

Mother was here.

Tazel had betrayed her. Sora too. If Kah'Sheen had ever been a friend, she certainly was not now.

But Ayla . . .

Flowridia shut her eyes and thought of that damn staff. She swore she knew it, had read of it, had seen it somewhere . . .

. . . In a painting. In Solvira. Not as consort-to-be, but as Lara's friend, in the library. The God of Death had wielded it. It could control all the dead, including vampires and their ilk.

Flowridia shoved her anguish aside, survival her most pressing purpose. She continued with her sobbing but fought to keep her head clear as she felt along the wall, seeking more shattered wood. They would serve well enough as knives— even better as stakes, if the opportunity arose.

Mereen would pay. They all would. But first she had to save Ayla.

First she had to save herself.

"How many fucking ballrooms can one city have?!"

Etolié glared at the map she'd stolen, holed up beside Casvir outside the library. Sure, they'd broken a window to steal the map of the city, but plenty of ruckus was afoot—there were undead about.

Fortunately, they were already at war.

"Look, here's the Rose Garden Ballroom, and the Cityside Ballroom, and the gods-damned Chaos' Flame Ballroom—it'll take all night to search all these!"

Casvir was as blank a slate as Etolié had ever met, but she hadn't spent the past twenty-something years with a different stoic, pupilless demon just to falter now. She'd studied for this test.

As it was, he seemed unimpressed by her tantrum. "Fortunately, I have limitless dead," Casvir replied, which . . . was actually quite fortunate.

"I'm more worried about the airship flying Flowers away than running out of dead, but I suppose I see your point. Though someone will try to clean up the giant wolf corpse at some point."

"Not if they are distracted by undead."

"You know what? You're completely right."

"Do you recall what they were wearing?"

"I was a little more worried about getting shot point blank."

"Mereen's dress was meant for a ballroom, and Tazel was dressed as a servant. Perhaps we should track down an event schedule—"

"Shut the fuck up—Tazel? As in Tazel Fireborn?!" Realization struck Etolié like that damn bullet. "That's the man who locked himself in the library!"

Confusion furrowed Casvir's brow. He was never this expressive back at home. "Yes, and he owes me money for it."

"Well, fuck me—he's my hero! Gods, I wish that were me. When Flowers told me about him, I saw my retirement flash through my eyes. What was that about an event schedule?"

Casvir seemed to flounder over that shift in subject, despite being the one who'd brought it up to begin with. "Yes. An event schedule. We need to find where a ball was hosted."

"Smart. Maybe we could bully it out of someone."

"Bully?"

"We ask random citizens on the street if they know anything about a ball until one of them fesses up. We can't be caught. We can literally change our appearance."

Currently they appeared as normal, due to Etolié's own laziness, but with a zombie hoard lumbering through the city, no one was looking at suspicious glowing wings lighting up alleyways.

And if they did—well, they were already at war.

"It is not my favorite plan, but it will work in the interim."

"Interim of what?"

"Of me thinking of a better one."

Etolié shoved the book at him.

"Could you not ask your goddess mother?"

"My momma isn't a magic tracker. I mean, she sorta is, but Demitri is a wolf and not, say, a dragon, for example. If he prayed to her, she'd know, but he's dead." Could familiars pray? Etolié mulled over the thought until Imperator First and Last spoke up.

"That is fine, because I have thought of a better plan."

Something in his flat tone made her roll her eyes. "All right, genius, lay it out."

"If I bid my dead to fall, it will allow me to more clearly pass across what dead things lie in this city. If I sense a wolf and it is in the direction of one of the ballrooms on the map, we have found our quarry."

Though perturbed, Etolié wanted to find Demitri more than she wanted Casvir to be wrong. "Lead the way, then."

Sparks of purple seeped into the ground as Casvir stood. In the distance, the screaming lessened. He shut his eyes, an aura of blistering power radiating like heat from his skin. Invisible but potent, and Etolié summoned her flask to dampen her headache.

When he opened his eyes, Casvir said, "Give me the map." She presented it; he pointed at the Chaos' Flame Ballroom. "Demitri is there."

Thank Alystra's Ass—it was the closest one.

A short walk, and no one stopped them. The ghouls had stolen the attention of anyone capable. They came across no patrols when they reached the building housing the ballroom, despite the numerous shattered windows. Etolié floated over the broken glass to peer inside.

Her heart broke in two, a gasp escaping unbidden.

In the abandoned ballroom, a massacre lay before them, albeit with very little blood; instead, signs of violent magic lingered, and residual necromancy bit at her skin. Amid the carnage was the corpse of a friend. "Casvir, it's him," she said, and she had no trouble floating through the broken window, tucking her wings in to avoid any remaining glass.

He had grown in their time apart, easily longer than Casvir was tall, his bulk monstrous but housing a good heart. Demitri could have been sleeping, until she saw his eyes. One was glassy; the other was bloodied and black. The back of his skull held a matching hole—where the bullet had gone.

When she touched him, he was cold beneath his thick fur. Tears stung her eyes. Whatever Etolié's distaste for Flowers . . . Demitri hadn't deserved this. He was just a pup.

Armored footsteps echoed closer. Casvir entered the ballroom from the proper entrance, his stare unremitting when it settled upon Demitri's corpse. "Unfortunate," he muttered, and Etolié swore she heard an actual glimmer of rage beneath it.

"So what do we do?" Etolié wiped her eyes on an illusionary tissue. "We found his body, but we lost Flowers—"

An underground *boom* pulsed through the room as purple light filled Demitri's corpse.

Etolié scrambled back as colorful smoke billowed around him, swirling in tendrils to caress his limbs, then his body and face. Though his good eye remained cloudy, it suddenly snapped into focus.

Demitri twitched. He rose in unnatural measures, his body a puppet on eerie strings as he stumbled upon his four legs. Etolié backed away, something ineffably wrong in his pose, in his gaze, in every tremor of his body. He took a clumsy step, then raised his hackles, his gaze set to Etolié.

"Demitri, it's me. Etolié." Etolié held her ground as he came forward, holding up placating hands. "Remember when we were friends? I never stopped loving you specifically."

Demitri charged. Etolié shrieked, mind blanking in the split second before death on every spell she knew, when Casvir's mace struck him with a horrible *crack*. The wolf stumbled as he rose, no recognition in his broken gaze as he snarled and inched back.

Despite the clear danger, she snapped her fingers, drawing the wolf's attention. "I have an idea."

Once upon a time, Etolié had tamed a berserk Bringer of

War, fueled by magic and technology that had been too much for even her ancient self. The memory evoked fear, those teeth never so threatening, but her momma's inheritance had saved them both.

And if she could calm a literal monster, surely she could do the same for a wolf. From Etolié's core came a tuneless, lilting song. No words, simply music; simply magic that she still barely understood or grasped but whose results were uncontestable. If she could calm the Bringer of War, surely she could settle the mind of a wolf.

He watched her as she sang, shifting from predator to a wary watcher. Though his hackles remained raised, he did not move. *"He doesn't seem to know us, Casvir,"* she sang.

"I feared this. Demitri's intelligence is magical, granted because he is a familiar. With his connection to Flowridia's severed, it is difficult to say what memories he still holds. It is possible he regards you as a friend, but given the violent nature of his death, he is disoriented."

Etolié hummed between phrases, the wolf well under her spell. *"What if you restore him as her familiar?"*

"That is my hope. There are conditions that I fear must be met first, but that is for the future. First, we return the body to Nox'Kartha. Then, I find her."

Something shoved against her magic, resisting the mesmerizing song. *"You can't just return him from a distance?"*

"No. If I tried, she would absorb him instead—and that is only a final resort."

Again came that shove. *"Demitri is fighting. Can you please put him away?"*

The purple smoke dissipated from Demitri's body. The wolf collapsed.

Though the sight broke Etolié's heart, she swallowed her grief. "You're gonna take the body away and find Flowers?

"Correct."

"That's fine, but I feel like there's a massive unknown between those two sentences. Also, you—alone? The imperator of the country these people are at war with? You're just gonna . . . walk around?"

"Who else would I send? I do not know what state Flowridia will be in when I find her. I am one of very few with reliable access to portal magic, and I suspect she will need to be transported quickly."

The initial question was rhetorical, but in that moment,

Etolié was struck with a foolish plan, the likes of which certainly risked death, but Flowers might be in some pretty dire straits.

And who was Etolié to forgo such a blessed opportunity for justice? "I could go."

"Your portal magic is unreliable, by your own admittance."

"I could go with you. Clearly we're a dream team. Then you aren't wandering elven lands like a beacon of evil—you'll just look like a vaguely evil elf who can't speak elven and relies on his handy translator."

If Casvir suspected bullshit, it didn't show. In fact, he seemed legitimately thoughtful. "I will consider it. You would be a valuable asset."

"Me and my ass are quite valuable, thank you."

There came the predicted twist in her stomach as Casvir summoned his portal. Etolié half expected him to do the necromancy thing and make the wolf walk out, as macabre as it sounded, but instead the massive De'Sindai hefted the wolf up as much as he was able, dragging him through the portal with little struggle.

The portal lingered. Etolié's conscience spoke in the silence, further sickening her stomach. Momma wouldn't approve, but Momma didn't need to know.

Flowers was a fucking monster, and that baby . . .

It wasn't difficult to illusion knives, and sometimes even simpler to illusion crimes.

Etolié couldn't say what sensation burned through her at the rise in resolve, but she spoke her creed aloud, only the dead to affirm it. "Let's go, Etolié. You're gonna fucking kill Flowers."

Chapter 10

When daylight came, sleep threatened to steal Sora's vision.

Exhaustion weighed at her eyelids as she sat with the guarded door to her back, but anytime she managed to nod off, a muffled whimper or cry would sound from behind.

Or perhaps it was all in her head. Behind every blink was Demitri's dead eyes. One glazed, one shattered.

Sora wondered, had she the nerve to have slit the wolf's throat all those years ago, whether it would have stopped all this in its tracks. Would Solvira be independent? Would Flowridia have stumbled down this path of darkness? Perhaps Ayla might still be dead . . . or perhaps have never fallen at all. Sora could not say.

Would Sora have become Sol Kareena's Champion? Or would she be six feet under, put to rest? Had she slit the wolf's throat, Ayla would have returned the favor, no question of that.

Sora was a decade Flowridia's senior. The girl was a child, though not one to underestimate. Sol Kareena accepted all, but she had extended her hand to Flowridia countless times before. Perhaps she truly was past redemption.

. . . No. If Flowridia's heart was sincere, Sol Kareena would accept it, though with penance.

Sniffling came from within, interrupting Sora's wandering mind. From her satchel, she withdrew her pipe, her matches, and a tied bag of Spore. With the first breath of the cloying concoction, serenity filled her mind, smoothing the edges of her guilt.

This was for the best.

Footsteps from above meant it wouldn't be Mereen. Mereen was secluded somewhere below, hiding from the deadly sunlight. Instead, Odessa's perfect figure appeared as a silhouette in the stairs. "Sora, you're still awake?"

"I've dozed off a few times."

"Oh, go upstairs and see the sun. Do your prayers. You'll be as pale as me at this rate." She laughed pleasantly, and Sora still found it strange that she could be so . . . kind. "I'd love a moment alone with my Flower Child. Mereen won't mind."

Though her limbs were limp from Spore, Sora did manage to stumble into standing. "I won't say no to a break. Thank you. Do you know where Tazel is?"

"With Ayla. We're taking shifts, he and I. I kept her plenty comfortable during the night." Odessa raised her voice; Sora suspected she hoped her 'Flower Child' overheard it. "Ayla is snug in her new home, fighting less and less. Funny, how pain will tame even the wildest of monsters."

Sora recalled the sensation of stabbing Ayla through her sternum, the visceral *crunch* of bone, and then her laughter as she'd dragged it down herself. Ayla Darkleaf didn't fear pain.

Which meant this was something a little deeper.

"You really ought to sleep," Odessa continued, jarring Sora from her horrid thoughts. "You can take my room, if Mereen didn't give you one—not like I need it. This body comes with wonderful advantages; such nasty things necromancy can do to the living."

"Thank you. I appreciate that."

Sora went upstairs, grateful to leave her conflicted feelings behind.

Crisp air invigorated her senses, chilled by the altitude yet warmed by the sun. She went to the edge and gasped at the expanding scenery below. It terrified her, the knowledge that one push would bring her doom. Yet she had never been nearer to her goddess' domain, so she forced herself to remain and bask in the frightful view, knowing it was rare and precious.

She was not alone. The occasional airship deckhand passed her by, ignoring her entirely. These elves would likely ignore her even if she spoke, but Sora was used to being invisible. Safer that way.

In silence, Sora performed a small prayer, making a circle with two fingers, then crossing it with one on her opposite hand—the Sun and her spear.

Sol Kareena, bless us this day.

As usual, she felt nothing at all.

In her ear, Leelan gave a sweet chirp. Sora took another draw of her pipe, savoring the dulling of her senses, until a strange sound interrupted the peaceful morning. Faint, yet clearly in distress.

Sora's stomach churned, but whatever Odessa did to Flowridia was on Odessa's head.

Again, the faint scream sang across the wind. Not even the peace the Spore brought could drown it. With memories of Odessa's last tortured victim ringing through her head, Sora steeled herself and made her way back to her post.

Sunlight had finally filled her room, and Flowridia sequestered herself in a corner, hiding seven splintered shards of wood in her voluminous skirts.

With the growing light, she had managed to make small rips in her dress and tie the stakes to her petticoat—accessible but difficult to perceive—and when she had jumped to test its security, she had resumed her weeping. Sora need not suspect a thing.

And given she was the most likely to be stabbed—well, she supposed they had never been friends anyway.

With eyes shut, she thought of her books, of the diagrams she had read of airships and knew this one was similar enough. The engine room was deep below—and Mereen would also be deep below—but a proper distraction could surely—

"Ayla is snug in her new home, fighting less and less."

Everything Mother said was a nightmare. Her mere voice, even without the face Flowridia knew, caused her blood to run cold.

"Funny, how pain will tame even the wildest of monsters."

Flowridia quietly removed one of the stakes from her skirt and slipped it into her glove instead, uncaring of the splinters threatening to pierce her flesh.

The lock clicked, and when Mother entered, she held no key. Magic, then. Such a kind and vicious smile she held. "Sweet Flower Child, how are you holding up?"

Flowridia managed to match her expression, her own

smirk false. "Tell me more about my wife. You said something about pain. Is that why you've come, to mock me? Get to it."

"Contrary to popular belief, I don't revel in your pain." Mother came closer, no fear in her posture as she sat before her—and why should she? She was an ancient witch, restored to a new and powerful form. She held a different face, yet not, for subtle similarities made Flowridia's blood run cold. Her smile, her laugh, even the glint in her eye—all was the progenitor Flowridia knew and feared. "But since you asked— only a small bit of torture. Currently she's in stasis. A reprieve before the storm." When she offered a hand, Flowridia simply glared.

"Losing a familiar is the worst pain a witch can experience," Odessa continued. "And to think you've experienced it twice? Flower Child, to be anything other than a weeping heap upon the floor means you are so strong."

Her words were intoxicating, but Flowridia hadn't become the sworn enemy of Nox'Kartha's viceroy just to be lured in by honeyed bullshit. So strange, to look at Mother, to hear her maternal voice, and feel nothing. To not need her at all. "Funny that you would be involved both times."

"Sweetheart, can you blame me? I would have preferred to hold a knife to his throat to control you, but what choice did we have? I commend you for gaining the upper hand." Mother's gaze became less kind, and Flowridia fought the instinct to wither beneath it. "Forgive my skepticism, but do you truly hold my grandchild?"

Her sneer said it all; she did not believe a word. "Which would help my cause?"

"The truth, whichever it is. You always had a tender heart for babies, but I have a difficult time believing your wife would let something like this happen." Odessa eyed her with intrigue. "Unless you found a spell, in which case I would love to discuss that further."

Truthfully, the idea of discussing any topic at length with Mother sickened her. "I'm not pregnant."

"Pity."

Flowridia's opposite hand casually fell to the glove with the sequestered stake. But could she kill Odessa's body? She would have sworn it was alive, yet she knew so little. "Do you know where she's taking us?"

"Of course I do, but why spoil the surprise?"

Mother said it with a smile. Flowridia refused to return

the favor, even in mockery. When Flowridia moved to stand, Odessa joined her. Flowridia spared a glance for the window, at least as large as her head—though she would not fit through, with her hair. But she was unique in that. The bars stuck out, leaving a bubble. "We can stop pretending you love me. We both know the truth."

Mother fell into silence, her false airs fading to quiet acrimony. "You were my most difficult labor. You didn't cry when I held you, and I am not so calloused to deny that it terrified me. My little girl with her tiny red curls, slowly turning blue—I spanked you until you finally shrieked. Against all odds, I don't regret that I saved you. Perhaps that's not love, but it's something."

"Funny—my crying is still soothing to you," Flowridia said, vitriol rising where there would have once been heartbreak. "Those are bold words from someone who murdered my baby brother."

"Flower Child, you are unruly enough. Can you imagine what kind of monster he would have become?"

Gods, Flowridia wanted to scream. The ruse demanded she didn't. Survival demanded she breathe, but how she cursed the angry tears welling in her eyes.

"Against all odds, you haven't broken," Odessa continued. "I do admire that. While you are by far my most irritating child, you are also my most accomplished. Seducing a monster? Becoming the empress consort of *Solvira*? Inspiring, truly. I don't have to love you to admit that I'm proud."

Once, the words might've warmed Flowridia's tender heart, but today they merely burned. As she stared again at the window, Flowridia forced herself to consider Demitri, to replay the moment of death in her head, over and over until the tears in her eyes finally fell. "Then may I beg for some kindness, even if it's a lie?" she finally asked, and it took no effort at all to sound pathetic—her anguish was true, even if her mind calculated every word.

She expected a trick, for Mother to cast some wicked spell. But she made no move to avoid Flowridia's hug, even returned it. And though Flowridia felt sick in her arms, she withdrew the stake from her sleeve.

With her remaining strength, she plunged it toward them, straight into Odessa's back.

Mother gasped, becoming slack from shock. Before she

could scream, Flowridia yanked her toward the wall by her dress, grabbed her hair—

And missed the window first, instead smashing Mother's head against the wood with a horrid *crack*. Mother did not struggle; she stumbled, balance wavering. A second chance, and Flowridia did not miss her target—she thrust Mother's head into the window, leaving her skull bleeding and jammed into the porthole.

That bloody stake remained in her back. Mother twitched, perhaps her shock stilling—she wouldn't die quite yet, even if the blow were fatal. From her dress, Flowridia pulled out a second stake, adrenaline coursing, hate pulsing in her blood. How she longed to stab her anew, but the clock ticked. Mother struggled mutely, and Flowridia did not even know if she *could* die. But she was trapped, too disoriented to cast.

Flowridia ran from the room.

Away from the light, though the location of the parachutes was sealed in her brain. She met a second set of stairs and frantically stumbled down.

The deafening sound of steam rose the nearer she went. She entered the engine room, and she wished she could stop to absorb its grandeur. How incredible it was, to see the diagrams she had studied in person—the great shifting gears, some as massive as she, hundreds, if not thousands interlocking together, along with the many pipes containing the steam keeping them moving. But she could only take passing glances, her racing heart a reminder of her quest. The temperature rose. A furnace would be near, she knew, but the fact that she could see meant she was not alone.

In fact, she heard distant chattering, and as she peeked beyond the wall, two women stood near a massive furnace, shoveling coal into its fiery maw. Flowridia ducked back, knowing time was scarce. She had only incapacitated Mother with luck and surprise—she doubted she could fight two women used to manual labor.

Be that as it may, she faced an intricate arrangement of gears, each and every one responsible for the longevity of this ship. She took two more stakes from her dress, one in each hand, and she considered all the hours she had spent reading, sought any memory from the diagrams to lead her.

Out of sight from the engineers, Flowridia thrust the stakes at opposite sides of the same gear, which memory said powered the fans. The wood creaked, the iron protested, but the gear slowed—and when Flowridia heaved one down with all her might, the gear loosened, slowly sliding forward as it turned.

It would fall. Flowridia ran.

As she sprinted up the stairs, she heard the first evidence of commotion below, curious shouts of, *"What is that noise?"*

Now, to find Ayla.

This was a small ship, meant to transport people and not cargo., Surely the engineers were paid handsomely to look the other way when Sora had dragged her on board, screaming—even for a human, it would be barbaric.

Behind one of these doors was Ayla. Behind another was Mereen. Or perhaps the same door, knowing her luck. She withdrew the fourth stake from her dress.

She faced a dim hallway, still torn on if stealth or pure berserker would be the best route, when a door opened ahead. Flowridia spotted a quick flash of steel and darted behind the nearest door—landing in a supply closet.

She held her breath, fearing Mereen would hear her pounding heart, but there came a distant cry: *"Mereen!"*

Sora. The figure that was Mereen darted away.

Then, from afar: *"All hands in the engine room!"*

Frantic footsteps sounded beyond, and Flowridia's hope surged. One thing had gone right.

With no one in the hall, Flowridia peeked out, then ran to the door Mereen had left.

She burst in, stake raised. There sat Tazel, the box, and in his hands—the damned staff. Shock showed in his eyes, but when Flowridia brought the stake against his chest, he batted her arm aside with his. "How did you—?"

She swung again; he grabbed her arm, his strength far surpassing hers, but when she reached for the staff, he evaded—but faltered.

Within the box sounded movement.

"Dammit, Flowridia," he said, because all she had to do was distract him, and then her weapon would come. Ayla would be free—

His foot met her chest. Though protected by the corset, she stumbled back, then threw the stake at his face.

Tazel batted the stake with the staff, but in the moment of weakness, Flowridia dove and yanked it from his grasp.

She so nearly felt something, yet it was trapped behind

a wall. The damn maldectine remained a weight, even as she swung the staff's skull at Tazel. He dodged with grace, perfection in his spin, then countered by wrenching the staff from her hand. "You won't win this," he said, his bloodshot eyes holding misery. "So get the hell out of here while you can. There are parachutes in—"

"I know where the parachutes are." She scrambled to her feet, gripping her stake.

The ship suddenly jerked, sending them stumbling against the wall. Commotion rose beyond, cries of engineers meeting her ears.

Beside her, Tazel smiled. "You sabotaged the ship. Brilliant."

"What game are you playing?"

"You're just a kid, Flowridia. Without Ayla and Demitri, you're harmless. She has to answer for her crimes, but I'll make a petition to anyone who asks that she got her claws deep in your head."

How she cursed his kind visage, the pleading in his words. "I won't abandon my wife."

"Then return with an army, but you're powerless and thousands of feet in the air. You won't win—"

A sharp rap echoed across the shut door. *"The girl has escaped!"* came Mereen's voice. *"Defend the coffin at all costs!"*

"I will!" he yelled back, and outside, Mereen's footsteps disappeared. "Flowridia, that's your one chance. Get out of here."

But though Flowridia inched toward the door, her stare lingered on the silent coffin. "I don't understand."

"And you can't."

"What are you planning?"

"Something more horrible than you can ever imagine, so run."

"And if I don't?"

With his free hand, Tazel grabbed her collar. "Flowridia Darkleaf," he said, vehemence in his words, "I don't want this. I never wanted any of this. But I can't hide in that damn library anymore and pretend the world isn't turning. I will fulfill my family's pact to slay Ayla, but don't make me throw you off this ship to save you."

His crazed eyes seared like a brand. She gasped when he shoved her against the door. Once more, she sought the staff, yet lost her footing as he pushed the door open and kicked her to the ground.

Collapsed against the wooden floor, she stared upon a desperate man, horror etched upon his scarred face. "I taught you elven. Use it to get home."

He slammed the door, and Flowridia knew it would not budge again. Though it tore her soul in two, she climbed to her feet and ran.

She sprinted up the nearby stairs, meeting no one, and across an equally empty deck. The sun cast brilliant rays across the sky, the cool air stinging her skin. Every bit of her was alight, her nerves burning, but there was the line of parachutes along the barrier.

No one was here. All were below deck.

Like walking through fog, she approached her quarry and slipped her arms through the straps, hand trembling as she took the rope that would release it. She stumbled as the ship lurched. It slowly descended, though if they fixed it, it would not descend for long.

As she stared upon the earth below, blinding reality struck her—she might never see Ayla again, if she jumped.

She climbed upon the railing, holding a rope for support. Casvir and Etolié had been in Velen'Kye looking for her.

"*Return with an army,*" Tazel had said.

With a final glance back at the cabin, Flowridia softly said, "I'm sorry, Ayla. I love you."

She shut her eyes and fell forward.

Chapter 11

"**O**h, fuck it *burns*!"

Odessa shrieked as the healing magic flowed through her, and Sora prayed it didn't harm her ghostly form. But the human body she possessed did heal, the blood stanched from her bleeding head.

When the golden light from Sora's hands faded, Odessa heaved labored breaths. Scarring remained, but she would live. In Flowridia's former prison, Odessa clung to Sora's shirt as she steadied herself. "I swear on every dead god, I will gouge her eyes out if I see her again."

Sora ignored the horrid words, more focused on saving the woman's life. There remained the splintered wood in Odessa's back, and Sora feared the damage she would find. "If your body dies, what happens?"

"Then I'm dead forever. This is what anchors me to the world now."

Mereen entered, her aura permeating cold. Fangs elongated from her mouth at the proximity of blood; she stayed in the doorway, though Sora didn't miss how her hands tapped against the doorframe. "How is she?"

"Not out of the woods yet. Is there any way Tazel could assist?"

"No. Though I can send one of the engineers in if you need a partner."

"Unless one of them is a medic, no point. Can you find me tweezers?"

Mereen's sharp jaw clenched, her beauty marred by frustration. "I'll send word around for a medic, but they're scrambling to fix the ship and find Flowridia. There is no sign, but a parachute is missing."

Sora knew whose fault it was yet also feared who Mereen

would decide to blame.

"Do whatever you must," Mereen continued, a clear threat in her tone. "I'll return with supplies."

She slammed the door as she left.

Odessa gave a pained cough—thankfully free of blood. "I hate that we're so compatible. I don't find many women as scary as I am. If she'd let me remove the rod from her ass, we could rule the realm."

Not the most comforting idea. Sora's kept her focus on the wound, knowing it would be a rough road ahead. "I'll have to pick out the splinters before I can heal this. If the wound becomes septic, we're in trouble."

"I've been through worse pain. I'm a screamer, but I can handle it." Odessa chuckled, though she winced when it rocked her torso. "You ever given birth?"

"I have not."

"It's so much worse than this."

Mereen returned and wordlessly tossed a medical bag into the room. The gulp in her throat suggested hunger; her fangs remained. "Do you need anything else?"

"No—"

Again, she slammed the door.

"Such drama," Odessa muttered, her laughter returning.

Sora controlled her tone, but tension radiated from her very essence. "She's a vampire. She is literally trying to not eat you."

"Oh. She can be insufferable for that, I suppose. What a strange creed she has. No eating people. Can't relate." Odessa released a groan, her hands twisting the fabric of Sora's trousers. "Get to it. If I'm going to be miserable, might as well front-load it. Don't worry about my feelings."

Sora opened the medical bag and withdrew tweezers and a scalpel. "Do you want something to bite?"

"Yes, please. If you wouldn't mind."

The bag contained nothing to assist with that, so instead Sora cut the leather strap of the bag itself and offered Odessa a long strip.

Once Odessa secured it between her teeth, Sora gripped the protrusion of wood in her back, noting how Odessa winced. "I'm going to say a prayer, and—"

"A prayer for me? Sol Kareena wants me dead. Why would she help?"

Sora swallowed her discomfort at that. "O-On the count

of three, then."

Odessa nodded, her fingers bunched in Sora's shirt.

"One ... two ... three—"

Odessa's scream filled the cabin, muffled by the leather. Sora's life for a smoke, and her smoke for a prayer—for the truth was, she had felt nothing in a year.

Sol Kareena, guide my hand, she silently prayed, but was anyone listening at all?

Sora progressed into bitter work.

Flowridia had expected falling to hurt, to make her ill. Instead, as she plummeted toward the earth, arms spread wide, the exhilaration was akin to flying.

Though she did wish she had done something to keep her hair from her face. The curls threatened to choke her, and there was little she could do for it.

Though the wind in her ears threatened to deafen her, the world spread out in an array of gorgeous colors, with a dense forest ahead, a river far away, a field below, and mountains all around. Sensational, truly, to see the world from afar.

Flowridia tugged the parachute's rope, releasing the tarp into the sky. She expected a horrid lurch—but was met with something milder.

Instead, her fall slowed, the world becoming quiet. She was left to contemplate how one landed and prayed she did not break her legs in the process. Yet despite it all, there was peace among the clouds. Flowridia swore she breathed for the first time in days.

The ground came ever closer. Flowridia trembled, her peace dissipating, replaced with the panic of potentially breaking a bone or several. An expansive field surrounded her, and it was merely a leap away, Flowridia's feet skimmed the foliage—

Her feet caught beneath her, taking a few running steps before she toppled to the ground. But she did not skid, simply collapsed into the grass. When she rolled over, she faced the blue sky, the burning sun. A fit of laughter overtook her, the residual energy too much. By every god—she had *lived*.

And so she remained in the field, hysterical laughter wracking her body, relief and adrenaline and anguish stirring all into one. She did not stop—not even when tears seeped from her eyes, when the laughter became sobs. With this single victory had come a vast, empty future. What now?

When she had finally calmed enough to think, Flowridia sat up and removed the parachute straps from her shoulders. In slow measures, she gathered the tarp and ropes. No use wasting what might be lifesaving supplies, but she did discard the crinoline, having no use for the extra weight.

But she had no inkling of how far north she was. She had seen no evidence of a city during her free fall. It could be weeks on the road . . .

But Casvir knew she was gone. Why had he been in Velen'Kye? Had he sensed their severance? She supposed he must have felt *something* when the bullet murdered her Demitri. Did he seek her?

She had already sold a child for Lara. She feared what she would have to give for Ayla, but so long as it was not Ayla herself, she would pay. Perhaps a second one. Apparently she wasn't much more than a vessel to him, anyway.

Try as she might, she could not stuff the parachute back into its pack, unable to get the folds quite as tight as before. Instead, she stuffed it as well as she could and carried it in her arms. The canvas would be useful for sleeping—she knew how cold the woods could be, especially the ground—and there were always reasons for rope.

Aura had taught her many things. Aura had taught her to survive.

A mother of sorts, yes, and Flowridia wished she could have known that at the time. So many wasted tears for Odessa, who had broken her heart, instead of seeing the wonderful figure she already had. But children were foolish. Aura had loved her, nevertheless.

Aura had been strict, but Aura had also been kind. She didn't need to wonder if Aura had loved her as she would a pup; a warm assurance from within said *yes*.

Flowridia looked to the sun, measured its place in the sky, and walked south.

"First we find water," she said aloud, recalling Aura's teachings. She had spotted a river from high in the air; she could not be more than a day away. "Food is second." The woods would be promising for that, though she knew little of elven plants. "And finally—shelter."

She carried shelter in her arms. As dire as her circumstances were, she could be much worse off. Her clothing was fanciful, but thick and layered. It might be colder in the north, but it was not winter. The canvas was damn heavy, however. She would be terribly sore in the morning.

Hours of walking meant too much time for contemplation. For all the tears she had shed for Demitri, they now fell for Ayla. Tazel had said that whatever they planned was more horrible than she could imagine, but she could imagine quite a bit.

The sun was noticeably lower in the sky when Flowridia faced the edge of the woods.

Perhaps she might leave the woods and find a town. She had no money, but if she could find a cart to procure passage on, she could use the maldectine for bartering.

Flowridia's stomach grumbled. As a rule, she avoided meat, but even if it were an option, she had no weapons. Humans could survive weeks without food, but it wouldn't be comfortable.

She stopped and shut her eyes, letting the sounds of the forest enrapture her. How muted she felt. How empty, to not feel the blessed life around her, to not breathe in the sensations of spirits and magic.

Instead, she listened for water. No evidence met her ears, but something else promising did. Chirping insects were familiar wherever you went.

Flowridia placed the canvas and ropes down, arms aching from the weight, and listened again, the prospect of eating a cricket harkening to her younger days with Aura. Not the most pleasant thing, but if she could do it when she was six, surely she could do it now. She had caught countless insects in her days, and soon found the location of her quarry—a resting insect, sequestered at the juncture of a branch and a tree trunk.

With careful steps, Flowridia crept upon it, no hesitation as she cupped her hand over it. She held the little thing by its body, grimacing.

"For Ayla," she whispered, and she stuffed it in her mouth, crunching it as quickly as she could to end its panic. The taste wasn't disgusting; it was the act itself, but it did not harken to her days in Mother's home, so she swallowed with a wince but nothing more.

"I can't believe you used to chase these for..." Flowridia's words faded away as she looked to the empty space beside her. Demitri was not there to jest with; she swallowed that awful truth.

She returned to her parachute and hauled it deeper into the woods, periodically dropping it to catch more crickets.

As the sun set, there rose the ambient light of fireflies. Flowridia stopped a moment, enthralled by their lovely presence. Aura had said to never eat them, that they were toxic, but their coming meant darkness would fall soon—and so Flowridia found a collection of trees and set up her camp.

It had been a long time since she'd tied a proper knot, and so she struggled as she wrestled with the rope and branches, eventually coming up with something passable. Knots would be the first thing she studied when she returned home—*when* being the key word. She would return home. She had to.

She managed to string up the other end on a second tree, and when she placed her weight on her clumsy hammock, it held. Darkness fell, and Flowridia saw only fireflies and the barest outline of her hand.

Tomorrow night, she would try to light a fire, but for now, she curled up in her hammock, anticipating soreness from a second night of sleeping in a corset, and covered herself in the remaining canvas layers, creating a cocoon.

Yet as she tried to sleep, all the memories of the previous night bombarded her with cruel precision. Over and over came the blast of the gunshot before Demitri fell. Ayla's desperate screams were an echo. Flowridia tried to stanch her tears, knowing she couldn't spare the water, but they fell, nevertheless.

In the dark woods, Flowridia cried alone, haunted by memories of death.

In her room in Nox'Kartha, as she feigned packing an illusionary bag with clothing that wasn't real, Etolié listened to Zorlaeus prattle on about issues that simply didn't affect her.

"You're going camping with the imperator?!"

"I volunteered."

"Are you worried at all?"

Instead of actually placing things in the bag, she stuffed them into an extra-planar space—but not dresses, no. She didn't need those. Extra flasks and booze for special occasions. The good wine. "I respect that you're terrified of Cassie. I suppose I am too, in an existential way. But on a personal level? Naw."

"Do you know when you'll be back?"

"As soon as we find Flowers. Casvir handed me some advisers to run the Solvira show while I'm gone, but I have Zoldar tasked to prevent them from doing anything beyond keeping people fed. Thankfully, things have been stable." She paused, reflecting on her conversation with the imperator—wherein he had finally agreed that she would be useful. "Casvir mentioned something called a 'bloodhound' to help search out Flowers. Do you know what that is?"

Zorlaeus' cringe was less than reassuring. "They're dogs, of a sort."

"I don't particularly like dogs, unless they're magically intelligent wolves."

"Well, these aren't exactly dogs, so I can promise you won't be neutral on them."

How lovely, for her palms to suddenly be drenched in sweat. "Great. I'll just find out for myself."

"Did you say Sora was involved in this?"

"Yes, and I'm not over it. Sora helping Mereen? Last I saw them together, Mereen literally tried to sacrifice her to a swamp witch, so I'm not sure what's going on."

"Family can be complicated," Zorlaeus replied, and Etolié hated how much it changed the whole mood of the room.

"I'm a fan of killing shitty progenitors, personally. But . . ."

Etolié thought of her momma, of the rekindling of friendship and maternal love in her life. Forgiveness could be warranted for some faults, she supposed, even egregious ones. Momma had done nothing but show her sincerity and love, but Etolié herself still held back.

"If they show they've changed, I guess it can be all right," Etolié continued. "But something tells me Mereen is exactly the same manipulative bastard as before."

"I suppose you'll have to ask Sora when you succeed."

"See, that's the kind of positivity I need in my life." Quite a lot of booze had been 'packed' in her 'bag'—far more than any bag of its size could reasonably carry. But a darker thought occurred then, that sometimes summoning knives didn't work. In her guest bedroom, she withdrew a boring, non-magical dagger from her bedside table and stuffed it into the extra-planar space as well.

Hopefully it wouldn't be boring for much longer. Hopefully it would be sheath-deep in a particular necromancer's stomach.

Etolié swiped her hand and let it all vanish. "I'd better go."

Zorlaeus offered a hand. When Etolié accepted, he squeezed it in comradery, a 'hand hug' as he had affectionately named it. "Good luck, Etolié."

"Stay busy, Zorlaeus."

As established, Casvir waited in the vast throne room, though what accompanied him made her stomach churn. Sure, there were the undead horses, saddled and ready for a rider, but standing near him were three hairless, disgustingly pale ... things. Vaguely dog shaped, so she assumed these were the bloodhounds. They reached her waist, which was entirely too big for a dog, and held obvious scarring along the seams of their limbs, their necks, their skulls. Red eyes, not unlike Casvir's, stared straight into her fucking soul, and Etolié knew she'd never sleep again.

She kept her distance. "Please tell me these are the bloodhounds."

"They are."

"Oh, thank Alystra's Ass. These are the worst things I've ever seen, and I don't want to risk there being something even nastier crawling around the inner mechanisms of this castle. What the fuck even are these?"

"They were dogs."

"Yes, and now they're what would happen if you handed Ayla Darkleaf a pile of raw chicken and said to sew a dog."

"That is not quite their origin, but she is the inventor."

Not even out of the castle, and Etolié felt critical meltdown approaching. "I assume they sniff things?"

"They do." He gestured to the obviously dead horse beside him. "Do you ride?"

"Under threat of death, yes."

He frowned, apparently not fluent in hyperbole.

She approached the feral beast, its soulless eyes even more alarming when dead. "I hate horses, but I'll suck it up. Do dead ones ride any smoother?"

"They do."

Perhaps she would survive, then. The horse carried a bedroll and other supplies on its saddle, and Etolié supposed there simply wasn't a weight limit if it was dead. "Where *are* we going?"

"First, we go to the outskirts of Velen'Kye. I have in my possession a dress Flowridia left behind. I am hopeful the bloodhounds will catch a scent. We do not know where our quarry is going, only that it is far enough to justify an airship. Unfortunately, our best hope for success is by riding. You are here to assist me primarily in camouflage, but I do not know what sort of abyss we ride into. I expect you to be resourceful, which time has shown you are capable of. There is no one on this mortal plane who can do what you do."

"Aw, I thought you hated me. I'm flattered."

Casvir struck his claw through the air; Etolié's stomach flipped, but she managed to keep her lunch in check. "I do not have to like you to acknowledge your use."

Etolié did not reply. She did not even give a facial expression in response. Not like he deserved it—or cared.

On second thought, the freedom to not be constantly policing her thoughts and expressions sounded rather nice. Politics could fucking burn. Perhaps this would be a vacation after all.

"Just for your information," Etolié said, "I still haven't calculated how you do that."

"Do what?"

"Create portals. You told me I'd figure it out—congratulations, I haven't."

Casvir's raised eyebrow conveyed how many shits he gave about that.

He handed her the horse's reins and stepped through the portal with his own. The bloodhounds followed, and thank her few remaining lucky stars for that. Left alone with the perilous beast, she cautiously tugged on the reins; it moved. "Here goes nothing."

They stepped through the portal. Again came the horrible, stomach-churning heave of teleportation.

She landed on her knees. With the sun too bright and the

breeze too cheerful, Etolié heaved out residual chunks of breakfast, soiling the luscious grass beneath her. "Please promise we'll do that as little as possible."

A shadow covered her. Silhouetted by blinding rays, Casvir stood beside his own skeletal steed, towering above her. "I promise nothing. We will do it as necessary."

"Boo to you too, you bastard."

As she gathered herself, Casvir removed what appeared to be a large ream of cloth from one of his saddlebags and offered it to the bloodhounds, who swarmed it like angry wasps. They had no tails, but their sudden spike in enthusiasm meant they'd surely be wagging if they could. They yipped in a way that was almost endearing, then circled around each other, eager to move on.

With a groan, Etolié spread her wings and allowed magic and gravity to do its job of lifting her up. She found her footing, though her head still spun, and again she rose, this time landing on the horse. She braced herself for it to panic—but no. It remained perfectly still. "At least dead horses can't be spooked. Right?"

"Correct."

Etolié took the reins, begrudgingly accepting that this might not be the worst experience of her life. "I see the appeal."

Surely there were silent commands being issued, the hounds controlled by necromancy, but Casvir gave no indication except to mount his own horse. The bloodhounds howled into the wind, the omen echoing across the field before they bolted forward—and Casvir's steed charged ahead.

"Goddess Momma, protect me," she muttered.

Her horse followed Casvir's into the impending unknown.

Once Sora had washed her hands of Odessa's blood, she joined the search for Flowridia, careful to stay above deck.

Below, she would have Mereen to contend with. Castigation was inevitable.

But when evening fell and there remained no sign of Flowridia, the mood had shifted. Their prisoner had gone, and she feared what it would constitute for the rest of them.

Sora stared up at the stars, and though it was not a domain she worshipped, she thought of Etolié, thought of her cry as the airship had lifted, leaving her behind: *"Whatever they're paying you . . ."*

At the edge of the ship, Sora released a scoffing laugh, because it was so unbearably Etolié, one of her few friends. If she knew, she would understand. Etolié had no love for Flowridia either, anymore. She had always despised Ayla, even before she was a proven monster.

What she wouldn't approve of was Demitri's demise, and Sora had no excuse for that. Yes, it made Flowridia less dangerous. Yes, it was for the greater good. But Etolié would never let it go.

Was that bridge burned? Sora looked to Leelan, her constant companion. "What do you think? Does Etolié hate me now?"

Leelan hopped along her shoulder to her cheek, where he rubbed his soft feathers.

Etolié had to understand. If nothing else, Etolié had also sacrificed her morals for the greater good.

The sun fully set, drenching the world in darkness. Mereen still did not emerge. Below, the world had become a sea of black, and Sora stared into the abyss, seeking resolve anew.

With light steps, Sora paced the perimeter of the ship, but when she passed the space above Flowridia's failed prison, she heard a faint whisper of rage.

Curious, Sora crept to the stairs leading below deck.

". . . and now she's missing because of your moronic impulsivity! What if she's dead? Everything we've done so far will have been in vain!"

"I understand," came Odessa's pacifying tone, *"but who could have predicted—"*

"Who could have predicted that the wife of the most famed villain of our era would have a few clever thoughts in her head? Certainly not her own mother, apparently!"

Whatever Odessa said in return was lowered to a whisper. Sora stepped on silent feet down the stairs and placed her ear to the door.

". . . go personally to retrieve her."

"Oh, will you?"

"I will. And this time, no mercy. Once we land, I shall go. It will take no time at all."

"Fail me, and that coveted body of yours won't be much longer for this world."

When footsteps sounded within, Sora took that as her cue to dart away, as soft-footed as she could. Mereen had placed her blame, but gut instinct said to stay out of sight.

Instead, she stopped where she knew Tazel was sequestered with the coffin. She knocked; no sound emerged. She peeked through the seams of the door and saw evidence of flickering lamplight but nothing more.

Footsteps neared. Sora took the plunge and slipped inside.

As predicted, there sat the coffin at the far side of the room and Tazel seated on the floor, his head propped up against it. He gripped the staff, the only sign of distress his white knuckles and stiff jaw—though he did smile at her entrance.

"Hello, Sora." His exhaustion entangled the words. "Something tells me there's no sign of her."

"Flowridia is gone." Sora sat opposite from him on the floor. "I overheard Mereen reprimanding Odessa for letting her escape."

"Mereen has never underestimated an enemy in all her days. It's how she's gotten this far. It's also why she has no patience for incompetence."

"If Flowridia really did jump from the ship, she's far braver than me." Sora shuddered at the thought.

"It's also possible she faked jumping from the ship and is still hiding, even now."

"I suspect Mereen would have sniffed her out already."

Tazel nodded in agreement, something labored in his breathing. In his hands, the staff trembled—nigh imperceptible, but Sora worried.

"Are you all right?" she asked, and immediately his smile rejuvenated, highlighting his handsome features.

"I've been better."

Sora spared a glance for the box, finding it strange to think the very core of wickedness lay within, hopefully docile. "Will the staff not aid us as much as we thought?"

"No, it's strong enough, and I have the talent to maintain it. But it's . . ." Hesitation stilled his words, a grimace twisting his lip. "Uncomfortable."

"Odessa mentioned something about feedback." His scowl remained, his eyes refusing to meet hers. "Yes, I suppose that's the word for it. This staff wasn't meant for me. It was meant for the God of Death. When you wear a shoe that's too big, you get blisters."

"So Ayla is as much in your head as you are in hers?"

"It's only little things," he said, not quite confirming it. "I'll catch a glimpse of something I haven't seen before, or think of something I shouldn't know as if it were my own memory. It's . . ." He shook his head, growing pale. "It's hopefully nothing to worry about."

Sora looked pityingly upon him, hating to watch him in pain. "If you need a break, I'm happy to try. I'm not as proficient in magic as you, but I've had Leelan for a few years now. I've used magic devices before."

Though Tazel cringed, he said, "It might be wise to have you try, just in case Odessa or I can't for whatever reason. If anything tries to rise, stomp it down."

Sora presumed she'd know what that meant once she was holding it. When she approached, his hesitation nearly offended her, but he offered it all the same.

Upon contact, her awareness of the world expanded, even as consuming darkness flowed through her veins. Like seeing new colors, it saturated her whole perception, and she felt with clarity the being in the box—

Upon the slab, the victim writhed, though with so little skin left, it was a wonder she even breathed at all. How euphoric, to unravel her, to watch each piece come apart—Sora?

Sora blinked and stood before Tazel, yet the unmistakable sensation assaulted her of something . . . *rising.*

The blunt-eared bastard struggled in her grasp, screams muffled by her own severed tongue. Ayla stuffed it farther down, reveling in her gag, the stream of blood from her mouth. Even half-breed blood smelled euphoric. "This city will never forget you, Sora Fireborn—"

Sora broke from deep water when Tazel wrenched the staff away. She stumbled backward against the wall, heart thumping in her ears. Within the coffin, the monster stilled. Sweat pooled at Sora's brow, her whole body cold. "What . . . I . . ."

"It's all right, Sora," Tazel said, his voice grounding.

Not trusting her legs, Sora slid down the wall,

consciously stopping her trembling. "I saw me."

"Her memory of you?"

Sora managed to nod.

"Odessa and I both experienced that same thing." But despite his painted smile, Tazel's eyes became soft. "Have I told you lately how much you remind me of your mother?"

Grasping the segue, Sora said, "Oh really?"

"Altruistic and confident, yes. And a little bit nosy." He winked to soften that blow, but Sora's cheeks flared red. "She was a dear friend. Mereen would often train us together. But she disappeared after she met your father. I didn't see her again until she was sick."

Fifteen years had passed, and the memory still haunted her on sleepless nights. Nearly delusional from fever, Sora had wandered to her mother's room where she languished in bed. *"I'm shivering, Mom. Will you hold me?"*

Sora had awoken with a broken fever in a cold, stiff embrace.

She steeled her voice, willing it to not waver. She managed to breathe out her anxiety, finally shaking off the scare from the staff, though absently withdrew her pipe and Spore. "I remember when you came to visit us at the Fireborn Estate. You weren't afraid of the fever at all."

"I hadn't traveled north of the Highlands and south of Ku'Shya's Realm just to die of sickness." His painted smile became sincere and sorrowful, and Sora was struck by his empathy. "And I'd heard from Mereen that Mari and her daughter were dying. Of course I had to come."

"You were the only person in that house who would talk to me." Sora chuckled, because what else did you do when contemplating bigotry?

But Tazel didn't join in, his expression remaining the same. "You were a child whose mother was dying. You were dying, as far as they knew. Horrible of them. You didn't deserve that."

"Barely a child. Sixteen is an adult in Solvira."

"Not in Zauleen. Not by any elven standards."

Strange, for her age to make her feel small. Thirty meant she was an adult now, but she hadn't considered that Tazel saw her as a child. Sora brought the pipe to her mouth, anticipating sweet relief.

"I know your mother ran away because of Mereen," Tazel continued, reminiscence in the words, "but when I spoke to her on her deathbed, she expressed that she feared I hated her as well, for loving a human man. I'm grateful every day we were able to speak before she died, but I do regret never having the opportunity to meet your father."

Familiar yearning returned, the sorrow that came from something lost and never found. "I have a picture, if you want."

At Tazel's nod, Sora withdrew a pendant of infinite worth from her pocket. Sized to the palm of her hand, it never left her side, as carefully hidden as her knives. She clicked the mechanism at the top. It smoothly opened, revealing two faces. Sora's smile came unbidden, for her mother's countenance was unendingly lovely. She liked to think she had her mother's eyes, always conveying joy. And there was her father, with his broad smile and treasured locs, inspiring her own.

When she offered it to Tazel, her heart went fondly with it. So strange, to remember stability. But Tazel stared sweetly upon it, immediate brightness coming to his tired gaze. "I haven't seen Mari's face in years." He gave it back, his dusty smile so reminiscent of her mother. "Your father has a very kind face."

"He had a heart to match."

"His death was why you came across the sea, right?"

Was it strange to pray her father was dead? When she stood before Sol Kareena in the afterlife, there was only one mystery she longed to know. "A few years later, but yes. And he's the reason I returned to Solvira when my mother passed. I searched for signs—of his death," she quickly added, because Tazel could not think the contrary.

"You don't know if he died?"

She hadn't meant to tear that wound open. No turning back, but Tazel was a safe space. "My father often traveled for months at a time. He was a paladin of Sol Kareena and had devoted his life to her. But one day he didn't come back. He had promised to return for my birthday, but I turned ten years old, and he wasn't there. I never saw him again."

However, months had passed before she finally walked in on her mother weeping in her bedroom, coaxing Sora into her arms. "*I can lie to myself no longer,*" she had said in her elvish tongue.

"Paladin of Sol Kareena? That's not a small title. Who bestowed it?"

"I don't know," Sora replied, the question making her cold. He had left so many questions behind. In the light of day, she recalled his voice, his laugh, how it shook his entire body, rumbled against her when they hugged. A thousand cherished memories, living on only in her head.

But in darker moments, the cruel truth remained—that he had kept secrets, even from her.

"I returned to Solvira seeking...anything," Sora continued. "I spent years investigating, asking if anyone had even heard of him. But it was like he had been wiped from the face of the realm. No one knew his name. My quest ended when I was captured by slavers in Moratham."

"Slavers?" Tazel said, intrigued despite his exhaustion. "And how in the world did you manage to escape from that?"

Sora's chuckle came unbidden. "I was rescued by the Savior of Slaves herself. Etolié was Magister of Staelash back then, but she would still assist in liberating camps—with the Bringer of War, of course."

Tazel stared as though she'd spoken dwarven. And so Sora explained—of Staelash, and of Etolié, her friend. "I might've lived a normal life as a citizen, but their high priestess spotted me and told me to come with her. She didn't give me much of a choice." Sora smiled to think of Meira, though her memory was bittersweet now—her death a spectacular, tragic end. "She always saw more than anyone really believed. Etolié thought she was crazy, but a part of me wonders if Meira saw that...well, that I'd be chosen by Sol Kareena. I wish she were here. Perhaps she might've had answers as to why."

"I always questioned why the goddess chose me," Tazel replied, then with a wink, he added, "though I hope you stay more resolute than me."

"It was Etolié who mentioned I had a cousin living in a library." At Tazel's ensuing chuckle, she joined, though a certain sadness settled into his eyes. "Flowridia had told her. Etolié was jealous of you, wished she could run away and live in a library for the rest of her days."

"No, she doesn't."

"Why did you do it?" Sora dared to ask.

Tazel remained silent a moment, his brewing thoughts palpable. Bitterness filled each chosen word. "Mereen became too much."

Sora glanced at the door, but Tazel said, "She knows."

"Then why . . ."

Her words trailed away as Tazel's shook his head. "I'm here to finish what my family started. I'm here to kill Ayla Darkleaf once and for all; perhaps then I can find peace."

Sora did not understand but managed to nod.

"Do you still seek your father?" Tazel asked, compassion even in his pained expression. He was hurting. She offered the pipe, but he shook his head. "I can't risk not being sharp."

Sora brought it to her lips instead. "Not actively. But I've never truly stopped, no. Sometimes I dream about his smile. I'd give anything to see it again."

"Tell me about him," Tazel said, but there was a layer to it, some desperation she saw straight through.

Sora could be a distraction. "He was my hero. He taught me everything I know about animals and hunting," Sora began, and she spoke easily of it for hours.

Flowridia awoke to chirping birds and sunlight peering through the thickly woven strings of her canvas hammock.

With care to not tip it, she pushed away her covering, prepared for the blast of cold. Whatever her anguish, she had no soreness in her back—though her arms were a different story—and the rustling leaves and animal sounds were a welcome ambience. Daunting, however, was the dryness in her mouth.

Her quest for water continued.

With a handkerchief she had in her bodice, Flowridia carefully wiped it across the vegetation around her, collecting every bit of water she could. She sucked on it intermittently, wasting nothing, but water remained in meager supply.

Soon, Flowridia had her small camp packed, this time tying a piece of rope around the parachute's pack to keep it confined. Though the thick canvas was heavy on her back, her arms would thank her, and she continued walking south.

She kept half an eye out for insects, and the deeper she went into the forest, the more earthworms she found slinking in the mud—worse to swallow than crickets, but edible. Aura would be proud of her ingenuity, and Flowridia could not help but drift off into memories, of hours spent in the woods with her beloved first familiar.

She wandered south through the trees for a few quiet hours, until a road cut through the dense forest.

Though vacant, it was clearly well-used, the packed dirt comfortable beneath her bare feet. Roads meant civilization. Civilization meant water and food—and perhaps passage to Velen'Kye.

Don't mention Ayla. Don't mention Casvir. But she had plenty of skills as a baker, as a gardener—if they wouldn't accept maldectine, surely she could still barter.

The day continued, and when the sun was directly above, tension formed a headache at the base of her skull. The dryness in her mouth became irritating. She supposed she could awaken early and lick the morning dew—which, in her current state, didn't sound too awful.

By nightfall, there was still no sign, not of water or civilization. Her stomach rumbled from her diet of insects. Sleep evaded her. Try as she might, she could not stop her tears.

In the morning, she repeated her tedious task of collecting all the water she could, but now her head pounded.

She returned to the road, stopping frequently to *listen* for sounds of civilization. Were there any gods who would accept her call for aid? Could they hear her with maldectine? Did it matter at all?

. . . It struck her that there was one who yet might.

Despite the cheery day, Flowridia stepped off the path and knelt in the darkest shadow she could find. She found a rock, pulse racing as she struck it against the bracelet's latch. When it scratched the maldectine, it left no mark, but the thin metal bent—bent—

Crack. The metal broke free, the bracelet falling open.

The world did not change, the reminder a heavy burden. She had no magic; she had nothing at all.

She stuffed it into her bundle of canvas, then clasped her hands together. "Izthuni, God of Shadows . . ."

Nothing changed, nothing shifted, yet dread filled her.

"I am lost and alone. Ayla is trapped. I don't know what aid you could deliver. I don't know what to ask for. But if there is anything . . ."

Within her rose the uncanny knowledge of being watched. He was a demon god; no matter what he felt for her, he would not do it for free.

"Tell me the price for aid—"

All the world went dark.

Flowridia gasped, still kneeing beside her chosen tree, but she knew that only by touch. Terror rose, and then came a voice she knew, as deep as thunder, permeating the air like fog. *Flowridia Darkleaf, lost and alone.*

Frozen, she listened to the taunting words.

How heartbreaking. How foolish. A just reward for leaving me.

All the air left Flowridia's lungs. "What?"

She put me aside. She left me behind. Always researching. Always spending time with you. No need for me—her maker. No need to become The Endless Night once more.

Flowridia remained perfectly still, fearful the predator would strike.

But that is not your fault. I feared you would corrupt her with kindness. Instead, you are an oblivious enabler of her disrespect. I will help you—after you perform a task for me.

Trepidation slowed her speech, for this may have been a terrible mistake. "What do you want?"

There is an artifact I left in this world. It is not far from where you sit and weep. Ku'Shya would strike me down if I set foot in her realm, so I cannot retrieve it myself. Find it, and I will assist you on your journey to Nox'Kartha, where you may leave it in my temple. You will not starve. You will be protected. You will find money as you need it.

Technically, it was all she wanted. "What of Ayla? Can you help?"

I can only possess Ayla's body if she calls for me. Until she does, I do not know her bearings and therefore cannot assist. But once you have succeeded in returning what I've lost, I will send my servants to find her.

Everything about it screamed of a trap, of danger, yet he would not betray his promise; it was not Demoni way. "What is the artifact? How will I know it?"

You will feel the pull in your soul.

The darkness seeped away, along with the pervasive echo of his voice. Flowridia knelt in a bright forest, hungry and thirsty, but filled with a jagged hope.

And somehow, like a compulsion from within . . . she knew to forge ahead.

Thank Eionei's disgraced Asshole—the hounds eventually slowed.

The endless fields continued, though clouds had gathered to block the sun. Casvir sat stoic upon his steed, following at a leisurely pace behind the bloodhounds—who led them straight north, occasionally stopping to sniff the dress half-hanging out of his saddlebag. Still weird as fuck that he had it, but in a sentimental dad way as opposed to a stalker way.

That said . . .

"So, you and Flowers had a falling out, right?"

Casvir kept his eyes firmly on the horizon. "My current standing with Flowridia is not your business."

"I just assumed because she ran away in the night and never calls. Also, she ended up on the other side of the war—"

"As I said, it is not your business."

That sharp tone said more than any confirmation. Etolié tucked that away for now, silent as she contemplated a second mystery.

She waited until his palpable menace faded, then said, "You weren't surprised at all to hear Flowers was pregnant."

"You have come around to the idea."

"I went through the stages of grief and landed on acceptance, yes." Did he know about the scroll? Etolié burned to find out—because what a fucking disaster that would be. "Did she ever mentioned the idea of wanting babies? Those aren't as easy to come by if you're a Daughter of Neoma."

"It was simply a surprise it happened so quickly."

That . . . meant nothing. Etolié chose something a little more straightforward. "Any idea who the father is?"

"No, though I intend to inquire when we meet again."

It seemed he didn't know about the scroll, though the weirdness of the situation remained.

It was then that three humanoid silhouettes appeared on the horizon. "Leave this to me, Cassie."

With a mere modicum of focus, the bloodhounds appeared as regular dogs—far friendlier and less dubiously dead. Casvir became an uncommonly broad elf, while the horses gained skin. Etolié lost her wings and became just a bit more elven.

"We should talk to them," she said.

"Why would we do that?"

Etolié glanced between him and the distant travelers, struggling to explain such an obvious connection. "Because they might know something?"

"Doubtful."

"But what if?"

"Then you may speak to them."

Was Casvir the most socially ill-adjusted person she had

ever met? Absolutely. "Bitch, I will."

Bracing her stomach, Etolié smacked her horse's illusionary rump and sent it into a gallop. To her surprise, Casvir followed, the dogs in pursuit, until the distant figure—*figures*, that was—gained substance.

A family, she presumed—a father and two sons. "Hello!" she cried, then recalled she sounded like a Solviran royal, and so she frantically tried to organize her words into an elven cadence. "Might we ask you fine folks a question?"

The man stopped his horse, his skepticism apparent. The rusted sword at his belt had seen better days, but his frame suggested he knew how to wield it. "You may, lady."

"My companion and I have heard some strange rumors coming out of Velen'Kye—regarding Ayla Darkleaf and her wife." Immediate alarm fell upon the man's face. Etolié quickly backtracked. "Apparently there was trouble."

"Yes, lady. A massacre. The two haven't been seen since, but the Imperator of Nox'Kartha was. Executor Faeborn was one of the only survivors, and their account doesn't mention the imperator in the massacre itself, but we fear we witnessed his revenge. What's worse is that with Executor Yewblade having lost his mind, Executor Faeborn is the only one left."

"Well, damn," Etolié said, noting Casvir's utter lack of reaction. "Strange times. Be safe on the road."

"You as well, lady."

Etolié waited until the man and his sons were out of earshot to say, "Well, good job. Your best crime wasn't even yours."

"I have far more impressive feats." Casvir withdrew a small mirror from his saddlebag, the design of which Etolié immediately recognized. When he tapped it, the mirror glowed, and then came . . . a truly beloved face.

Etolié beamed at the glimpse of Khastra's face. "Imperator," his general said, and Etolié clung to even that despicable word.

"I have received word that Executors Stormforged and Desertblessed are dead. Rumors say Executor Yewblade is incapacitated. Send our full force to Heivyr. We will strike down the Highland Elves in their confused state."

"Yes, Imperator. This is a promising path."

"Can I?" Etolié asked, surprised when Casvir acquiesced; he handed the mirror with no hesitation.

How lovely, to see Khastra set aside her mantle of

general and become the woman she loved. "Hello, Etolié."

"Hi." She looked to Casvir. "We can keep walking. Can I just ..?"

"Fine."

With Khastra's company secured, Etolié giggled like a besotted virgin—not that she'd been one of those in a while—as she spoke of the horrors of bloodhounds and the annoyance of never-ending fields. But the miserable things became just a little bit less that.

All that mattered was Beefcake was here.

By evening, Flowridia had found no water. She simply walked, compelled now by a sensation she found oddly familiar. Years ago, at fifteen, when she had wandered to Mother's home, drawn by a force she couldn't name ...

The beckoning in her heart felt similar. It gave her no peace of mind.

Darkness neared. When her keen eyes began to fail, distant flame rekindled her hope. She hadn't the energy to run, but she did limp ahead with renewed vigor. The light became brighter, even multiplied—a village.

Flowridia stuffed the maldectine into her bodice and stashed her parachute in the trees, knowing it would draw more questions than she wanted—more questions about a human girl in a ruined ball gown, splattered in droplets of blood. Might as well spare herself a little bit of pain.

Savory scents wafted across her senses, causing her empty stomach to rumble. Lights shone from the few homes she passed, and Flowridia wondered what their livelihood would be, so isolated in the woods. Or perhaps she was closer than she thought.

The cottages were not dissimilar to Velen'Kye's architecture, but instead of bricks they bore rougher stone, with wood filling in the gaps. Her stomach rumbled as she caught a whiff of something sweet from the window, but when she lingered, the door suddenly opened—

And she faced the barrel of a large gun.

"Get out of here, monster!" the woman at the other end

shouted, the silhouette of her home casting her in darkness. "Get back in the woods where you belong!"

Flowridia held up defensive hands, taking slow steps back. "I'm no monster. Simply a woman who lost her way."

She shrunk further, wondering what monsters she spoke of, when the woman said, "You're not from here. What is your accent?"

"Solviran. I-I'm from across the sea, in Solvira."

With trembling hands, the woman fumbled in her pocket, then withdrew something small—a coin? "If you're no monster, pick this up." The woman tossed in the air before her, where it glinted silver in the light.

It landed at Flowridia's feet. Keeping careful eye contact, Flowridia crouched and picked up the coin. It seemed like normal currency, but the silver sheen could not be dismissed.

When she offered it forward, the woman noticeably relaxed, lowering her gun. "Not a monster, then. Human?"

Flowridia finally breathed, no longer facing imminent death. "Yes, my lady."

"Never met a human before. What are you doing in Hyall?"

"It's a long story, but the short version is that I'm trying to find my way home."

"Come closer so I can look at you."

As Flowridia approached, the silhouette gained detail, and she saw her clearly. A Sun Elf, assuredly, her features softer, shorter than the residents of Velen'Kye, with brown hair and eyes and rich, suntanned skin. "I assume you won't eat my son if I let you in."

"No, I won't," Flowridia said, a hint of a laugh in her throat. "And I'll happily offer work in exchange for water and a meal."

"Too late. Dinner is already done. Pity—you'll have to eat for free."

Flowridia hadn't expected kindness, attuned to the Iron Elves and their own biased views of humans. She swallowed a sob as she thanked the woman, who beckoned her inside.

A quaint little home, lacking the technology of Velen'Kye, but signs of sophistication remained—the boiler was very different from home, and a little boy built a tower with blocks. Surely no older than four, the sweet child left his toys behind and came forward curiously, his features shared by his mother. "Hello."

229

"Hello, young man," Flowridia replied, her smile genuine in the child's presence.

"What is your name?" the mother asked, and Flowridia's mouth watered at the serving of stew she placed on the table. "But come sit first, you and your bloody ball gown. You look half-starved."

Flowridia spared a glance for her audacious dress, accepting a spoon when offered. "Flow—ra. My name is Flowra."

"I'm Eyal. My son is Mati. My husband is attending a town meeting. Should be home soon, though."

Flowridia had to stop herself from drooling at the first sip of broth, the vegetables not any she had seen before. "I can't thank you enough."

"Once you've eaten, I'll accept the story behind why a Solviran woman is lost in the woods in a bloody ball gown as payment."

Flowridia looked down at her dress, the reminder of Demitri's death welling a lump in her throat. "That's a fair trade," she replied, mulling over what lies she could use to avoid the truth, but nearly sobbed for joy when the woman placed a tankard of water before her.

Her stomach sang at the sustenance, her head stopped spinning at the blessed water, and beside her, Mati sat himself at the table to watch.

"You'd best not talk her ear off, Mati," Eyal said, patting his plump cheeks. "Let her eat first."

He wouldn't stop staring, particularly intrigued by Flowridia's hair. "Yes, Mother."

Flowridia wished she had flowers. Alas, she had not seen any in the woods yet, so her hair was free of its usual décor, all the remaining petals from the party having blown away in her free fall from the airship. She supposed she could mention that bit to Eyal—that she had been kidnapped from a party and made a dramatic escape. It would certainly entertain the child.

When she finished her stew, Eyal took her bowl. "A second serving for you, starving one?"

"If you're offering, I won't say no, but I can't possibly repay—"

"Think nothing of it. Travelers are rare."

As Eyal served up a second bowl, Flowridia asked, "Forgive the naïve question, but is Hyall in Falar'Sol?"

"It is."

So she was in Sun Elves lands—farther from Velen'Kye than she had thought.

When Eyal placed down the steaming bowl, the front door opened. In came a man bearing the same sun-beaten skin, but his eyes and hair were akin to Tazel's blue and blond. "Terrible things are happening . . ." His words trailed off when his eyes landed on Flowridia. "Who is this?"

"Her name is Flowra, and she isn't a vampire—I checked."

So that was the sort of monster they feared. Flowridia's pulse quickened at that, but far worse was the horror in the man's eyes. "Flowra?"

"Tomen?"

Before Flowridia could blink, the man grabbed the gun by the door and pointed it directly at her head. She froze, heart pounding in her ears now. "I-I haven't meant to—"

"She's the necromancer!" He backed away from the open door, positioning himself between her and his wife and son. "Get out, or I'll shoot!"

Flowridia's mind reeled at his words, but she stumbled into standing, hands raised as she went to the door.

"Tomen, what are you talking about?"

"You've heard who's returned to Velen'Kye. Not many humans match the wife's description. Grab Mati and run."

Dread filled the woman's countenance. "Flowridia Darkleaf," Eyal whispered, and she did as implored—grabbed her boy and fled into a back room.

Flowridia kept her hands up as she slipped from the door, not daring to remove her stare from the man and his gun. When her feet touched dirt, she found her voice. "I'll leave your village. You have nothing to fear—"

A shot fired. The wind shifted as the bullet sang beside her ear. Flowridia darted away.

"*Monster!*" she heard the man yell. "*Monster in the woods!*"

The bare beginnings of angry cries stirred behind her. Flowridia kept to the road and ran, bombarded with memories of a lifetime past— "*Witch!*"

Twice was too many times to have been run out of town by an angry mob.

Darkness quickly enveloped her, but the approaching lights beyond meant she could not slow. Though the full moon shone bright, thick trees blocked the celestial light. She ran on pure instinct, praying the dirt path wouldn't betray her.

"*Beware The Endless Night!*"

She couldn't reason with them, even if she could prove she was harmless. Of course word would have come out of Velen'Kye of Ayla Darkleaf. Of course they would hear of her human wife with her dark complexion and red hair.

Flowridia's thighs burned as she ran, but still the distant lights followed. She tried to slow when her feet touched the grass, but branches tore the side of her gown. She toppled, scraping her arms on a fallen tree, and crawled deeper into the woods, utterly blind.

She prayed she met no predators, and when she found a large log, she managed to fall over to the other side of it. With heaving breaths, she collapsed, desperate to silence herself as the mob neared.

When firelight touched the opposite side of the tree, Flowridia's tears flowed freely from her eyes. She pressed herself to the ground, horrified to be faced with a spider as large as her hand, but she could not scream, could not weep, lest the mob come.

And so she lay as still as a cornered mouse, biting her tongue to make no sound as angry men passed her by.

"*Does this mean The Endless Night will come?*"

"*Should we evacuate?*"

"*We should alert the executor!*"

Terror colored their words. These were brave men, expecting a monster; how pitiful, for her to only be a small girl now.

Eventually, the fire faded. Flowridia inched away from where she knew the spider waited, then stood and cautiously hiked deeper into the woods.

Her parachute was far behind, but she couldn't go back. Yes, that compulsion within her soul remained, but hopelessness filled her as she gathered a pile of leaves to rest her head on. The cold ground mocked her. She settled upon it, nevertheless.

"*Monster!*" the man had cried, and Flowridia knew it well.

But how horrid it felt, to watch Eyal's kindness become fear. Not hatred. Fear.

This . . . this was who she was.

Soft tears continued falling from her eyes, her stomach taunted by the memory of warm stew and water. She fell into a fitful sleep, aching both in body and heart.

Sora awoke to an errant light blinding her from the doorway. Alert, her hand went to the knife at her hip, the other to shade her eyes, only to see—

Odessa. Holding a lamp.

"Sorry to disturb you, but we've arrived. Prepare yourself for a hike. Do you need help?"

"I'm ready once I've pulled on my boots."

"Efficient. I admire that. Mereen is insistent we hurry—which for once I am sympathetic toward, given she will burn at sunrise. In the meantime, I'm off to unload our special package."

Odessa left, the flickering light disappearing with her.

Sora dressed to the light of holy magic summoned in her hand—just a spark. She could not conjure much more, unless it was in service of someone. Soon, she slung her pack over her shoulder, and with Leelan perched on the other, she left for the deck of the ship.

The full moon would light their path, and Sora admired the beautiful scenery around them. A massive forest expanded one way, a mountain to the other. The plank was readied, and Sora caught a glimpse of Mereen handing a bag of clinking gold to who was probably the captain.

"Your discretion is appreciated," she overheard Mereen state. "Once we've disembarked, I want this ship gone immediately. There can be no sign."

"Nothing except the imprints in the grass, Dark Slayer," the captain said, a weathered woman of middle age.

Mereen made her own way off the ship, passing Sora by with her lengthy strides. She carried her own bag of supplies, irritation sneering her lip as her boots stepped into the yellowed grass. "I would have preferred there be no mortals to remember our presence here," Mereen muttered, and there was no one to hear except Sora—so she listened well. "They are lucky I do not know how to hide an entire airship."

"Too much metal to burn," Sora replied, heart beating rapidly enough to feel against her chest. Mereen spoke to her, and there was nothing dismissive in it.

233

"Fortunately, there are not many who live near here. Perhaps hermits, but nothing more. There used to be a town at the base of the mountain called Tsilia; perhaps you knew that."

"I'm afraid I don't know where we are."

"You will soon," Mereen said, her tone as wistful as the night breeze. Her attention fell upon Odessa and Tazel, the former of whom directed a floating coffin with her hand, coaxing it to follow like a dog. Tazel held Staff Seraph deDieula, the sweat on his brow reflecting the moonlight.

Odessa raised her arms to the sky. "What gorgeous scenery!"

"*You* won't be staying long," Mereen spat, and she began trudging up the mountain.

To Sora's surprise, Odessa held her tongue at the remark. "And we couldn't have stopped at the top of the mountain? We have to climb it? If I didn't have the coffin to contend with I'd fly, but will I risk it? No. Not after losing one prisoner."

Her final phrase held resignation. However, as she looked to the levitating coffin, a bit of mischief twisted her pretty lips. With a snap of her fingers, she lowered it back to the ground, then climbed atop it, sidesaddle like a noblewoman, and lifted it once more. "Much better. Tazel, do keep a firm grasp on Ayla's mind. The last thing I want is to tumble off."

The coffin floated to keep pace with the rest of them, and Sora had to suppress a chuckle at her ingenuity.

As it was, Sora's athleticism made it an easy journey, though the anticipation within her kept her silent. They hiked with a coffin—to where? Mereen said she would know this place, but while Sora recognized northern air and plants, she could pinpoint nothing. Were they in Sun Elven land? Highland? Could be either.

And so an hour passed in silence, until they reached a plateau near the top.

There lay their destination, unquestionably.

A magnificent building stood before them, a strange bit of civility on an otherwise-untamed mountain. Though darkness obscured the details, the mansion held an archaic design, with emphasis on beautiful stonework and pillars. Time had taken a toll, cracks clear even beneath the starry sky, and plants grew along the outer walls, sprouting amid the foundation.

But though Sora knew little of magic, there emanated something truly vile. She caught a glimpse of Mereen up ahead, fearless as she entered the ancient building.

Odessa slid off the levitating coffin and gracefully smoothed her skirts. "What a lovely ride. Highly recommended."

The bags beneath Tazel's eyes appeared as twin bruises, aging him past his middling years. The staff in his hands appeared to be a heavy burden, not quite dragging but still weighing him down.

"What is this place?" Sora asked, awed by the structure.

"Did Mereen really not tell you?" Odessa gave a *tsk tsk*. "We are in the Mountains of Kaas, and that ancient relic is where a certain Lady Darkleaf conducted business for a few hundred years of her reign of terror."

That certainly explained the dark feeling. No magic required—the place was unquestionably cursed by nature of the crimes it had once housed.

As they neared, Sora summoned a spark of holy light in her hand, revealing an ominous entryway. The wooden doors were chipped from weather, any smoothness to them long gone away. Mereen had left them ajar, thus leaving no need to touch the metal knockers. Sora stopped a moment to make sense of the design yet found nothing strange about it—an innocuous doorknocker to a beautiful home in the mountains.

Perhaps this was the honeytrap. Sora could not shake the image of carnivorous plants who secreted sweet, enticing substances—only to snap and consume their prey.

She entered a portal into another world.

Though it was dilapidated from age and covered in dust, Sora gasped in shock at the garish décor. Her magic illuminated a great chandelier in the foyer formed entirely of bone, predominantly featuring elven spines. When she peered closely, she saw evidence of melted candles, where the flame would have been cast. Yet it was not the end of the horror—merely the grand beginning. The peeling wallpaper held shades of red and gold, chips of paint suggesting the owner had perhaps put her own artistic touch onto it, but the sconces upon the wall were ribs assembled to form expanding cones. Sora stepped slowly forward and flinched when her boot crushed what she knew in her heart was bone.

Worse than the ambience, however, was the seeping filth

upon her skin, a sickness sinking deep.

"Wow!" Odessa said, marching as though entering a ballroom. "All right, say what you will about my Flower Child's taste in women, but Ayla Darkleaf definitely knows how to make a first impression. Color me impressed."

Sora supposed she agreed.

Mereen appeared from around the corner. "The dungeon is below. Follow me, and we'll find a place for her."

'Her' was surely Ayla, but when Sora tried to follow, Odessa slowed to stand between her and their path. "Sora, dear, if you have any trust in my judgment, you will wait."

Sora glowered at the statement. "Why?"

"Just wait," Odessa said, her pleasant tone holding no malice. Sora's objection died at the touch on her forearm. "Explore the upper reaches instead. Return and report." At that, she followed the now-vacant path, the coffin floating eerily before her.

The imprint of Odessa's fingers lingered like static. Despite her misgivings, Sora was surprised to find . . . she did trust Odessa's judgment. So she went her own way, slowly navigating a dark hallway, led by morbid curiosity. The stone floor shifted in places, the tiles unsettled from a few hundred years of abandonment. Though the light in her hand illuminated the space, it did not ward away the pervasive aura of dread. It engulfed the place like fog, ever-present, and Sora stopped at the first door she came to.

Though the hallway continued, revealing other doors along the path, she twisted the resistant handle, breath held to see what was on the other side.

A dusty bedroom, not spectacular enough to be for the former mistress of the house. It bore similar designs as the foyer, with sconces of bone and a few skulls embedded into the wall. The rich accents of red and gold were muted by grime and age, but Sora imagined this room had once been spectacular.

She went onward, finding a few similar rooms. What did it mean, that Ayla Darkleaf kept guest rooms in her home? Did she entertain her victims before subjecting them to torture? Did she invite influential folk to come and see her work? Sora knew bedtimes stories—the ones every Sun Elf mother told to keep their children tucked in their beds.

"The shadows of demons live in the woods, Sora. Just because The Endless Night is gone doesn't mean there isn't danger."

Sora came upon a set of stairs leading upward. They creaked with each step, the ancient stone precarious here. The rail looked in well enough condition to cling to, but despite the shifting tiles, Sora kept her balance with ease.

The top floor seemed more of the same, though the aura of dread was lesser here. She came upon a large parlor room, the couches decayed and eaten by moths, which opened straight onto a balcony, framing a sky filled with beautiful stars. A splendid view, showing the whole valley below the mountain, surely providing a gorgeous view of the sunrise, though the stone guardrails were all that stood between her and a precarious fall. Dust escaped with each breath, replaced by fresher air. How strange it was, to stand on the same ground as the Scourge of the Sun Elves and admire the same sights.

Back in the entertainment space, a set of grand double doors were set directly facing the open balcony. Sora's stomach tightened as she twisted the knob, unsurprised to find it led to yet another bedroom—but this one was of magnificent design.

Magnificent, yes. And so subtle in its horror.

The four-poster bed held posts as high as the ceiling, the translucent maroon curtains just as long. No windows, but there were sconces of gilded bone, the gold dusty but once brilliant.

On the desk was an open book, beside it a half-disintegrated quill. With care to not damage the ancient paper, Sora gently blew on the pages, the dust swirling into the stagnant air. A drawing half-completed—at first glance, of a beautiful woman, her face twisted in ecstasy, but Sora gasped to realize she had no limbs, the remains of tattered, ripped arms and legs attached to a pristine torso. She could not look away; so lifelike was the artistry, though her very soul recoiled. By the Light—what had driven Ayla's depraved mind?

Upon the same desk was a candleholder of strange design—hollow, for the light to emanate, yet the glass was oddly thick around it. Sora withdrew a handkerchief and carefully dusted off the odd trinket, revealing the first hint of red liquid and bone inside. There floated a small preserved skeleton, perhaps of a kitten or rat, any light shining through surely casting the room in eerie shades.

Then Sora spotted the skull. Not a rat—an elven fetus.

Sick, Sora stumbled back, torn between curiosity and revulsion. Of course she should not be surprised to see horror manifested as art, but Sora didn't have to like children to not want to witness . . . that.

Yet so much more lay untouched. Sora held her breath and opened the drawer of a nearby dresser to find innocuous art supplies, collections of ink and paper, even cloth and thread. Embroidery lay in some—most of anatomical figures, some combined with floral images, an accidental homage to the woman she would someday marry. Astonishing, to think she bled creativity.

Sora was faced with the decision between the bedside table or the armoire. First, the table.

Meticulously organized, like everything else Sora had found. An embroidery half-done, perhaps for times of rest—a highly detailed animal skeleton, which Sora identified as a bear—a dusty, ancient book—*Moments of Passion*, which Sora quickly learned was an erotic novel—as well as a smaller book with no label.

Sora took it and sat on the old bed, perfectly made with rich sheets matching the curtains. Upon opening it, she balked to realize the words were handwritten, and though the language was archaic, the penmanship was perfection:

> *Finally met with Count dePonte from Solvira. My reservations were founded—the dolt wanted the assassination of a political opponent, and said it was worth the trip across the sea for the hope of my aid. Apparently I am the best. True. He offered money. I said no. He offered land. I said perhaps, but he did not have enough. I told him my price was sacrifice, but neither of those were a sacrifice for him. A life for a life, preferably.*
>
> *All ambitious men are the same, content to sell their daughters like cattle for slaughter. Funny, how I never have to propose it. She will be delivered within the week.*
>
> *Why is no one decent in this world?*

The page ended. Sora set the book aside, sicker now than from the candleholder. Some mysteries could stay mysterious.

After shutting the drawer, Sora opened the decorated armoire doors, coughing as a layer of dust puffed in her face. A collection of dresses, largely in shades of black.

Chills shot down her spine as her hand brushed across leather. The collection of boots and fancier shoes were lined up at the bottom, and the dresses were gaudy, the sort an actress might wear on stage. All were perfectly suited for Ayla's tiny physique, but when Sora withdrew one, she caught a glimpse of something odd tucked behind. She brought her light forward, then gasped when it illuminated a face.

Forever preserved in shock, though its eyes had been long ago eaten, was a woman's desiccated body. Yet the limbs were gone, torn away, displaying bone and parchment flesh.

Sora recalled the drawing and ran.

At the balcony, she finally stopped, heaving in the night air. What was she thinking, exploring the home of a monster? *Sol Kareena, can you even hear me here?*

Sora felt nothing at all. Perched safely on her head, Leelan remained perfectly still.

When she had regained her breath and bearings, Sora returned to the first floor, finding it comparatively tame. But as she neared the entry hall, she heard terse words.

"*. . . As I've said, I'll be going immediately. I've left Tazel with a few rejuvenating potions, so he'll have no need to sleep while I'm gone.*"

Sora knew the voice as Odessa's, placating in her motherly way.

"*This will give us time to prepare her,*" came Mereen's reply. "*But do not push the limits of my patience.*"

Footsteps signified the end, and Sora caught a glimpse of Mereen leaving down the opposite hallway.

Sora returned to the entryway, where Odessa smiled at her appearance. The light cast from Sora's hand revealed her frightful shadow, of a monster instead of a woman, but Sora did not mention it. Instead, she voiced an unexpected heartache. "You're leaving already?"

"My Flower Child has proven resourceful. I should be proud, but instead I'm annoyed." In a dramatic fashion, Odessa slouched and sighed. "I won't give her any benefit of the doubt this time."

"Do you think she might be dead? The woods here are dangerous."

Odessa shook her head. "She may not be as keen a huntress as yourself, but she knows how to survive in the woods. I'd be more worried about her hiding until the end of her days." From a pouch in her belt, she pulled out a strand of coarse auburn. "Fortunately, she seems to have removed the maldectine. This will do perfectly well."

Odessa tucked it away, then offered a hand. Confused, Sora placed her own upon it, which Odessa then covered. "There is a saying about monsters, Champion of Sol Kareena: to stare upon them is to know they're staring back. Monsters beget monsters. I know the irony, for me to be telling this to you, but that is precisely why I must speak up—because I worry it will be too late otherwise. We are in the calm before the storm, and it would be best if you leave before the hurricane strikes."

"Leave?" Sora reeled at the words, pulling her hand back. "I can't leave. This is my duty."

"There are dark times ahead, but I am a dark soul. You're not. And despite what values have been nobly instilled in you, you owe your family nothing. Despite what she'll tell you, you owe Mereen nothing, and I say this with all the appropriate self-awareness—some family will never love you, so love yourself more."

Odessa cast light upon truths Sora was not ready to face, blinding her instead. "You know nothing of family loyalty. You can't understand."

"I suppose not. But unlike the rest of us, you still have a soul. That's a terrible thing to lose."

Sora sought a reply, desperate to fight—but what did it mean, for Odessa to care? "You have been kind to me from the day we met," Sora admitted, the bitter remark leaving her shaking. "Even when I've judged you. Why?"

"You're a self-righteous ass sometimes," Odessa replied, her pretty features soft, pleading, "but I see right through you, you poor lonely child."

Sora balked at the statement. "What? I'm not—"

"Mereen offers breadcrumbs when you deserve a feast. I would say you don't need a family at all, but you can't comprehend it. Instead, I will simply say that there are better causes for your loyal heart. But I do care for you, Sora Fireborn. You are my friend, and I don't want you to get yourself killed when you don't have the spine to do what must be done."

"Are you saying I'm not strong enough?"

"I am. I'm saying you will leave this quest dead at Mereen's hands or at your own. Monsters beget monsters—and I implore you to leave before my return. Farewell, Sora."

Odessa's words held finality, her pristine dress swooping around her legs as she walked into the unknown, awaiting no reply. Sora barely balanced, her very foundation shaken.

What did it mean? Sora feared to look, every nerve alight from the lingering echo of Odessa's ominous plea. They were not friends, could not be friends, so why did Odessa care?

. . . Were they friends?

Sora ran for the door, cold for reasons she could not comprehend, suppressing the urge to scream, to fight.

Instead, she witnessed a frightful transformation.

Odessa stood beyond the reaches of the porch, her figure expanding beneath her dress, ripping it at its seams. She grew feathers, spread her arms only for them to transform into magnificent wings ending in gnarled, bird-like claws.

"Rulan!" Sora cried, for she knew who this was; Odessa had spoken plainly of it.

The monster turned, her beautiful features a memory. Not quite owl, but far from human, the feathers at her brow were reminiscent of horns, her beak far more expressive than the average bird's. Though her face was covered in feathers, Sora knew it.

"Farewell," came the melding of voices, feminine at its core yet bearing the soothing coo of an owl's dark sound. "Should we meet again, I pray it is not here."

The monstrous owl launched into the air. Sora lingered in paralysis as the owl flew higher, farther, eventually a dark star—and then nothing at all.

Only then did her breath return. Numb, Sora stumbled from the porch, into the moonlight. Something soft fell upon her shoulder.

A feather, as long as her forearm. Ombre brown to tan, as fine as silk, and Sora clutched it to her breast for reasons her mind couldn't touch.

Was this friendship?

Sore gazed into the night sky, seeking any sign of the departed witch, her loyalty torn in twain.

Flowridia awoke shivering at dawn. With sore arms and a sorer back, she sat up and groaned, that dry stickiness having returned to her mouth. Every part of her was damp, the dew having collected around her hair and dress.

Her hair would be a nightmare to fix when she returned to Velen'Kye.

Though every part of her ached, she managed to stand, using a branch for support. The birds sang to greet the morning, but Flowridia felt no joy in their presence, shivering instead in the slight breeze. She had no idea where Velen'Kye was, or her parachute, or even the road . . .

She withdrew the maldectine from her bodice and dropped it, relieved when the stirring in her soul returned, compelling her to wander. Surely it was close. Izthuni would not send her to die, right?

Her better judgment said that had never been a guarantee.

She ripped a strip from her ruined dress and wrapped the maldectine inside, noting she was fine so long as it didn't touch her skin. Summoning every ounce of spite and stubbornness she had, she trudged forward through the damp forest, knowing it would dry within an hour or two.

Her mind reminded her of an errant thing—that Eyal had implied vampires were in these woods.

At least daylight guaranteed safety in this one thing. All she would have to bargain with was Ayla's name; she prayed they believed her. The elves certainly had.

"*Monster!*" he had cried, and they were good people. She could take pride in evil men's fear, but this was a father. This was a family.

"I've killed good people before." She spoke it to the trees, who gave no response. They didn't need to. The statement lingered in the air as a damning truth, and she wondered why she cared today.

Flowridia Darkleaf—wife to Ayla Darkleaf, The Endless Night. She was too exhausted to feel any pride.

For hours, she walked. Then came a break in the trees.

Flowridia wished she still knew magic, as she gazed upon the ruins before her. A warning stirred in her gut, but nothing more.

A vast field, overgrown with grass but bearing evidence of stone ruins—sophisticated structures, though she could not gauge their age. Countless ruins, yet nothing fully standing;

Flowridia swore she stood upon the remains of a city. The sun cast its rays, but there was no comfort in it. The compulsion in her gut said straight ahead. Perhaps her quarry was here; perhaps it was why she felt so sick.

But something beautiful sprung up among the ruins—moonlilies, large and vibrant, the palest blue. The Silver Fire had overtaken the once-icy shade of Ayla's eyes, but Flowridia felt fondness for them, nevertheless. Sprouting up among the grass, they seemed so natural here, and Flowridia sprinted toward a large patch sequestered in the shade of a stone wall, adjacent to another.

She plucked one blossom and tucked it behind her ear, uncaring if it were comically large, and forced the stem to weave into her tangled locks. One beautiful thing. One thing of purity in her life.

Only then did she realize . . . the world was silent. No breeze, no birds, simply her own rustling.

Hair rose on the back of her neck. Flowridia stood, nerves alight, when one of the darker shadows within the shade moved.

She stumbled back into the sun. A figure stood. Flowridia stared upon a feral smile and dirty hair—this elf had not seen a bath in years.

Fangs grew from his mouth, but he stopped at the edge of the sunlight, scarcely an arm's reach from where Flowridia stood frozen. How thin he was, sickly for even an undead creature, and his voice grated like gravel. His dialect was old, but Flowridia understood him well enough. "It's a beautiful day. Won't you join me in the shade?"

Despite her shock, she managed derisive words. "Your starvation has led you to have no subtlety at all."

He laughed, sending a chill through her blood. "Night will come. Can you run far enough?"

The sun remained low enough to give him considerable shade. It would be many hours before sunset. "Are you alone here?" she asked instead, because a small part of her did feel pity.

A second shadow moved within the dark corner, revealing another man lurking behind. "Not alone," replied the first.

"What is this place?"

"Once, it was Fallanar."

"I can't imagine you find much prey here," Flowridia

said, settling back onto the ground, far enough that he could not reach her. Her fear dissipated, replaced with curiosity. "Why do you stay?"

"No hunters come here," the vampire replied, sitting to match her pose in the shadow. "They are afraid. Even the Dark Slayer dares not return to this place. Yet you are at ease."

Mereen was the Dark Slayer, Flowridia recalled—but what did it mean, return? "You're not the first vampire I've met. I've even met Mereen Fireborn."

They recoiled at the name.

"Why won't she return here? What does that mean?"

"Mereen Fireborn was a good woman, once," the second man said, his voice unexpectedly light compared to the first one's rasp. "Married to the judge. Loved this town."

"You knew Mereen before she was turned—"

The words dried up in her mouth. If Mereen was turned here—

"This is where The Endless Night first manifested." Flowridia scarcely breathed the phrase, acutely aware of how the vampires bristled. Despite the bright sunshine, the world became cold. "Ayla Darkleaf turned you."

"You know much of elven history, for a human," said the first.

"Are you a hunter?" asked the second.

"I'm not a hunter. But I'm versed in elven history, particularly about The Endless Night."

The second came forward, yet nothing predatory showed in his stance. Curiosity, perhaps. "Is that why you have come here? To learn?"

"Not expressly. But if you wish to talk, I'll listen. I'll even write it down so others can know your story."

And to her surprise, the one who had come forward sat by his companion, as dirty and matted as he, and began to speak. "I have not thought of my name in so long. It was Regev. I am Regev. I was a traveling merchant, only stopping in Fallanar once a month. You mentioned Mereen—she was a regular customer, always coming to admire the scarves I would bring from the capital. I always looked forward to her energy and light."

Hatred had calcified in Flowridia's heart toward Mereen, yet small bits chipped away to think of her as mortal once. "Did you know her son?"

"She brought Eldrin on most of her visits. A delightful

little boy."

"I knew Mereen as a gossip, but a friendly one," the first man said, his hesitation apparent, but Flowridia felt his yearning to speak. "I was a keeper of the peace, working under Constable Lightblade. She would often be outside with Eldrin and Natan during my nightly patrols and always stopped me to talk. She knew everything about everyone, but never said anything she would not say to their face. She uplifted Fallanar."

Natan must have been Eldrin's father. How strange, to think of Mereen as someone kind. She knew Mereen as a mother, but she had also been a wife.

She had also been a sister, and the thought made Flowridia's stomach clench. "What is your name?" she asked instead.

"I . . ." The vampire stopped. Beside him, Regev placed a hand on his shoulder. "I don't remember."

"Give yourself one. Everyone deserves a name."

"What is yours?" Regev asked, earnest now.

The name died in her throat as she weighed the likelihood of them knowing it. She doubted they received news from the executor, but why risk it? "Flowra."

"Is it a common human name?"

"I have never met another, but my mother was eccentric." At Flowridia's smile, Regev returned it, though his companion remained conflicted. "Would you like help with a name?"

"No," he replied. "I think I have chosen. I shall be Ofir— my lover's name. He died in the flames the night the monster turned us."

He did not say 'the monster' with any affection. Flowridia made a note of that. "Tell me more of your lives," she asked, and part of her softened to watch light return to their black eyes.

Regev and Ofir spoke with love of Fallanar, of the lives they had led. Regev had never married; Ofir had left behind a lover who he had hoped would become a husband. Neither had children, but both had wanted them. Regev wistfully spoke of his travels, of cities Flowridia did not say were long destroyed in The Endless Night's rampage. Ofir was shy but spoke of romance, of buying little gifts for his lover.

They spoke long enough for the sun to shift, for Regev and Ofir to retreat farther into the shade, for Flowridia to have to inch closer. And she loved to hear it, of this time long ago, yet it came with an immutable foundation of sorrow.

All they had loved was gone. All their hopes and dreams—destroyed. Turned into monsters instead.

When the mood felt right, Flowridia spoke her own inquiry, though casually. "You both mentioned fondness for who Mereen once was. Did you ever know her sister?"

Regev looked confused, but Ofir's demeanor became dark. "Never met her personally. But most of us knew of her. Sarai loved the monster."

"Did you know Ayla Darkleaf was a monster?"

"Children were missing. We wondered."

Flowridia had blocked out all she had read of Ayla's crimes against children. "Sarai loved Ayla Darkleaf?"

"She skipped off into the woods each day to see her, then skipped town the day Ayla slaughtered us all."

Flowridia supposed that made sense, but she did not mention Sarai had killed her, lest it evoke further questions. "That is suspicious."

"The constable was infatuated with Sarai—and then he was found dead in the woods, not a week before The Endless Night came to murder us. Suspicious, yes."

Flowridia supposed that was a very Ayla thing to do when someone else held affection for someone she loved. And Ayla had unquestionably loved that damn minstrel. Flowridia had never forgotten what light had filled her eyes to speak of Sarai, to wax poetic of her beauty and voice. That bitterness rose anew, but Flowridia squashed it down.

"But you fear Mereen now?" Flowridia asked, careful as she chose her words.

"She is the Dark Slayer," Ofir said. "Seeks to kill us all as she pursues her revenge on The Endless Night."

"I have reason to believe that Mereen Fireborn will be dead soon enough, if that makes any difference."

Interest filled both their faces. Regev spoke first. "How do you know this?"

"Because I'm going to kill her."

That intrigue faded into wariness. "But you are not a hunter."

"No," Flowridia said. "Just a simple necromancer with a grudge. She hurt someone I love."

"Will you return and tell us when?" Ofir asked.

"I'll try, but I don't know how long it will be. I have a long journey ahead. I will warn you, though, I don't know precisely where, but she's in Falar'Sol. I wouldn't risk leaving quite yet."

"Thank you," Regev said. "Is this you taking your leave?"

Flowridia looked to the sun, high above. "I suppose I should. But you two have been an unexpected delight. Thank you for not trying to eat me."

"Thank you for listening," Ofir said, yet so much weight was held in those simple words.

Flowridia smiled, her heart brimming. "Goodbye. I will do all I can to send a message once Mereen is dead."

"There are others in the shadows," Regev warned. "Be careful. But if you cross the river, none of us can follow."

Flowridia nodded and went on her way, not feeling quite so cold anymore, despite the dark history around her.

Her mind replayed their words, committing all she could to memory. She would write it down. She would tell their stories, even if it were simply in a letter to Etolié. She passed ruins and wondered what they once were, which was Ofir's home with his lover, which was the inn where Regev stayed, which was Mereen's . . .

But she could feel no true peace; the pulling in her soul denied it.

In shadows, she spotted makeshift coffins and figures cowering from the light. Pity filled her, to think they had been here for seventeen hundred years, but she was vulnerable. And . . . she was wed to the one who had destroyed their lives.

The woods approached, and Flowridia wondered if these had been the same woods Ayla had lived in when she had met Sarai, seventeen hundred years ago. The dense trees closed around her, though as she left the peace she had found in the condemned village, she was reminded of her gnawing hunger. How lovely it had been to talk, but she had wasted precious hours—

The thought was so appalling that she stopped in her tracks. "Not wasted," she whispered, though vehemence bled into the words. "They needed it."

Yet it came soured with the knowledge that if they'd known who she truly was . . . they might've called her the same cursed title.

Monster.

The sunlight flickered low upon the horizon and trees when Flowridia heard a blessed sound.

Water.

Though the light quickly dimmed, she ran through the trees and thick foliage, desperate to parch her thirst. Her stomach cramped, but water was essential, and dew collected from leaves would not save her life.

Moist air caressed her, tantalizing her senses. She tugged on her skirts when they snagged on branches and bushes, uncaring of the damage.

She broke through the line of trees and faced a great divide.

The river rushed, the spray cooling her skin even on the shore. Sunset shone upon its rapids, casting fiery hues upon it. It spanned several homes wide, no peace in the scene, and while Flowridia's parched throat rejoiced, a greater part of her panicked.

Darkness fell, but only a fool would try to swim across this river.

With care, Flowridia crept to the bank, mindful of the shifting, slippery rocks. On hands and knees, she put her face to the water, unprepared for the splash of cold. She flinched, then cupped it with her hands instead and gulped the blessed water with greed. She drank and drank, elated at its clean, refreshing taste.

But when her stomach ached and her thirst was satiated, the last vestiges of sunlight disappeared on the horizon.

The trees became black silhouettes, illuminated by moonlight. Flowridia stared upon the shore, apprehension filling her. Regev's warning remained.

In the waning light, she searched for a log, a bridge— something to assist her in crossing this wide, turbulent river. But unless there were a man-made bridge somewhere near, it would be a long night.

Perhaps the dirt and distance would obscure her scent. But they had been listening, hadn't they? These starving vampires knew where she was going.

"Izthuni," she said, but her dread only rose. The magical

compulsion bid her to walk along the river, but she heard only the barest whisper of wicked laugher, softer than the night breeze.

He would not help. Not yet.

Scattered amid the moonlight, millions of stars twinkled above, casting their gentle beams upon her. She was no friend to Staella, she knew, having been responsible for her kingdom's downfall. But it did not mean she couldn't be grateful for the celestial light—enough to prevent her from falling into the river.

Nevertheless, she took careful steps, mindful of the rapids. She did not dare to stop, simply let the feeling lead her on, praying it did not also bid her to cross. Perhaps if she found whatever she sought, she would live through the night. If not . . . could she wield Izthuni's name as a weapon? It would just as likely get her killed as mentioning Ayla's.

Strange, to be safer in anonymity than with her name.

As she wandered, she noted the moment the night creatures suddenly silenced.

She stilled, listening to the trees beside her, and heard the quietest rustling of brush. "Hello?" she said, but her gut already knew.

The noise did not cease or slow.

A part of her prayed it was simply a bear, but she knew, she knew. The faint silhouette was humanoid—and not alone.

One by one, they emerged from the trees, their eyes reflecting the bright moonlight. Flowridia took a step back, but her heel touched damp mud. Despite her fear, she summoned all the false courage she could muster—she had not been an empress consort only to learn nothing. "You don't want to do this."

In the same ancient dialect as the two she had spoken to, one of the silhouettes said, "It's so rare, for fresh meat to wander here."

"You don't know who I am."

"Your name is Flowra," said another. "You're a necromancer. You're off to slay Mereen Fireborn, or so you claimed. Many of us heard you. Ofir and Regev tried to stop us from finding you."

At Flowridia's feet, they threw two severed heads. She gasped, the dead eyes familiar. She trembled as she bent to pick up the head of one friend, his eyes set in horror at his final fate. She cradled it, hatred surging as she faced the predators. "My name is Flowridia Darkleaf. I married The Endless Night."

At that, a few of the silhouettes did falter, but the ones in front remained still. "All the more reason to feast on your blood, assuming you're telling the truth."

"She'll avenge me," Flowridia replied, knowing it was the only weapon she had left. "I am favored by Izthuni, the god who created her, and he will tell her what you've done."

"She'll keep spouting lies all night," said a voice, and Flowridia swore time slowed.

From the corner of her eyes, she caught the subtle motions of one preparing to pounce, backlit by the stars and the horizon. More crept forward. There was nowhere to run.

Flowridia leapt into the river.

Icy water crushed her. The undertow dragged her down by her heavy skirts. She released the severed head and frantically pushed through the rapids, stealing a tiny breath when her lips touched air. But the current dragged her beneath, the power of it sending her tumbling deep into the river.

Darkness obscured her vision. The river tugged her along at breakneck speed, yet she did not know up or down. When she tried to tread water, her hands touched only the rocks at the bottom, and when she tried to swim up, her dress tangled around her legs.

Her head pounded, vision swimming. Panic compelled her to thrash about, but nothing could stop her tumbling. She tore at her underskirts. Her lungs burned. She swore her chest would implode, but breathing meant death.

Her hand touched air, yet she could not find the way. When she tried again to touch the surface, her hand remained submerged.

Her strength failed. In a final sprint, she pushed toward sparkling light, only for pain to ricochet like lightning across her forehead when she hit a rock. Her mouth opened to scream. Water rushed in to fill the space.

The pressure outside expanded within her body. Blood pounded in her ears. Though her mind screamed to fight, her arms and legs ceased their flailing. Her head spun, and the darkness around her slowly closed in.

So this was how it ended—drowning in a foreign land.

As her mind embraced unconsciousness, a prisoner inside herself, there shone a pinprick of light, blurred by her own waning life.

Darkness fell, all sensation ceasing—

Save for a song that caressed her in her dying moments, as beautiful as the morning sun.

To Flowridia's surprise . . . she awoke.

She blinked into consciousness, touching her face to confirm she lived—and winced at the developing bruise on her forehead. Though sore and exhausted, she sat up, realizing she could see.

How magnificent, this secluded grove of trees. The river had become a trickling, gentle stream, a pond of sorts, though a small bit of water filtered away, leading out. Willow trees covered every bit of the sky, blocking the stars completely, but fireflies floated to fill the space. Fluorescent mushrooms emitted light—enough for Flowridia's keen eyes to see it all. Though mushrooms made her ill, the aura of this place did not leave her soul covered in the filth of wicked deeds. Instead, despite the ethereal beauty of this place, she couldn't shake the pervasive sorrow seeping into her skin.

How had she come here? Pain meant she lived, but she had drowned . . . right?

With care, she rose to her feet and crept toward the curtain of willows. When she parted them, there lay the dark forest. This was no mystical plane. This was certainly not the Beyond.

Strange omens remained, however—unnatural disruptions in the trees, some split down the center of their trunks, and fallen boughs, thicker than she. Something violent had happened here, but the moss growing inside the shattered trunks meant it had not been recent.

She shut her eyes and sought Izthuni's path, yet . . . nothing radiated. She removed the maldectine from her blouse, miraculously still in place, but when she dropped it—nothing. Instead, in the melancholic peace, there was safety and warmth.

All of her was soaked. She grimaced at the nightmare ahead, of drying her corset and skirts and hair, and slowly shed herself of layers for the first time in days. She hung the various pieces upon branches, creating a second curtain between her and the world, soon leaving her in only her chemise. After a glance around to see if she were truly alone, she removed it too, then wrung it out as well as she could, creating a small puddle at her feet before she slipped it back on. When the trees parted, she felt the chill of night, yet here in this space, warmth encircled her, bidding her to rest and unburden her weary, broken heart.

Memories of Demitri came. Oh, the wound was tender. Fresh tears welled to think of him torn so cruelly away. Flowridia inched toward the bank of the serene pond and sank to her knees, uncaring of the fresh mud covering her gown. His body lay in Velen'Kye, perhaps taken by Casvir and Etolié instead of being cruelly discarded by the elves.

And Ayla, sweet Ayla—would they ever meet again? Her heart lay suspended, drowning in grief but still wishing, grasping onto any hope to see Ayla again. The first of her sobs came. Awful reality descending anew—that she was lost, that she did not even have a direction anymore, that her life had been shattered irrevocably. She wept into her hands, for the world seemed far away. The trees blocked every bit of exterior light, and when Flowridia glanced into the pool of water, her reflection showed a little girl, scared and alone—

Until another face joined it.

Flowridia gasped, scrambling back on her hands and feet. From the pond emerged a ghostly figment, soaked to the bone from the pond's water. The figure emanated her own light, a haunting, serene blue, her stunning face marred by tears, flowing in sparkling droplets from her eyes.

She did not truly drip water—those same droplets eternally trickled from her wet figure, only disappearing because they hit the pond's surface. The woman—an elf, Flowridia saw—wore commoner's clothing, trousers and boots and a shirt that might've been loose in life but now clung to her wet figure. And like the droplets of tears, like the water, there flowed blood from her slit wrists, disappearing in shining streaks.

All ghosts appeared as they had upon their death, and this ghost's cause of death was clear. Flowridia's heart might've broken, were she not frozen from shock.

Short wet hair, no longer than her cheek, clung to her face, highlighting her strong jaw and pointed ears. But she held gentler features than those in Velen'Kye—more akin to Mereen, a Sun Elf. Those lips looked so keen to smile, yet they remained as mournful as the rest of her. "I did not mean to startle you," the ghost said, her dialect of elven identical to the vampires of Fallanar.

Wary, Flowridia forced herself to her feet, prepared to run if this ghost proved malevolent. "Who are you?"

"I'm the one who saved you from drowning." The ghost floated forward, moving as though walking once she hit the shore. Taller than Flowridia, though not by much, she stopped a small distance away. "Did you mean to fall in?"

Flowridia sensed no trickery, but if this were the ghost of this grove, then the sorrow pervading it was surely unnatural, brought on by the elf's tragic death. She could trust nothing she felt. Ghosts were capable of magic. "No. Well, yes, but it was to escape a coven of vampires. I didn't mean to almost drown. How did you save me?"

"It is what I do," the ghost replied, as though that were as clear as day. "Who are you crying for?"

"I beg your pardon?"

"You did not throw yourself in, but this place attracts the brokenhearted all the same."

Again, no malice at all, but Flowridia's jaded self did not know reality from fear anymore. "Why do you care?"

"Because I'm alone," the ghost replied, and how soft her eyes were, the brightest part of her. "All I know is sorrow. It never fades."

Whatever her failures, Flowridia clung to the hope that Ayla was somewhere out in the world. "I lost someone dear to me. Half my soul, you could say. Perhaps you won't understand it as an elf, but he was a familiar. I am—" Her voice caught. She suppressed a sob at the heartbreaking phrase. "I *was* a witch."

"Of Ku'Shya?"

"No, of someone else."

The ghost did not press. Instead, she said, "I am sorry for your loss. Truly."

"His name was Demitri." Flowridia choked at the name; how raw the wound was, how horrible it burned. "He was murdered."

"By whom?"

"By a vampire. It doesn't matter. I . . ." Her words stopped, suspicion rising toward the magic pervading this place. "I'm saying a lot."

In a mortal gesture, the ghost sat upon the ground, hands clasped as she resumed an unassuming pose. "It is the nature of this place. It reveals the wounded pieces of your heart."

"Is it possibly you?"

The phrase evoked something new within the ghostly elf, something spurring her to stare. "I suppose it could be. There was nothing magical about this river until I came. Now it compels people to throw themselves in. Terrible. Another log for the pyre of my legacy. I save who I can. The rest are down below."

A chill coursed through Flowridia's blood.

"So many failures," the ghost continued, and what a curse it must be, Flowridia thought, to relive your tragedy in others, time after time. "But look at you—you're a lovely person. I think I could talk to you for hours and never bore. What is your name?"

The question took Flowridia aback, especially from the melancholic ghost. "Flowra. Though with as few visitors as you get, you might simply be starved for company." Flowridia smiled in jest. "What is yours?"

Despondence sank the ghost's shoulders as she glanced back to the river she haunted, peering to where the water disappeared beyond the draping trees. "I've long forgotten. Would you believe that?"

"I would."

The ghost's tears never ceased, flowing even as she gave a wistful smile. "You could give me one."

Flowridia joined her gaze upon the water, her mind drifting away from the horrors of the past few days. The river did not rush here, merely trickled by in silence. "How about River?"

"I like that. I shall be River." The ghost—River—seemed taller somehow, something different in her sorrowful eyes. "Where are you going, Flowra?"

With slumped posture, Flowridia contemplated the very same question. "I want to go home. That's the short answer."

"Where is home?"

"The outskirts of Nox'Kartha."

"I've not heard of it."

An ancient ghost, then. "Have you heard of Solvira?"

"I know of Solvira, though I've never been across the sea."

Flowridia sighed, searching again within herself to find what Izthuni sought . . . Nothing. What did it mean? "I've lost my familiar, I've lost my wife, my friends, I . . ." She swallowed her sob, though another tear did fall. "I'm sorry. To be honest, my life has completely fallen apart."

River seemed so intrigued at her words. "You have a wife?"

"I do, though I fear I may never see her again."

"What happened?"

Again, hesitation stilled her tongue, but this ghost had saved her life—and her resolve remained weak. "The same vampire who killed my familiar captured her. But with my powers taken away, I can't fight her. I can enlist help if I return to Nox'Kartha, but luck hasn't been on my side."

"How does one get to Nox'Kartha?"

"I-I suppose one finds a way to cross the sea. My intention was to charter passage in Velen'Kye. They know me there. They might help."

"Velen'Kye is the Iron Elf capital," River said, no less serene than before. "You are in Falar'Sol—Sun Elven land. It is a long journey."

Flowridia resisted to urge to sob, but to hear those words destroyed what shallow faith she'd clung to. "I know."

"I can take you."

Hope surged through her anew. "Really?"

"Yes. Before my death, I traveled many places, including Velen'Kye."

Yet Flowridia's heart just as quickly sank. "Have you ever left this place, though? Are you able to?"

River floated up from her seat, returning to the empty air above the pond. Curiosity overshadowed her sorrow, a small spark igniting within this pitiful figure. "I have never tried."

"Are you tied to this place? Ghosts linger because they've tied themselves to something—and even if the pull is emotional, there's still an object or place it'll manifest as."

River remained silent a moment, then whispered, "I do not believe it is this place. It is the knife."

"The knife?" Flowridia stood to join her, then focused on the horrid gashes on River's wrists. "Oh. Where is it?"

"Down there," River said, gazing into the peaceful abyss.

256

"I do not know for how long or how deep it is buried. I fear it may be impossible."

Flowridia went to the pond's edge, hoping she could see the bottom—alas, it was deeper than that. "Might as well try. I've done worse things in my life." Yet as she contemplated how best to approach this, something new settled with her resolve. "Why, though? Why help me?"

"Is it enough to say that I genuinely wish to?"

Taken aback, Flowridia's arms fell, her chemise slouching around her body. "Something I've learned in my life is that those who've known the most sorrow often have the kindest hearts." *Or become monsters,* she did not say, for River seemed like a tender soul. "So, yes. It is."

She did not admit that she had no other choice. If River led her to her doom, at least she led her. But what a waste, to save her life just to drown her here. Flowridia knelt to touch the water, finding it as warm as the air. Surely not natural, but ghosts could provide a powerful influence.

To look at River, it appeared she did not know what magic she wielded—not entirely, aside from the ability to mysteriously rescue people from the river. Flowridia wondered what else the specter was capable of. Perhaps a great many things, depending on her age. "Would you be offended if I removed the rest of my clothes?"

When River shook her head, Flowridia first ripped a long strip of already-torn fabric and gathered the thick locks of her hair to tie them back—unruly, but better than risking blindness beneath the water. She then bundled the chemise over her head and held it to cover her front as she peered again into the depths. "Can you sense the dagger at all?"

"I . . ." River floated to be beside her, then shut her eyes. A few moments passed in silence. "There is something, like a pull in gravity."

"Can you dive with me and light the way?"

In response, River floated serenely to the water and sank half her body into the crystal depths. Illumination sparkled across the surface, and beneath, her cerulean glow was an ethereal sight. But most importantly, when Flowridia studied the water, she could clearly see the bottom.

"I don't swim well," Flowridia admitted, recalling a childhood spent in the woods. "If this goes wrong, can you rescue me?"

"I believe I can."

Flowridia dropped the chemise upon the shore, though kept herself demurely covered by her hands. Sure, she had gained confidence with Ayla, savored her wife's eyes upon her, but strangers were another thing entirely. Though she struggled to preserve her modesty, Flowridia sat herself at the edge of the pond, her legs dipping in the warm water. River very pointedly did *not* look at her, which Flowridia appreciated, and though apprehensive, she slipped into the water.

It enveloped her like a hug, so gentle it was. With the water up to her shoulders, River finally met her eye. After a shared nod, Flowridia took a deep breath and dove.

Crushing waves of panic threatened to overwhelm her. Not hours ago, she had nearly drowned, but the reassurance of ghostly blue light calmed her enough to keep her focus. Flowridia swam down with inexperienced arms, though it took only a few strokes to reach the bottom.

Her fingers brushed across smooth rocks. She hardly knew what she sought—a knife, but that meant little, only that she feared to grasp the blade too tight and lacerate her skin. Surely it was rusted and ruined. But that precluded the knife was even capable of being reached. Who knew how long it had been buried?

Flowridia aimlessly tossed dirt about until her lungs burned, then pushed off the ground with her feet, propelling her to the surface.

The water broke. Flowridia gasped and managed to reach the pond's edge. She heaved a few deep breaths before returning to equilibrium.

River sat her ghostly self upon the shore, feigning a corporeal form as she kicked her drenched legs in the pond's depths. "Nothing, I assume?"

"No."

"I fear it is hopeless."

River's features were always sorrowful, yet despair now mingled with the ever-streaming tears upon her face. With her body hidden beneath the water, Flowridia placed a hand upon River's, prepared for the icy sting of her touch. "We won't know unless we try. Let's try again."

Flowridia dove into the pond, that blue light following behind.

Every day, the sun called to Sora. But some days, curiosity called louder.

It was wrong. She gave in anyway and found herself back on the frightful upper floor, nose buried in gruesome writings.

> *Lord Omri shall be arriving today. Informants say he's bringing his daughter. I'm told she's nine. I am suspicious.*

> *No amount of foreplay could compensate for the wretched stench of those cigars. But he offered a thousand troops in exchange for my cunt, another for my throat, and to double it all to cut a new hole and fuck that too. I told him triple. He accepted.*
>
> *As he dressed, he offered his daughter for my assistance in slaying Magistrate Elid of Einav. I asked in what regard. He said in whatever regard I liked. I described my tanning methods in detail. He said it was fine. Told him he could have offered troops for her instead. He said he wanted to say he'd fucked the Scourge of the Sun Elves and laughed.*
>
> *I aspire to the audacity of men.*
>
> *Not sure what to do with the daughter. He seemed too cheery at my tanning speech. I watched her cower at dinner. I suspect he does quite a bit worse to her than he did to me.*
>
> *The world is cruel to little girls. Leaves a grime that never goes away.*

> *I am ashamed to say I lost six thousand troops.*
>
> *Again, I could wax poetic on the audacity of men, but he approached me a second night—and when I declined, he begged, then said he'd love it if I'd fuck the girl and let him watch.*
>
> *I said no. He was insistent, even said he'd already sent her to my room to wait.*
>
> *I consider myself slow to anger, but perhaps it*

259

makes my decision worse. As I said, I am ashamed to have lost the troops, but I changed the terms of the agreement and fucked him instead—though I may have cut a few too many new holes.

I sent the girl away, down the mountain to Tsilia. Her death would have been too gratifying for him—

Sora's ears twitched at a distant, odd sound.

Leelan perched contentedly by the open windowsill, basking in the sun's light. Sora had nearly buried her nerves when a scream echoed faintly below her feet.

"Stay here, Leelan," she said as she drew a knife from her boot. Sora crept out the door and pressed against the wall of the staircase when the scream echoed once more.

In the basement, unquestionably.

Sora had yet to explore the forsaken underground, and as far as she knew, Tazel and Mereen had yet to leave it. Odessa's warning sang in her head, as opaque as it was ominous. Never in her life had she considered herself prideful, but the insinuation that she was not strong enough for this . . .

Something wasn't right. The feeling defused. Sora preferred to not think about the warning or the witch who'd given it.

Gathering her courage, Sora stepped through the vacant corridors to where the stairs awaited. Darkness rose until Sora summoned holy magic. The light cast shifting shadows across the stone walls, the steps beckoning her to join whatever horrors awaited below.

Another scream sounded. Sora did not know it, but truthfully, she did not know what any of her companions' screams sounded like—save for Odessa's, but she was no longer here. Though every instinct within her urged her to run, Sora descended into the dark unknown, curious above all else.

The faintest glow shone beyond when her feet touched the ground. She faced a vast hallway, various doors lining the sides. Sora snuffed out her magic. The screams sounded once more.

Sora's suspicions rose as she followed the feminine shriek, visceral and pained. She lurked in the shadows as she peeked around a doorframe into a dungeon cell.

Within, Ayla writhed like a worm on the floor, bent in unnatural degrees as holy light radiated from inside her body. Trapped in a barred dungeon cell, her box lay open beside her, vacant. Her claws sank into the floor, cracking the stone, though remains of chipped fingernails were scattered about. When the magic faded, Ayla's tension left with it. Tears streamed down her face, eyes crazed as they narrowed upon Sora herself—The Endless Night missed nothing. "Come to watch the show, blunt-ear?"

Near her were Tazel and Mereen, the latter of whom had some sort of cloth stuffed into her ears. Tazel gripped the cursed staff, the bags beneath his eyes sunken and skeletal. The duo looked to Sora, though Tazel's attention quickly returned to the vampiric creature on the floor—who sought to rise, only to fall into a heap of screams as light burst inside her once more.

Sora stared transfixed as Ayla shrieked, untold damage ravaging her from inside. When it faded, the eyes of the demonic skull glowed as Ayla fell limp upon the floor, utterly still.

Mereen removed the cotton from one of her ears. "Yes?"

A monster lay helpless before them, and Sora couldn't tear her gaze away. "I heard screaming and came to investigate."

"Now you've seen it."

Mereen's dismissal was clear. Already she stuffed the cotton back, but Sora dared to push. "What are you doing?"

Tazel spoke up, exhaustion in his soothing voice. "Following Odessa's instructions." The words were cryptic, but Sora wondered if it were as far as Tazel understood as well.

Although wary of the torturous sight, Sora lingered. Before her, Ayla's fingers flexed, her stress apparent, and when the skull's eyes flashed, she whimpered against the stone. "Don't," came Ayla's soft plea, her tears puddling upon the floor.

"What's going on?" Sora whispered, but at the words, Ayla's petition of mercy faded in favor of a rancorous glare.

Ayla curled into a fetal ball, her hatred curtailed by falling tears. Her eyes lost focus and shut tight as she embraced herself, claws splitting the skin of her arms.

"It's not something I want to describe," Tazel said. "But she's slipping in and out of awareness. She needs to be plunged as deep into her memories as we can get her."

"Why?"

Hesitation caught Tazel's breath, his trembling hands the only sign of pain. "Odessa's instructions."

"Sol Kareena, dry my tears," came a plea—yet it was from Ayla, curled upon the floor. "The light shall burn away all my fears."

Sora knew those words. They were a children's prayer, taught by her father who sang them as a song.

Ayla continued. "Protect me with your holy light, and guard my bed all through the night."

Mesmerized, Sora did not dare move during Ayla's recitation, her small voice speaking the lines in rhythm. Strange, to hear them from a monster's lips. If Sol Kareena could even be in this awful place . . . would she? Would she listen to a monster's prayer?

When Ayla had completed the lines, her quiet cries remained, the puddle of her tears expanding. Whispered words left her lips: "Bring her home, please. Bring my momma to me."

Pity was not an emotion to feel toward so depraved a being, a creature as dark as her deeds. Yet something within Sora twisted uncomfortably as she watched the monster weep. "Carry on," she muttered, and she left them all alone.

On the seventh or eighth or perhaps even twentieth attempt, Flowridia broke the surface and resisted the urge to faint then and there.

Every part of her ached, muscles burning as she hoisted herself up with a final spurt of strength and collapsed upon the pond's shore. She rolled onto her back, lest she drown in the drenched locks of her hair, and shivered in the moist air.

Blue light shone beside her. Flowridia no longer cared about her nudity, exhausted beyond belief. "All right," she managed between deep breaths, "perhaps it is a little hopeless."

She smiled, but River's voice came despondently. "I suppose I can try to give verbal directions to Velen'Kye, but I fear my memory will betray me."

Flowridia stared up at the covered sky, the barest hints of daylight beyond. But the density of the trees created a timeless void. "How long have you been here?"

"I don't know."

River gave no hint of being defensive, so Flowridia gently pressed for more. "I know a little of elven history. Perhaps I could help you figure it out. What do you say?"

"All right."

Flowridia considered all she knew, wondering how far back to go. Her ghostly companion had never heard of Nox'Kartha, so at least a few centuries. "Do you know about the Scourge of the Sun Elves?"

"Every Sun Elf knows that, even us dead ones."

She supposed that hadn't narrowed it down then. River might've heard it even after death. However, it affirmed Flowridia's instinct to keep her identity hidden. "What about Dark Slayer? Mereen Fireborn."

"I know of Mereen Fireborn. She is a famed name."

"Did you know the name when you were alive?"

"Yes."

So River was younger than Mereen's transformation. But too old to know of Nox'Kartha. "Currently, I'm estimating you're between seventeen hundred and . . . nine hundred."

Beside her, River laughed—the most joyful sound Flowridia had heard from the sorrowful ghost. "Congratulations on narrowing it down so fully."

Flowridia noted River's smirk—what charm it conveyed, even in mockery. This woman had been terribly charismatic in life. "At least we know you're not young."

"I suspected not. But you are."

It left a lingering question. "I'm nearly twenty-one."

"Do you all marry so young?"

The ghost was highly inquisitive, and Flowridia's exhausted self found it amusing. "It depends on where you're from. I was nineteen, which in Solvira is young. But when you know, you know. Though I know elves don't generally marry for love, so perhaps it's confusing to you."

"Sun Elves sometimes do. It depends on their wealth and the weight of their name and whether it's worth preserving that legacy. Or we did, at least. I don't much of how my people are now."

River knew of the monster who had committed genocide against her people, but did she fathom the scope of it? Perhaps, if she knew of Mereen, but just as likely not. "I haven't met many married Sun Elves," Flowridia said, though her eyelids began drooping, "so I wouldn't know."

"You should sleep," River said, "though you might want to put your dress back on first."

Flowridia managed to stumble into standing, though her strength waned with each motion. "I'm sorry if I'm making you uncomfortable."

"Not at all, but you're much more susceptible to cold than I am."

Flowridia wrung her hair out as well as she could into the pond, then dried off with one of her hanging skirts. Once she slipped into her chemise, her legs threatened to collapse. Another layer was bundled and placed beneath her head as she laid upon the damp earth, soothed by River's light.

"Are you prone to nightmares?" came River's voice.

"Not so much anymore."

"If you become fitful, I can sing to you."

Flowridia drifted off to sleep.

Yet within the realm of dreams, there was no rest—only pounding fists upon her skull.

"You are so close," came the pervasive voice. "So close, so close— yet you sleep! Only in darkness will you find what you seek."

Mists of black consumed her. Flowridia screamed at the rush of corporeal shadow.

"Be wary of this interloper. You need not her aid—only mine!"

Flowridia saw nothing at all, could barely breathe. When she shrieked, it sounded far away.

"She is not what you think! Beware her crimes!"

"Flowra!" cried a distant voice, yet she swore it deafened her all the same.

"Beware! Beware—!"

Flowridia awoke screaming in the peaceful glen.

Sweat drenched her figure. Her breathing came in fast spurts. River knelt beside her, looking helpless as she brought her incorporeal hand to Flowridia's brow—though it passed straight through, sending a cold jolt through her skull. "Flowra?" Ghosts could not look pale, yet everything in River's countenance bespoke horror. "The shadows came for you. They retreated when I came near, but . . ." She stared upon the darkness of the grove. "It covered you. Are you all right?"

Flowridia sat up, finally catching her breath. "I'm fine," she said, though her mind reeled from the dream—and she would be a liar to say she did not know the voice.

The memory sounded as loud as any whisper: *"Only in darkness will you find what you seek."*

River floated between Flowridia and the darkness, terror on her features. "I fear whatever monster has come to this grove. It is morning, and yet . . ."

Whatever River said, it was lost behind the incessant words in Flowridia's mind. Without a word, she stood and removed her chemise.

"Flowra?"

"Guard the pond, but don't follow me," Flowridia said, and before the ghost could ask, she jumped into the water.

Shock stilled her, though the water was warm enough. She wasted precious seconds of breath finding her bearings, but soon dove deeper, plunging herself into darkness.

Izthuni, she said in her head, *you'll have to lead.*

She touched rocks, and all the world became black.

Dig, said the darkness, and Flowridia obeyed.

Time slowed as she pushed aside layers of churned dirt, yet it seemed softer now, more malleable. She saw nothing at all, simply trusted the god who compelled her, little more thought to anything but that. Though exhausted from fractured sleep, she pushed onward, digging until her nails chipped and bled, until her lungs burned from emptiness.

Deep red glinted in the darkness. Flowridia touched something smooth and polished. Careful now, she uncovered the space around the red stone, revealing a hilt. Her hand wrapped around it and tugged.

The world returned to color. Flowridia's head grew faint.

With the last of her rational thoughts, she pushed off from the ground, vision blurring when her face broke above water. Flowridia coughed, frantically treading. Though every motion was agony, she managed to return to shore and collapse. Tears fell from her eyes, lost in the droplets of water. Every part of her trembled.

Held within her hands was a knife.

Her gaze centered upon it, for it drew her like the heart of a star. With a hilt of polished red and black, it appeared to be of stone, but the blade was metal, dark as midnight, and though she no longer felt the magical world singing in her head, something wicked radiated like heat.

No question that it was Izthuni's artifact. But it was also River's anchor.

The ghost in question stared from beyond, motionless as her arresting gaze fell upon the knife. "Not hopeless," she whispered, yet her light did not touch Flowridia; she had frozen in time.

Flowridia finally caught her breath, releasing the knife with some relief—though it called to her, revulsion followed with it, not unlike standing before the demon god himself. "What does it do?" she asked, then recalled Izthuni's warning:

"Beware! Beware!"

"It is a wicked thing that should have stayed hidden." River drifted closer, though her stance remained hunched, fright in her features. "Do not use it. Not even for defense."

"She is not what you think. Beware her crimes!"

Flowridia gazed warily upon the ghost, for now the pieces no longer added up. "Then why have me find it?"

As River seemed to contemplate this, Flowridia studied her for any sign of betrayal, any hint of subterfuge—yet found only that same sorrow, that regret. "Because it is the only way to help you," River finally whispered. "I am choosing to place a lot of trust in your character, but I want to help you."

Flowridia resisted the urge to laugh at the word 'character,' given there was no better proof of this ghost's lack of judgment. Here this ghost faced the wife of the Scourge of the Sun Elves, the impostor Consort of Solvira, someone the world would see as evil, and this ghost had not a clue.

"Beware! Beware!"

She lifted the wicked artifact, fearful of its presence. "What history do you have with this knife?" Flowridia asked, for if Izthuni said to be afraid, who was she to not tremble?

She saw her wariness reflected in River's gaze. "It is a painful thing."

"What history do you have with a knife belonging to a demon god?" Flowridia made no attempt to hide her accusation, gave no care to what it revealed about herself. Izthuni said to fear; who was this woman?

"How do you know—"

"I didn't, but I do now. I've met Izthuni. Why does he have a grudge against you?"

River frantically shook her head. "I do not know any demon gods. I-I didn't know the knife was his."

"Then why would he tell me to fear you?" Knife in hand, Flowridia approached the cowering ghost—who did not budge. "What are you not telling me?"

The ghost recoiled at the words, face covered when Flowridia stopped not a step away. "There is so much I'm not telling you. But you have nothing to fear from me."

"Then explain—"

"Flowridia, I beg of you to listen. I've kept nothing from you maliciously."

"What does—"

Flowridia's voice died in her throat. She tried to breathe yet was met with nothing, the echoing refrain of the name ringing in her head.

"If Izthuni has a grudge against me, so be it," River pled. "Goddess knows, I deserve it. But if—"

"How do you know my name?!" Flowridia found her tongue, bid it to be sharp and deadly. "What trick is this?"

"Mereen told me your name," River said, and Flowridia felt faint, unable to summon any response at all. "And your story matched what little I knew of the awful plan she had. There are not many human women who cross these lands, and when you said a vampire had stolen your wife, I knew." The tears in her eyes, forever floating away, fell faster now. "You're Ayla's wife. And I am begging you to trust me."

Flowridia looked again at the ghost's scars, her tears, her body and face, sought patterns within them. Suspicions welled in her gut, but she asked, "Who are you really?"

Such heartache in River's countenance, and Flowridia's own heart threatened to crack for empathy—but no. Not if this ghost was who she feared.

In stifled tones, the ghost spoke a truth Flowridia already knew. "My name is Sarai Fireborn."

Chapter 14

Flowridia stared upon the ghost—upon Sarai Fireborn who had stabbed Ayla Darkleaf right in her heart, had murdered her in cold blood. Ayla had loved her; Ayla *still* loved her.

Sarai awaited castigation if her wary stance were any proof. But shock stilled Flowridia's tongue, caused every part of her to freeze. The knife fell from her hand, caught in the soft earth.

"You do know of me, then," Sarai said, uncertainty in those frightened eyes. "I was not sure. Ayla was always secretive—"

"Don't!" The word tumbled from Flowridia's lips unbidden, roused from a place beyond thought. Old hatred welled, and Flowridia let it fuel her. "Don't say her name. Don't speak of her."

Sarai shrunk as she held herself, nodding her agreement.

Anger pulsed heat through her, thawing her shocked limbs. Uncertain of what else to do, Flowridia picked up her chemise from the ground and marched away, slipping it on as she left the trees.

The stark sunlight blinded her as she emerged from the curtain of branches. Morning had come, and the sun fought to cut through the thick forest. Yet it brought no joy. Flowridia clenched her fists, resisting the urge to scream.

Instead, she knelt to pray, finding a shady spot among the trees. "Izthuni, I understand now. You hate this woman too."

The light beyond Flowridia's closed eyelids faded. There again came that voice, like mist across the landscape. *Wicked, wicked woman. Murdered my protégé.*

Flowridia had not considered how the few other

companions Ayla kept might've felt about her murderer. Why would Izthuni not despise this ghost too? "She's attached to the knife. I can't leave her behind."

Bring her along. Keep her appeased. I will dispose of her upon your arrival. His laughter echoed inside her head, a nightmare in the darkness. *But perhaps keep that to yourself. You are an actress, are you not? The false Empress Consort of Solvira.*

"I will try," Flowridia said, and when she opened her eyes, the predictable blackness had settled. "Is there no way to separate her?"

Ghosts are tricky, as you well know from your mother. Nor are they anything to trifle with, especially one so ancient. A proficient necromancer could banish her, but you are without power, and I am forced to be far away. As I said—bring her here.

Flowridia nodded, then realized she did not actually know if he could see that. "I'm not happy about it, but I will do it."

Good girl.

The words twisted in her gut, causing sickness to course through her. But she shoved it aside; he was an evil god. Flowridia supposed she deserved him. "Do you know why Sarai killed her?"

She supposed she already knew the answer, for if Ayla did not, why would he? And so she was not surprised to hear him whisper, *No. All I know is what Ayla spoke of in life—how she wept to me of Sarai's games, her soft manipulations. She was a breaker of hearts, leaving strings of shattered lovers behind.*

A message from long ago stirred in Flowridia's head; Mereen had said the same, to Tazel in a letter.

But murder? Appalling. She will say what she must to sink her influence inside you, a spinner of beautiful words and songs. She did so for Ayla; she will do the same for you. You know of the monster, Eva—after her death, Ayla was a shell, vulnerable to the next predator to strike.

Flowridia could not think of Eva without revulsion and rage. Ayla had spoken so fondly and sweetly of Sarai, despite her death at her hands. Flowridia had hated her.

I remember her well, Flowridia. Beware of her wicked intentions. Beware of her lies.

Yet even filled with ire, she could not help but think of Sarai's brutal end—the cause was crystal clear.

What did it mean?

"If she tries to steer me wrong, will you protect me?"

I will do all I can.

The finality of the words was apparent, and the darkness around Flowridia faded.

Before her, placed lovingly in the grass, was a platter of carved wood, bearing a collection of fruit, bread, and nuts, as well as a pitcher of water. Starved, Flowridia fell upon it like an animal, uncaring of the mess. She drank until her stomach ached; she ate until it would surely burst.

But it came with relief. Izthuni would protect her.

When she had finished her meal, Flowridia rose carefully, mindful of her overfull stomach. She returned to the grove, emersed in moist, tranquil air.

The knife remained, as did Sarai, unmoving. Such kind eyes she had, a lion masquerading as a doe as she stilled her quiet cries.

"I will let you lead me," Flowridia said, unnerved at Sarai's sudden gasp of hope. "No tricks."

The ghost nodded in earnest. "No tricks. I will take you to Velen'Kye."

As Flowridia gathered her clothing from the tree branches, she considered Izthuni's warning. It all rang true and added to the picture she had begun painting of Ayla's once-beloved. Yet from the corner of her eye, Flowridia watched Sarai's wistful visage, caught a glimpse of the eternal streams of blood from her wrists.

Something was not right.

But she said nothing of it, still contemplative of this strange twist of fate. Instead, she returned the maldectine to her bodice and retrieved the dagger last, slipping the blade into the waist of her skirt. "Let's see if you truly can leave this place."

Sarai led her out. She did not vanish beneath the sun, but wonder did part her lips to gaze upon it. "It has been so long since I've seen Sol Kareena's light."

Flowridia said nothing, for she could say nothing good of the goddess Sarai worshipped.

They traveled in silence.

For three days, Etolié had stared at a seemingly infinite forest.

"I'm gonna need spectacles by the end of this," she muttered when the sun rose, further illuminating the endless fucking sea of trees. Ahead, the bloodhounds led the way, their pace lulling Etolié into sleep. Birds sang, aggravating her brewing headache—which meant it was time for more booze. She summoned her flask, brought it to her lips—

"Why?"

And fucking choked because she'd forgotten she wasn't alone. Casvir could lapse into silence for literal hours—days, probably—before startling her senseless with a single word. Etolié hacked up the noxious liquid, ripping her throat raw. "Fucking hell—you restarted my heart."

"You would be in much worse pain if—"

"Oh, shut up. I'm gonna need spectacles because my vision is blurry from these damn trees!"

"I find the view refreshing."

The sun's rays filtered through the trees, blasting her with its angry light. "Good for you."

That's when she realized that Casvir, while maintaining his default unapproachable aura—it was difficult not to on the fucking undead horse—was hardly menacing in the moment. Simply . . . quiet. "You seem agitated," he said, which startled her even more than her actual start.

"And you're saying a lot of words. I'm confident this is the most you've spoken in four days."

"Would you like me to stop?"

"Fuck, no. I'm bored." Etolié flopped forward, forgetting her horse didn't have nice soft hair and narrowly avoiding gouging her eye out on a spinal knob. "Sure, I'll pray to Momma sometimes, but there's a limit to how much I want to bother her."

"Given the legends surrounding your mother, I suspect she is not easily bothered."

Damn, he was downright conversational today. "That's true, but consider this: I'm insecure."

"That is unfortunate."

They lapsed into silence because Etolié didn't want to explain the nuances of her mommy issues to her third-worst living enemy. Loyalty to Momma said Morathma would always be the first, even though she had never met him. An unmentionable motherfucker had killed her beloved Lara, making him an easy second.

Murishani was a high contender for that third-place trophy, but he had been an irritating fly at worst lately.

"Do you have a mom?" she finally asked.

"We all do."

Casvir's tone never wavered, but that didn't mean he wasn't being fucking cheeky. "All right, smartass—is your mom alive?"

"No."

"Did you kill her?"

Etolié reveled in the slight twitch in his frown. "No. She passed in my infancy."

"Oh, that's sad. Sorry. What about your dad?"

"He passed in my childhood."

"My dad is dead too," Etolié said, but unfortunately, Casvir spoke before she could clarify the fucking party that fact was.

"I am sorry for your loss."

"Fucking don't be. I dedicate only my worst shits to him."

And to her surprise, Casvir gave a tiny scoff that sounded an awful damn lot like a laugh.

"If the higher powers that be handed me a gun with two bullets and locked me in a room with you, Murishani, and that bitch, I'd shoot the bitch twice."

"Impressive. I sense there is a story here."

"I don't really want to tell it, but needless to say, he was a downright bastard to my sweet mother, so he had to die."

"This an acceptable reason to kill a father."

"I stabbed him several times," she said before she could stop herself. No one knew that—except Sora and Khastra and Momma.

And Eionei, unfortunately. But now Casvir. Fucking dammit—apparently this was the consequence of boredom.

"Given you maintain positive relations with your mother," Casvir said, "I presume this is not a sore spot between you two."

"You presume correctly."

"Then I am also glad he is dead."

Had Etolié any real control over the horse, she would have stopped it in its tracks at that oddly affirming statement. "Thanks."

"I simply speak the truth."

Etolié had nothing to say to that.

How . . . how fucking dare she be having a pleasant time.

"What of your grandfather?"

The question jarred her from her offense. "What about Eionei?"

"You killed his son. I am curious if that affected your relationship."

"Naw, Eionei doesn't care about his kids, which sounds really calloused when you say it out loud."

"It does."

"Eionei and I aren't talking right now anyway," Etolié said bitterly. "He meddled where he shouldn't have fucking meddled."

"I am sorry to hear that as well."

"Momma says I should see him and let him explain, but I'm not ready for that."

"Do you want to see him?"

What the fuck kind of therapy was this? Etolié glared at Casvir, absolutely furious about falling into this non-trap. "Sometimes. He did take care of me for . . . you know, twenty-four years. Sometimes it's sad that his tiny wine body doesn't accost me when I'm trying to take a drink anymore."

"I suppose the question is whether or not he has changed."

"Motherfucker—I don't know! I haven't spoken to him. My momma says he's sorry, but he really fucked me over."

Whether or not he was sorry wasn't exactly the issue on that one. Thirty-four years without Staella was a goddamn crime.

"Also! He hates Khastra. That's its own issue."

"Indeed."

"He doesn't especially like what you made her do in the Theocracy, yes offense."

His ensuing sneer boiled her blood. It was for the best, given they had been getting along. Strange, to speak so idly of genocide, but this was apparently who Etolié was now.

They fell again into silence as she contemplated how to further stir the pot—conflict was necessary—when a new sound joined in with the distant birds and occasional whirring insect. A dark baritone drifted quietly along the wind. Upon investigation, Casvir's hand idly motioned a four-by-four time signature.

Fucking twit.

Etolié prided herself in knowing most songs yet couldn't

place the melody. She listened in silence, mulling over the tune, and as he entered a verse, she joined him and sang:

Casvir wants to be a god
He dresses dark and gloomy
But underneath, he's just a sap
Who misses his dead mommy.

At the conclusion of the—in Etolié's opinion—masterful composition, Casvir gave what she could assuredly call the blankest stare to ever assault her vision. She had never seen a man show truly no emotion before, but there was nothing decipherable in those unblinking red eyes.

He returned his attention forward, the world silent save for the trilling birds above. Etolié rode a little taller, feeling triumphant, when a deeper voice matched the meter of her bullshit song.

Empress Etolié, unruly pest
Her jabs are quite unbearable
She earns her keep by charming guests
And fucks my favorite general.

Etolié struggled to lift her jaw off the ground. "Holy shit, you're savage."

"I have my opinions."

"Did you seriously say fuck? For me?! I'm fucking flattered."

"I will indulge in crass language for a good cause."

"Are you calling me a good cause? Well, by Goddess Momma—that's the nicest thing you've ever done."

Casvir seemed thoughtful, then resumed his song:

All day, she cons the lesser folk
Out of their hard-earned gold
Even though she's sitting on
Her boundless wealth untold.

"Asshole." Etolié stuck out her tongue. "You're right, but you shouldn't say it. How the fuck did you even know?"

"Murishani has informed me of your pastimes with his servants."

"Ah, so Zorlaeus was the rat. I guess I can't blame him.

Poor idiot."

"I believe it is your turn, lest we be unbalanced."

"My turn for what?"

Casvir had the polite sense to actually face her. "Song banter."

"Oh, it is *on*, Imperator Cassie." Etolié didn't even think, she just stole a breath.

"Wait."

He held his arm out in front of her like a protective parent, which was weird given they were both adults and because they were on horses. Her own smoothly stopped. Though it pained her, she managed to withhold a quip. "Should I illusion us as elves?" she whispered instead.

The bloodhounds paced, as alert as their master. Casvir's mace of dark matter appeared in his hand, held at the ready. "There is something . . . lurking."

Etolié summoned a quarterstaff, prepared to bust some heads. "An invisible something?"

"It is familiar—" His frown deepened. "It is not in this world."

Etolié readied her staff, stiffening at the warning. "Is it a demon—"

A girlish voice spoke from behind. "Hello, Etolié—"

Etolié shrieked and swung her staff, nearly busting a familiar and beloved head—or tried to, given she would have to float to reach the statuesque figure's face. Instead, the half-demon's many hands stopped it, grasping the staff with relative ease.

"Kah'Sheen?!"

Kah'Sheen, Youngest of Ku'Shya, released the staff and held up her arms, backing away on her many legs as she stared at Casvir. The bloodhounds snarled but kept their distance.

"I am not wanting trouble," the half-demon said. "I am curious why you are here."

In response, Etolié slid from the horse, struck at just how fucking *tall* her sort of sister-in-law was. Taller than even Khastra, and lankier by far in her upper half. Etolié faced her taut stomach. "Fucking hell, Kah'Sheen—you nearly killed me. Just say hi next time."

"I did. I am saying 'Hello, Etolié.'"

Damn demons and their literalism.

Kah'Sheen looked past Etolié. When Etolié followed her eyes, Casvir still held his weapon readied, clearly ready to charge with his mount. "Relax, Imperator. She's my sister, remember."

"She is also The Coming Dawn, and we do not know why she is here."

"She's gonna explain, so calm those enormous pecs of yours."

For some reason, he obeyed. The bloodhounds silenced. His mace disappeared, though Etolié didn't doubt he could summon it again in an instant. He stepped down from his skeletal horse with surprising grace for his size, a few heads shorter than Kah'Sheen even with his horns.

"It is lovely to be seeing you as well, Etolié. And not unpleasant to be seeing you, Imperator Casvir, even though we are not friends."

Etolié fought a snicker at that.

Despite Kah'Sheen's frightful features, nothing of the legendary *Coming Dawn* showed in her stance—simply defeat, those four eyes filled with grief. "I am making a big mistake, Etolié. I am trusting Mereen Fireborn. Now she has something I need to take back."

Etolié barely heard anything after that damn name. "Mereen, you say?"

"Yes, Mereen. You are knowing her?"

"Casvir and I are on our own quest to find the bitch. We're looking for Flowers—Flowridia."

Incredible, to watch both horror and light fill her demonic visage. "The small one?! Yes, yes—Mereen is killing her dog!"

"We know. We actually have him in custody."

"It is sad. She is not telling us she is going to shoot the dog. And now Mereen has Mother's staff, and I cannot go home—or I am in big trouble."

"What staff?"

"I am a fool, Etolié. Mereen is coming to *Daemenacht* to steal Staff Seraph deDieula, and Mother—she is saying no. But Mereen is wanting it to kill Endless Night—"

"Hold the fuck up," Etolié said, unable to not interrupt at *that* nasty name. "Are you telling me that Mereen Fireborn has the *God of Death's staff?*"

Shame filled Kah'Sheen's countenance. "Yes."

"Well, this got exciting. Continue."

"Mereen is not saying how, but she is saying she needs it to kill Endless Night. And so I am taking it for her, because I am wanting to kill Endless Night. But then she is killing the dog, and I am getting angry, and so we are fighting, but suddenly I am asleep." Kah'Sheen crossed her four arms and pouted, clear distress in her quivering lip. "I am waking in Sha'Demoni. Mereen is gone."

Etolié's brain took a moment to comprehend Kah'Sheen's disjointed words. "Clearly, the answer is to team up."

Kah'Sheen perked up, but better yet, Casvir did not seem displeased.

"You need the staff," Etolié continued. "We need Flowers. We're going to the same place, and I like you."

"Oh, very good!" Kah'Sheen actually clapped in delight, her own little round of applause with her four arms. "Yes, yes—I will help."

"I assume Mereen said nothing about where she was going?"

"No."

"Did she say anything about her plan?"

"She is not. I think only she and the witch are knowing."

The word pinged an unfortunate recognition. "Witch?"

"Odessa. She is the small one's mother."

When Etolié met Casvir's eyes, never had she met a more kindred look of dread. "Well, fuck."

"Indeed," Casvir replied.

"You are knowing her?"

"Long story, but yes. She was a ghost, but I'm not surprised to hear she's apparently transcended that."

"She is having a body when I am meeting her," Kah'Sheen said. "She is the one having the plan and the one interested in the staff."

"My mom might have a meltdown if she knew," Etolié said, but then came a strange and impossible thought—yet was it? Had Casvir not gone on a road trip seeking an artifact of death before? "Casvir, you can sense necromancy, right?"

"Well enough."

"If I said 'let's look for the most potent source of undead magic on this continent,' is that something you could do?"

His frown conveyed nothing, as was typical for his expressions. "I do not know. Often I need something to hone my search with. In my quest for the Dark Orb, Flowridia was my beacon. I will meditate and see what I can feel, but I do not promise perfect results."

"Might as well try."

"If you are finding a direction, I can take us through Sha'Demoni," Kah'Sheen said. "Faster that way."

Casvir gave an affirming nod and stepped into the woods alone.

Etolié turned a scathing eye to Kah'Sheen. "You seriously gave the God of Death's staff to Mereen."

"She is providing a compelling reason—the reason being to slay Ayla Darkleaf. I should still be there helping, but I am getting too angry."

"As someone whose temper frequently gets the better of her, I understand."

"Would you and the imperator help to slay her?"

The burning rage within Etolié toward the false former Empress of Solvira remained a nasty driving force in her life. A predictable evil, however. Flowers was a greater threat, but if she and the baby had to go, might as well add to the body count. "I can't speak for him, but it's the least she deserves. Between you and me"—she looked toward the woods where Casvir had vanished and saw no sign—"I wouldn't be sad if 'the small one' were offed as well."

"I am seeking no harm to her. She has no quarrel with Sha'Demoni."

"I mean, she did for a while there—"

"Yes, yes," Kah'Sheen said, clenching her words, "but Khastra is not being dead, remember?"

Etolié stared a moment, forever mystified by the apparent megalomania of their mother, the Goddess of War. This was the lie they told her to prevent her from rampaging against the world—that Khastra hadn't been killed by The Endless Night, instead faking her death to run from Staelash, all to avoid a massive war and consequentially sparing Flowers the crime of being complicit. "Right."

Plenty of accidents could happen in a fight against an ancient evil vampire. Flowers had to go.

Casvir's steps crunched foliage and branches, his voice soft as it came steadily nearer. ". . . taking a detour up north."

"All will be well," came Khastra's reply, and Kah'Sheen perked up at the sound. "There are sightings of a large battalion of airships at the Cliffs of Khovav, but it should not be a difficult fight if we . . ."

The little mirror flashed past Kah'Sheen.

". . . Murishani and I are more than capable, is my point.

278

Pardon me, but am I seeing Kah'Sheen?"

"You are!" Etolié's said, only then realizing that Kah'Sheen had become a rather pale shade of blue.

"I apologize if this is below you, but may I speak to her?"

Casvir wordlessly handed the mirror off to Etolié, who pointed it toward Kah'Sheen.

Khastra's demeanor became something Etolié had never seen before, sharp and terse. "Kah'Sheen, Mother is asking everywhere for you. Go home."

Submission showed in Kah'Sheen's apologetic smile. "I cannot be doing that."

"Is it true you have taken Staff Seraph deDieula?"

"Uh—"

"Mother is furious! You must—"

"No, listen, listen—Mereen Fireborn is using the staff to kill Ayla Darkleaf forever."

Rapid words left Khastra's lips, and Etolié realized this was the persona of *sister*. "And when are you trusting Mereen Fireborn?"

"I am not needing to trust her to know she has a plan! It is her life mission—"

"A mission she has failed for a thousand years—"

"It is mine as well!"

"So you are also a failure."

"*Khastra!*"

Gone was Kah'Sheen's stilted Solviran, replaced with sputtering, furious Demoni. Khastra matched it, and all around, the shadows slowly rose, consuming the cheerful day. Etolié glanced to Casvir, within whom she saw the same uncomfortable solidarity of being a witness to someone else's fight.

When corporeal shadow caressed Etolié's foot, she screeched and dropped the mirror—and dove to catch it, lest it shatter on a rock.

She caught it but tapped the image of the irate Khastra in the process, accidentally shutting her up.

Kah'Sheen still fumed, but with the absence of Demoni words, the shadows dissipated. "I am fixing this myself."

"I know," Etolié said. "Not judging your fuck up."

"I am not regretting stealing the staff. I am regretting not knowing where Mereen is."

"I hear you, Sheen Bean." Etolié offered the mirror to Casvir. "Any luck?"

"I have found a potential source of power," Casvir said, though his uncertainty was clear. "I am unable to identify it from this distance, but it is dark magic."

"If it's that far away, it must be powerful."

"Indeed."

He gave Kah'Sheen vague directions—*north*—and thankfully, the half-demon seemed confident. "We will go through Sha'Demoni, as I am saying. Then it will not take weeks if we are lost. And if we are wrong, we can try again."

Casvir summoned a portal and bid the bloodhounds to go through, claiming they would not be well behaved in the demonic realm. Etolié was more focused on holding in her lunch.

When the portal had closed, Kah'Sheen offered two of her hands. Despite her petite figure, her slim hands somehow engulfed Etolié's. Casvir's were broader though a comparable match. In their other hands, they held the horses' reins.

When they stepped into the nearby shadow of a tree, Etolié was prepared for the gentle tug into the alternate plane. The last time she'd seen it, it had been in a brief moment of panic from avoiding Mereen's bullet, but now she had a moment to savor the sights. A lush purple sky hung lower than in the mortal plane, the light filtering down like fog, dissipating before it could touch her. The heat sank like a blanket, already weighted against her skin. What she presumed were plants held primarily warm tones, though some had accent shades of deep blue. But they swayed too much to be mere foliage, and when Kah'Sheen shooed a few from their path, they fucking *crawled away with their roots.*

"So is everything here a multi-limbed mon—creature?" Etolié amended that last word as she, realizing it would be terribly rude to call her new sister a monster.

Kah'Sheen seemed thoughtful, ignoring the scrambling plants. "Perhaps yes. Many limbs means many weapons. I am surprised you are having so few."

"Khastra has expressed her frustration at only having two arms, yes."

"More limbs would be useful," Casvir muttered, and Etolié decided to withhold any jests.

With merely a thought, Etolié illusioned two extra arms to rest on her hips, much to Kah'Sheen's clear amusement, then recalled a terrible thing. "Oh. I shouldn't use magic. Demons are drawn to it, right?"

"We are less hungry on this side of the world. You can keep your clothes, Etolié. They will not attack a daughter of Ku'Shya or her entourage."

"I appreciate that," Etolié said, letting the extra arms vanish. "Not that Cassie cares, but it gets a little drafty."

"You are immune to cold," Casvir said, as plainly as though commenting on the weather.

"Don't make me justify why I don't want my tits hanging out."

"Fair enough."

"It is not cold here," Kah'Sheen said, "but what about heat? Are you tolerating heat?"

"I'm pretty hardy, and Imperator First and Last is dead."

"Very good. You must drink water."

Kah'Sheen beckoned them along, and Etolié marveled as the plants parted for their passing, revealing stone in deep shades of red.

"It will be a few days' journey," Kah'Sheen said, "but that is much faster than weeks."

They followed Kah'Sheen into the foreign world on foot, leading their horses along. Etolié absorbed every bit with curious eyes, fascinated by the strange realm.

Exhausted from swimming and minimal sleep, Flowridia's steps faltered far earlier than usual.

She found a clearing in the secluded forest, deeming it ideal for sleep. Were there danger here, she had a ghost to keep watch, and while her distrust remained, Sarai could have slain her last time she slept.

All day, she had considered this strange development. All day, she had sought meaning in Sarai's willingness—nay, *eagerness*—to help. But anytime she had thought to speak, there came simply the memory of Izthuni's words and Ayla's shattered heart.

Though Flowridia's dress was soiled and dirty, it was the only warmth she had now. But as she cleared a space to sleep, in the shadow of a tree was another slab of wood, this time with cheese and various fruits and vegetables—as well as matches.

Flowridia resumed her task with more vigor, the cool night already threatening to chill her to the bone. Soon, a small fire flared in her camp, and Flowridia ate her dinner in comfort.

Sarai's voice startled her. "Do you generally trust stashes of food and supplies found in suspicious shadows?"

"I do."

Flowridia resumed her meal, put off when the probing questions returned. "Who leaves them?"

"Izthuni."

"Are you pledged to him?"

"No. But he likes me."

Sarai floated down to the opposite side of the fire, looking nearly alive in the blended light. But subtle translucence remained in her figure. "Are you pledged to anyone?"

It seemed odd to admit that she was technically pledged to her own wife as a goddess, but the act had been mutual—and necessary. "Yes, but she didn't grant me my familiar."

"Being a witch means your powers come from demons."

Flowridia did not know what to make of Sarai's inquisitive nature but supposed there was no harm in the truth. "That is correct."

"But not of Ku'Shya."

"No. And if you haven't heard of Nox'Kartha, you haven't heard of my patron."

Though her tears forever flowed, Sarai's gaze held no sadness, only wonder. "It makes sense that Ayla would marry someone so unique—"

"I don't want to talk about Ayla with you," Flowridia snapped, anger surging. It was irrational, yes. But something about it felt so wrong. A violation of trust, perhaps. Ayla wasn't here, so she could not guess how Ayla would feel to think she had met Sarai . . . whom she loved.

Sarai retreated into herself, growing quiet. Crackling fire filled the silence, and Flowridia ate until her stomach was full—but not bursting this time.

In the ensuing tension, however, came many questions. Flowridia finally let one seep out. "How *did* you rescue me? I have never heard of a ghost doing anything like that."

The ghost perked up to be acknowledged, and Flowridia cursed her endearing nature. "It's strange. It's more instinct than knowledge. I sing, and the currents slow. In those moments, I can touch the world in ways my incorporeal form shouldn't allow. I lifted you from the river and led you to the grove."

"I suppose I'm not surprised." Flowridia was torn—how desperately she wanted to know every little thing about her, but her hesitation remained. Curiosity won this day. "I heard you were a . . . a *minstrel* in life."

Sarai laughed at that—and how strange and lovely it was, to hear this tragic ghost expel such joy. A beautiful sound, and Flowridia did not know how to feel about it. "Yes, I was. I actually gained considerable fame. My songs were often silly, but a few became renowned. I would sing in grand halls and amphitheaters, traveled all over the country—even left the country, for a few performances. I thought I had found my calling . . ." Her expression fell, a shadow passing over it. "But when Mereen's husband died, I left to be with her. Mereen and I weren't particularly close—she was so much older, you see— but Eldrin, my little nephew, was the truest extension of my heart. Mereen teased that he was the only boy I could ever love, which wasn't wrong."

"That was kind of you," Flowridia said and thus she found it suspect. "Giving up everything for your sister."

"I don't know if it was all altruistic. Fame was tiresome, but that doesn't mean my family wasn't important. Do you have any siblings?"

Flowridia had once found a family, supposed she might've once called Marielle or Etolié sisters, but rumor said Marielle was far too wrapped up in Murishani, and Etolié had made it very clear where they stood.

But there was one. Not a sister, but . . .

Flowridia's heart seized at the memory. "I had a brother," she said, though her gut twisted at the memory of the knife. "I would have done anything for him."

Including slay him to ease his passing. On sleepless nights, she repeated the necessary refrain of *"It's not my fault, it's not my fault . . ."* but it ached. Perhaps it would forever.

She was surprised to meet compassionate eyes. "I'm sorry for your loss."

Flowridia had lost so much. The conversation had taken a turn. Desperate to hide her welling tears, she spoke the first thought she had. "Would you sing for me?"

Such a charismatic grin Sarai had. "All right." The words

held laughter, and Flowridia despised her easy charm. Bliss filled Sarai's countenance, and when she stood and opened her mouth, there rang a spectacular sound:

I often go walking alone in the dark
And sing all the beautiful songs in my heart.
I'm as blessed by the Moon as I'm loved by the Day
And I trust in her light to not lead me astray.

Flowridia was struck, jaw slack as she listened. Marielle's voice had been silk, blending seamlessly with her harp. Etolié's had been a gorgeous spectacle, her range and talent mesmerizing, a born performer.

But this . . . Sarai's soprano voice echoed across the whole forest, her vibrato a powerful force. Not alluring, but uplifting, the sort of voice to lead a battalion to war. Yet there was beauty in it—unearthly beauty. Flowridia's despondent soul received new life, intoxicated by the resplendent sound.

The Moon and the Stars sing their chorus by night
While the Goddess of Sunshine awaits the dawn's light.
The angels are watching, so why should I fear?
So I'll sing all my songs, and know that they're near.

Speechless, Flowridia simply stared as the final note faded, struggling to gather her thoughts as Sarai bowed. Perhaps her talent was enhanced by death, yet Ayla had fallen in love with it—and Flowridia begrudgingly supposed she understood why. "That's a lovely song," she finally managed to say.

"Thank you." Sarai returned to her seat, her weeping odd with her smile.

"I've never heard a worship song for more than one goddess."

"I wrote it myself. I didn't see why we could not give praise to Neoma and Staella as well as Sol Kareena. Blasphemous, though not in a way that would get me into trouble. Remember what I said about sisters? Neoma didn't have to be worshipped to be begrudgingly accepted."

"Why, though?"

"I won't lie and say I'm not enamored by scandal." Sarai's laughter resumed, and it seemed so natural for her. "But I also always loved Neoma and Staella. I know the former is dead now, but not when I was born. I always loved the idea of a goddess who loved like I did—though I assure you, the comparisons ended there. If I had truly detoured from Sol Kareena, I would have likely found the most friends among Eionei worshippers."

Flowridia thought of Etolié and could not find a single point to argue. "I can see that. I . . . I know a granddaughter of Eionei. She also sings."

"There you go."

Discomfort rose within Flowridia at this rising kinship, uncertain of what to trust as a lie or as truth. Sarai seemed so radiant, so sincere, but there remained tangible proof of her evil deed—and what a betrayal it would be, for Flowridia to decide she liked her wife's murderer. "I should try and sleep."

"Of course. I'll watch the woods."

Flowridia laid her head on her corset, which was uncomfortable but better than dirt, and hoped the night would not be long. Night was when the sorrow came, and she could not cry again of Ayla in front of this ghost.

Quieter now, Sarai trilled a gentle lullaby. Flowridia clung to the sound.

They emerged the next day from the haunted woods, a massive field spreading before them.

Flowridia savored the sun's warmth, grateful for this mercy after so many days in shadow. Her arms spread to embrace it, and though she held no affection for the Sun Goddess, how she cherished her domain.

Sarai's light dimmed beneath the bright sun, but her countenance softened to gaze upon the brilliant sky. "There is a town if we continue south, only a day or two more. Though, I had a thought. I know Velen'Kye is your destination, but we might be able to hire a carriage in Kachul to get there. Where is Nox'Kartha anyway? If it's anywhere near the sea, we may be able to charter a ship. We can hire a carriage to take us to Vulun—a port city. It might save us weeks or even months if we avoid Velen'Kye."

Whatever her reservations regarding Sarai, having a

guide continued to be invaluable. "Nox'Kartha is across the sea. How far is Kachul?"

"Just a few days south of Pe'er, past Ganat Canyon—and we can be in Pe'er by tomorrow night if we hurry."

"I'm willing to try—"

A great shadow eclipsed the sun.

Flowridia gasped to see . . . a dragon.

No question of it—the massive skeleton dragon flew overhead, gravity holding nothing to the magic it wielded. What omen was this? Was it fate?

Shock stilled Sarai, but Flowridia waved her arms and cried, "Help!"

"What are you doing?"

"I know her." And what had Etolié called her? "Kitty!"

By some miracle, the dragon deviated from its northbound course.

"You know a dragon?"

"I've known two dragons."

Mesmerized, Flowridia could not look away as the skeletal creature grew larger and larger, her descent revealing her massive size.

'Kitty' dominated Valeuron in size, her wings spread wide as her feet touched the ground. The earth trembled, dust rising to consume and coil around the great beast. Those gaseous globes within her sockets flashed as they fixed upon Flowridia, paying the ghost no mind.

Yet while those eyes held intelligence, there was no kindness here. The dragon's might could not be denied, her jaws capable of snapping Flowridia up in a single bite. She paced, a panther stalking her prey—but Flowridia grasped this hope with all her strength. "Etolié told me the name she gave you. I hope you don't mind that I used it."

Could this 'Kitty' talk? Etolié's eccentric account meant it could go either way. Flowridia held up defensive hands and chose a soft approach. "This is an astounding convergence of fate. I would be remiss to not talk to you."

Kitty's stance remained aggressive. Had she fur, it would bristle along with the bones of her spine. Her wings remained tucked to her body, protective of her hollow core—or not so hollow, given the orb embedded into her spine.

Still, Flowridia's more prominent memories of the dragon were of her being enslaved. "I want to say that I'm sorry."

Kitty's menace did not lessen, but her relentless stare meant she had heard.

"I was young and foolish when I found you with Casvir. I didn't know anything about dragons. I assumed you were mindless undead, but I know now how wrong I was. I met your brother, Valeuron. I was there when he was killed. I-I understand now what crime was done to you, and I'm sorry for being complicit."

Nearby, Sarai kept her curious gaze, but Kitty stopped her prowling. It was impossible to decipher any expression from her skull, but radiant waves of *judgment* washed over Flowridia—yet this shame was not from within. Kitty extended a claw, bidding Flowridia to touch.

Though hesitant, if the dragon wanted her dead, it would be trivial. She accepted this strange boon and grabbed the dragon's nail.

Tell me of my brother's fate. Is he still enslaved by the imperator?

Flowridia recoiled at the bombardment of words in her head—like Demitri, but feminine. "No. His body has been set free. It was burned in the battle against Solvira."

Kitty's leer welled dread in Flowridia's soul, and she feared this had been a mistake. *I do not understand you.*

"I suppose I am enigmatic at times. Why?"

Etolié said my brother gave you the Earth Orb. Why?

"I don't know," Flowridia said, and with every breath, her body became colder. "I was hoping you might be able to tell me. He decided I was worthy after we touched. He said his duty was fulfilled. Does that mean anything to you?"

No.

Flowridia waited, prayed for more. This mystery had plagued her for years, but Kitty offered nothing. "I should warn you," Flowridia said, desperate to cut the tension, "the God of Order is hunting you."

I know. We have met a few times. We fight. I fly away. He hunts me anew. I cannot be far from my Mother's grave, and so I circle around it. Sometimes I return, but he knows to find me there.

"Your mother's grave?"

Yes. Her coming is soon. Is there anything else?

Flowridia summoned what courage she still held to. "I wished to beg for your aid. I'm lost in this strange land, and while I have my companion here to help me, you could take us to Kachul in only a few hours. Everything has been taken from me—my wife, my familiar—I have nothing, but if you would be willing to help, I would be forever indebted to you."

You are not a woman used to consequences, are you.

Flowridia reeled at the statement. "I beg your pardon?"

You have some audacity, pleading to me for aid after what you did. I was a slave. I was a prisoner in my own body as I was ridden like a common steed into battle and forced to murder innocent people. I am a being of Death, but death is not destruction—yet I was forced to destroy. And you? You are complicit, as you said. Your ignorance does not dismiss the monstrousness of your actions.

Her judgment did not relent; shame welled from deep within Flowridia. "I simply thought—Valeuron said—"

My brother was wise, but my brother is dead. So I shall not repeat his final act, which apparently was trusting you.

Flowridia struggled to speak, struggled to even gather her thoughts. "I-I understand."

No, you do not. But I am not a being who deals in justice. When my mother returns, I shall tell her of your crimes so she might judge you herself.

Kitty spread her wings wide, catching air despite the hollow spaces between the bones, and launched with hardly a dash of wind at all.

Flowridia stood transfixed upon her silhouette in the sky, until she vanished upon the northern horizon.

"So was she talking to you?"

It jarred Flowridia from her stagnation, forcing her to collect her thoughts. One minor mercy in this hellish moment—Sarai did not know the depth of her shame.

"Yes. My gamble was . . . foolish."

Sarai followed her gaze to the horizon. "Your gamble wasn't foolish, because you've come out even. Gained nothing but lost nothing. Take my advice as a former gambler—so long as you have fun, you've come out on top."

"I can't say I had fun."

"But you also aren't dead. What did she say?"

Flowridia wallowed a moment in wonder, the depths of her crimes expanding. "She reminded me that we have an uncomfortable history and that she has no interest in assisting us."

"Disappointing. I'm here to listen if you'd like."

So earnest, this damn woman. Flowridia gritted her jaw and shook her head.

Sarai's sigh bespoke . . . not pity. Something near it.

Something kinder. Sarai was . . . kind. "Our plans have not changed. I'm taking you to Velen'Kye, or to Kachul, or wherever you need to go."

Kind . . . or malevolent. Izthuni had maligned her, yet Flowridia sensed nothing like it, nothing wicked at all in this woman.

But perhaps she was not ready to reconcile that. "Lead the way," she said instead, and Sarai soon filled the silence with song.

At the setting of the sun, Sora treaded back to the ghastly abode in the mountains.

Leelan circled around her, darting about in the air. The untamed grass caressed her trousers, at times threatening to cling and keep her there. But Sora loved the outdoors, and with her duties suspended until Odessa's return, she spent the days wandering freely beyond. She swore the sun burned the filth from her veins, the grime of the mansion slowly escaping as she breathed the cool mountain air.

Odessa's warning remained, but she had time to decide. Though the thought gave Sora pause; she turned her head to the horizon, seeking an owl's silhouette.

How long would it be? Should she have gone alone? Perhaps Sora should have begged to go along, forced Odessa to elaborate on her cryptic warning, chosen for herself whether to go or stay . . .

Odessa had been her companion for a year, and as Sora stared at the ominous sunset, an odd truth struck her—that though this was a family affair, it felt colder without her.

Her steps resumed. Sora despised the grand mansion, but there was no danger there—assuming Tazel remained well. There were enough of Odessa's potions to keep him sustained. The witch was innovative, if nothing else.

The familiar dread seeped into her skin, stealing all the comfort the outdoors had brought as she passed through the doorway. Leelan settled upon her shoulder, becoming languid as he always did. Did the aura affect him too? In moments like this, she wondered what it might be like to be a witch and hear actual words from her familiar. Instead, Leelan remained a conduit, a comfort, but little more.

As she traversed the path to her bedroom, content to eat a few rations, she heard the strangest thing—laughter.

Emitting from the darkened corridors, it cast a baleful aura, and Sora found she preferred the screams. She released Leelan into her room, then went to the basement beneath.

It did not matter how familiar the corridors were. The hair rose on the back of her neck, warning of imminent danger. Sora kept her ears keen and knife readied. She peeked into each cell as she passed, finding them precisely as they'd been left—some with ancient blood upon the floors, one even with dusty skeletal remains strapped upon a table.

"Will you pray with me? I love the way you sing it best."

The voice was Ayla's, yet not—for it was nearly cute, and 'cute' was not a word Sora would have ever used to describe The Endless Night. There came no response, but Ayla's laughter resumed in a conversational cadence.

"Yes, I know. It's as you always say—the light shall burn away all my fears."

Sora peeked inside Ayla's cell and immediately met crazed, blind eyes. But the monster moved on as though she hadn't seen her at all, the typical fluidity of her motions gone, replaced with apprehension, innocence in her vacant gaze.

Tazel sat alone on the floor, the bags beneath his eyes bruised and hollow. Yet his tension had lessened, rare serenity upon his features. He smiled weakly at Sora's entrance, then beckoned for her to sit beside him.

She obeyed, grateful for company. The staff lay across his lap—held without any stress.

"What—" Sora began but Tazel lightly shushed her.

"Why does Sol Kareena only answer when it's you?" Ayla said, staring at some unknown entity. "When I was little, I would pray for my momma to save me, but she never came."

Tazel whispered between Ayla's lines. "She's living in a memory."

"But if my momma is dead," Ayla replied to the invisible figure, "Sol Kareena could bring her back, couldn't she? Oh." Heartbreak settled upon her ageless features, a rare glimpse of vulnerability. "She still never answered. Not even once."

So unnerving, to watch the monster be so . . . childish. Yet even deeper than that, Sora recognized the yearning for a lost loved one, felt it stir deep within her soul. "How?"

"Odessa began the process on the airship," Tazel replied. "She showed me how to use the staff to dig deeper into her head. I can see glimpses of what she's seeing. This memory is peaceful—"

His words cut off at Ayla's sudden sinking posture. "I'm sorry. I didn't mean to disrespect the goddess." A pause, then Ayla whispered, "Yes, I'll go to bed now, but . . . it's my birthday tomorrow—did you know? You did!" Ayla's smile beamed, its innocence startling, radiant in the way only small children could be. "Really? I've never had a birthday surprise before." Ayla's arms came to wrap around herself, pure adoration in her gaze. "I love you, Eva. Good night."

In as natural a motion as the manipulative magic could muster, the demon skull's eyes flashed purple, and Ayla returned to her box. The lid shut.

"How strange," Sora muttered, and beside her, Tazel's blinks became heavy. "Do you want me to give that another try? Perhaps you can nap."

Tazel shook his head, as weak as it was. "I have those potions to sustain me."

Sora returned her attention to the quiet box, contemplating what she had witnessed. "So Ayla was seeing the past."

"Correct. I'm not currently controlling it, though I have funneled it away from unpleasant things. I rarely let them play out like that, but seeing glimpses of kindness is a nice change."

"Who is Eva?"

"I don't know. Someone who cared for her."

Sora struggled to articulate her thoughts, seeking to unearth the source of discomfort inside her. "As a child, whenever my papa was gone, I'd ask Sol Kareena to send him home. My mom eventually found out and reprimanded me, saying Sol Kareena works miracles, yes, but not in that way. She doesn't control people, though she can prompt them. Asking her to control my father was wrong."

"You were a child. I think it's exactly what any one of us would have done."

"Be that as it may, I did stop. He came home just as often as before."

"I hear many conflicting accounts," Tazel said. "Mereen claims Sol Kareena was distant back then and became more so when her sister passed away."

"Sol Kareena often speaks," Sora said, recalling wisdom

of long ago, "but not in words. She speaks in promptings. She speaks in feelings. She brings miracles to our lives, but through other people. That's how my father described it. He said that sometimes we are the miracles others pray for; we just have to listen when Sol Kareena bids us to act."

"That's a beautiful sentiment."

Her next words were vulnerable; she said them with care. "When I ended up in Staelash, I always hoped it was the miracle that would bring me back to my father, but no. Instead, it was the miracle that gave me a new purpose in life, which I suppose is better. Sol Kareena sent Meira to pull me from my rut and give me something new to live for." She stilled, pained to admit the rest. "Perhaps it's wrong, but I still pray to find him, or some sign of him."

"I have no doubt he was a wonderful man."

Despite Tazel's reassurance that all was well, Sora could not dismiss his sudden grimace. He shut his eyes, recoiling at nothing.

"What's wrong?"

"It's nothing, little dove—" He flinched, biting back words.

Tazel had always been a melancholy soul, his aura one of calm and sorrow. But here, his bloodshot eyes watered, that careful balance he held suddenly shifting. Sora's gaze slipped to the staff, tempted to steal it, when Tazel added, "If Sol Kareena sent someone to help Ayla, it went horribly wrong."

"Tazel—"

"I don't care what you talk about—just say something."

Tazel gripped the staff with white knuckles. The first of his tears fell down his scarred face. Though worry welled in Sora's heart, she spoke memories of light and joy, of quiet times in Staelash, and prayed it could be enough.

The fields ended at a road. Flowridia's tired feet touched trampled dirt. The breeze lifted her matted locks.

"Forgive me if this is too much," Sarai said, having done little more than sing the whole morning, "but would that god of yours be able to give you some money?"

A slight weight suddenly weighed down Flowridia's skirt. When she slowed, she was confounded to realize coins had appeared in the seams. "That answers that."

With Sarai's cursed knife, Flowridia ripped the seams, and while she had no concept of how elven money was valued, Izthuni would not leave her wanting.

"Pe'er is ahead. You might be able to buy a few supplies. A bedroll, perhaps a new dress."

Flowridia glanced down at her shredded attire. The gown had been meant for parties, not for extended wear in the woods. Still, though the idea was logical, Flowridia shook her head. "The last time I went to a town, they ran me out when they discovered my identity. Apparently word has spread from Velen'Kye that Ayla Darkleaf and her wife are about, and unfortunately, there are only so many humans in this land with my description."

"I see the dilemma." Sarai floated leisurely along, thoughtful as she added, "Could your god give you a new dress and a bedroll?"

"I don't see why not. I'll ask next time we stop."

If nothing else irked her while on this strange journey, it was the fact that Sarai continued to be . . . charming.

"If you do decide to go into town, we could adjust your hair to hide your ears and pass you off as a half-elf."

"Would that actually be better than appearing human?"

"Look, we Sun Elves have our failings, but we're much kinder to our half-elven kin than the rest of them."

Flowridia had a funny suspicion that "we" extended as far as Sarai and not much more, though Tazel had at least learned empathy for his half-elven family. His memory came with darkness now, however, her mood shifting to think of him and his betrayal. "I'll think on it," she finally said, not meaning it at all.

"Well, might as well stay on the road for now, anyway. We can avoid the town once we near it if you like, but this way *I* won't lose my way."

Amazing, how time in the sun had caused the despondent ghost to blossom into someone entirely new. Flowridia said nothing, merely continued following the road, grateful for the firmer foundation beneath her feet.

Sarai, of course, could not stay silent for long, the songs in her heart too loud to keep to herself. But this time, the lyrics piqued Flowridia's attention.

Flowridia, with her auburn hair
The color of leaves in the autumn air
The speckles of freckles upon her skin
Makes my heart sing again and again.

Flowridia stopped and stared, much to Sarai's amusement. "Oh, you're too easy," the ghost said with a laugh. "I used to write songs for people all the time—all of equally poor quality, I assure you."

Flowridia did know that, quietly living with the knowledge that Ayla had been sung a song for her legacy. Ayla had forgotten the words; Flowridia wondered if Sarai had too.

"It's cute." Flowridia wrestled with her thoughts, uncertain of how to feel about her wife's murderer trying to win her over. "And a little more flirtatious than I appreciate."

Dismay slumped Sarai's posture. "Oh. I apologize. Most of what I wrote were love songs—simply a habit. I promise, I meant nothing by it."

Flowridia continued treading onward, uncertain of how to salvage the awkward turn in conversation, or if she even wanted to.

Fortunately, Sarai decided for her. "Do you sing?"

"A little. Nothing special. I was once described as a 'lackluster mezzo-soprano.'"

Sarai's laughter resumed at that. "How rude!" Still, she remained in good spirits. "I don't believe that at all. Oh, sing a bar or two—I love duets!"

Hesitation flooded Flowridia, given Sarai had been renowned in her life because of her voice. "I don't know. I'm not—"

"There's nothing to be self-conscious about. In fact, there's no one to hear you but the dead."

A shadow passed over, and Flowridia flinched at the memory of Uluron, fearing she might've returned. She held a hand up to shade her face from the sun as she caught a glimpse of . . . not a dragon—a large bird high above.

"Fine, fine, you don't have to," Sarai continued, but Flowridia barely heard it, scowling at the bird as it circled back, like the vultures at the outskirts of the Abyssal Swamp.

It was far away, but it seemed uncommonly large.

"How far away did you say the town was?" Flowridia asked, unnerved for reasons she couldn't place.

"Very near. Did you change your mind?"

Flowridia's pace increased. "Yes."

It was likely nothing, but her gut stirred in warning. Flowridia hurried along.

The town of Pe'er approached, as told by the distant houses, and Flowridia repositioned her hair at Sarai's instruction, guiding it to hide her ears. "Yes, you will still stand out, but I've met half-elves who looked a bit like you," Sarai said, though she grimaced at the state of the dress. "I'm more worried about your clothes."

In addition to being stained in wolf's blood, torn by trees, and scuffed from dirt, now it held clear water damage—which had dulled the bloody marks, at least. "It's definitely suspicious. I'll see if I can purchase a new one from the inn. Perhaps gets some oil for my hair while I'm at it."

"I can't help much on that part, but I'll take your word that it's important."

"Well, in case you hadn't noticed, I'm a mess all over."

"Nearly drowning will do that to you."

As they neared, a different dilemma arose. Flowridia asked, "What will we do about you?"

Confusion marred Sarai's features. "What about me?"

"You're a ghost. I don't feel comfortable leaving the knife outside of town, so that's not an option."

Understanding came to replace her bewilderment. "I forget sometimes that I'm dead." She cast a glower to her wrists, pain coming to replace her good mood—but it was gone just as quickly. "You're a necromancer. What do you know about ghosts?"

"I know you're not easy to banish," Flowridia muttered, but smiled behind gritted teeth. "Silver Fire can destroy you, unless your anchor is particularly strong."

Upon consideration, Sarai's anchor was certainly strong enough to withstand even the Silver Fire. But what if the anchor was destroyed by Silver Fire instead?

"Look at you, so focused on my banishment." Sarai winked, but something odd lay with it. "Could I occupy . . . you?"

"I beg your pardon?"

"Ghosts sometimes go inside people, don't they? I could hide in your body."

"Ghosts can only possess people who are near death— which will stop them from dying. But no. Absolutely not."

Again, Flowridia gave that bitter smile, less keen this time to hide it.

Sarai had been a bit too friendly lately.

"I suppose I could meld into the dirt," Sarai said, more subdued this time. "I would have to pop up here and there to check, but I can be subtle."

"I think that would be our best option." Flowridia looked again to the sky and found it vacant. What had she to worry about in the daylight? Perhaps she was being foolish. Still, the idea of purchasing a new dress was much too enticing, as well as spending the night indoors. "Come on."

Sarai sank into the earth, disappearing from sight. Flowridia traversed cautiously into town. Larger by far than the first, she hoped anonymity would be to her benefit—that, or everyone already knew the wife of Ayla Darkleaf was afoot. Upon her finger was her wedding ring, which thankfully bore no distinguishable marks.

She passed a few carts, the occupants of which watched her curiously. She kept her hair near her face, hiding her features as well as she could as the buildings became more and more dense. This was nearly a proper city, with a town square and everything. Children laughed and played with each other near a well, while townsfolk went along their way, exchanging friendly greetings.

Flowridia adopted her best elven accent as she approached a woman lingering by the road. "Pardon me, lady, but can you direct me to the nearest inn?"

The woman wore clothing not unlike those Eyal had worn in Hyall—in good repair but not nearly so rich as in Velen'Kye. She cast her scrutinizing gaze to Flowridia and her ruined dress. "You're near it. Take a turn to the right, and it's the third building. But are you all right, dear?"

Flowridia summoned her politician's smile from the depths of her memory, praying it was charming enough to offset the spray of blood on her dress. "I have been traveling for some time. Do you know if I would be able to purchase new clothing there?"

"You should. If not, the clothier is on the same street."

Flowridia thanked her, then hurried away before the woman could ask further questions.

The inn held two stories, and Flowridia withdrew the coins in her pocket before she entered, lest she be kicked out for being a street urchin. Within, the décor was modest and neat, conveying no riches but no debauchery either. This would be a safe place, and Flowridia kept her charismatic smile as she approached a man at the desk. "Good afternoon. How much for a room?"

The man gave her the same study as the woman on the street had, though with less concern for her well-being. "Can you pay?"

Flowridia placed a coin on the desk, unwilling to reveal she did not know how to count elven money. "More or less than this?"

"You'll need three times that . . ."

His voice trailed off as she placed the appropriate funds upon the desk. With a silent prayer of thanks to Izthuni, she said, "I'm told I might be able to purchase clothing here."

The man said he would send his wife up.

Within half an hour, Flowridia sat in a tub in a small room, a clean dress and underclothes waiting for her on the bed. To soak in the water was bliss, dirt rising to the surface as she scrubbed it from her skin.

"This is a nice stroke of luck—"

Flowridia gasped at Sarai's voice, then covered herself when the ghost floated in from outside wall. "Where were you?"

"I was watching the people downstairs. If I focus, I can become more translucent, nigh invisible. I didn't know that."

Flowridia relaxed, though sank deeper into the tub.

"I used to love places like this," Sarai continued, a wistful smile twisting her lip. "I would sing for the patrons—not for money, for fun—and inevitably I would find a beautiful girl to take back to my room. It always brought such a rush, spending the night with a stranger. No commitment. No strings. Just fun."

Something in Sarai's features fell, some memory uncovered.

"I don't know if I could open myself up to a stranger like that," Flowridia admitted.

"Of course you couldn't—you were practically a baby when you married. You would still be a child if you were an elf."

The statement was . . . unsettling. "Would I?"

"We live long lives, and our minds and bodies develop a bit slower than humans. We're considered children until we're twenty-six. Then the world is open to us."

The first horrid thing to come to Flowridia's head was a memory of Ayla herself—who had committed her first murder at fourteen, yes, but far more horrifying was everything that had come before. "Oh."

"Don't worry. You're an adult by human standards, so you would be an adult here."

"Good to know," Flowridia said, shoving all other miserable thoughts aside—save for regret. She was no longer a necromancer, a thought that brought anguish, but no one could enact torture upon the dead quite like a necromancer, and brutal thoughts of burning priestesses floated through her head. She couldn't say she was generally keen to cause suffering, but she also couldn't say she had ever hated a stranger quite so vehemently as Eva. Not even Sarai.

"Do you want me to leave while you finish up?"

"It's your choice. The water is starting to cool, but I have hours of oiling and brushing my hair ahead of me. It might bore you."

"I doubt it, but I'll at least leave until you're clothed again."

Sarai remained unflappable, disappearing down into the floorboards.

The thought occurred to her that Sarai might be watching from the walls, and Flowridia would have a few stern words for her if that were true. Was Sarai the sort to watch unsuspecting young women as they bathed?

The darker thought came that Flowridia was simply inclined to think the worst of Sarai, but was that really so wrong when the woman in question had murdered her wife?

When Flowridia emerged from the water, she quickly dried and slipped a fresh chemise over her body. How heavenly it was, to wear something clean. A knock sounded; Flowridia opened the door to find a tray of food—not unlike the ones in the woods.

Izthuni would provide even here. Flowridia brought the offering in and began to feast.

After, Flowridia had only her fingers to brush her hair, so with meticulous care, she applied oil upon different segments and slowly worked her fingers through. Below, she heard faint sounds of revelry—not Sarai's voice, but songs coming from the tavern. How lovely it would be to join them, but no. She was lucky to have come this far without too much suspicion.

Instead, she contemplated what Sarai had said about elven adults and wondered again of Ayla, realizing she had no idea how old Ayla had been upon her death. Long enough to gain a reputation as a monster in the woods, long enough to have to be something of a nomad lest she be caught, but . . .

Ayla was a vampire—of sorts—twisted by dark magic to be alluring, to be ageless. By Flowridia's human standards, Ayla truly could be any age. Yet curiosity made her wonder, made her . . . sad.

A haunting blue filled the space. "What a party! I'm jealous, honestly."

"May I ask you something?"

Flowridia regretted her tone; everything in Sarai's pleasant demeanor shifted into unease. "Certainly."

With her fingers busied by her hair, Flowridia kept her focus there, instead of staring upon Sarai's visage. "You killed Ayla on her birthday. How old was she?"

Flowridia could decipher nothing at all from Sarai's sudden stillness. "Twenty-seven."

That explained a whole damn lot.

The room tensed at the discomforting question. Flowridia returned to busying herself with her hair, an uncomfortable plethora of emotions pounding at her head. So many questions; this small one had struck a crack in the dam.

In the deafening silence, Flowridia took a breath. "Sarai, I—"

A knock sounded from the door.

Flowridia wiped oil from her hands upon her soiled dress, wondering if Izthuni had brought more gifts. Sarai had sat upon the floor, looking nearly mortal aside from the wounds and the ghostly hue. "Do you want me to check who it is?

"No need." Flowridia opened the door

Before her, a nightmarish mirror grinned. "Hello, Flower Child."

Flowridia slammed the door shut. "Sarai, how high up are we?!"

Sarai floated to the window. "High enough to break a leg. Who—?"

Purple smoke seeped from the bottom of the door. A tendril caressed Flowridia's leg, burning through her skin. She yelped and stumbled forward.

The door blew open of its own accord, and there Odessa

stood. The very picture of victory with her grin and confident pose, yet malevolence radiated from the darkness behind her and the necrotic smoke swirling from her figure. "You would lock out your loving mother? Shame on you."

Flowridia ran to the window and thrust it open—only for it to shut and nearly crush her hands. In tandem, the door shut behind Odessa. "And who is . . ?" Odessa gasped, glee in her outburst. "Sarai. Friends with my Flower Child? What a funny little twist of fate."

"You two have met?" Flowridia put her hands up, clinging to the knowledge that if there was anything her mother loved more than revenge, it was talking.

"This is your mother?" Sarai looked from Flowridia to Odessa, jaw falling slack. "How can you do this to your own child?"

"She did kill me once. I wouldn't say we have a typical mother and daughter bond. What I want to know, though . . ." Odessa's eyes flashed with intrigue, one hand held toward Sarai—who flinched. "How did you leave the river?"

"Spite," came Sarai's reply, and Odessa's cackle cast chills across Flowridia's skin.

Izthuni, help, Flowridia cried in her head.

The response was immediate: *Use the knife.*

Odessa's vindictive joy seeped into her grin. "Does that mean you'll be coming along? I would love to have you watch the show. An awkward reunion, though. I wonder what Ayla would think of you looking like . . ." Odessa motioned with her hand, the magic lingering as a fog. "Well, that."

Flowridia kept her hands up as she knelt humbly upon the ground beside her dirty dress, within which was the cursed knife—and the maldectine.

"Hopefully nothing," Sarai replied, though anguish stained the phrase.

"What do you—" Mother cut off when Flowridia threw the maldectine with all her strength, her hand raising to swipe it away with magic—

Only for it to bash her forehead. She reeled, blood welling from a thick cut on her forehead. "Damn you, Flower—"

Flowridia bombarded her with her own body.

They toppled. Before Odessa could breathe, Flowridia raised Izthuni's knife, the pathway clear to her throat—

"Flowridia, no!"

Ice engulfed her. Flowridia stilled as blue light colored her vision—then yelped when she was flung across the room. Pain coursed through Flowridia's head and body, battered against old wood.

Sarai knelt where Flowridia had been; purple engulfed her. The ghost shrieked as Odessa rose, smoke caressing her translucent figure.

And in Odessa's hand, lay the knife. "Please, Flower Child. I'm not going to die the same way twice . . ." Her focus fell to the knife alone.

Flowridia tried to rise, but an invisible hand crushed her, leaving her crumpled in a heap on the floor.

"What is . . ?" Odessa's grin twisted with delight. "Oh, this is delicious."

Sarai managed pained words amid her unnatural torture. "You don't know what you're dealing with."

"No, I know exactly what this is. Don't worry—I'm not stupid enough to use it on her. I need my Flower Child alive."

Pain pulsed with each beat of Flowridia's heart. Again, she commanded her legs to stand, but a greater force held her down.

The maldectine had landed hardly a reach away, droplets of blood marring the rich green. Flowridia scooted toward it.

"Leave her out of this," Sarai pleaded. "You have the knife, so you have me. If you want Ayla dead, I can do it again."

"See, to your sister, that would be tempting. But I am a woman of simple wants, and currently those wants center around gruesome revenge on my sweet girl. Besides, you're incorporeal, which does put a bit of a damper on things like wielding knives."

Flowridia touched the maldectine. The crushing force relented. She burst into standing, running to her old dress— still hiding a few stakes.

But Odessa seemed unbothered, unimpressed when Flowridia held up her shard of wood. "You're a clever little bastard," Odessa said, paying no mind to Sarai—who suddenly floated through the floorboards. "Maldectine won't stop Rulan from grabbing you. We'll be flying out just as soon as I wrangle you out of this inn—"

"*Help!*" came Sarai's scream from the hallway. "*Flowridia Darkleaf is trying to kill us!*"

When commotion sounded outside, hope surged

through Flowridia's veins.

With a swipe of Odessa's hand, the door flung open, revealing Sarai.

"Oh, shut up." Purple lightning shot from Odessa's hand, crackling across Sarai like a second skin. The ghost gasped and buckled, floating as she clutched herself in fetal position. "All you've done is condemn everyone in this tavern to die."

Angry footsteps stomped up the stairs. There came the sound of foreign screams and bodies toppling. Odessa burst with light, though it circled to avoid Flowridia. "Fine, fine," Odessa said toward the downstairs, "I'll be Flowridia Darkleaf. The resemblance is uncanny, I know . . ."

Something soft echoed from Sarai's lips—a song.

No lyrics, simply a tune, somber and small. Below, the commotion continued, yet Odessa stared . . . warily. "Do not—"

Odessa cut off when Sarai's song became loud, then two toned. A dissonant chord rang from her core, and Flowridia's ears ached—though she remained frozen. The discordant sound became higher, higher, until Sarai unleashed a *scream*.

A scream so sharp, Flowridia heard nothing at all.

She dropped to the ground, muscles aching, ears burning. The magic swirling around Odessa ceased; the witch pressed her hands to her ears, visibly pained as she tripped backward. The pain in Flowridia's head increased with each decibel. Death would be a welcome relief from this awful sound. Yet Odessa seemed worse off, blood dripping from her ears. Whatever frantic spell she tried to wave was silenced by the dreadful scream.

The floor shook. The building swayed. Walls cracked. Timbers fell beside Flowridia, the roof shredding in response to the unnatural shriek. Though her vision blurred, her final blinks beheld Odessa's wicked transformation—a nightmarish memory from a time long ago. Feathers burst from her skin, hands twisting into claws, her arms into wings. Odessa launched through the shattered roof.

Flowridia clutched the maldectine, praying it protected her from whatever force Sarai had unleashed. Blue light appeared, even as her vision threatened to fail. "Flowridia, come on! It isn't safe!"

Flowridia sought to grab the ghostly hand, though of course her own fell straight through. Chaos rose, the building collapsing at its base. She stumbled into standing, holding her head as her eyes steadied upon the crumbling floor. Smoke rose from cracks in the floorboards. "Sarai—"

"She dropped the knife—grab it, and come with me."

Flowridia obeyed, compelled by her words alone. She swore with each blink, time zipped by, feeling drunk as her feet found the stairs, found the floor, as fire from the chimney spread across the first floor.

"Stay with me, Flowridia," came Sarai's entrancing voice, and soon, night air enveloped them. A crowd of elves had gathered, their faces a blur. Some had collapsed. Some healthy folk ran inside to fetch those who had fallen.

"Did you hear it?" she heard from the crowd. "The call of a banshee."

"Those are but legends—"

"There it is!"

Flowridia met no resistance as she stumbled into the woods, still following that ghostly blue.

Within a copse of trees, she finally fell to her knees, then to the dirty ground. Her oily hair cushioned her, surely attracting dirt and more, but she could no longer keep her eyes open.

"I'll protect you. You can rest now."

Flowridia shut her eyes, and an enrapturing song whispered in her ear as she drifted off into sleep.

Flowridia awoke to faint light beyond the trees and trilling birds high above.

Morning would soon come, but the world was quiet here. Her fingers brushed the hilt of the knife, but her head was clear when she sat up and surveyed the scene. She unclenched her fist—there fell the bloody maldectine. A chill sunk into her skin, the brisk air cutting through her wet hair and thin chemise. She had even less than when she'd started, though in the dark shadow of a nearby tree was a platter of food and a soft blanket.

Sarai floated near, seated, though not quite on the ground. She faced the sun, shifting only when Flowridia wrapped herself into the offered comfort and sat beside her, food in her lap.

No hunger stirred in her stomach, but she did not want to sacrifice it to the roaming insects. Instead, she placed it before her, then said, "What was that?"

"There is magic in my songs," Sarai said, though she would not meet Flowridia's eye. "I have quelled storms, and I have caused earthquakes."

"As we were leaving, they called you a 'banshee.' I've never heard the word."

"I have." Sarai kept her gaze to the sun, her flowing tears sincere, matching her tragic countenance. "As far as I know, it's only an elven phenomenon, that when an elf passes on, their anguish may cause them to manifest as something different than a typical ghost. It's speculated to be because of our Chaos-worshipping ancestry, but no one knows for certain. There is power in a banshee's screams. Apparently, I can topple buildings."

No pride in the words; merely sorrow. Sarai's face fell

into her hands.

So many questions filled Flowridia's head, evoked from all she had seen. She finally settled upon one—the most virulent of all. "What are you thinking?"

A sob came from Sarai's throat. "I'm thinking I should have never been born. My legacy is death."

Whatever Sarai's lies, whatever her villainy, there was no question of her agony. Flowridia contemplated a response, uncertain of anything anymore. Her life had forever changed, her future stolen by a bullet, though perhaps her wife could still be saved.

Flowridia voiced a dangerous thing, something that had haunted her from the moment she learned Sarai's true name. "You ended your life after killing Ayla, didn't you."

Amid her soft cries, Sarai nodded.

The picture Flowridia sought to complete had so many missing pieces, so many holes. *Beware,* Izthuni had said, but she could not lie to herself and say this woman was cruel—not anymore. "Why did you do it?"

Sarai looked again to the sun, her eyes gushing tears. "You said to never speak of Ayla."

Within Flowridia stirred the beginning of something she had never thought to feel for the woman who had slain her wife, who had betrayed her, destroyed her—a monster. Yet compassion rose, for Flowridia held softness for monsters. Though she did wonder . . . if that label fit Sarai at all. "I'm taking that back. I want to understand."

When Sarai's arms came to wrap around herself, Flowridia wished she could hold her—how pitiful the woman was. How broken. Something, somewhere, had gone tragically wrong. "I loved Ayla with every part of me," Sarai whispered. "I had been with many women, But I had never been in love. She was different, so shy, so *scared.* She hid it beneath armor, but she was such a delicate soul. I fell for her quickly, and she for me too. Ayla meant everything to me—"

Sarai's voice cut off, stolen by a gasping sob. Her tears sparkled as they disappeared, and Flowridia listened, finding it surreal to hear. "But there had been disappearances in Fallanar—where Mereen and I lived. Children lost in the woods. One day, Eldrin, my nephew, vanished as well. He was three years old."

Flowridia's gut clenched at the statement. Yes, Ayla had murdered children, even before she had become a monster.

Izthuni had directed her; Flowridia remembered that too.

"Mereen and I were desperate. We searched everywhere in the woods, got the city guard involved. But that night . . ." Sarai's breath hitched, though she needed no breath. "A traveler had come into town. That night, he told me he was hunting her. He told me horrid things, accused her of wicked crimes—and I didn't believe it. He said she had surely stolen Eldrin, and I told him no. And so . . . he showed me. He showed me what hid in her cellar. Perhaps you can guess. I don't know."

Flowridia recalled a laboratory from years ago, attached to a cathedral of horror—her shock, her dismay, her anguish to find out the truth of what Ayla was.

Now, in their cellar at home, that horror had been recreated. "I can imagine what you might've seen," Flowridia said, her words a gentle stream.

"It was pure horror. I was shaken. But it was her, all her, and then the traveler handed me a knife."

Flowridia clutched the knife in her hand, the story slowly falling together.

"He told me he had been hunting her for years but she had evaded him. He told me I was the only one who could get close enough to do it. He pleaded with me to do what was right, that perhaps I couldn't save Eldrin, but I could save the next child."

Sarai hesitated, hands trembling as she wiped tears from her eyes, though it did nothing to stanch their flow.

"You killed her," Flowridia whispered.

Anguish wracked Sarai's body, her sobs rising anew. In the quiet morning, she wept, and Flowridia's mind reeled from it all. Something was wrong, yet she struggled to find the lie. All of it rang true—but no. No.

"When I returned to town," Sarai said, muffled by sobs, "Eldrin was playing in Mereen's yard."

The words sank like a stone.

"The traveler came to me as I watched through the gate. He apologized for taking my nephew. He said it was the only way. He thanked me for my service to the world, assured me that no one would link the murder to me, but refused to accept the knife. Instead, he said to do with it as I would. He wanted it left in the world.

"Ayla was buried in the cemetery in town that same day," Sarai continued, resolute now, though the strength behind it was thin. "I claimed to have found her dead."

"You sang to her." Saying it aloud settled something in Flowridia, for the story matched the pieces Ayla had once tearfully revealed. "Ayla had asked you for a song, and you sang it after she was buried."

"Did Mereen tell you that?"

"Ayla hums it. She said it was from you."

For the first time, Sarai looked at her, her waterlogged face cast in shock.

"She doesn't recall the words," Flowridia continued, "but she sings it for comfort. She calls it 'a song for her legacy.'"

Sarai said nothing at all, her astonishment remaining even as she returned to facing the sun.

"A-And then Ayla rose as a monster," Flowridia finished, her mind still racing to comprehend all Sarai had said.

Sarai remained quiet, the only sign of turmoil her trembling lip. "No. First, I went to the river."

"And you used the knife. It's why you're connected to it."

"I sought to bury it with me, but I wouldn't have dared to use it. The dagger I used to end my life was nothing, long since rusted and gone."

Flowridia repeated a question of before: "What does the knife do?"

Again, Sarai stared at the sun, the light not blinding to a creature such as her. "It creates monsters. If you had stabbed Odessa, she would have become like Ayla."

It explained Odessa's interest. It explained why Izthuni wanted it back. This dagger contained unfathomable power, and Flowridia stared upon it with new clarity. "Did you ever find out the identity of the traveler?"

"No. He appeared as an elf, but he also claimed to be a priest, so who knows what magic he wielded to conceal himself. When I asked him why, he gave no reason. Simply thanked me and disappeared."

Flowridia's mind danced upon a thousand different things, desperate to assemble these pieces into a picture she could make sense of. But Ayla had never solved this tragic mystery. Neither had Sarai. Something was missing.

But who . . . who would want . . .

And then came words of long ago, from a night stained in tears and confessions, when Ayla had laid bare her heart: *"I would have left my whole life behind for her and become someone new."*

The answer came so gently, so cruelly. Flowridia asked but one thing. "I can only speak for what Ayla has said on the matter, but you would have committed to her, yes?"

Sarai nodded. "I wished for nothing more than a future with her."

All I know is what Ayla spoke of in life, Izthuni had said, *how she often wept to me of Sarai's games, her soft manipulations. She was a breaker of hearts, leaving strings of shattered lovers behind . . .*

This was not what Flowridia saw. This was not what Ayla had said that tearful night: *"She saw me immediately as a broken person and sought only to build me up."*

Flowridia studied the knife—Izthuni's knife—knowing he was wicked, knowing he was the sort of monster to groom a little girl and twist her mind, who would lurk until invited and compel her to burn the world.

And Ayla had burned the world. Only one woman had ever stood in her way—this shattered ghost, who instead had unknowingly struck the match to the flame.

Flowridia's entire core sank, breath shallow as the final pieces of the Lurker's subtle manipulations fell into place. "No . . ."

"No?" Sarai replied, but Flowridia barely heard it.

Ayla was everything Izthuni had wanted, groomed from childhood, her mind warped through abuse and lies—all she was missing was power.

Izthuni had created his own monster.

When her limbs failed her, Flowridia dropped the knife onto the soft earth. "We can't return this knife," she whispered, yet even as she spoke it, she feared.

If not Izthuni, who would help them?

"You'll hear no arguments from me," Sarai replied, wariness in her visage. "But why?"

With Flowridia's next blink, mist obscured her vision. Yet a sudden spark of rage pulsed with it. "When I was stolen from Velen'Kye, I saw something impossible—old acquaintances of mine. I don't believe that's coincidence. And while they have every reason to hate me now, I would trust them over . . ."

All the lies. All the trickery. Nearly two thousand years of betrayal in the making.

"I shouldn't say it."

But as the wind rustled the trees, the shadow of a branch fell cold upon her skin. She froze. Then came a dark voice in her head: *Precious little fool.*

Flowridia stood and stumbled forward into the sunshine. Her breath came labored, heart pounding in fright.

"Flowridia—!"

Sarai's voice cut off. When Flowridia turned, the food upon the platter was nothing but ash. Around her, the blanket she clung to suddenly crumbled. Flowridia gasped as the remnants floated away with the wind.

"What is happening?" Sarai asked, her incorporeal form coming closer.

The truth of how damned she was settled upon her heart, but Flowridia's anger rose above all. "Izthuni is withdrawing his help."

From the cover of trees, the shadows crept closer, unnatural. Flowridia dove to grab the knife, successful, but a cold shadow caressed her foot before she could dart away. From the darkness echoed a deep, ominous laugh. *It does not have to be this way.*

Sarai came closer, fear on her ghostly face. "Why?"

"Because he tricked you. He stole your nephew." Flowridia clutched the knife to her chest. "He killed Ayla Darkleaf."

Then came his final words, rumbling across the earth in warning: *Good luck, little girl.*

The presence disappeared, but the feeling of dread lingered.

When the sky displayed the barest preamble of sunrise, Sora woke from an uncomfortable sleep. No nightmares but no dreams, simply tossing and turning, unable to shake the dreadful sensation this building perpetually permeated.

That, and Odessa's warning. It sang like a cave echo, fading but only just.

Leelan languished on the windowsill, gazing forlornly upon the word beyond. He no longer gave his morning chirps. She feared this place affected him more than he could convey. She dressed, for the mountains awaited.

Against her will, she contemplated Odessa's parting

words more and more as the days passed. Her return harkened a great unknown, a coming storm she claimed would sweep Sora away.

Sora had not been raised to back down from challenges, yet . . .

There sat Leelan by the window, sickened. How long until this poison infected Sora too? She held one comfort, that Sol Kareena was not omnipotent. She would not know what transpired in this awful place if Sora did not speak of it.

As Sora left her room, she kicked the rug centered in the hallway, revealing a scorched line. As Sora knelt to right it, she saw the line continued . . .

A swirl of magic, resembling a snake, wrapping around a dagger—a symbol of Izthuni. At the brush of her finger, it sparked.

Sora reeled back, sickened at the proximity of something so vile. The very antithesis of her goddess, and she covered the mark back over with the rug.

Before she could make her way outside, she heard distant yelling. *"The audacity of that woman!"*

Sora knew its source. She crept to the dungeon, quiet as a mouse. Into the darkness, the very air suffocating, until she peeked into the first cell, not surprised to see Ayla standing, and Mereen leaning against Tazel's side on the floor.

". . . absolutely insufferable. All Mereen does is tease. I nearly regret killing the judge—perhaps if her husband weren't dead she wouldn't be such a cunt."

Sora looked to Mereen, whose countenance had become grim, indeed. Her husband's murder was not a secret, but surely it was jarring to the woman, to hear it so starkly stated.

"But if I hadn't, Sarai wouldn't have come."

Childlike wonder filled Ayla's face, stars in those vibrant eyes. "I'm sorry. I didn't come here to rant. In fact, I've been . . . afraid. I came to say that things must be different now. I haven't brought you what you asked for. I hope you can understand that . . . I can't.

"I wanted to thank you for caring for me, all these years. I know we've had our disagreements, but in the end, you're the reason I'm here. You're the reason I survived. But I want to move out of the woods. Sarai asked if I would live with her in our own little house, and how can I say no? You understand, right?"

Fear rose, a child awaiting castigation, but just as quickly, her expression softened, that smile returning. "I knew you would. Sarai isn't meant for all of this. She's kind and good, and it makes me wonder if . . . if Sol Kareena sent her just for me. Perhaps she listened after all."

What was this? Sora knew of Sarai, she supposed. Knew she'd written a song. But this was so poignant, so pure. Ayla's dirty visage did nothing to cloud the sunshine she radiated from merely speaking the name.

"Sarai means everything to me," Ayla continued, those silver eyes sparkling, nothing like the cruel gaze Sora had faced when this same creature had slit her throat. "Can you believe I wanted to cut out her voice box? How silly of me. I love her, Izthuni. And she loves me! I can hardly believe it." Her eyes filled with tears, arms wrapping around herself. "I think she wants to be wed. I could dismiss my bastard name and be hers. *Ayla Fireborn*—what do you think?"

Sora thought it reprehensible, but was who she faced the same monster who had burned the world? No, this was someone different.

"Of course I will tell you of the wedding. If you're subtle, you can even attend."

None of this came to pass. What tragedy had come between this and the genocide of Sora's ancestors?

Mereen muttered beneath Ayla's effervescent monologue. "I tire of this." With vampiric grace, she stood and marched toward Sora, who stepped aside for her exit.

At Mereen's disappearance, the staff in Tazel's hands flashed. Ayla quieted and crawled into the coffin. The lid shut.

"She's deep in," Tazel said. "I felt no resistance at all."

"What do you mean?"

"Sometimes she fights, even when she seems serene. Odessa described it as plunging her underwater but not deep enough for the ocean to crush her. It's a balance."

"Why, though?"

"Simply following orders. Though I pray Odessa returns soon. She would be better than me."

"If Ayla is serene, would you be able to relax a little?"

"Perhaps." Though marred by fatigue, Tazel managed a charming smile. "I would benefit from your blessing, priestess."

He held out a hand. Sora came to his side and grasped the calloused appendage. Not the first time they had done this, but every occasion seemed fraught with tension.

"May the Light be your guide," Sora recited, as she had a hundred times before for countless folk, "and may your heart be guarded from the darkness of the world."

Small spots of light flowed from her to him, and though his grip on the staff tightened, white even in the dungeon, something in his gaze became softer. As the spell ebbed, he squeezed her hand; she released upon its conclusion.

"Is there anything more I can do?"

"You'll be outside today, right? If you happen upon any vegetation, it's been too long since we've had anything but rations. I know I would benefit from a good meal."

Sora considered the mountainous terrain. "My cooking isn't nearly as adept as Odessa's, but I'm functional. I'll find something good, I promise."

She left, though reluctant for him to be alone. Mereen had vanished, but Sora supposed if anything went wrong, the vampire could not have gone far.

Sora did not realize how near Mereen truly was until she came upon the entryway of the cursed home—for there, seated in the doorway, her grandmother had become one with the stone gargoyles. The first flickering of sunrise appeared in the distance, not quite reaching the porch. But the light shone near, dangerously so.

And Mereen did not move an inch.

Sora took a step back, content to slip out her window instead, but Mereen's pervasive voice came upon the scene. "I won't stop you."

Not quite an invitation, but Sora did come forward. Mereen's dyed leather had accumulated dust from the dungeon, the white marred by flecks of brown, her blonde hair disheveled in its once-perfect braid. Yet upon her face, Sora saw unmistakable yearning.

"I heard rumors of your resurrection even before I came across you in Nox'Kartha," Mereen said, staring into the distant horizon. "Not every day you hear of the goddess you love granting resurrection to an acolyte, much less a half-elven Fireborn."

They had never spoken of it. They rarely spoke at all. "I avoided attention as much as I could in the aftermath. I did my best to fade back into Staelash and do my job."

The sunlight neared, and Mereen lifted a leather-clad hand toward it, even letting the tips of her fingers touch the dazzling light. Beneath it, her glove trembled. "Tazel was once

312

chosen, but life broke his gentle heart. I did everything I could to keep him near, but it was not enough. I often wonder why Sol Kareena chose such a fragile soul to be her champion. Even now, I curse that it was not your mother instead."

At the statement, Sora became rooted in place. "Do you think she would have done better?"

"I do. Mari's fierce heart would have brought glory unbound—both to herself and to Sol Kareena. Instead, her fierce heart gave her the courage to rebel and abandon her family." Mereen withdrew her hand, though her stare remained forlorn toward the dawn. "I fear you have also inherited that rebellious spirit. You would not abandon us, would you?"

"I have no intention of it," Sora replied, yet a shadow of doubt remained; Odessa's words had sunk deep. "With all possible respect, you're the one who drove me away the first time."

Amid threats of violence, Sora, weak from a broken fever, had gathered what she could before she fled. *"I have no place for half-breed bastards in this house! Crawl back to your swine of a father!"*

Mereen's gaze left the horizon, those blue eyes disarmingly bright. "Grief does vicious things to a person's tongue. It is far too late, but I am sorry. It is hurtful to confess that there is not a single person in my lineage I have not driven away eventually, though a few have returned. Even Eldrin, though . . ." And there it was once more—that twitch in her eye, that chink in her stoic armor. ". . . Though it was cruelly necessary."

It was a story told with admiration among the Fireborns, and in whispers among the elves who knew of her—that Mereen, newly turned as a vampire, had managed to avoid the temptation of eating her toddler son, despite Ayla throwing him at her feet.

But so few knew the tragic aftermath. So few knew that Mereen had left her little boy on the doorstep of a stranger to save his life, for even one moment of weakness would have meant the end. Sora had been young when she learned; Mom had hugged her a little longer before putting her to bed that night.

"I had never thought Mereen could cry, until I heard her tell that tale," Mom had said. *"There's no force on this realm more vicious than a mother with a broken heart. If you are not at Mereen's*

side, you had best be out of her way."

"My mom only ever spoke of you with respect," Sora said. *And fear,* but she did not speak that aloud. She struggled to speak at all, breathless at Mereen's apology. "And whatever else transpired between us when I was a child, I will say this— you lived up to the legend."

Her grandmother's gaze returned to the sunrise, for the line of light crept ever closer. "What a tragedy it was, her death, your sickness. At least she was able to see her home one last time. She was raised in the Fireborn Estate, did you know?"

Since tender years, Sora's head had been filled with stories of elven lands. "I did."

"When this business is done, you should visit. Her grave could use some tending, I'm sure. Perhaps bring Tazel along. He is a sentimental man."

"What about you?"

Mereen remained silent a moment, a quiet longing in her stare. "For seventeen hundred years, I have hunted—and I have failed. Yet victory approaches; I feel the end as viscerally as I tremble in the presence of blood. And soon I shall have to tremble no more." As the sun shifted higher, Mereen scooted back, the tips of her boots at the edge of day. "I am a woman of my word. I shall grant Odessa her payments, for they are small. Revenge and few Demoni plants— laughable, given the magnitude of the service she is doing for the realm. But you must understand, I do not intend to see the Fireborn Estate again."

Sora lost her breath at that.

"I only pray it is enough," Mereen continued, "that my means may be justified by her death, and that Sol Kareena will accept a disgraced daughter back into her light."

"She would. I doubt she's even left you." Yet the weight of it welled emotion in Sora's throat. All her life, Mereen had been a figure on par with gods, a legend who had slain a thousand vampires, who had devoted her undeath to nobility instead of depravity.

Here, Sora beheld a mere mortal clutching regrets and shattered dreams.

"You are kind to say that. Wrong, but kind." Mereen inched back into the shadows. "I will not discuss it more until the time comes, lest I curse myself further. But I did not mean to keep you. Enjoy your time in the sun."

Mereen slipped into the forsaken dark.

Sora stared a moment after her, a new conflict brewing. For though Odessa had implored her to run, Mereen needed her here.

"You owe Mereen nothing."

Sora owed Mereen her very life, for without her, there would be no blood in her veins.

She stepped into the welcoming sunlight, savoring its blessing.

With the cursed dagger, Flowridia carved a point into a broken half of her maldectine bracelet. Shattered at the hinge, it lay in pieces, and Flowridia was unsurprised to find that the dagger didn't dull, even rubbing against the hard stone. Chip by chip, she recalled Thalmus and his glass, how he had formed edges in the delicate material. She was not strong, but the day was young, and a sturdy length of wood notched by the same dagger lay waiting, along with braided grass to attach it all together. Though she had little talent with weapons, she had not practiced for months in the woods with a spear for nothing.

It was crude, but it would do. Casvir would approve.

Sarai kept an eye on the sky, though the cover of trees made it difficult. "So Odessa is your mother?"

"Yes." Though Sarai's question sparked a few more. "How do you know her?"

"She came with Mereen to the river to interrogate me. Mereen sought the knife because she believed it would kill Ayla, so she brought Odessa to torture the truth out of me."

Flowridia's blood boiled at that. "I didn't know she could torture ghosts, but I'm not surprised." Though her focus remained on her task, the stone sharper with each stroke of the knife, memories of Odessa came unwillingly to her head. "You said they want to kill Ayla with the dagger?"

"Odessa decided there was another way. I don't know what."

"Whatever it is, they want me there."

Sarai floated serenely along, though her wary gaze still studied the sky. "Mereen is vindictive. Even if you don't play

315

a part, she'll likely want you to watch."

All Flowridia had seen of Mereen confirmed that image of her spiteful heart—desperate enough to aid her in bringing about Ayla's return for the chance to slay her forever. Yet she recalled the conversation with the vampires in Fallanar, for they had known a very different Mereen Fireborn. "But she wasn't always this way, right?"

"Vindictive? Yes." Sarai's wistful smile juxtaposed oddly to her tears, lost in a memory well over a millennium old. "But if she was on your side, there was nothing that would stop her from tearing out someone's throat for you."

"How did she find you, after you became a ghost?"

"Luck and determination, I think. Survivors in my river spread the word of a ghost who rescued suicidal souls. Mereen followed the legend. She was kind, at first. We confided our sorrows to one another. I . . . I suppose I told her too much. I watched her slowly shift from my sister with a stick up her ass to a warrior who slew vampires, but grief and undeath twisted her into something different." A pause, then Sarai asked, "Was your mother ever kind?"

The words would have once paralyzed Flowridia. Now, she wouldn't say it was indifference, but in the utter and complete absence of hope for love, she was left with both a level head and simmering, quiet rage. "There were little moments, but little moments don't justify the rest. I think she was born good. I'm sure I don't know the whole story, but I know a Solviran prince killed her familiar and raped her. I know it changed her. I suppose I wouldn't be any better." She glanced up to add the rest. "She did kill the man, though."

"As happy of an ending as the story can have."

"I was raised in an orphanage until I was fifteen, but I was forced to run away after I was discovered to be a witch. That was when I met her. Three years in hell, and then I killed her."

Kindness lay in Sarai's gaze. "I'm sorry."

"I'm at peace with it," Flowridia replied, supposing it was true, "though it took a few years. Ayla was . . ." Her words trailed away, for they prompted a more important question. "Do you want to hear about Ayla?"

To her surprise, Sarai nodded.

"Ayla helped me reconcile my feelings for my mother. She was the first person I told, and she told me I wasn't a monster for all the terrible things I did. I was a victim." The sentiment held so much more poignancy now, knowing Ayla's history of abuse. The truth of it struck Flowridia hard. "A monster came to claim me," she whispered, an echo of the past, "and I survived. I needed someone else to say it for me to believe it."

"That's good," Sarai whispered, hesitance in her words and stance.

Flowridia sought meaning in Sarai's countenance, the sudden weight on her shoulders, and asked, "Do you want to hear more of Ayla?"

"If you want to speak, I'd happily listen."

Flowridia moved to tie the two sharpened maldectine shards to the spear, slipping the stone and braided grass into the notches. It held when she shook it, as sturdy as she could manage. "Let's start moving. My mother will come back. We have to be ready."

"Ganat Canyon is near." Sarai pointed south, toward the distant horizon. "There are bridges to cross it. After that, we'll be near Kachul. We can find supplies there."

Flowridia's stomach rumbled, and she grimaced at the prospect of eating crickets again. "How far is 'near?'"

"Two days, if we take time to rest at night."

She could survive on insects until then, though there remained the issue of her distinctive features, especially now that 'Flowridia Darkleaf' had attacked an innocent tavern. Word would spread.

But Flowridia swallowed that fear and took the first step forward. "Ayla and I fell in love quickly," Flowridia said, watching Sarai carefully for her reaction—but the ghost immediately softened to hear it, "though not before an uncomfortable beginning. She hated me because I'd embarrassed her, and she wanted to hurt me. Break my heart; break my spirit. But then she fell in love, even if she hadn't intended to."

The memory was not a pleasant one, of Ayla's tearful confession. But to think of her beloved wife then, compared to now . . . It was as Casvir had once said—Ayla Darkleaf had begun to change. "She told me everything, expecting me to leave. And perhaps it was foolish, but I forgave her instead. I wanted to believe she was sincere. But then . . ."

No matter how many years passed, Flowridia's body still became cold to think of it.

"She was killed. By Sol Kareena herself."

Flowridia contemplated the memory and all that

317

followed. Instead of despair, there came pride. "And I think that's when my life truly began. It's quite the story, certainly long enough for us to reach Ganat Canyon."

"Good. We have a long day ahead of us."

They headed toward the canyon, and Flowridia spun the tale of a journey with a man who sought to become a god.

In pure darkness, a cold aura enveloped every part of Flowridia.

"Flowridia?"

Her eyes snapped open at the familiar voice, and within the swirls of black mist, there emerged a nightmare.

Empress Alauriel smiled with vacant eyes and a torn throat, the smell of her rotting body welling nausea in Flowridia's stomach. "I gave my life to save you," Lara cooed, yet nothing in her tone suggested the late empress—where she had been gentle in life, this phantom's tongue conveyed seduction. "You repaid me by burning my kingdom to the ground. Thousands dead because of you."

Flowridia tried to step back yet found her body frozen solid. Lara came closer, too close, her blackened, raw lips ghosting across her ear. "And you feel nothing at all, do you."

Lara's lips caressed her neck. Her kisses stung like needles. A gruesome hand groped Flowridia's breast, and though she tried to scream, only silence rang. She could not fight. She could not move at all.

"I loved you. You betrayed me."

Flowridia shut her eyes as those hands touched her over her dress, visceral violation rising as they caressed her thighs. Her tears fell. When she whimpered, it came out as only air.

Then, the voice changed, a wicked one melding with Lara's gentle, sultry tone. "Face your sins—"

"Flowridia!"

Flowridia gasped, sweat soaking her body, tears falling from her eyes. When she sat up, her head spun, but she gripped her knees and sobbed.

The darkness parted for ghostly blue light; there floated Sarai, whose hand came to touch her cheek. It brought an icy burn. "You were thrashing in your sleep."

Flowridia wept into her hands, a wash of grief falling upon her. Her body remained cold, mind shrieking though it had all been a lie. "I saw—I saw—" She clutched her body, Sarai's light her only comfort. "It was so vivid." Realization struck like a slap to the face. "Did it become darker?"

"Hard to say because of my light. I was watching the sky until I heard you move."

"I think . . ." Flowridia sought the memory of voice, the words—*"face your sins"*—a nightmare. "I think it was Izthuni."

Sarai's countenance fell into grief. "He can't hurt you. If he could, he would have already. But it seems he can torment you. Do you want to talk about it?"

Flowridia frantically shook her head.

"Lie back down. I'll stay beside you and sing, all right?"

Flowridia obeyed, falling upon the cushion of her hair. The hard ground did nothing to soothe her. She curled into herself and trembled.

But Sarai joined her, her ethereal hand miming calming gestures upon Flowridia's skin, the gentle touch of ice a welcome distraction. Flowridia's mind filled in the rest, imagining a comforting touch.

"I used to sing at weddings," Sarai said sweetly. "Would you like to hear a love song?"

Flowridia nodded, supposing anything was better than her virulent thoughts. Behind each blink, Lara's visage awaited, mocking her with her presence.

I saw the world in hues of grey
My heart was just as dull
Until the day you came to me
And entranced my very soul . . .

The words became a tranquil stream, soothing Flowridia's addled mind and soul. Despite her best efforts to stay awake, her eyelids became heavy . . .

And she awoke to chirping birds and distant sunlight.

Chill had seeped into her bones. Flowridia rubbed her arms as she sat up, shivering in the fresh air.

Beside her, Sarai serenely watched the sky, a smile upon her lips. "Good morning. Did you sleep better?"

"Yes. Thank you." Her stomach rumbled, and Flowridia sighed as her dry mouth struggled to cough out words. "We'll reach Kachul tomorrow, you said?"

"If we get started now, yes. I think we'll be at the canyon within the hour."

"You don't happen to know if there's any water near, do you?"

Sarai shook her head as she floated up, miming standing. "Only what cuts through the canyon itself. But you won't want to go down there."

Though her body ached, Flowridia forced herself to stand, head swimming from the motion. With her spear in hand, she followed as Sarai led. "Hopefully, we can find some charity in Kachul. Or at least a cozy prison cell. They feed you in Sun Elven prisons, right?"

Sarai scoffed as they wove their way through the trees. "Well, yes. But let's try to avoid prison, shall we?"

Perhaps if she was imprisoned, word might spread. Casvir could find her, if he still sought her.

"Yesterday you were going to tell me about a wedding," Sarai said, interrupting her flow of thoughts. "The queen of . . . Staelash, I think you called it."

Marielle and Zorlaeus' wedding—a memory tainted by a kiss with an empress and all that followed. Lara's vision assaulted her, the cruel phantom from her nightmares lurking behind her eyelids. "I would rather not today. But I can tell you . . ." Hesitation came with her next words, a question too. "Do you want to hear more about Ayla?"

Such tenderness in Sarai's features, to hear the precious name. Flowridia still couldn't decipher how she felt about it. "If it isn't too strange to you, then yes."

Was it? This woman knew her wife intimately, was still loved by her in the broken recesses of Ayla's heart. Yet the Ayla of a thousand years ago was but a shadow of the Ayla who walked the realm now. Sarai didn't love the woman Flowridia had married.

And Flowridia wondered, like a chill upon her skin, if she would have loved the Ayla of all those years ago. Her romantic heart said yes. Yet introspection made her wonder.

"What do you know of Ayla now?" Flowridia asked, her tongue finally catching up to her thoughts.

"Mereen taunted me on countless occasions regarding the Scourge of the Sun Elves' crimes. I know enough." They left the expansive forest, coming onto an open field. Sarai's translucent blue hue became washed out in the bright sunlight.

In the distance, Flowridia saw the barest edges of what was surely Ganat Canyon, a great gash upon the world. Magnificent, and despite her hunger and exhaustion, Flowridia yearned to see it.

Sarai's words were cold, however. "May I ask . . . what you think about all of it?"

A dangerous query. Chills rose along her spine, but Flowridia had processed it well enough. "I don't condone it. But I love her, and true love means acceptance. I can accept it even if I don't like it. At the same time, I think the most rewarding part of being her partner is watching her grow as a person. It's incredible, to think of the woman I met compared to the woman I married. Ayla has so much to overcome, but I watch her choose every day to be better than her past.

"What about you?" Flowridia continued. "You loved Ayla then, but she was still . . . She *had* killed those other children." She hated to speak it aloud, her motherly instincts strong even in the absence of a little one to love.

It brought the harsh memory of her bargain with Casvir—which she promptly shoved aside.

Sarai floated serenely along, resignation upon her countenance. "I ended my life because of this question. I'm not ready to face it. And I still haven't processed what it means, to think I was manipulated into murdering her. So I can't speak for that either." She slowed, her floating figure no longer feigning touching the ground. As though regressing back into the spirit by the river, floating along the stream. "I think that saddest truth of all is that my greatest regret isn't killing her. It's that I couldn't save her.

"I *can* say the Scourge of the Sun Elves was a depraved monster," Sarai continued. "And no matter what Izthuni's part in it, I still did it. I created her. I didn't genocide my people, but I'm still the reason my entire culture died."

"That's not true—"

"I don't want to hear about that Ayla," Sarai interrupted, her voice wavering at the name. "But I would like to know about the Ayla who fell in love again."

"You still love her, though," Flowridia said, for there was no question of it. "Doesn't it hurt to hear of her loving someone else?"

Sarai's smile was tragic but true, her beautiful features masked behind sparkling tears. "All I want is for her to be happy."

As Flowridia studied the woman before her, seeking to understand, the truth unsettled her very foundation. This was kindness with no shadow. This was charity without bounds. In matters pertaining to Ayla Darkleaf, Sarai had been selfless from the start, and were there justice in the world, she would have her prize—which could not even be called that. There had been nothing to earn.

Yet Flowridia, selfish to the core, had won.

"I could tell you of our wedding, if you'd like," Flowridia offered, and with that same sorrowful smile, Sarai gave a small nod.

But as Flowridia took her first breath, a shadow passed far too near.

The only warning.

Large talons sank into her shoulders. Flowridia screamed, flailing as the monster yanked her from the ground. Blood bloomed across the white chemise. Flowridia gripped her spear as a lifeline. Above, Odessa's transformed visage hid behind a beak and feathers, her familiar's shadow made manifest.

The canyon appeared, the vista a magnificent sight. Her pulse might deafen her, no thoughts except *flee*. The green glow of maldectine offered hope, this weapon's purpose hopefully not wasted.

She plunged it upward—into Mother's stomach.

The owl that was her mother screeched. Not human, not beast—some unholy amalgamation. Odessa flapped those great wings, yet the ground came ever closer. She banked away from the canyon, her hold on Flowridia waning—then gone. Flowridia tumbled as she hit the earth, feeling nothing besides the pulsing adrenaline in her veins.

Sparse grass covered the ground, the cliff's edge dangerously close. Odessa crashed, the spear impaling deeper into her core. She remained a monster, and when she ripped the spear from her stomach, feathers and flesh fell with it. She coughed. It expelled blood. "Damn you, Flower Child."

Only one maldectine half had emerged from her stomach. Bits of bloodied, severed string dangled from the stone.

Though bruised and battered, Flowridia stumbled into standing, catching a small glimpse of ghostly light rapidly approaching—but not fast enough. As Odessa heaved another cough, Flowridia darted forward and managed to grab her spear before the monstrous bird could right herself.

"I feel nothing," Odessa muttered, and the voice was not merely her—something deeper melded with it, perhaps the owl. The monster met her eyes—this same wicked woman who had stolen years of her life, who had murdered Aura, who had taken her wife—and clutched her stomach, pressing into the gaping wound.

Flowridia kept a readied stance, spear held in defense. Mother seemed helpless. Was she helpless?

Another cough. Blood dripped from her strange mouth, staining the feathers around her chin. Yet it remained Mother, that malevolent stare unmistakable. "You were always a clever little bastard—"

An awful gurgling sounded from her throat. Odessa leaned forward, blood hurling from her mouth and stomach.

Flowridia did not dare to move, paralyzed at the gruesome image. "I'll ease your passing, if you ask."

"A mercy?" From Odessa's mouth came blood and a weak cackle. "No. I shall grant one to you instead. My final gift—to die by my hands instead of Mereen's."

The monster's feathers spread wide. With a final shriek, she charged.

Years ago, Flowridia had wielded a spear against a necromancer far more powerful. She stood firm in the path of the beast, bracing herself for impact. At the final moment, she raised her weapon, then pivoted.

Flowridia dropped to the ground as Odessa drove herself through the spear. The witch's momentum did not cease.

Flowridia braced herself against the ground, inhaling dust in her heaving breaths as Sarai's figure became clear—

Until claws snatched her leg. Flowridia felt sharp rock—then air.

In the gnarled grasp of her progenitor, Flowridia tumbled off the canyon wall.

Once, Flowridia had jumped from an airship, her survival unassured. The fall had been exhilarating, the world gorgeous as it spread boundless beneath her.

But now, nausea lurched in her stomach. Flowridia twisted, her mother's body falling under her. The beginnings of transformation occurred, the owl disappearing to become a woman once more. From the corpse, the ghost within was thrust out, and Flowridia watched a figment claw the air and split in twain—an owl as one; a hated woman as the other— and shriek as both pieces faded away . . .

The ground struck.

Upon impact, Flowridia felt nothing, simply stared at the dead woman beside her—Odessa's vessel, free of its inhabitant. Flowridia's vision became white, then black, and finally blurred as she took a single, heaving breath.

Pain seared through her body. She screamed, yet heard nothing.

"Flowridia!" A friendlier ghost appeared, her words muffled, as though underwater. "Oh, by the Sun—keep your eyes open! Just stay awake!"

Amid her silent screams, Flowridia glanced down her body—only to see bone.

"Your leg is, um, a little mangled," Sarai said, stark panic in her words. "Both of them, actually."

Flowridia forced herself up on her elbows, horrified at the bone jutting from her thigh, her other twisting at an angle too violent to stem from her hip.

Tears streamed down her face, mingling with the blood dripping from her head. "Sarai, I . . ." Her words faltered, the pain only rising. "*Fuck*, I'm dead!"

"You're not dead. I'm dead—"

Flowridia howled, and Sarai's words were lost.

Glinting just out of reach, Flowridia caught sight of Izthuni's knife.

Darkness coated her soul at the thought, but what choice did she have? She would die here of exposure, infection—or perhaps simply from pain. Though her vision blurred from tears and blood, Flowridia reached for the dagger, only for her hand to fall. "T-The knife . . ."

Sarai's ghostly hand passed through it. "Y-You want to— Flowridia, no—"

"I don't *want* anything!" Flowridia managed to scoot a mere twitch before the pain in her leg exploded anew. Her scream echoed across the canyon, the river before them carrying it away.

Her words faded as a beam of light shone from around the bend.

The approaching figure was both miracle and man, accompanied by a foreign beast Flowridia had ridden upon, years ago. His impossible appearance could only be fate, or perhaps the surest of luck—for she had known he'd come this way. She'd known he explored the elven lands, seeking a dragon he called 'daughter.'

Soliel met her gaze, his confusion fading into horror. He ran the rest of the way, his strange steed following behind. "Oh, gods," he whispered, falling to his knees beside her. "Lie down. I have to set it. Scream all you need to."

Flowridia did not hesitate, clinging to this unexpected savior. New pain ricocheted across her body. A pop sounded like gunfire. Warmth seeped down her leg.

"Just a few moments more. Try to breathe."

Radiant light shone even through her eyelids. Flowridia sobbed at the final coursing of pain, then simply at the memory of it.

Her blood thumped wildly, but her breath came without pain. When she opened her eyes, she stared upon bloody but solid flesh.

Trembling, she curled into a ball, adrenaline manifesting as further tears.

"Thank you, kind sir," she heard Sarai say. "You wield Sol Kareena's power."

Flowridia nearly laughed at the understatement.

"I do." The Old God's haggard visage held concern. She had never seen him so close, curious at the subtle lines upon his face. How did a god age so starkly? "Flowridia, let me help you sit up. I want to check your head."

With his assistance, she sat, forcing her breath to steady as he inspected her hairline. "Look at my finger," he said, and when she obeyed, he sighed. "There's bruising in your head. May I lay my hands on you?"

Trepidation rose to replace her panic, but she nodded. Large hands settled upon her hair. Dirtied and tired, the God of Order looked nearly as mortal as any other, aside from his unnatural stature. His golden hair hung matted upon his head, weighed down by sweat, and now blood stained his worn clothing. But warmth filled her head, radiating through her body, and dizziness she hadn't recognized faded, leaving her vision solid and bright.

He lingered, and in the wake of the healing wave came . . . calm.

When he pulled away, her breath came easy. "Thank you," Flowridia said, the only sign of trauma her blood-soaked chemise.

His weary smile was familiar, and despite her hatred of his morals and quest, she had never been so grateful to see him. "Let us pray you have no infection. That requires a different kind of help than what I can offer."

"Do you two know each other?" Sarai interjected, floating down beside Soliel.

"We do," Flowridia said, resigned to tell the tale. "Do you remember me telling you about the God of Order and his quest for the orbs?" Flowridia motioned with a flourish to Soliel.

Realization flashed across Sarai's features. "Oh. How . . . interesting."

Her confusion might've been humorous, had Flowridia not recalled that, last Sarai had heard, he had slain Valeuron. And she knew none of the rest. "He and I are at an understanding."

Soliel chuckled fondly, and Flowridia grimaced to hear it. "That is a good word for it." His eyes fell upon the knife, brow furrowing with it. "What is that?"

"An evil dagger," Flowridia replied, unwilling to mince words. "This is Sarai. She's attached to it. She's not evil, just a guide."

Soliel reached to grab it; Sarai stiffened but made no move to stop him. "An abomination," he said.

"I'm accepting advice on how to destroy it, but for now, it's more useful traveling with us."

"Your wife wields Silver Fire. She could absorb the magic and be done with it." Something in Flowridia's expression must have spoken the truth, because Soliel frowned and added, "Where is your wife?"

"What a lovely twist of fate—I finally know something you don't." Flowridia looked to Sarai. "You'll be amused to hear that he has quite the grudge against Mereen."

"You know my sister?"

Soliel's confusion seemed permanently etched. "Mereen has a sister who is a ghost?"

Perhaps fate truly had been twisted—never, in all her cursed interactions with this man, had she seen him so lost. "It's a long story," Flowridia said. "But what matters is Mereen captured Ayla. She has a small but powerful team, and they . . . they killed Demitri too. I have nothing. Sarai and I are trying to get to Kachul and charter passage to Nox'Kartha."

"You are many leagues from Nox'Kartha." Soliel frowned at the corpse beside them. "Was this a member of Mereen's 'team?'"

"Yes." Flowridia did not elaborate. Shock hadn't let the death settle. "I can't thank you enough. If you can spare a few rations or coins so we can get to the capital—"

"Forgive me if this is news to you, but you are not pregnant. I would have felt it."

Oh, she had forgotten that. "I never was. It was a ruse. If Casvir thought I was pregnant, he wouldn't retaliate against me to hurt Ayla."

Oddly, Soliel seemed to accept this, his amusement apparent on his rugged features. "A wise plan. Be that as it may, your travelling plans will take months to enact. Where will Ayla be by then?"

The words struck a blow. Flowridia considered her quest; she considered the distance. She sought Kachul and Nox'Kartha, for what choice did she have? "Presumably wherever Mereen is."

Soliel studied her bloodstained self, then gazed upon Sarai, surely noting her tragic end. "I have many questions still." His attention fell upon his camel. The knobby creature, loyal and inquisitive, watched idly from beside the water. "But I will take you to Kachul, if you wish."

"What?" Despite the generosity, her entire world

threatened to upend at those simple words. "Why?"

"Because your quest is hopeless, but perhaps no more hopeless than mine. I am here, so I may as well help. We will travel together to Kachul. The Sun Elves may not worship me, but they will not undermine me. From there, we will travel until—"

"No, no—your reason isn't good enough." Flowridia cut herself off, realizing rudeness was unacceptable given the circumstances. "I apologize. Soliel, I'm incredibly grateful for what you've done. You have literally saved my life. But you have no reason to abandon your quest to help me. I trust you with my life, but I don't trust *you*. So, explain yourself."

His scoff only fueled her frustration. "I am offering you the chance to save yourself, and you would turn it down for spite? You are inexplicable."

Flowridia prayed her glare was vicious enough. "I don't think my terms are unreasonable. I simply wish to know why. You can't use me as a bargaining chip for orbs this time, so what is it?"

"You are not in a position to negotiate."

Though she seethed, she bit back her threatened anger. As she contemplated her next words, Sarai spoke up softly. "Do you mind if she and I discuss this a few paces off?"

Soliel agreed. Flowridia followed Sarai away from where the God and his camel awaited. "Last I heard," the ghost said, "this man tried to kill you in the woods and slew his son."

"His crimes reach far higher than that," Flowridia replied, for Lara's death remained fresh in her mind.

"Would he kill us if we tried to run?"

"He would think we were fools, but he's shown he has a vested interest in keeping me alive." Flowridia glared back at the man waiting beyond, his focus with the creature he doted on. Such a gentle man in his quiet moments. A pity he hadn't offered that same care to Valeuron.

"Why?"

How Flowridia despised that question, the mere thought irking her anew. "I don't know. He has heavily implied that in the future, Ayla holds some influence in the fate of the world, but he won't say anything more of it. He says to tell me my future will take it away—which is frustrating given the many times he's alluded to my impending death. His interest in me is strange but not . . . creepy, if you follow."

"You don't have to accept his aid, but I do see the merit.

I can lead you, but he can protect you. I have no doubt Mereen will send someone else once she realizes Odessa won't be returning. It may even be Mereen herself who comes."

Mereen had undermined Soliel before, managing to detour him from capturing her, even stealing an orb from his possession and leading him on for weeks . . . but he held more power now, for better or worse.

"Mereen will come," Flowridia echoed, the phrase sending a chill down her spine. "I'll try and swallow my hatred."

"For Ayla," Sarai said, the words weighted and true.

"For Ayla."

They returned. Humility was not her strong point—not anymore—but Flowridia swallowed her pride. "I accept your aid. Thank you."

Soliel kept near his beast, but approval fell upon his visage. "There is no trick, I swear." He dug into one of his saddlebags and withdrew what appeared to be an oversized shirt. "You may decline, but your clothing is covered in blood."

She accepted it wordlessly.

"I will leave you alone to change. Once you are done, tell me everything you know of this team Mereen assembled. If this corpse is any indicator, they may come for you again."

Soliel led his camel away. Sarai glanced between them, following Soliel at Flowridia's beckoning.

Flowridia stripped from her bloody chemise, horrified at the gashes from Mother's claws, and cut a strip from the bottom to tie around the waist of the oversized tunic, easily a dress on her small figure. She cut a second strip to wrap around the cursed knife, replacing its temporary sheath.

As she tied the makeshift dress together, Flowridia's eyes froze upon the corpse. Not Odessa's body—some unfortunate soul worn by a ghost as a shell. Yet while it was not Mother, it bore her memory.

The maldectine remained embedded in her stomach, still tied to the spear, but though Soliel had not presented his orbs, they were present upon his person. And whatever worth the stones had, it was not worth the risk of the Old God finding it—and masking his presence.

The maldectine would stay behind, its final act one of salvation.

Flowridia had cried enough for Mother, had yearned for her love but resigned herself to a lifetime without it. She had even mourned her death, yet Mother had returned as vengeance itself. Flowridia felt no sorrow; instead, simply . . . finality.

A chapter closed, three years of hell paid for—or as much of that debt as her abuser could return. "I can mourn what you weren't," she whispered to the body, recalling a sentiment from years ago, "but I can't mourn what you were. Goodbye, Mother. And good riddance."

Soliel and Sarai waited by the camel. Flowridia took another step upon a strange and perilous journey.

Countess Windfall, heir to Highland Estate, requested a clandestine evening with me. I do not know quite in what capacity, but I am prepared to entertain her.

She was a gentle lover and asked that I be gentle too. I indulged, curious to know her purpose. Is it strange to admit I cannot stand to lower my guard around women? At least men are honest in their depravity; women are snakes, content to strike when your eyes are closed.

She finally did reveal her price, though it was not what I expected. Requested I bite her while we fucked— and I obliged. Tasted sweet, like her perfume. I cradled her at the brink of death, found it endearing. Strange, that just when I think my heart cannot feel, it pangs in odd moments. I nearly would have called it love until she begged me to make her like me. Told her it was torturous. Told her she would never stand in sunlight again. She claimed she didn't care—she was much more afraid to die.

When I asked her of her husband and child, again she did not care, insisting that the child was better without her. Her husband was cruel. Told her my price—once she was turned, she would bring me

their heads, lest I hunt her down. She agreed. A
bargain is a bargain.
  No loyalties. No love in this world. I am tired.

Sora wondered if it were masochism or her own cursed curiosity that kept her turning pages in this awful journal. Sol Kareena would not approve, but Sol Kareena did not know her thoughts.

Though . . . the reminder did set her on edge, but as she gathered the will set it aside, she spotted a familiar name.

As much as I despise her, I am impressed by the
ingenuity of Mereen Fireborn.
  The Coming Dawn and I shared a violent
altercation in my own bedroom. Flirted, of course, bid
her to join me, said if she were so insistent, to simply
ask and I'd oblige. No, no, it came to blows. She
thought to catch me off guard—poorly, or so I
thought.
  Meanwhile, Mereen awaited in the shadows,
prepared with a sword and a sharpened stake.
Jumped me when my back was turned—managed to
shove the stake into my heart, but she did not succeed
in chopping off my head.
  I ran them out. They escaped.
  Is it even possible for them to succeed? I have
removed my own head before. I have ripped myself to
pieces. No matter how hot the flames rage, I cannot
seem to become only ash.
  I wonder what it would be like to burn and
become nothing.

Though Sora braced her stomach for more, unmistakable motion from below prickled at her senses. Sora set the book aside and glided on silent feet to the stairs.

"She should have been back by now."

The words sunk like a stone. Sora crept down, mindful of the creaking steps.

"You'll enlist Sora to stay by your side. I know you tire, Sunshine. Do whatever you must to keep on. When I return, I hope to have this business done with quickly. Then, we can rest."

Sora stepped faster, not caring if she were overheard now. "Wait!" she cried, and in the entry hall, she found them.

Mereen stood spectacular in her white leather, braid flawless in the hints of light, whereas the presence of sunlight only enhanced Tazel's disheveled appearance. More cave creature than man, his skin ashen, face gaunt and weary. Shackled to that damned staff, he had gone far too long without reprieve.

"What happened to Odessa?"

"I don't know," Mereen snapped, "but I hope to find out."

"There's no way Flowridia could have hurt her. We should give Odessa more time."

"Do not forget, Flowridia has not only outsmarted her before, but killed her before—without magic."

"What if she returns and you're gone?"

"Then she helms the next phase of our plan as I had hoped, and I eventually return unsuccessful."

Panic rose. Sora could not name its cause. "But—"

"Sora, in this family, we do not deny the truth just because it is inconvenient."

Mereen hadn't blinked even once, her stare demoralizing. Sora's fist clenched behind her back. Gods, she hated what Mereen could do to her.

"You could send me instead," Sora said, but already Mereen shook her head. "I'm an excellent huntress. Then you don't have to abandon Tazel. If anything happens, you're better equipped to protect him."

"True on all counts, but what would take you weeks might take me hours if I know my destination in Sha'Demoni. Days, at most. The shadows don't love me, but if I'm on my own, I will succeed. Don't forget where you inherited your talents."

Sora had nothing to say, simply watched as Mereen slipped into a shadow and vanished without a trace.

Tazel seemed small as he clutched the staff, a child lost without his mother. Sora could not protect him; they both knew it.

Be that as it may, she came up beside him. Her feelings lay behind a dam; her question would break it. "Do you really think Odessa is dead?"

"I don't know."

Sora's tears came fast, and she did not understand them, could not explain why she cared. She shouldn't; she couldn't. Yet the first of her sobs sent her stumbling against the wall. She shoved aside her tender, awful feelings, lest they consume her—yet consume her they did.

"She can't be dead." Sora barely felt Tazel's embrace, hardly heard the kind words he whispered as she fell into sobs. But Odessa might be dead, and Sora could not even offer a prayer to mourn her. Sol Kareena could not know. Her goddess would not seek salvation for Odessa's soul.

Oh, goddess—would she wander the Beyond alone for eternity?

"She was a friend to you, I know," came Tazel's soothing voice. "And perhaps it truly is nothing. Perhaps Flowridia is adept at hiding. I would believe it."

"I wish Mereen would let me go. If Odessa is out there, I'll find her."

"I won't stop you if you want to follow."

If Mereen sprinted in Sha'Demoni, she would be miles away. "I would never catch Mereen in time."

But why oh why did it matter? Odessa was wicked. The world was better without her.

Tazel held her, one of her few remaining relics of family. Yet it was nothing to the touch of Odessa's hand. Amid her tears Sora realized, perhaps, that her own small world had been better.

I see right through you, you poor lonely child.

"Before she left," Sora said, desperate for answers, for stability in heartbreak, "Odessa begged for me to leave, but . . ."

Odessa had *seen* her, had drawn back the curtain covering her darkest truths and shown them the light.

". . . I didn't even say goodbye." Sora ached too much to say anything more.

"Why did she beg you to leave?"

"She wouldn't quite say, only that I wasn't . . ." Strong enough? No, her first words of Odessa would not be cruel. "Only that she feared for my soul."

"Impressive, to actually find decency in this world," Tazel replied. Through her tears, she heard his exhaustion, felt it seeping.

The memory of old words came, and Sora swallowed fresh grief. "She was more than decent. She was my friend."

The word rang as a bell in the ensuing silence, damning and true.

Tazel groaned; vacancy filled his expression. Sora tried to pull away, but his grip had become iron. "Tazel?"

He went lax, his countenance twisting despite his glazed

333

eyes. "Do you ever wonder what it would be like to burn and become nothing?"

Sora opened her mouth but shut it just as quickly, the statement far too familiar. "What do you—"

"I don't know," he snapped, his rapid blinking bringing lucidity once more. "I . . . I-I'm sorry. I need to sit down."

He left too quickly, that horrible staff meeting Sora's eye as he rounded the corner.

Chills crawled up her arms. Amid her tears, Sora recalled the damning words: *I wonder what it would be like to burn and become nothing.*

But the shadow of grief hung too low for her to contemplate the full implications of magical feedback. Instead, she ran to her room and locked the door. There on the windowsill was Leelan, who chirped at her entrance. He flew to her hands; she clutched him to her heart.

In private, Sora's tears flowed anew, softer now as she forced the ancient window to open, coughing at the puff of dust. But the blessed breeze was worth it, the mountain air bringing hope despite the awful aura. She took her pipe from her pack, a pinch of dried Spore, and that sleek brown feather.

With her private indulgence, she sat upon the windowsill, absorbing the view of the mountains. Immediate relief filled her soul as she breathed the sweet smoke. She gazed upon the sky, searching . . .

Such was the way of her world, to attach herself to those who vanished.

"*But why do you have to go?*" Sora had asked, at nine years old. "*You always go!*"

"*And I'll always come back,*" Papa had said. Yet he'd hesitated, holding the reins to his beloved horse, the pack at its side carrying his polished armor—armor she had never seen him wear. "*Sora . . .*"

Heartbreak twisted his expression—even then, she had recognized it—as he looked to her mother behind her. "*I'll be back in six months, for your birthday. I haven't missed one yet, have I?*"

Sora shook her head, though tears spilled down her eyes. "*And perhaps . . . perhaps then I can explain.*"

He hadn't returned. Sora had never seen him again.

Caught in the cloying fog of smoke, Sora withdrew her beloved locket and gazed upon Papa and Mom's faces, both eternally frozen in smiles.

She had forgotten Meira's smile in time. Would she forget Odessa's too?

Sora shut the locket and tucked it away, searching the horizon through misted vision. Though implored to leave, she lingered. Her family needed her. Surely Odessa would understand . . .

But Sora's heart spoke the bitterest truth: Odessa was gone.

Sora stroked the feather and descended into tears.

In a haunted world of black mist, Flowridia wandered an aimless path. Cold crept along her skin, like icy fingers from the void. She shivered, then called, "Hello?"

The void replied behind her back. "Flower girl?"

Flowridia gasped and spun around, stumbling away from the half-giant. With vacant eyes, no sight at all, Thalmus came forward, nevertheless.

"All I ever did was love you," he said, yet no matter how far Flowridia ran, he was only a step behind. "All you ever did was run."

"No!" she screamed, whirling around at the accusation. "That's not true!"

His arms wrapped around her. She fought, but his strength held no bounds. "I watched you become a monster. I couldn't save you."

His embrace became a cage. "Thalmus, let me go!"

"That is what you said, isn't it. You said I was not your father."

Gods, the regret punctured like a knife.

"All I ever did was love you."

Tears welled in Flowridia's eyes, along with fury, as she struggled to escape—but he crushed her tighter, tighter . . .

"All I ever did was love you."

"Thalmus, please."

Then came that horrid melding of voices, the earthen rumble joining with Thalmus' lighter tone: "Face your sins."

"Flowridia!"

Light washed over them; the Thalmus figment screamed—

"Flowridia!"

Though night still reigned, Flowridia awoke to dual hues of light—blue and gold. Sarai peered from above, fear upon her lovely countenance.

Soliel knelt beside her, his golden glow casting aside all shadows. "Flowridia, are you all right?"

Tears stained her face, mingled with sweat. Flowridia wrenched herself into sitting, wiping her face on her blanket. Reality descended, along with memory: she was traveling with Soliel now. They had set up camp when night fell. She had eaten. She was warm. She was safe here, against all odds.

"When you started convulsing, Sarai informed me that you have been having nightmares," Soliel continued, "but what I sensed was not natural."

"It's Izthuni." Flowridia wrapped the blanket around her, ashamed to be so vulnerable before the man she hated. "He's punishing me for turning my back on him."

"That fits his character."

Though she hated to be near Soliel, his light brought comfort.

"Do I dare ask what you did to earn the wrath of The Lurker?"

Flowridia wrapped the blanket tight around herself, haunted by the lingering curse of Thalmus' embrace. "I trusted Sarai instead of him. I don't want to say more than that."

Silence settled. Soliel remained a stable presence, yet Flowridia's mind would not relax, instead bombarded with the memory of this man rising from a crater of black sand, healing from the brink of death, bringing his knife to Lara's throat, and—

"In Velen'Kye," Soliel said softly, "you asked me of Casvir's phylactery. Why?"

"Because you told him—"

"No, no—why for you?"

There was nothing to lose from the truth, and Flowridia swallowed a choking sensation as she considered the price of her bargain—and the cause. "I need him dead. I made a bargain, but I can't fulfill it." She didn't say it was Soliel's fault, in a way. There would be no need to bargain for Lara's soul if Lara had lived. "But I can't back out either. Ayla's plan was to slay him."

Gods, the truth stung like a lash. To say she did not love Casvir was a lie. At her lowest, he had helped her to soar. He was a mentor, a confidant, and despite it all, she supposed he loved her too, in his arrogant way. And here she was pleading to Lara's murderer for help killing the man who had given her everything.

"Do you often break your contracts with gods?" Soliel asked.

Flowridia supposed it was a valid question, when stated in those terms. Not that she would admit it. "If you knew, you'd understand."

"Perhaps." His visage remained kind through it all, despite his despondent words. "Flowridia, I truly have no inkling to where his phylactery might be. I can tell you where it was not, if you would like."

"Anything helps."

His gaze became distant, falling upon the shadows beyond the bounds of his holy aura. "It is assuredly not in Sha'Demoni. Magic from this realm attracts demons. We enlisted Ku'Shya's servants for help, but there was simply nothing.

"I highly suspect it is not in Celestière," he continued, quiet acrimony settling upon his face. "It is a broken world, and while to lose something in the mists is final, no one knows where they lead. The phylactery could be in danger, and he would never know.

"He is not a man who gives his power away, nor would he give any hint of weakness to those around him—so it is not in any extra-planar space, because he cannot reliably reach those on his own. If it involved any spells outside his repertoire, it was the kind of spell one can purchase. Wherever it is, he placed it there himself.

"What haunts me most is the knowledge that wherever it is—it is near. He would not risk it being abandoned where he could not reach."

Flowridia considered his palace and those many catacombs. In witnessing Khastra's torture, she had seen but a glimpse of its many secrets. Built into a mountain—so how deep did it go?

"I did not know him on any personal level," Soliel continued, "and so my thoughts end there."

"It saves us the trouble of scouring Sha'Demoni." However, her mind still dwelled upon Nox'Kartha's Palace and its depthless mysteries. He had constructed a secret labyrinth below a secret bathroom. Anything was possible. "Did you ever look inside Casvir's palace in Nox'Kartha?"

"Among countless other places, yes."

Defeat colored his words, but Flowridia could not shake the notion. "If Ayla and I find his phylactery, you would stop your quest to separate the realms."

"I would."

"Then why not help us?"

It was no surprise when he shook his head. "You are still desperate for me to abandon my quest."

"Don't ask me to give a proper answer to that. You've made me conflicted—congratulations."

He laughed, but she kept her glare. "What are your loyalties, Flowridia?"

"To Ayla. She's all I have left."

"I cannot besmirch you that, given she is your spouse."

They lapsed into silence, though it held no peace. Flowridia recalled one truth, though could not say if it were comforting—that if Soliel's future was true, then Ayla's fate surely did not end with Mereen.

Or perhaps it was not a comfort at all. "I'm not keen to forget that Ayla would apparently kill herself to run from her fate. Does my quest to find her have anything to do with that? Should I abandon everything?"

To her surprise, Soliel did pause at that, his stare toward the distant stars above. "I do not believe there is any connection, and if that has been plaguing you, I do apologize."

"I don't know how else any reasonable person would act. This is my wife."

He looked to the earth, his soft eyes the same hue as the rich dirt. "If I can offer you any peace, it is that you would be proud of all she does—both in villainous pursuits and in altruism. Whatever my own feelings on the matter of Ayla Darkleaf, there is no question that she does right by you."

Though it led to more infuriating questions, she supposed it did help. "Was she one of your allies in the fight against Casvir?"

"In a way, yes."

In a way . . . She slumped, too exhausted to discern what it meant.

"Do you think you can sleep again?" he asked.

"If you stay near enough for your light to banish the shadows, yes."

Flowridia returned to her bedroll, her mind buzzing from his tales. "*You would be proud of all she does*" could only mean Flowridia was not there.

"Is my death truly so inevitable?" she said aloud, for despite all she had lost, despite her broken heart . . . she did not wish to go.

Demitri might be in the afterlife. But what of Ayla?

"You make me wonder that myself, at times."

Flowridia struggled to reply to that, until a blue light grew before her. Confusion lay upon Sarai's pretty features, but she said nothing of it, simply ran her ghostly hand along Flowridia's hair—emotionally soothing but holding the cold touch of death.

"I also have questions," Sarai whispered, "but I don't think it would comfort you to ask them. You should sleep."

Flowridia nodded, warding off tears.

A lullaby trilled from Sarai's lips. To Flowridia's surprise, she knew it—Ayla had hummed it a time or two in quiet moments at home.

In breathy, choked tones, she joined Sarai in the gentle song. Quiet joy softened Sarai's pretty features. Flowridia clung to her solace.

An eerie feeling set Flowridia on edge as they approached distant ruins.

The evening trailed a pleasant day, the sun having been bright and bold, with the breeze cool enough to balance it. Yet the sunset did not silhouette a grand city—instead, ancient ashes upon a flat landscape. Flowridia sought civilization but found nothing. "This is the capital?"

"This is Kachul, yes," Sarai said, wistful and soft. Her tears never ceased, but there was something truer to them now. "Or it was."

"I know less than I should of the history of The Endless Night in these lands," Soliel said, leading his animal by a loose bridle, "but I recall learning that it destroyed the capital city in a night, massacring every citizen it could find. Maagi has been the capital for over a thousand years."

"Then I have led you wrong." Sarai clutched her ghostly form, those sparkling tears falling faster.

"You have not led us astray," Soliel replied, as though to

soothe a despondent child. "This is not even a detour. We simply have farther south to go."

Flowridia's heart ached as they neared. A millennium had passed, yet a pervasive feeling of sadness remained.

Plants had overrun this forsaken place, sprouting from the ruins of stone structures. Mostly grass, but a plethora of moonlilies lay among them, casting beauty upon the oppressive terrain. Flowridia knelt to pluck one, savoring the small bit of peace it brought. How precious, this reminder of her love, the blue a perfect match to Ayla's eyes before Silver Fire had pulsed through her veins.

"Chaos Tears," Sarai said, fondness in her words. "Mereen used to cultivate them in her front yard."

"Across the sea, we call them moonlilies." Flowridia attempted to string the stem into her hair but struggled to find an opening amid the matted locks. Frustrated, she ripped a hole in a particularly matted sector by her scalp, wincing in pain, but managed to thread the stem through. Yes, the flower was large and audacious, but today she didn't care.

"The legend says they sprouted following the Goddess of Chaos' first heartbreak, an homage to someone she dearly loved."

Flowridia looked to Soliel, who, to her surprise, also bent to pick his own. "Is that true?"

He placed it as an emblem upon his armor. "Yes."

"But it couldn't have been you."

Thoughtfulness stilled his words. "When Demitri died, did it break your heart?"

Though said in kindness, the words struck like a blow, the reminder enough to choke her. "Yes."

"Not all heartbreak is romantic."

Flowridia followed when Sarai led, mulling it over as she asked, "But if she comes in the future, how are the flowers here now?"

"The sorrow and regret never left her. When we were sent back to the beginning of the world, she created them to heal her loneliness. She was a Goddess of Creation in a literal way and could breathe life into more than dragons."

Any mention of dragons stirred unwell in her gut, to think this man had slain who he might've once seen as a son— or perhaps still did. She thought of old words from the Old God: "*I loved her, and at times, she loved me too.*"

"You've gone through considerable trouble to get her

back."

He said nothing, merely scanned the horizon.

"Would you sacrifice her to stop Casvir?"

Nothing changed in his demeanor, but subtle signs of anger rose beneath his skin, felt only on the wind. "I wish I could say yes."

Beside her, Sarai floated leisurely along. How strange, Flowridia thought, to think Sarai had done the very opposite— and condemned the world. Yet Soliel would condemn his quest for his own selfish heart.

Flowridia did not think aloud, lest Sarai be hurt, but was there any cause she would sacrifice Ayla for? Her very soul reeled at the thought.

The final flickers of sunset disappeared over the horizon, but between Soliel's effulgent light and Sarai's ghostly hue, Flowridia kept her footing through the ruins. "Is it safe to stop here for the night?"

The answer came when Soliel's camel suddenly grunted and lurched. As Soliel calmed the beast, Flowridia peered into the darkness, pulse spiking to see light reflected back—from predatory eyes. "Vampires," she whispered, and Sarai came close to her side.

"He can protect you, right?"

Soliel's camel became increasingly erratic, fighting against her bonds. He murmured calming words, his patience never failing, but Flowridia feared to get too close, lest she be kicked in the head. "Hush now," he soothed. "There's no danger if you stay."

The creature yanked. Shadows shifted beyond the bounds of light, coming nearer. Sarai held up pacifying hands as she approached. "Let me try something."

A gentle tune trickled from her lips, a faint whisper upon the wind. Flowridia barely heard it, but the camel kept eye contact with the ghost as her movements steadily slowed.

Soliel dropped the rope; the camel stayed put, mesmerized by Sarai's song. He drew his sword instead. "Stay in my light. They cannot harm you."

When one vampire came near enough for light to reflect upon his face, some flash within Soliel's satchel illuminated. His sword caught flame. "If you value your life, you will turn back. I am the True God of this world, and this woman is under my protection."

And to Flowridia's relief, the vampire took cautious steps

back.

Click.

Flowridia's breath seized.

A great *boom* tore across the night.

Soliel cried out, blood spurting from his neck. He fell to his knees, hand clamping over the bullet wound.

In the moment of confusion, a gloved hand gripped Flowridia's collar. *"Hello, sweetie."*

Flowridia failed to escape, tugged beyond the line of light.

"Mereen, no!" Sarai cried. Behind her, Soliel struggled to rise, not dying but certainly wounded.

Flowridia pulled Izthuni's dagger from her makeshift belt, but Mereen's reflexes proved faster. "I have so many questions and no hope to find answers." Mereen ripped the knife from her grip. She threw it to the ground. "As well as no wish to risk her interfering."

"Flowridia!" Sarai cried, and Flowridia heard the first violent note of her banshee scream.

"Sarai!"

The world changed. Flowridia no longer faced a shrieking ghost or desolate ruins. Instead, she stood in an alien world, the purple sky revealing the shift in planes.

"Sarai!" she screamed, but it was no use, the words lost in the sprawling world of Sha'Demoni. When Mereen tugged her along, she followed from pure shock.

Silence settled between Flowridia and Mereen as they traversed the world of Sha'Demoni.

Flowridia did not know their destination, nor could she find a way out of Sha'Demoni without Mereen's assistance. So she bided her time, occasionally stretching the ropes around her wrists, slowly loosening the loops.

Yet the loudest part of her said her world would crumble.

Her legs burned as they climbed a mountain in the alien realm, the plants shuffling to move as they passed. Were they truly alive? Did they react to necromancy like the plants in the mortal realm?

There was no hope to know. She had no magic. She was helpless.

Mereen stopped partway up, her keen eyes surveying the landscape surrounding them. "Close enough." Mereen tugged on her rope, sending Flowridia stumbling into her arms.

Though Sha'Demoni had been endless light, they appeared in the shadow of a mountain blocking the moon's silver glow. Night air caressed Flowridia's cheek, sending a chill across her skin. As her bearings returned, she summoned all her strength. She pulled from Mereen's grasp—

Only to gasp when Mereen's claws dug into her arms. Blood welled. Fangs grew from Mereen's lips, eyes becoming black. "Nothing funny, sweetie. I can make this so much worse for you."

With her nails piercing Flowridia's skin, Mereen dragged her along. Only then did Flowridia see the great building before them.

Dilapidated and worn, the mansion did not look quite near collapsing, but it might within the decade. The stonework on the outside had crumbled in parts, though darkness obscured most of the damage. Mereen dragged her up an ancient porch, toward a set of doors—which she kicked open with her foot. "Sora!" Mereen yelled, the sound echoing through the entryway. Flowridia's eyes failed her, staring only into enveloping blackness, but the sound of footsteps signified that someone had heard.

Light shone from beyond the hallway. Sora appeared, a holy spark held in her hand. "You found her."

Mereen withdrew her claws, then shoved Flowridia to the floor. Flowridia landed hard on her elbows, skin stinging against the cruel stone. "Take her." Mereen stumbled back. Flecks of blood stained her fingernails. Only then did Flowridia recall her vow against feeding. "Where is Ayla?"

"In her coffin."

"Keep her there. Lock Flowridia in an empty cell. Tazel will know which one."

Mereen dashed out of the foyer, disappearing deeper into the halls.

Flowridia struggled as Sora lifted her to her feet, failing to wrench herself from the half-elf's grasp. "I don't want to hurt you," Sora snapped.

It was not a feeling at all, but knowledge—that she would never leave this place if locked inside. Flowridia struggled, stomping on Sora's boot with her heel.

"Dammit, don't *make* me have to hurt you," Sora said, and her grip did not relent.

But Sora did not, even as Flowridia lost strength with each useless tug. Days of travel, hours of walking today alone, and Sora dragged her down the hallway, then toward a foreboding set of stairs.

Flowridia froze at the precipice. "What is this place?"

"The Mountains of Kaas."

History books of long ago, ones she had shared with Tazel Fireborn, had spoken of a place of nightmares—where Ayla Darkleaf had once set up her home.

"Why are we here?"

Sora did not answer.

Flowridia took each step down the stairs blind, her eyes ill-adjusted. A gallows march; a lamb to the slaughter.

Their feet touched the bottom. From the half-elf's hand burst holy light. "Tazel!"

From a distant room emerged a wraith.

Flowridia knew Tazel well, had found him a comforting friend during her more difficult times of mourning. Yet this was not the same man who had come to greet her at her wedding. This man was haggard and pale—paler than even six years in a library had done. Sunken eyes; hollow cheeks; a sickly creature. In his hand, he held a frightful weapon—Staff Seraph deDieula.

The demon's skull watched with empty eyes, yet Flowridia felt its stare like an omen. "In here," Tazel said, not meeting her eye.

Flowridia did not fight as Sora led her forward, heart thumping in her chest as they passed what appeared to be ancient prison cells. Dusty and worn, many with doors showing signs of rust, a few bearing evidence of ancient bones within. With each step, her dread rose, yet she sought signs of Ayla in every shadow.

Flowridia was shoved unceremoniously into the final cell. A large room, and the light in Sora's hand revealed a table—significantly newer than anything else in this building. Upon it waited what appeared to be a dagger in a sheath.

Sora withdrew a knife from her sleeve and cut Flowridia's bonds. The ropes coiled like snakes upon the floor.

Wordlessly, Sora stepped back. The door rattled as it shut.

Only then did panic fall upon her. Flowridia rushed to the door, a barred window letting in the distant light. "Tazel!"

The man did not turn, but Sora did.

"Please, whatever Mereen told you, I . . ."

Her words trailed away at the horrid truth—that whatever Mereen had told them was true.

But Sora waited. She had to say something. "I have powerful friends. I can pay you."

Sora studied her pleading countenance a moment more, then tore her eyes away and followed Tazel. They disappeared into a different cell, drenching Flowridia's world in darkness.

"Please!" she cried but was met with merely the void. Flowridia sought a seam along the door, a knob, a lock, yet found nothing. Exhausted, she felt her way to the table, managing to find the sheath—and then withdrew the dagger.

Not one she recognized. It likely bore no magic at all, nothing special about it. With care, she felt the sides, confirming it was sharp. This had been deliberate . . . but why leave her with this?

"I see you found your weapon."

Flowridia gasped and whirled around.

Mereen's leather and skin practically glowed in the minimal light, a specter of white. Flowridia held the knife aloft, prepared to stab.

"No need for fear, sweetie. Not from me. Though this may be the last time we speak."

Mereen lingered by the opposite wall, coated in shadow. "Welcome to the Mountains of Kaas. Before Ayla was locked away in her coffin, this place was synonymous with her presence. The Sun Elves still refuse to climb this mountain for fear of bringing evil to their homes, but you don't care about that, do you? This is practically a honeymoon home to you. A little worn down, but there is beauty here if you look through the lens of a monster—and I assure you, Flowridia Darkleaf, one who would marry The Endless Night is a monster."

Flowridia remained stiff.

"You've gone through so much," Mereen continued. "Losing your familiar, traversing the wilds—more than any little girl should experience. You've proven yourself clever. Congratulations. You killed one of the most powerful witches to walk this realm and convinced my nitwit of a sister to help you. I am so impressed, and since I am no longer tied to Odessa's terms, I shall offer you a single mercy: a full pardon. Do as I ask, and you shall walk free."

The hairs on Flowridia's arms rose in warning, the ones on her neck following suit. "What do you want from me?"

"I want you to kill Ayla Darkleaf."

The statement panged like a drum against her heart. "No."

"Of course you would say that. But she won't stop you. She won't even see it."

Anger surged at Mereen's indifference. "Why in the world would I possibly kill my wife?"

"Because you're the only one who can."

The words meant nothing, yet some aspect rang true, like a shriek lost in the wind.

"Ayla was cursed through Sarai," Mereen said, her tone sensuous and sweet. "I wondered if the knife was the key, but it can only create. Not destroy. To destroy, you must fulfill the terms of the knife's curse. It is not true vampirism. Those cursed by the knife create true vampires with their bite, but vampires do not create creatures like Ayla. The knife creates something different; vampiric, but the undeath is a curse—one that can only be broken by intention. Whatever motivation drove that dagger through its victim is what will destroy them—and in Ayla's case, it was love. The weapon does not matter—only the one wielding it.

"It was why Izthuni could not kill her as a mortal himself or enlist some hero to curse her in violence and hate. A pity, for my work would be so much easier. He anticipated enemies, those who would seek to destroy her. She is immune to all that. Ayla can only be destroyed through love, for he never anticipated her loving again. And she didn't, for seventeen hundred years."

Mother had often bemoaned the vagueness of curses, the spirit of the law far more important than the letter. All of it fit with Izthuni's wicked mind. All of it completed the puzzle of Ayla's longevity, her immortality.

Flowridia held the key to end it all, and Ayla had never even known. "I won't do it."

"Of course you won't. But let me lay down some rules, just in case."

Flowridia knew the dark would not hide her trembling from this predator. Surely Mereen heard the rapid beating of her heart.

"As I said, if you kill Ayla, I will let you go. I will even deliver you to Nox'Kartha, or whatever destination you choose. Or I shall slay you painlessly, if you wish, if you cannot live without her. Consider the greater good—not that you ever have before.

"If you kill yourself, woe be unto Ayla Darkleaf. Your fate shall be hers instead. If you somehow succeed in escaping—again, your poor bride. You'll imagine well enough in time. Otherwise, you will die here, whenever fate decrees you go. Might be tomorrow. Might be today. Or it might be years from now, as a wrinkled old hag. And then it is as I've said—poor Ayla. She has gone through so much already."

"What have you done to my wife?" Flowridia said, bolder at that. Her spirit might yield, but not for her wife.

"She is physically unharmed."

"Mereen, answer me."

But in the darkness, Mereen shook her head. She stepped back into the darkest parts of the cell, scarcely more than an outline. "The choice is yours. You know my terms. In the meantime, reap the consequences you've sown. It is the least you deserve."

"Mereen—!"

"Good night, little girl. Now the nightmare begins."

Flowridia threw the knife with all her might, only for it to clatter against stone.

Mereen was gone.

In the ensuing silence, Flowridia trembled in the dark, spotting phantoms in the corners of her eyes. They remained when she shut them, mere figments of her mind.

Kill Ayla? No. Mereen was mad to even propose it.

Nearly as mad as the parameters of the curse. Ayla could only be killed by someone she loved? Outlandish. Impossible.

Yet gut instinct spoke of its truth. Curses were as cruel as they were vague.

Flowridia took careful steps back to the wall, finding comfort in having something solid behind her back. Her breathing danced across the stone, echoing her muted terror. Was this Mereen's plot—to drive her mad from isolation? She might succeed in that. With each blink, details in the darkness became clear, finally able to decipher the shapes of the stones in the wall, the table, even the dagger in the far corner.

"*Keep this one alive, they said,*" came the whisper on the walls.

Flowridia's heart jolted at the words. "Ayla?"

An unmistakable figure sauntered from the shadows, her skin and fangs aglow, her black eyes reflecting the light. "Simple enough," Ayla whispered, and those vacant pupils consumed what little courage Flowridia still held. Not a speck of silver or blue, though Ayla's voice held enough ice to compensate. "I've kept hearts beating for weeks without a vessel. What harm could I possibly do to you?"

Her laugh was maniacal glee. Flowridia yelped when a vicious hand gripped her hair, dragging her. She clutched the wrists of her captor, her love, desperate to relieve the pain. "Ayla, what—"

Cold metal slammed her forehead. Pressed against the table, Flowridia could not speak for shock, freezing when something sharp touched her back.

Metal caressed metal. Fabric ripped. The chill of the underground cell assaulted Flowridia's bare back as Ayla cut the tunic from her body.

Ayla tore the rest aside, leaving Flowridia nude. "You're too thin to make a perfect specimen," Ayla said. Familiar hands stroked along Flowridia's skin, yet there was no devotion behind it, no sensual intent. Flowridia shivered, tears welling in her eyes, but then came a hitch in Ayla's breath.

"Ayla, I don't understand—"

Ayla gasped and twisted Flowridia's hair. Pain tore through the sensitive nerves of her scalp. Flowridia bit her lip to keep from crying.

"Much too thin, too tight to your bones," Ayla said, a strange monotone to it. "A few weeks of starvation will loosen your skin."

Flowridia said nothing. Surely this was a dream, a nightmare. Mereen had called it that, yes?

Metal sang anew, cutting what sounded like flesh. The pain in her head vanished, tension releasing. Perhaps she was free. Perhaps this depraved prank had run its course.

"Beautiful. I'll embroider it into a gown."

In the faint light, Ayla tied a knot around a thick bundle of matted auburn, the moonlily falling to the floor.

Flowridia's breath came shallow. Her blood turned cold. Nausea grew as she reached to touch her hair, her precious hair, but found only short, jagged ends.

A nightmare, yes. It had to be. Yet she shook as she tugged on the chopped locks, breathing erratic. Tears welled in her eyes. A sob wrenched from her core. It could not be. It could not be real. What little hair remained could not even be gripped in her fist.

Merciless hands grabbed her wrists. Flowridia batted them away—

Only to be stopped by a sharp slap on her face.

The skin tingled, residual pain pulsing. Flowridia trembled as she touched the raw skin, numb as the shears rained the remaining locks to the floor, cutting her hair to the scalp.

Flowridia's voice was hardly more than a sob. "What are you doing?"

"It is best you don't know beforehand," Ayla said—the sound of her love yet crueler than she had ever heard. "Wouldn't want you to panic. Panicked hearts are more difficult to keep beating."

Unbidden, a memory came of a mutilated figure on a slab—whose throat she herself had slit—disassembled, hardly a person. And there, in the center, a raw, exposed heart, kept beating by some melding of dark magic and science. Inscribed gently in the sinew was a precious name—*Flowra*.

Flowridia's shock melted into fear. "You don't know me."

"I intend to know you intimately before the end, darling."

The shears left her head. Flowridia touched the remaining fuzz, reality slowly descending.

She tried to run; Ayla yanked her back by her throat.

Flowridia struggled, no match for her unholy strength. Ayla forced her onto the table, held her down with a knee on her chest as she reached below the table and lifted leather straps.

"What did they do to you?" Flowridia cried, desperation driving her words. One strap tightened around her wrist. "Ayla, you must remember me!" The second latched around her opposite one. "Say my name, please! Flowridia Darkleaf—your wife!"

As Ayla's nails scraped against the bare skin of her thigh, again came that hesitation, that hitch, the still before the storm.

"Ayla, say it. Flowridia. My name is Flowridia—"

"Yours is a face I could fall in love with," came the mocking reply. Ayla's visage leered, shrouded in the dark. There was no recognition here, no memory of the woman she loved. This was a monster. "Perhaps I'll cut it off and frame it."

"Ayla, please, no."

Ayla ignored her, instead hopping to the ground. More straps were hidden beneath the table, these ones for her ankles.

"I don't know what they've done to you," Flowridia said, her tears falling fast, pooling on the metal slab beneath her. "But you know me. You married me—"

Her sob stole her words. Ayla tugged her ankles tight against the table.

Flowridia choked on her tears. She managed to gasp the precious name. "Ayla—"

She yelped when that dreadful face came near in a blink. Too near. Here she saw Ayla's disheveled hair, falling in limp strands, her black eyes bespeaking madness. Thin fingers grabbed Flowridia's face, squeezing her cheeks. "Speak again," Ayla cooed, "and I'll stitch those pretty lips shut for good."

Mere inches away, and Flowridia surged up with all her remaining strength and kissed those precious lips. Her tears fell as Ayla's tongue slipped into her mouth. Desperate, she kissed with all the passion she could muster, praying it conveyed what words could not. For this was real. A kiss was no nightmare.

Ayla suddenly recoiled. The monster's pupils receded, revealing precious silver. "You smell so . . ."

She cried out, lurching as though in pain, then ducked away and disappeared into the shadows.

Silence. A draft of air blew through the room. Flowridia remained frozen, bound far more by fear than the straps. Her breath echoed across the stone walls.

Footsteps shuffled beyond the door. Did she imagine the faint flash of light?

Elsewhere, water dripped . . . dripped . . .

A sharp prick cut her sternum. Flowridia screamed at the monster's return, at Ayla who knelt upon the table, studying her naked body with vacant eyes. Blood pooled beneath the scalpel, a searing line splitting Flowridia's skin. She shrieked, terror far surpassing pain.

Ayla set the scalpel aside, then licked along the split line. How obscene, her ensuing moan, and Flowridia wept—for this was a nightmare, but it was no dream.

Blood dripped from Ayla's lips. Metal sang against metal as she withdrew something new—something larger. It glinted in the faint light.

At the first touch of blade and bone, Flowridia screamed.

"We nearly lost Ayla. This bespeaks an ill omen."

Sora sat in a dark cell, unable to face Mereen and her clinical words. Sickness twisted her stomach, and Tazel fared no better, it seemed. Within the box beside them, a monster lay dormant. But along the walls, there echoed the memory of screams.

This was the hurricane Odessa had foretold.

"I didn't anticipate . . ." Tazel wavered, clutching the staff as a lifeline. But Mereen waited, her stare relentless as he struggled. "The response."

"You have spent days reeducating Ayla's mind, and you didn't anticipate her fighting? What this tells me is you haven't

S D SIMPER

broken her enough, but we don't have time."

"I did my best," Tazel snapped, jarring Sora from her self-pity. Never had she heard anything so virulent from the man. He calmed then, more akin to what Sora recognized. "If I break her mind entirely, she won't have enough of herself left to torture Flowridia."

So this was Mereen's master plan. To torture Flowridia until she was too weak to resist slaying Ayla Darkleaf herself— or until she died a horrible death, and Ayla was brought back to witness the aftermath.

And then be subjected to the same.

Sora knew it was justice, knew it was right. Yet sickness struck her down to her soul. *Sol Kareena . . .*

No. The goddess could not see this. Shame flooded Sora, even as she clung to the mantra of the greater good.

"Pity," Mereen said. "And a pity Odessa is gone. Hopefully, this business will be done quickly, Sunshine. We are nearer to the end than the beginning. The girl will crack."

Sora felt Mereen's stare but kept her own fixed to the floor. Not even insects crawled along the walls. Nothing dared live in this cursed place. "You will be Flowridia's guardian," Mereen said. "You will be stationed outside her door by day. I will take over at night."

But Sora was weak, so weak, and shook her head. "I can't live in darkness."

"Then I will put a torch in the hallway. Go check on her and see that she lives. Heal whatever is left so she is fresh for next time."

"What about infection?"

"Let's hope nothing has set in."

Mereen would not accept a no. Sora managed to stand, unable to meet anyone's eyes as she left. The walk through the lines of cells twisted as her imagination ran rampant, fueled by screams far too recent. Images of blood and torture played through her head as she glanced between the bars of each, for the history of this condemned place had never felt so near. Even with her summoned spark of holy light, the haunting aura did not relinquish.

Sora peered through the bars of Flowridia's cell, her magic casting stark light within.

Blood on the floor. Blood on the table. Blood on the straps hanging beneath. All of it coagulated, sticky and fresh.

Sora had to adjust the light to find the motionless body

352

on the floor, naked and sprawled. Like a cross on her chest, horrid stitches marked the damage done. Enough blood covered her to hide the extent of the carnage, yet any fool could see that she had gone through a torturous affair.

The door did not lock, but it could only be opened by a mechanism on the outside. Sora twisted the low knob and entered the gruesome chamber.

Flowridia was either dead or asleep. When Sora knelt beside her, she did not stir. But a touch upon her warm skin confirmed she was alive, as well as the pulse in her wrist.

With care, Sora placed a hand on an untouched part of her sternum and sent sparks of light into her body. The wound sealed around the stitches, but it was more important that it sealed at all. Sora felt deeper damage right itself, cracked bone knitting together, minor lacerations within her organs healing like new. But it was not quite right—the bone was displaced, the skin held ugly scars.

But Flowridia breathed easier, her lungs rising and falling with no hesitation.

Beside the table, stained in blood, ruined clothing lay in a pile, a flower beside it. Sora gathered the cloth, cringing at the fluid, and returned to Flowridia's side to place the driest parts beneath her shaved head.

Sora backed away, only then noticing the blood staining her trousers, seeping through to her knees. Yes, there had been days in her youth spent splattered head to toe in animal blood, treasuring the time with her father in the aftermath of their hunts as they cleaned the meat, but this was humanoid. This was . . . still alive.

Where Flowridia's clothes had been, something tiny glinted in the light.

A ring.

Sora picked up the delicate piece, heart panging to realize what it was, what bond it represented. It would only be ruined if it stayed here, already saturated in blood. Sora slipped it into her pocket.

When she shut the door, she collapsed against it, sliding down to the floor. If this worked, a monster would be put to rest forever.

"To stare upon them is to know they're staring back."

The light in Sora's hand extinguished, and she cowered in the dark, fighting nausea.

"*Mom?*"

Flowridia ran through a vacant void, each labored breath searing pain across her ribs. But the ache was nothing compared to the desperate tugging in her soul. She sought him. She sought . . . her.

"*Mom?*"

"*Flowridia?*"

She knew them both, but dark fog covered all. "*Demitri?!*"

Her voice echoed across the abyss.

Softer, she said, "*Aura?*"

When the oppressive loneliness threatened to crush her fully, three golden eyes peered from the mist. Aura, her mentor, her friend, whose desiccated body still smoked from necrotic magic. And Demitri, her boy, the dearest piece of her heart, bled from his skull, blood dripping from his shattered eye socket.

There was no safety in their presence. The hair on the back of her neck rose in warning, in tandem with their ominous growls. "*My friends—*"

"*I waited for you,*" *came Aura's voice, dark and feminine, wise and assured.* "*I searched for you. And you lured me in, only to let me die.*"

The words cut as deep as her heart, for they were what she had told herself in the months following. "*No, it wasn't me. It was my mother—*"

"*You couldn't protect me,*" *came Demitri's voice, boyish and sweet, childish and adored.* "*I always protected you, but you didn't protect me.*"

They circled her, stalking as predators would. "*That isn't . . . Demitri, you know I would have tried.*"

"*You didn't take the bullet.*"

"*You have forgotten all I taught you,*" *Aura said.* "*I steered you toward light, yet you have embraced dark. How could you.*"

"*Mom, we were in a bad place. You should have known.*"

"*How could you.*"

"*You should have known.*"

Flowridia's tears fell, obscuring the vision of the wolves circling closer, becoming a blur. "*I . . . I'm sorry.*"

She screamed when they lunged, shocked as great teeth tore into her flesh. Ripped apart; Flowridia shrieked as Aura swallowed the bite whole. Demitri's jaw sank into her stomach, consuming her entrails. Crunching bone sounded like gunfire. Her dismembered limbs were strewn about. Flowridia became nothing, nothing at all.

Amid the rising pain and shock, there echoed a refrain in her mind, their voices conjoining with a darker third one: "Face your sins, face your sins, face your sins . . ."

Chapter 18

"Imperator, I think we are nearing what are you are describing."

After several hours of hiking through a dense and far-too-living jungle, Etolié celebrated the offered reprieve.

Sha'Demoni was pretty in a murderous sort of way. Filled with untamed foliage—though the foliage moved, and Etolié instinctively tucked her legs against her floating form as the next thicket of creeping plants crawled away to evade them.

The sky hadn't shifted, and Etolié was quite certain by now that there simply was no night—it would explain the oppressive heat. Though by and large immune to temperature, her illusionary clothes hid the swamp of sweat her body had become.

Rather than risk exercising, her wings had gently floated her along. Beside her, her poor horse struggled with a sudden descent, its boney legs slipping on loose pebbles. Thankfully, it had no feelings, but Etolié's habit of emotionally attaching herself to random objects—and this certainly counted as an object—betrayed her this day.

"Come on, ya stupid animal," Etolié said, but she considered her abuse affectionate. "Casvir and I have a quest to do, and my comfort hinges on you not snapping your leg."

"I can acquire a new mount if necessary," came Casvir's voice.

"No, because I've imprinted on this one."

At the base, Kah'Sheen stopped and surveyed the land. "It is safe to phase out of Sha'Demoni here." When she offered a hand, Etolié wiped her own sweaty one on her skirt before accepting.

She was bombarded by dry, cool air.

Sha'Demoni had been colorful at every turn—but here, the landscape nearly resembled the world across the sea, bearing shades of grey. Yet there was no mist, no incorporeal figments. It was simply monochrome. Even the sky had greyed, as though filled with virulent clouds.

Something about it pinged as familiar in Etolié's head, but she could not name it. "And this is where the necromancy led—"

Oh, shit.

Amid the grey scene, the dying trees were sparce upon the horizon, the ancient stone ruins too crumbled to study. But it was not the view that swelled familiarity within her, but a pulsing, vibrant magic, a brewing semblance of *something* in the air.

Chaos' grave. But Etolié would have bet a considerable amount of Khastra's money that the staff wasn't what brought them here.

"This place feels odd," Casvir said, but before he could march ahead, Etolié stumbled in front of him. "I beg your pardon—"

"This is a terrible place. I've been here. It's supposedly the grave of the Goddess of Chaos, and it's a big bag of bad news so we should just leave." Etolié grinned just a little too wide, so she opted on illusioning a more stoic expression.

Casvir's frown suggested it had worked. "What kind of bad news?"

"The sort of bad news that means a staff?" Kah'Sheen asked, looking warily about.

The issue with lying, of course, hinged on Etolié having a lie to tell. "No. The sort of bad news that means, uh, imminent death."

"From what?" Kah'Sheen asked, not exactly being helpful.

"The legend doesn't say."

"But you are coming here before."

Casvir's expression became increasingly suspicious, and Etolié cursed her inquisitive demonic sister. "Listen, it's—"

Casvir strode forward, brushing past her with ease.

"Fucking dammit—Casvir!"

Etolié again came to stand in front of him, his annoyance quite apparent, though the man did stop. "Empress Etolié?"

"It's complicated. But we shouldn't be here."

"Give me a reason."

For a moment, Etolié contemplated the merit of illusioning Sol Kareena possessing her, just to give this fucker a scare, but perhaps there was power in the truth. "Uluron, the Dragon of Death, is here. And she understandably fucking hates you."

The words meant nothing to Kah'Sheen, all four of her eyes narrowing in confusion. But something changed in Casvir's countenance, that same hunger she had seen in the siege against Solvira—that lust for something more.

"Listen, buddy," Etolié continued, floating up to match his height. He met her eye, not blinking, and she refused to look away on principle. "I don't give a fuck what sort of contract we're under—not one line of it says I have to help you recapture that fine, upstanding lady, and it definitely doesn't say I can't try and stop you. I'm contractually obligated to not kill you, but you bet your ass I'll summon fucking black smog to blind you or make a second dragon for you to fight while Uluron flies away. And you know who's not under *any* sort of contract? Kah'Sheen. I think we both know whose side she'll take."

Casvir glared with those disconcerting red eyes, the subtle shift from annoyance to animosity admittedly quite terrifying to float across from. "You have strong feelings on the matter."

"After Khastra squished you into a pulp, Uluron and I became friends. She flew us back to Staelash. She's also actively guarding not only the Dark Orb but also the Earth Orb. Do you want the responsibility of guarding two orbs from the God of Order?"

"I would happily accept the task of—"

"Never mind, that's a stupid question."

"Empress Etolié, you clearly will not budge. I will not fight Uluron this day. The search for Flowridia remains our highest priority."

His scathing glare remained. Etolié tried her damndest to match it. "You're giving in suspiciously easily."

"I can always return without you."

"Fair enough, smartass." Etolié floated back down, her feet unsettling the ancient dirt, untouched for who the hell knew how long.

Kah'Sheen raised a shy hand, interrupting their spat. "Can the dragon help us? It is your friend."

Etolié thought a moment, considered magic and its

nature, and said, "It's a long shot, but potentially. She has the Dark Orb—if Cassie can't find the staff, perhaps it can point us in a direction. We might as well try, given we're running out of other options." She narrowed her stare at Casvir, her frustration remaining. "And you'll wait here. Kah'Sheen, if he tries to follow me, throw him into Sha'Demoni."

"I can do that."

Casvir said nothing, though his annoyance was palpable.

Good. The man deserved some damn disrespect every once in a while.

Etolié traversed the barren path alone, following her brewing headache. Inescapable, that growing sensation around her, some searching presence rising slowly from the earth. It radiated against her bones, invigorating as much as it caused her head to pulse in pain. This apparent graveyard held true power—no question of that.

When she was out of sight of her fellows, Etolié called, "Hello! Uluron!"

Her voice echoed across the wasteland, as prevalent as wind.

Opting for practicality, Etolié soared up into the air, relishing the aerial view—

And there Uluron was, curled up like a cat in the distance. Unmistakable, that great bone dragon.

Etolié guided her fall. When her feet hit the ground, she ran, deeming this important enough to risk getting sweaty.

When her lungs were burning, the first hints of Uluron appeared on the horizon. "Uluron! It's me, Etolié!"

Glowing purple light filled the dragon's eye sockets. Uluron stretched out her spine, her yawn authentic despite her lack of breath. With feline grace, she slinked closer, no threat in her stance, but Etolié wasn't prepared for the dragon's size—her memory hadn't let her recall the extent of it.

An absolutely fucking massive pile of sentient bones settled comfortably before her. *Etolié, Daughter of Stars,* came Uluron's formless voice. *How strange to see you again. But not unpleasant.*

"I didn't plan on this either," Etolié said, hiding her heaving breaths behind a pristine illusion, "but it may be a stroke of luck. How are you, first of all?"

Quite exhausted. The Great Father has chased me around this continent for months now, and I am frightened of the day he manages to surprise me. But I cannot abandon my Mother for long. I feel her stronger each day. I fear what it would mean to miss her return.

Etolié's heart hurt at that, knowing well how it felt to long for a mother who was not here. "I can't imagine she wouldn't look for you."

I simply do not know. The dragon presented her paw, and within it rested the Earth Orb. In her chest remained the Dark Orb. *But my orbs are safe. What of you? Why have you come?*

"Long story short, I'm on a quest to find a powerful artifact of necromancy, so my brilliant idea was to follow the source of the most powerful pull of necromancy on this continent. You can see how this backfired."

She swore she heard amusement in Uluron's words. *I do.*

"I was wondering if you might be able to offer assistance with that," Etolié said. "My party and I seek Staff Seraph deDieula, which was stolen from Ku'Shya's Realm." No need to mention that she was adventuring with the half-demon who had stolen it. No need to mention Casvir's involvement either. "Can your orb help us?"

Sadly, no. I am sorry.

Etolié withheld a 'damn' and instead forced a smile. "It was worth a try. Thanks."

Do you know anything of its location? I do know this continent. Perhaps I could fly you and your party.

"I . . . will have to politely decline the ride," Etolié said, choosing her words with care. "One of my party members gets . . . just ridiculously airsick. He would puke all over you. But I don't know anything about location. We only know that it's where someone we're looking for is being held captive— which is the other part of my quest, to find her." *And kill the bitch,* but those weren't words one said aloud. "You know her, sort of. The flowery girl Valeuron was going to give the orb to."

Strange, to be scrutinized by the great dragon. Etolié struggled to know if she felt threatened or not. *Flowridia is in Falar'Sol.*

The strangeness of the statement slammed Etolié's words into a wall. ". . . What?"

I passed her in a field. We spoke. Had I known you cared, I would have taken her.

Etolié's hand flew to her forehead, the news startling and . . . useful. "Well, shit. That's still a direction. Thank you."

She claimed to be going to Kachul to find an airship to

Velen'Kye. She had a strange ghost as her guide.

"How long ago?"

A week ago, more or less.

"Do . . . do you think she's reached it by now?"

She was far. I cannot say. It might be worth trying. Are you sure you do not want a ride?

Oh, her better judgment screamed, but there was a time and place for stupidity. "I think my friend can hold in his stomach for this."

I shall forgive him if he gets ill.

Etolié beckoned, frantically thinking through the factors of her plan. "Well, follow me."

They weren't close, but walking gave her time to actually formulate a plan, given she was leading Uluron straight to her former slavedriver. Etolié cursed her inability to whisper messages to her peers like Momma could. Magic and lies this would be.

As they trekked along the path Etolié had taken, she kept her eyes peeled to the horizon, desperately trying to spot Casvir—or Kah'Sheen, given the spiderous demon appeared first.

Goddess Momma, any help you can possibly give would be appreciated.

Etolié placed all the focus she could on the shorter figure beside her demonic sister and illusioned him to be the most boring-looking elven guide she could. Judging by the sudden start from Kah'Sheen's silhouette, it worked.

"I brought a friend!" she cried as they neared. "Uluron, this is Kah'Sheen and, uh—Reginal."

Fuck. Hopefully, Uluron didn't know elven names.

'Reginal' was relatively under-animated compared to Etolié's other creations, her panic dampening her magical luster. Kah'Sheen, however, made no effort to hide her wariness, looking prepared to dart into the nearest shadow should Uluron turn violent.

Is this friend dead?

"Yes, Reginal is an undead guide," she said, as smoothly as she could manage. "Uluron saw Flowridia. She said she was going to Kachul to take an airship to Velen'Kye."

"Kachul is not a place to find airships," Kah'Sheen said. "It is only death."

Etolié looked to Uluron for explanation.

I am simply repeating what she said.

"Be that as it may, she has agreed to give us a ride. Apparently Flowers had a ghost as her guide. Perhaps the ghost was mistaken."

At Uluron's beckoning, Kah'Sheen crept onto the dragon's outstretched claw, her many legs clinging to the ridges. Casvir followed, and Etolié silently praised his commitment to silence.

She looked to the two horses, which stood unbothered even in the face of a gargantuan dragon. "Uh, Reginal, will the horses be taken care of?"

Casvir nodded. Perfect.

Etolié settled upon Uluron's other hand, where the Earth Orb also lay sequestered. "I can't thank you enough."

You have proven your integrity to me. I do not have to understand your quest to want to aid you.

Etolié huddled in the safety of Uluron's claw, stomach heaving as the great dragon took off.

"Hello again."

Sora sat outside the cell door, grateful for the flickering torch down the hall. That cold voice pervaded the air, but Ayla was locked inside. Sora was safe. Physically.

"How is your blindfold? Helpful?"

Faint whimpering sounded from within.

"Gag too tight? I promise to remove it once we begin."

Begin. Sora's blood ran cold, but it was right. It was what must be done.

"My memory is hazy, but something in my mind tells me you've said my name. You know me? Good. My reputation precedes me."

Again came that whimper, the muffled words indecipherable.

"What gorgeous skin you have. I think it's fit for something fancier than a book cover. Perhaps a smart pair of shoes. What do you think? Your freckles would add a lovely design."

Sora grimaced at the cruel implications.

"Sadly, we must be patient. I shall need to keep you here a few weeks first. Starvation does wonders for skin elasticity. But I will embroider something lovely with your hair. Something floral,

perhaps. Do you like flowers?"

Whatever Flowridia said, it sparked laughter from Ayla.

"You smell like flowers," Ayla said, voice dripping with sensual delight. Shivers ran down Sora's arms. *"I wonder if you taste of it."*

Sora heard nothing for a long time. Worry settled. She trembled as she peered through the barred window.

The torchlight cast flickering shadows upon the scene. There, tied upon a chair, was Flowridia, nude and blindfolded, a gag spilling from her mouth. Ayla straddled her, her embrace nearly tender, but a faint dribble of blood down Flowridia's neck revealed her true act, draining her of life.

Flowridia held too much tension to be dead, but how much blood had Ayla taken? A tear dripped down from beneath the blindfold. Sora stepped from the line of sight and banged on the metal door.

"How rude of the world to interrupt our affair," came that rich voice. *"On with the show."*

Sora pressed her ear to the door and heard quiet weeping. Then, scuffling. Clinking metal. Louder cries, gasping terror—presumably, the gag removed.

"Did you know if you rearrange an elf's intestines, they slowly put themselves back together? Little wriggling worms with a mind of their own. Fascinating. I wonder if they do the same in humans." Childish delight colored her laughter, a stark change from her antics of before. *"I suppose we shall find out together."*

Sora had heard Flowridia's screams before, while sequestered in a cell with Tazel. But close now, so close, Flowridia's screams held anguish, tragedy in the pain.

Sora had never understood Flowridia's attraction to Ayla. She did not understand the pull between them, what twisted bonds of love they claimed to share.

But they had married.

They had gone away to live a quiet life.

And with every scream from Flowridia's throat, those bonds of love stretched at the seams. Somehow it seemed the most heinous crime of all.

All through the black void, Flowridia wandered alone, seeking . . . seeking . . . something.

There stood a figure in the distance, gaining detail with every step Flowridia took. Her religious garments were unmistakable, the tabard bearing the sigil of the sun and spear, the crown upon her head a precious treasure—gifted to Flowridia before her wedding, hidden safely in a drawer at home. Lunestra's grey locs were twisted in a thick bun atop her head, her umber skin withered from age, but her eyes—no, those were not right.

Vacant. Unseeing. Nothing moved at all save for her mouth. "You were a miracle. You were hope in my old age, that my legacy might continue."

Flowridia ran to her, yearning for her presence. "Lunestra—"

"Instead, you gave yourself to a monster and betrayed your forebearers. We love Sol Kareena, yet you forsook our name for her antithesis."

The words sliced deep gashes across her heart, severing the blood that bound them. "That wasn't my intention."

"Nor did you intend to kill me, but there was no other cause of death. The blood of our lineage is on your hands."

Tears shone in Lunestra's eyes; Flowridia's were a mirror. "You have destroyed us," Lunestra said, and Flowridia frantically shook her head. "You are our demise."

"Lunestra—"

She gasped when Lunestra's hand shot up and touched her forehead.

Flowridia could not run. She remained frozen solid, even as a potent blend of silver flame and purple smoke poured from Lunestra's hand.

"Face your sins," she said, but it was not her voice—not hers alone, that was.

The magic caressed Flowridia's head, sifting through her thoughts, plucking them out one by one . . .

She became nothing. All was dark.

In the ensuing hours of flight, Etolié had a silent conversation with Momma.

So is it unethical that I lied about Casvir's identity?

Little white lies are just that. So long as he doesn't hurt her, I see no harm in it.

Anxiety filled her, but Casvir hadn't spoken a word so far. Against all odds, the plan moved smoothly along.

Until . . . Uluron spoke. *Daughter of Stars, there is something wrong.*

Etolié peered through the cage of Uluron's clawed fingers as the dragon brought her up to her face. "What's wrong?"

The orbs speak. My Father is near. But we near our destination as well.

"Well, shit."

The idea of Flowers teaming up with the God of Order seemed questionable even for her dumb, betraying ass—given she and Etolié shared one regret, which was his murder of her moonbeam. Could he have captured her? What use would he have for her? Was this merely coincidence?

"Bring me closer to my friends. I need their thoughts."

If all else failed, they were equipped for a fight.

Uluron brought her claw to the other, revealing Kah'Sheen and the illusionary 'Reginal'—the former of whom shivered in violent measures.

"Sheen Bean, what's wrong?"

The half-demon had become a pale shade of blue, her lips and fingers—all twenty of them—especially so. "Very cold. I am not liking cold."

Etolié glanced to the disguised Casvir, prepared to berate his lack of chivalry but noted that all he had was metal armor. Instead, with a mere swipe of her hand, a fluffy blanket appeared around Kah'Sheen, who clutched it tight, engulfing her spindly arms and torso in warmth. "Soliel is close, says Uluron. We need to be prepared for the possibility that he and Flowers are working together."

Recalling that Casvir should be keeping his mouth shut, she continued, "I'm proposing we have Uluron drop us off at the outskirts of Kachul so we can continue alone and survey the scene. I know what you're thinking. A giant dragon would be useful. But while I'm still hoping for Soliel's head on my mantelpiece, our quest is to rescue Flowers. If Soliel has her captured and Uluron is here, he might try to use her as a bartering chip for the final two orbs. He'll be violent toward Uluron, so we can't have her near if we don't want to risk Flowers. Got it?"

Kah'Sheen nodded, and though she felt his waves of begrudging acceptance, Casvir did as well.

Etolié patted a boney finger, longer than she was tall. "Understood?"

I hate to abandon you with him, but I can begrudgingly agree that this is for the best. If trouble comes, can you escape?

"We can, I promise. We can even find you again."

Etolié fought rising bile at the tilt in Uluron's flight, swooping toward the ground.

Peering down, she beheld a great blight upon a plateau surrounded by deep canyons. A few stone bridges connected it to the rest of the world, but the terrain itself appeared different than its surrounding cliffs. As Uluron descended, more details slowly became clear—evidence of rubble, of plants growing among stone that might've once had a purpose. Kah'Sheen had said Kachul was not a place to charter an airship, and now she understood. No one had lived here in many hundreds of years.

He is here. He has surely seen me. I will have to place you and leave.

"I can't thank you enough."

It is my pleasure.

"Why though? You seem pretty fond of me."

The ground neared, and Etolié willed it to slow, to perhaps gain some semblance of answers. *To know your future is to take it away.*

"I mean, I might want that if this really is a cycle. Your words; not mine."

How soothing, the laughter filling Etolié's head. *My Mother spoke fondly of you to my past self. You have lived up to expectation.*

Definitely cryptic bullshit, but asking for more was just punching a brick wall. "Thanks, Kitty."

Again came Uluron's laughter.

Instead of landing, the dragon flapped her impossible wings and levitated as she carefully set her riders down. Etolié stumbled to find her footing, immediately distracted by the dark ambience, but then Uluron's shadow shifted.

Etolié looked to the sky, and already the dragon was flying away—back to her mother's grave.

Her focus withdrew from Casvir, revealing the imperator once more. "Ingenious," he said, though a certain bitterness colored the words.

Kah'Sheen swayed on her spindly legs. Her pallid hue was one Etolié recognized, and her own stomach churned in sympathy. "No judgment if you puke, Sheen Bean."

Kah'Sheen managed a weary *"Mmhmm"* and huddled in her blanket.

Clouds covered the sky, casting the ruins in a melancholic darkness. Etolié's senses prickled in warning. She surveyed the dilapidated scene, spots of green grass and pale blue flowers the only color. "Am I nuts, or . . ."

"There are vampires watching us," Casvir said, his mace and shield already summoned.

The clouds were thick enough to block all sunlight. She stepped nearer to Casvir and summoned armor and a quarterstaff, fully prepared to duplicate them all.

"Can you make us invisible?" Casvir asked.

"They can still smell us. Also, invisibility is actually extremely difficult because I have to illusion the constantly shifting nothing."

"I see the dilemma."

And then he appeared, the most hated sunrise in the sky.

Etolié's knuckles became white around her staff, her trembling unbidden but spiking with her anger. She hadn't stared Lara's murderer in the eye since knowing his crime, and nothing—not fourteen years of watching her mother be beaten and abused, not ten years as a vagabond slave liberator, not years and years of trying and failing to save the world—could have prepared her for the righteous surge of rage coursing through her blood.

She saw red. She felt red. And he'd be a red smear on the ground if she had anything to say about it. "You better do the talking, Cassie, because I'm one word away from cutting a bitch."

Casvir stepped forward. "Good afternoon, God of Order."

Soliel stopped, an unmistakable sight with that golden armor, sword sharp though soiled with grime. She saw no sign of orbs, but her headache meant they were certainly somewhere on his person. The light cast from his head resembled a halo, evidence of his so-called 'divinity.'

But he wasn't alone. The ghost was new. And she wasn't Flowers. In fact, she kinda looked like—

"Do you know Mereen Fireborn?!" she called before she could stop herself.

The ghost perked up, but Etolié froze at the sight of her . . . everything. "Yes. She's my sister."

Those slit wrists were quite the fashion statement, but Etolié knew better than to speak *every* thought in her head. Consequentially, she forgot all the words she'd ever learned and kept her mouth shut.

"Greetings, Imperator, Empress, and Daughter of Ku'Shya," Soliel said, and Etolié's blood fucking boiled. Kah'Sheen said nothing at the title, but she did summon a knife.

"We have reason to believe you know the whereabouts of Flowridia," Casvir replied. "We seek her."

"Then it is not coincidence that brought us all here," Soliel said, and with each cursed phrase, Etolié's struggle to remain silent only grew, in tandem with the temptation to tear out his throat with her teeth. "She was under my protection until Mereen Fireborn stole her. I suspect our motives are aligned. I seek only her safety."

"Indeed. What do you know of Mereen Fireborn?"

"Only what Flowridia told me, which was not much. I know Ayla Darkleaf is also in Mereen's possession—for what purpose, I do not know."

"If you and I both seek Flowridia for the purpose of her safety, it may behoove us to unite forces—"

"*What?!*"

The word came from Etolié, but she barely heard it, certainly hadn't controlled it.

She tore her gaze away from Soliel, directing her rage to Casvir instead. "No. I refuse. I fucking *refuse!*"

"Empress Etolié, this man—"

"*KILLED MY MOONBEAM!*"

With the explosion came furious tears, but Casvir did little more than raise an eyebrow. "You are under my orders."

"This man killed Lara! *He killed my baby girl!*"

"And he is currently a valuable asset in finding Flowridia—"

"Oh, *FUCK FLOWRIDIA!*" Etolié stilled her words long enough to sob, blinded by tears. "Fuck that cunt—she *burned Solvira!* She's a selfish fucking sadist who'd rather let her monster wife rampage across the country than risk growing a fucking moral backbone! I've never understood your fixation on her, but I at least fucking accepted it. But this? THIS?! This is too fucking far. You have some fucking audacity asking me to work with the man who *murdered my moonbeam*?! And who *almost murdered Khastra*?! Who was fighting alongside The Endless Night when it fucking *killed her the first time*?! Fuck you, I won't fucking do it!"

Curse her tears, she couldn't see his damn face. "I will command you."

"No."

"Then I will leave you behind. Thank you for your service on this journey."

Etolié wiped her misted eyes enough to stare into the very picture of indifference. To look anywhere else meant to face Kah'Sheen, who she would abandon, or face Soliel, who would kill her before she managed a single blow. "Well, fuck you too, Cassie. I nearly thought we were friends."

"That was your mistake."

And though the spell she cast was the most complex in her repertoire, though she anticipated being torn limb from metaphorical limb, to the passing observer, she simply snapped her fingers and vanished.

In reality, she ripped herself across unnatural planes, through broken worlds long forgotten. Etolié screamed as she became one with the stars, shattering into pieces as her bones ripped from sinew and sinew from skin—

Until she landed in a peaceful desert scene and vomited into a patch of wildflowers.

"It's just too much, Momma."

Etolié's tears splattered into her tea, but she savored it more for warmth than for drinking. A thick quilt had been tucked around her, the weight of it comforting her agitated heart, while Staella sat on the table in front of her, holding her free hand.

"And just fucking seeing him—Momma, he killed my baby girl."

"I know," Momma soothed, and though Etolié was attuned to the magic Staella wrought, it never ceased to amaze her how the burdens in her soul lessened with each word. They said Staella took on the pains of the world, and Etolié never liked to contribute to that.

Today, though, she threatened to collapse. "He burned Khastra."

"Oh, Starshine . . ."

"I feel like nobody gives a shit about him except me. He's literally trying to bring the apocalypse, and nobody cares! Lara cared, but now she's fucking dead. He fucking murdered her." She paused to sob, safe enough to do so in her momma's home. "I miss her, Momma."

"She's happy where she is, I promise. I told you I found her spirit, right? She has a mother and father who love her in the Beyond."

"You did, and I know, but I'm here without her and it fucking hurts."

"Would you like me to take you there someday?"

Etolié could hardly see from behind the thick mist of her tears, but still she studied Staella's face, seeking any understanding at all. "What?"

"It's a perilous journey for a mortal, but when you've gotten a better grasp on your portal magic, I can take you. I know it's prudent to mourn and move on, but most people don't have a goddess as a mother."

Etolié simply stared, managing little more than a nod.

"I'm surprised Casvir would work with the God of Order."

"I'm not. He has no fucking morals. Perhaps it's better this way, given we were starting to get along. It's not natural." Her scoffing laugh did nothing to elevate the mood, but Momma's smile certainly did. "I feel awful for abandoning Kah'Sheen."

"You had mentioned Ku'Shya's daughter was there, though you didn't say why."

"She's my friend, first of all—well, sister. That's what she calls us, and there is literally no end to how much I fucking adore that. But she's trying to find a staff she helped Mereen steal from Ku'Shya—uh, Ilune's staff, actually."

Etolié didn't have to see straight to recognize the stark horror in Staella's gaze. "Mereen has what?"

"Staff Seraph deDieula."

Etolié hadn't seen her momma go this dim in decades. "This is bad."

"I know."

"I don't think you do. Do you know what it does?"

370

Admittedly no, so she made an educated guess. "It controls the dead?"

"It controls *any* dead, even the ones necromancers normally can't touch, such as vampires or liches. Ilune created it in response to Izthuni creating vampires, in case they ever became a threat to Solvira, but I don't think any of us knew the full extent of its power, besides her. The only undead it can't control is her own blood, if potent, because she didn't want it to be used against her if stolen. If I were dead, for example, I would be safe, but her grandchildren or beyond could still be controlled. But what that all means is anyone wielding it gains the power of a master necromancer, even if they have no magical talent—and if that person is already a necromancer, that power grows beyond comprehension."

Those were not good words. "Fuck."

"None of us knew it was the skull of Ku'Shya's son until Ilune went to trial for Neoma's death. It was actually Khastra who revealed it. And that is why Ku'Shya was charged to keep it—by right of blood and because she has the resources to guard it. No one should have been able to take it."

"Except her own dumb kid with free rein of her house."

"We all have blind spots when it comes to our children. I'm certainly guilty of that. Why would she steal it, though?"

"Well, she's trying to get it back now. That's why she joined Casvir and me—because the staff and Flowers are presumably in the same place. But Mereen has some master plan to kill Ayla Darkleaf once and for all with it, and Kah'Sheen was originally intending to help."

"Mereen can control Ayla with it."

Fucking yikes. For some reason, that hadn't quite pieced together in Etolié's head.

"I'm not asking you to work with Soliel," Staella continued. "If there is any way for you to assist in returning the staff to Ku'Shya, however, I will offer whatever assistance I can. I don't know if it wields quite the same level power as the Dark Orb, but it can do things the Dark Orb can't. The world is in danger if it doesn't have a keeper."

"The world is always in danger," Etolié muttered, her bitterness quite apparent. "I should help Kah'Sheen."

"Perhaps you could break off with her and search on your own."

"But if they get a lead and beat us there . . ." The thought struck her like a bullet to the wing. "Fucking hell, Casvir might try to take it if he gets there first."

Staella, too, stared as though shot. "Oh dear."

Etolié detangled herself from the blanket. "I have to go back."

"What about Soliel?"

The name caused her blood to boil. "I'll just have to rip his throat out."

"That seems like a good way to get yourself killed."

"Momma, after all he's done, I think my life is a worthy sacrifice if it gives the world even a fucking chance of wiping him off it."

Once more, Staella took Etolié's hand and squeezed it tight. "My dearest Starshine, you hold so much anger inside you."

"How can I not?"

"I won't say you haven't earned the right, but that doesn't mean it isn't going to tear you apart."

Fresh tears welled with Etolié's blink. "Nothing is fair."

"No, it is not. And some anger can be healthy if directed to make a change, but your rage is poison, slowly eating you inside."

Though she despised introspection, she held the metaphorical mirror to herself and considered if Momma were right or wrong, if she were hurting herself . . . "I've been angry for a long time."

Perhaps . . . even longer than Lara's death, she realized.

"To let go of rage, you have to forgive."

The words slashed through her tentative good mood. "Absolutely fucking not. Soliel's a fucking monster."

"Etolié, forgiveness does not mean to like or get along with the person who wronged you. It simply means to accept and release your anger. That anger doesn't hurt Soliel. It doesn't hurt Casvir. It only hurts you. And to release it removes the power they hold over you.

"It may take time, and that is completely understandable," Momma continued, though Etolié already sought to reject her kindness, "but anger can warp even the most stalwart of souls. In order to heal from my wounds of long ago, I forgave Morathma. It doesn't mean I like him or spend any time with him; it means I don't spend my energy on him. He's simply nothing, because he holds no power over me. And I will say the same thing of Camdral, though I'm still working on full forgiveness—because it is so much harder to let go when someone hurt someone you love instead of simply you."

Staella squeezed her hand; Etolié clutched hers back. "I should work on that forgiveness thing."

"It's not easy. Many have wronged you. It is the bravest thing you can do, to accept and let go."

Etolié contemplated Soliel and Casvir, but beyond that, she contemplated Flowers, who had become the worst sort of manipulative person, Eionei, who had once been her savior, a supporter, a father figure when she had none, and then her own father, who the mere mention of had once sent her into shakes and despair.

And then there was Momma herself, to whom Etolié had never said those healing words. Deep inside, there were still knots to detangle, but fucking hell—she wanted to.

"How do you forgive?" Etolié asked, for she struggled to envision even that first step.

"You have to let yourself hurt, which you have assuredly been doing, and that is good. And you have to want to move on, though I'm not certain you're quite there yet. It's a process."

Etolié shook her head, lip trembling as she sought what message she wished to convey. "I don't want to forgive Soliel. I'm not ready. It's as you said—he hurt someone I love."

"And that's all right."

"But hopefully, I can push my anger far enough away to stand beside him and get the damn staff. I can do that much for you and the world, I think."

Staella beamed, her wings a lucent glow. "That would mean a whole lot to me. It's a good first step too."

The painful realization rose as well—that Etolié had a whole list of candidates for forgiveness, but none were as pressing as Staella herself. Something blocked her from just . . . *saying* it.

Yet another problem to drink to.

In the small moment of peace, Etolié wiped her eyes, wondering if she truly could align herself with this monster— this monster who had nearly taken everything she loved. Lara's blood stained his hands, and she supposed Khastra's did too, not to mention that he had come to finish the job by burning her alive.

Compared to those things, his quest to separate the three realms seemed like only a small thing.

The living needed her, though—her momma and Kah'Sheen. But could she stand by his side for them?

"I'm going to go back," Etolié said, no enthusiasm in the phrase at all. "If I can't do it, I'll grab Kah'Sheen and come back here. We'll go our own way."

"Normally I can't just find people, but the God of Order has four orbs. I can find four orbs, with some meditation. Should I drop you off with them?"

"Yes, please."

And soon, after a lingering hand hug with her momma, Etolié was whisked back to the mortal realm, Staella's magic much gentler on her stomach.

To her surprise, she appeared in a forest.

She recalled then that time was strange and much longer had passed here.

But approaching her, though shocked by her appearance, was Casvir back on his skeletal steed, beside Soliel with his stupid camel. "Hail and well met, assholes!" Etolié cried, and she bridged the gap between them.

Kah'Sheen beamed at her reappearance, and there floated that strange ghost—Mereen's sister. "You are back!" the half-demon said.

"I am surprised," Casvir said, "but not displeased."

"Indeed," said Soliel. "You will be invaluable—"

"Absolutely fucking *not*, you godly shit!" Etolié spat at Soliel's mount's feet, her blood pressure back to lethal levels just by breathing his same air. Momma had called her anger poison—well, for now, she'd just have to die. "Oh, I'll be here. And we won't be talking. You even so much as fucking look at me for too long, and I'll stab out your eyeball, got it?"

He nodded.

"I hate all of you. Except you, Sheen Bean." She looked at the ghost, her violent image still shocking. "I guess I don't know you well enough to hate you. What's your name?"

"Sarai."

"Hi, Sarai. I'm Etolié, Empress of Solvira. My mother is Goddess Staella. Anyway." She looked back to the rest. "I'm here because I need Staff Seraph deDieula. Cassie, may I have my horse back?"

"If you say please."

Etolié's jaw snapped shut, her irritation reaching new heights. "No, I'll float." And she did, to punctuate her point. "Where are we going?"

"North," Casvir replied. "It is the best we can discern, given what we know."

"Lead on. I'm fucking tired."

They did, but Etolié fell back with Kah'Sheen. Much better company.

In the evening, Etolié and Soliel resumed the function of illuminating their paths, like holy fireflies.

"Next time we stop, I'm making tea," Etolié said, her mind still dwelling in Celestière, with her momma and her advice. Staring at Soliel's back, she clung to Staella's message, let it prevent her from exploding once more.

Kah'Sheen's pointed teeth showed in her smile. "Oh, I am loving tea!"

"I'll even make it for you assholes," Etolié said a little louder, vindicated by the annoyance in Casvir's glance. "It's only fair."

Then she recalled the ghost, who illuminated their path in less-than-holy shades. "Not for you, sorry. I would, though."

Sarai smiled despite what was technically a somber statement—acknowledging her death and all. "I appreciate being thought of."

"So how are you here? Aren't ghosts tied to fancy objects? Places?"

"The God of Order has my knife. Mereen didn't want me to follow, so she took it from Flowridia."

"You must have quite the stories, being Mereen's sister."

"One or two," Sarai replied, a sparkle in her eye. "What do you want to know?"

"Was she always so intense?"

Sarai laughed, and it bore subtle hints of a melody. Etolié knew a musician when she heard one. "Yes, always. Though she used to direct it toward fighting for her loved ones instead of hunting vampires."

"So she wasn't always a shitty person, got it."

Again came Sarai's laughter, though it concluded with hints of remorse. "No, not always. She was a tease, but I suppose I was too."

"And, uh, you're still here," Etolié said, sparing a glance for the gashes on Sarai's wrists.

Which . . . unfortunately Sarai noticed, her smile fading by small degrees. "I am still here."

"Seems like a fate worse than death, to kill yourself and then not escape." At Sarai's increasingly forced smile, Etolié fumbled as she sought to pull her foot from her mouth. "I'm sorry, truly. I'm just a fucking idiot."

A few feet away, a laughing snort escaped someone.

"You can shut the fuck up, Casvir."

He did not, in fact, shut the fuck up. "As someone who technically killed himself and did not escape this life, I found your statement amusing."

Damn fucking liches—carving out their hearts like it was normal.

A few moments passed in torturous silence. Even Kah'Sheen looked appalled by the slip. Etolié's heartbeat thumped in her eardrums, her face burning hot. "So who wants to break for tea?"

To her surprise, there were no objections.

With a snap of her fingers, she illusioned a campfire, complete with artificial warmth. Another snap—only for flair—and several chairs fell around it in appropriate sizes. Only then did Etolié consciously realize she was the shortest person here. Not a phenomenon she was well acquainted with.

She ignored her comrades in favor of boiling the water and assembling a few teacups.

"Many thanks, Etolié," Kah'Sheen said as the teacup floated into her hands. Casvir gave his own nod of thanks at the gesture.

Etolié delivered the tea to Soliel but withheld it when he tried to accept. "One question first."

"I will listen," the God of Order said, sincere as far as Etolié could sense.

Etolié released a stabilizing breath, resisting the urge to rip that smirk from his face. But, no. No. Poison. She had to keep that anger directed into positive outlets—like plotting a murder she could successfully pull off.

"I had an interesting conversation with the dragon you call 'daughter'—not that the title means much, given what you did to her brother, but I digress. She's worried about the future, as we all should be. But she said something that's stuck with me—that she thinks it all might have happened before.

This is a cycle, and you're perpetuating it."

Soliel's smile came pleasant but forced. "An interesting theory, but what is your question?"

"Uluron told me that the world falls into some sort of darkness. Lara"—she bit back a sneer at the name, to speak it in front of this monster—"believed that if there was a catalyst to stop it, only you and Chaos might know it. So what is it? Be introspective. What could you do to save the world instead of fucking destroying it?"

"Perhaps what I am doing is breaking away from the darkness. I have a plan."

"The death of a billion people isn't a solution. My momma is one of them."

The thought made her sick—that there was someone else this monster could steal from her.

"Hell, so's yours," Etolié continued, her hatred flowing. Yes, definitely poison, and likely to shave a few years off her immortal life, and so she breathed out the worst of it, simmering instead of boiling over. She would work with him to get the damn staff. Nothing more. "So who do you save? Or who do you kill? What was missing? Have you even considered being creative?"

Ire showed in his stare, but Etolié held far too much of her own to bend. "I spent ten thousand years alone as a ghost being creative, Etolié. And in my future, you might've agreed with me."

"I would like you to not speak on behalf of future me."

"I would like to hear more about this apparent darkness," Casvir said.

Soliel said nothing, but judging by the rise in rage in his own countenance, she'd bet a considerable amount of the treasury that Casvir was involved. Something to think about.

"Nothing?" Etolié asked. "I gotta know—was killing Alauriel Solviraes just a whim, then?"

"Alauriel Solviraes' death was regrettable."

The ensuing silence carried all the peace of a held breath—and Etolié kept hers inside, lest she fucking scream. "That's all you have to say?"

"She died valiantly. It was a battle I only barely survived—"

"*You can shut the—!*" Etolié snapped her mouth shut, because she certainly felt that poison flowing once more. But this man held four orbs, and while he did not actively seek her

death, he'd certainly bring it if she tried anything stupid—
even if stupid was her favorite pastime.

Etolié held eye contact—painful as it was—as she
dumped Soliel's tea onto the ground. The cup vanished.
Goddess Momma, give me strength, was her silent prayer, and
while she wouldn't say she felt better, she did manage to walk
away.

She sat beside Kah'Sheen, swiping a hand to bring her
own cup. Though fuming, she looked to Sarai. "Do you want a
teacup so you can feel included?"

"No, but thank you."

Etolié had potentially botched any initial hope for
friendship, but perhaps it could be fixed.

At the first sip of tea, the warmth grounding after a day
of simmering, her thoughts fell once more upon her momma.
"Kah'Sheen, may I ask something personal?"

"You may."

"Have you ever had to forgive someone you love?"

Kah'Sheen appeared thoughtful, bringing the teacup
down from her lips. "Yes, a few times. Why?"

"I'm going through something. Just wanted to know if
you had any advice."

"When Khastra is not telling me she is alive, I am very
angry."

"Relatable, actually."

"But I am at peace in her company now. Mistakes are
made in our past, but I am loving Khastra very much."

Etolié thought of Momma and the difficult years she had
witnessed—from depressive states to full lethargy to her
almost manic states of joy when Camdral left the right herbs
behind. Etolié had let herself hurt before. She had let herself
rage. Within her, there was no wish or want to be angry
again . . .

Sarai's voice rose softly. "Sometimes, when we can't see
past a block, the person we have to forgive . . . is ourself."

Etolié held her breath at the ghost's tender words. The
poignant statement brought old memories, of days watching
Lara grow into a fine young woman before her very eyes.

And as Etolié considered Soliel, considered Casvir,
considered Flowers and Eionei and Sora and Camdral and
Momma and every person toward whom to held
resentment . . .

Not one held a candle to the burning rage she felt toward

herself.

Etolié stood from her place on the log. "Just a moment," she muttered, but before illusioning away her glowing wings, she stopped at the cusp of the tree line. "Casvir, may I borrow that mirror?"

Wordlessly, he offered the magical device, and for all his faults, she could be grateful he asked no questions. With the mirror in hand, she trudged into the woods, far enough that she could no longer see the campfire. Her wings disappeared, allowing her to vanish.

Amid dark trees, Etolié wept.

For Lara, who she missed with all her soul, who even now she feared to fail—yet had she not already? Etolié worked with her murderer. The quest for the orbs was at a standstill.

For Flowers, who she had once held love for, who had betrayed them and married a monster. Etolié hadn't seen it coming, blinded by affection for the once-innocent child. She hadn't protected the naïve, flowery diplomat—not from Ayla or Casvir, and look where it had led.

For Eionei, who had once been her staunchest supporter, protector—who she hated to still love, but she did, she did. His sins were unquestionable, but he was not all to blame . . .

And so most of all, she cried this night for Momma, who she could have never protected, yet had never quite forgiven herself for not. The ghost had ripped the curtain away, and Etolié looked back upon fifty years of life, of a young freedom fighter who fought slavery, of a magister who had the chance to give those people a life. She screamed on behalf of the voiceless . . .

"Leave her alone! Don't touch my momma! Don't touch her!"

And though she'd sought to slay the dragon . . . the dragon would simply shove her aside, saving his fire for momma.

Etolié shut her eyes, tears streaming hot down her face. She grasped onto the image of Lara, once a little girl. How small she was, how helpless she was to monsters—monsters she never had to fight, for Malakh was there. Etolié was there.

Little Alauriel could breathe fire, but she could not have slain dragons.

Etolié knelt upon the pine needles, avoiding the cones, holding herself as she thought of a tiny Etolié who could illusion visions of fire, visions of dragons, but fight one? No.

Momma had said she should have never been in that home, but Etolié still cried for her and for her tiny self who had witnessed far too much.

And when she did succeed in slaying her momma's tormenter, a piece of her had died as well.

Etolié wept, but it released a dam, fifty years of heartbreak flowing freely. But through her veins flowed catharsis, an understanding of the past. Little girls were not meant to fight dragons; they were meant to be protected. They were meant to be loved.

. . . Eionei had protected her. He didn't know everything, but he had done what he could.

She shoved that thought aside, unwilling to unbury it yet. Instead, she wiped the wetness from her eyes and steadied her breath. Within her rose a foreign peace, a comfort she had sought to bring to others but had never allowed herself.

She thought a final moment of that little girl in the dragon's lair—not a hero; a victim. Etolié wrapped her arms around herself and hoped it would be enough. "You're a piece of work, kid. But you're perfect. And you're going to be all right."

That little girl deserved better. Etolié released those shackles and felt she'd finally thrive.

The yearning for her mother's presence threatened to overpower her, but no. No, this was a conversation to have in person, when she could hold her sweet momma's hands and deliver this new message of hope.

Instead, though her face had swollen, she tapped the mirror's surface, prepared for the blinding light. Khastra would understand. Khastra had lived countless lifetimes. Perhaps she could help Etolié unravel the rest—for there was more to forgive herself for, though today might simply be for Momma.

And there came Khastra's face, exhaustion marring her smile but not the joy in her glowing eyes. Canvas and candlelight was her backdrop; she lay in a tent. "Hello, Etolié—" Concern stole that happiness. "What is wrong?"

"Weirdly, nothing. I just had an emotional breakthrough and hoped I could tell you about it."

She did—she spilled the tender truths in her heart to Khastra, a safer space than any other, even her momma. Though she wept anew as she spoke of dragons and those foolish enough to fight them, that clarity clicked together with new vigor. "I'm wondering if telling Momma will unleash a flood. I'll just be forgiving everyone, left and right. I'm even..." She swallowed, bracing herself for the truth. "Thinking about Eionei. But I can't let go of what he said about you. He called you a fucking monster—I can't just let that go."

"You do not have to, but you also do not need to hold a grudge on my behalf."

"I just don't know how he feels about you, and that's important, you know?"

"You know you can speak to him without forgiving him, yes?"

The statement stopped Etolié's mind in its tracks. "Yes, I could."

"I am indifferent to Eionei, if it matters."

"A little, yes."

"Who I have not forgiven is Soliel," Khastra replied, her sneer fully apparent. "Perhaps when he is dead. For now, it is fueling me to kill him."

"You haven't mentioned that grudge in months."

"I have had no time to think of other grudges. I am fighting a war I do not care for." Khastra's good humor returned, and Etolié blushed beneath the affection in her gaze. "But I will support you in whatever you choose."

Despite her lighthearted words, Etolié wished to hold her, kiss her, be whatever support she could. "The war taking its toll?"

"I have fought much longer wars, and I suppose the challenge is worthwhile. I do not have to consider the lives of my soldiers or even the enemy's, so I can focus on tactics instead—and that is a good change. But while I am loyal to Imperator Casvir, it is not a fight I would have chosen. We are much closer to the beginning than the end, I fear."

"Once we're back, I'll get to stay with you again."

Khastra's lazy smile brought comfort. "Someday this war will end, and then I will insist on a vacation. I am thinking somewhere quiet. You will come, yes?"

Elation filled Etolié, heart soaring at the idea. "You couldn't stop me. I'm pretty familiar with Sha'Demoni now. You could show me all the best spots."

"There are many beautiful sights to see ..." Khastra looked past the mirror. In the background, Etolié heard what sounded a fair bit like Murishani muttering. "Can it wait?" More muttering, and a frown furrowed Khastra's brow. "You are certain? That is not . . . Yes, yes—I will come out." She looked back to Etolié. "I must go. We will talk again soon."

"Everything all right?"

"It will be."

"Love you, ya big lug."

And there again came that boundless love. Etolié soaked it up like a sponge. "I love you, Etolié."

Her image faded from view, leaving Etolié in darkness.

Chapter 19

*I*n that world of darkness, Flowridia walked alone, urged onward by the sound of a pitiful cry.

The black mist parted for her steps, her heart aching with each sob. She yearned for the source, yet her mind could not place it, could not remember it, though her soul knew it, nevertheless.

She swore it grew louder. Faster, she raced through the mist, not caring for her aching chest, her burning lungs. Her body protested each motion, pain rapidly escalating, but this . . . what she sought was precious. Precious beyond compare.

And there he lay, within a pool of light.

The baby screamed, and already Flowridia saw the cause. Not simply the cold. Not simply the lonely atmosphere. Instead, he bled from a gash in his stomach, sure signs of a stab from a knife.

Flowridia sobbed, falling to her knees beside him. She took him in her arms, careful not to jostle and cause more pain. With welling tears, she pleaded silently for her magic to rise, to let her heal this infant—her final connection of blood. Her brother without a name.

But nothing came.

The boy cried, and she with him, for agony would be his life, and then a painful end. He bled, and in the crevices of his wound, she saw split flesh, signs of fragile innards severed and ruined. Even if she could heal, he was well beyond repair.

"I'm sorry," she said, the words stained in tears. "Gods, I'm so sorry. I couldn't save you."

She held him close, his screams a nightmarish refrain.

No voice this time. There did not need to be. Flowridia wept in the darkness.

On the fifth day of torture, Sora held a small platter with a pitcher of water, a slice of bread, and a side of meat, despite her own protests.

"*She doesn't eat meat.*"

Mereen had simply scowled. "*She'll be grateful for whatever she gets.*"

Tucked under her arm, she had a blanket rolled as tight as she could make it, lest Mereen see. Before the door, Sora checked the hall and found it vacant, then slipped a small bag of nuts from her pocket and placed it on the tray. She peered through the bars and saw nothing.

When she opened the door, the flickering light did little to illuminate the chamber. But though Sora had been instructed to leave the food and go, she lingered, searching for any sign of life.

Trembling in the corner, curled like a frightened kitten, lay Flowridia.

She had lost weight, though Sora sought to right that. "Food's here," Sora said softly, lest the girl startle.

No reaction.

Sora set the tray on the ground. "I brought you a blanket too. Don't tell anyone."

Nothing. Sora placed the blanket near the wall and left. At the door, she pressed her ear to the seam and listened for familiar scuffling, relieved when it came. More so when quiet sounds of chewing ensued.

She kept her mouth shut. Yesterday she'd spoken and scared the doe away.

Instead, Sora waited, uncertain of this gentle instinct within her. But Sol Kareena would not condone cruelty to prisoners, so why should Sora?

The irony settled then, and Sora refused to think on it a moment longer.

Sudden retching sounds came from inside. Sora remained still, only daring to shift when quiet weeping followed.

Sora peeked through the bars, aghast to see her prisoner *eating* what she'd expelled.

She threw open the door to meet the gaze of a pitiful creature.

Tears streamed down Flowridia's face, the tray empty save for the splatters of half-chewed excess mixed with bile. She tried to cover her exposed self with her hands, stumbling as she stood and crept back. Five days, and her cheeks had thinned, her eyes had sunk. Not a corpse, but the poor girl didn't have much to lose.

"Don't eat that," Sora said, as soothing as she could. "Drink the water. I'll get you more food, all right? Try to eat it slower." With care to hold her eye, Sora set the pitcher aside and took the vomit-covered tray away. "I'll be back soon."

Sora left, unable to cope with Flowridia's palpable shame, though her own threatened to match.

She was met with empty halls, empty rooms. No one stopped her as she procured rations from her bedroom; no one questioned why she was bringing her prisoner more food. Were they even here?

"Hello?" she called, and it echoed through the halls of the ground floor.

Silence.

Though dread filled her to return, Sora carefully navigated the underground with a tray of bread and nuts—not meat this time, and she wondered if that had been what made the starving girl sick.

But something was amiss—she was not met with silence.

"*Please stop,*" came the tearful phrase, though there was no bite to it.

"*You taste of vomit, you nasty thing.*"

Ayla was not supposed to be awake.

Morning was when Tazel rested. It was when Flowridia ate and had a small respite. Sora hurried, setting the tray on the floor before the door.

"*Ayla, stop.*"

"*I don't like my women coy.*"

"*Then say my name. Say my name, and I'll do whatever you want.*"

"*I don't like taking orders either.*"

"*Flowridia. Just say it. Flowridia—*"

Sora banged on the door then, though could not bring herself to look.

"*Stop fighting, or I'll strap you to the table and fuck you anyway.*"

That was different. Sora ran.

Up the stairs, and all the while she screamed, *"Tazel!"*

It bespoke ill if he had fallen asleep, but it was the only cause she could think of. She bolted to his room and banged on the door. "Tazel!"

Something moved inside. Sora threw open the door.

And there he sat with Mereen in his lap, both of them nude, her bare breasts in his face. The ecstasy twisting their countenances quickly shifted—for Tazel, to stark horror. Mereen simply glared.

Sora immediately looked away, but the image had seared into her head, reappearing as she blinked.

Mereen's smiled through her growl. "Close the door, half-breed."

"Ayla is out of her coffin," Sora said. All of her was numb, body and mind. "She's with Flowridia."

"Close the door," Mereen repeated, each word precise and cruel. "We'll be there soon."

Sora obeyed but stood frozen in the hall, staring upon a decorated door until the muted sounds of passion resumed.

Though shock remained, anger surged through her. Justice was justice, though she questioned even that anymore, and as she mulled over five days of witnessing horrors unmatched, something inside her cracked.

Sora threw open the door, prepared for slapping skin and sickness. "I haven't sat in a dungeon for a week just to risk losing her because of whatever degenerate thing this is. Flowridia is in danger. You will do your *fucking job!*"

She held up a hand to block the sight of Mereen rising, too disgusted to move. She simply stood aside, gaze to the floor as Tazel stumbled into his trousers and ran for the dungeon, that damned staff in his hands.

The ensuing sensuous tone filled Sora with rage. "Sora, sweetie, you—"

Sora ignored her, marching to her bedroom instead. There was Leelan upon the windowsill, for the little bird did not need to wallow in this grime.

Sora had no name for this dread, this awful, depthless depravity coating her skin. Odessa had warned her of this, and Sora remained the fool. Sickness rose in her stomach, every part of this day stained in debauchery, and despite herself, despite the horrors below, Sora's legs buckled.

Curled upon a dusty carpet, Sora wept.

When Sora finally left her room, the sun had shifted, beaming high above.

She went first to the entry hall and stared a moment into the sunny day, wondering, not for the first time, what she was doing here.

"Family does not have to be blood," Papa had said, *"but even when it is, you have to work for that love. You have to choose."*

"Do you choose me, Papa?"

"I choose you every day."

Except one day, he hadn't. He hadn't returned.

Sora stood in the edge of the doorway, every thought one of turmoil. How beautiful, the sunlight—so cruel a juxtaposition as she stood in this oppressive place. From her pocket, Sora withdrew her treasured locket, her parents' smiling countenances only filling her with shame. "I always prayed you were alive," Sora said to her father's image, "while hoping all along that you were dead—so that at least, perhaps, you loved me in your final days instead of abandoning me."

"We only have one family," Mom had said, *"but some family takes precedence over others."*

"Is that why you choose Papa?"

"Papa and you."

Meanwhile, Mereen had no qualms about manipulating her own blood while blotting them from the family tree.

"Sol Kareena . . ."

She could not finish it. The goddess could not know what happened beneath this roof.

". . . I hope you're well."

The idea of stepping back inside made her ill, but to run away . . .

Mereen wouldn't hunt her. Mereen wouldn't care.

Odessa had known. Odessa had tried to steer her away.

"Monsters beget monsters."

Sora's tears fell fast because the witch was dead, her only friend among this damn, horrid crowd. The witch was dead, and she could not even mourn her. Not with ritual. Not with song.

And down in the basement was Odessa's child, whose fate had been plotted by the witch herself.

An evil woman . . . and a friend.

The one unshakable thought remained, that to leave meant to abandon Flowridia to this house of sadists—yet was Sora any better?

She returned, thoughts of finally feeding the poor thing all that steered her steps. The tray of food had been left in the dungeon. Hopefully, someone had delivered it.

As Sora traversed to the lower floor, a small voice stopped her as she passed the first cell. "Sora, can we speak?"

Sickness welled anew in Sora's soul to hear Tazel's voice—now spoiled by the memory of his body and impassioned voice. "I'm not ready for that."

She tried to continue, already spotting evidence of her offering scattered across the floor. But his voice sounded behind her, stronger now. "Do you think this is easy for me?"

Sora whirled around, startled at how withered he appeared. Spells could sustain a person indefinitely, but lack of sleep still took a toll. Thin and pale, a near match to Mereen, and a foreign, ugly hatred twisted his once handsome features.

"I have been in that sadist's head for weeks now," he continued. "I'm trying to survive, so let me have one gods-damned vice."

Anger simmered within Sora's blood. "You knew she was out of her coffin. You knew what she was doing to Flowridia. She was in danger."

"Ayla knows she's not allowed to kill her. If anything, this was a reprieve for them both."

Sora stepped back, skin crawling at the words. "You're sick."

"Torture is fine, but you draw the line at rape? Don't pretend you're better than me."

The statement struck like a slap to the face. "I've never thought I was better than you," Sora seethed. "On the contrary—I saw you as a hero. Someone to aspire to be like."

"I haven't been a hero in a long time, Sora."

As much as Sora wished to scream and bring her knife to his throat, that horrible staff stared with the same vacancy as Tazel himself. More powerful than them all, for it had been created by a god, and Sora feared who was truly in control.

She stepped around Tazel, who said nothing at all.

When she returned with more bread and a stash of nuts,

he had gone.

Instead, Mereen leaned in the doorway of the same cell, a huntress staring upon her prey. "Tazel says you're a little shaken from our encounter, sweetie. I wanted to apologize."

So sincere, her eyes bearing evidence of a woman who was once kind, of the legendary vampire who had resisted the siren call of her son's blood. But Sora could not summon a response; her anger burned bright.

"Forgive Tazel," Mereen continued. "He is a good man, not suited for this grime. All I can do is comfort him through this awful business. Before you ask—it was not the first time, though we only recently rekindled what we had. We've tried to keep our affair quiet for what I think are understandable reasons, but the secret wasn't kept from you out of malice."

Her kindness was an insult. "What game are you playing, Mereen?"

"No games. You're my family. You're Mari's daughter. I'm trying to be nice."

"I thought I was a half-breed."

"That's objectively true."

Sora prayed her glare was scathing enough, but knew in her heart Mereen was immune. "You're right. We're family. And I'm here because I believe in our family's quest—to kill Ayla Darkleaf once and for all. But once it's done, none of you will see me again."

Mereen's smile remained as charming as before, even as she gave a nod and sauntered past, returning to the world above.

Alone, Sora went to the blighted cell at the end of the hall, her boots crunching the scattered nuts. When she peeked through the bars, there was nothing.

Sora entered, the torch's light casting farther inside. Tucked away in a shadow, wrapped in the blanket Sora had left, was a cowering figure.

The smell of vomit lingered, along with remnants of the putrid pile. Sora set the tray away from the mess.

When she left, she listened at the door for scuffling—and was surprised to hear it. As quiet as she could, Sora sat against the door, back to the cold metal, and listened for munching— but that never came.

Instead, from the other side of the door came a dusty voice. "Who is Mari?"

Sora nearly forgot how to speak, shocked to hear herself

addressed. "M-My mother. Mariam."

There came a gasp. "Mariam Fireborn."

"Yes."

A quiet sob sounded from within.

Sora waited, uncertain of what it meant, torn between asking and leaving the girl alone, when Flowridia tearfully said, "Your father's name was Zanoram."

Sora's breath hitched. "Yes. How did you know?"

Flowridia cried beyond the door.

"Flowridia, how do you know my father's name?"

The words came muffled through tears. "He was the only child of the late Archbishop Xoran, heir to the Theocracy's throne."

"No," Sora replied, every part of her growing cold. "He was just a paladin—"

"Paladin of Sol Kareena. Lunestra said there was a girl he had loved who he wasn't allowed to marry. Her name was Mariam, and Lunestra wondered if he'd ever let her go."

The words were impossible. Yet it was just as impossible for Flowridia to know her father and mother's name. She had no witchcraft anymore. "How do you know this?"

"Twenty years ago, he was traveling south to visit his family," Flowridia said, her sobs barely controlled. "As he passed a town called Ilunnes, he met a demon who told him of a maiden captured by a witch in the swamp. He went, because he was a hero, and he slew the witch and rescued the maiden, who enchanted him, seduced him—and murdered him."

The story rang like a bell, a distant memory from a campfire long ago. "You're lying. You told this story back in Staelash. It was about—"

Odessa.

Every part of Sora became numb.

"He was my father too."

"No."

"Sora—"

"You're lying!" Sora rose to her feet, the urge to flee rapidly growing. "My father isn't your father. That would mean we were . . ."

Family. Sisters.

Sora's voice came rough from panic. "You're lying."

"I'm not."

Sora fled, unwilling to hear the rest.

Her footsteps echoed across the stone, revealing her to

anyone near as she bounded up the stairs. To her room, to Leelan, and to the secret pack she kept beneath her bed for if ever there came a need to run.

The bird tweeted to chime in her entrance, but Sora's tears fell fast. When Leelan came to her side, she stroked his precious feathers, wept to the tune of his song. It couldn't be. Flowridia lied. Odessa hadn't killed her father.

Odessa . . . her friend . . .

Sora had never felt kinship to Flowridia—a protective instinct at best, for how young she was, how vulnerable to monsters who would corrupt her. No longer. She was selfish and wicked, responsible for the deaths of thousands in Solvira, and she walked a path Sora's goddess condemned.

She deserved every cruel thing the world could offer, yet Sora felt so sick to be a part of it. When had justice become corrupt?

Sora looked to Leelan, her constant friend. "She can't be my sister."

Was it truly so impossible?

She thought of Papa, who had loved every creature, who had healed with light. She thought of Flowridia, who was once chosen by Sol Kareena, who walked a necromancer's path but wielded light in tandem with death.

And she thought of herself, chosen by Sol Kareena as well, to be a champion—but not now. Not with this storm swirling above her head. Not with this swamp engulfing her heart. Sol Kareena preached of justice, but this was no longer justice.

Monsters begot monsters, and standing in the eye of this hurricane, Sora understood. Twenty years ago, she had waited on her doorstep for days, for weeks, praying for a father who was already gone. Fifteen years ago, she had wept in her mother's arms as her own fever broke—and as her mother's had consumed her.

What had Mereen done then? She had cast her out—a child, helpless and alone.

And what had Tazel done? Nothing, she realized. He had been there yet had simply stood nigh.

"You poor lonely child . . ."

In the basement, her father's blood stained the floor— the very blood that flowed through Sora's veins.

Sometimes family was who you chose. Sol Kareena had loved a sister too.

With no other rational thought, Sora grabbed her pack, grabbed Leelan, and ran to the basement.

No sign of Tazel or Mereen. Perhaps they were fucking. She hoped so, this time.

In the dank basement, she heard Flowridia's tragic weeping. When she threw open the door, the girl's face glistened with tears, shock beneath them.

There brewed within Sora an instinct she'd never known before, and she wondered if this was what it meant to have a little sister to protect. "We're leaving."

"What?"

"We're leaving. Now."

Frantic, Flowridia shook her head. "If I go, Mereen will torture Ayla."

"Mereen can't kill her, but she can kill you."

Flowridia hesitated. "How do I know I can trust you?"

From her pocket, Sora procured Flowridia's wedding ring and offered it forward. "We'll find help," Sora implored, "but I'm begging you. Come with me . . . sister."

Flowridia took the ring, slipped it on as a wedding band. Their hands touched, and Sora swore she felt the strings that tied them, willingly or not. Flowridia rose at her lead, unsteady on her feet. Sora brought Flowridia's arm over her shoulder and helped her to walk.

Up the stairs, Sora's senses remained on high alert all along. At the first floor, they picked up their pace, banking around the hall, stumbling into the entryway, the first rays of sunlight cast over them—

"SORA!"

"Run," Sora said, shoving Flowridia ahead. She withdrew a knife from her boot just in time for Mereen to rush with her dual swords. From her sleeve came her second knife, but the game was to avoid, defend—not fight.

Mereen would kill her.

Sunlight burst through the room. The great doors opened wide. Mereen screamed and stumbled back, her exposed parts charred from the blast of light, but Flowridia's silhouette only lingered a moment before she disappeared beyond. Sora held her daggers in defense as she stepped backward toward the door, but Mereen's hand surged out to grab her boot.

Sora toppled, her head smacking hard against the wooden floor. Her vision spun as Mereen dragged her back, soon faced with her grandmother's furious visage.

"Changed your loyalties, half-breed?" Mereen spat. "And here I thought you had the spine to do what must be done. "

Sora struggled against her grip, too dazed to summon a coherent thought. Mereen's image shifted from two to three and back again.

"You really are like your mother. Fortunately for you, your end will be a little faster than hers."

Though Mereen's sword glinted, the threat apparent, the statement jarred Sora from her shock. "What?"

But Mereen brought the sword down—

In time for Sora to glow with her own burst of light. In the far distance, a bird chirped; Sora's energy surged. Mereen shrieked. Sora shoved her off and darted into the sun, head spinning as her boots stomped against the wooden porch.

A distant cry destroyed her rising hope.

Forgetting Mereen and her poisoned words, Sora ran toward the mountainous terrain. Tazel wrestled with the fragile girl, overpowering her with ease. Sora rushed him, daggers readied, but even with Flowridia subdued in one arm, he whipped the staff through the air, smacking Sora across the face with the demon's skull.

Her head spun, but she refused to fall. The skull's eyes flashed. Beneath her feet, the ground sizzled, a blight burning through her boots. "Don't make me kill you," Tazel said, and it was far more a plea than a threat.

Again, she rushed, then screamed as pain burned across her arms, black, necrotic lines consuming her flesh. She dropped the daggers to grip the dying skin.

"Sora, go," came the quiet plea—but this time from Flowridia. "Don't die for me."

The staff's glowing eyes held more life than the gaunt man wielding it. "I'll tell Mereen you died. Run away. Don't come back."

The pulsing heat of failure coursed through her veins. Flowridia wept, but her eyes screamed to *go*.

"You could come with us," Sora begged, her final chance. Her arms stung, the flesh still raw, but Flowridia's life was at stake. "You're a good man."

"Sora—"

"You don't have to do this."

"It's the greater good."

"It's not! We're no less monstrous than—"

She screamed as the necrotic blight spread once more across her arms, decaying the skin of her forearms.

It stopped. "Next time, I'll let it eat you. Now go."

Sora met Flowridia's gaze and swore she'd seen those hazel eyes before, smiling in her father's countenance. But here, they silently begged.

Sora stumbled back, leaving her fallen knives behind, and bolted down the mountain.

Before the shadow consumed her anew, Flowridia savored the blistering sun upon her naked body.

It disappeared as Tazel dragged her back into the oppressive mansion. When he shut the door, her eyes held spots of sunlight, leaving her blinded.

"We won't have to worry about Sora anymore," Tazel said, and the tightening grip on her arm conveyed a warning— that to speak up would condemn Sora to die.

Mereen's white outline approached from the darkness. "Damn that blunt-eared bastard. Take the girl to the basement. Send Ayla to keep her company."

Flowridia did not fight as Tazel led her away, disoriented in the dark. The world became colder, and her prison returned.

Yet she felt no panic. She clenched her fist, feeling the subtle pressure of her wedding ring. This . . . this was hope.

Tazel brought her to her cell, and gently lowered her down. From the ground, she met his eye, still astonished from his lie, and dared to ask a dangerous inquiry. "Why are you doing this? You don't want to be here."

"It's what's right." His voice came monotone, recited from a script he hadn't written.

"Sora didn't think so."

He opened his mouth to speak, yet whatever excuse he might've summoned died in his throat. Instead, he left her alone in darkness.

They had been so close, but had there even been hope at all? Would Sora come back for her?

Sora . . . her sister. Mariam had been a Fireborn, and of

course her family would never allow her to wed a human man, no matter his esteem to Sol Kareena. Nor would his family fight for it—half-elven royals were unheard of.

What were the bonds of family? Flowridia still wept for the baby brother she'd never had the chance to know. Would Sora weep for her?

"And how is my favorite little girl?"

Flowridia's blood froze at the once-beloved voice.

She emerged, the monster from the shadows. With matted hair and a dirty, tattered masquerade gown, Ayla had no awareness of the blood staining the fabrics and her skin, no concept of her dirty fingernails. This was no civilized creature.

Flowridia clutched her own body, her skin, terror spiking at the anticipation of pain, of tears, of utter violation. Her lungs screamed for air, yet she could not breathe. "You're back."

"I can't leave my favorite girl for long."

In her hand, Flowridia hid her wedding ring. "So you remember me?"

"You're talkative today," Ayla said, ignoring the inquiry. "Now will you get on the table yourself, or do I have to make you?"

In her moment of hesitation, Ayla barged forward. Panic rose in Flowridia's blood as she strained herself to stand, but she was weak, so weak . . .

She gasped as Ayla wrenched her up by her arm. She stumbled against the table, catching her heaving breaths.

Every part of her revolted when sharp nails ran along her back. "Hmm . . ." Ayla's curious hum raised the hair on Flowridia's neck. "Not perfect, but perhaps good enough."

The sensation of fingers tugging at Flowridia's skin was a cruel reminder of the threat.

"Such lovely shoes you'll make. What do you say?"

Though her movements were slowed from terror, Flowridia managed to turn around.

She swore she lived beyond herself, an observer of her pitiful form. Her body recoiled at her predator's presence, heart thumping loud enough for Ayla to hear, surely. "I have a gift for you," she whispered, forcing a smile. "Would you accept it?"

Confusion marred Ayla's features. "And what disgusting thing have you found for me in a place like this?"

"Let me see your hand."

"No. Get on the table. Lie on your stomach."

Flowridia took her final leap of faith—and held up the ring.

A shuffling sound came from beyond the door. Fear coursed through Flowridia, but Ayla didn't react, focus narrowed to the beautiful ring. "What is that?"

"It's a gift, as I said."

"Where did you get it?"

"Found it. One of your previous specimens must have left it."

Ayla simply stared. When Flowridia tried to take her hand, Ayla batted it away. Yet her eyes remained fixed upon the ring.

"Is it familiar?" Flowridia asked, hope returning despite her panic.

"Yes."

"Where have you seen it?"

So close. Ayla stiffened against her. Her jaw became steel. "I helped make it."

"Did you? Who was it for?"

Even in the dank atmosphere, silver appeared at the edges of Ayla's vision, reflecting the subtle light. "My wife."

The words were like the sunrise after a nighttime monsoon. "Who was she?"

"She . . ." Ayla suddenly gasped, gripping her hair as she backed away.

"Ayla," Flowridia implored, but beyond the window, she saw a flash of purple light. "Ayla, my love, she was Flowridia. I'm Flowridia!"

Ayla's face twisted in anguish, tension revealed in her hands. When she tore them away, they ripped out patches of matted hair. "No!"

"Ayla, fight it!" Flowridia stumbled forward, weak but pumped with adrenaline. With all her strength, she took Ayla's hand—

Only for Ayla's to grip her wrist with bone-crushing strength. In her shock, Flowridia dropped the ring, heard it clink against the stone. The silver disappeared from Ayla's eyes, replaced by a void of black.

"Darling, stop playing games."

Flowridia wept as Ayla dragged her to the table, cutting her skin against the corners as she forced her up.

"On your back. I've had a change of heart. I can't say"

why, but I have a strange fixation with hands lately."

Flowridia fought as Ayla strapped her in, but it was useless. Panic rose, chest burning in anticipation of pain. "Ayla, please don't!"

But Ayla ignored her, instead taking careful study of her left hand. "I think I could create something gorgeous from this. You like flowers, don't you?"

Flowridia could not comprehend that awful question— not until Ayla bought her scalpel to her finger and slit slowly up the center.

"Such lovely flowers . . ."

Flowridia screamed and entered the nightmare anew.

"Such a beautiful flower it will make. Perfect lines, slit up the seams."

"It still moves when I pluck on the tendons, good."

"We just need to stitch it in place, better than before . . ."

Upon the floor lay the remains of a soul stripped of dignity and personhood. Flowridia Darkleaf clung to her name with every shred of her remaining sanity.

Clung to her name . . . and to the wedding ring in her fist.

Her other hand bore countless stitches, pulsing pain with every beat of her heart. Slit in the center of each finger, following up the line, through her hand, curved to become a macabre bouquet . . . Ayla had called it art, rearranged it all, and sewed it together—*better than before.*

Her chest ached with each breath, the memory wrought far more with fear than with pain.

Footsteps sounded beyond, a reminder of her tormentors. But not two feet away, scrubbing the table of blood, was Ayla.

Flowridia curled around her mutilated hand, protective of the ruined appendage. For better or worse, her heart still beat.

Her thoughts circled and floated with nowhere to land. She held hope in one hand, yet her body refused to let her live within its cage of skin and bone; the pain was far too much.

"I remember the night you proposed," Flowridia

whispered, to no one at all. Even in the darkness, the outline of the wedding band cast a gentle ring. "You were so nervous, even though I had already asked *you*, and you'd accepted. You rambled your way through your proposal and forgot to ask the most important question." Despite the agony of her hand, despite the horrors of her environment, she managed to smile. "You cried when I said yes. You wept for joy. And I felt . . ." Mist rose to cloud her vision, her face still sticky from torturous tears. "I *still* feel so blessed that someone can love me so much.

"I don't know if what I'm saying means anything to you anymore," Flowridia continued, tears streaming calmly down her face. "But I love you. If I close my eyes, I can still see your face at the altar. Even under your façade of the empress, you were always you. Our wedding was perfect. It was perfect because of you."

"I made your dress," came a wistful whisper. Flowridia stiffened at the sound, caught somewhere between panic and hope. Ayla leered above her, countenance curious. "It was long enough to cover your feet."

Flowridia's lip trembled as she spoke. "It was. Long enough to cover my silly bare feet. It was embroidered with—"

"Flowers," Ayla finished. Her eyes remained black, but her stare held new life. "A-And your hair . . . your hair, it was braided with—"

"Flowers," Flowridia said, in tandem with her love. With her mutilated hand cradled against her chest, she managed to sit up, ignoring the shooting pain.

There came that ring of silver, Ayla's eyes becoming brighter, nearly human. "Flowridia?"

"Yes!" Flowridia stumbled as she stood, but adrenaline proved the strongest force.

Ayla had no need to breathe, yet the hitch in her breath convulsed her whole figure. Tears and terror filled her eyes, but when Flowridia cupped her face, gave a gentle *shh*, realization came as well.

From beyond the door came that cursed flash of purple. Ayla screamed, hands flying to her ears. "Stop it! Stop!"

"Ayla, my love, listen—give me your hand—"

Flowridia's words disappeared in Ayla's soul-wrenching shriek. Her fingers dug deeper, deeper, breaking skin as they sought to clutch her ears, soon cracking bone.

"Ayla, don't—!"

Bone shattered. Ayla's fingers plunged into her skull. A horrible *snap*, and Ayla's hands lashed away, bits of skull and brain matter splattering the ground, along with her pointed ears. No blood. Simply viscous, clear liquid. Flowridia's hand flew to her mouth, horror filling her as Ayla teetered, eyes glazing. She collapsed to the stone floor, utterly still.

Flowridia sank down beside her, sicked by the display, by her own hand, by every aspect of this chamber. Within seconds, Ayla's brain began refilling the hollow spaces. Her bones steadily regrew. Flowridia brushed Ayla's matted locks from her wounds, mesmerized as the skin and bone pieced together, fueled by her unholy existence.

Flowridia hummed a quiet tune—Sarai's song, which she prayed might soothe her love, even in her dream-like state. With her good hand, she dared to take Ayla's, and she slipped the ring onto her middle finger.

A loose fit. An idle fling, and it would fall away. But Flowridia had a chance.

Assuming this worked at all. Would this game continue, of Flowridia pleading, speaking of love and all her cherished memories, only to be thwarted? A stronger force, more powerful than even Ayla's love for her, enslaved her wife's clever mind.

Discarded against the wall, the knife remained. It had all along. Ayla lay vulnerable, and one quick stab would guarantee an end.

It might be a mercy to free Ayla's tortured mind.

Footsteps signaled intruders. The door creaked open, revealing Mereen. Flowridia wrapped protective arms around her love, praying it might be enough. She would awaken—but to what?

Mereen stared down, and Flowridia knew what the woman must see, how pathetic and small she had become. Mereen had to see the mutilated stump of her hand, the raised scars on her chest.

Her beautiful face held pity. "You could end it."

Behind her, Tazel stood in the doorway, the hated staff held tight in his hands. His ashen face saw nothing at all.

Flowridia stared at the blade, a hitched breath rubbing her throat raw. "Not today," she whispered, and when Mereen knelt to steal Ayla from her protective embrace, she let her go.

In Mereen's arms, Ayla hung slack, her hand dangling as she was taken from the room. The ring remained, inconspicuous and unseen, liable to fall with a single misstep. The door shut. Alone, Flowridia wept.

Chapter 20

Sora ran until her lungs were aflame. Her head burned from dehydration, brought on by her tears. With every blink, she was plagued by memories of all she'd seen and done. Flowridia weeping, Flowridia cut open and mutilated, Flowridia pleading through the door for Sora to believe they were *family*.

It was too much.

Sunset fell by the time Sora finally collapsed into a heap of exhaustion. If Mereen were to come for her, distance would make no difference. Yet whatever part of Tazel still clung to goodness would not betray her. She oddly trusted that.

Flowridia was her sister, and the thought still sent her reeling.

And Mereen . . . what had she meant? That she would die faster than her mother?

Mereen hadn't . . . had she?

Beneath the cover of pine trees, nestled upon needles, Sora rested her weary self. Every muscle in her body was hot. Sweat poured down her forehead, stained her clothing. Even her beloved locs were disheveled. Sora's face fell into her hands.

What had her life become?

She knew only one thing—she could not give up.

Odessa had gone before her, and a piece of Sora still hoped . . .

But Odessa had killed . . .

Fresh tears welled in Sora's eyes. Odessa had killed her father.

Etolié and Casvir had been in Velen'Kye. Surely they searched for Flowridia. Perhaps she could seek them, get them to help. She cared not for Ayla, and she suspected they did not either, but if saving Ayla was the price of Flowridia's life, so be it.

Shame remained the strongest force—for failing. "But what can I do?" she whispered aloud, for her thoughts had become too loud.

Leelan tweeted frantically. She watched as he flew up high and circled the sky.

"It's a clear night, but be careful of owls."

Yet Leelan would not stop chirping, drawing her eye to the clear spots between trees, the first stars of night.

Etolié was of the stars, but she was not the Stars. Goddess Staella was difficult to pray to, but surely she could send a message to Etolié—

Dammit all. Sora's pack had been dropped in the fight with Mereen, so she had nothing . . .

From the corner of Sora's eye, with the last semblance of sunlight, she caught sight of something strange and familiar. Mushrooms. She crawled toward where they lurked beneath the bed of needles, their orange hue unmistakable—Chaos' Spore.

Dried and powdered, it was Sora's relaxation method of choice. But in large amounts, it risked a hallucinogenic sleep. A fine line between relaxation and the risk of horrid nightmares, but Sora knew how to walk it.

She sought Etolié. Spore brought waking sleep. And Goddess Staella spoke in dreams.

Sora dug out the mushrooms by their mycelium, the odor sweet and serene. "Goddess Staella," she whispered, "I seek your guidance. I seek your presence. Please, as Etolié's friend, I'm begging you to talk to me."

Typically, just a pinch of powder in her pipe would do. Today, she bit a chunk off the mushroom.

At the first touch of Spore to her tongue, a familiar tingling formed in her mouth. It spread across her skin, coating every limb and surface, seeping deeper, pulling her down. Sora lay upon the forest floor, the brief worry for predators disappearing beneath the weight of her eyelids.

Yet though she blinked, the world remained the same. Until . . . a glowing light appeared before her.

Staella faded gently into view, kind and beautiful, her wings casting radiant light across the forest. "Good evening, Sora Fireborn. This is unexpected."

"Goddess Staella," Sora said, yet the word was heavy on

her tongue, "can you deliver a message to Etolié? Or can . . . can you tell me where she is?"

"You're slurring quite—" Staella glanced at the sliced mushroom beside her and laughed. "Oh, I see. Drastic times. Well, Etolié is mighty furious with you."

"I'm not surprised."

"Regarding your request, I can do a great many things, including take you to Etolié if you're so desperate. But you will have to convince me."

Sora chose her words with care, for Staella was a goddess of mercy, but this was regarding a couple she might view with vengeance. "If you know Etolié is looking for me, that means she must be seeking Flowridia, right?"

"She is."

"I can take her there. I know where she is. I've just escaped there."

Staella looked oddly upon her, confusion in her lovely face. "Why?"

"Because what's happening there is evil. There's no other word for it. Sol Kareena may hate The Endless Night, but even she wouldn't stoop so low as what I've witnessed. I have to stop it, and I think Etolié and Casvir actually have a chance, especially with my help."

Staella studied her, visibly mulling over her request. "So you would save Flowridia?"

"I would."

"What I will do is speak to Etolié. If she will see you, I will take you."

And Staella faded from view.

Sora's head became heavy, falling back into the dirt. With Staella's absence came crushing darkness. Shadows swirled beyond, surely hallucinations, yet dread oozed into Sora's soul.

Sora had reaped the consequences of too much Spore before, even experienced the nightmares, but something here felt . . . darker.

Be careful, little Fireborn, came a damning voice on the wind, as deep as earth's core—and though she had not heard it before, she knew it, knew it as the perfect antithesis to the goddess she loved.

If you come, I will warn them.

The light returned, Staella's face reappearing. She frowned a moment, her stare sweeping across the landscape, but immutable peace settled upon Sora in her presence. "Etolié has agreed to see you, though I feel the need to warn you of the impending verbal assault. Shall I take you to her?"

"Yes," Sora said, still fixated on the horrid warning.

"Would you like me to wait until the Spore has worn off?"

"No. Take me now."

Staella's hesitation felt so oddly out of character, but her words gave the answers. "We are not alone, are we."

"No."

"Warn Etolié of that too."

Staella gave a light touch to her forehead, and Sora's world became swirling mist.

Her vision blurred, the night turning impossibly dark, yet a sea of stars flurried past her vision, tilting even as she landed.

What had once been Staella's light was replaced by something new, but hazy, as though staring beneath the ocean.

Something yelled, yet Sora didn't hear it. Fire burned, but Sora didn't feel it. She simply plunged in and out of awareness—

Then suddenly blinked into wakefulness.

Sora sat up, feeling no hangover, no aftereffects—only to see Etolié collapsed beside her, groaning.

She was not alone.

The four-eyed stare of Kah'Sheen leered above her, a knife in each of her hands. "Hello, Sora Fireborn."

Yet she was not the only presence. A campfire crackled nearby, but standing beside it, radiating his own light, was the God of Order. Near him, what Sora recognized as a ghost floated serenely by, her appearance ghastly and violent. Casvir was the least daunting figure by comparison, or at least the only expected factor.

"Etolié is saying you are coming," Kah'Sheen continued, jarring Sora back into focus. "And I am preparing. She is taking your sickness away. Why are you here?"

"I can take you to Flowridia."

The entire mood shifted, the suspicion rising. "Why?" Casvir asked.

Sora bit her tongue against the reveal of her sisterly bond, lest there be any question. But while it was the final nail in the coffin, as she had told Goddess Staella, there were other valid reasons. "Because what's happening to Flowridia is worse than any of you can fathom, and I will no longer be a part of it. I've been complicit in a horrible crime, and upon my honor, I must rectify what I've done."

Etolié let out a particularly loud moan, rolling over as she puked into the grass. "I somehow believe you," came the Celestial's pitiful reply, and Sora relaxed at the words.

"I swear, I'm telling the truth."

"Then where is she?" the God of Order asked.

Sora looked to Kah'Sheen. "Am I allowed to tell him?"

"Yes. We are agreeing to be friends for one quest."

Sora had many questions, but there was little time. "She is in the Mountains of Kaas. Mereen and Tazel are there. Odessa is dead."

The words felt final and true.

"And they are having Staff Seraph deDieula?" Kah'Sheen asked.

"Yes, though I fear Tazel may waste away because of it."

"That is helping us, so I hope so."

Beside her, Etolié struggled to sit up. Kah'Sheen tucked away a knife to offer her a hand, but the Celestial fell back into the grass. "Fucking hell, what did you do?"

"Spore. I had to talk to your mom somehow."

"You're clever, and I hate you."

"We leave once Etolié is well," Casvir said, and already he moved to pack up their camp. "The mountains are near."

Kah'Sheen's focus remained on Etolié, her worry clear. "Sha'Demoni is faster, but Sarai cannot come that way."

"If it is for the greater good, leave me behind," the ghost said. "Flowridia and Ayla are the priority. Nothing can harm me here."

The ghost's name sparked immediate realization. Sora surveyed the phantom and assuredly recognized her face. "Sarai Fireborn?"

The ghost smiled as she approached. "I am. And you are Sora Fireborn? Then we are family."

Disbelief filled Sora, for this explained so much, yet led to further questions.

"Absolutely fucking not," came Etolié's slur. When she sat, she managed to remain upright. "Even if I approved of leaving you behind, which I don't, if we're as close as Casvir says, there's no point."

"Agreed," Soliel said.

"We are," Kah'Sheen affirmed. "Mountains of Kaas is

Ayla Darkleaf's old home. We are within hours. Perhaps arriving before sunrise if we are leaving now."

Again, Etolié vomited and, this time, washed it away with a chug from her flask. "Then fucking carry me."

Kah'Sheen took the initiative, her four arms having no trouble lifting the bedraggled Celestial.

Such strange bedfellows. But if Etolié could work with Soliel, Sora could work with Casvir.

As they walked, Sora recalled the condemning story Kah'Sheen had told beside the campfire. She jogged to meet the arachnoid half-demon. "Kah'Sheen, did you say before that Mereen had poisoned Raziel Fireborn?"

Kah'Sheen had no trouble with the rapid pace, her many legs moving in succession. "I am saying this, yes."

Sora peered back in her memories, upon days spent in delirious fever, recalling so little. But she had been helpless . . . how simple would it if have been for Mereen to have . . . "Why did you think that? What were his symptoms?"

"Fever and delirium. Poison from staphyn root, I am thinking. Why?"

But Sora suddenly felt ill, steps slowing as her breath became shallow.

She hardly noticed Kah'Sheen's presence, hardly noticed Sarai's light as she slowed beside her. Sora stood still, her vision blurring in a blink.

Her mother was dead, had been dead for years, but that grief washed over her anew—for her mother had been taken, her father had been taken, and all by people she trusted . . .

"Sora?" came Kah'Sheen's voice.

Sora's tears saturated each word. "Does it hurt humans?"

"I do not know, but Mother is telling me that humans are not killed by many elven poisons, only makes them sick."

Sora choked back a sob. "Go ahead. I'll catch up."

Kah'Sheen obeyed, keeping with Casvir and Soliel. But beside her remained that blue, soothing light. When Sora fell to her knees, Sarai sank down with her. A small cry escaped her lips, tears falling fast as the horrible truths bombarded her. Her family had been stolen, her mom and papa both.

"May I sing for you?"

Sarai's voice startled Sora from her spiraling thoughts. Though surprised at the request, she managed to nod, supposing it wouldn't hurt.

Only one question remained . . . why had Sora lived?

A rich song filled the air, in a cadence of elven far older than Sora. Sora cried, but the warmth of Sarai's music washed over her like a hug.

Not all her family had abandoned her. She could persevere for them.

Flowridia awoke from a silent sleep to throbbing pain and a vision of holy light.

She blinked fitfully, clutching her ruined hand to her chest. Gods, what was that smell? Was it she herself? Before she could look, she reeled back in shock, eyes adjusting to the figure seated upon the bloody table.

Unmistakable, for her image saturated Solvira, the Theocracy, even some streets in Nox'Kartha. Depicted in artwork, celebrated with song, none could walk this realm and not know her godly grace, her golden wings floating peacefully behind her, a hood covering golden hair. A spear leaned against the wall, casting its own light.

Sol Kareena did not look at her, instead idly plucking the petals from a flower—Flowridia's flower. She had left it at her altar, years ago.

In the quiet, one floating petal landed upon the floor, its glowing light fading into the darkness.

The goddess removed her hood, staring upon Flowridia with eyes she knew—she had seen them before, but also in her son. How similar they were, both in face and in radiant aura.

"Flowridia Darkleaf. We meet again."

Flowridia struggled to speak, a thousand questions flooding her mind. "How can this be?"

"We can see strange figments in our fevers," Sol Kareena replied, and her voice was the breeze on a sunny day, bright and soothing. "And sometimes gods may appear to us when we are not all in ourselves."

Fever. Flowridia looked to her hand, stomach lurching at the macabre sight, the bones shattered and curled back, black stitches holding the noxious 'petals' into place. Pus welled from the seams, the skin bearing hints of green and blue.

"You were supposed to be mine," Sol Kareena continued,

with no anger, but . . . disappointment. "I chose you. I called to you in the voice of my servants, but you did not listen."

"What's your point?" Flowridia said, her rising shame threatening to surpass even the pain permeating her body.

"My point is I could save you, if you forsake it all."

The words lingered like a fog. "I led to the death of thousands."

"True."

"I have betrayed so many who loved me. Even many who loved you."

"True."

"I am far past redemption."

How sweet was Sol Kareena's smile, and Flowridia knew not what to make of it. "It is far more powerful to live with your sins and repent than to run."

Perhaps there was honor in that, but Flowridia could not release her hesitation. "Why?"

"Because you still have goodness inside you. You could do great things in my name, as the heir to my kingdom."

The words were kind. Perhaps even sincere. "It would mean to abandon Ayla."

"I can promise her a swift death, but as I said, you must forsake it all."

"She has my wedding ring."

"But will it work?"

The words plunged her hope into dark waters.

It was an escape. It was the promise of life. And she would not have to slay the woman she loved—perhaps she could bring her back again, using the moon's blood.

And yet . . .

"I don't trust you."

Sol Kareena frowned, a mar upon her beautiful face. "Why not? I have never hurt you. I have never betrayed you."

"No, but you abandoned Ayla."

A strange malevolence filled the goddess' countenance, the raise in her brow lowering the temperature of the room. "Did I?"

"She lived in your home, in your *cathedral*, and you never once answered her prayers."

"You would trust the memory of a child?"

"I would trust the results. Monsters came to claim her."

Curt words came from the Sun Goddess, and Flowridia felt darkness behind them "I sent a supposed savior to act in my stead, who chose to hide her wickedness behind devout rituals and closed doors. No god is omnipotent, Flowridia. We only know what we are told. I drove Izthuni out through Eva, and I did not condemn Ayla for slaying her. Instead, I sent one of the kindest hearts among my worshippers to find her, only for Izthuni to come again. Did I not try?"

The words were . . . wounding. Perhaps even true.

"Come with me, Flowridia. We can start your life anew."

Flowridia stared upon the goddess' visage, seeking flaws, seeking any explanation for the familiarity plaguing her soul.

Her very center shifted at the realization, sending her off balance. "I'm not the heir to your kingdom."

"Were you not Lunestra's pride?"

"Sora is the heir to the Theocracy."

Flowridia met a vacant stare, the goddess' smile returning. "But you are *an* heir—"

"What did you say to me on the steps of the cathedral?" Flowridia glared, her suspicions ever rising. "The exact words, or close enough."

Something cruel twisted Sol Kareena's smile, chilling Flowridia's blood. "You expect me to remember every word I've spoken?"

"You wouldn't, because you're not Sol Kareena. You'd been banished seconds before, *Izthuni.*"

At that, the false Sol Kareena's smile became eerily broad, but her lips did not end. Wider, taller, her mouth spread to consume her beautiful visage, leaving only a gaping maw, teeth lining the inside. Sinister, the laughter evoked from that vicious mouth, echoing across the walls. Izthuni stood, grabbed the spear, and took firm steps toward her.

Flowridia screamed as she scrambled back, but that mouth only grew, elongating well past the reaches of the impostor Sol Kareena's face. Cowering, she sobbed as the mouth spread around her, swallowing her whole, plunging her into darkness . . .

"Face your sins . . ."

Flowridia wailed as she bolted into sitting, soaked in sweat. She knew her cell even in darkness, but the burning in her hand surpassed all other sensation. Gasping, she sought to see it in the dark, but her hand was merely a pulsating mess of red. Gods, the smell. Bile rose in her stomach.

Even in the dark, her vision tilted, disoriented by the light flashing beyond the barred window. Her mind shifted slowly back into her head. Sweat coated her skin like slime. Oh, how she shivered.

Beyond, a battle sounded. A scream—Ayla's scream.

Flowridia stumbled as she sought to rise, her good hand clutching the table as she balanced on shaking legs. She peeked from the doorway, flashes of silver lighting the room, though she could not quite see the source, nor the ensuing battle. "Ayla!" she cried, her voice cracking from disuse.

A glint of steel, and Mereen steered nimbly down the hallway, swords clashing to block a swipe from Ayla's claws. A blast of holy light; Ayla screamed, skin sizzling as Tazel appeared, the staff in one hand, rapier in the other.

Flowridia knew her wife's motions, her grace and perfect poise, but here she stumbled, tripping on her skirts, her own feet. Disoriented, yes, but the wedding ring glinted on her finger. Her feral eyes held a silver band at the edges—and recognition when she met Flowridia's gaze. She bolted, slamming Mereen against the wall, and Flowridia stepped back in anticipation of her ripping open the door, hope surging—

But it did not come.

She peered again through the window, gasping to see a great shadow, its corporeal claw holding Ayla down. Ayla shrieked as a second emerged from the darkness and gripped her left arm—

Ripping it from her body.

It repeated the act, leaving a pitiful torso to shriek on the floor.

Mereen stood frozen, swords raised in defense, but Tazel wasted no time; the skull atop the staff glowed, the magic rising to steal Ayla anew.

Flowridia felt nothing, too shocked to even comprehend—until a booming voice permeated the room like thunder. She knew it well.

Izthuni had come.

This place was cursed in my name long ago, consecrated as a temple by the dark deeds pledged in my name. I have seen everything. Flowridia can tell you—I have been here all along.

Writhing on the floor, the mutilated Ayla gasped and sobbed as her limbs regrew, fresh bone elongating inch by inch, followed by muscle and flesh.

Ayla abandoned me, and so I thought to let her be punished. But now her wife knows too much—and so whether it be by Ayla's hand or yours, she must die. If Ayla falls, so be it; I shall make a new champion in time. You are a plague, Mereen Fireborn, but in this one moment, we are aligned. Danger is coming. Tell me Flowridia will not leave this place alive, and I shall deliver a warning.

No hesitation. "Flowridia shall die."

Imperator Casvir and the Empress of Solvira are coming to rescue Flowridia. They are accompanied by The Coming Dawn, the God of Order, your sister, and your half-blooded descendant. They will be here before the night is through.

"Sora is dead," Mereen said, and her stare fell upon Tazel. "Sora is *dead*, right?"

Tazel's words came utterly muted. "Perhaps she lived. I-I don't know."

Sora Fireborn assuredly lives. I was drawn to her prayer to the Goddess of Stars.

Upon the floor, Ayla wept, the staff's glowing eyes more powerful than any undead could ever be.

But if you swear Flowridia shall die, I will defend this place from their onslaught.

Panic pursed Mereen's lips, her cool demeanor fully cracked. "I will see that Ayla is dead before that." Her steel gaze fell upon Flowridia, who clung weakly to the bars, her legs shaking against the door. "But if not, I accept your offer."

When it is done, we part as enemies. In the meantime, take the ring upon her finger and be immune to her power.

The shadow withdrew, but the malevolent aura remained.

Flowridia's heart skipped when Mereen suddenly appeared at the door, falling as she yanked it open. At the woman's feet, Flowridia yelped when Mereen ripped her up by her arm, all but throwing her against the table. The metal banged her mutilated hand; she shrieked as fresh pain seared through her blood.

"Flowridia Darkleaf, I can make your life so much worse."

Flowridia managed no words, simply cried against the cruel metal.

"Tazel, bring Ayla in here!"

Upon the floor, Ayla crawled like a dog, resisting every motion. Her hair had become a matted mass against her neck, clotted blood binding it. Every part of her was dried blood, cracked and old—all of it Flowridia's; all of it stolen. But ice clung to the edges of her black pupils, glistening with unshed

411

tears.

Cold hands gripped Flowridia's neck, forcing her focus to Mereen alone. A knife glinted in the vampire's grasp, the leather hilt pressing against Flowridia's good hand. "Stab me if you like," the vampire spat, "but you won't succeed. Stab Tazel, and I'll make a few fresh cuts in that stump of yours."

At the release of her neck, Flowridia dropped against the table. The weighted threat vanished with the shock of Mereen kicking Ayla in the head.

Ayla gasped but did little more, even as Mereen's boot split her lip. Flowridia swore she felt the blow in her stomach. "What are you doing?"

Mereen's malevolent smile revealed a glimpse of dark soul, her façade of sanity fracturing. "Feel free to interrupt anytime. I won't stop you."

Ayla's face repaired in time for another kick. Bone cracked beneath Mereen's boot as she held it to Ayla's skull, the dried blood on her face streaking beneath falling tears.

Ayla didn't care about pain, or at least it was what she said. But the knife trembled in Flowridia's hand, caught between weakness and rage as Mereen kicked Ayla again and again . . .

And when Ayla's face had become pulp of distorted flesh, Mereen paused. "I could do this for hours. Feels cathartic."

When Ayla twitched, the skull in Tazel's hand flashed anew. She curled into a ball, smaller than Flowridia had ever seen, smaller than any image she'd ever had of a tiny elven child lost in the world.

Flowridia swayed on her feet, desperately clinging to consciousness. "Why are you doing this?"

"Because torturing you isn't working fast enough. Perhaps torturing her will speed this along."

Mereen withdrew a knife.

"Wait!" Flowridia staggered forward, collapsing when the table ended. Gods, every motion wrecked her as she crawled toward her love with her broken hand tucked away, the knife in her other. Sweat poured down her face, the effort draining what little energy she had left.

But she managed to touch Ayla.

Flowridia did not know what she could do, only prayed this staved off Mereen's onslaught a moment more. Her thumb caressed the thin skin of her love's arm, and beneath it,

Ayla's body fell slack.

Tears spilled from Flowridia's eyes as she scooted herself near, mindful of her hand as she took Ayla in her arms from behind, shielding her with what little of her body remained. "I love you," she whispered, the words drenched in tears.

She breathed, simply breathed, smelling nothing of familiarity—no clean soaps or lingering traces of blood. Instead, the blood was overpowering, the dirt and filth nauseating, but Flowridia was surely no better.

Gods, there was no dignity in death.

Mereen's cold voice seeped like poison through the air. "What are you doing?"

Flowridia did not reply, simply clung to Ayla with all she had left. And Ayla did not move, did not react—save to melt against her body, and it was enough.

Before sunrise . . . and hope might come. But a horrid sensation of doom permeated her being. Her hand . . . oh, her hand . . .

Even if they did come, was there hope at all?

"Flowridia!"

Flowridia gasped, tears flowing when Mereen wrenched her away, forcing her to stand. "I know I can't fight you," Flowridia said, "but if there's anything . . . anything at all—"

Pain ripped through her hand, vision white as Mereen took the mutilated appendage and squeezed. "Go on."

Mereen released; Flowridia sobbed, for it lingered like fire, stealing her sight and sanity. Her head spun, her vision tilting with it. Amid her cries, she managed small words. "Not her. I'm begging you."

"Then you'll have to kill her, sweetie."

At Flowridia's hesitation, Mereen shoved her toward the wall. She collapsed to the floor, anguish rising when Mereen held her knife anew. "Tazel, hold Ayla steady."

At the first plunge of Mereen's knife, Flowridia screamed, for Ayla could not, utterly stiff—except her eyes, suddenly wide in shock, before they shut, forced serenity in her countenance.

Again . . . and again . . . Flowridia felt too sick to count. "Please, no," she managed instead, pleading through her tears.

She tried to move, but weakness weighed her down. Gods, she was so *cold*. Above her, Tazel's misery radiated, but something in Mereen's reticent visage, in the flecks of flesh and grime spraying across her face, in the grim twist of her lip, showed a person who had left their soul far behind.

"Mereen, stop," she whispered, but there was no power behind it. Oh, she hurt, and not just in her mind.

Mereen did pause, callous as her gaze fell upon Flowridia. And though Ayla lay in pieces on the floor, bit by bit she reformed, cursed into consciousness by immortality.

"Something tells me you're going to stall again." Mereen looked to Tazel, that wicked glint in her eye a sure cause for nightmares. She took the wedding ring from her pocket and slipped it on her finger. "Loosen your hold, just a little. I want Flowridia to hear her cry."

Ayla suddenly seized, the hacked pieces of her flesh still reforming. But instead of weep, she growled like a wounded animal. "If only I could bleed," Ayla said, tremulous and pained, "I'd spit it in your damn face."

"It's so lovely to actually speak with you." Mereen sliced a line down Ayla's arm, who hissed but nothing more.

Despite each repeated motion, Ayla stayed perfectly still, save for the slight clenching of her fists. "Flowra won't last. She's dying. Can you not smell it?"

"What does it matter to me if she dies? Her death is already promised."

"You care. All she has to do is outlast you and your opportunity to kill me ends forever—and it'll be mere hours now."

Mereen paused in her onslaught. "What do you want?"

"I want my Flowra to live, obviously. If you leave her for the others to find, she might have a chance."

"Adorable, your empathy for her. And how sickening, that you don't hold it for a single other creature to walk this realm. You took everything from me—my life, my country, even my son. Forgive me if I relish taking away the one thing that matters to you."

Ayla managed to turn her head, her silver gaze settling upon Flowridia—and how it broke her heart, after so many nights of pain, of monstrous, vacant eyes, to look upon her love's visage and know she was *seen*. How deep was Ayla's anguish; it twisted her features, streaked with blood and tears. "Darling, darling, close your eyes. You don't need to remember this part."

"Tazel!" Mereen spat, and the man's haggard face fell upon her. "Use the staff. Hurt her like you did before. Perhaps that will convince Flowridia to make up her mind."

414

"I'm sorry," Ayla said, her voice finally breaking. "I'm so sorry, Flowra—"

But the name cut off, replaced by a wail.

It did not stop, merely ebbed and flowed. Flowridia failed to silence her tears. She shut her eyes as Ayla had implored, caught in the torturous loop of sound.

There was no one to pray to. Her goddess was here, screaming on the cold dungeon floor.

E tolié finally stopped seeing stars—rather, stars she didn't wish to see.

"You must be drinking more water," Kah'Sheen kept reprimanding, but Etolié just took another swig from her flask, savoring the rising inebriation.

"Who says this isn't water?"

"I do." Kah'Sheen thrust a waterskin into Etolié's hands, which was impossible to avoid, given that the spiderous lady was actively holding her.

A little strange, to be cradled by a naked half-demon who wasn't Khastra, but everything Kah'Sheen did conveyed sisterly affection and nothing more. And if sisters carried you when you were coming off a secondhand high and dehydrated as fuck, well, Etolié kinda loved it.

The moon cast the world in silvery light, easily seen once they reached the mountain's base. "I can walk now, theoretically," Etolié said, and Kah'Sheen helped her balance on her feet. Etolié's wings spread wide, supporting the rest of her, and she walked without trouble through the wild grass. "Sora, I swear on my estranged Granddaddy's Whorish Dickhole, I will gouge out your eyes with a spoon if you ever make me do that again."

"I didn't make you do anything," the half-elf said, her honesty frankly perturbing.

"You're right, but fuck you. You're still on thin fucking ice."

"I told you—"

"You accept that, yeah, yeah."

Nearby, Casvir watched the exchange with a smug sort of amusement, the general emotion of *I don't understand you, but it's funny when the abuse is being thrown at people who aren't me.*

Etolié took another drink, forgetting that it was a waterskin. It wasn't that the fresh water was nasty—it was that all water was fucking nasty. But beneath the watchful eye of Kah'Sheen, Etolié chugged it like she would her booze, gagging all the while.

"What should we expect to find up there?" Casvir asked, aiming that domineering stare toward Sora.

Sora seemed surprised to be addressed and stumbled through her first few words. "Ayla's old home is large. Flowridia is kept in the underground dungeon, along with Ayla. Ayla is being controlled by Tazel—I suspect we'll have to fight her. Tazel is vulnerable. Mereen is who I'm most afraid of."

"Tazel is far more effective than I expected," Casvir said.

He didn't follow it up. "What did you expect?" Etolié asked.

"I expected him to behave like a coward who hides in a library for six years and runs away from his debts."

Casvir was choosing violence today. "That's a fair assessment," Etolié replied, "though I still find him iconic." She looked to the rest, noting that half of them glowed. Great for navigating, not so great for stealth. But was there even a point in illusioning them away? Sora had said Izthuni would warn their foes. "Just so we're all on the same page—does anyone here give a shit if Ayla Darkleaf lives? Or, rather, is destroyed?"

The God of Order had the fucking audacity to speak up. "I care."

Beside him, Sarai raised her hand. "If we're taking votes, I also would prefer she live."

"Well, you're outvoted, but it won't be a priority."

"Leave her to me," Soliel said. "The rest of you focus on finding Flowridia and killing Mereen."

"So, ghostie," Etolié said, "what fight skills do you have?"

"I scream and destroy buildings."

Not what Etolié had expected. "You might be too dangerous for this battle. We do need the building intact if we're going to save Flowers."

Sarai nodded. "I can only be so far away from the knife, but I will keep away as much as I can. At the very least, I can make myself difficult to find."

"Use your head. If you find a place to insert yourself,

fucking do it." Etolié looked to her half-demon sister. "Sheen Bean, we'll all be focused on Mereen, but you're the only one of us who can also stalk her in Sha'Demoni. I need you to be on full alert."

"I can be doing that," Kah'Sheen replied, her knives already readied. "And I am knowing this is a bad time, but I must know in case you are dying—why am I a bean?"

Etolié's words died in her throat. "What?"

"Sheen Bean. I am a bean? You are saying it many times."

Damn demons and their literalism. "It's a pet name. No affiliation to any actual beans. Just a cute rhyme."

The smile on Kah'Sheen's face was nothing less than adorable. "Oh. Well, thank you."

Back to business. Etolié pushed aside all thoughts of sisterly bonding. "Casvir, I know we all want Ayla dead, but if you can play backup to Soliel and agree to not kill her, be in that role. Sora, back up Kah'Sheen. You did a damn fine job evading Mereen way back in the swamp, and I need you to do that again now." Etolié glared up the mountain. "I'll take care of library boy."

All agreed to their roles. They began their climb.

Casvir couldn't get winded, and Sora had boundless stamina, it seemed, given she had run down this same mountain earlier that day. Kah'Sheen had an extra pair of legs and navigated the steep slopes with ease. Soliel was slow but never faltered.

Etolié, however, took the Sarai route and opted to float. Why work harder than you had to?

The chill of night rose the higher they climbed. The vegetation steadily shrank. There was no clear path, simply the precarious slopes and rocks. *Goddess Momma,* she thought, for apprehension clenched her stomach tighter and tighter, *just keep half an eye on me, all right?*

A few seconds passed before a gentle whisper sounded in her head, bringing a familiar presence. *Always, my Etolié.*

Etolié swallowed the sudden lump in her throat at the motherly phrase. *Thanks, my momma.*

Laughter chimed in her head. The presence withdrew.

With Etolié too nervous to speak, they traveled in silence. Time became elusive, and when Sora spoke, it jarred Etolié from her wordless anxiety. "We're close."

"Remember the plan, kids," Etolié said.

Soliel unsheathed his sword. Casvir summoned his

mace. Kah'Sheen readied her knives, and Sora caressed the one at her hip. Sarai met Etolié's eye, then sank into the earth, her incorporeal body vanishing.

As they crossed a final slope, the moon illuminated a once-grand estate. Surely a spectacle in its prime, it now bore signs of termites, of mold, of the passage of time, yet Etolié couldn't deny the surge of dread in her soul to face it.

The world became quiet in unnatural ways. No owls. No insects. "Something's here," Sora said, and Etolié illusioned a quarterstaff, prepared to bash some elven heads.

When they stood approximately a hundred feet away, from the balcony came a familiar yell. "This is your only warning. Turn around."

Undoubtedly Mereen. "I didn't cross half a fucking continent, join with my worst enemy, and take on a Spore overdose just to turn around and have a picnic," Etolié cried. "You can keep Ayla. Give us Flowridia!"

No response.

"Well, that was our warning," Etolié said, her nervous laughter failing to lighten the tense mood.

From the shadow emerged a monster.

It expanded as it left the porch, elongating in gruesome measures, becoming a beast with glowing, silver eyes and an infinite maw with fangs and rows of teeth. Horrid claws gripped the earth, its hunched figure nearly humanoid, yet the unnatural proportions of its limbs and body revealed its demonic half. Sickly thin, and when it rose on two limbs, it towered nearly as high as the mansion.

The Endless Night grinned.

"You didn't mention that, Sora," Etolié muttered, because three times was too many times to stand at odds with this fucking creature.

The half-elf looked like a woman two seconds from pissing herself. "I don't know anything anymore."

"Forget my plan," Etolié said louder. "Let's kill The Endless Night!"

And with that battle cry, they charged.

Etolié quickly fell behind, never prepared for athletic pursuits. The monster roared. Silver flame erupted at its feet.

Only then did Etolié remember she was useless here. "Gods-fucking-damn Silver Fire bastards."

Casvir stayed the farthest away from the monster, purple mist emanating from his feet and spreading across the ground like lightning. The earth shook. Ancient bones unearthed, clawing through the packed dirt. From the dilapidated home, other creatures emerged, that same mist caressing their beings, bidding them to come. But these were not simple bones, no—these were abominations, not unlike what Etolié had once seen in the war with Solvira, when Ayla had waved the white flag. Yet these were cruder, messy, some falling apart even as they shambled forward. Nothing more than bones and dust, so ancient they were.

They joined the fray, swirling to surround The Endless Night.

Sora stayed at the outskirts, clearly apprehensive to come close. Kah'Sheen, however, whipped in and out of darkness, appearing long enough to throw a knife at the monster and vanish. Etolié had never seen The Coming Dawn fight and was shocked at her fluidity, her size and shape not suggesting she'd be graceful. Yet weren't spiders elegant? She supposed it made sense.

It was Soliel who brought the literal thunder—or lightning, rather. High above, storm clouds gathered, blocking the moon and lingering stars. A bolt of light shot down to decimate The Endless Night, whose fire only burned brighter. Piercing laughter sounded from the monster, and Etolié realized how fucked they were.

Orb magic could be absorbed. Fuck.

But Soliel did not cease, perhaps capable of overpowering it with pure, relentless might. Fire burned, ice crept forward, all of it seeping across the monster's skin, penetrating its thin flesh. The monster swiped its claws, attempting to toss Soliel away, but the God of Order merely stumbled, managing to hold his ground. He drew his sword instead and charged.

From his hip, Casvir grabbed what appeared to be a simple silver rod, daring to approach the beast. In tandem, he and Soliel battered The Endless Night, landing blow after blow—successfully, for there was no magic here. The monster roared and attempted to grab Casvir—but a glancing swipe from Soliel detoured its path. When it sought to bite the Old God, Kah'Sheen vaulted beneath it and sliced a gash into its ribs.

Kah'Sheen landed—only to scream as a new figure appeared for a flickering moment. Blood spurted from the half-demon's arm as Mereen's sword lacerated her skin. The vampire disappeared.

Etolié's panic spiked, but with it came a plan. She couldn't fight The Endless Night, but she could royally fuck with Mereen. "Everyone, ignore what I'm about to do."

And appearing on the battlefield were numerous Casvirs, Soliels, Kah'Sheens, and Soras.

The figments joined the fray, harmless as they swung their weapons at The Endless Night—who of course saw straight through them. But Mereen reappeared to slash at Kah'Sheen, only for the illusion for sparkle and ignore it.

"Take that, bitch," Etolié muttered, then soared high into the air, wings aglow. Best not tempt the vampire wielding twin swords.

The chaos escalated with these new false competitors. The Endless Night's flame intensified, pouring from its mouth. Soliel evaded. Kah'Sheen grabbed Casvir, dragging him into Sha'Demoni just in time. They reappeared when the flame dissipated.

Again, they drove back the monster, Mereen's spontaneous appearances useless.

Until . . . the real Casvir faltered.

The dead fell. Casvir froze, pain twisting his countenance. He clutched his head at the base of his horns, confusion joining with grief, until . . .

His visage relaxed. He dropped the silver rod, summoning his mace instead—

And struck an unsuspecting Soliel across the face.

Soliel stumbled back, hesitant as he met the imperator's gaze, and parried the ensuing blow from Casvir. The dead rose anew—this time swarming Soliel and Kah'Sheen.

"It is Staff Seraph deDieula!" Kah'Sheen cried. "It is controlling Casvir!"

Shit. Fuck. NO. "Gotta find Tazel!" Etolié yelled, then swooped nearer to the battle. The illusions remained, but the real Soliel was forced to fight both Casvir and The Endless Night. Flame poured from the monster's body, this time engulfing Soliel. His cry filled the night, soon fading in tandem with the roaring fire. And though his charred form healed before Etolié's very eyes, he slowed—and received a wicked bash to the head.

The illusionary Casvirs turned on their doppelgänger, immediately swarming the true Casvir. "I'll hold him off!" Etolié cried. "Focus on The Endless Night!"

Where the hell was Tazel? Etolié's headache burned wherever she flew, the monster a fucking generator of magic, so no sense in following that—

She screamed when The Endless Night suddenly grabbed her by the wings, dragging her toward its horrible maw. With no time to even contemplate her doom, Etolié stared at rows of terrifying teeth—

Then recalled she could plane shift. Etolié screamed and made the tiny jump into Sha'Demoni.

Unimpeded, she fell to the porous ground, then screeched as numerous plant . . . *things* scattered from around her. But as she caught her breath, the shadow of that same fucking claw swiped without the hindrance of planar barriers.

She barely dodged, bolting away from the fray.

Tazel's staff had stolen Casvir. The Endless Night was too much.

Time moved slower in the mortal plane, so Etolié spared a moment to panic and contemplate their doom. Sure, she could escape, but what of her friends? Her enemies? She would essentially be leaving Sora to die, the mortal that she was—and The Endless Night could pursue them, no question.

But as Etolié contemplated the impossibility of their quest, she realized there was someone else to call, someone who had fought both The Endless Night and Soliel before. Not that Soliel was the threat, but it was a comfort.

Etolié grabbed a bottle of wine from her extra-dimensional space, very few thoughts in her head as she popped off the cork.

Instead of downing it, she frantically sang: *"Oh Eionei, please bless this cup, I pledge my revelry to thee—"*

Within seconds, a teeny tiny figure appeared from the wine bottle, bearing deep maroon shades. Unmistakable, with his wings and slim physique—the only thing wrong was his less-than-gallant stance as he stared at her. "Etolié?"

Fucking fuck, Eionei sounded so damn sweet. "Look, no time to explain. In exchange for your help, I promise to have an entire conversation with you, all right?"

"What do you need?"

"*We* need to fight Izthuni."

Eionei perked up. "Why are we fighting Izthuni?"

He didn't exactly sound displeased. Excited, actually. "Because he'll kill some of my sworn foes if we don't, which today is actually a bad thing. Some of my friends will go down with them."

"Then what are we waiting for, Starshine?"

The name sparked a surge of old affection within her, the part of her that was forever a little girl cherishing every visit from her grandfather. "Let me just pop back into the mortal realm, and we're doing this thing."

As Eionei's form swirled back into the wine, she took a long sip for luck. She phased back into the world just in time to watch The Endless Night slam Soliel into the ground and laugh as lightning struck its figure.

Ready?

Eionei's voice filled her head. *This looks like fun.*

Etolié braced herself for the odd sensation of being worn as a glove, her grandfather's spirit filling her limbs. She controlled herself, yes, but just as easily, he controlled her, her skin stretching to accommodate him. Her glow expanded, her resplendent wings gaining a fractal pattern, shifting with every motion. From her mouth came Eionei's familiar laughter, yet her own voice rang with it.

Let me lead, Starshine. I have this.

Etolié was simply a puppet as Eionei flew high into the sky, then dove. He drew his rapier and landed easily before The Endless Night, significantly taller than Etolié alone. "Hello there," he said, sounding like the splendid figure she had known all her life.

With Soliel at his side, Eionei battered back the unruly monster. "Fancy seeing you again. You're prettier without the helmet."

All she heard was a groan, but Soliel fell in line beside him, his motions matching Eionei's in ways his bulkier form shouldn't have allowed. Yet every step seemed practiced, his sword swinging to defend Eionei against The Endless Night's assault as naturally as the rising sun.

What's wrong with the imperator? Eionei said in her head.

He's being controlled by the staff.

You know, your mother mentioned something about you delving into song magic. I'm something of an expert as well. Would you like to make it a duet?

If Etolié could calm the Bringer of War and dead wolves, how different could a god and imperator be? *Can we spin the song to only control the undead?*

You just sing and leave the channeling to me.

Strange, for not once voice, but two, to belt from her

core:

Izthuni slinks around the dark
Some say the sun is caustic
But others claim it's 'cause his face
Makes little children nauseous

Power flowed through the words. The song cut through the noise of battle, for Etolié knew how to fill a stage even without magic. She controlled the words and voice; Eionei pulled her body's strings, striking at their foes as she continued her blasphemous ballad.

His legacy is mostly death:
To cause it and create it

The Endless Night watched her like an irritating fly, its consuming gaze oddly vacant. It swiped, but Eionei dodged, and Soliel's sword managed to make impact instead.

But cowards do as cowards will
And from fair fights—he'll split.

Casvir slowed. The dead followed suit. His red eyes fell upon her too, though with clear fascination—as the spell would do. His mace vanished. The dead did not fall, but they, too, watched.

The Endless Night slowed. Its fire receded. Though it swiped with fearsome claws, the lackluster blow met only air. No sign of Mereen. Perhaps the woman had run.

A quick glance revealed Sora, knives readied but her distance kept. Kah'Sheen whirled into sight, blinking in and out like a flickering candle as she cut the monster with her knives.

We haven't touched upon his smell
I'll try to do it justice
Fetid, musty, putrid, rank,
Vomitous, vile and viscous.

As the ballad continued, Eionei swooped in with his rapier once more, slashing a particularly brutal wound upon the monster's ribs.

Click.

Etolié heard it even amid the thunder and lightning, the flames and clanging swords—

Boom.

Etolié felt nothing, merely fell from the sky as all sight vanished. Each blink held the heaviness of teleportation, the world shifting anytime it went . . . white?

Liquid dripped to block her vision. Something soft cushioned her. Grass? When had she landed?

"Etolié!"

Kah'Sheen?

Etolié!

Eionei?

She blinked—there came a sisterly face.

She blinked—Etolié was floating, no, held.

"Etolié, no!"

Etolié tried to speak, tried to say she was fine yet could not seem to move her jaw.

Stay awake! Eionei screamed in her head. *Don't let me fade!*

"Breathe, Etolié!"

She blinked—and the chaos of the world disappeared, replaced by the familiar, warm colors of Sha'Demoni. She felt nothing from beyond, only a sharp grip inside her as Eionei clung with all his spiritual might.

"No sleeping. Just breathing. Etolié, please!"

The wind rushed. Each blink brought pure light. "Sheen Bean?"

It was the worst sort of drunken slur. Etolié tasted metal.

"I am saving your life, Etolié. Breathe."

Each blink brought time forward. The wind never ceased. Darkness came to overtake the light, and Etolié drifted away . . .

Stay awake, dammit!

She managed another blink . . . and another blink . . .

The thunderous bullet broke through the cacophonous night. Sora's breath caught as the amalgamation of Etolié and Eionei fell like a bird shot out of the sky.

The song ceased. All illusions vanished. Kah'Sheen appeared, screaming. Blood splattered the grass where the possessed Celestial landed, dripping from the bullet lodged in her skull.

They vanished into the shadows.

Shock stilled Sora's emotions. No time to cry. No time to panic. But the *boom* of the whirring bullet echoed in her head, signaling what she prayed was not her friend's final moment.

She remained on the edge of the battlefield, debating how best to aid the God of Order when The Endless Night, again, erupted into silver flame. Casvir's mace reappeared, quickly bashing the Old God, the dead soon following.

Sora wielded knives. She was adept with a bow. Sora fought beasts in the wild and sometimes robbers on the road. Her talents were in stealth and speed—but this? What could she do here?

"Sora?"

Sora gasped at the sudden hint of ghostly blue.

"What happened?" Sarai asked. "Can I help?"

"If Tazel senses you, he'll try to control you too. Stay out of..."

The barest flash of necrotic purple shone from the second floor of the mansion. Tazel was there—and Tazel controlled The Endless Night.

Sora sprinted to the mansion.

Along the outskirts, over rocks, away from the elemental onslaught beside her. The God of Order froze Casvir in ice, only for The Endless Night to shatter it with its grip, freeing the lich. Fire coated Soliel's sword; The Endless Night laughed and absorbed it. Lightning flashed, but The Endless Night shielded Casvir, and all along, the dead swarmed the Old God.

Soliel was God, but he was not yet a god. But why was Izthuni helping Mereen? Even if the staff could control him—which she could not confirm—why would he be here? Gods came when bidden, but they could easily refuse.

Either way, her only chance lay in subduing Tazel.

Something prickled against her senses. Pure instinct drove Sora to duck—just in time to evade Mereen's sword. Sora spun with her knife, only for Mereen to vanish anew into the shadows.

Again, came that tingling instinct. Sora's knife caught Mereen's blade. "You're fast for a blunt-ear," the vampire spat.

She swung. Sora caught it once more. "My mother

426

taught me all her tricks."

Mereen's grin leered, near enough to bite as she withdrew. "She was incredible. Could have been my protégé."

The statement sparked anger within Sora, coursing red hot through her veins. "So why did you kill her?" Sora gasped as she failed to dodge. The sword sliced across her cheek.

"Rage, Sora," Mereen said, voice smooth in the absence of breath. "She left me, then had the audacity to come crawling back with a half-breed bastard and expect me to take it in."

Sora's blade stopped a blow to her neck. Their weapons sang at contact, Sora's strength relenting to Mereen's unholy might. She staggered back and drew a second knife from her sleeve, but Mereen remained calm as she sauntered forward, swords readied.

Words simmered in Sora's throat. She barely saw Mereen's swords. "You poisoned her. But it didn't work on me."

"I didn't account for you to inherit that damn human constitution of yours. Still, with Mari dead, there would have been no witnesses to slitting your throat if Tazel hadn't come to visit."

"You're a monster," Sora seethed.

"How I wish I could say you're wrong." Mereen charged.

Sora faltered a moment too long, dodging instead of parrying. The earth shook as The Endless Night bashed Soliel against the ground, sending her stumbling.

Even if Mereen didn't succeed in killing her, Soliel was running out of time. Yet all of that faded as Mereen's horrible truths struck her like lightning. "You murdered my mom." Heat burned through Sora's blood. *"Do you feel anything at all?!"*

"Regret. Every day—"

Sora screamed and rushed. Mereen's words disappeared with the clash of metal. Fury drove her actions, thoughtless as she slashed at Mereen with her knives. All these years of yearning for parents. All these years of seeking to belong . . .

Anger kept her sharp. Pure adrenaline fueled her. Mereen matched her motions with perfection, yet when she vanished and reappeared, Sora sensed it like the breeze, like prey stalked by a predator. "Sol Kareena—"

Light appeared. But it was not holy; instead, a gentle blue.

Mereen faltered as a ghost rose from the ground. Sarai's sorrowful countenance held peace. "Hello, Mereen."

"Sarai—"

Sora screamed as her dagger struck Mereen's throat. She wrenched it forward, slicing tender skin and veins. A ghastly croak escaped Mereen, her swords dropping—one of which Sora caught. Before Mereen could dodge, Sora sliced with all her might across the vampire's thigh—

Which severed, skin and muscle and bone. Her legs fell in separate pieces. Mereen toppled, seeking to crawl away, but Sora set the sword's tip to the back of her neck. "Any final confessions?"

Mereen stiffened, and Sora felt her like a dying animal, the split moment of choosing whether to fight or flee. Yet she did neither. Merely gasped despite needing no breath, her wounds seeping clear, viscous ichor. "Seventeen hundred years, Sora." Her voice gurgled from her severed throat, hardly audible. "My greatest regret should be that I've failed, but no. My regret is that I've become no better than her."

"*Monsters beget monsters,*" Odessa had said, and *her* could be only one.

"You don't deserve a merciful death," Sora said, resolve in those final words, "but I'm not you. I never will be."

"One mercy, Priestess of Sol Kareena," Mereen whispered. "Let my body burn in the sun. I wish to leave this realm behind."

Sora brought the sword down upon her neck. Mereen's body slumped, head rolling to the side.

Heaving breaths shook Sora's core. Sora grabbed the head by its disheveled braid, leaving it far from its mutilated body. Only then did she look to Sarai, who stared forlornly upon her sister's severed head.

"Sol Kareena will judge her," Sora muttered, but bitterness stained each word.

Sarai's tears fell faster, sparkling before they disappeared. "I only pray she is judged for who she was in life as well."

The earth shook. The Endless Night suddenly roared, the flame it wielded dissipating. It tore at its face, wrenching itself away from the weakened Soliel, away from Casvir—

Who also froze. The undead fell. Casvir teetered on his feet and slowly lowered himself as his head fell into his hands.

Soliel glanced rapidly between the two, his armor charred, sword blackened. "What is . . ."

"*Get out!*" The Endless Night screamed, the discordant

tones enough to make Sora's ears bleed. It did not look at them. It shook and tore its own skin. *"Get out!"*

Sora ran to Soliel, accompanied by the ghost. Beside him, Casvir remained disoriented, swaying even as he sat. "Mereen is dead," Sora said, "but why is . . ."

Tazel.

"Tazel withdrew control. So why is The Endless Night—"

The Endless Night shrieked and erupted in flame. Soliel charged, sword in hand.

The battle resumed. Yet the tides of war had shifted.

The Endless Night remained a threat, but it clawed at itself as much as Soliel and Sora. At times, it would breathe fire and seek to tear the God of Order's head off, and other times, freeze and allow his sword to cleave its thin flesh. It fought itself just as it fought the Old God, and Sora remained warily in the background, standing between the creature and Imperator Casvir.

A small part of her longed to slit the man's jugular. Sol Kareena might condone it, though her own honor said no.

Common sense said it would fail anyway.

Sarai's ghostly light rose beside her, but faintly. Only her head appeared from the ground. Such grief in her features as she stared upon The Endless Night, and Sora felt she knew so little, only that whatever else was true or false, whatever had been lost with time, Sarai had a complicated history with this monster.

"Sora, look at the house," Sarai said.

Sora obeyed and saw nothing amiss, except . . .

Light. Orange light flickering from a window. It shone as an omen, for something was terribly wrong.

Smoke. From the open window, a bird flew into the sky and disappeared.

Ferseph?

The Endless Night screamed, its claw swiping wildly at Sora—and missing, for Sora was no longer there.

No thoughts. No sanity. In a dark and putrid dungeon, her sister would perish to smoke and flame.

Sora ran into the inferno.

Flowridia knew only fever.

Against the wall of the dungeon, she shivered, tears mingling with sweat and spit. "Tazel . . ." she managed weakly. "Tazel!"

Though she tried to yell, it hardly even echoed.

Something was wrong. Instinct screamed that it stemmed from the fire burning in her mutilated hand. The pain throbbed with her pulse, and though the room was dark, the raw lines had become white, viscous fluid seeping from the stitches. It smelled as putrid as Ayla's basement in their secluded manor home.

The memory of it lurked behind each blink. Mere weeks ago, life had been bliss . . .

She tried to crawl to the door, but weakness stilled her. Dirt from the floor clung to her damp skin. Gods, she couldn't stop shivering.

"Tazel?"

As though summoned by her prayer, rapid footsteps echoed against the stone. Muttering filled the halls. "*This ends. This ends. This ends . . .*"

"Tazel!"

How weak she was, but the door opened. There shone no life in Tazel's eyes, no recognition. He shook, his muttering never ceasing—not until he knelt before her. "You're dying."

"I'm freezing," she whispered.

She gasped as he withdrew a knife—and sliced it across his own skin. "I seal this sacrifice in flame," he muttered, a strange power stirring in the words.

Flowridia winced as he cut the knife across her arm, enough to well a line of blood.

"Blood of the dying."

He stared upon the knife, his and her blood mingling upon the blade. "This ends."

"Tazel, what are you doing?"

"This ends, this ends, this ends . . ."

With the mixed blood, he dragged the knife along the wall, using it to write a symbol Flowridia did not recognize. It glowed. "No atrocities shall touch this place again."

Dread welled in Flowridia's soul. "T-Tazel—"

The knife clattered to the ground. From his pocket, Tazel withdrew something small—a match, casting light upon the room.

430

Flowridia winced, blinded by the bright light. Yet the flame revealed a skeleton of a man, sickly and pale, eyes half-blind. Nothing of a soul lay in his visage; he was merely a shell.

"I'm sorry, Ferseph." He stared a moment upon the match, the moment a held breath. "With this flame, I seal myself as a revenant. No Fireborn shall hunt the undead again." He set the match to the bloody symbol.

The flame spread, the blood catching fire. Flowridia cowered, for something was wrong, so terribly wrong—

Blood of the dying rang like an echoing bullet in her ears. The memory of a curse of years ago, spoken of by Tazel himself, used to bind a witch to defend the lands she'd once terrorized—

So he would curse himself instead?

Tazel touched the burning symbol.

Fire spread across his figure, scorching his clothing and skin. He screamed yet did not move, did not seek to escape this gruesome end. Heat rose—though weak, Flowridia managed to scoot back in horror, watching as Tazel's skin burned away, first red, then visceral white. Flesh parted for bone, which blacked beneath the flame. The stench left her reeling—for burning humanoid flesh had been her hell for three years.

His screaming stopped, yet he remained, sealed in his spot even as a ghostly blue figment peeled away from his cage of flesh.

Flowridia gasped as she stared upon the ghostly visage of Tazel Fireborn, gruesome in death. Yet he did not look at her, merely upon his own corpse—which only then collapsed into a pile of flesh and ashes.

"This ends," came his discorporate voice.

The burning symbol spread, fire coating the stone walls. It should not be, yet Flowridia stared in horror upon the growing inferno, this magical flame eating even the stone. The walls became a hellish cage, rapidly expanding. Though every breath was pain, Flowridia forced herself to crawl, cradling her disfigured hand to her chest as she dragged herself from the burning room.

All the cells had caught flame. Smoke clogged the air. The sweat at her brow evaporated from sheer heat, the light blinding.

Inch by inch, she dragged herself, the endless stone floor merciless. The fire spread far faster than she, soon coating the ceiling. Far away, she heard falling timber, felt the building shake.

Her breath became labored, the air stale, hot, burning her lungs. Flowridia coughed, each breath shallower than the previous. Her vision spun. The fire raged. Flowridia crawled forward, weaker with every motion.

Her head ached, blood pounding in her ears. Smoke obscured her vision, air scarce, breath shallow—

She touched a stone step.

No strength remained.

Flowridia blinked, yet darkness crept along the edges of her vision, despite the blinding fire. If Tazel were dead . . .

"Ayla?"

Nothing.

Darkness crept in and did not fade. Flowridia's head rested gently upon the stone, her funeral pyre rising.

Her final moment of sight passed. Perhaps she would not feel her death after all.

Yet in the seconds before her mind fell into oblivion, rapid footsteps came down the stairs.

Noxious odors bombarded Sora's senses as she ran through the entryway, a dense cloud of smoke blinding her. She need not see; she knew the path, had walked it more times than she wished to remember, and she cut a thick slice of her shirt with her dagger to wrap around her mouth and nose.

She crouched, pacing her limited breaths as she skirted the corner. Already the heat wafted toward her. Ancient wallpaper coiled against the walls. From the basement, fire rose at unnatural speed.

Yet were the sides of the stairway not stone? Sora barreled forward. Whatever magic this was, if she dithered, it would be the end.

The steps led to a level of hell.

The stone walls glowed red hot, leaving the staircase as an oven. Sora coughed at the smoke, eyes burning.

But at the bottom of the staircase, a silhouette lay prone on the floor.

Sora all but fell to the bottom, the hairs on her arm singing from mere proximity. Flowridia lay upon the ground, still as death, naked yet untouched by flame. No time to check for a pulse; Sora lifted her frail body, finding it pliant at least, and heaved Flowridia over her shoulder before climbing the stairs, slower now with her sister's slight weight.

Flame consumed the hallway. Sora fled from the inferno, praying she could outrun a fiery death. The stench of scorched hair caught her nose. She ran faster—

But skidded to a stop at the bend in the hall, faced with a gruesome specter.

A macabre mass of open flesh and bone, each layer of skin held charred edges, his skull exposed. Even in shades of ghostly blue, the raw flesh pulsed, the burns glistening and fresh. No eyes in those putrid sockets, yet she felt his stare as fiercely as the growing heat.

Despite it all, Sora knew him. Shock stilled her. She all but retched the name. "Tazel?"

The spectral man, her flesh and blood, withdrew a ghostly rapier. His voice echoed from nowhere, for he had no mouth with which to speak—only a nightmarish tangle of flesh at his jaw. "If she does not die, the spell is incomplete. This feud must end."

"Mereen is dead. There's no need for a feud—"

"Leave, Sora. But Flowridia must stay behind."

Sora frantically shook her head, panic rising. To see him like this, to feel the heat of this place, the burden of her sister on her shoulders—her mind raced to comprehend it. "Tazel, this isn't you. This isn't who you are—"

"It's the only way."

From Sora's shoulder, Flowridia's slight gasp sounded louder than the crackling wood, louder than her own pounding heart. Sora gripped her sister tighter, her limp body burning from more than simply the hellish atmosphere. She glanced past Tazel—

The specter lunged. The tip of the ghostly weapon stung where it lacerated her arm. Sora stumbled back toward the inferno, head spinning as she gasped a toxic breath.

"Drop her, or die as the last Fireborn."

Sora's heartbeat pounded in her ears. Tazel seemed to absorb the light, his translucent blue somehow a pit instead of radiant. Yet far beyond, Sora heard a familiar bird's chirp. Beckoned by power beyond her comprehension, Sora whispered, "Sol Kareena—"

Light burst from her skin, coating her flesh. Sora rushed forward, shielded by divinity, a torrent of gold as she rushed straight through the ghostly figment. Burning cold enveloped her body—and then she felt nothing at all.

No time to stop. Sora's eyes burned as the golden light vanished from her skin. The entry hall stood as her final hurdle. Wood creaked as a segment of the ceiling collapsed before her, sending a spray of sparks. She spun, shielding her sister, and cried out as the flame caught the edges of her clothing.

"Guide me," she said aloud, for divinity was all that could save them now.

Sora shut her eyes and charged, screaming all the while—

Until she burst from the inferno, feet pounding against the wooden porch, and tumbled into the grass beyond.

Fresh air burned, but her tears welled from relief instead of pain. On the ground, she pulled Flowridia into an embrace, clinging to consciousness with the same desperation to which she held the limp girl in her arms. Sunrise was imminent. Nearby, the gods fought, the sounds of violence distant behind the deafening pulse of Sora's blood. Gone was the warm amber of Flowridia's skin, instead sallow from darkness, her scars and open wounds far ghastlier in the light. Abominable in that underground hell, yes. Yet illuminated by the first hints of day beyond the mountain, Flowridia appeared as the monster she truly was, unfit for mercy, but Sora sobbed, desperate to deliver it.

She set a trembling hand to her sister's neck. By the Light, she was so cold. "Flowridia—"

"*FLOWRA!*"

Beyond, The Endless Night tore apart its own skin. It fought to come near, but equally pulled away, claws striking deep gashes across its flesh to drive itself back.

Soliel ran to stand between them, becoming a barrier. Even Casvir, who had apparently found his bearings, ran on uneasy feet.

Then came beautiful song.

No source; no words. It simply emanated, one with the mountain. Sora had heard legends of banshees, sirens capable of grand destruction . . . or of peace, some even said. The Endless Night ceased its flailing, its wounds sealing shut. It fought halfheartedly, stumbling on all fours as the angelic song wafted like the wind.

Faint, so faint, came Flowridia's pulse. Only then did Sora notice the mutilated mess of Flowridia's hand, the stench of smoke yielding to the rot. Deep bruising blotched the skin around it, yet it was but one of many mutilations. Scars left horrible memories across her chest; the positioning of her ribs was off.

Sora followed the line of infected blood in her arm, found it traveled all the way to her chest. Beneath the residual heat of the fire, Flowridia burned, yet all of her was clammy and cold to touch. Sora could not fix this. She could only heal wounds.

"Soliel!" she cried, and the God in question stared at her. "She's dying! I need help!"

Soliel and Casvir shared a glance, the former rushing to her as the latter stood his ground, keeping a watchful eye on the calming monster. Soliel knelt beside them, a grimace overtaking his features. He touched her head, the sheared locks singed.

"Sepsis is a sickness holy magic cannot cure," he said, yet his expression did not shift. "She would be mutilated if I heal the rest of her just yet. She has broken ribs that would heal inside punctured organs. Not to mention her hand. It might condemn her to a slow death instead."

Sora's tears came faster, grief surmounting. "There must be something else we can do."

"Yes, but we must move swiftly."

Beyond, the monster suddenly froze, then shrank as it turned into shadow. Spirit separated from body as the shadow parted and dissipated, leaving only a small woman.

The song ceased as Ayla Darkleaf collapsed into a pitiful heap. But Ayla's wail sounded to replace it. Pity rose even in Sora, to hear her agony.

Casvir dropped his weapon and ran to her, but when he knelt, she lashed out, claws leaving deep gashes in his face. He remained stoic, nothing more than a twitch in his lip as he met her gaze.

She screamed and fell into sobs, clutching her hair as she rocked. Her motions were erratic, never ceasing, shaking like an injured dog—and just as liable to bite.

Whatever Casvir said, Ayla did not hear it, instead tugging at the grass as she screamed. The imperator abandoned her, instead sprinting to where Flowridia lay dying. "What has happened?"

"Flowridia is septic," Soliel said gravely.

"She will come to Nox'Kartha for healing. We have surgeons and healers."

"But will she survive the process?" Sora asked. "She literally has minutes, perhaps seconds."

"And we stand here bickering?"

"*Wait!*"

Ayla stumbled, pupils blown, hardly a ring of blue around them, but something of recognition lay in them. She fell to her knees beside Sora, seeking the dying woman. Sora let her, even helped Flowridia settle into her wife's embrace.

Ayla said nothing more, simply plunged her fangs into Flowridia's neck—

Only to be battered across the face by Casvir. "Do not."

"She'll die!" Ayla shrieked, managing to keep hold of her wife. "But this will save her!"

"She owes me a debt."

"*You would rather have her die?!*"

"I would rather try to save—"

Ayla tried again—and Casvir smacked her anew, bone cracking beneath his mace. But Ayla did not fight, simply curled around Flowridia, her tear-stained face falling into sorrow.

Then came a ghostly blue, rising from the earth. Sarai stood a ways off, shy as she floated forward.

Ayla Darkleaf froze, shock in her gaze. She said nothing at all as Sarai approached, did not move a modicum as the ghost knelt beside her. "I can save her."

Ayla's voice was small, smaller than Sora thought possible from the indomitable woman. She was power, she was fury, but here she was merely a whisper. "Sarai?"

Sora knew so little yet felt like an intruder as the world faded to merely their mutual presences. Ayla kept her protective embrace but made no move at all as Sarai touched Flowridia's forehead, her hands passing through. All of her fell inside the vessel, and Sora recalled what Odessa had said—that a ghost could possess a body near death.

And keep it alive.

All was still, even the sunrise muted as they waited . . . waited . . .

Flowridia's eyes fluttered open, yet there was something

different there. "She hurts," Flowridia said—or was it Sarai?

"But she will live through healing," Casvir said, approval in the words. "We should not delay."

When Casvir ripped his claws across the air, a sizzling line appeared. It spread wide, revealing an array of stars. He waited beside the portal as Ayla stumbled to her feet, clutching Flowridia's body as she stepped through.

She disappeared.

Casvir lingered, his red eyes landing on Soliel. "Our truce ends, unless there are any bargains we might make."

"Our quest is finished," Soliel replied, a certain darkness behind it, "as is our alliance."

Casvir's gaze fell upon Sora next, who felt too weak to fear it. "Will you join us?"

"Yes," she said, the reply as natural as breathing.

Casvir stepped through the portal without another word. It lingered, waiting.

Soliel offered a hand, helped Sora's weakened body to stand. "Before you go . . ." From his belt, he withdrew. . . a knife? A gorgeous weapon, forged with gems in the handle, the black steel a work of art.

Yet Sora stared warily upon it, something wicked in its aura. "What is that?"

"It does not matter what it is, except to say Sarai was attached to it until moments ago. It must be destroyed, but one of the few with Silver Fire left in this world just stepped through that portal. Bring it to Ayla. I will trust her to choose the right path in this one thing, given what horrors it has caused for her."

Sora accepted it, repulsed by the mere touch. "I will."

"Do not let Casvir see it."

She slipped it into her trousers, only the hilt showing. She put her fingers to her lips and released a great whistle into the wind.

A few peaceful moments, then a familiar tweeting responded faintly. Leelan's shadow appeared in the sky. He quickly joined her, settling upon her head. "As Imperator Casvir said, our truce ends. If I thought I had any chance of killing you myself, I would try."

The God of Order smiled, the kindness within it dusty and old but there, nevertheless. "Your bravery is commendable."

He trudged down the lonely mountain.

Sora offered her finger to Leelan. When familiar claws gripped the skin, she brought him down. "What secrets do you hold?"

Leelan stared with intelligent eyes, the yellow bird suspiciously dirtied with smoke and ash.

He could not speak. But how often had he spoken anyway? She set him on her shoulder, for time was short, but this would not be forgotten.

True to form, Sora lingered, staring upon the dilapidated building, still burning within. There Tazel's body would incinerate, no evidence except for charred bones.

Sora glanced to where Mereen's body had fallen. There lay white leather, covered in ash.

The Dark Slayer had truly gone, blessed to feel the sun's light one final time. A creature of rage, of obsession . . . and of grief.

From her tunic, Sora withdrew the salvaged feather. Tears prickled in her eyes. Odessa had killed Sora's father; Odessa had abused Sora's sister; Odessa was a witch of depthless evil, known for centuries as a depraved and vile creature . . . and she had been Sora's friend.

All those statements could exist as truths.

Sora pressed the feather to her lips, holding the image of Odessa in her mind as she emblazoned that face to memory. Sol Kareena would say it was wrong, but Sol Kareena did not know her thoughts. Thoughts did not a define a person; actions defined a person and their legacy, who they were to the people left behind.

And so it would be a secret only for her. Sora kissed the feather, grasping Odessa's image one final time, and released it into the sky, where it became a speck and then nothing.

And so they were gone, the great conspirators of this nightmare, the Mountains of Kaas a final resting place. Sora shut her eyes and voiced a final prayer: *Give me the strength to forgive.*

Perhaps someday. She stepped into the portal.

Chapter 22

Etolié's eyelids weighed more than Khastra's hammer—
though comparisons were useless. Both were impossible
for her to lift.

Yet she stirred into consciousness, freed from her prison
by a beautiful song. She knew the voice, grasped it tight, let it
lead her back into the land of the living.

And though it took time and pain, Etolié finally blinked
awake, met with vermilion walls and her mother's treasured
face. "Momma?"

Staella's smile held light. "Eionei! She's awake!" Fresh
tears welled in her eyes, joining the dried ones glistening on
her face. "Hello, Etolié."

A familiar presence joined Staella—Eionei and all his
topaz glory, his face damp and puffy. "Oh, thank the Suns,
Starshine."

She felt no pain, simply grogginess, like a hangover
without the headache. "Where am I?"

"We are in the home of Goddess Ku'Shya, in
Sha'Demoni," Staella said. "Kah'Sheen brought you and
Eionei, and her mother called for me."

Etolié's surroundings steadily swirled into view—
notably the impossibly high ceilings and cave-like walls. Her
bed was built for someone her size, however, the blankets
spun from silk. The heavy stack was grounding, though
perhaps overly warm. Staella's hand fell into her hair, gently
stroking the silver strands.

"How am I alive?"

"Your grandfather kept you awake and refused to leave
even when your body tried to banish him." Staella blinked,
grief filling her lavender eyes—a mirror to Etolié in so many
ways. "It's because of him that you're still here."

Panic filled Etolié to see her momma cry. "Momma, it's all right—"

"Shh, relax." Staella continued her soothing gestures, her touch sending pleasant chills across Etolié's scalp. "As your mother, I reserve the right to worry for my baby."

Something about being her 'baby' filled Etolié's heart to the brim. Her other hand came to find Eionei's, who simply held it. "How's your head?" he asked.

"Light."

Perhaps it was her shaky consciousness, or simply the aftermath of bodily trauma, or more likely the fear of never being able to speak her next words, but her own emotions rose.

She withdrew her other arm from the blankets and took Staella's hand from her scalp. "Momma, I need to tell you something." Etolié's voice trembled, her mind still finding its bearings. She gazed upon Staella's tearstained face, seeking the familiar bonds of blood, and the words burst forth like a stream. "In case I almost die again, you should know—I forgive you."

Staella said nothing, instead bringing Etolié's hand to her cheek and cradling it like a cherished newborn. She placed a small kiss upon the back of her hand, and with it came a smile, the hope it conveyed unmatched.

She managed to look to Eionei, feeling weak and sore— but alive. Sore meant alive. "I'm still working on that with you, but I did promise to meet with you in exchange for help."

Eionei nodded, clearly holding back a sob.

But the warmth within her faded as the ground shook.

Nearly draconic, yet arachnoid as well, a gargantuan figure entered. Four yellow eyes leered above her, blinking in succession, and Etolié only knew from interacting with the Bringer of War that her monstrous grin was indeed a grin and not a hungry leer. But she was far larger than the Bringer of War, perhaps three times over.

This could only be one person. Goddess Ku'Shya spoke in an accent Etolié mostly deciphered. "You are awake!" Her voice boomed across the room, her trunk-like legs nimbly evading them. "Very good. Kah'Sheen is hoping you are awake when she returns."

With Staella's help, Etolié managed to sit up. "You must be Goddess Ku'Shya."

"No, no—well, yes, but you are not calling me goddess.

440

You are calling me my name—or mother."

When Etolié caught Staella's eyes, her sweet momma visibly suppressed a laugh even as she wiped her tears. "Well, who could turn down an offer like that," Etolié said, oddly charmed. "It's nice to meet you, uh, Mother."

"It is the least I can do for my Khastra's wife."

This time, Staella shared her look of confusion. Eionei, too, seemed to be fighting shock.

"Yeah, Khastra's wife," Etolié said, not wishing to disagree with her apparent mother-in-law on their very first meeting. She gave a quick shake of her head to Staella and Eionei. Inevitably, this would begin a hole of lies she wouldn't remember to keep digging, but she would leave this one for Khastra to fix.

"You are having enough blankets, yes? Angels are easily cold."

Etolié opened her mouth to object but caught her momma's slight shake of her head. *It's a long story. Go along with it,* spoke a voice in her head.

"Perfectly warm, thank you. Where is Kah'Sheen?"

"She is finding Staff Seraph deDieula. I am told you are knowing her great betrayal to me." Ku'Shya said it so offhandedly, despite the condemnation.

"Yes, I heard."

"She is fixing this, but I understand leaving to save family. She is making the correct choice, because what would I do without Etolié?"

She said the name with the same endearing mispronunciation as her daughters, and Etolié supposed it was simply the Demoni way. "Probably die," Etolié replied to the woman she had met not one minute ago.

Ku'Shya burst into . . . laughter? It sounded not unlike a braying donkey, but it wasn't entirely unpleasant—endearing in a monstrous sort of way. "You are so funny, Etolié. To think of me *dying.*"

Etolié shared a quick glance with Staella, whose voice again floated through her head. *Yes, this is Demoni humor.*

"What even happened?" Etolié said.

"You were shot," Eionei replied, his eyes as wide as the apparent bullets.

Etolié stared into space, seeing the battle in memory. "I was fucking shot?"

"Yes, you were fucking shot," Staella said. The swear was

mockery; it showed in her smirk.

Still, Etolié couldn't appreciate the inherent humor in her sweet momma uttering a swear. "Then Mereen Fireborn fucking shot me."

Ku'Shya immediately bristled at the name. "Mereen?!" she cried, and it boomed across the walls, echoing through the tunnels, repeating the cry.

"*Mereen is dead!*" came a familiar voice. Kah'Sheen appeared in the enormous cave entrance and immediately gasped. "Etolié!"

Kah'Sheen scampered on those spider legs, and before Etolié could object, she stole as much of her as she could reach into a hug—which wasn't much, given the excessive pile of blankets, but apparently she didn't get the memo about touching. As it was, though Etolié instinctively cringed at the sensation of those spindly arms around her, Kah'Sheen's tears of joy made it all right just this once.

"Thanks for helping to save my life, Sheen Bean."

"Mereen is dead!" Kah'Sheen proclaimed. "I am finding her ashes."

"What about everyone else?"

"I am finding a corpse in the basement. I am thinking it is Tazel, but his body is burned. Everything is burned."

Etolié reeled at the statement, struggling to fathom it. "Burned?"

"The house is burned! And everyone else is gone."

"Yes, yes, Etolié is alive," came Ku'Shya's guttural brusque. "Where is Ko'Khan?"

Kah'Sheen stiffened. In careful measures, she retracted her touch, and Etolié didn't have to be empathic to anticipate her next awkward words: "I am still searching."

"Yet you are home."

"To see Etolié."

"And now you are seeing."

"Mother, I am worried. I am not seeing it in the ruins."

The monstrous exoskeletal face was difficult to decipher, but the slow blink of those four eyes was not something to dismiss. Etolié suspected annoyance, and non-humanoid empathy *was* a talent of hers, as she'd learned from Zoldar.

"Rest for a while, Kah'Sheen," the Goddess of War said, resignation in the words. "Enjoy Etolié's company. Then you are going back out."

Etolié snaked her opposite hand out from the covers and

took one of Kah'Sheen's many. "Seriously, thank you."

"You are more important than revenge, Etolié."

"I'm not more important than saving the world, though."

"In a battle for the world, we can decide. But I am rather having you alive than Endless Night dead."

Etolié shook her head at that sappy bullshit. "Kah'Sheen, The Endless Night killed a hundred thousand people."

"And are you not saving that many in Solvira?"

Damn, that was actually logical. "Fine."

They spoke of lighter things, she, Kah'Sheen, Momma, Eionei, with the occasional quip from the terrifying Goddess of War, who was apparently now her second mother. History said Khastra would have a few words to say about that, but as terrifying as Ku'Shya had been reported to be, if Momma liked her, there had to be something redeeming there.

Etolié supposed family was simply meant to be messy. And perhaps that was all right, even if it boggled her black-and-white sort of justice.

She had given Momma space to grow. Perhaps she could give the rest that grace as well.

Just breathe. I have you.

Flowridia blinked in and out of awareness, occasionally haunted by visions of color, by the stench of blood—her blood. She knew it all too well.

Just breathe. All is well.

The soothing voice echoed within her head, not unlike how Demitri's had. But even her subconscious knew it was Sarai, whose essence filled every part of her.

So many foreign voices. So many foreign words.

"... rebreak her sternum for it to sit right ..."

"... going to have to amputate ..."

"... may have nerve damage, but ..."

Just breathe.

Flowridia knew not how much time had passed before the fog lifted around her mind. Awareness of warmth soothed her body. Something soft enveloped her skin.

"Flowridia?"

Sora?

Flowridia tried to open her eyes, yet could not seem to find the path. How did one move a limb? She thought the command with all her might, but nothing happened.

Oh, sorry. It seems I have to move you.

Flowridia's eyes opened by a compulsion that was not her own.

Seated at her bedside, Sora Fireborn offered a kind smile, relief in her sharp exhale. "Oh, thank Sol Kareena's Light. You had us frightened."

Flowridia tried to speak, but her tongue was a prisoner. She summoned all her will, her thoughts, and screamed them as loud as she could: *Sarai?*

"Don't worry," Sora said. "Odessa—your mother, sorry—once explained how ghostly possession works. Sarai is in control, but you're aware of everything. And she needs to stay in control for a short while longer, in case something goes wrong."

That would explain it. But let me know if there is anything you need me to say.

"Your surgery lasted half a day, and you've been asleep for half a day more. There's someone Casvir wants you to meet, but first I should warn you of something. Your hand . . . it isn't quite the same."

Her left hand hid behind layers of bandages. Sarai sat her up, revealing her nightgown, and settled her back against the headboard.

"The doctors did the best they could, but many of the nerves were severed or irrevocably damaged." Sora beckoned for her hand. Flowridia's body obeyed, the ghost leading her as a kindly puppet master, yet she was surprised at how tender it was as Sora cautiously removed the wrapping.

A mass of scars, two fingers missing, the skin gnarled in sections like old scar tissue. The fingers the doctors had managed to save hardly appeared as fingers at all—no nails, perhaps no knuckles either. Ghastly, hardly attractive. When she tried to move, it remained still.

I can't move it either.

"The doctors will explain what exercises you'll need to do to regain full control. It'll be a long road to recovery. I spoke to Imperator Casvir and asked if he could find any Priestesses of Staella to come and speak to you—they're trained to aid with emotional wounds." Sora's voice caught, a rim of redness

444

lining her eyes. "And on that subject, I know it means so little, but I'm sorry."

Please take her hand, Flowridia pleaded to the presence inside her. Her body did so, squeezing Sora's hand with her good one.

"It doesn't matter what you've done in the past," Sora continued, her smile bringing quiet tears. "Not right now. And with Mereen and Tazel's deaths, you're the only family I have. What was done to you was a crime in which I was complicit. If you'll allow it, I would like to stay by your side and help you heal."

Though her body was not her own, Flowridia's throat choked. *Tell her yes, please.*

"Yes," came the words from Flowridia's tongue, not spoken by her, nor was it her voice. This was Sarai.

Sora seemed to understand, her smile marred by falling tears. "In other news, I encouraged your wife to wash up and change. I'm surprised she listened, much less allowed me to stay unsupervised with you. She might be in shock, but she does want to see you, if you'll allow it."

Now Flowridia's own tears threatened to fall—yet they were not hers. This was Sarai's sorrow. *Please nod,* Flowridia said, and her body obeyed.

"I'll go find her."

Sora, her sister, the last of her blood, released her and left.

Only then did Flowridia truly get a look at her private space, sparse and meant for healing. The white sheets would show any blood. The blank walls would echo, to amplify sound. The minimal décor could be cleaned. This was a medical ward, surely in Nox'Kartha.

The doorknob turned, and in came Ayla Darkleaf.

For a moment, Flowridia's blood reacted, pulsing loudly in her ear. But this was not a monster. Those eyes were silver. Her stance was small. This was her wife, who wore her shame like a scarlet stripe across her black dress.

Ayla stopped at the foot of the bed, jaw trembling. "You're not Flowra."

"No," came Sarai's voice, "but she's here. She's listening."

"Why are you here, Sarai?" Ayla's voice broke at the name, a glistening sheen filling her eyes. "How can this be?"

Flowridia felt Sarai's apprehension, her shame, her sorrow. *Tell her,* Flowridia said. *It would bring her peace to know.*

"I have waited seventeen hundred years to tell you I'm sorry, and that I—" Sarai's voice cut off, but Flowridia knew the truth like the ghostly presence in her soul.

Flowridia felt no animosity, no jealousy. *Tell her. It's all right.*

"That I love you."

Ayla's eyes fell downcast, the first of her tears streaming down her sharp face. "You saved Flowra's life."

"I suppose I did."

"Why?"

"Because I consider her my friend, and . . . because you love her."

Hesitation stilled Sarai's tongue before she began her somber tale. All she had told Flowridia. All she had said of the stranger, of the knife, of Eldrin, of the lie . . .

And of Izthuni.

When it was done, Ayla had not moved an inch, had not made a sound, save for the gentle splattering of tears upon the floor.

"I could not live with what I'd done," Sarai said, calm in her own quiet sorrow, "so I ended my life. But it did not bring me peace, or even oblivion. I was cursed to mourn for all eternity." Sarai was quiet a moment, then her words came softer. "What an honor it has been, to meet the woman you married."

Ayla's gaze snapped up, though silent she remained.

"She's brave, she's kind, and she's fiercely protective of you. I love her stories and her heart. All I ever wanted for you was peace; she brought you that, and I know how much it means to you."

All serenity in Ayla's countenance disappeared with her sob. She brought her arms around herself, tension clear in her grip.

"Ayla . . ."

The name faded away as Ayla crawled onto the bed before her and stole Sarai into her arms.

Desperation came in that embrace. Flowridia felt it returned, these two lovers torn apart. A future destroyed before it could come to pass. What a different world it would have been, had they been granted the life they deserved.

"Do you remember the day we met?" Sarai whispered, and Ayla sat back, though she kept hold of her uninjured hand. Their fingers intertwined, the innocence bringing elation.

"I do. You sang to wake the whole forest."

Sarai laughed, a melodic sound, joined by Ayla's darker tones. "And I am so glad I did."

"You don't regret it?"

"I regret so much, but I don't regret you. Every day of my death, I mourned that I could not save you—but I think I would rather mourn for all eternity than have never met you."

"You showed me what love was," Ayla replied, her small voice quivering. "I mean it when I say no one had loved me before I met you. And I clung to that, even after my death. Even though it broke me to think of it too hard. Somewhere deep inside, I knew what love was supposed to be. When I met Flowra, it frightened me to face it again. But I knew it—and instead of run, I let myself be vulnerable and love her too." Her words stilled as she brought Flowridia's hand to her lips, her kiss as gentle as sunrise. "Whatever else transpired, never think you did not save me. Because of you, I knew how to save myself."

A strange something occurred within Flowridia, within Sarai—a severance Flowridia did not recognize yet knew like the sensation of water, like the first breath of spring air.

Sarai was . . . ready.

"I don't think I can stay much longer," Sarai said, but the words were not said in sorrow—but in hope.

"Before you go," Ayla said, her composure falling away, every part of her trembling, "will you sing? Please?"

Sarai's voice wavered. "What would you like me to sing?"

"The one for me."

From Sarai, there rose hesitation, a question. "It is a song for heartbreak. Not for happiness."

"It was my final memory of you for so long. Of course it hurts, but if this is the end, I would like to hear it one last time."

Within Flowridia, Sarai asked silent permission. Flowridia said, *Yes. She needs it.*

Sarai sat up taller, pulling in as steady and deep a breath as she could. There came a soft beginning:

In death there's redemption
I pray that is true
But I hope there is peace for the monster in you.

With beautiful words came a melancholic tune, a sweeping soprano to tell the tale.

By moonlight at midnight I watched your sweet breaths
How I long for those moments of lost innocence.
Eternity seemed but a small reach away
When we kissed, or you listened and watched while I played.
I'll cherish those times 'til the end of my days.

My mind's so conflicted; Oh, is there an end
To the torment I'm living, to the hell that I'm meant
To go on and suffer for doing what's right?
Oh, what I would give to look in your eyes and see light?

Sarai's voice fell away, yet the note echoed across the white walls. It lingered as a phantom in the air.

Your gaze that once froze the fire in my veins,
Lifeless;
Barren.
A star gone away.

I'll write no more music but sing all my life
Of that moment of peace, eclipsed by a knife.
Our dream has been shattered, yet I'm left to bear
The shards of a future that I can't repair.
But it's better than lies.

Is it better to lie than give into despair?

Her final words came soft, a requiem of regret.

In death there's redemption
For someone like you
I'll hold to that hope. Ayla, I love you.

The great mystery came to rest. Sarai's song had been a confession all along.

Ayla's tears fell fast, yet she nearly smiled in the ensuing silence, a mere whisper. She again offered an embrace; Flowridia's body came closer, compelled by a tentative force.

Leave her with peace, Flowridia said, and she faded as small as she could be. This was not her moment.

Sarai Fireborn blinked, not quite alone, but her hostess was silent.

Ayla wept, clinging to Sarai with all her might. Sarai's tears fell like rain upon her black hair, holding her close, for it would be the last time.

"I don't need you to say it back," Sarai said, because Ayla had moved on, she had married, and finally, *finally*, she lived, "but I have never stopped loving you."

Ayla's small hands cupped Sarai's face, her touch cold but true. "I—" Her word cut off, and instead of speaking, she leaned up, her lips close.

At Sarai's hesitation, a sweet voice within her said, *It's all right.*

They kissed, curtailed passion beneath it, a release. In the soft motions of Ayla's lips, Sarai felt love unbound.

When Ayla pulled away, there came that precious smile Sarai adored, her large eyes vulnerable and seeping tears. Memories came, a lifetime ago, of dreams they'd once written, of love they'd once shared. Gentle moments in the forest. Jests they'd swapped and kisses they'd stolen. Passionate moments and innocent gestures of affection.

Ayla's words were more healing than any affirmation of love. "I forgive you."

And though it was unbidden, the strings binding Sarai to Flowridia's body severed one by one. Sarai faded, so she pulled away—

Flowridia's head spun, gasping as she emerged from deep waters. She touched her face, her body, and when Ayla grabbed her, she collapsed into her lap.

In her final moments of consciousness, each blink heavier than the last, she saw Sarai floating before them, her smile pure and true. The ghost faded away, off to the Beyond, the prospect of peace assured.

Before darkness overtook her, there was only Ayla.

Chapter 23

Sora kept her ear to the seam of the door, at first enthralled by a rich tune, then muttering, then . . . silence.

A minute passed before she knocked. When she heard nothing, she dared to enter.

There lay Ayla, curled like a cat beside Flowridia, who had fallen asleep again. She did not move even a flicker at Sora's entrance, save for her eyes, menace in her unblinking gaze. Dried tears had left shiny streaks upon her face, detracting from the image of evil.

And evil she was. Sora had not forgotten that.

"Hello, Sora," Ayla said, her disdain thinly veiled.

Sora shut the door, only mostly confident Ayla would not snap her neck. But she trusted more that Ayla would do nothing to disturb her wife's rest. "Hello, Ayla. We need to talk."

"No, we do not."

"I have something for you," Sora replied, ignoring the obvious threat. From her belt, she withdrew the mysterious knife, noting the curious frown upon Ayla's features. "Soliel had this. Sarai was attached to it until she possessed Flowridia. But he said it must be destroyed and to bring it to you."

The curiosity in her silver gaze became steel. "Sarai, you say?"

"It belonged to her, yes. But you're one of the only ones left in the realms to wield Silver Fire—which means you can destroy it."

Ayla retracted like a feline claw from Flowridia's side, slinking to Sora's side with as much grace. Her presence sent chills across Sora's skin, her very aura radiating hatred—how else could it be, with so much blood on her hands?

Sora had the grand honor of calling her sister-in-law.

The slight caressing of their fingers brought revulsion, Ayla's skin unnaturally cool, but she accepted the knife. "What does this do?"

"Soliel didn't say. He only warned to keep it away from Casvir."

Ayla remained unreadable, a closed book in every respect. She held the knife near her chest. "Anything else?"

There was, unfortunately, though it was not a conversation Sora particularly wanted. "Your wife said I can stay for the duration of her healing. I wanted to know if there would be a truce between us or if I should watch my back."

"I must begrudgingly admit that you risked your life twice to save her," Ayla replied, contempt in the words. "So while I hold great hatred for you and your blood, I know you pose no threat. Besides, are we not family too?" Scorn twisted her lip, leaving a mockery of a grin.

"So you know?"

"I remember far too much."

The door opened. At Casvir's entrance, Ayla slipped the knife behind her back.

Casvir studied the sleeping Flowridia. "You told a servant she awoke?"

"She did, Imperator Casvir," Sora said, though it irked her to grant him respect.

"Wake her. I have brought Demitri."

Shock stole Sora's response, the feeling mirrored on Ayla's severe features as numerous De'Sindai guards dragged in the wolf, his quiet growling pervasive. He was collared, muzzled, subdued by the chains, and he bore the same wound, one eye missing, the orbital bone shattered. That single eye fell upon Flowridia, and though he did not quite become docile, he stilled.

Ayla stood warily between them, but at her offered hand, he bumped against it, the gesture familiar for how she smiled. "Of course you went and found him."

"There has been far too much investment in his well-being," Casvir said, coming to the foot of the bed, "and in hers. When they touch, he should become hers again."

Yet Ayla hesitated to rouse her. Sora recalled the knife she hid. So she went to Flowridia's side instead and gently shook her shoulder. "Flowridia—"

Flowridia gasped as she awoke, quickly gathering the blankets to her chest, legs flailing, until she met Sora's gaze, revealing blown pupils. A few deep breaths, but then she noticed the wolf beside her bed. Tears filled her eyes, and she trembled as she sat up, letting the blankets drop.

"Touch him," Casvir said. "He can be yours."

Flowridia's sudden sob held her back, hand flying to cover her mouth as her tears came faster. Demitri remained subdued, a statue for how little he moved. There came the first touch of fur and flesh—

And if anything happened, Sora didn't see it. Judging by Flowridia's falling visage and Casvir's sudden frown, there had been nothing to see.

"I had feared this," the imperator said, subtle fury in the words. "It is said that a witch and a familiar cannot be in separate states of life. Either you must both be living or both be undead."

Flowridia's sobs overtook her as she fell into Demitri's side, weeping into his fur.

"Be that as it may, he can be chained to your bedside for now. I do not trust him alone, however."

Sora glanced to Ayla, whose subtle shake of her head conveyed a clear message. "I will stay by her for now," Sora said. "I'm good with animals."

"That will do."

When Sora looked again, Ayla had disappeared into the shadows.

Casvir and the servants left. As Flowridia clutched the undead wolf, Sora was struck by the memory of his death, at the sight of her wailing over his bloodied body.

If she'd known then what she knew now, could she have stopped it?

When Flowridia drew back, her eyes swollen and wide, panic bled into her voice. "Where is Ayla?"

"I don't know. She must have left with Casvir."

Flowridia said nothing.

"Sarai is gone?"

The girl nodded.

"What does he feel like?" Sora asked, fearing she would cry anew.

"Nothing. Like an animal." So cautious, her touch as she caressed the finer hairs on his face. He gave no reaction. "I barely had time to mourn him, so it's . . . surreal."

Sora thought upon the words of a friend, of the heartbreak of losing a familiar.

"So, we're family?"

She hadn't noticed Flowridia's stare, her gaunt cheeks a daunting reminder of what she'd survived. "If you'll have me," Sora said, "I want to try."

"It means Lunestra was your great-aunt. Did you consider that?"

The words fell heavy upon Sora's chest, the connection lost amid the panic of the last few days. "I . . . you're right."

"Casvir orchestrated my conception," Flowridia said, her tone sobering and soft, "because he wanted Odessa's child— the child he would give a familiar to—to be the heir to the Theocracy. Someone he could train and later groom to take that throne. But all of that unravels, because I'm not the heir. It's you."

Sora had hardly heard a word after the reveal of Casvir being her patron—but, *heir*?

"Not that it means much anymore. It's ashes now. But you should know."

Sora's breath became shallow, for it fell together in a perfect puzzle. Her papa's disappearances, her mother's secrecy, even Sol Kareena's decision to return her to life and give her a chance as her champion . . .

"Sora, do you know our father's family name?"

Our father . . . "No. I didn't make the connection as a child that he wasn't a Fireborn. When my mother passed, the secret died with her."

"I decided to take Ayla's name when we married because it was the name I'd longed for. I saw it as a reward for all I went through to get her back. But the revelation of having a name by birth instead of just by marriage meant so much to me, after growing up as an orphan. You have the Fireborns, but . . ." Flowridia kept her damaged hand on her chest, her other never leaving Demitri. But how kind was her smile; and how powerful was the swelling in Sora's chest, for she had seen that smile before. "His family name was Makosa. It's yours too."

Tears welled in Sora's eyes. She dabbed them with her sleeve, struggling to parse this new revelation. *Fireborn* had been her legacy for so long . . .

For thirty years, Sora had sought to piece herself into the Fireborn puzzle, rejected and belittled at every turn, granted *decency* at best, but not love. Never love. Her mother had abandoned them but faltered at the end. Returning had been her downfall.

But Makosa . . . The name fit like a glove, the sensation enveloping her soul as comforting as a father's hug.

"My father was Zanoram Makosa," Sora said, voice breaking at the final word. "And I . . . I shall be too. I shall be Sora Makosa."

She did not mean to cry, but the grief she'd felt in trying to stand up to the waves of her family name crashed over her, washing away the name she'd clung to for all those years. But she was a Fireborn no more. The line died with her.

Flowridia pulled Sora into her arms, embracing her through her tears. Sora forsook her name but found something new. Her papa's smile lived on in her sister, and Sora knew family was complicated, knew the ties that bound could be abhorrent, could connect you to wicked people.

But the difference, she supposed, was she wanted to try. And Flowridia did too.

"Will you tell me about my father?" Flowridia asked, and Sora pulled away to withdraw the beloved locket tucked into her shirt.

When she offered the small relic, Flowridia stared upon the picture of his face, mirroring so much of who he was. At her blink, her eyes filled with fresh tears.

Sora spoke healing words, telling tales of their father's legacy.

Fairly uneventful, the walk through the Nox'Karthan palace. As much as Etolié wanted a nap, there was an employer to appease.

Night had fallen. Etolié stepped through vacant hallways, seeking the imperator's office. Any servants she passed bowed but did little else—apparently her death had not been announced, which she supposed was best.

"Thank the Great Spider—you've returned!"

Zorlaeus ran to her in the hall, but stopped inches away. He offered a hand, though the impulse to hug was clearly there.

Etolié squeezed it, touched that he remembered at all. "It

takes a little more than a bullet to put me down."

From behind her scurried Zoldar. "What are you doing out of the library?" Etolié asked, but the Skalmite ignored her in favor of taking her hand and rapidly shaking it.

He then took back his spindly digits and signed.

"Flowers is here, you say?"

Zorlaeus confirmed it. "She has been here for about a day, yes. There was some uncertainty as to whether or not she would have a good prognosis, but as far as I'm aware, she is doing as well as she can."

Etolié hadn't intended to face Flowers here, in the relative safety of the castle, but technically her quest culminated in this moment. Flowers was weak. Flowers was vulnerable. "I suppose I should see her."

"I'll escort you."

She followed Zorlaeus, trailed by her Skalmite friend. Etolié didn't need to be armed to be able to kill, and she had been fantasizing about staining her hands in this traitor's blood for years. Flowers had proven her loyalties. Flowers had damned a whole country to die.

Yet . . . Etolié felt no glee, no vindication. In fact, she felt a little ill.

She was taken to the medical ward. Zorlaeus knocked on the door before peeking his face inside. "Etolié is here."

He wouldn't so casually use her just her name to just anyone. Etolié failed to hide her shock when he opened the door to reveal Sora at Flowridia's bedside.

The duo glanced over, the ends of Sora's locs looking a little singed, but otherwise she appeared in good spirits.

The same couldn't be said of Flowers.

Surprise came to see her chopped hair, no individual strand longer than her pinky finger. Though she didn't quite look to be at death's door, her cheeks were cutting, her sunken eyes exhausted and broken. Hints of scarring peeked from her collar, though Etolié could not see it all, and her hand was wrapped in bandages.

And for all Etolié's hatred, for all the shattered promises between them, the tinest pang of pity struck her.

Shock flooded Sora's face. "Etolié, thank Sol Kareena." Mist softened those brown eyes as she ran to Etolié's side. She offered her hand; Etolié accepted it, not quite able to tear her gaze away from Flowers. "How did you survive?"

"Kah'Sheen brought me to her mother's house. She

called my momma. The rest is history. What happened?"

Sora spared a glance for Flowers, whose hesitation spoke volumes.

"You know what—tell me later." Etolié passed her by, approaching Flowers. The girl remained small in her bed, though it was difficult to say if it were from fear or pain. "You've looked better."

Flowridia's voice was even smaller. "I was told you were part of the group who came to save me. I can't thank you enough."

"It wasn't my idea."

Flowridia nodded, presumably understanding.

Etolié had a few uncanny talents, and instinctively sensing pregnancy was one of them. However, one look at this frail mess, and it didn't take a damn sorceress to know the uncomfortable truth. Either she never had been pregnant— which was hilarious—or had been—a tragedy—and Etolié chose the tactful approach and said nothing about it. "Is Ayla around?"

Sora frowned, as though reminded of a cake she'd left in an oven. "Yes. Though I'm not sure where."

"That's comforting. I'll watch my back. But do you mind if I have a moment alone with Flowers?"

No doubt Sora sensed something amiss. The half-elf hesitated, and Etolié had about a thousands questions, mostly revolving around why Sora gave two shits about Flowers at all. "S-She's not quite stable," Sora said, which was a lie; mortals always lied with their eyes. "I'd be more comfortable staying here."

"Are you friends now?"

"We . . ." Sora glanced to Flowers, whose nod cleared up absolutely nothing. " . . . It's a long story. I owe you a drink anyway—we can talk over that."

"You absolutely owe me a gods-damned drink." Etolié returned her attention to Flowers as she considered her quest, her resolve, the ethics of charming Sora into sleeping or leaving with song—or if it even mattered at all. "Sora, if you're not gonna fucking leave, can you at least step out of my line of sight so I can think?"

Though clearly wary, Sora obeyed. Etolié didn't miss how the half-elf's hand skimmed across one of her knives.

But it didn't matter. Etolié had magic enough to drop on anvil on Flowers' bed and convince Sora that Casvir himself had done it—or something. Sora knew it, and Sora knew Etolié knew it. There were perks to being nearly a demi-god.

It didn't stop fucking bullets, but everyone needed a weakness, right?

"Etolié?"

Flowers herself drew Etolié back to the present, everything in her pitiful expression reminiscent of the girl Etolié had plucked from the woods years ago. Had it been a mistake? Would Flowers have found her way, or would she have died alone?

Would it rectify that mistake to slay her now? Gods knew she deserved it, and with her wife nowhere in sight, there was no better opportunity—and perhaps never might be again.

. . . So why did she hesitate?

"They aren't exactly saying the nicest things about you in Solvira," Etolié said. "I'd suggest you stay away."

"I understand—"

"Do you though?" Etolié bit back her sudden rise in anger, mindful of Sora's presence and her own precarious resolve.

To her surprise, Flowers spoke quiet but true. "I do."

Not an apology, but an apology would have been hollow. Etolié couldn't quite guess what horrors had befallen the former flowery diplomat, but something in it curtailed her rage.

Or perhaps her rage had already been curtailed. Etolié had forgiven herself, and the ramifications still unfolded.

"I fucking hate you," Etolié said, but her anger had quelled.

Flowers said nothing, gave no excuse. She simply nodded.

"I joined Casvir in searching for you because I was going to drive a knife through your throat," Etolié continued, yet felt no vindication to say it, "and you're damn lucky I apparently grew as a person because I'm not going to. And that's a fucking promise."

Flowers remained silent.

"You don't deserve forgiveness, but I'm going to work on it anyway, you fucking bitch. Don't squander it. That said . . ." Etolié despised this bit of compassion inside her, cursing her genetics for sharing half her blood with the empathetic Goddess of Mercy. But she was working on forgiveness. "I know a sorceress in Solvira who specializes in hair. Hair's just a spell. I could bring her here."

Flowridia teared up, her non-wrapped hand coming up to touch the short locks of auburn. She managed to control her wavering voice well enough. "Yes, I'd like that."

"A little bit of normalcy in a chaotic world. I get that. I'll take care of it."

Etolié stepped to the door then, worried she'd try and do another good deed. "I'm off to see Imperator First and Last," she said to Sora, "but afterward I want a full account on why the fuck you're here—with *her.*"

Sora glanced to Flowridia, a strange energy between them—the sort even Etolié's political senses couldn't interpret. "Come find me when you're done," Sora said. "We'll get that drink."

Etolié left, returning to her friends in the hallway. "We both know you're terrified of Casvir," she said to Zorlaeus, "so you can wait in the library. Though I don't think he'll be mad. He might even be happy to see me."

A weird thought, yet it rang true. Damn that piece of shit, making her feel slightly friendly.

She continued on to Casvir's office, Zoldar in her shadow, the path winding in a way that was actually quite well-designed for avoiding assassins. But she had harassed him countless times in the privacy of his office, able to speak far more freely when they were alone.

"Wait out here—"

"*Are you fucking joking?*"

That was unquestionably Murishani, and it came from Casvir's office.

Etolié shared a conspiratorial glance with Zoldar, then crept closer, ear to the door.

"*. . . language is very unbecoming, Viceroy Muri—*"

"*You are kicking me out of my own house!*"

"*I am providing you alternative accommodations—*"

"*This is my house!*"

"*—for the duration of Lady Flowridia's stay.*"

Zoldar tapped her arm for attention, then quickly signed: *Why is he not allowed?*

She mouthed, "Not sure."

"*You have the audacity to place that little cunt on so high a pedestal that you would kick me out of the palace?*"

"*Again, your language.*"

"*You already lost the war because of her!*"

Lost the war?

"*The war continues. We are simply set back—*"

"*IS THAT WHAT WE'RE CALLING IT?!*"

Again, Etolié matched eyes with Zoldar, thoroughly enjoying every moment of Murishani's pain.

"*You will calm yourself.*"

"*And how am I supposed to do my job?*"

"*When do you do your job?*"

"*Don't pretend you don't keep me for a reason!*"

Murishani devolved into screaming, a few of his obscenities impressing even Etolié, when what could only be described as a *smack* cut off his words.

There was silence. There was muttering. And then there were footsteps.

Etolié grabbed Zoldar's arm and tugged him back, feigning steps toward the office. "And we had the best time ever in the woods, Kah'Sheen and I—"

Casvir's office door opened, and out came Murishani. A large red splotch covered his cheek, but Etolié pretended not to notice. "Oh, hi, Murishani."

He smiled at her as wide as the sea and gave a small foppish chuckle. "Hi." He left without another word, which was officially the oddest thing she had ever seen the man do.

Etolié waited until he was out of sight to whisper, "Well, damn."

Zoldar gave a few quick clicks. *Indeed.*

She counted to sixty, deemed it enough time for Casvir to have calmed down, and bid Zoldar to stay. She opened the door with no preamble, then froze.

Casvir sat at his desk, and in his hand was Staff Seraph deDieula. His frown could have curdled milk, but Etolié had no time for that shit. "Empress Etolié—"

"You fucking *didn't!*"

"I did. And you will say nothing of it."

She stomped inside, slamming the door behind her. "That thing isn't safe! Only Ku'Shya can guard it!"

"Look how well that went."

"Dammit, Casvir—this is bad business. It controlled you!"

His glower darkened. "Yes, and I am seeking ways to combat that."

Only then did Etolié notice the ring sitting idly on the desk—a unmistakable silver band, bearing a pattern of filigree and a single diamond. "Is that Flowers' wedding ring?"

In response, he slipped the ring into his desk. "It may be the solution I need."

Fury rose within her, in tandem with panic. This was the worst of partnerships: Imperator Casvir and the God of Death's staff. "I really fucking hate this."

"And you may continue to do so, though I assure you that I have no intention of flaunting its presence. It will be kept under strict guard, incapable of being accessed even by those who walk in shadows."

The implication was clear. "You're a bastard."

"We need to discuss something."

"If it's my use of language, I regret nothing."

"Etolié, sit down."

Her rage extinguished. He had never used only her name.

She sat cautiously on the nearest seat. "What's going on?"

Casvir set the staff against the wall, then took an opened letter from his desk. "You have previously expressed dismay at chronological stories, so I will tell you the ending first."

The space between his words was filled by her rising pulse.

"General Khastra has been captured."

Etolié's ears suddenly rang. Cold caressed her skin, seeping into her veins.

"Her battalion was cornered against the Cliffs of Khovav and fought to total destruction against a volley of airships and tanks. All were destroyed except for her."

Etolié hardly felt her tears. She felt nothing at all.

"She is a prisoner of war, though I know not where. I only know because of Murishani's account and this letter, intercepted between Executor Faeborn and the vice executor of the Iron Elves."

He offered it forward. When Etolié did not move, he set it on the space beside her.

Khastra . . . she was . . .

"Empress Etolié, I assure you that I will do all in my power to retrieve her. She is a servant of great use to me . . ."

Whatever else he said, it faded behind her ensuing sobs. Etolié's face fell into her hands.

Khastra wasn't here. She might never be again.

"I . . . will leave you alone."

Through her parted hair, she saw him take the staff from

the wall. The door remained open as he passed, a few quick words exchanged, and Zoldar entered, clicking in confusion.

But Etolié could say nothing. She felt nothing, became nothing as the horrible truth rose to choke her. Zoldar placed his insect hand upon her back, gently clicking comfort.

She couldn't speak, so instead she offered him the letter. His crystalline eyes skimmed whatever horrid words were written.

Once done, he sat beside her, taking her hand in his, becoming merely a presence.

Etolié wept, for the world was falling apart.

There were no windows in Flowridia's sterile room, and so time became a distant thing as she fell back into a lull of conversation with Sora.

So strange, to see the half-elf as a friend. But it felt right to find that connection of blood. Lunestra had been a grandmother, and Flowridia told Sora tales of their few weeks together. Sora was family, disconnected from her mother's cruel legacy, and for now, they had tabled any discussions of Flowridia's crimes.

"*I've always seen you as a kid,*" Sora admitted, and at last they understood why.

Demitri was . . . distant. He paced, restless after a time, raising his hackles in warning when Sora tried to bring him back to Flowridia's side. Though the wolf had his face and body, this was not her familiar.

Yet . . .

When she said his name, he turned, even if it broke her heart to not hear that little voice in her head. When she called for him, he came, though he seemed ineffably less keen for touch, merely tolerating it instead of cuddling her back. He knew her. Somewhere in his head, he remembered her face, her name, her scent . . .

While swapping tales with Sora, a knock sounded to interrupt them.

Still in his muzzle, Demitri's hackles raised, his growl emanating when the door swung open to reveal Casvir.

"Flowridia, I wish to speak to you in private and discuss your future here. Are you well enough for that?"

"Yes, now is fine." Flowridia gave a small smile to Sora, who returned it as a mirror.

"I'll be nearby."

Casvir left Sora distance enough to leave, and Flowridia watched with curiosity to see what Sora would do—which, it seemed, was keep as far away as possible and slip around the doorframe.

Demitri's growl permeated the room, rising to a snarl when Casvir took a step forward. "Past experience shows he will strike. Would it disturb you if I dismissed him for the duration of this conversation?"

Of course it would, but it somehow seemed a small drop in a bucket now. "Do what you need to do."

With no grandeur at all, Demitri collapsed to the floor, eerily still.

Casvir came to her bedside, the subtle clanking of his metal armor echoing across the walls. "I need to state something that I suspect will not be a shock to you, but it must still be stated—per the surgeons, you are not pregnant."

Flowridia made no effort to hide her impish smile. "I never was."

"Clever. But if you play that game again, I will not be so amiable to being tricked."

Her smile became steel, for she felt no remorse at all.

"How do you feel?"

"In what regard?"

"We shall start with physically."

Flowridia gave it thought, considered her head, her hand, and her permanent exhaustion. "I feel like I could sleep for a year, and it wouldn't be enough. My hand is numb, which is incredibly unnerving, but I think in every other regard, I'm fine. Your healers did their work well." She hesitated at her final phrase: "Thank you."

"You may be reassured to hear that Viceroy Murishani has been temporarily relocated."

Flowridia merely blinked, startled at that.

"I would not ask you to live in his vicinity, especially in so vulnerable a state."

"I'm not vulnerable."

"No? Then how are you emotionally?"

Her breath hitched at the question, having been lulled

into comfort by her visit with Sora—but reality did remain. "Fine. I am vulnerable."

"I am seeking physicians who specialize in surgical recovery in hopes of hiring the best help possible for your hand. There remains the option of amputating it if becomes a source of pain, but with as much as the surgeons could salvage, I am confident you will be dexterous again."

Flowridia said nothing, merely unwrapped the bandages, this time without Sora's protective presence. Gods, it was ugly, pale scarring down the center of the three remaining fingers, her palm a mess of flesh with no lines. At least she had a thumb, a small victory. She set all her focus upon it, determined for it to twitch . . .

Nothing.

"I will have gloves made to your measurements," Casvir said, his red eyes following hers. "I understand that aesthetic recovery is often vital for psychological recovery. Priestesses of Staella have already been called from Solvira to come and assist you."

"I don't know if I'm ready to talk about it," Flowridia said, despising how easily her words came. Casvir was the enemy. She plotted his death. Everything she had done was to spite him.

Yet he remained a friend.

"Perhaps not. You may speak of lighter things to them instead. But I must insist you speak."

"Why, though?" Flowridia held her mutilated hand to her chest, still dizzy at the memory of pain. Though all was quiet, her body was not used to safety. "Why are you helping me?"

"It is prudent to invest in your well-being—"

"Oh, that again." She forced a smile. "I could leave."

"You have that freedom. But Nox'Kartha has the resources to help your hand and your mind."

"You're very insistent on claiming you know the state of my mind."

"Am I wrong? You said you were vulnerable."

He did not talk her in circles, no; instead, he remained an immovable mountain; she walked in circles, and he remained firm. "I did."

"The surgical report was harrowing."

He said nothing else, for which she was grateful. Yet shame filled her, to think of all he knew. "Ayla didn't mean to.

They forced her—" Damn her voice; it shattered. She quickly swallowed tears. "W-With the staff. Do you know about it?"

"I do."

The truth was a betrayal, and so she spoke a lie instead. "It was done to punish me and Ayla. Mereen's the villain. She's the one to hate."

"Mereen Fireborn is dead."

"Yes, that's what Sora . . ." Yet she burst into tears to hear it stated so plainly. Relief flooded her, as well as hatred. There would be no catharsis. Mereen was simply dead and gone with nothing left.

"I returned to investigate the ruins and saw the remains of her corpse. Tazel has passed as well."

"I knew that," she managed, but it was more tears than word.

"Forgive me if I was calloused," Casvir said, his words cutting through her sobs. "There are logical reasons to assist you. But I do care for you. And it would bring me peace of mind for you to spend your recovery here."

Flowridia wiped her eyes, seeking to purge her sobs yet failed at every turn. Instead, she simply nodded. "I'll consider it."

Mereen was gone, but there was no finality. A swift death surely, for vampires were not easy prey. Gods, for all the pain, for all the terror-ridden dreams, Ayla's screams sounded loudest of all, the memory of Mereen mutilating her love's frozen body a nightmare.

Where was she? Ayla was gone . . .

"You have drifted away," Casvir said. "What are you thinking?"

She contemplated the question, for it was easy to say she might drown in despair. It was easy to say she was shattered. Yet as she sat in silence to consider herself and all she had been through, there came an errant realization. "May I say the worst thing?" she whispered, and she sniffed as she wiped away her tears.

"Of course."

"Mereen and Izthuni both sought to punish me for what I'd done, and I suppose they succeeded. I can't look in the mirror and say I didn't deserve a single moment of it. And obviously I hate that it happened. I can't fathom the path ahead." She looked down at her ruined hand, spared a glance for the vicious scarring on her chest. "But Izthuni told me to face my sins, and now I have, truly. I've stared them in the face . . . and gods, they're awful, but I can't take them back.

"It frightens me, how easily I can lie to myself," Flowridia whispered, and to speak the words brought power. "I lie to say it was not so bad, that what I did in Solvira was not so bad, that The Endless Night was not so bad . . . But I faced the Sun Elves. I saw their fear. They called me a monster, and though I knew it was true, I didn't know what it truly meant. I opened myself up to monstrosity, but I was blind to the consequences. But I understand now. I faced the visions Izthuni cursed me to experience, and I understand.

"I don't know what path I'm on anymore, only that Izthuni has perhaps made me a better person, in that single, bitter way. Mereen, too, I suppose." Flowridia nearly laughed, so awful it was. Instead, amid her quiet tears, she smiled. "No more lies, Casvir. It's as you once told me—damn myself and have no regrets. But I do have regrets, and that's precisely what Izthuni weaponized against me. I think the only way to move forward is to let them go."

Curse her tender heart. It only led to pain.

Mereen had said she was harmless on her own, had offered to let her go—but no. Flowridia did not need Ayla's legacy to carve her name into the history books.

No, no. She would forge her own legacy.

Approval showed in the small smile on Casvir's lip. "You are a powerful person, Flowridia. From ashes you have risen before, and from ashes you shall rise again. I believe in you, and I do not make poor investments."

The words came with a terrible sting, that Casvir, her friend, could still inspire her so. Once she had plotted his death, but now, if she killed Casvir, she could not have Demitri back. She could not have her magic back.

"Would you accept a new familiar," Casvir asked, an echo of her inner nightmare, "or do you wish for Demitri?"

She could not find her words, struck by this new torture.

"If you wish for Demitri, you would be protected here for as long as it takes for you to find a safe path to undeath."

"By which you mean, while I fulfill the terms of my contract." Her smile became bitter.

"To fulfill the terms of your contract, you would need to have a child before Demitri is returned."

The walls closed in around her, smothering her in the final strike of those bitter, cruel consequences. "Then . . .

would you allow something else instead?"

Insanity had brought her here. Insanity could forge the path out. Casvir waited for her words.

"When my mother's familiar was killed, you brought his spirit back so she could absorb it and become one with him. Her magic was returned. Could you . . ."

Already, he shook his head. "It would stunt your growth."

"My mother was powerful enough to become a legend."

"It would drive you mad, as it did her."

"I would rather be mad than lose Demitri."

"I will not do it."

She glared, for there was nothing to say to that.

Casvir remained frustratingly stoic. "I will do all I can to keep you comfortable during your recovery and then pregnancy. I will even assemble candidates to be the child's father, so you—"

"For the sake of us remaining civil for the duration of my stay, you need to leave now." It took all her will to not scream in his face—even if he deserved it. Still, her rage rose. "I don't want to discuss this ever again. The baby will happen when it happens."

His frown came suddenly, though it held no ire. "I have not meant to offend you."

"And you never do. But please send Sora in on your way out."

There came his subtle anger, and how gratifying it felt, a small victory in these hellish times. He left, but it did not change the cold pulsing through her veins.

Consequences came. She had survived this far, but still there came dreams of Lara, of Thalmus, of all the rest . . .

Did she fight the future or leave it? Would she sacrifice Demitri to escape this horrid fate?

As though in response to that awful question, a subtle mist of purple descended upon him, waking him from his unnatural sleep. Demitri roused himself, shaking like the canine he was, and when she beckoned, he came.

And though she held his face in her hands, he was not the same. He was the boy she loved, but he was wrong. Emptiness showed in his missing eye.

But love shone in the other, familiar shades of gold.

She hugged him tight and wept.

But I hope there is peace for the monster in you...
Within a shadowy realm, Ayla Darkleaf stepped silently along a familiar path, savoring the sweet embrace of home—
We just need to stitch it in place, better than before.
Sha'Demoni had always been home.

The outline of Nox'Karthan buildings filled the landscape, mere figments, incorporeal to touch. Ayla passed hapless mortals, unaware of the monster just a world and a breath away.
Yours is a face I could fall in love with...
No pride in her stance. She knew it. She didn't care. Not today.
...Perhaps I'll cut it off and frame it.

When the world became darker, she knew she had reached her destination, the unnatural melding of worlds. The space became solid, her feet echoing across the stone floor. Pure darkness remained, even to her keen eyes. Ayla Darkleaf, a predator, a monster, a *legend*—
Perfect lines...perfect lines...slit up the seams...
In darkness, she waited.

"*Ayla Darkleaf,*" the voice finally said, and Ayla did not need to have blood in her veins for it to boil, "*my grandest and beloved.*"

"Show yourself. I have a question."

He rolled in from the shadows, his spindly features a nightmare, but not to her. She felt no fear to face his endless maw, for he was as familiar to her as her own body, her own soul.

Now she knew the truth. He had stolen both—
You taste of vomit, you nasty thing...

"Go on," he said, and she knew enough of demons to know he was pleased.

How delightful, to ruin his day. Ayla held out her hand and summoned the image of a particular knife. "What does this do?"

Immediate interest shifted his stance, his pleasure rising. "I did not expect—"

"Sarai was tied to it. What does it do?"

"So you have met."

"Answer my question."

"If you are coming to me, you already know."

Ayla looked down at the knife, careful to envision its swirling pattern. A work of art, truly; she could appreciate it. "It creates monsters like me."

"Yes. And any favor you have lost shall be restored since you have returned—"

His words cut off when the dagger vanished.

"The real dagger is not here," Ayla said, refusing to let her stare waver. Not for a moment. "I came with that question and to deliver a final message: You will leave me alone. You will leave my wife alone."

How disgusting, his rumbling laughter. "Deliver me the dagger, and I shall leave you and Flowridia alone."

With the release of her breath, Ayla's pores seeped silver flame. It rose at her will, coating her body, illuminating even his ghastly form—pale and sickly, not so menacing when cast in light. "You tried to kill Flowra. If I thought I could kill you, I would. But I have more than that to offer—because you cannot kill me either."

Her fire burned bright. She stepped forward; he stepped back.

Anger simmered, for he had ruined her. He had ruined everything. "If you ever come near me or my family, I will destroy everything you have gained. My life's mission shall be to murder every vampire to walk the realms. I will kill every follower you have. I will rampage through Sha'Demoni and slay every demon I find on this continent. I will make you *nothing*."

A pause; a whisper. "A weighty threat."

"You cannot stop me. You created me."

A pause, then laughter. "Your threat is received, Ayla Darkleaf. I shall play your game, for now."

"Forever."

"For now." He stepped farther back, melding into the darkness. "I am eternal, for I am a god. But who are you, Ayla Darkleaf? Bastard orphan who came from nothing. You are correct—*I created you.*"

Such cruel and wicked words. Ayla did not even allow herself to twitch.

"Who are you, without me?"

His booming laughter rumbled across the conjoined realms, the insult as clear as the message.

Such lovely flowers . . .

Ayla stood alone.

The journey to the castle was slow.

Quiet was torture. She refused to blink, despite the residual instinct to do so. Over a thousand years of undeath, closer to two, and still she was plagued by the damn need to blink.

The image of the victim lurked in darkness—

"Say my name . . ."

In the shadowy landscape, Ayla stilled and pressed her claws into her arms, savoring the sweet release, the return of control. Deeper she plunged, the flesh splitting, tearing, euphoric in its burning. She sliced the skin in twain, the gashes deep, revealing bone, releasing wicked thoughts—

"Say my name . . ."

Ayla gasped as she withdrew her hands, and watched the pallid flesh seal and mend, becoming perfect, polished glass. She blinked, for she could not stop it in time, and there lay the victim's precious body, gashes revealing tender things beneath—

Ayla cried out as she slashed her claws across her own face, shutting the memory up.

There was no peace at Flowra's side—not for either of them. Ayla's vision misted at the memory of her beloved's panicked eyes, at how she flinched to even hear her voice.

Whatever compulsion led her underground, she could not say. But Ayla appeared in a stone labyrinth, to a path she had mapped herself. Some part of her savored the stagnant stench of old blood, and another saw it splattered on the ground, staining the stone beneath the table where her victim lay—

"Say my name . . ."

The light shall burn away all your fears, the sign said, written in her own bloodied script. Ayla stepped into a monument to madness, a project meant to last for centuries to come. It was not complete. Empty patches on the wall were meant for art, for fun. Empty pews needed filling.

She had not seen it since her return with Flowra, when she had walked in to find her love standing in the very center of hell—distraught, but not because this. Flowra had accepted every part of her.

And what had Ayla done in return?

Such a beautiful flower it will make . . .

She made no sound as she came forward, the macabre image of Sol Kareena filling her with . . . shame. Not for the blasphemy. Not for the desecration. But she remembered every victim, every scream to get that leather. Every cry of pain and terror—and all for art, all for fun—

"Say my name . . ."

The patches could have been darker. They could have been Flowra's precious skin.

Ayla stared upon the altar, the blood old and chipped. It flaked as she dragged her nail across it, lost in the memory of its conception. This blood had belonged to a child. She had found it fitting. A lost child on the street, missing her mother, until Ayla came to coax her home.

She could not even drop the body off, lest Casvir suspect her crime. All that remained of the child was blood upon the altar.

Ayla stared upon the face of the goddess, the abiding betrayal welling from the basest parts of her being. "Where were you?"

The words were met with silence, not even an echo on the decorated walls.

"So many speak freely to gods, but you did not look at me. Not even once."

Sol Kareena did not speak. She never did.

"One could say you brought me Eva—who fucked it up in spectacular ways. One could say you brought Sarai—"

To say the name brought fresh anguish to her heart, yet with it came the memory of a kiss too sacred to speak of.

"Who you had best care for. She deserves the damn world."

The fresh memory of a song stirred in her heart: *"But I hope there is peace for the monster in you . . ."*

A few preserved victims sat in their pews, the names of the ones she knew flittering through her head. What a legacy they had, eternal supplicants in a cathedral of the damned. Upon the wall, depictions of demons—of Ku'Shya, who she feared, of Onias, who intrigued her, of Izthuni, who brought a tangle of hatred with no end. Her very soul felt gnarled.

Her history—lies.

Her legacy—ruined.

All she thought she knew . . .

She remained The Endless Night, the Scourge of the Sun Elves, the Gaping Maw—all those terrible, glorious names—but what was a monster without terror? What was a monster who felt only horror at her own actions? When did this terrible feeling of shame become synonymous with her name?

She left the cathedral, moving on to the back room.

Less grand, yet no less meticulous—the diagrams she had drawn, some labeled down to the individual blood vessels in their arms; the array of surgical instruments, organized by size and function; the variety of dress forms, most for her, some for Flowra; a dirtied table coated in old blood, bookshelves and fabric and leather and bones.

The collection of a madwoman.

"What are you, without me?"

Upon the floor were remnants of a discarded veil.

How gorgeous, the final display. How perfect, her Flowra on their wedding day. Ayla knelt before the scraps, a few pieces rejected where she had erred, and gathered them in her hands, finding them precious even in ruin.

And what had she gone and done? She had destroyed everything—

"Say my name . . ."

Ayla clutched the discarded scraps to her chest, shaking as tears fell silently down her cheeks.

She blinked and saw the mutilated form of her subject, relived the girl's screams as they sang in her head. Her skin had parted so smoothly under her knife, another nameless victim shrieking her name. Ayla had kissed those lips and reprimanded her, the smell of her blood utterly intoxicating. A beautiful specimen; a beautiful face to carve away and hang from the wall. Over time, the smell of flowers upon her skin had been replaced by blood and grime.

But those words, those sweet words that had caused her to falter, caused the haze of her mind to clear: *"I remember the day you proposed . . ."*

Even in the depths of hell, Flowra spoke of peace—

Stop fighting, or I'll strap you to the table and fuck you anyway.
Ayla screamed and threw the scraps away, clawing anew at her face. She severed the skin, split it in two, the sensation of pain a release. Yet she could not escape the shame, the grief—oh *gods what had she done*?!

Flowridia flinched at the sound of her voice, so how could she ever return?

Ayla withdrew her claws from her flesh, willing her body to remain mutilated, to savor the sting a moment longer. Flowra hated this habit, had bid her to stop. But it was hardly her worst betrayal.

Yet amid the memories of torture and pain, despite the violation of her own mind, her memory settled somewhere tender.

To think of Sarai, their final goodbye, that tragic, bitter song . . . she felt peace.

And what was a monster of lust and rage to do with peace?

Ayla looked within herself and sought to know what was missing, what madness Sarai's kiss had wrought. Her head fell into her hands, and she wept at the tender wounds Sarai had left.

"I forgive you."—but what did that mean?

This tangle of hatred . . . what if it did not have to be?

But no—she could not let go. Not yet. Gods, she despised introspection, the pain of it all. It hurt, it *hurt*—

Ayla cried out as she plunged her fingers into her ribcage, shattering bones, tearing them out. Left with a hollow wound, she dug until she reached her dead heart, the radiant pain a godsend—at least it meant she did not have to *feel*.

The organ was pale, moist, stagnant. It did not beat, so how could it ache?

Already she felt the regrowth of her broken organs and bones, a new heart filling the gap in her chest. She could not be killed, except for love. She dropped the heart to the floor, wishing she had no need for it.

Eternity alone. Ayla had resigned herself to such a fate, of filling her hands and heart with pretty girls to carve to pieces and sew together better than before. Knowledge and creativity. Work before play. But Flowra, sweet Flowra, whose smell intoxicated her senses, whose form danced behind her eyelids, igniting her cold veins, and whose body split so delicately beneath her knife—

Perfect lines, slit up the seams.

Ayla's eyes shut, and in the darkness, she saw the slab and the nameless victim filter in and out of recognition. She saw the weeping, pitiful figure who lay mutilated on the floor yet still spoke of love—

Stop fighting, or I'll strap you to the table and fuck you anyway.

A cry tore from Ayla's throat, shame drowning her thoughts at the compulsion to ruin that beautiful creature, nameless yet precious even in obscurity. Ayla's hands had ruined her body, yet Flowra spoke of love. Ayla's hands had carved her to pieces, disfigured her beyond repair, yet Flowra spoke of love.

"Who are you, without me?"

And it occurred to Ayla, as she sat weeping on the floor, that to tear open her skin and peer into her soul would reveal only a hollow shell. For she was nothing.

Nothing at all.

What did that mean?

Ayla shook upon unsteady legs, managing to balance somehow. Her lab bespoke horror, bespoke knowledge, bespoke the mind of someone damaged. Ayla's fingers traced the walls, the drawings pinned to the surface, the detailed musculature of her dearest Flowra before her.

From memory, she could fill in the blanks on the parchment, finish with what she had seen with her eyes, felt between her fingers—

No.

She crumpled the drawing in her hand, the pencil strokes smudging into disrepair. First her hand caught flame, and then the parchment, flickering from silver to orange.

She let it fall.

Patterns created by her own twisted mind were torn from the walls, shredded by her elongated nails. Ayla ripped books from their spines. She crumpled research and threw it aside. What she had carefully constructed, her treasure in another life, she wrecked and left strewn at her feet.

Blood and dried entrails, patterns and leather—

"Say my name . . ."

Silver Fire burned at her feet, rising to consume her body. It swirled from her pores, held in perfect control. "Flowridia Darkleaf," Ayla whispered, gazing upon her once-beloved laboratory, "all of my growth, I have done for you."

It was the breath before the storm.

"But this, I am doing for me."

Fire expanded to touch every destroyed thing—the patterns, the dress forms, the books, years of research and projects burned at the seams.

And Ayla felt . . . free.

She left the blazing room, entering her palace of horror, machinations of macabre built by her own hands. With her first breath, the flame flowed slowly from her hands, seeping against the walls, but it was not enough.

"I will not be no one," she said, her voice pure steel despite her falling tears.

A second breath, and all the world erupted into flame.

Ayla screamed as fire burst from her body, a swirling inferno across the walls. The leather decorations did not catch the flame, instead coiling from sheer heat, charring and becoming small. The image of Sol Kareena disintegrated into macabre curls of ruined skin. All the fabric, the pews, and the curtains held to the flame, burning bright. Heat rose, yet Ayla did not relent, unleashing a thousand years of lies and hatred and pain.

Within the inferno, she was bombarded with images of her crimes, of screaming victims upon her slab, of lovers she'd murdered in the midst of passion, of burning cities filled with crying survivors left to clean up the aftermath of genocide— and all bore Flowra's face. It could've been her; it had nearly been her; by god—*it was her.*

What was this pain? It was far deeper than guilt.

Her own fire extinguished, but around her the cathedral was consumed in flame. How glorious, to feel its heat. How euphoric, to feel it char her skin.

Behind her, in the laboratory, a little embroidered flower sat upon the floor, slowly stained in smoke. Ayla ran to it, immune to the poisoned air, and plucked it from sure destruction, holding it to her chest instead.

What did she want? She was well and truly beyond forgiveness. There was no redemption for monsters like her. Would there be no escape for Ayla Darkleaf? She was The Endless Night, the Scourge of the Sun Elves, the Gaping Maw—all those terrible, awful things, granted by a god who had groomed her from tender years. Was it cowardice to run from who she was?

. . . Or was it weak to stay?

Small explosions fired as glass bottles burst, spraying the

air with their noxious chemicals. Ayla returned to the cathedral, leaving it all to burn. Such beauty in the destruction, a graveyard of her broken dreams, of the lies she'd been sung for over a thousand years.

When the fires burned out, what would she find? What was a monster without monstrosity?

Ayla paused in the entryway, gazing upon the burning pyre of a former life. Years of work, gone in minutes, left to waste away, to blacken and burn. In her hand, she studied the embroidered flower, the only survivor to this madness.

"Who are you, without me?"

"I don't know," she whispered, the sound lost amid the crackling flame, "but I will live to find out."

She clutched the flower to her heart and turned her back upon the burning cathedral, clinging to this hope found among the ruins of a former life.

From these ashes, she would rise.

At the cusp of sunrise, Flowridia stepped into the glorious morning.

The gardens in Nox'Kartha were truly a sight, cultivated to impress foreign royals. Sora stood at her side, supporting her weak body as they walked. She had atrophied during her time in prison, each step a difficult task, but there was hope for healing, hope for regaining her strength once more.

All seemed better in the sun. She smiled and whispered its name. "Good morning, Kedira."

Nearby, the missing piece of her heart remained unnervingly quiet. Sora held his leash—not that it would do much. Demitri lacked intelligence, his once-vibrant eyes now down to only one, glassy and distant. He wasn't the same, and some wicked part of Flowridia rejected him.

There was hope to hear her little boy's voice again, to hear the beloved name: *Mom.* And whatever the cost, she clung to the conclusion, that perhaps her life might find joy with him once more.

"Demitri," Flowridia said, and her wolf met her eye. He still knew her, and she clutched to that with all her might.

"Come with me, won't you?"

Sora helped her onto the grass, the morning dew staining her medical gown, but Flowridia savored the sensation of cold, the brisk air. Demitri sat himself beside her, his attention not quite here.

Despite the perfect ambience, Flowridia worried. Where was Ayla? Of course she would be erratic after all Mereen had done—so where had she gone? What would she do to herself? The fact that Ayla was incapable of killing herself was a small comfort, but what if she ran? She could hide for all eternity if she wished, and where would that leave Flowridia?

Sora sat beside her. "Do you want to talk about whatever's bothering you?"

"Am I that transparent?"

"You've always been that transparent."

Of course to think of what had transpired caused her blood to race, her eyes to well with tears. Her body reeled at the memory of pain, exhausted despite being healthy enough. "Everyone is worried for me. I suppose rightfully so. But no one is worried for Ayla. She was tortured too."

"I know," Sora whispered, though she struggled to be sincere in it.

Flowridia had found a sister, but that sister understandably hated her wife.

As though summoned by her will, Sora turned toward the castle. "She's here."

Flowridia's heart leapt from joy and relief. She followed Sora's gaze toward a forlorn figure avoiding the reaches of the sun.

"I'll leave you two alone," Sora said, though she left a pause for Flowridia to object.

Instead, Flowridia simply asked, "While you're gone, would you find me parchment and something to write with?"

No sense in explaining the promise she had made in Fallanar, to write down forgotten men's stories. One more string to tie up.

Sora nodded as she handed Flowridia the leash, then passed Ayla by, who ignored her entirely. All was the same, though a satchel hung on her shoulder. Yet something different shone in her stance, a softness Flowridia so rarely saw. She smelled strongly of perfume and soaps, and she hesitated before sitting a little farther away than normal—able to be reached by hand, but not close enough for Flowridia to rest her head on her shoulder.

"Good morning," Flowridia said.

Ayla offered a crumpled scrap of fabric, and Flowridia gasped to see what it was. An embroidered flower, and she remembered the pastel tone. This was from her veil. She took it, immediately noticing the strong smell of smoke, and held it to her heart. "Thank you. Where did you get this? I thought it was destroyed."

"The veil was, yes. But that's a scrap from my laboratory. Something I never threw away."

Flowridia smoothed the embroidery, the translucent fabric leaving nothing to distract from the meticulous pastel flower in the center. How beautiful, this memory—a treasure to cherish.

Ayla's attention was on the grass. She idly plucked at the individual growths. "I will only say this once, I promise. But if you ask me to leave, you will never see me again. I would understand."

"Ayla, no," Flowridia replied, aching at the words. Ayla Darkleaf, typically a closed book, had revealed her entire heart. "I'm still your wife. I'm still Flowridia Darkleaf. I think we have some challenges ahead of us, but I want to try. Our marriage is worth it."

A ghost of a smile came to Ayla's face.

"I love you," Flowridia whispered.

Ayla's hands clutched the other, her twitching revealing her nerves. "I love you too."

"Do you need to talk?"

"No."

Flowridia had feared that, but there was nothing she could say of it today. Both of them were hurting. Ayla needed time. "I'm always here for you."

Ayla nodded.

Beside Flowridia, Demitri laid himself in the grass, sunning his fur. She wondered what instincts remained. He did not breathe, which was certainly alarming, but he did still love the sun.

"You have to be dead to have Demitri back. And Casvir has to be alive to restore him."

Ayla's voice startled Flowridia from her musing, her monotone in stark juxtaposition to the cheerful morning.

"Casvir might not restore him as your familiar if you turn your back on your bargain."

She spoke the bitterest of truths.

"You could accept a new familiar," Ayla continued, "but I know what he means to you."

The implications were clear. Flowridia's gut clenched.

"Sora gave me Izthuni's knife. She asked me to destroy it. I shall, but not before I turn you to be like me. You could walk in the sun. You would be powerful, unkillable. Immortal."

Intrigued, Flowridia forgot the nausea of before. "It's perfect."

Ayla nodded, yet tension lingered in the air, the unspoken, damning truth remaining.

"I have to have a baby," Flowridia said, and to speak the words aloud brought fresh tears.

Again, Ayla nodded.

"Ayla, I'm sorry. I'm so sorry. You can leave for it all if you want. I know how sick it makes you . . ."

Ayla held up a hand. From the satchel at her hip, she withdrew a scroll—

Goddess Staella's scroll. The golden string faintly glowed.

"I read it before the wedding," Ayla said, that monotone returning. "My curiosity got the better of me. I slipped it into Sha'Demoni to hide it from Etolié, who was far too interested in its contents. Consequentially, it survived the blast, and—" Ayla's voice caught, lip trembling as she fought sudden tears. "And you shall hate me when you read it. I hid it from you, and I'm sorry. I'm so damn sorry, Flowra."

Ayla looked away as she offered it.

Flowridia's blood pulsed loudly in her ear as she accepted the godly gift. She pulled the golden string and carefully unraveled the parchment, revealing beautiful script written in perfect Solviran:

For the Creation of New Life—

Shock stilled her. "What?"

The joining of the Silver Fire and your beloved's womb.

"Goddess Staella gave birth to Ilune," Ayla said, depthless shame in the words, "who was the literal daughter of Neoma. She was not created by biology but by magic. By Silver Fire."

Flowridia's breath became scarce. "Goddess Staella gave it to us because Lara was the last of her line." All the pieces fell into place, creating a puzzle both hopeful . . . and damning. "And you hid this from me?"

Ayla's head fell into her hands. "I was afraid—"

478

"Afraid of what?!"

"We had already discussed that you did not want a child with me, but this would have changed everything—"

"And so you made the decision for me? Right before it would have been irreversible?!"

Ayla said nothing at all. Beneath her hands, tears fell into the grass.

Flowridia looked again to the scroll, then rolled it back up, too furious to try and decipher its words. Angry tears welled in her eyes, and she gripped the scroll tight, protective. "I'm not going to leave you because of this. But this isn't a small slight. I would have said no to this for all the reasons we already discussed, but how dare you."

Ayla remained silent.

Under normal circumstances, Flowridia would have marched away. Instead, she was imprisoned by her own weakness, her body exhausted from the exertion of walking this far. And so she, too, remained quiet for a time, fuming at the audacity of her wife, heartbroken for all she'd been through, all of it bombarding her mind at once.

Eventually, she spoke a practical truth. "We'll have to wait. I don't think my body can carry a baby right now. Not until I gain some weight."

Ayla nodded.

"Besides, I . . ." She swallowed the lump in her throat, dreading her next words—but knew they must be said. "I'm not ready to be intimate with you."

Cold seeped into her veins at the thought. She fought her rising panic, unwilling to cry—not to Ayla. Tazel had done the wicked work of breaking Ayla's mind, and she deserved no extra guilt for that.

Yet beside her, Ayla began to sob.

Flowridia scooted carefully forward, shattered at her wife's heartbreak. "It was not your fault, Ayla."

Ayla wept, hyperventilating as she clutched at her hair, her clothes.

Flowridia wrapped her arms around Ayla, holding her as she convulsed. What demons lingered in her mind? What memories remained to torture her?

"It was not your fault," Flowridia repeated, her own tears falling to match. "You were violated too. I still love you, I swear it. I love you, I love you . . ."

All the while, Ayla wept in her arms, and Flowridia

wished Mereen an eternity of loneliness for what she had done to them both.

Ayla stained her shoulder with tears, and the horrible, tragic truth emerged: there was no promise of happiness in life. There was no promise of joy or blissful endings.

"I love you, Flowra," Ayla whispered, and the simple phrase brought hope.

One day at a time.

Across the sea, Soliel stood upon a shattered arena. Lightning struck the great dragon. Uluron's pained roar echoed across the landscape. Any guilt was swallowed by adrenaline, by the burst of dark magic she released. It coated her bones like static, armor from his elemental attacks. When Soliel sent a blast of holy light toward her, the dark energy deflected it, the magic stronger when wielded by its mistress than when wielded by him.

As long as she had the Dark Orb, she was untouchable.

The land was barren, void of life, not even ruins to dot the area. All was grey, even the sky, and nothing provided cover. Soliel set his sword aflame and charged the dragon he had once called daughter, narrowly dodging when she swiped with her claw, and managed a shattering swing to a rib before she caught him and threw him aside.

Uluron had always been her mother's favorite, frail in her infancy. As she had grown, her strength surpassed the rest of her siblings, perhaps because of that extra devotion. Soliel could not say, only knew that, like her mother, she was not above dirty tricks.

Uluron welled a ball of dark matter in her mouth and shot it toward Soliel. Not unlike fire, yet more solid, weighted, and though Soliel summoned what holy light he could, his skin still burned as the necrotic magic disintegrated his shield of light.

Amid her onslaught, the ground beneath Soliel opened up—

Damn that Earth Orb.

He plunged into the underground, his last glimpse of sunlight shadowed by a dragon's flying silhouette. Darkness consumed him as the earth closed and swallowed him.

Down he fell, smacking against jutting rocks, bruising against the cave walls. He landed with a groan, but Gods did not break limbs for long—their wounds healed nearly instantly. By the time Soliel stood up, he was battered and disoriented, but far from broken.

His light revealed a massive cave. But it had not always been.

There was artistry here, the ruins of a civilization of long ago, harkening back to the era where he and she had ruled together. He took careful steps, wary of a deeper plunge, but found remnants of statues, of mosaics whose details were lost in the stale cave air. But he knew who it must be, far too many emblems of her colors scattered about.

Still, the nostalgic beauty would not provide an exit. Soliel's armored boots disrupted dust untouched for ten thousand years, swirling as an ancient cloud.

It was undeniable, the residual presence here.

Soliel recalled his own imprisonment as a ghost of ten thousand years, the slow maddening of his mind, the loneliness that had followed all along. His spirit had been tied to a single object—a pendant bearing his godly mother's sigil. He had worn it until its destruction by the empress' flame.

A particular mosaic drew his eye, largely intact. How beautiful, her fire, and what bitterness filled him to see it. The artwork was cracked, damaged by time, great gashes through it—

Inside one, something reflected his aura of light.

Soliel removed his glove and reached into the crevice. Shoving aside ancient dirt, he unearthed a small pouch, revealing the metal beads that had caught his attention.

He knew this emblem.

"Where are you?!" he cried, the words echoing all across the cave, shaking against the walls. Again and again, the walls returned his query: *Where are you . . . Where are you . . . Where are you . . .*

Then came laughter.

Soliel could not say if his blood burned or chilled, for that laughter haunted him on sleepless nights, an omen of mischief, of joy—or of sadism unmatched.

She burst from the pouch itself, glowing in pale shades of blue.

The woman matched his height, her ghostly hues revealing the truth—that she was dead and would remain so for a time. Fire coated every part of her being, her silhouette merely shadow within it, but as the flames died at her command, it unveiled a face the world did not dare to gaze upon, lest it be a sacrilege.

But Soliel found her beautiful. He had loved her from the start. Speechless, he swore his tongue had been caught in a trap, enthralled by merely her visage. She touched his face in a manner her incorporeal form should not have allowed, her caress welling madness within him.

The Goddess of Chaos smiled, revealing pointed fangs and wickedness unbound. "Hello, Soliel."

Coming Soon

Fallen Gods 6: Chaos Undone

"Love redeems . . . or love destroys."

Whispers from across the sea warn that the Goddess of Chaos walks the elven lands once more, and Sora and Etolié find themselves victims of her wrath. However, Chaos' loyalties are as mercurial as her name, and only she holds the knowledge of how to break the cycle of destruction and stop the God of Order once and for all. But her current form is but a shadow of her true power—and helping her means to place all the realms at her mercy.

Meanwhile Flowridia languishes as a prisoner in her own body, burdened by bargains and her own chronic pain. But Flowridia discovers she doesn't need the temptation of magic to embrace her inner darkness, and when a new destiny calls, to answer means to regain all she has lost . . . at the cost of her heart.

Pasts and futures collide, dead deities rise, and all that is earned is delivered in the sixth and final installment of FALLEN GODS.

Join S D Simper's newsletter to be the first to hear news about *Chaos Undone* and receive two free Fallen Gods novellas! Find out more at sdsimper.com.

Keep turning pages for an excerpt from my upcoming Patreon exclusive story *The Monster and the Minstrel!*

Dear Reader,

Thank you so much for reading! I hope you've enjoyed the ride (or at least as much as this book can be called "enjoyable"). Eve of Endless Night comes in the aftermath of a difficult few years for me, so it's a bittersweet feeling to have it out in the world. Lots of struggle, but lots of triumph to go with it. It's difficult to believe there's only one more book in Flowridia's story, but I'm excited to be able to share it with you soon.

If you loved what you read, please consider leaving reviews on Amazon and Goodreads. Reviews are the best thanks you can give to a book and help me out immensely.

If you're itching for more Fallen Gods content, considering following me on social media (I'm @sdsimper on all major platforms) or joining my Patreon! For a small monthly donation, you not only support an author, but you get access to exclusive stories, art, erotica and more! Just go to patreon.com/sdsimper <3

Once again, thank you so much. You, dear reader, are the reason I get to do what I love most. I hope you'll join me for Fallen Gods 6.

-S D Simper

THE MONSTER AND THE MINSTREL

A FALLEN GODS NOVELLA BY S D SIMPER

Coming August 2022 to Patreon!

Morning sun peeked through the seam of curtains, casting errant light across Sarai Fireborn's face.

She groaned and tried to drag her pillow to cover her face—only to touch soft blankets instead. Unwillingly, she blinked, the morning sun doing the cruel work of bringing her mind to wakefulness much too early. Her pillow lay on the ground. By the time she had pulled it over her face, she was wide awake.

Sunrise was not a time for sane people to be conscious.

Yet her mind would not stop buzzing, and so Sarai rose and dressed, cursing the curtains she swore she'd put in place before bed. Breeches and boots and a loose linen shirt—Sarai even did the quick work of styling her cropped hair.

But what to do so early? Her sister was not awake, nor her nephew. Sleeping in ran in the family, it seemed, yet apparently fate insisted Sarai get her ass out of bed at an ungodly time.

Well, not an ungodly time, *technically*. This was Sol Kareena's time, though Sarai had not sung a prayer in years. The birds, however, sang a delightful tune. Sarai supposed she could join them.

She crept through the silent house, cursing the hardwood floors for creaking. Mereen had always been a decorator, her home reflecting the creative mind who owned it. Sconces and art, rugs and lace-trimmed curtains—Mereen's hedonism showed in every detail, both large and small. Sarai grabbed an apple out of the elaborate kitchen on her way to the front door.

Almost a week into her stay in Fallanar, and Sarai had never visited the woods. Not much else to do at sunrise.

The town was predictably sleepy, though Sarai passed more than a few well-wishes, returning their greetings politely.

"Good morning, Lady Fireborn!"

"Beautiful morning, isn't it?"

"Give my best to Mereen!"

Small town types were friendlier than cityfolk—a culture shock when Sarai had first left her home—but there was something pleasant in knowing she was seen. Her grumpy mood abated to the kind greetings and fresh air. The sunshine cast a welcome warmth upon her skin, and Sarai savored it until she reached the edge of town and disappeared into the woods.

Once alone, she did what she did best—sing.

The whispering of trees sang a magical song, a lovely harmony to Sarai's own tune as it fluttered from her lips. Her words mixed with the wind and the birds, responding in kind to their orchestral cacophony. Morning sun flickered through the thick forest leaves, and Sarai basked in the perfect scene, her only wish that she had brought her harp.

She followed no path, but what did she have to fear? The village could not be too difficult to find. No animals but birds and squirrels had crossed her path. No wolves, no bears, no predators—

Yet a strange sight pulled her focus. Sarai's song died on her lips. She squinted as she stared into enormous oak tree tree—perhaps she had imagined the flash of black in her peripheral. Sarai stepped off her wayward path.

Indeed, there was someone—a woman lounging with feline grace upon a branch. Too bony to be beautiful, her thin form practically swam in the black dress, a perfect match to her chin-length hair. Yet her eyes were magnetic, vivid and icy blue. Her grin sent a shiver through Sarai's blood.

"What a beautiful voice you have," the woman said, and any condemnation one could give to her looks vanished in the luxury of her words. The voice was downright sinful, dark and sultry.

Sarai stilled her salacious thoughts, instead laughing at the opener. "Thank you." She peered upward to where the woman sat, nearly ten feet above her head. "What are you doing up there?"

"Listening. I didn't want to disturb you." The intensity in her tone grew with each word. "You're something to watch, nearly as lovely as your voice."

A forward one. Nothing to complain about. Sarai let practiced flirtation guide her, a charming grin twisting her lip. "Thank you. Do you live in Fallanar?"

"No." Her grin widened, and Sarai was struck with the image of a snake about to envelope its prey. "Sing more."

"Only if you come down from that tree."

What Sarai expected, she didn't know, but it certainly wasn't for the woman to suddenly backflip from the tree and land perfectly balanced on the forest floor. She looked up with enormous eyes, which starkly juxtaposed how small the woman was in every dimension. Surely not a child, but her head didn't even reach Sarai's chin.

On the ground, the woman's proud stance withered away, and she stood as though faced with the gallows. Sarai offered her a hand. "My name is Sarai Fireborn."

"Ayla Darkleaf," came the reply, though she delayed a moment before accepting the outstretched hand.

So tentative a grip from those delicate hands—but the odder part remained that Ayla gave no reaction to the name. "A deal is a deal," Sarai said. "I promised you a song. What would you like to hear?"

Ayla responded too quickly, too eager. "What was it you sang earlier?"

"Oh, something I made up." She laughed, and Ayla leaned in at the sound, hesitant but clearly mesmerized. "I love writing songs."

"Do it, then." Ayla stared, unblinking. "Make up a song."

An insistent little woman, but Sarai had always been weak to women who bossed her around. "All right, then." She hummed, putting herself into the proper key to match with the wind. *"I met an odd girl in a tree. I caught her as she stared at me. And to my surprise, right before my eyes, she managed to backflip* ... down?" Oh, it was terribly stupid, and Sarai laughed. "Most of my songs are silly."

But Ayla's expression remained deathly serious, never wavering. "I think that was wonderful. Do you write them down?"

"Only if I'm trying to write something serious. I have a few love songs in my repertoire. A few hymns."

"Do you perform?"

"I've performed all over ... a few places." No need to mar the interaction with the truth—not when Ayla stared with such earnest intent.

"Is that why you're here?"

"I'm on hiatus." Sarai gave her most charming smile, praying Ayla didn't ask her to elaborate. How strange, to not be recognized. "I've come to Fallanar to stay with my sister. Do you know Mereen Fireborn?"

Ayla shook her head. "But won't you sing more? What would you sing if you were performing?"

Perhaps not strictly forward—perhaps a little socially awkward. But there was something so endearing in her earnest intensity. "I don't often do private solos. Consider yourself special. I'll sing you my most popular." Sarai winked, keen to notice Ayla's slight blush, and drew a deep breath.

I often go walking alone in the dark
And sing all the beautiful songs in my heart.
I'm as blessed by the Moon as I'm loved by the Day
And I trust in her light to not lead me astray.

She gauged Ayla's mood all the while, fearful of boring her with a hymn—but Ayla remained enraptured, her severe countenance softened by her smile.

The Moon and the Stars sing their chorus by night
While the Goddess of Sunshine awaits the dawn's light.
The angels are watching, so why should I fear?
So I'll sing all my songs, and know that they're near.

At the final refrain, Ayla burst into applause. "I can't imagine Goddess Staella herself matching that."

Sarai set a hand on her heart. "High praise."

"I have never heard a hymn to three different goddesses. Never thought that was allowed. Do you worship Sol Kareena?"

"I suppose yes, technically. I'm a bit of a sinner by most definitions." She shrugged, though kept it light. "Does sneaking into the chapel to kiss pretty girls on the altar count as devout?"

A little more was done than 'kiss,' but the implications were laid out, and Ayla made no attempt to hide her intrigue. She bit her lip, struggling to meet Sarai's eye. "No, but it does make a statement."

Ayla was too easy. "Shall I sing something else?" Sarai asked. "A love song, perhaps?"

"Yes. Please."

The *please* was an afterthought, and Sarai bit back a chuckle. "Have a seat and relax, my lady."

Ayla obeyed, and Sarai's show began.

Read the rest in August of 2022 – only on Patreon!

About the author:

S D Simper has lived in both the hottest place on earth and the coldest, spans the employment spectrum from theatre teacher to professional editor, and plays more instruments than can be counted on one hand. She and her beloved wife share a home with their many four-legged housemates and innumerable bookshelves.

Visit her website at sdsimper.com to see her other works, including *The Fate of Stars,* the story of a mermaid, a human princess, and a love that will shape the future of the world.